Sacrifice

WRITTEN BY COLIN GEE

The Fifth book in the 'Red Gambit' series.

25th DECEMBER 1945 to 24th APRIL 1946

Those of you with a clear eye will realise that the name of this book had changed from the preview in 'Impasse'. I abandoned 'Counterplay' early on in the piece, but it was too late to change the details in 'Impasse'.

I hope there is no confusion as a result.

ISBN-10: 1505458110
ISBN-13: 978-1505458114

Series Dedication

The Red Gambit series of books is dedicated to my grandfather, the boss-fellah, Jack 'Chalky' White, Chief Petty Officer [Engine Room] RN, my de facto father until his untimely death from cancer in 1983 and a man who, along with many millions of others, participated in the epic of history that we know as World War Two. Their efforts and sacrifices made it possible for us to read of it, in freedom, today.

Thank you, for everything.

Overview by author Colin Gee

If you have already read the first four books in this series, then what follows may serve as a small reminder of what went before. If this is your first toe dipped in the waters of 'Red Gambit', then I can only advise you to read the previous books when you can. In the interim, this is mainly for you.

After the end of the German War, the leaders of the Soviet Union found sufficient cause to distrust their former Allies, to the point of launching an assault on Western Europe. Those causes and the decision-making behind the full scale attack lie within 'Opening Moves', as do the battles of the first week, commencing on 6th August 1945.

After that initial week, the Soviets continued to grind away at the Western Allies, trading lives and materiel for ground, whilst reducing the combat efficiency of Allied units from the Baltic to the Alps.

In 'Breakthrough', the Red Army inflicts defeat after defeat upon their enemy, but at growing cost to themselves.

The attrition is awful.

Matters come to a head in 'Stalemate' as circumstances force Marshall Zhukov to focus attacks on specific zones. The resulting battles bring death and horror on an unprecedented scale, neither Army coming away unscathed or unscarred.

In the Pacific, the Soviet Union has courted the Empire of Japan, and has provided unusual support in its struggle against the Chinese. That support has faded and, despite small scale Soviet intervention, the writing is on the wall.

'Impasse' brought a swing, perhaps imperceptible at first, with the initiative lost by the Red Army, but difficult to pick up for the Allies.

The Red Air Force is almost spent, and Allied air power starts to make its superiority felt across the spectrum of operations.

The war takes on a bestial nature, as both sides visit excesses on each other.

Allied planning deals a deadly blow to the Soviet Baltic forces, in the air, on the sea, and on the ground. However, their own ground assaults are met with stiff resistance, and peter out as General Winter spreads his frosty fingers across the continent, bringing with him the coldest weather in living memory.

In the four previous books, the reader has journeyed from June 1945, all the way to Christmas Eve 1945. The combat and intrigue has focussed in Europe, but men have also died in the Pacific, over and under the cold waters of the Atlantic, and on the shores of small islands in Greenland.

Battles have occurred from the Baltic to the Adriatic, some large, some small, some insignificant, and some of huge import.

As I did the research for this alternate history series, I often wondered why it was that we, west and east, did not come to blows once more.

We must all give thanks it did not all go badly wrong in that hot summer of 1945, and that the events described in the Red Gambit series did not come to pass.

My thanks to the family of John Thornton-Smith, who gave me full permission to publish his reports, without interference or direction. I am deeply indebted to you all.

Thus far, I have avoided writing anything that could be attributed to Sir Winston Churchill and President Truman. The requirements of 'Sacrifice' make me tackle the introduction of these statesmen head on. It is my hope that I can do both of these men justice.

My profound thanks to all those who have contributed in whatever way to this project, as every little piece of help brought me closer to my goal.

[For additional information, progress reports, orders of battle, discussion, freebies, and interaction with the author please find time to visit and register at one of the following-

www.redgambitseries.com, www.redgambitseries.co.uk, www.redgambitseries.eu, Also, feel free to join Facebook Group 'Red Gambit'.]

Thank you.

I have received a great deal of assistance in researching, translating, advice, and support during the years that this project has so far run.

In no particular order, I would like to record my thanks to all of the following for their contributions. Gary Wild, Jan Wild, Jason Litchfield, Peter Kellie, Mario Wildenauer, Loren Weaver, Pat Walsh, Elena Schuster, Stilla Fendt, Luitpold Krieger, Mark Lambert, Simon Haines, Greg Winton, Greg Percival, Robert Prideaux, Tyler Weaver, Giselle Janiszewski, James Hanebury, Renata Loveridge, Jeffrey Durnford, Brian Proctor, Steve Bailey, Paul Dryden, Steve Riordan, Bruce Towers, Victoria Coling, Alexandra Coling, Heather Coling, Isabel Pierce Ward, Hany Hamouda, Ahmed Al-Obeidi, Sharon Shmueli, and finally BW-UK Gaming Clan.

One name is missing on the request of the party involved, who perversely has given me more help and guidance in this project than most, but whose desire to remain in the background on all things means I have to observe his wish not to name him.

None the less, to you, my oldest friend, thank you.

Wikipedia is a wonderful thing and I have used it as my first port of call for much of the research for the series. Use it and support it.

My thanks to the US Army Center of Military History and Franklin D Roosevelt Presidential Library websites for providing the out of copyright images.

All map work is original, save for the Château outline, which derives from a public domain handout.

Particular thanks go to Steen Ammentorp, who is responsible for the wonderful www.generals.dk site, which is a superb place to visit in search of details on generals of all nations. The site has proven invaluable in compiling many of the biographies dealing with the senior officers found in these books.

If I have missed anyone or any agency I apologise and promise to rectify the omission at the earliest opportunity.

Author's note.

The correlation between the Allied and Soviet forces is difficult to assess for a number of reasons.

Neither side could claim that their units were all at full strength, and information on the relevant strengths over the period this book is set in is limited as far as the Allies are concerned and relatively non-existent for the Soviet forces.

I have had to use some licence regarding force strengths and I hope that the critics will not be too harsh with me if I get things wrong in that regard. A Soviet Rifle Division could vary in strength from the size of two thousand men to be as high as nine thousand men, and in some special cases could be even more.

Indeed, the very names used do not help the reader to understand unless they are already knowledgeable.

A prime example is the Corps. For the British and US forces, a Corps was a collection of Divisions and Brigades directly subservient to an Army. A Soviet Corps, such as the 2nd Guards Tank Corps, bore no relation to a unit such as British XXX Corps. The 2nd G.T.C. was a Tank Division by another name and this difference in 'naming' continues to the Soviet Army, which was more akin to the Allied Corps.

The Army Group was mirrored by the Soviet Front.

Going down from the Corps, the differences continue, where a Russian rifle division should probably be more looked at as the equivalent of a US Infantry regiment or British Infantry Brigade, although this was not always the case. The decision to leave the correct nomenclature in place was made early on. In that, I felt that those who already possess knowledge would not become disillusioned, and that those who were new to the concept could acquire knowledge that would stand them in good stead when reading factual accounts of WW2.

There are also some difficulties encountered with ranks. Some readers may feel that a certain battle would have been left in the command of a more senior rank, and the reverse case where seniors seem to have few forces under their authority. Casualties will have played their part but, particularly in the Soviet Army, seniority and rank was a complicated affair, sometimes with Colonels in charge of Divisions larger than those commanded by a General. It is easier for me to attach a chart to give the reader a rough guide of how the ranks equate.

Fig# 1 – Table of comparative ranks.

SOVIET UNION	WAFFEN-SS	WEHRMACHT	UNITED STATES	UK/COMMONWEALTH	FRANCE
KA - SOLDIER	SCHUTZE	SCHUTZE	PRIVATE	PRIVATE	SOLDAT DEUXIEME CLASSE
YEFREYTOR	STURMMANN	GEFREITER	PRIVATE 1ST CLASS	LANCE-CORPORAL	CAPORAL
MLADSHIY SERZHANT	ROTTENFUHRER	OBERGEFREITER	CORPORAL	CORPORAL	CAPORAL-CHEF
SERZHANT	UNTERSCHARFUHRER	UNTEROFFIZIER	SERGEANT	SERGEANT	SERGENT-CHEF
STARSHIY SERZHANT	OBERSCHARFUHRER	FELDWEBEL	SERGEANT 1ST CLASS	C.S.M.	ADJUDANT-CHEF
STARSHINA	STURMSCHARFUHRER	STABSFELDWEBEL	SERGEANT-MAJOR [WO/CWO]	R.S.M.	MAJOR
MLADSHIY LEYTENANT	UNTERSTURMFUHRER	LEUTNANT	2ND LIEUTENANT	2ND LIEUTENANT	SOUS-LIEUTENANT
LEYTENANT	OBERSTURMFUHRER	OBERLEUTNANT	1ST LIEUTENANT	LIEUTENANT	LIEUTENANT
STARSHIY LEYTENANT					
KAPITAN	HAUPTSTURMFUHRER	HAUPTMANN	CAPTAIN	CAPTAIN	CAPITAINE
MAYOR	STURMBANNFUHRER	MAJOR	MAJOR	MAJOR	COMMANDANT 1
PODPOLKOVNIK	OBERSTURMBANNFUHRER	OBERSTLEUTNANT	LIEUTENANT-COLONEL	LIEUTENANT-COLONEL	LIEUTENANT-COLONEL 2
POLKOVNIK	STANDARTENFUHRER	OBERST	COLONEL	COLONEL	COLONEL 3
GENERAL-MAYOR	BRIGADEFUHRER	GENERALMAJOR	BRIGADIER GENERAL	BRIGADIER	GENERAL DE BRIGADE
GENERAL-LEYTENANT	GRUPPENFUHRER	GENERALLEUTNANT	MAJOR GENERAL	MAJOR GENERAL	GENERAL DE DIVISION
GENERAL-POLKOVNIK	OBERGRUPPENFUHRER	GENERAL DER INFANTERIE*	LIEUTENANT GENERAL	LIEUTENANT GENERAL	GENERAL DE CORPS D'ARMEE
GENERAL-ARMII	OBERSTGRUPPENFUHRER	GENERALOBERST	GENERAL	GENERAL	GENERAL DE ARMEE
MARSHALL		GENERALFELDMARSCHALL	GENERAL OF THE ARMY	FIELD-MARSHALL	MARECHAL DE FRANCE

* OR ARTILLERY, PANZERTRUPPEN ETC

1 CAPITAINE de CORVETTE   2 CAPITAINE de FREGATE   3 CAPITAINE de VAISSEAU

ROUGH GUIDE TO THE RANKS OF COMBATANT NATIONS.

Book Dedication

I once read that for every Medal of Honor, Knight's Cross, Hero Award, or Victoria Cross presented, a score of similarly noteworthy actions will have gone unnoticed.

When you read the citations for bravery awards, if you are anything like me, you will conjure up pictures of valiant actions and superhuman courage on behalf of the recipients, many of whom so often paid the full price for their actions.

If you visit war cemeteries, you will find a nation's young lying in neat rows, often alongside comrades who fell in the same fight, and occasionally find the grave of a soldier who has received such an honour.

Of course, such headstones will attract attention.

However, I also spare some thought for the soldier alongside, whose headstone carries only a name and some numbers, and perhaps an inscription chosen by a grieving family.

Maybe the bones laid to rest there belong to one of the score who died, but whose valiant contribution went unnoticed?

Perhaps it is fitting that this book, Sacrifice, is dedicated to such men, and women, who died for their country and comrades, and whose deserving actions will forever remain a secret.

Although I never served in the Armed forces, I wore a uniform with pride, and carry my own long-term injuries from my service. My admiration for our young service men and women serving in all our names in dangerous areas throughout the world is limitless. As a result, **'Soldiers off the Streets** is a charity that is extremely close to my heart. My fictitious characters carry no real-life heartache with them, whereas every news bulletin from the military stations abroad brings a terrible reality with its own impact, angst, and personal challenges for those left behind when one of our military pays the ultimate price. Therefore, I make donations to **'Soldiers off the Streets,'** and would encourage you to do so too.

In Impasse, I made a mistake in the name of the island on which the B-29 crashed. It should have read Østerskær Island, which is part of the Christiansø Archipelago, also known as Ertholmene. Perhaps the greater sin was in stating sovereignty belonged to Sweden, whereas in fact the island belongs to Denmark. My apologies.

Book #1 - Opening Moves [Chapters 1-54]
Book#2 - Breakthrough [Chapters 55-77]
Book#3 - Stalemate [Chapters 78-102]
Book#4 – Impasse [Chapters 103 – 125]
Book#5 - Sacrifice [Chapters 126 - 148]

TABLE OF CONTENTS.

Series Dedication 3

Overview by author Colin Gee 4

Author's note. 7

Book Dedication 9

TABLE OF CONTENTS..11

Chapter 126 - THE OPPONENTS.................................24

The Soviet Union. 24

The Red Army. 24
The Red Air Force. 27
The Red Navy 28
Soviet Allies. 29
Imperial Japan.. 29

The Allies...32

Allied Ground Forces. 32
Allied Air Forces. 34
The Allied Navies 35
Allied technology 36
German designations for Republican Forces. 37
German Republican and Austrian Forces 37
The French Army.. 38
Author's note on the forces- 39

Chapter 127 - THE ANNIHILATION 42

1317 hrs, Wednesday, 25th December 1945, airborne above North-West Eire. 42
2002 hrs, Thursday, 26th December 1945, Camp 5A, near Cookstown, County Tyrone, Northern Ireland. 44

Chapter 128 - THE WASTELAND 47

1627 hrs, Monday, 30th December 1945, Lough Erne, Northern Ireland.. 47
1633 hrs, Monday, 30th December 1945, OSS base, Inishmakill Island, Northern Ireland. 48

2358 hrs, Tuesday, 31st December 1945, Lough Erne, Northern Ireland. 52
0000 hrs, Wednesday, 1st January 1946, Glenlara, County Mayo, Eire. 52
0034 hrs, Wednesday, 1st January 1946, airborne over the Atlantic, 35 miles north of Llandavuck Island. 53
0049 hrs, Wednesday, 1st January 1946, off the North coast of Eire. 54
0142 hrs, Wednesday, 1st January 1946, Building Nine, Glenlara, Cork, Eire. 72
The facts about the Robert Hastie. 76
0817 hrs, Wednesday, 1st January 1946, RAF Castle Archdale, Northern Ireland. 77

Chapter 129 - THE BASES 79

1331 hrs, Wednesday, 1st January 1946, Camp 5A, near Cookstown, County Tyrone, Northern Ireland. 79
1355 hrs, Wednesday, 1st January 1946, airborne with 34th Bombardment Group, approaching Prague, Occupied Czechoslovakia. 81

Chapter 130 - THE FREEZE 84

January 1946, Europe. 84
2013 hrs, Monday, 20th January 1946, 3rd Guards Mechanised Corps headquarters, Bargteheide, Germany. 89
2111 hrs, Monday, 20th January 1946, OSS British Headquarters, 70-72 Grosvenor Street, London. 95
0401 hrs, Tuesday, 21st January 1946, Headquarters bunker, Motorised Anti-Tank Company, 1st Motorised Battalion, 9th Guards Mechanised Brigade, Fahrenkrug, Germany. 97
Relative to the events within the Headquarters of 'Camerone', Gougenheim, Alsace, on Sunday 8th December 1945 97
1854 hrs, Tuesday, 21st January 1946, Former Headquarters of 'Camerone', Gougenheim, Alsace. 102
0310 hrs, Wednesday, 22nd January 1946, the Cemetery, La Petite Pierre, Alsace. 104
0413 hrs, Wednesday, 22nd January 1946, Headquarters, 16th US Armored Brigade, Fénétrange, France. 106
0418 hrs, Wednesday, 22nd January 1946, Drulingen, France .. 107
0502 hrs, Wednesday, 22nd January 1946, Drulingen, France. . 110
0504 hrs, Wednesday, 22nd January 1946, Drulingen, France. . 111
0513 hrs, Wednesday, 22nd January 1946, Headquarters, 16th US Armored Brigade, Fénétrange, France. 114

0525 hrs, Wednesday, 22nd January 1946, Drulingen, France.. 115
0533 hrs, Wednesday, 22nd January 1946, Headquarters, 16th US Armored Brigade, Fénétrange, France...................................... 116
0529 hrs, Wednesday, 22nd January 1946, Drulingen, France.. 117
0601 hrs, Wednesday, 22nd January 1946, Drulingen, France.. 121
0643 hrs, Wednesday, 22nd January 1946, Headquarters, 16th US Armored Brigade, Fénétrange, France...................................... 125
0647 hrs, Wednesday, 22nd January 1946, Drulingen, France.. 126
0649 hrs, Wednesday, 22nd January 1946, Soviet-held treeline, east of Drulingen, France.. 128
0900 hrs, Wednesday, 22nd January 1946, Hangviller, France. 131
1101 hrs, Friday 24th January, Ward 22, US 130th Station Hospital, Chiseldon, England.. 144
1157 hrs, Saturday 25th January, L'Eglise Saint-Hippolyte, Thonon-les-Bains, France... 146

Chapter 131 – THE LULL..150

February 1946, Europe. 150
2054 hrs, Sunday, 3rd February , Der Brankenwald, one and a half kilometres south-east of Hollenbeck, Germany.......................... 150
2054 hrs, Sunday, 3rd February Three hundred metres south-east of the Soviet supply base, Hollenbeck, Germany. 152

Chapter 132 – THE RETURN 156

0551 hrs, Wednesday, 6th February 1946, airborne over Russia.156
0701 hrs, Wednesday, 6th February 1946, GRU Commander's office, Western Europe Headquarters, the Mühlberg, Germany.157
0852 hrs, Wednesday, 6th February 1946, Office of the NKVD Deputy Chairman, Lyubyanka, Moscow. 161
0900 hrs, Wednesday, 6th February 1946, The Georgievsky Hall, Grand Kremlin Palace, Moscow... 162
0937 hrs, Wednesday, 6th February 1946, GRU Briefing room, Western Europe Headquarters, the Mühlberg, Germany. 165
1203 hrs, Wednesday, 6th February 1946, Bois Neuf, Moselle, France. 166
1607 hrs, Wednesday, 6th February 1946, la Mairie, Troisfontaines Moselle, France. 169
1700 hrs, Wednesday, 6th February 1946, Office of the General Secretary, the Kremlin, Moscow. 170

Chapter 133 – THE PROTOTYPE 175

1104 hrs, Saturday, 9th February 1946, on board S-22, off the coast of Sweden. 175

1607 hrs, Saturday, 9th February 1946, Ramenskoye Airfield, USSR..............176
1903 hrs, Saturday, 9th February 1946, on board S-22, Østerskær Island, Denmark. 180
2159 hrs, Monday, 11th February 1946, Temporary Office of the Deputy Chief, Deuxieme Bureau, Heming, France................184
0218 hrs, Tuesday, 12th February 1946, astride Route 58, one kilometre east of Ascheburg, Germany......................185
0859 hrs, 12th February 1946, the Mühlberg, Nordhausen, Germany................192

Chapter 134 – THE CIRCUS 194

1000 hrs, Friday, 22nd February 1946, Chateau de Versailles, France................194
1430 hrs, Friday, 22nd February 1946, Chateau de Versailles, France................197
2030 hrs, Friday, 22nd February 1946, Chateau de Versailles, France................203
0939 hrs, Friday 1st March 1946, Headquarters of 3rd Red Banner Central European Front, Hotel Stephanie, Baden-Baden, Germany. 205

Chapter 135 - THE PREPARATIONS................211

0942 hrs, Tuesday 5th March 1946, SHAEF Headquarters, Hotel Trianon, Versailles, France. 211
1122 hrs, Tuesday 5th March 1946, Wittensee, Bünsdorf, Germany. 212
1442 hrs, Tuesday 5th March 1946, Headquarters, 1st Guards Mechanised Rifle Division, Torgelow, Germany................215
1102 hrs, Wednesday 6th March 1946, Disembarkation point 1192, east of Rullstorf, Germany. 217
2042 hrs, Thursday, 7th March 1946, Den Gyldene Freden, Österlånggatan 51, Stockholm, Sweden................221
Friday, 8th March 1946, 1843 hrs, GRU Commander's office, Western Europe Headquarters, the Mühlberg, Germany. 222
0840 hrs, Saturday, 9th March 1946, Castello di Susans, Majano, Italy. 224
0905 hrs, Saturday, 9th March 1946, Rivoli, Italy. 229
0909 hrs, Saturday, 9th March 1946, Castello di Susans, Majano, Italy. 230
0910 hrs, Saturday, 9th March 1946, Rivoli, Italy. 233
0921 hrs, Saturday, 9th March 1946, Castello di Susans, Majano, Italy. 236

0925 hrs, Saturday, 9th March 1946, Rivoli, Italy..................... 240

0930 hrs, Saturday, 9th March 1946, Castello di Susans, Majano, Italy.. 241

0925 hrs, Saturday, 9th March 1946, Rivoli, Italy..................... 242

Chapter 136 – THE DECEIVERS 244

1554 hrs, Tuesday, 12th March 1946, the Billiard House, Hameau de la Reine, Versailles, France.. 244

0917 hrs, Thursday, 14th March 1946, Map room, GRU Western Europe Headquarters, the Mühlberg, Germany. 246

Chapter 137 – THE COUNTDOWN 251

1600 hrs, Friday 15th March 1946, Meeting Room 3, The Kremlin, Moscow. 251

1843 hrs, Friday 15th March 1946, Scientist's residential block, Los Alamos, New Mexico. 255

1912 hrs, Friday 15th March 1946, Office of the NKVD Deputy Chairman, Lyubyanka, Moscow... 256

1737 hrs, Friday 15th March 1946, House of Madame Fleriot, La Vigie, Nogent L'Abbesse, near Reims, France........................... 258

1011 hrs, Saturday 16th March 1946, Headquarters, Legion Corps D'Assaut, La Mairie, D'Essey les Nancy, France. 260

1521 hrs, Saturday 16th March 1946, Headquarters, 501st Parachute Infantry Regiment, 101st US Airborne Division, St-Hilaire le Grand, France. 263

1526 hrs, Saturday 16th March 1946, Ward 22, US 130th Station Hospital, Chiseldon, England. 265

1530 hrs, Saturday 16th March 1946, the Billiard House, Hameau de la Reine, Versailles, France.. 266

1318 hrs, Sunday, 17th March 1946, Bickenholtz area, France. 268

1339 hrs, Sunday, 17th March 1946, Route 46, eight hundred metres north of Bickenholtz, France... 271

1350 hrs, Sunday, 17th March 1946, the copse, nine hundred metres north of Bickenholtz, France. 275

1401 hrs, Sunday, 17th March 1946, Rue D'Eglise, Bickenholtz, France. 277

1423 hrs, Sunday, 17th March 1946, base of fire position, east of the copse, Bickenholtz, France. 282

1021 hrs, Monday, 18th March 1946, The Kremlin, Moscow, Russia. 288

1100 hrs, Monday, 18th March 1946, The Kremlin, Moscow, Russia. 289

2200 hrs, Tuesday, 19th March 1946, Old Town Square, Torun, Poland. 295

2200 hrs, Friday, 22nd March 1946, 15th Transportstaffel, Avno Airbase, Denmark. 301

2258 hrs, Saturday, 23rd March 1946, Task Force X-3, the North Sea..304

0009 hrs, Sunday, 24th March 1946, Red Army Senior Officers Dacha, Moscow, USSR..304

0022 hrs, Sunday, 24th March 1946, GRU Commander's office, Western Europe Headquarters, the Mühlberg, Germany. 305

0903 hrs, Sunday, 24rd March 1946, Headquarters of 1st Guards Mechanised Rifle Division, Jatznick, Germany. 306

1230 hrs, Monday, 25th March 1946, OSS safe house, Thompson's Farm, Doddinghurst Road, Shenfield, UK. 307

1602 hrs, Monday, 25th March 1946, Temporary Headquarters, Camerone Division, Schleiden, Germany. 310

1722 hrs, Monday, 25th March 1946, GRU Western Europe Headquarters, the Mühlberg, Germany. 311

1735 hrs, Monday, 25th March 1946, GRU Commander's office, Western Europe Headquarters, the Mühlberg, Germany. 313

1802 hrs, Monday 25th March 1946, office of the Chairman of the NKVD, Moscow, USSR. 314

1833 hrs, Monday, 25th March 1946, Flat 3, 2 Franciskánska, Torun, Poland...316

2004 hrs, Sunday, 24rd March 1946, Rail bridgehead at Torgelow, Germany..317

2201 hrs, Monday, 25th March 1946, 1002nd Mixed Air Regiment, Pütnitz-Damgarten airbase, Germany. 319

Chapter 138 – THE REVELATION 321

1002 hrs, Friday, 22nd March, The Thatched Barn, Borehamwood, England. 321

1945 hrs, Friday, 22nd March 1946, SOE Headquarters, 64 Baker Street, London, England..323

1312 hrs, Saturday, 23rd March 1946, MI6 Headquarters, 54 Broadway, London...327

1201 hrs, Sunday, 24th March 1946, MI6 Headquarters, 54 Broadway, London, UK. 330

1557 hrs, Sunday, 24th March 1946, 7 Leinster Mews, Bayswater, London, UK. 331

1616 hrs, Monday, 25th March 1946, 12th US Army Group Headquarters, Arlon, Belgium. 333

Chapter 139 - THE LANDINGS 337

0028 hrs, Tuesday, 26th March 1946, the night skies over Northern Europe.. 337
0047 hrs, 26th March 1946, seven kilometres north-west of Naugard, Pomerania. 343
0204 hrs, Tuesday, 26th March 1946, Drop Zone around Konnegen, Poland.. 344
0149 hrs, Tuesday, 26th March 1946, two kilometres north-east of Cierpice, Poland.. 346
0252 hrs, Tuesday, 26th March 1946, Joint Command Headquarters, Cierpice, Poland. 347
0303 hrs, Tuesday, 26th March 1946, Joint Command Headquarters, Cierpice, Poland. 351
0500 hrs, Tuesday, 26th March 1946, Kolberg, Pomerania....... 361
0600 hrs, Tuesday, 26th March 1946, Factory Rinat, Chaiky, Kiev, Ukraine. 363
0602 hrs, Tuesday, 26th March 1946, Beach Zulu, Kolberg, Pomerania. 364
0833 hrs, Tuesday, 26th March 1946, ten kilometres east of Bärwalde, Poland.. 365

Chapter 140 - THE BEGINNING..366

0844 hrs, Tuesday, 26th March 1946, Europe. 366
0909 hrs, Tuesday, 26th March 1946, Operation Heracles-I, above Nordhausen, Germany. 367
Author's note on the remaining chapters of Sacrifice................ 369

Chapter 141 - THE FIFTEENTH 370

0958 hrs, Tuesday, 26th March 1946, the grounds of Schloss Maria Loretto, Klagenfurt, Austria. 370
1058 hrs, Friday, 29th March 1946, St Ruprecht district, Klagenfurt, Austria. 374
Author's note - The Heracles Missions 376
1008 hrs, Monday, 1st April 1946, the Kremlin, Moscow. 378
1209 hrs, Friday, 5th April 1946, Headquarters of 1st Alpine Front, Stainach, Austria.. 381
1238 hrs, Friday, 12th April 1946, Headquarters of 1st Alpine Front, Stainach, Austria. 383
1109 hrs, Wednesday, 17th April 1946, Headquarters of 1st Alpine Front, Klaus an der Phyrnbahn, Austria. 384
1301 hrs, Friday, 19th April 1946, headquarters of British Fifteenth Army Group.. 386

1101 hrs, Monday, 22nd April 1946, Headquarters of 1st Alpine Front, Klaus an der Phyrnbahn, Austria. 387
23rd April 1946, Area of operations for the British Fifteenth Army Group, Austria and Italy..388
1009 hrs, Tuesday, 23nd April 1946, Headquarters of 1st Alpine Front, Klaus an der Phyrnbahn, Austria. 388

Chapter 142 - THE SIXTH 390

0758 hrs hrs, Tuesday, 26th March 1946, Toul-Rosières, France.390
The journalistic reports of John Thornton-Smith, War Correspondent for the Daily Sketch newspaper. 390
With the United States Army Air Force, somewhere in Eastern France, 8:42am, 26th March 1946. 390
With the United States Army Air Force, somewhere in Eastern France, 9:13am, 26th March 1946. 392
With the United States Army, somewhere in Eastern France, 11:13am, 28th March 1946. 393
With the Allied Army, somewhere in Eastern France, 3:17pm, 29th March 1946. 395
With the United States Army, somewhere in Eastern France, 11:13am, 30th March 1946. 397
With the United States Army, somewhere in Eastern France, 12:33am, 1st April 1946...399
With the United States Army, somewhere in Eastern France, 12:33am, 2nd April 1946. 402
With the United States Army, somewhere in Eastern France, 12:33am, 5th April 1946. 404
With the United States Army, somewhere in Eastern France, 12:33am, 6th April, 1946. 408
With the United States Army, somewhere in Eastern France, 12:33am, 8th April, 1946. 414
With the United States Army, somewhere in Eastern France, 12:33am, 11th April, 1946. 416
12th to 20th April 1946, Area of operations for the US Sixth Army Group, Germany..418

Chapter 143 - THE FIRST 420

1558 hrs hrs, Tuesday, 26th March 1946, Ahlen, Germany.......420
1632 hrs, Tuesday, 26th March 1946, two hundred metres from the Werse River, Ahlen, Germany. 422
1645 hrs, Tuesday, 26th March 1946, two hundred metres from the Werse River, Ahlen, Germany. 423

1744 hrs, Tuesday, 26th March 1946, Werse River Bridge, Ahlen, Germany. 427

1814 hrs, Tuesday, 26th March 1946, Werse River Bridge, Ahlen, Germany. 429

1825 hrs, Tuesday, 26th March 1946, St. Bartholomäus, Ahlen, Germany. 432

1920 hrs, Tuesday, 26th March 1946, St. Bartholomäus, Ahlen, Germany. 434

2058 hrs, Tuesday, 26th March 1946, Hamelin Jail, Hamelin, Germany. 438

2328 hrs, Tuesday, 26th March 1946, St. Bartholomäus, Ahlen, Germany. 441

2359 hrs, Tuesday, 26th March 1946, St. Bartholomäus, Ahlen, Germany. 445

0639 hrs, Saturday, 30th March 1946, III/899th Grenadiere Regiment Rest Area, Gütersloh, Germany. 448

1549 hrs, Saturday, 30th April 1946, 899th Grenadiere Regiment Headquarters, Gastatte Dalbker Krug, Lippereihe, Germany. ... 453

2046 hrs, Sunday, 30th March 1946, 14th Guards [Ind] Engineer-Sapper Btn HQ, the Menkebach, Oerlinghausen, Germany. 456

0757 hrs, Sunday, 1st April 1946, the Teutobergerwald, Germany. 459

0809 hrs, Sunday, 1st April 1946, III/899th Grenadiere Forward Headquarters, on the Schopkettalweg, Lipperreihe, Germany. . 461

0924 hrs, Sunday, 1st April 1946, the Teutobergerwald, Germany. 473

0925 hrs, Sunday, 1st April 1946, the Teutobergerwald, Germany. 474

1703 hrs, Sunday, 1st April 1946, 899th Grenadiere Regiment Headquarters, Gaststatte Dalbker Krug, Lipperreihe, Germany. 476

1st April to 17th April 1946, Area of operations for the 1st German Republican Army Group, Germany. 477

Chapter 144 – THE TWENTY-FIRST 479

1600 hrs, Tuesday 26th March 1946, Schafstedt, Germany. 479

0502 hrs, Wednesday, 27th March 1946, Headquarters of 10th Guards Army, Bad Oldesloe, Germany. 483

0745 hrs, Wednesday, 27th March 1946, Field Headquarters of Prentiss Force, Bad Brahmstedt-land, Germany. 486

0850 hrs, Wednesday, 27th March 1946, Astride Route 111, Germany. 492

0939 hrs, Wednesday 27th March, 1945, 23rd Hussars HQ, Bauernhaus Holzbein, Bad Brahmstedt-land, Germany. 496

1005 hrs, Wednesday 27th March, 1945, Prentiss Force HQ, Hill 73, Bad Brahmstedt-land, Germany. 500

1015 hrs, Wednesday 27th March, 1945, Prentiss Force HQ, Hill 73, Bad Brahmstedt-land, Germany. 501

1015 hrs, Wednesday 27th March, 1945, Route 206, Bad Brahmstedt-land, Germany. 502

1111 hrs, Wednesday 27th March, 1945, Route 206, west of Bad Brahmstedt-land, Germany. 509

1121 hrs, Wednesday 27th March, 1945, Hill 79, adjacent to Route 206, Germany. 512

1232 hrs, Wednesday 27th March, 1945, Headquarters, Prentiss Force, Hill 73, Germany. 518

27th March to 14th April 1946, British Twenty-First Army Group's advance into Northern Germany. 522

1209 hrs, Sunday, 15th April 1946, 1st Baltic Front Headquarters, Heiligengrabe Abbey, Germany. 525

1312 hrs, Sunday, 15th April 1946, Guards Division positions, WittenbergerStrasse, Lützow, Germany. 527

1408 hrs, Sunday, 15th April 1946, 15th Motorised Rifle Brigade forward headquarters, west of Gottesgabe, Germany................. 535

1318 hrs, Sunday, 15th April 1946, Guards Division positions, WittenbergerStrasse, Lützow, Germany. 537

2020 hrs, Sunday, 15th April 1946, former Guards Division positions, WittenbergerStrasse, Lützow, Germany. 544

2040 hrs, Sunday, 15th April 1946, 15th Motorised Rifle Brigade forward headquarters, Gadebusch, Germany. 546

Chapter 145 - THE PANTOMIME 552

0259 hrs, 26th March 1946, Wollin and Hagen, Pomerania. 552

0921 hrs, Tuesday, 26th March 1946, Wollin, Pomerania. 553

0954 hrs, Tuesday 26th March 1946, Second Battalion CP, near Klein Mokratz, Pomerania. 556

1000 hrs, Tuesday 26th March 1946, Second Battalion front, near Grosse Mokratz, Pomerania. 557

1200 hrs, Tuesday 26th March 1946, Second Battalion front, near Grosse Mokratz, Pomerania. 559

1348 hrs, Tuesday 26th March 1946, HQ of 63rd NKVD Rifle Division, the woods west of Neu Kodram, Pomerania............... 565

2055 hrs, Tuesday 26th March 1946, Second Battalion front, near Grosse Mokratz, Pomerania. 567

2113 hrs, Tuesday 26th March 1946, Second Battalion front, near Grosse Mokratz, Pomerania. 575

0304 hrs, Friday, 29th March 1946, shoreline of the Vilm-See, Pomerania. 581

1001 hrs, Monday, 1st April 1946, Treptow Palace, PLAG Headquarters, Treptow an der Rega, Pomerania....................... 583

1236 hrs, Monday, 1st April 1946, HQ, 7th Guards Tank Assault Brigade, Wollchow, Pomerania. 588

1259 hrs, Monday, 1st April 1946, Naugard, Pomerania. 589

1331 hrs, Monday, 1st April 1946, HQ, 1st Guards Mechanised Rifle Division, Farbezin, Pomerania.. 592

1249 hrs, Monday, 1st April 1946, HQ, 7th Guards Tank Assault Brigade, Forward positions, Schwarzow - Naugard road, Pomerania. 599

1636 hrs, Wednesday, 3rd April 1946, Treptow Palace, PLAG Headquarters, Treptow an der Rega, Pomerania....................... 607

Chapter 146 - THE TWELTH 610

1400 hrs, Tuesday, 26th March 1946, US Third Army Headquarters, Hamm, Luxembourg.. 610

1803 hrs, Tuesday, 26th March 1946, US Third Army Headquarters, Hamm, Luxembourg.. 611

2323 hrs, Tuesday, 26th March 1946, US Third Army Headquarters, Hamm, Luxembourg.. 612

0723 hrs, Wednesday, 27th March 1946, Point units of the 35th US Infantry Division, Alf, Germany.. 615

0939 hrs, Wednesday, 27th March 1946, US Third Army Headquarters, Hamm, Luxembourg.. 618

1238 hrs, Thursday, 28th March 1946, US Third Army Headquarters, Haserich, Germany. 620

0621 hrs, Monday, 1st April, 1946, US Third Army Headquarters, Rheinböllen, Germany.. 621

1714 hrs, Saturday, 13th April 1946, US Third Army Headquarters, Ducal Palace, Wiesbaden, Germany.. 622

1117 hrs, Wednesday, 17th April 1946, outskirts of Reiskirchen, Germany. 624

Chapter 147 - THE RAMIFICATIONS.....................................628

1202 hrs, Wednesday, 24h April 1946, SHAEF Headquarters, Hotel Trianon, Versailles, France... 628

1209 hrs, Wednesday, 24h April 1946, Meeting Room 3, the Kremlin, Moscow. 629

Chapter 148 - THE DEVELOPMENT 636

0545 hrs, Monday 29th April, 1946, White Sands Bombing Range, New Mexico, USA. 636

Glossary.. 637

'Initiative' - the story continues. 649

Read the opening words of 'Initiative' now. 649

Chapter 149 - THE POWER 649

1000 hrs, Tuesday 30th April, Frankenberg an der Eder, Germany. 649

1100 hrs, Wednesday, 1st May, 1946, Red Square, Moscow, USSR, and the Oval Office, Washington DC, USA. 650

List of Figures within Sacrifice. 654

Bibliography... 657

'Sacrifice' and its contents have, of course, been dictated by the events of WW3. That has meant periods of relative inactivity militarily, followed by intense combat shoehorned into a few weeks.

Whilst I have tried to bring some breaks into the different passages of history, it may well be that the reader may find areas top heavy with either type of content.

I can only apologise but, for the most part, it has been important to follow events chronologically.

Fig# 117 - Map of Europe

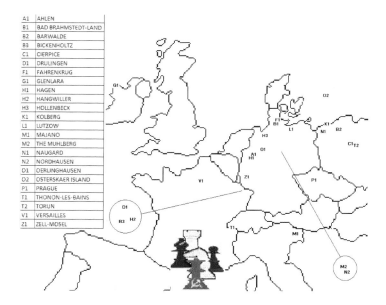

A1	AHLEN
B1	BAD BRAHMSTEDT-LAND
B2	BARWALDE
B3	BICKENHOLTZ
C1	CIERPICE
D1	DRULINGEN
F1	FAHRENKRUG
G1	GLENLARA
H1	HAGEN
H2	HANGWILLER
H3	HOLLENBECK
K1	KOLBERG
L1	LUTZOW
M1	MAJANO
M2	THE MUHLBERG
N1	NAUGARD
N2	NORDHAUSEN
O1	OERLINGHAUSEN
O2	OSTERSKAER ISLAND
P1	PRAGUE
T1	THONON-LES-BAINS
T2	TORUN
V1	VERSAILLES
Z1	ZELL-MOSEL

*It is forbidden to kill, therefore all murderers are punished, unless
they kill in large numbers, and to the sound of trumpets.*

Voltaire.

Chapter 126 - THE OPPONENTS.

The Soviet Union.

The Red Army.

At the start of the new war, the units of the Red Army's
ground forces had been at different strengths. Some had received
reinforcements before 6th August, mainly those with specific and
important tasks in the new plan, whereas others that had been
decimated in the heavy fighting of the final days of the German War
were left in a reduced state.

The overall effect of the constant fighting against their
new adversaries had been to remove a number of formations from
their order of battle, and to make others shadows of their former
selves. The Red Army at the start of 'Sacrifice' is not as numerous
as it was at the start of the war, as casualties had been extreme.

By example, Artem'yev's Guardsmen, the 179th Guards
Rifle Regiment, of the 59th Guards Rifle Division, of the 34th
Guards Rifle Corps, of the 5th Guards Army.

5th Guards Army was still an effective fighting formation,
as other units were slipped into its order of battle to replace some of
the casualties it had sustained. However, 34th Guards Rifle Corps
had been virtually destroyed, along with the 59th Division, and most
of Artem'yev's regiment. Admittedly, the 179th saw some brutal
fighting, and was virtually in constant action for weeks on end. By
the time that the unit was withdrawn from combat, post
Muggenhausen and Strassfeld, taking into account men returning
from hospitals, the 179th cadre consisted of 467 capable men, which
meant that it had lost 2147 men killed or so severely wounded that
they could not return to combat. That represented an incredible loss
of over 81% of the regimental strength. Whilst the 179th's war was
unusual, it was by no means the only example of 80% plus casualties
in the Soviet OOB.

By February 1946, the cold had also taken its toll, and there were very few frontline units from August 1945 that were at anything like full strength in manpower, weapons, and supplies.

Soviet ground force morale had been excellent in August, and had continued at a high level, except where heavy casualties and local reverses made themselves known. Such drops in morale tended to be temporary.

Two of the major factors that started to reduce morale permanently were the initial supply problems and the growing power of the Allied Air forces. As the advance slowed or was halted, morale started to decline across the board, assisted by the worsening weather.

The Soviet infantryman in Europe, during the early months of 1946, was not a happy soul. His kit was sufficient to keep him relatively warm, and food, although often a meal went missing, was enough to keep him on his feet and about combat effective, although the rations did not put meat on a man's bones.

Small arms ammunition was in plentiful supply, but there were decided issues with large calibre rounds, and the replacement of lost vehicles and weapons. The appearance of older tanks, removed from frontline service during the German War, gave sufficient warning that all was not well, although new types were also available and arriving with prime formations. Soviet artillery, for so long the powerful arm of the Red Army, was proving much less effective than previously, as Allied counter-battery fire, air attacks, and lack of ammunition combined to reduce their power. With regard to the artillery arm, casualties far outstripped replacements that made it to the front.

The Soviet Engineer forces had received good quantities of bridging gear, explosives and associated engineer equipment, and were probably the nearest to full strength of the military arms of the Red Army

Some new weaponry reached units in the west. SKS carbines made an appearance in numbers, but not enough to supplant the standard Mosin. The promising weapon was issued out to regiments all in one go, although, for some reason, this process started amongst the reserves and rear-line troops first, depriving most of the frontline units of an excellent weapon.

A new infantry weapon, one with great promise, had not yet entered production, as teething problems remained unsolved. However, the AK47 was being made a priority and facilities were already earmarked for its mass production.

The relative lull in hostilities should have given the ground forces time to recuperate, but Allied air and partisan attacks continued to play havoc with the system, although the latter were much decreased in effectiveness and frequency.

T54's, rushed through the approval process, were churned out as quickly as possible, and, although many were lost en route to the front, enough arrived to fully equip a few units. The vehicle had the potential to be a class above pretty much anything that the Allies could field, but production issues, quality control, and basic errors caused their new crews many headaches.

IS-III and IS-IV production picked up the pace but both types were not particularly numerous amongst frontline units, and for some reason, pre-delivery losses amongst these tanks were higher, well over 50% being lost in transit.

Numerous obsolete tanks, mostly the old 76mm equipped T-34's, were either field or main workshop converted to mobile AA guns, in an effort to counter the Allied air superiority. Tables of equipment were changed to provide increased AA protection across the spectrum of Soviet units, particularly adding more mobile AA defence to ground formations.

A factory production T-34m46 model with a 100mm weapon was produced in significant numbers, but suffered from lack of proper development, the turret size restrictions and ammunition size alone reducing its effectiveness.

Soviet production of a direct copy of the Panzerfaust placed a good quantity of the effective tank-killer in the infantry's hands, although there were occasionally some issues over the quality of explosive and with a lack of detonation, which made them unreliable at first.

A copy of the Rheinbote long-range artillery rocket was being tested, the Soviet version ramped up to carry an effective warhead.

So, in summary, the Red Army was less numerous and possessed less hardware in February 1946 than when it rolled across the battle line in August 1945. It had lost a lot of experienced soldiers on its way to the Rhine, and replacements of everything from men to machines arrived in dribs and drabs at the front.

New weapons that could give their soldiers an edge were arriving slowly.

The artillery arm was a shadow of its former self, and was increasing hampered by serious supply issues, as was all of the Red Army.

One simple crucial problem was oil, more specifically fuel. The absence of sufficient quantities of it, or the absence of quality stocks, afflicted every arm of service.

Even the most 'bull at a gate' Soviet Generals understood that their machine was broken and no longer the all-conquering force it had once been.

None the less, driven by both professional pride and political pressure from Moscow, the Red Army developed plans to renew the offensive in the spring of '46.

Perhaps some of the political will in Moscow derived from claims made by the scientists working on the USSR and Japan's joint enterprise, Project Raduga.

The Red Air Force.

After its spectacular success with the sneak attacks of 6th August, the Air Force had done extremely well, but the capacity of the Allied air arm to absorb its losses, recover, and reinforce had been hugely underestimated.

Soviet control of the air was brief, if it ever happened at all, and it was only a matter of weeks before the growing Allies established relative control of the European skies.

Again, there was serious misinterpretation of the capabilities of the aircraft that they opposed, and Soviet pilots found themselves at a technical disadvantage across the board.

Before winter set in, the Red Air Force had been totally dismantled as an effective unit, rarely flying across No Man's land, and generally used solely to respond in defence of Allied incursions.

Specifically, the greatest defect in Soviet thinking, accompanied by a gap in Red Air Force capability, was in the inability to meaningfully intercept the large formations of bomber aircraft that roamed across Soviet-held Europe. Despite a one-off savaging handed out to the RAF night bomber force, and that achieved mainly by flak it should be noted, the remaining interceptors proved unable to prevent attacking formations from reaching their targets, exposing the logistics and infrastructure networks to great harm.

Even pressing every single captured heavy AA weapon into service proved little inconvenience to the Allied swarm.

During the air battles over the southern Baltic, the Allied trap had removed whole regiments of aircraft from the Soviet inventory, as well as savaging elements of the Baltic Fleet.

Soviet pilot training programmes were accelerated, and new aircraft types were pushed forward as quickly as possible, but it would be some time before the Red Air Force had any hope of meeting their opponents on equal terms, if ever.

Surprisingly, morale amongst the pilots of Soviet Aviation remained high in the face of extreme adversity and heavy casualties.

In summary, the Red Air Force had been crippled by its efforts to support the Red Army and would, for the foreseeable future, only achieve air superiority by concentrating large numbers of its remaining aircraft in one operation, leaving other areas exposed and defenceless.

There was next to no thought given to developing a heavy bomber that could hit back at their enemy.

Standards of pilot training inevitably lowered but there was no shortage of personnel wanting the opportunity to fly in defence of the Rodina.

Slowly, aircraft of worth would arrive but, in the interim, those that flew would be always outnumbered and mainly outclassed.

The Red Navy

In the initial stages of the new war, the Red Navy's submarine force had enjoyed an incredible run of good fortune and luck, sinking some important Allied naval and merchant assets. In particular, the type XXI U-Boats, captured from the Germans, had been ultra-effective.

The Allies had been slow to effectively respond, which enhanced the Soviet rewards, but they slowly started to sink the Atlantic submarine force.

By late-November, the Red Navy's serious assets were all lost or interned in various neutral ports on the Atlantic seaboard.

The Soviets considered the Baltic their sea, and rose to the challenge of the trap set by the Allies. Hand in hand with their Aviation colleagues, the sailors of the Baltic Fleet lost heavily in the deception operation in the Southern Baltic. This reduced the Baltic Fleet to defensive duties, with the exception of a few submarines still functioning.

Given the needs of the Army and Air Force, Soviet thinking did not encompass reinforcing the fleets, except for modest efforts to replicate the German process of building the type XXI submarine in separate sections in different locations.

28

It would be no surprise that the morale of the Baltic Fleet was extremely low as 1945 moved into 1946.

In summary, the Baltic Fleet was a spent force, barely capable of policing its own shoreline, its only ability to take the fight properly to the Allies lying with its remaining submarines, who would have to operate under effective Allied airborne coverage, and against the once again effective anti-submarine groups of the Royal and United States navies.

The Northern Fleet and the Pacific fleet had their own problems. The former was blockaded by U-boats and British submarines, the latter confined to its ports by the huge presence of the United States Navy, whose carrier aircraft attacked on a daily basis.

In essence, the Red Navy was a spent force, except for the Black Sea Fleet, whose geographical location meant its ability to influence matters was not high.

Soviet Allies.

In general, forces from Rumania, Bulgaria et al, mirrored those of the Red Army in terms of morale and supply. The exceptions were the Poles who, despite the ransacking of their inventory by Soviet officers keen to resupply the damaged Red Army formations in Western Europe, still enjoyed high morale, possibly because they were, more often than not, garrisoned on home or friendly soil, and were not the subject of heavy air attack.

Imperial Japan.

Mainland Japan was suffering at the commencement of hostilities, and its position has not improved, save that the Allies have lowered the number of offensive bombing missions, simply because there is little of value left to bomb. The nation is slowly starving, despite desperate agricultural measures and rationing that borders on starvation.

In clandestine raids on 6th August 1945, seemingly innocent merchantmen carried the war to the US Navy in a way that the Imperial Navy no longer could. Sneak attacks on US naval installations had been fruitful and damaged Allied efforts in the Pacific area.

At the start of the renewed hostilities, the Chinese-based military forces of Imperial Japan had enjoyed a resurgence and a change in fortunes, ground attacks being generally successful as units equipped with Soviet supplied weapons used their increased firepower to good advantage. Those units equipped with German tanks and vehicles proved extremely effective on the appropriate terrain.

The Communist Chinese, at the behest of the Soviets, and against their better judgement, permitted the Japanese units to advance into contact with the Nationalist forces unopposed.

However, the Chinese Nationalists rallied and managed to halt most of the assaults, and reinforcements started to arrive from the States, bringing large well-equipped formations to the battle, albeit units that had been destined for the Japanese home islands. Soviet units were committed in small numbers, more to maintain the façade of Soviet goodwill and full support, rather than to achieve military success.

Military activity to the south accelerated the advance of the British and Dominion troops, pressing ever northwards to threaten the southern borders of China, squeezing Japanese land forces into a reduced area.

Most of the Soviet military strength assigned to eastern areas was concentrated on opposing any Allied landings on the coast of Mother Russia and in preservation of national boundaries, and Vasilevsky, the Soviet commander, faced enquiry after enquiry regarding forces that could be transferred back to Europe.

Occasionally, an enquiry became an order, and a unit would entrain for the Western Front, leaving the east more and more exposed.

In general, the Japanese soldiers engaged on the mainland were tired and underfed, but still enjoyed good morale, despite some recent reverses.

Similarly, the pilots of the Imperial Air Force maintained their esprit de corps, despite the dwindling supplies of aviation fuel and aircraft spares.

Put simply, there was no Imperial Japanese Navy anymore, and the Allied rode the seas with impunity.

Japanese efforts to produce an atomic weapon had virtually ground to a halt, as scientists moved east to work alongside Soviet colleagues, all for the greater good.

In summary, the Imperial Forces were less supported and less well-equipped than at the start of the new war. The Soviet Union had much less to send in any case, plus Allied bombers also turned their attention to the Chinese infrastructure, causing similar problems to those wreaked in Europe.

There was no reinforcement available for Japanese units, and stocks of munitions and weapons were constantly reduced by fighting or by destruction from the air.

In essence, the Pacific War was already lost, although it would take many months and many more deaths before it was acknowledged by those in power in Tokyo.

The Allies.

Allied Ground Forces.

At the start of the new war, Allied forces in Europe were singularly unprepared for a restart of hostilities, and early Soviet results illustrated the Allied units' generally reduced effectiveness, with a few notable exceptions.

The Americans, in particular, had moved back large numbers of veteran soldiers, ready for demobbing or, in many cases, to be sent to the Pacific, earmarked for the Invasion of Japan. This had left their European units short in both numbers and quality.

The flow of men and materiel to their home countries was stopped quickly, and reversed, ensuring that units quickly recovered some of their fighting strength.

The Red Navy's success with its small submarine force made inroads into the reinforcement efforts during the opening weeks, further assisting the Red Army's advances.

POWs were absorbed into units, helping to bring numbers up to TOE levels, although the ex-prisoners were often weakened and less fit.

Despite some valiant defensive work, the Soviet advances continued and Allied casualties mounted, with some divisions struck from the order of battle due to combat casualties.

Slowly the Soviet advance was halted, as much by air attack and supply difficulties as by steadfast defence.

Units of the new German Republic gathered themselves and soon became a significant part of the order of battle, taking over the Ruhr and a part of the Italian Front.

Similarly, Spain had committed a number of divisions to the Allied cause.

Other Allies sent men across the Atlantic and, combined with troops from the States, the UK and dominion states, France and the German Republic, the Allied armies started to recover their numbers.

As the supply effort cranked up to higher levels, larger numbers of German POWs made their way to Europe from Canada and the USA, swelling the ranks of the German Republican Army even further.

Equipment-wise, the production lines recently turned over to civilian goods again churned out the chattels of war, and tanks, vehicles, guns and ammunition once more flowed in incessant lines from factory to front line.

New equipment, or variations on old, started to appear in numbers that could make a difference.

Conversions like the T20E2 Garand, which put even more firepower in the hands of the US infantryman. Additions like a regulation issue of Winchester shotguns to infantry platoons, a decision made as a result of the high levels of close-quarters fighting encountered since August 1945.

Other technology started to arrive, such as infra-red sights in numbers that could directly affect infantry and tank tactics.

The need for heavier armed and armoured tanks was quickly identified, as the Sherman found itself at a huge disadvantage, much the same as it had against the late German tanks, except the Soviets seemed to have superior vehicles in greater numbers. Much of the Sherman output that arrived in late '45, early '46, was the M4A3E2 Jumbo version, with the 76mm gun and considerably more armour. Production of the Super Pershing was stepped up and, yet again, development projects were pushed along quickly to provide the man in the front line with a weapon of war to do the job.

The Invasion of Japan was put on hold indefinitely, with the Soviet incursion into Europe being made the focus of all Allied efforts, save small numbers of troops sent to reinforce the Chinese Nationalists.

The air war against Japan and mainland China was intensified.

Whilst improvements and technological advances again benefitted from the imperatives of active warfare, the decisions made ensured that priority was given to tried and trusted hardware, which was to be delivered in the numbers needed to throw back the Communist hordes.

Thinking started to change when numbers of newer model Soviet tanks made their presence known, and existing tank types were suddenly found wanting. Development projects shelved as the Allies basked in the glory of the German defeat were restarted and given increased impetus by the imperatives of the front.

The Allied infantryman in Europe, during the early months of 1946, was much the same as his Soviet counterpart. Whilst kit was reasonably functional, in general, the Allied soldiers were less hardy and found the freezing conditions less bearable, a higher number succumbing to temperature related conditions.

Supply was generally good, although there were occasional local shortages, caused mainly by the extreme conditions, and occasionally by pro-communist groups ambushing supply convoys.

That the Allies had command of the air was a boost to morale, but the Allied ground troops were battered and bruised by the hard defensive fighting of the later months of 1945, and morale had become a problem amongst some of the more junior formations, especially those that had seen hard fighting.

Those that were new and recently arrived steeled themselves for the horrors to come.

Allied Air Forces.

Having taken a very real beating in August 1945, the Allied Air Forces bounced back surprisingly quickly, re-establishing their numbers quickly and seeking domination of the skies in short order.

However, the effectiveness of the force had taken a severe knock, and it was not until October 1945 that domination went hand in hand with fully effective air operations across the spectrum of air combat.

The ground attack force, which had taken a deliberately higher hit from the initial Soviet attacks, recovered least quickly, part of the reason that the Red Army advances continued into November 1945.

As 1946 was ushered in, aircraft and pilots available began to approach January 1945 numbers, without taking into account the experienced pool of ex-Luftwaffe air crew that was steadily being retrained on available Allied aircraft types, or being returned to the fray in captured German machines.

Morale in the Allied Air Forces was extremely high. They knew that they had achieved mastery of the air, and had inflicted grievous losses on the opposition.

Morale was further boosted by the arrival of decent quantities of superior new aircraft, such as the F80 Shooting Star, Gloster Metoer and de Havilland Vampire, enabling the Allies to stay ahead of their enemy across the spectrum of disciplines.

Whilst the report of the attack on Maaldrift highlighted some unfortunate circumstances, poor judgement, and incredible luck on the part of the small attacking force, no chances were taken. Security at all air force establishments was greatly increased and the few further attempts made were nipped in the bud, without the loss of a single Allied aircraft.

A weapon used in limited quantities in the German War, namely napalm, found itself further developed and refined. It began to be used in increasing quantities, as its effectiveness against the mass formations favoured by the Red Army was realized, as well as its capacity against fixed positions or, indeed, to demoralize anything in the vicinity of an attack.

It was estimated that, by 26th March 1946, 40% of all munitions delivered by ground attack aircraft were napalm-based.

The Allied Navies

Having been troubled by the surprisingly effective Soviet submarine efforts in the early stages of the war, the Allied Navies accepted criticism that they had not responded effectively for far too long, particularly in regard to the threat of the type XXI.

The anti-submarine groups were quickly re-established and worked up to peak performance, establishing domination of all waters in which they worked.

There had also been some glaring errors in intelligence, that had permitted interned Soviet shipping to function as supply vessels in neutral ports, and serious errors of judgement regarding the possibilities of established Soviet bases beyond the mouth of the Baltic.

Some excused the issues, given the lack of serious threat from the Kriegsmarine in the closing months of the German War, but it was generally accepted that the Navies, across the range of nations, had been caught well and truly on the hop.

However, the problems were addressed, with more than one senior commander finding himself sailing a smaller desk, in a new job with less responsibility.

By the time of the Baltic phase of Operation Spectrum, the Allied Navies were back functioning at top level, and the results of the 'ambush' of Red Air Force and Navy assets in the Baltic illustrated that in spades.

In the Pacific, the USN adopted responsibility for blockading Japan, Manchuria, and the Soviet Eastern seaboard. Two excursions by Soviet Pacific fleet submarines enjoyed little success and the losses had sent a clear message to Soviet naval command, ensuring their assets stayed in port.

Battleships and cruisers launched the numerous forays into Chinese waters, cruising off-shore, taking out an airfield here, a bridge there. Smaller warships moved in closer, patrolling up and down the Chinese coast, seeking targets of opportunity, all of which ensured that the seas in the east remained very firmly under Allied control.

The lack of any Soviet or Japanese naval presence of note meant that there was no pressure to encourage further Allied naval development, although the Midway, Coral Sea and Franklin D. Roosevelt heavy carriers had been completed and sent to persecute the Siberian mainland.

Allied technology

The failure of the programme's plutonium test in July 1945 caused a rethink of the plans to invade Japan, although that rethink had not prevented the exodus of units from Europe until the Soviets attacked.

Scientists assured their political masters that a device would be ready by summer 1946; indeed, the uranium bomb was considered ready to go, and had been for some time. It was the plutonium bomb that awaited a successful trial in the desert at White Sands.

Given the limited amount of suitable fissionable material available, the decision had been made not to deploy any devices until the military situation in Europe became more or less favourable. If the Soviets produced a surprise, then the weapons could be deployed as strategic weapons capable of destroying huge numbers of soldiers. If, when the Allies advanced, stubborn pockets of resistance grew, they could be used to eliminate such positions. Should Soviet defences prove insurmountable, or should the political will of the people falter, then they would be delivered on top of political targets in the Soviet Union, to break the enemy's will first.

That was the basic plan, in the limited circles that knew of the existence of the weapons.

However, it was the political objections of others, mainly from the Allied nations, which made the use of such devices in continental Europe a political hot-potato.

Whilst the senior Allied leaders had not been told the full technical details and facts, the general outline of what was possible had been revealed, and most had recoiled from idea of using such 'big' bombs.

German designations for Republican Forces.

German Army – DRH – Deutsches Republikanisch Heer.
German Air Force – DRL – Deutsches Republikanisch Luftwaffe.
German Navy – DRK –Deutsches Republikanisch Kreigsmarine

German Republican and Austrian Forces

By the time of the meeting of the Allied Powers at Versailles on 22nd February, German and Austrian forces in Italy totalled fourteen and four divisions respectively, most of which were considered combat ready.

German forces in Germany and France totalled thirty-seven divisions, of which twenty-nine were considered combat ready.

German forces in Norway had been reduced during the early months of the war, partially by transfers to the mainland and partially by combining units to increase effectiveness. Eight divisions remained, all of which were in full fighting order.

In addition, Luftwaffe strength had risen to thirty-eight Staffel, although the lack of German aircraft meant that many were equipped with Allied aircraft or were still retraining on various Allied types.

German production had been partially restored, mainly by the superhuman efforts of Speer and his staff, and some items were being produced in France and the Low Countries, under an agreement that was beneficial to all countries.

The ST-44 and MG-42 both rolled off French and German production lines, mainly the former in truth, and other facilities commenced manufacturing the ammunition, although immense quantities still remained from the previous war.

Initial attempts by France to manufacture Panthers were mainly failures, but the relocated German production lines, although few and slow at first, started production of the Panther II, the tooling for which had been mostly saved from Allied bombing.

Eventually, France also produced the hastily upgraded 1946 design for the Ausf F Panther, which became universally known as the Jaguar

Priority was given to the production of 88mm and 128mm tubes, the former to equip the Jaguar that was expected to be Germany's battle tank for the coming years, and the latter for a redesign of the Jagdpanther and for heavy anti-tank guns, both of which were already under construction in Belgium by FN and Imperia respectively.

There was no aircraft production of note in early 1946.

The Kriegsmarine found itself contributing submarines and coastal vessels to the war effort, surplus manpower being sent for training in the Army.

The French Army

Mistakes had been made, and De Gaulle's attempt to field a large force of poorly organized divisions, which had some limited success against an already defeated German Army, fell foul of the fighting skills of an organised Red Army on the offensive.

Divisions which were, to all intents and purposes useless, were withdrawn and the dross weeded out, leaving enough manpower to initially field seven reasonable divisions, not including the expanding Foreign Legion. An intense period of training started integrating POWs and new blood together, the plan being to field a total of thirty divisions for the Allied order of battle.

The target was viewed with a jaundiced eye by Allied commanders, who had seen France's desperate efforts to get numbers in the field, and had observed as the project failed miserably.

A reasonable amount of French industrial capacity was restored as quickly as possible, sometimes to introduce new all-French designs, such as the ARL-44, or to churn out tried and tested weapons of war, such as the ST-44 and MG-42.

Initial attempts by both Renault and Berliet produced Panthers, but the marriage of French engines and the cut-down 17-pdr to a proven German design failed, so none were made operational in the first instance. The restoration of equipment hastily salvaged from the Maybach plant at Friedrichshafen ensured proper engines eventually became available, but most were assigned to German produced vehicles.

A number of the Maybach-engined French versions, called the Panther Felix, made their way into forward units and performed surprisingly well. However, once Speer had rejuvenated the German industrial base, albeit spread throughout the low countries and France, as well as Germany, the proper combination of Maybach, 88mm L/71 and Panther chassis started to appear from German industry and facilities spread throughout free Europe.

Development, refinement and production of the X7 wire-guided missile system was undertaken in a specially constructed facility near Sassy, France, chosen because of its nearness to the Legion depot for ex-SS personnel, who were the only troops with the experience of using the weapons in the previous conflict.

Given the large numbers of aircraft available from US and UK factories, France undertook no serious aircraft development.

Author's note on the forces-

I have redrawn a basic order of battle for the European front. That can be found either in the Sacrifice biographies, or can be downloaded as an xls file from the website, free of charge.

www.redgambitseries.com
www.redgambitseries.co.uk
www.redgambitseries.eu

Also included in either location is the European map I have posted under this entry, which gives the approximate frontline positions of the two armies that are preparing to make 1946 one of the bloodiest years in history.

Fig# 118 – Explanation of Military Map Symbols

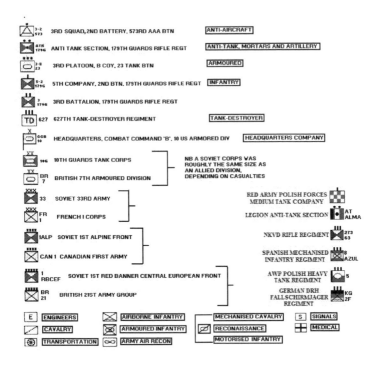

3RD SQUAD, 2ND BATTERY, 573RD AAA BTN — **ANTI-AIRCRAFT**

ANTI TANK SECTION, 179TH GUARDS RIFLE REGT — **ANTI-TANK, MORTARS AND ARTILLERY**

3RD PLATOON, B COY, 23 TANK BTN — **ARMOURED**

5TH COMPANY, 2ND BTN, 179TH GUARDS RIFLE REGT — **INFANTRY**

3RD BATTALION, 179TH GUARDS RIFLE REGT

627TH TANK-DESTROYER REGIMENT — **TANK-DESTROYER**

HEADQUARTERS, COMBAT COMMAND 'B', 10 US ARMORED DIV — **HEADQUARTERS COMPANY**

10TH GUARDS TANK CORPS

BRITISH 7TH ARMOURED DIVISION

NB A SOVIET CORPS WAS ROUGHLY THE SAME SIZE AS AN ALLIED DIVISION, DEPENDING ON CASUALTIES

SOVIET 33RD ARMY

FRENCH I CORPS

RED ARMY POLISH FORCES MEDIUM TANK COMPANY

LEGION ANTI-TANK SECTION — AT ALMA

IALP SOVIET 1ST ALPINE FRONT

CAN 1 CANADIAN FIRST ARMY

NKVD RIFLE REGIMENT

SPANISH MECHANISED INFANTRY REGIMENT — AZUL

SOVIET 1ST RED BANNER CENTRAL EUROPEAN FRONT

BRITISH 21ST ARMY GROUP

AWP POLISH HEAVY TANK REGIMENT

GERMAN DRH FALLSCHIRMJAGER REGIMENT — KG 2F

E — **ENGINEERS**

CAVALRY

TRANSPORTATION

AIRBORNE INFANTRY

ARMOURED INFANTRY

ARMY AIR RECON

MECHANISED CAVALRY

RECONAISSANCE

MOTORISED INFANTRY

S — **SIGNALS**

MEDICAL

40

Fig# 119 - The Military Map of Europe, March 1946.

Additionally, I have created a sheet that will show those who wish to know which weapons are either arriving or will become operational in 1946. This list may not be for everyone, so it is not included in the books and will solely be available on the website or facebook.

God rest ye merry Gentlemen
Let nothing you dismay
Remember, Christ, our saviour
Was born on Christmas Day
To save us all from Satan's power
When we were gone astray
O tidings of comfort and joy
Comfort and joy
O tidings of comfort and joy.

Anon.

Chapter 127 - THE ANNIHILATION

1317 hrs, Wednesday, 25th December 1945, airborne above North-West Eire.

Smoke poured from the two outboard engines, leaving parallel lines in the sky as the crippled B-24 Liberator tried to make the nearest friendly territory.

Despite the obviously fraught situation, everyone aboard the Coastal Command aircraft was calm, and there was even laughter amidst the serious activity of their real mission.

It fell to the navigator to bring failure or success, for his skill would bring the Liberator directly to the precise point where they would achieve the task set them… or they would fail.

There would be no repeats, so it was imperative that the B-24 hit its mark right on the button.

He thumbed his mike.

"Navigator, Pilot. Come left two degrees, Skipper, course 89°."

"Roger, Nav."

After a short delay, the navigator, sweating despite the extremely cold temperatures, spoke again.

"On course, Skipper. Estimate seven minutes to game point."

"Roger, Nav. Bombs?"

"I'm on it, Skipper."

The bombardier shifted to one side of the modified nose and checked for the umpteenth time that the internal heating circuit was functioning.

"Bombs, Pilot. Ready."

The pilot looked across to his co-pilot.

"Time for you to play."

It was Christmas Day, and most of those still asleep bore all the hallmarks of heavy encounters with the local brews, Russian and Irishmen alike.

A few, an unlucky few, had literally drawn short straws and found themselves sober and alert, providing the security whilst others spent the day acquainting themselves with their blankets or, in the case of a few, the latrines.

Seamus Brown was one of the selected few, and it was he who first heard the sounds of an aircraft in trouble.

The staccato sound of misfiring engines and the drone of their fully working compatriots mingled and grew loud enough to be a warning in their own right.

The camp was occasionally overflown, so there were provisions for this moment, and Brown instigated them immediately.

A large bell was rung, only a few double blows from a hammer were needed to warn the base what was about to happen. It was a question of keeping out of sight for most, but balancing that with having a few bodies in sight so as not to make the place seem deserted which, quite reasonably, they had all agreed might make the camp suspicious, even though most of it could not be seen from the air.

Brown dropped his rifle into a wheelbarrow, and started to move across the central open area, his eyes searching the sky for the noisemaker.

"Nav, Pilot. Thirty seconds."

"Roger. Bombs, over to you."

The Bomb Aimer looked through the unfamiliar sight and decided that he could proceed.

The finger hovered above the button pressed hard and the shooting commenced.

Brown kept walking, his eyes taking in the smokey trails from two of its engines, his ears adding to the evidence of his eyes.

'The fucking bastards are in trouble'.

"Crash, you fucking English shites! Go on! Merry fucking Christmas, you bastards!"

A couple of his men chuckled and shared the sentiment, although not quite as loud as Brown.

His raised voice brought a response from some of those aching from the night's exertions and windows were opened, the oaths and curses directed his way not always in Irish brogue.

The Liberator, for he was sure that was what it was, kept dropping lower in the sky and eventually flew below his line of vision.

In his mind, he enjoyed the image of the mighty aircraft nose-diving into some Irish hillside and promised himself that he would find out what happened at some time.

Turning to the nearest open window, the small hut hidden under a camouflage of turf roof and adjacent shrubs, Brown tackled the aggressor.

"I don't know what the fuck you are saying my little Russian friend, but if you don't fuck off, I'll shoot you."

The words were said as if he was apologizing for waking the Soviet marine; his smile was one of sincere regret.

The Matrose nodded and closed the window, happy that the stupid Irishman would not repeat his error.

The Liberator continued on for some miles before the navigator gave another change of course, this time turning northwards and put to sea.

Once clear of land, the smoke generators were turned off, the co-pilot stopped palying with the throttles, and the B-24 resumed its journey to RAF Belfast. There it was met by two members of the SOE Photo interpretation section, specially flown in from the Tempsford base to look at the stills and movie footage shot by the special duty crew as they passed precisely over the IRA base at Glenlara.

2002 hrs, Thursday, 26th December 1945, Camp 5A, near Cookstown, County Tyrone, Northern Ireland.

Wijers helped the female officer carry her stuff from the car into the lecture room.

Section Officer Megan Jenkins, and one other, had been rushed from RAF Tempsford to RAF Belfast, where they joined up with the film produced by the B-24 Liberator pass over Glenlara.

The stills were easier to produce quickly, so Megan Jenkins had already examined them and found a great deal of information that would be of use to those present.

She had not waited to view the film footage before she left for Camp 5A so, once everything was set-up and introductions were made, the movie footage from the fly by was shown for the first time.

The others in the room looked at surprisingly good clarity shots and were surprised, allowing that surprise to mask what the film contained.

Not so Jenkins and her assistant, who made notes and, when the short film had ended, compared them.

The assistant, a male Sergeant, removed the film from the projector and took it away to make some copies of still frames that they had selected during the show. A small suitcase contained everything they would need, Wijers showing the Sergeant to a suitable dark place.

The room had been set up to her requirements, so Jenkins moved across to the table, spread with white paper, and started to draw her map.

The others in the room gathered round, careful not to get between her and the maps and photos.

The speed and accuracy with which she worked was seriously impressive and, before their eyes, a map of the whole IRA camp started to appear.

The Sergeant reappeared, holding some of the images selected from the movie. In the manner of specialists throughout the services, he enjoyed his moment in the limelight, taking the main map and annotating it with the reference number of one of the new pictures.

Two in particular were of great note, and Jenkins moved between her hand drawn map and the new photographs, comparing and adjusting.

Wijers was the first to voice doubts.

"Officer Jenkins, these two positions here… and here… the new ones… they are not in these photographs."

Megan smiled, knowing that not everyone could grasp the science of photo interpretation.

"Here, Sir, these are from the movie. When we watched," she indicated the smug looking Sergeant, "Both of us saw a flash, small, but there for sure. The new pictures prove it. The flashes were caused by reflections… something moving in the light, such as a window, a mirror, a glass, anything like that."

She moved back to the original photos and selected one that covered the new 'position' nearest the water's edge.

"Here. If you look carefully, that flash would come from this point here. See?"

He didn't.

"Look here, Sir. Here is a shadow band. The sun is to the south east, so this shadow is on the northern edge of the position. The bushes muddy the waters a little… and I'll have to study them a lot closer, but my experience tells me that this position is roughly eleven foot tall from ground level."

Wijers looked at her and the photograph without comprehension.

"To be honest, Sir, I'm a little annoyed that I didn't see it first time. Still, got it now."

The Dutchman still didn't see it.

Neither did Sam Rossiter, head of OSS Europe.

Michael Rafferty, top man in Northern Ireland's Special Branch couldn't either.

Much to his surprise, the last officer in the room could see it perfectly.

Turning his attention back to the hand drawn plan, he found himself well satisfied.

"Offizier Jenkins, can you put everything down on this map here. Find every position and put it here?"

"Yes, of course, Major. You tell me what you want, I will put it there.

De facto Sturmbannfuhrer and leader of the OSS's special Ukrainian force but, for the purposes of Megan Jenkins, Major Shandruk of the US Army, nodded to Rossiter.

"More than enough, Colonel."

He turned his eyes back to the plan, his mind already assessing how the job would be done and how, at the end of the operation, Glenlara would be nothing but a wasteland.

Revenge is barren of itself; it is the dreadful food on which it feeds;
its delight is murder, and its end is despair.

Friedrich Schiller.

Chapter 128 - THE WASTELAND

In the short period of time available, they had moved the proverbial mountain.

Having a friendly RAF base commander with a vested interest in the mission's success had helped a lot.

The close availability of the necessary assets was also instrumental in making the rapidly constructed mission possible.

Set close to Castle Archdale, the uninhabited Inishmakill Island, with its western side bay, had proved perfect for the task, and an old facility there was, after a little work, sufficient for temporarily housing a group of forty men. The thick woods that covered the whole area provided both shelter and cover, guaranteeing secrecy.

There could be no second photographic run over Glenlara, so Megan Jenkins and her Sergeant worked over and over again on the evidence to hand, bouncing interpretations off each other, adding to the map, and building the fullest possible picture of the layout of base, and what problems might present themselves to those tasked with its destruction.

On Inishmakill, the assault group quickly reconstructed the old metal structure, adding their own embellishments, and made themselves comfortable, spending their time working on the weapons, sharpening the more silent tools of death, checking battery packs and personal equipment.

Alerted by a brief radio transmission, six of the men were at the water's edge when one of 201 Squadron's motor boats grated ashore.

Three passengers leapt onto dry land, and four bags were handed over by the RAF boat crew. A helpful shove freed the keel, and the small craft disappeared back into the descending night.

Fig# 120 – Forces involved at Glenlara, Monday, 1st January, 1946.

GLENLARA RAID 1ST JANUARY 1946.

MARINE SPECIAL
ACTION FORCE 27

IRREGULAR UNIT.
MAYO BTN. IRA

OSS SPECIAL
ACTION GROUP

Jenkins and Viljoen were impressed, although both also felt a little out of their depth, surrounded, as they were, by men who looked like their sole purpose in life was to kill. The uniforms and weapons also told them that Shandruk and his men were not as had been presented.

The Ukrainian group had been smuggled onto Inishmakill on the night of the 28th, and had remained hidden since then.

Shandruk, who had made the short journey over from Castle Archdale with the two RAF officers, had called his men to order and a quiet circle formed.

Viljoen was introduced and swiftly went through his part in matters. His cooperation had never been in doubt, given the death of his brother. In fact, it had taken direct intervention from Sam Rossiter to hold him in check, so enthusiastic was he for revenge.

The flight plan was simple, and there were no questions for him to answer.

Jenkins' presentation was more detailed, and had required more setting up.

Four oil drums and some planks made up a table, on which a large plan was unrolled, and various box-like structures were added to show where buildings lay, so that the circle of men could better appreciate the wall plan that Jenkins used. Shandruk, a broom handle in hand, mirrored Jenkins' brief with his own movement over the table model.

Whilst the photo reconnaissance mission had been rushed, the interpretation had been excellent, and the secrets of Glenlara were laid bare in front of the watching group.

Building usage was an issue, but, again, experience came to the fore, and the interpreters made a good case for which ones were store areas, barracks, et al.

Even so, some buildings and bunkers had no purpose that could even be guessed at, which had added complication to the planning.

Jenkins and Viljoen sat back, ready to answer any questions that might arise, as Shandruk and Kuibida, his senior non-com, swung rapidly into the tactical plan.

Surprise was key.

Silence was key.

Speed was key.

The plan was simple and straightforward, as all such plans should be, but, as in all plans, they expected things to change, so contingencies were discussed.

There had already been one forced change. The Ukrainian's medic had tripped and broken his ankle whilst they were setting up the island base.

He was already back at Camp 5a, and a replacement present for the briefing at the Inishmakill camp. The fit 63 year old man wore nondescript white camouflage clothing, which neatly matched his hair.

When the question had been posed to him, Doc Holliday had leapt at the chance, glad to be able to get involved in the operation that would avenge the slaughtered men of 201 Squadron.

It would not be his first time in combat either.

When he was a much younger man, he and his comrades had landed on W Beach at Cape Helles, Turkey; part of the ill-fated Gallipoli landings.

His venerable Webley Mk V service pistol, his constant companion since his first day in uniform, had drawn some ribbing from the Ukrainians, although they knew a cared-for piece when they saw one, and none underestimated it, knowing that such a weapon was still a lethal thing.

Fig# 121 – Joint IRA-Soviet Naval Camp, Glenlara, Eire.

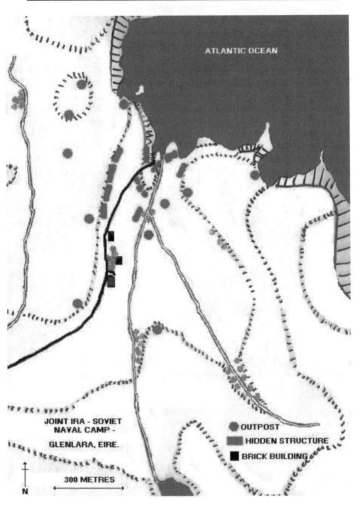

The whole force, forty-two strong, was split into five groups, each commanded by an officer or NCO, and equipped with two SCR-536 handie-talkies [HT].

On landing, each group had tasks that required it to split up into smaller sections; taking out guard posts, providing security, and setting up the specialist kit.

Once the initial phase was complete, the group would come back together and, on the order, make the assault.

Shandruk's headquarters group, with the only main scheme radio, was where the orders would come from; four men strong, including the venerable Holliday. In close support, but initially uncommitted, would be a larger group of ten, under the command of Kuibida, acting as a reserve if things changed.

'For when things changed'.

A four man section, each soldier expressing open disappointed as he was selected, was tasked with providing security at the rear, to ensure no surprises.

The remaining twenty-four men were equally split into three groups, each one tasked with the silent killing of the occupants of Glenlara.

Occasionally, Shandruk ceded the floor to Jenkins, needing her to clarify a point for one or other of his men.

Although her Welsh accent and strong looks had long since captivated her listeners, it was her professionalism that they respected most.

Shandruk again took the lead, emphasizing the group mission.

"Comrades… we take no risks to get prisoners here. Any risk, they die. If we can secure a Soviet officer, then our masters will be happy."

He turned to the board and, with a definite flourish, pinned two pictures up.

"Now then."

Pointing at each in turn, he announced their names.

"Reynolds… Brown…"

Catching Viljoen's eye, he nodded his silent agreement to the RAF man's earlier plea.

"If you can take these two alive, then do it. The Intelligence Services want them very much. Our Air Force friends also have business with them, which will take priority."

They all knew what that was. At first, the story had been an ugly rumour, until the combination of Holliday and an excess of Irish Whisky had laid bare the full horror of what had happened to the Sunderland's crew. Each of the Ukrainians understood perfectly, and made an unspoken promise to the RAF officer.

'If it's possible, you'll have your revenge, comrade.'

The briefing complete, the group waited on the one essential piece of information not yet made clear.

"Boys… we go tomorrow. All in order for 2300. Clear?"

It was.

"Happy New Year."

2358 hrs, Tuesday, 31st December 1945, Lough Erne, Northern Ireland.

The three Sunderland Flying boats had dropped anchor in the small bay at the west end of Inishmakill, where they silently waited for their human cargo to arrive.

Quietly transferred by RAF tenders, the assault force climbed aboard the dark, silent aircraft, and each man was immediately ushered to a specific position within the airframe, to ensure good weight distribution for take-off.

Each Sunderland carried only a partial crew of six, and no heavy munitions, all to allow the aircraft to cope with the additional weight of the Ukrainian soldiers and their kit.

There had been only one opportunity for a practice take-off, and that was without the full weight that now resisted the straining Wasp engines, as the leading Mk V full-throttled westwards across the lough.

Reluctantly, NS-F, Viljoen's aircraft, rose into the night, followed, at one minute intervals, by the remaining two flying boats. Second to take off was NS-D, its crew given the opportunity, at their request, as it was they that had made the gruesome discovery off the coast of Éire. Lastly, NS-J, crewed by more angry men, all with friends amongst the dead of NS-X.

0000 hrs, Wednesday, 1st January 1946, Glenlara, County Mayo, Eire.

"Happy New Year!"

Discipline and good sense ensured that some of the Soviet marines remained sober and alert at their posts.

The same had been intended of a dozen IRA men, but their personal need to celebrate took priority, and only two of the men posted on lookout remained in situ, the others having sought comfort and companionship in the main barracks blocks, where the stoves glowed hot as the fires were stoked up, and where the alcohol flowed freely.

Potchine, that most Irish of drinks, made from potatoes, and vodka, sometimes both in the same container, oiled throats that sung familiar tunes in unfamiliar tongues; Russian, English, and Gaelic speakers combining to welcome in the new year.

Some were already collapsed on their bunks, the ushering in of 1946 wasted on them in their unconscious state.

Belching before speaking, Dudko leant forward conspiratorially.

"You will understand, Comrade Reynolds, that I, as a true communist, can't be seen to observe religious festivals of any kind... but," he looked around to make sure his point was noted by only the one pair of ears, "We're in your country, so it's only proper."

"That it is, Dmitri, that... it is!"

Clinking bottle to bottle, Reynolds and Dudko sealed their agreement on the important point.

So, a second night of revelry was set in place, this one for the Gregorian calendar's Orthodox New Year on 14th January.

Looking around at the men around them, Reynolds frowned with mock severity.

"Let's hope we can replace the booze in time!"

The bottles clinked again, and both men drank their fill, as around them an excess of alcohol stood victor over many a man's efforts to party long into the night, replacing raucous laughter and singing with the gentler snores of the happy drunk.

0034 hrs, Wednesday, 1st January 1946, airborne over the Atlantic, 35 miles north of Llandavuck Island.

Viljoen leant across to his passenger, removing his face mask so that the soldier could hear him clearly.

"The weather's a problem, Major. Wind's whipping up the surface fierce, man."

Shandruk eased the weapon at his shoulder and brought his mouth closer to the pilot's ear.

"Are we off?"

Ordinarily, Viljoen would probably have waved the mission off, but this was not ordinarily. He needed no time to think.

"No, we're still on, bloke. Just warn your boys that the run in will be... ," he smiled in the way that professionals smile when describing difficulties, "...Interesting."

Shandruk disappeared back down the ladder, already anticipating one hell of a landing.

Clipping his mask back on, Viljoen spoke briefly.

"Pilot to crew. Make sure our guests are secure, and then brace yourselves. Pilot to Nav, give me a course for touchdown point. Pilot to tail gunner, send standby to execute."

The flurry of orders brought about responses throughout the Sunderland.

In the rear turret, the gunner flashed his Aldus lamp, sending the agreed signal in the direction of the two barely visible shapes in NS-F's wake, which, in turn, sent their brief acknowledgements.

With the new course ready, Viljoen gave his last command.

"Pilot to tail. Send execute."

NS-F and her two companions turned due south, and headed towards the Irish coast and a bloody rendezvous with the occupants of Glenlara.

0049 hrs, Wednesday, 1st January 1946, off the North coast of Eire.

NS-F had been the least fortunate of the three, slamming into a rising sea as hard as a brick wall, or at least that's how it felt to the men inside. One of the Ukrainians was spark out and minus three front teeth.

Of greater concern was the condition of the radio that had removed them, the casing clearly heavily deformed by the impact.

A quick check by Shandruk's radio man was sufficient.

"No good, Sturmbannfuhrer."

No use moaning about it, and besides, the planning had allowed for a spare.

Shandruk smiled.

'Correction. That was the fucking spare.'

"Check the other set, Wasco."

The man moved off quickly, hampered by the wallowing movement of the flying boat.

Two men had already summoned up the contents of their stomachs, much to the disgruntlement of those around them.

Shandruk moved to the ladder, climbed halfway and shouted up into the glasshouse.

"How long before we go?"

Quickly making the calculations, Viljoen extended three fingers, receiving a nodded acknowledgement before thumbing his mike.

"Pilot to crew. Standby portside hatch."

The Ukrainian commander moved amongst his men as they readied their weapons, unhappy when one of the vital T3 carbines was found unusable following the heavy landing, its infrared lamp more closely resembling a waxing moon than a full circle.

54

Slapping the unfortunate infantryman on the shoulder, Shandruk laughed the matter off.

"You've still got your pistol, Yuri. That'll have to do."

The man produced one of the US Army blades that equipped many of the group.

"And my knife, Sturmbannfuhrer!"

Ruffling the young man's hair, Shandruk looked around his men, who were clearly in good spirits, showing confidence in their faces, as they grinned back at Shandruk in response to his unspoken inquiries.

The display of comradeship held sway for the briefest of moments before Shandruk was business again.

"Attention!"

The group became cold killers again.

"Ready the dinghies, comrades."

Space had dictated that the number of dinghies was limited, and that the assault force would have to be ferried ashore in two stages, but the presence of three wooden boats on the slipway at Glenlara had been noted, and every man was under strict instructions not to damage them.

Plus there would be other help to hand... when the time came.

The first wave of dinghies had discharged their contents, and, already, were nearly back to the waiting flying boats, each crewed by two men from the second wave.

With anchors in place and engines switches off, the three flying boats rose up and down with their silent crews, whilst in the dinghies the sounds of wind and sea were enough to drown out the rapid plunge of oars.

The first party ashore was not idle, fanning out from the small landing area, closing the distance to the outposts that marked the secure perimeter of the Glenlara base.

On a nearby hillock, lying to the west of the landing area, two small positions had been earmarked for immediate neutralization.

Four man groups were used. Two men at the back, one illuminating the area with an infra-red Vampir or T3 carbine, the second with a silenced Sten gun or Winchester M69, ready to silently remove any threat.

Fig# 122 – Glenlara Camp, IRA codenames.

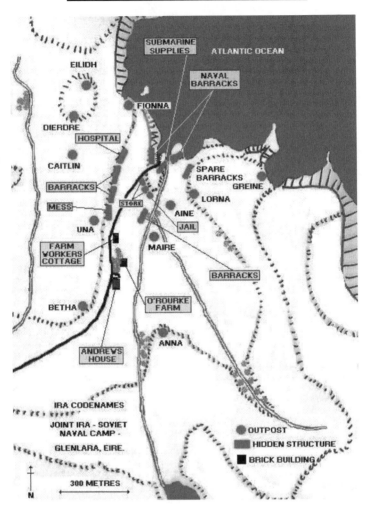

The other two men moved in front, armed with edged weapons that would have graced battlefields a thousand years beforehand, and that were still every bit as lethal as their more modern cousins.

Some had selected the Fairbairn-Sykes; the classic Commando knife, but only the British-made version. OSS had initially issued them with the US-manufactured copy that was, simply put, totally inferior. Most of those were at the bottom of the

Ballinderry River near Camp 5A, inexplicably 'lost' when the British version became available.

A few were content with the M3 Trench Knife.

The handful of KA-BAR USMC knives available, courtesy of Rossiter, were considered the finest for close work of the kind that commenced at the outpost furthest north.

[Author's note. I have made all references to the bunkers numerical, removing the IRA labels to avoid confusion, except where it is wholly relevant to maintain the Irish code name.]

Two Soviet marines in 'One' became the first deaths of 1946; bloody, silent, instant deaths at the hands of men without mercy.

They were followed by two more sons of Russia, both asleep in the vital 'Three', the position chosen by Shandruk as his headquarters for the initial assault.

'Two' and 'Four' were cleared in good time, and one of the assault groups was ready to go, sending a brief message on the HT.

"Sestra, four, clear, over"

The acknowledgement was even briefer.

"Tato, out."

Shandruk took the report, understanding that Group Sestra was gathered at position 'four', and waiting on the order to push forward.

Each of the Sunderlands had their own HT, and the crews followed the progress of the Ukrainian soldiers as the radio spoke in whispers of the fall of each position in turn; the RAF airmen understood that each message represented the deaths of men.

"Babushka, all clear, over."

"Tato, out."

The Ukrainian officer could not help but smile, as even the smallest of messages could not conceal the young NCO's disgust at being in the cover party.

"Brat, clear, over."

Shandruk raised an eyebrow at that, and spoke softly in reply, silently impressed that the group with the most difficult task had made their initial position in such good time.

'A pat on the back for Panasuk after this is over.'

Having been sat still for a few minutes now, Shandruk started to realize a simple flaw in his planning.

'Idiot! How could we forget the cold?'

Without the benefit of activity, it was eating away at him, consuming his energy, the lack of movement allowing the weather its moment of victory.

The same would apply to his men, more so for those who lay outside the bunker positions.

'Fuck it!'

Fig# 123 – Glenlara Camp, Ukrainian location codes.

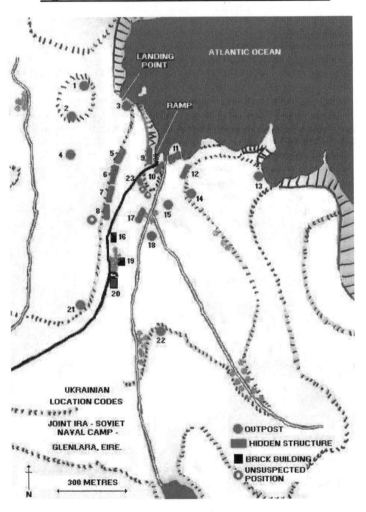

The HT broke into his doubts.

"Dedushko, two, clear, over."

Another of the assault groups, one from the second wave, had made good time.

Shandruk made a decision and keyed the HT.

"Mama, time, over."

Kuibida's voice responded immediately.

"Four, over."

'Time enough. Give the order.'

"All units, Dagga, repeat Dagga."

Aboard NS-F, Viljoen heard his dead brother's name without emotion. When a codeword had been needed, 'Dagga' had been his suggestion; it seemed only fitting.

On shore, frozen limbs protested as they propelled bodies forward.

First for attention were 'Five' and 'Nine', earmarked for visits by Dedushko and Brat respectively.

Both huts were full of the sounds of contented snoring, and then they weren't.

Moving stealthily, the knifemen glided through the positions, terminating lives with simple thrusts and slashes, gloved hands pressing on mouths to stifle any noise that might escape.

'Five' was full of IRA men, and the detritus of their excessive drinking. One empty bottle toppled over and rolled across the floor, accidentally knocked over by an eager Ukrainian.

One of the last two living Irishmen in the hut woke up and reacted surprisingly quickly, grabbing for a weapon, an act that earned him a small burst from a silenced Sten. The clacking of the bolt was enough to open the eyelids of the last man, but a commando knife punched through his neck and into his brain, ending Connolly's interest instantly.

"Dedushko, five, over."

"Tato, out."

'Nine' contained Soviet submariners, relief crewmen in the main, for whom boredom had lent additional impetus for the drinking session.

One man had already died, frozen to death outside the hut, where his drunken state had led him to believe that a toilet awaited his full bladder.

Nine more perished as the 'Brat' group worked away efficiently.

"Brat, nine, over."

"Dedushko, six, over."

"Tato, out."

Fig# 124 – Glenlara, Assault.

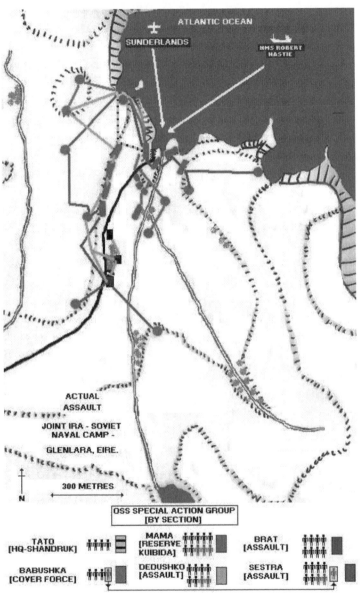

[Author's note. This map clearly requires colour to properly interpret. The colour version is available on the web site

Thinking for just a second, Shandruk decided to move on immediately.

"Tato, moving to five, Mama, move up, out."

The plan called for every location west of the track, except position 'Twenty-one', to be purged of enemy before moving further eastwards.

The plan was going well.

"Sestra, unknown position located, fifty metres west of eight. Delayed, over."

The plan started to unravel.

On the evening of the B-24's photo-reconnaissance mission, one of the IRA's new recruits, formerly a soldier of the Great War, had spotted the fact that the distance between 'Betha' and 'Caitlin', 'Twenty-one' and 'Four' respectively, was a definite security problem.

Approaching Reynolds, the man sold the IRA commander on the need for a new position, also commenting on the exposure of Reynolds' own quarters, and 'Una' was born, one of three positions not recorded on the Ukrainian's maps.

As 'Una' was the closest position to the warmth of the kitchen hut, Naval Lieutenant Dudko, having left the snoring Reynolds in his own quarters, selected it for a comradely visit with coffee in hand, an act he felt sure would be spoken of by the grateful men, and his reputation would be enhanced as a result.

He approached, unsteady on his feet, the scalding hot coffee lapping over the edges of the mugs and burning his hands.

Dudko yelped.

Heads swiveled in his direction, and both friendly and murderous eyes made a quick assessment. The former relaxed as the familiar figure of the political officer approached; the latter, narrowed and calculating, made a swift and lethal decision.

A silenced pistol spat four bullets in quick succession, with three finding soft flesh.

The noise of the standard HDM was sufficient to register in the brains of the two Marines, but their main focus of attention was the metallic clang as the errant .22 round deflected noisily off one of the enamel mugs.

The .22 was not a hi-power round, and its killing ability was not brilliant but, none the less, the combination of the three bullet hits suddenly robbed Dudko of his strength, and he dropped to his knees, hardly noticing the pain in his hands as the hot coffee flowed over them.

One of the marines reached for a rifle, the other knew his own weapon was too far away, so his hand sought his bayonet.

A Ukrainian junior NCO, the foremost of the silent killers, stumbled in his haste to get at the two men, bringing down the man behind, granting the Russians a temporary reprieve.

The Marine rifleman worked his bolt, but the action proved stiff, and the weapon remained silent.

Untangling arms and legs, the two fallen Ukrainians picked themselves up and moved forward, with fatal consequences.

Without warning, the Lance-Corporal sprang forward at the precise moment that the silenced Sten opened fire, perforating the Ukrainian NCO's back with half a dozen bullets, and dropping him lifeless into the snow.

Shocked at his error, the gunner did not continue to fire, granting a second stay of execution to the Soviet rifleman.

Sergeant Demchuk turned his attention from Dudko to the two marines, placing a pair of his remaining bullets in the side of the nearest man's head.

Low power or not, the .22's ripped through delicate brain tissue, killing the man instantly.

The HDM moved to the surviving marine and clicked.

'Mudaks!'

The Soviet bayonet is not a throwing weapon, but the desperate man got lucky, and the point caught Demchuk in the left eye, burrowing deep enough to drop him instantly to the ground.

Grabbing up his PPSh, the surviving Russian screamed a warning to his comrades, pulling the trigger without a meaningful target in his sights.

Frozen urine, deposited by himself some time beforehand, the act of a man wishing to remain in cover as he exposed his genitals, had virtually cemented the trigger and bolt in place, rendering the weapon useless.

The Sten gunner, now recovered from the shock of his terrible error, ended the marine's resistance.

The survivors of 'Sestra' dropped into the new position and caught their breath.

Corporal Tkachuk, now in charge, was a steady man and rapped out orders.

"Grab the HDM and the HT from our Demchuk, and get him into cover."

He grabbed an old soldier by the arm.

"Do what you can for him, Roman."

Lance-Corporal Roman knew exactly what was expected of him.

Tkachuk gestured at the kneeling Russian, softly moaning on the snow path ahead.

"Get that in here out of the way... and kill the fucking bastard."

Men moved off quickly to do the tasks.

The Corporal accepted the HDM and HT without a word, noting that Roman was not moving the wounded sergeant.

Two men dragged the bleeding Russian by his arms, leaving a small red smear behind all the way to the edge of the bunker.

"Fuck me, Pjotr. This one's an officer!"

The stroke of luck was accepted, although the price had been high.

"Don't kill him. Gag the bastard...plug his holes... tie him up... you've got a minute."

His radio message had to convey everything so that Shandruk could make a decision.

"Tato from Sestra. New position taken. Two men dead," as he spoke, the corpse of his Sergeant was dragged past, confirming his suspicions, "One wounded enemy officer in hand. Over."

"Tato, out."

Shandruk carefully placed the HT on the edge of the position, his mind working overtime.

'There's no alarm yet... so why change anything?'

The HT was back in his hand.

"Tato, all units. Proceed with plan."

'Sestra' was supposed to be outside number 'Eight', the largest building on the site, positioned at the end of a line of structures that were assumed to be barracks. Building 'Seven' had been the one whose open door had surrendered the presence of both Reynolds and the Russian officer to O'Farrell's observation, and was to be visited by 'Sestra' after the larger structure.

Improvising, Shanduk contacted 'Babushka', and ordered two of the four men providing rear security to double up to 'Sestra', and bring up their numbers; 'Sestra' was ordered to hold and not move into Building 'Eight' until reinforced.

The Ukrainian leader justified the change in timetable in exchange for a full assault team on 'Eight'.

"Brat. Ten, empty. Ammunition store, torpedoes and such... over."

"Tato, out."

Jenkins' stock went up again, as she and her Sergeant had suggested that, given its location, 'Ten' was most likely to be a store for submarine replenishment. That meant that 'Brat' would be moving onto 'Eleven' more quickly, which Shandruk was happy to permit.

None the less, there was something that was troubling the commander, and he made a decision that went against everything that had been put in place.

"Tato, Mama. New orders... take Twenty-three and Seventeen... send the MG42 to me... over."

Kuibida was surprised by the order, but acted immediately, dispatching the machine-gun team, and moving his own men up towards building 'Nine'.

'Twenty-three' had not been spotted originally, and its existence was only found when Jenkins' Sergeant went back over the film evidence for the umpteenth time. Even then it was difficult to be certain, but the 'whatever-it-was' got a number, just in case.

"Tato, Brat... did you understand... over?"

"Brat, out."

Men from the Brat group were already moving into Building 'Eleven', where more naval personnel lay ripe for the slaughter.

Dedushko's silent killers moved on to 'Seven', dealing with a half-conscious man in the latrine, before moving through the hut with deadly efficiency.

From the cover of 'Nine', Kuibida sent a group of four men forward, their classic group for small and silent assaults, infrared and silenced weapons covering the two edged weapons leading.

As they approached target 'Twenty-three', it materialized into what was very obviously a camouflaged structure. The grass and snow-covered building was suddenly revealed for what it was. The door frame became illuminated from inside as a light was switched on, and the silence was broken by the loudest of belches, as an occupant stirred to answer a call of nature.

Whilst the building was a store room, a guard had been placed in the building to reduce pilferage, and it was the guard commander who had awoken.

The man opened the door, clad in a greatcoat and already exposing his genitals, so as to rid himself of his weighty burden in as short a time as possible.

He saw death approaching and shouted loudly...

... and briefly...

The leading Ukrainian drove the commando dagger home with all his force, knocking the man off his feet. With his assailant lying on top of him, stifling any further noise with his free hand, Lieutenant Masharin died quietly and quickly.

The second attacker leapt over the mass of arms and legs and into small hut, where he stabbed twice into something that was just starting to stir from under thick blankets; fatally so.

Evancho, one of the covering men, laughed loudly, creating more noise, but did so deliberately. To add to the consternation in the 'Mama' group, the quick-thinking man shouted in Russian.

"Get back in here and shut that fucking door, you clumsy fuck!"

At first, Kuibida wanted to throttle Evancho, the idiot, but quickly understood the man's reasoning, and nodded his agreement.

Less than sixty metres away, a marine on guard, wrapped in a greatcoat and blankets, was reassured by the outburst. He closed his half-open eyes, cradled his SVT rifle closer, and dropped back off to sleep.

'Mama' moved on and immediately ran into another unexpected obstacle.

Kuibida raised his clenched fist and the group melted into the ground.

Whispering to his second-in-command, he gestured at some lumps to the right.

"Blyad. I think there's actually three locations here, Konstantin. See there? One... two... three?"

"You're right, Sturmscharfuhrer. Our little bird missed two... look there."

The keen-eyed man pointed out the smallest wisp of cold breath adjacent to the furthest end lump.

"A guard?"

Kuibida nodded unseen, but added a comment.

"Guarding something... what?"

The light in the hut behind them had long since gone out, and the assault group was reformed.

Kuibida dropped back and pulled his force in around him.

Firstly, he slapped Evancho's shoulder.

"Good work."

Pointing back towards the previously unsuspected structures, he whispered his instructions.

"Your group will take the first two," he touched one of his NCO's on the arm.

65

"Watch out for sentries. Something there's worth guarding so it seems… that position has a man outside. That's down to your group, Evancho."

The men prepared to move off.

"I'll stay here and keep an eye on Fifteen and Seventeen."

The two assault groups slipped away as Kuibida quietly briefed Shandruk on the change.

Completing his brief conversation with his senior NCO, Shandruk waited a moment before cursing.

"Koorva!"

He looked at his watch, and knew it was going wrong. He attracted the radio operator's attention.

"Wasco, tell Shark to hold."

Shark was an integral part of the escape, and could not be risked to a failing plan. Shandruk had decided to keep the vessel out at sea a while longer.

Other reports had come in, and only 'Seven' was left to purge, at least, as far as the west side of the track was concerned.

"Brat, twelve and fourteen empty, over."

Shandruk welcomed the advantage that offered, but the professional in him felt disgusted that his enemy was so inept as to leave important positions unmanned, no matter what the circumstances.

"Dedushko, Seven, over."

'Excellent'.

He toyed with the idea of sending 'Sestra' to sort the stone buildings out, but checked the thought, knowing that Building 'Seventeen' was still an issue.

Instead, he kept 'Sestra' and 'Dedeshko' holding in place, and moved himself forward.

"All units, Tato moving to Nine, out."

He reasoned that he could best use the MG42's cover from 'Nine' if there was an issue with either the farm buildings or the final wooden structure at 'Seventeen'.

Shandruk simply didn't realise that the new locations, recently discovered by Kuibida's force, would be in his line of sight.

The snow crunched gently underfoot as the teams moved forward, this time seemingly more loud than before, their senses enhanced by the known presence of an enemy.

Evancho, his infra-red goggles revealing everything, found the sleeping sentry with ease, and he gestured his knifemen forward. Inside the small building, voices were mumbling, not in alarm, but seemingly in quiet conversation.

The sentry's SVT-40 clattered noisily onto the wooden verandah, causing those inside to abruptly stop talking.

Recovering his knife, the lead killer moved quickly to the doorway, part of his mind registering metal bars on the windows, the other part indignant that the door was padlocked and resistant to his attempt to enter.

Evancho saw the problem from his cover position, and gestured at his companion, who placed his silenced Winchester on the snow and started looking through the dead sentries' pockets.

"Here."

The keys were tossed to one of the waiting knifemen, but he missed the catch, the distraction of something landing in the snow in front of him proving too much.

Evancho reacted the quickest and threw himself forward, landing on top of the grenade as it exploded.

Whilst he muffled the explosion, and protected his men, the dull noise rolled through the silent camp, and redoubled as the sound of automatic fire followed the grenade.

"Bastards! There's fucking English bastards in the camp, lads! Wake up, you fucks! Wake up!"

The Irish voice summoned the camp to arms, although the owner didn't realize that he was mainly calling to dead men.

Three of Evancho's group were down hard; Evancho and the key catcher were both dead. The Winchester man had taken a round in the shoulder, and was screaming in the red snow.

Scrabbling around at his feet for the dropped key, the surviving Ukrainian unlocked the padlock and sought cover inside, his pistol readied for any problems.

A chair leg, swung by a very muscly and tattooed arm, felled him immediately, and a pair of hands grabbed the inert figure, dragging him inside before pulling the door closed.

One occupant, who had been subjected to regular beatings, was in no fit state to offer resistance, but the other was fighting fit, and ready to take advantage of whatever was going on around him, as the camp burst into frenzied life.

Shandruk realized his positional error and quickly shifted the MG42 to where it could flay Hut 'Seventeen'.

Surprise was just a distant memory now, but most of the work had been completed, although there had yet to be any sighting of the two specific targets, 'Kolobok' and 'Ryaba', or Brown and Reynolds as they were known to their peers.

"Wasco, get Shark moving again. Tell 'em not to worry about silence."

He spoke rapidly into the HT as his radio operator passed the message to the RAF rescue trawler, HMS Robert Hastie.

"Bird, Tato, stage two, out."

Busy taking in the tactical situation, part of Shandruk's brain registered the sound of aero engines bursting into life, as the three Sunderlands responded to his order.

To his front, Kuibida had flanked Building 'Seventeen', coming at it from the east side, where it was set against the trees and bushes, and where there were no openings.

The MG42 was spitting bullets at any part of the structure that showed signs of movement.

Across the track, part of 'Dedushko' had joined in the firefight, whilst the other part had teamed up with 'Sestra', and that joint force was closing on the stone farm buildings at speed.

With part of the group covering, the rest of the attack force pressed hard on the farmhouse they knew as Building 'Twenty'.

It seemed they had got there without problems until a burst of fire from a downstairs window put two of the attacking Ukrainians down, sparking a firefight with the covering force.

Back at 'Seventeen', Kuibida was in position.

"Mama to all, no fire on Seventeen. Assaulting now, out."

Whilst all stations received the message, Shandruk made sure the 42 team fully understood, and took the opportunity to check their fire.

"Tato, Sestra… report… over."

Nothing.

"Tato, Dedushko… report… over."

"Dedushka, Tato, Sestra inside Twenty… there is resistance… at least four men down… waiting, over."

"Tato, Dedushko… leave Sixteen to us… stay away, out."

The MG42 was given another target and started peppering the windows of building 'Sixteen'.

Back at 'Seventeen', Kuibida's assault was heralded by grenades. It also came in from the south side, whilst the IRA defenders were oriented west and north.

One Irishman, a veteran of the Great War, realised the presence of enemy to their rear, but died as the first of six grenades exploded inside the wooden hut, setting fire to a number of flammable items, and bathing the area with an intense orange light in seconds.

The Ukrainians swept in and over the stunned defenders, shooting the wounded and stunned survivors without mercy.

"NO!"

Kuibida's shout rang through the hut, giving everyone a moment's pause.

"Not him," he pointed at the unconscious man who had been about to travel to his maker at the hands of Konstantin Lach.

"Him, we want, Konstantin. He's your responsibility. Make sure he gets back alive."

Lach took the order for what it was, realising this was a man whose face he should have recognised. He tried to kick the unconscious man awake, without success.

"Gimme a hand."

He and another dragged the large man outside and dumped him in the snow, where the cold brought him round quickly.

Kuibida watched as the man was helped to his feet and taken away.

"Mama, Tato. Kolobok, over."

The message was received by a number of listeners, but none welcomed it more than the listener on NS-F.

"Skipper."

Viljoen, concentrating on moving his Sunderland around the island and down to the Glenlara slipway, grunted to show that he could hear.

"From the lads ashore... Kolobok."

For the first time in many days, Viljoen smiled.

It was not a pleasant smile.

'Seventeen' had been bloodily cleared, the IRA men inside wiped out almost to a man, and that surviving man was being escorted away to the slipway, the effects of blast, shock, and alcohol all combining to ensure that he didn't comprehend that the doors of hell had just swallowed him whole.

In 'Twenty', 'Sestra' had cleared the building, but not without further cost. The farmer, the same as had killed one of Bryan's agents by running him over with a tractor, had used a shotgun to defend himself, spreading one of the Ukrainians up the wall of the staircase. His resistance had earned him little respite, and he and his family were slaughtered in their bedrooms, the screams of young and old ignored by men with specific orders and no mercy in their hearts.

'Dedushko' had rolled through 'Nineteen', the two men inside so incapacitated by alcohol as to both be slaughtered like lambs, and with as much comprehension of events.

"Tato, Dedushko…report."

"Dedushko, Tato, Nineteen cleared…over."

Shandruk could see the muzzle flashes from the windows of the last farm building and instantly made the call.

"Tato, Dedushko… attack Sixteen immediately, out."

"Tato, all units, fire on upper floors of Sixteen only…repeat…upper floors only…out."

As he studied the position, the rush of feet to his left gave him a moment's concern. He turned and saw Wijers and the 'Shark' contingent at the wooden boats, setting their part in motion.

'Dedushko' was inside the final building now, and the group leader called for a ceasefire from the supporting groups, until only an occasional shot and flash came from with the dark stone shape.

The conversation, like all their conversations, was in Russian.

"What the hell are they speaking?"

Through battered lips, his cell mate spoke one word.

"Ukrainian."

That made Sveinsvold think hard, and he spoke his thoughts out loud, as his hands moved over the senseless form, seeking identification.

"Well… judging by what's going on out there, no way are they buddies with the Irish… or your lot."

He pulled open the man's snowsuit.

"What the fuck's that?"

The camouflage was unknown to him, but then, the Navy wasn't strong on camouflage.

Nazarbayev couldn't see properly in the dull, almost quarter-light, provided by the oil lamp and the orange glow of a nearby fire penetrating the sacking at the windows. Scrabbling over on all fours, he looked hard and gasped, suddenly pulling the camouflage jacket aside and searching for what he suspected was round the man's neck.

And, even though Nazarbayev half expected it, the metal oval was still a shock.

"Blyad! German soldier's metal tag."

"German?"

"Yes, Bee," the Marine had long since given up trying to pronounce his fellow prisoner's name.

"German… here?"

Suddenly, feet crunched across the snow-covered wooden decking and, just as suddenly, came to an abrupt halt.

Nazarbayev acted on instinct, and shouted in Russian.

"We're prisoners here. No guns. We surrender!"

Outside a whispered conversation took place, as Kuibida weighed up the pros and cons of letting his man throw the grenade inside. Clearly the men were prisoners, hence the locked door.

But…

"Lev?"

It was a fair guess that the voice outside was speaking to the insensible lump on the floor of the prison.

Sveinsvold tried his own Russian language skills.

"We're prisoners in here. Your man… we're sorry…we hit him… he's unconscious… he'll be alright but… we didn't know what to expect… sorry."

The muzzle of an ST44 made itself known as the door creaked opened, permitting more light to enter the cell.

Half a head appeared behind it, the single eye calculating and unblinking down the sights.

The half head spoke in Russian.

"Talk fast."

Sveinsvold took up the offer.

"I'm an American sailor… US Navy."

Grasping his companion by the shoulder, he continued.

"My friend is a Soviet marine… a prisoner. He's been badly treated, as you can see."

The calculating eye flicked between the two men as the brain that received the information made its decision.

Relaxing, Kuibida stepped backwards, but maintained a line of sight on the two men.

"Then this is your lucky day, Comrade."

A nod was sufficient for his back-up to swoop forward and help both men away. As the Soviet prisoner staggered past, the NCO snatched a familiar object from the man's neck.

Pausing to scan the cell for a final time, Kuibida noticed the merest hint of a uniform jacket in the straw that had been the men's mattress. He shook the chaff clear and took in the sight. On instinct, he ran his hands through the pockets, liberating the standard Soviet ID book and a not so standard brown leather wallet. A quick look disappointingly revealed it to be a Communist Party

71

membership. Slipping the items inside his pouch, he elected to rip one interesting part of the Russian's jacket away, and quickly followed his men.

<u>**0142 hrs, Wednesday, 1st January 1946, Building Nine, Glenlara, Cork, Eire.**</u>

Kuibida arrived at the temporary command post with two wounded men and unexpected news.

Holliday examined the more seriously wounded man and helped him inside the building.

Shandruk grasped his NCO's shoulder in welcome as the HT brought messages from 'Sestra' and 'Brat', confirming the occupation of 'Twenty-one' ,'Twenty-two', and 'Thirteen', none of which had an enemy presence, and no sign of any men running from the scene.

"Sturmbannfuhrer, Kolobok and two others are prisoners. Herr Wijers men are looking after them for now. Charges being laid, timed for 0230."

"Two others?"

"Yes, Sturmbannfuhrer. They were prisoners under guard, so I kept them alive. One is an Amerikanski, or so he says."

Shandruk's attention focussed.

"Amerikanski? Is he?"

Kuibida made a gut call.

"I think so, Sturmbannfuhrer. He speaks pretty good Russian though... but I think he's what he says he is. The other doesn't say much. He's been badly beaten."

The NCO held out the necklet he had snatched from around the beaten man's neck.

"I took this off him."

The Soviet Army did not have dog tags as such, rather favouring a small vessel with a hand-written note inside, a poor system that ensured that many a dead Soviet soldier remained unidentified after a battle.

"Haven't opened it. The American is doing enough talking for the two. From what he says, seems the other one's a Soviet Naval officer."

Kuibida removed his last finds from his overalls, passing over the ID book and party wallet, and then fishing out the epaulette of a Captain-Lieutenant of Soviet Marines.

The two shared the briefest of silent moments before all three items disappeared from view again.

"Very good, Oleksandr. We've exceeded our wildest dreams tonight. How many?"

Kuibida shrugged, mentally listing those comrades who were already stiffening in the snow.

"Can't speak for 'Sestra' and 'Dedushko' yet, but we have three dead and three wounded amongst the rest of us, Sturmbannfuhrer."

Both knew the final count would be higher.

The HT made a final announcement.

"Dedushko, Tato, Sixteen. Ryaba... over."

The exhilaration ran through both seasoned veterans, pulsed like an electric shock through the Ukrainian force, and coursed through the veins of the RAF Sunderland crews.

Turning to Wasco, Shandruk could not conceal his triumph.

"Send full house... full house... clear?"

Wasco was, and had the message on the airwaves in seconds.

In a small Irish fishing village called Bundoran, two quiet men shook hands and silently toasted the message with a nip from a hip flask. Back in Castle Archdale, men from a range of interested organizations celebrated and patted each other on the back, as the stunning news arrived. Reynolds and Brown, Ryaba and Kolobok respectively, were in hand, and would soon understand that their lives were very precariously balanced.

The capture of two Soviet officers was a definite bonus.

Back at Glenlara, men swept through the silent huts, picking up anything that looked like it could conceivably have intelligence value. Sacks of papers, letters, maps, and books, were piled at the top of the ramp, ready to make the short journey to the trawler.

The three wooden boats were already down at the bottom, their keels wet, each with an experienced brace of crew members from the Robert Hastie to guide the passengers through the short journey.

Holliday collected the more grievously wounded, ready for transfer to the Robert Hastie, on which waited two RN medical ratings and a hold space converted for surgery and higher level medical intervention.

The Ukrainian's lighter casualties were respectfully handled aboard with the sacks, and made the journey to the nearest Sunderland.

Once the cargo was transferred, the launch pulled away and was quickly replaced by the next in line.

Again, the HT was in brief use.

"All stations, Tato... recover... recover...out."

Across the wasteland that was Glenlara, the Ukrainians moved swiftly backwards, all focused on the top of the slip way.

The 'Sestra' group, assisted by the men of 'Dedushko' struggled back with their dead and wounded.

The boat waited at the bottom of the ramp as next came the prisoners, both the healthy and the injured. Kuibida detailed three men to provide security, although each man was securely bound. Doc Holliday was also aboard, fearing that the wounded Dudko was not long for this world.

With them went another of the boats, with the badly wounded soldiers and a few men for extra security on the trawler.

Shandruk spoke softly to his senior man.

"Eight of our brothers are dead, Oleksandr. A high price."

Kuibida nodded and passed a small flask, encouraging his leader to take a draught.

"Irish. It warms nicely."

Both men took a slug before it disappeared back under the layers that were keeping Kuibida warm.

Wijers had the responsibility for ensuring that every man got away from the raid, one way or another, and he had counted heads as men moved down the ramp and away to safety.

Kuibida gestured to the group huddled next to Building Ten, sending them away past the counting Wijers.

"One more load after that, and then it's us, Sturmbannfuhrer."

The excitement of combat was wearing off now, and Shandruk could feel the cold seeping into his legs, despite his layers.

"Koorva."

He wasn't angry; it was just surprise, but Kuibida recognized something in the voice.

"Sir?"

Whatever it was that had caused the damage had struck Shandruk in the upper thigh, just a few inches short of the hip.

The cold he felt was the first indication he had been injured, so intense had his concentration been. The sensation was that of his blood starting to chill in the night air.

74

"Koorva! I'm hit."

The leg gave way, dropping Shandruk into the snow.

"Wasco, Lach... the boss is hit. Get him on the next boat to the trawler... and make sure he gets seen by the Sanitäts-Offizier. Move!"

Wijers counted off the departing three men, registering the identity of the man leaving the trail of blood as he was carried down the ramp.

"Move to the ramp, comrades."

The NCO chivvied the Ukrainian soldiers along, wishing to get clear of the Irish coast as soon as possible.

Distant lights caught his eye, and he quickly understood what the source was.

"Vehicle!"

"Next group," called Wijers, as much to give Kuibida a choice as to get the men away.

The senior NCO made a judgment call.

"Go!"

The RAF trawler, with Shandruk aboard, was already pulling away from Glenlara, heading for a special rendezvous at Bundoran, where Colonel Bryan, head of Irish G2, waited to ensure that the transfer went without hindrance from the local IDF and Garda units.

There were, including Wijers, ten men left ashore from the OSS operation.

Each of them made the calculation of ramp and boat versus approaching lorry.

There seemed little choice.

Kuibida whistled once, drawing attention on himself, and his hands pointed out men and angles, sending three soldiers towards Hut Six, and another three across the stream towards Fifteen.

Checking that Wijers had a torch, he gave the Dutchman an order, and the OSS officer moved quickly to carry it out. It was no time for the niceties of rank.

Settling in behind the MG42 gunner, the NCO held a steadying hand on the man's shoulder and waited for the right moment.

Behind him, hidden by the curve of the ramp, Wijers played his torch on the rock, its irregular movement teasing, almost inviting the new arrivals forward.

A dozen IRA men, in a truck normally used for picking up milk, moved slowly closer until, as Kuibida judged, it lay in the centre of the triangle formed by the three little groups.

He slapped the gunner's back and the 42 immediately spewed bullets at the IRA arrivals. Those in the cab were ripped to pieces, the highly effective machine-gun putting its bullets on the money from the off. Those in the back suffered too, and only six survivors touched their feet to ground.

Before they could organize themselves, the two flank parties took them out, and the briefest of affairs was ended, with not one shot fired in return.

A simple hand signal from Kuibida stopped one returning ambush group in its tracks, and they moved over to the smashed lorry to finish off the work, finding two men and a woman who exhibited signs of life, albeit briefly.

Wijers waited to usher the final group down the ramp, having satisfied himself that everyone, living, wounded, or dead, was now away from Glenlara.

None of them were near enough to the camp when the timers ran out, and everything was turned to fire.

The facts about the Robert Hastie.

The HMS Robert Hastie was a very unusual craft, more so for its unique role in World War Two than anything else.

The vessel started life as a nondescript British trawler, SN189, first tasting the salt water of North Shields in 1912. It served as a minesweeper in the Great War.

Returned to civilian control between the wars, the demands of the new conflict saw Robert Hastie again hired to the Royal Navy, when it was converted to an air-sea rescue vessel, and, officially at least, based with the Naval fleet at Foyle, Londonderry, Northern Ireland.

In reality, and with the full agreement of the Irish Government, the joint RN and RAF manned vessel spent most of its time based at Killybegs, Éire, on the condition that the eleven man crew wore no caps, and were kitted out in common working rig, not uniforms.

As the war progressed, cooperation between the Irish and British authorities grew, despite Éire's official neutral stance, so much so that by the end of hostilities, officially sanctioned journeys from Killybegs to Castle Archdale, and other locations within Northern Ireland, were not unheard of.

My thanks to the website naval-history.net for filling in some of the gaps.

0817 hrs, Wednesday, 1st January 1946, RAF Castle Archdale, Northern Ireland.

At first, the listeners had heard a frenzy, a veritable maelstrom of furious blows and raised voices.

Or rather, one voice, one very angry and merciless voice.

But the noises had slowly subsided until there was a silence that drew them in, and encouraged their minds to speculate.

There was a gentle tapping on the door and, with a nod from Blackmore, the RAF policeman unlocked the cell door, permitting Viljoen to emerge.

Without singling out any specific recipient, the disheveled pilot spoke softly.

"Thank you."

There was no joy in his heart; no warm feeling of a need for revenge well satisfied, or a brother appropriately avenged.

There was nothing.

Some of them understood, indeed, some had told him beforehand. None the less, Viljoen had wanted his time alone with Brown, and wouldn't accept anything less.

Initially, he had pummeled Brown, working out the death of his brother on the perpetrator, hurting his hands as he struck blow after blow on the defenceless man.

Then he had stopped, as inside him a different struggle took place, occasionally lashing out as revenge gained the upper hand, more often stood immobile, as his own self-worth triumphed.

Dan Bryan exchanged nods with two others present and stepped forward, placing a calming hand on Viljoen's shoulder.

"I think we might get these scum away now, Squadron-Leader."

Viljoen nodded, although Bryan needed no permission.

The division of spoils had been decided well in advance.

Any IRA men taken would enjoy time in the company of earnest men with enquiring minds, all members of Éire's G2.

Any Soviets would find themselves in the hands of US intelligence services, confronted by a long list of indelicate questions and expectations of honest answers, with no hope of salvation. The death of Dudko had been seen as a problem, until Shandruk revealed that another Soviet Marine officer had been taken, one who would probably have an interesting story to tell.

Any information gained by either side would, where appropriate, be shared.

The physical intelligence haul was to be examined by SOE, and, as with any by-products of the operation, the expected harvest would be shared with any interested party.

By the time that the sun broached the Irish sky, Reynolds and Brown were on their way south, Shandruk was out cold as Holliday operated to remove the two bullets that had struck him a centimetre apart, Nazarbayev and Sveinsvold found themselves again imprisoned, although in a guarded hospital ward with food and proper beds, and Section Officer Megan Jenkins had made the first of a number of startling discoveries.

Diligence is the mother of good luck.

Benjamin Franklin.

Chapter 129 - THE BASES

<u>1331 hrs, Wednesday, 1st January 1946, Camp 5A, near Cookstown, County Tyrone, Northern Ireland.</u>

Dalziel had enjoyed precious little sleep, most of which had been during the car journey from Castle Archdale to the OSS camp near Cookstown, but he was awake now, and waiting to hear what had been so important as to rouse him ahead of the allotted hour.

Jenkins, almost out of her feet, had insisted on staying awake to deliver the vital information.

"Bases, Sir, their submarines were being supported from a number of concealed bases."

'Blast it! Glenlara wasn't the only bloody one.'

Jenkins felt Dalziel's silent anger.

She had a map of the Atlantic out, already marked with the information she had first found some hours ago.

"Here, at Glenlara, we know about. But there are more."

The pencil, acting as a pointer, moved to east coast America. She stayed silent, allowing the enormity to sink in.

"Bloody hell! I mean to say... bloody hell!"

The normally calm naval officer was overtaken by the thought that Soviet submarines had been supported from a covert base on the American mainland.

He recovered his composure before continuing.

"Our cousins will be rather embarrassed."

The pencil moved up to Nova Scotia.

"I see. Oh dear...that's rather closer to home. One for HMG and the Canadians."

The pencil journeyed across the Atlantic in the briefest time before coming to rest.

"Well, you have to admire their style, if nothing else."

The base on Renonquet Island was laid bare.

Malpica was next.

"Our Spanish allies will be delighted, I'm sure."

The final point came to rest at Lisbon.

"How?"

79

"According to the documents, one vessel... err...," she looked for the appropriate piece of paper and found it with ease, "... the Doblestnyi, surrendered herself to the Portuguese at the beginning of the war, Sir."

Dalziel completed the statement.

"Most of the crew interned, I daresay, all except a maintenance group. Enough men to pass supplies and equipment to any nocturnal visitors."

Jenkins was beyond her comfort zone, but the captured documents suggested that the old destroyer was acting as a supply point, so maybe Dalziel was on the money.

However, she did put forward another suggestion.

"And probably intelligence gathering, Sir?

He frowned, thinking the matter through.

"Hang on. A bloody Russian warship in Lisbon port would have been reported surely? I remember no such reports."

"The ship is an old Town Class, a familiar sight, and not one to draw too much attention. Not flying the Soviet ensign, I bet, Sir."

"A fair bet, Section officer. Anything else?"

"Yes, Sir. We have an interesting naval code book."

"We broke their code some time ago, Jenkins."

"Not this one, Sir, least I don't think so anyway."

She proffered a thick pad with very official looking binding, official government notations on the top edge, covered from top to bottom with a series of five random letters.

Dalzeil swallowed as the Holy Grail was handed to him.

"Do you know what this is?"

"Not really, Sir."

"Well, unless I'm mistaken, it's a Vernam's cypher."

"Sir?"

"A one-time pad."

He looked meaningfully at the Soviet radio transmitter sitting proudly on a small table.

"Anyone else know about these pads," he had already spotted two more with the same impressive binding sat with the priority intel that had been recovered from the radio room.

"Not yet, Sir, but more people will be arriving shortly to document and interpret this haul," She indicated another six large bags worth of paperwork, spread across the tables of the old mess hall.

"It could take weeks to wring everything out of it all, Sir."

"Yes it could, couldn't it?"

As he spoke, Dalziel reached across and added the other two pads to his briefcase.

"Make a note of the frequencies on those dials if you please, Jenkins."

She quickly made the necessary notes and passed it to the excited naval officer.

"No need to bother anyone about these," he indicated his briefcase, "Are we clear, Section Officer?"

"Yes, Sir."

"Thank you, Jenkins. Now, get yourself some shut-eye time."

Her objections fell on deaf ears as the Admiral turned to summon the senior of the three guards.

The door opened and the immaculately dressed MP NCO strode in.

"Ah Sergeant. Section Officer Jenkins is just leaving. Please secure this room, and permit no one to enter without the correct authority or, in the Section Officer's case, before 1800hrs."

The USMC officer acknowledged the order and opened the door, allowing the two British personnel to leave, only for them to be replaced by gallons of freezing air.

Solomon Meyer, no more an MP than the two other OSS personnel in USMC uniform, positioned his men, one at each door. Then, as directed by Rossiter, he enjoyed the opportunity offered to rummage through the paperwork, in search of something to confirm his commander's suspicions about the latest Russian guest, something Rossiter wanted to keep quiet, if at all possible.

Agreement or no agreement, something's were just too valuable to share.

He had no idea that Dalziel shared that view too.

1355 hrs, Wednesday, 1st January 1946, airborne with 34th Bombardment Group, approaching Prague, Occupied Czechoslovakia.

The New Year marked a new start for Allied air power, and it was being demonstrated across the length and breadth of Europe, as Allied squadrons took to the skies to rain down high explosives on the logistic and communication routes of the Red Army.

The basic principle of the Allied air war was now to apply the maximum possible force as often as possible; whilst avoiding civilian casualties was important, the exiled governments all understood that many of their civilians would die before they could return home.

Across Britain and Western Europe, aircraft of all types and sizes had filled the skies from early morning, all under the ever-watchful eyes of hundreds of fighters. Streams of ground attack aircraft, intent on making the Soviet frontline soldier's life a misery, followed by more of the same with the light bombers, who visited themselves on reserves and supply dumps behind the lines. The heavy bombers, including RAF units more used to night work, flew deeper into enemy territory, either to level the infrastructure of the enemy war effort, or to undertake intelligence driven missions, requiring the precision placement of tons of bombs on STAVKA reserves.

The US 34th Bombardment Group was one of those fully committed to action.

The 391st Bomb Squadron had taken off from RAF Mendlesham earlier that morning, intent on delivering its payload to the woods north of Weilerswist.

The 391st was also to be the first of the Group's squadrons to return to a newly assigned home base; Beavais-Tille, in Picardy, France, an old Luftwaffe base that had been heavily extended and refurbished over the past two months, ready to accommodate heavy bombers.

Many of the 34th's ground crew were flown over from Norfolk by DC-3, and were already working to receive the returning bombers.

Allied planners were now moving many bomber squadrons across the channel and into Europe, ready to extend the range of targets available, and hoping to carry the battle further into the Soviet heartland.

The 391st's remaining B-17's, from the 4th, 7th, and 18th Bomb Squadrons, escorted by Mustangs of 2nd and 4th Fighter Squadrons, swept down upon the vulnerable Czech capital, intent on destroying the remaining bridges and railway infrastructure.

Defensive Soviet fighter regiments, already worn down and exhausted, were almost universally brushed aside, and, from the Baltic to the Adriatic, only five Allied bombers were prevented from reaching their targets, with only two of those shot down by interceptors.

Flak defences were more effective and, over Prague, took their toll of the leadership of the three bombardment squadrons.

First to go was the 18th's senior man. A 105mm shell, fired from a German mount, cut through the lead aircraft's wing spar.

Whilst many of the crew, including the Lieutenant Colonel, died instantly, those at the two ends of the fuselage were condemned to ride it to earth. The wings folded together and the Flying Fortress dropped twelve thousand feet onto the residential area of Lodénice, obliterating a huge area as the bomb load exploded, spreading flaming aviation fuel across the flammable buildings.

The Colonel leading the 4th Squadron, senior man and mission commander, took a lump of shrapnel in the chest. Despite the flak jacket, the hot piece of metal demolished enough of his vital organs that he died before he could speak, leaving his co-pilot to handle the damaged Fortress to the target and back again.

7th's commander had fallen out with a serious mechanical problem, and he was already back at the new base, watching his damaged aircraft being unceremoniously towed off the metalled landing strip.

The three bomber squadrons were formed for the attack, and the 4th, leading the group, deposited its high-explosives over the Balabenka district, wrecking the railway lines and sidings.

Behind them, the 7th destroyed their own target, but some bombs went astray, adding the Jerusalem Synagogue and the Prague State Opera House to the list of destroyed buildings.

Bringing up the rear, and south by three miles, the 18th Squadron turned northwards and in behind the lead aircraft, intent on attacking the Štvanice Islands bridges, as well as the road and rail crossings at Vitava, less than a mile north of the island, and also taking out the Bubny railway sidings in between the two.

The 18th successfully took out the main road bridge at Štvanice, and the marshalling yards at Bubny were heavily damaged. The rail bridge at Štvanice remained untouched and, although damaged, the road bridge at Vitava was back in use before the day was out. Again, the rail bridge was unscathed, and the Soviets were able to use both rail bridges to move vehicles, although the damage to rail systems was considerable.

The 7th and 18th each lost another aircraft to flak, although both managed to partially control their landings, permitting some of the crews to escape

Allied planning already allowed for another visit on the 4th January.

'Sleep comes inevitably, and to sleep is to die. I tried in vain to save a number of these unfortunates. The only words they uttered were to beg me, for the love of God, to go away and permit them to sleep. To hear them, one would have thought that sleep was their salvation. Unhappily, it was a poor wretch's last wish. But at least he ceased to suffer, without pain or agony. Gratitude, and even a smile, was imprinted on his discoloured lips. What I have related about the effects of extreme cold, and of this kind of death by freezing, is based on what I saw happen to thousands of individuals. The road was covered with their corpses.'

Armand-Augustin-Louis, Marquis de Caulaincourt, Duke of Vicenza. Personal aide to Napoleon Bonaparte, and witness to the Grand Armee's retreat from Moscow.

Chapter 130 - THE FREEZE

<u>January 1946, Europe.</u>

Thousands died.

Whether they wore green, or brown, or khaki, or field grey, or white, they died as soldiers in extreme conditions had done for millenia beforehand.

Thousands upon thousands suffered as plummeting temperatures, combined with supply difficulties, brought some Allied combat units to their knees.

The Red Army was not immune to the awful effects of that terrible winter, and their own supply lines, already creaking under the strain, were made worse by Allied air attacks across the breadth and width of occupied Europe.

The civilian populations suffered equally, many communities bereft of food perished through hunger, simply melted away, unlike the snow and ice that presently gripped the continent.

Occasionally, some enthusiastic officer would suggest a raid or a reconnaissance, and a bloody fight would break out, but mostly the casualties that filled the dressing stations on both sides of the line were caused by the lowest temperatures ever recorded on mainland Europe, except for the 1932 dive to -52.6°c, registered at Grünloch in Austria.

USAAF meteorologists at the Bolzano fighter base incredulously recorded a new record Italian low temperature of -49.5°c.

At Butgenbach in Germany, -49.9°c wreaked havoc on the US Army personnel stationed there.

In Denmark, Danish and American personnel downed tools at Karup, unable to achieve anything of value in -50.1°c.

On the other side of the line, in the small Czech town of Křemže, the supply soldiers of the Red Banner Forces of Soviet Europe didn't know the temperature; just that it was cold enough to freeze the blood in their horses' veins, and their own, for that matter. The cold prevented the tired and hungry men from eating any of the carcasses, and the unit just gave in to the cold.

The valuable supplies remained deep frozen in their carts.

A Czech science teacher and amateur weather forecaster later confirmed that Křemže had descended to a record temperature of -51°c.

Of course, warmer weather, or more accurately, less freezing weather, came and went, sometimes lasting as long as forty-eight hours.

Exhausted Allied engineers and pioneers labored long and hard to keep open roads that seemed to attract drifting snow in huge quantities. Bulldozers, tanks converted to snow ploughs, and plain old human muscle moved tons of snow and ice out of the way of the vital supplies of war. Many men were hospitalized, and over three hundred engineers died in the first four weeks of 1946, but their efforts kept the roads and rail lines open.

Across the front lines, a different story started to emerge, as fuel rationing, at least at first, prevented the use of non-military vehicles in most of occupied Europe.

Many local commanders saw the foolishness of the orders, and made other arrangements, often siphoning fuel from their tanks and trucks in favour of civilian snow ploughs, in order to keep the roads open and permit their supplies to get through.

The difference between the two huge armies was clear, as the Red Army, cleared roads or not, was delivering so little to the frontline troops by comparison to the Allied soldiery.

Mostly, this was the result of the Allied air campaign, but often, rear line units 'claimed' supplies passing through their territory, depriving the frontline troops of their rightful allocations of fuel, munitions, medical supplies, and, above all, food.

Many Soviet units went days without a delivery of rations, and foraging had very quickly taken precedence over any organized military activity.

Sometimes there were clashes between different hunting parties, and many often ended in violence, with groups of soldiers firing at each other in an effort to secure a farmer's hidden store of grain, or a newly discovered cache of vegetables.

Men died in such encounters.

Supply officers found themselves without suitable supply units, as often horsed units delivering to starving units would not return, the carts left redundant as the frontline soldiers filled their bellies on fresh red horse meat.

That in turn created more supply problems.

Soviet troops started to cross No Man's Land, some in organized groups, intent on stealing from their clearly better off enemy, others for the clear purpose of desertion and surrender.

Many of the latter were shot down as they ran, more often than not by their own officers, rather than a vigilant Allied soldier.

The life of the frontline Soviet soldier was truly awful, pushing their collective will to resist the cold and deprivation to the outer limits of human endurance.

But, in the main, they endured, a testament to the incredible resilience of the Red Army, as well as an endorsement of their German enemy's respect for their incredible capacity to absorb suffering.

Behind the lines it was little better, although the hideous temperatures mostly kept the few surviving Kommando and guerrilla groups in hiding.

And then, as fuel became scarcer still, Soviet efforts at maintaining the road network did not involve mechanical effort at all; fuel was now far too precious. Instead, local populations were driven from their homes; young, old, and infirm were all set to work with shovels and brooms. That most died in the process was of no import.

German civilian casualties were extreme.

For most Soviet officers, the released Russian POWs were still considered dishonoured vermin and an insufferable burden, but now they found them new work shifting tons of snow from A to B, often with nothing more than pieces of wood or their bare hands.

And finally they added the new wave of POWs. Allied soldiers, often still in their summer uniforms, were set to work to do their share for the motherland.

So, across Europe, thousands died.
Combat.
Starvation.
Exhaustion.
Frozen to death.

86

German women, Austrian children, Polish grandmothers, Czech grandfathers; all died.

Indian sepoys, Canadian riflemen, US aircrew, British tankers; all died.

The NKVD were merciless, driving the clearing work forward with a flurry of blows, or organizing working parties to place the frozen corpses of the fallen beside the roads, creating piles that marked the routes for vehicles and horses to follow.

And there was cannibalism.

The Baltic Sea was frozen, or at least most of it was. The Red Navy stayed at home, its ports locked by ice, with only submarines undertaking patrol activities to the south.

The ice extended to the Danish islands, although any reasonable size vessel would have been able to move it aside, not that any tried with the Allied air superiority so marked.

Whilst the Baltic itself saw next to no action, there was a flurry of political activity from the Finns.

From September 1944, they had concluded hostilities with the Soviet Union and commenced what became known to them as 'The Lapland War', fighting their former allies, the German Army, in the most northern of Finnish provinces.

Rather perversely, Finland officially found herself technically at war with Germany, the Soviet Union, and the United Kingdom.

Links forged in the battles on the Eastern Front ensured that quiet communications from German friends came to receptive Finnish ears, and they passed on high-powered assurances about Allied intentions regarding Finland

Per Törget, the head of Swedish intelligence services, again proved of great value, facilitating a number of clandestine meetings between members of the Finnish Foreign Ministry and representatives of His Majesty's government, which resulted in a secret protocol being established between Finland and the Allied nations.

On Thursday 9th January, Finland officially declared herself as adopting a neutral stance and openly declared her national borders on land, sea, and air to be inviolable to all sides, including other neutral nations, and without exception.

In Moscow, the immediate reaction was to turn on the upstart Finns, until calmer heads prevailed, and the advantages of a neutral bastion were appreciated.

'Calmer heads' at first consisted solely of Zhukov, who quickly ventured to suggest that Beria's idea of liquidating the entire Finnish state would require slightly more than the 'three panje carts and an old musket' that represented his uncommitted reserves.

Stalin enjoyed the moment as his man was put down by Zhukov's sarcasm, but pursued the military option with his recently appointed Commander of Soviet Ground Forces.

Zhukov laid the matter out simply and without frills.

Reserve units were needed for the Western Front, and there were few forces available for any action against the Finns, let alone sufficient for an expedition of any kind.

The Marshal, offering Beria a proverbial olive branch, spoke plainly.

"Comrade Marshal Beria's wish to punish the upstarts is wholly understandable, but we cannot… not now anyway. Surely we have more pressing matters to hand?"

The GKO members present grunted their understanding and agreement.

Eyeing Beria, Zhukov completed the rehabilitation of the NKVD leader.

"I share your wish, Comrade, but we must finish the job in Europe first. The Finns will keep, Comrades."

None the less, the new stance ensured that some units, both regular army and NKVD, remained stationed to cover any signs of belligerence or treachery from the Finns.

Besides, the Red Army was clearly short of supplies and quality assets, and any Russian with a memory knew that the Finns were no pushover.

The following day, the Swedish Government announced the establishment of minefields on the borders of international waters, and assured all nations, regardless of their allegiance, that Swedish national boundaries would be rigorously policed.

Two days later, Monday 12th January illustrated the end result of the 'new' Swedish stance, as they attacked and sunk an unknown submarine inside their territorial waters.

Saturday 18th January saw British newspapers record the sad loss of HMS Rorqual, N74, a Grampus class mine laying submarine. Of her crew of sixty souls, only fourteen had been saved, and the dejected survivors were publically displayed by the triumphant Swedes as they were taken away to be interned for the rest of the present hostilities.

In truth, only a handful of people knew that the obsolete Rorqual had been scuttled, and that her skeleton crew of fourteen were all volunteers, selected from men declared unfit for active service.

To all intents and purposes, it looked like Sweden's borders were not to be messed with, no matter which flag you rallied behind.

Which was the plan.

2013 hrs, Monday, 20th January 1946, 3rd Guards Mechanised Corps headquarters, Bargteheide, Germany.

Lieutenant General V.T Obukov and his deputy, Major General Viktor Klimentievich Golov, sat drinking pepper vodka as they vied for supremacy over a battlefield of sixty-four black and white squares.

After a hasty knock, the bunker curtain was dragged aside and a flustered Major stepped in, closely followed by a smaller anonymous figure.

Obukov was deep in concentration and, in any case, Golov was technically the officer of the day, so he stayed focussed on his approaching finesse.

Golov, however, had the benefit of seeing the newcomer and was already thinking about making the young Major's life a misery in short order.

"Mayor Barodin, you have a report?"

"Comrade Mayor General Golov. This person arrived at our rear picket and asked to be brought before the commanding General."

Obukov had half an ear cocked to the conversation, but had just spotted a possible problem with his intended strategy, so decided the board still had priority.

Golov rose to his feet, his impressive height falling millimetres short of the bunker's wooden ceiling joists.

Major Barodin was a new arrival with 3rd Guards, and had yet to impress either of the general officers with his abilities, which made him fair game.

"So, any fucking Boris or Bogdan who turns up with a request to see the Comrade General gets your fucking personal escort here, eh?"

"No, Comrade Mayor General."

Exaggerating his lean, he eyed the newcomer and reverted back to eye contact with the hapless Barodin.

"And yet, here we are, or rather, here you are, with some shitty civilian in tow, both of you stood in our bunker, Comrade

89

Mayor. Now, unless you want to find yourself with a platoon command fighting those SS bastards in Alsace, I suggest you fucking sort yourself out man!"

The nondescript arrival passed Barodin the paperwork for the second time that night, and the Major passed it on like it was red-hot, which, in a sense, it was.

Golov read it.

A wide-eyed and disbelieving Golov re-read it.

He held the paper out to Obukov, obscuring his commander's view of the board and breaking his train of thought.

"Comrade General."

"For fuck's sake, Viktor! I'm trying to concentr..."

Obukov's eyes widened as his eyes took in certain words that leapt off the paper.

"For fuck's sake!"

There was little that Golov could meaningfully add.

"You are dismissed, Mayor. And nothing is to be said about this matter, clear?"

"Yes, Comrade Mayor General."

"Remember that, Comrade Barodin."

"Yes, Comrade Mayor General."

Barodin saluted and made his hasty retreat, happy to be away from something way beyond his pay grade and understanding.

The three were alone in the bunker, and the silence was oppressive.

Obukov examined the document once more and handed it to the newcomer.

"Your credentials are impeccable. How may we be of assistance, Comrade..."

He left the question hanging, although he knew exactly who was stood in front of him.

With a flick of his eyes, he encouraged Golov to an ice-breaking move.

His CoS picked up the bottle and a spare glass.

"Vodka, Comrade?"

"Thank you, but no thank you, Comrade."

The new arrival removed the nondescript ushanka and military greatcoat in which she had travelled from Hamburg, revealing the uniform of a Major General of the GRU, and one with the Hero Award at that.

The arrival of an unfamiliar Major General was never a welcome thing for troops of any nation, as bad things tended to visit themselves on men of all ranks, but such an arrival was even less welcome when unannounced and unexpected.

Even for a Lieutenant General commanding a Mechanised Corps, such an arrival was filled with danger, especially in the Red Army, where such surprises often brought orders to report back to Moscow, and the almost inevitable unsavoury end that such returns entailed.

Gesturing the GRU officer towards a spare chair, one that was close to the small fire, Golov stuck his head out of the bunker door and growled at the young Lieutenant positioned at a small desk.

"Harruddhin. Tea… and some of that German cake. Bring it yourself. Not an orderly."

Obukov used the wait to discover more about the Army's true strategic position, rather than rely on what senior officers were spoon-fed by higher command. Nazarbayeva was as candid as she could be, which reinforced Obukov's view that the war was going to hell in a handcart, and that all he had heard about the GRU woman was true.

Lieutenant Harruddhin, unhappy at doing orderly's work, entered the bunker with a tray containing captured English tea and liberated German stöllen.

Golov was about to give the nervous young officer a piece of his mind and some advice on rumour spreading, but Obukov beat him to it.

"Thank you, Leytenant. You may go and consider yourself off-duty now. You will do well to remember that the Mayor General is here on important secret business, business that will remain secret… and unspoken of. Am I clear, Comrade Harrudhin?"

"Yes, Comrade General."

The Lieutenant's retreat was about as speedy as it could be, without the indignity of breaking into a run.

"Thank you for that, Comrade General."

Obukov waved the piece of paper gently and then offered it back to Nazarbayeva.

"I am assuming that, your clandestine appearance apart, anyone with complete freedom of movement and action, authorised by the Comrade General Secretary, may wish for some… err… anonymity?"

Nazarbayeva folded the paper and slid it inside her breast pocket, extracting another which she passed to Golov, although she addressed the senior man.

"Comrade General, I find myself needing to speak to the man on that piece of paper and, rather unusually, on a matter of huge importance to the Motherland."

The statement didn't really make sense until Golov passed the slip of paper over.

Then, whilst he didn't fully understand, he understood more... maybe.

Nazarbayeva also suddenly had a moment of light, as her mind clawed deep into its recesses and prompted her to bring forth a memory of words written on a piece of paper by her long-dead mentor..

'V.K.G.? Can it be him?'

The out of place presence of a Christmas tree gave her the opening she needed.

Nazarbayeva gestured at the thinning spruce.

"When this is all over, Comrades, I look forward to next Christmas with my family once again. Perhaps somewhere other than home. I've heard that there is nothing like Christmas in Krakow."

Only the silent nods of men with bittersweet memories of home returned her enquiry.

'Not him then.'

Obukov broke from his thoughts first.

"May we all have that opportunity, Comrade General."

It was ten minutes to midnight before the man named on the paper was shown into a small workshop that had been set aside for Nazarbayeva's use.

The escort moved away, as instructed by Golov, and left the two alone.

Salutes were exchanged, as they always were, regardless of their status in other surroundings.

"Comrade Starshina."

"Comrade Mayor General."

Saluting hands relaxed, as did the voices.

"Husband."

"Wife."

The two hugged and kissed before settling down on a padded bench.

"What are you doing here, my woman?"

Part of him feared the worst, the sudden sadness in his wife's eyes declaring her as the bringer of bad tidings before she uttered a word.

"Is it Ivan? Ilya? What is wrong?"

Tatiana shook her head slowly.

"As far as I know they are both safe and well, Yuri."

Confused that he had misread his wife's face, Yuri Nazarbayev looked again.

The pain was still present, etched all over her pretty face.

"My love, what is wrong? What is it?"

Taking his hand, and the deepest of deep breaths, Tatiana Nazarbayeva started her story.

Yuri Nazarbayev listened, without interruption, as his wife told him all that had happened on that December day, or at least, all she believed had happened...

...and only up to a point.

She spared him some of the more delicate matters, purely through her own embarrassment.

When she finished, the silence was oppressive, her eyes filled with tears and concern as she watched her husband wrestle with the enormity of her words.

Almost as if waking from a trance, Yuri frowned and looked at the woman sat beside him.

"So how did you manage this little enterprise then, wife?"

"Does it matter, Yuri?"

"I'm just curious."

She produced the document that had caused such an effect on Obukov and Golov.

It had once been issued to her husband by a magnanimous leader wishing to assist a concerned husband to reach his wife's side in timely fashion.

Yuri Nazarbayev read it aloud.

"In the name of the Soviet Government and the Bolshevik Party, I command all persons, civil, military, and political, without exception and distinction of rank, to assist the bearer of this document, ...Comrade Nazarbayeva ... in the carrying out of their proper instructions, and thereby guaranteeing the bearer's freedom of movement and action as they see fit to discharge any and all orders given to them on matters of extreme state importance.

Issued by my hand on behalf of the Soviet Government and the Bolshevik Party, 20th August 1945.

У. Сталин

He brought the paper closer to his eyes.

"You changed it, Tatiana."

She shrugged, unsure as to what was happening and why her husband was examining the minutiae of her tampering with the document when there was the enormity of her transgression to deal with.

"Just a single A, my husband."

Which had been all that was needed to make it applicable to her; the addition of a single A.

Handing the document back, he composed himself, as he had been trying to do since the mother of his children had revealed everything of her shame.

Taking her hand in his, he spoke softly, but with conviction.

"It is done, and we both wish it was not so, but it is. It cannot be undone, my wife, and both of us will carry it like a burden from now onwards."

Tatiana nodded.

"There was no intent, my love. You did not set out to defile our marriage. It just happened. The rich food... the company... the wines..."

A crackle of emotion stopped him speaking further, and he coughed gently, willing himself to a less emotional state so he could continue and say exactly what he wanted to say, and in the way he wanted to say it.

"Wife, we will put this behind us and never speak of it again."

Taking her face gently in both hands, he spoke his final words.

"We... you and I... we've already lost too much, Tatiana. We will lose nothing more to this. If you seek my understanding, then you have it."

Both of them cried.

"If you seek my forgiveness, then you have that too... both without condition."

He kissed her on the lips, and on her cheeks, absorbing her tears.

"You are my wife, and my love. This will not stand between us."

They hugged in silence.

2111 hrs, Monday, 20th January 1946, OSS British Headquarters, 70-72 Grosvenor Street, London.

The great man had only just arrived but, as was his dynamic style, instead of taking the opportunity to shower and eat, he had swung straight into action.

He sat at Rossiter's desk, listening to the latest snippets that had been added to the information that had brought him from the States to England.

"So no-one else knows what we got here, Sam?"

"Some of the RAF boys know the basics of the numbers, but not names, and I had my troops clean up the raw intel at Archdale, just to make sure the name wasn't mentioned. I believe we're clean, General."

Major General William J. Donovan, head of the OSS, trusted his man, but the prize was so tantalising that he had to ask some basic questions.

"A plant?"

"Not a chance, General. No way, no how."

It hadn't seemed likely in any case.

"And he is who he says he is?"

"The paperwork supports it. He describes his family as we know 'em, and clearly doesn't know about any promotions, probably 'cos he was sort of outta the loop where he was."

Donovan nodded his understanding, policing up the large folder that represented all they knew on their prisoner and his family.

"Right then, Sam. Let's get down to brass tacks. I know you've developed some pretty good ideas on how we can use this gift horse. I'm going to leave you to run with this ball, but we're going to share this with our cousins. That's why I'm here, to help smooth matters as to why we didn't let them know immediately."

He held up his hand, silencing Rossiter's protest in its infancy.

"I know you've worked hard to hang on to this, Sam, but it's got to be shared."

Rossiter held back his questions, but his expression spoke volumes.

"We have a God-given chance, one chance, to use this boy, and if we do it right, then we can affect how this war's going to run. If we do it wrong, then there'll be hell to pay, so bringing the British on-board means we get all the minds working on how to do this... and there'll be no finger pointing if it goes to hell in a hand cart."

Standing smartly, Donovan tapped the file.

"This is great work, Sam, and I want you to head up our side of this. I will brief the British in the morning, and sort out with General Menzies how we proceed."

"Sir, if we've gotta share then I'd like to bring in the French too. I know a good man high up in the Bureau."

Donovan was surprised but didn't show it.

"Give me his name and I'll run it past Menzies. Wait until I give you the word though, Sam."

"Yes, Sir."

Rossiter quickly wrote out De Walle's name and passed it to his boss, ending with a formal salute.

Replying in kind, Donovan also extended his hand.

"Good work, Sam. Now, I need something to eat... and a shower."

"The Sergeant will show you to your quarters, General. It's all sorted."

"Thank you. Good night, Sam."

"Good night, general."

As soon as the door closed, Rossiter flopped into his seat, still warm from its previous occupant, and reached into the bottom drawer, extracting the bourbon and a glass.

He carefully poured a good measure and threw it down his neck in one action.

"Goddamnit!"

He patted the file as he poured another.

The cover was nondescript, bearing only the names 'Achilles' and 'Thetis', as well as the insignia of a top secret file.

Ancient Greek history was a favourite of Rossiter's, so he had chosen appropriate names for those represented in the file.

Achilles was Thetis' son, or in real file terms, Ilya was the son of a Major General in the GRU, one Tatiana Nazarbayeva, which represented a huge opportunity for Allied intelligence.

Nazarbayev took leave of his wife and returned to his unit, his outer calm hiding an inner turmoil.

Something that was his, exclusively his, had been lost, and could never, no matter what he said or tried to think, be returned to what it was.

His mind flicked between emotions, seeking the one that caused him most pain, or the one that could give him most comfort.

Grief, betrayal, love, family, sons, betrayal, memories, betrayal... betrayal...

And then, in a moment, they were gone, and only anger was left.

[Stalin's signature was acquired from the public domain, under this attribution - By Connormah, Joseph Stalin [Public domain], via Wikimedia Commons]

Relative to the events within the Headquarters of 'Camerone', Gougenheim, Alsace, on Sunday 8th December 1945

Knocke had remarked how Weiss looked as white as a sheet on that early December Sunday evening.

Weiss was embarrassed inside, believing that his lack of colour and tiredness was due to the efforts of his 'removal' of Kowalski and the woman, and subsequent close shave with the room inspections.

He started to feel genuinely unwell, and pain spread through his head and eyes, growing every second.

Without examining the folder, Agent Amethyst had surrendered to the sudden onset of lethargy, using the continued presence of French Intelligence agents to justify his inactivity.

The midnight rapping on his door was most unwelcome, the more so as it yielded Sergeant Lutz, recently returned to light duties in the headquarters, who issued an immediate and non-negotiable summons to an interview.

Two members of 'Deux' trawled through Weiss' actions for the previous evening, cross-referencing with other testimonies. Sat at the back of the room was Knocke, there solely to observe. Adjacent to him was the very beautiful French Capitaine that Weiss had dreamed of conquering ever since he had arrived at the

Camerone headquarters, her attention clearly focussed on recording the full interview in shorthand.

Despite the fact that the German Officer was clearly unwell, the interview lasted for nearly forty-five minutes of detail, review of detail, and intense cross-examination, only being concluded when an orderly arrived with coffee. Encouraged to take his with him, Weiss had been permitted back to his room, where he took two aspirin and immediately collapsed onto his bed.

The arrival of coffee had been the pre-arranged signal that the task was complete.

In the office, De Walle could not spare Knocke's discomfort, so simply placed the recovered folder on the desk and invited his man to speak.

The orderly, actually a 'Deux' man, spoke swiftly.

"Sir, Agent Guiges and I searched the room thoroughly and discovered a bent nail on top of the wardrobe. As it was not dusty, unlike the furniture it was on, we found it suspicious."

Nervously coughing, conscious of the fact that he was the centre of attention for two extremely unhappy senior men, he tried to continue as quickly as possible.

"Guiges quickly found the under floor hiding place, which contained that folder, a silenced pistol, his documentation, and a copy of Thomas Mann's 'Der Zauberberg'. We replaced all the items, unloaded the pistol, and exchanged the contents of the folder for meaningless paperwork."

"Thank you, Denys. If that's all?"

It was, and Denys Montabeau beat a hasty retreat, nodding to De Valois on the way out.

"Scheisse!"

None of the room's occupants were used to outbursts from Knocke.

"So it is Weiss who killed the Russian... and the woman agent." Knocke's mind was working on what other damage Weiss could have brought about and immediately started wondering if the reverses of Spectrum Black had been authored in a small bedroom upstairs.

De Walle understood perfectly and offered up his own knowledge on the matter.

"This piece of rubbish was a late arrival at Sassy, Ernst. According to records, he arrived with your command on..."

The German officer completed the statement.

"On the 3rd of December."

De Walle was impressed.

Knocke also calculated that the timing would not have permitted Weiss to betray the operation to his masters.

However, De Valois had something to say on the matter.

"Mon Général, there is a problem here."

She produced her notes taken during a telephone exchange with the senior Deux officer at Sassy.

"Weiss left the main camp on November 28th. At his own request, his travel documents permitted him to proceed to Gougenheim via Pfalzweyer."

De Walle snarled immediately.

"And Pfalzweyer is close enough to Phalsbourg to make no difference, and a short hop to Sarrebourg eh? In that time he could have acquired a lot of information."

Knocke steepled his fingers in front of his face, tapping his lips with the central spire, his face growing darker by the second, so much so that his silence became oppressive and stopped De Walle and Valois in their tracks.

"Pfalzweyer."

Knocke's tone indicated that he had developed a greater understanding.

"Why Pfalzweyer?"

De Walle's question was partly answered by Anne-Marie.

"He told the Sassy Transportation Officer that he wished to visit the brother of one of his Hitler Youth soldiers, who was killed in Normandy. The TO is a former 12th SS man, so gave him the necessary travel permits immediately."

De Walle pushed further.

"Did he recall the name of the man that Weiss intended to visit?"

"Not accurately. He remembers Bart or Bert, nothing more."

Knocke sat forward in his chair, slowly unfolding his hands, drawing the others forward to hear his words.

"Norbert. Hans-Georg Norbert, Capitaine, Mountain Battalion."

He had their undivided attention.

"Pfalzweyer was Rettlinger's headquarters for the week before the attack."

Another thought occurred, and it sent him into one of the drawers in his desk, searching for a casualty report.

The paper flicked noisily as Knocke consulted the painful document, reading names of those no longer alive. He suddenly closed it with a flourish and a noise that marked a moment of supreme horror.

Passing the list to De Walle, Knocke shook his head in anger and disbelief.

"He's not there, Georges. He's not on the list."

De Walle checked for himself, which Knocke accepted was not an insult.

"Perhaps he is one of those as yet unidentified from the horror of La Petite Pierre, Ernst?"

"No, he is not. I am sure of it. His unit was at Neuwiller-lès-Saverne, and his body, and those of nine others, has not yet been recovered."

"Merde!"

Both men looked at St.Clair, thus far silent, whose contribution, although unnecessary, summed up the situation.

There was a silence that, by unspoken agreement between St.Clair, De Valois and De Walle, only Knocke would break.

"This cannot go on. We must find a way to purge any problems within our own ranks before we become a liability."

De Walle offered up a quick idea.

"There is someone who can help us, I'm sure of it."

Thinking quickly, he decided that Anne-Marie was trusted enough to hear a name and some highly protected information.

"You have heard of Gehlen, Ernst?"

"Yes, but is this his area of expertise now?"

"Général Gehlen is now head of the German Intelligence apparatus, and has already had some success with discovering agent-provocateurs within the new Republic's armies. He and I have... err... cooperated on some ventures, so he owes me a favour or two."

There was no time for outrage or posturing, something that they all understood.

"Then get your favours returned as soon as possible, and put the trust back in my soldiers!"

Immediately he raised his voice, Knocke's hands were on the way up in a placatory gesture. It was not necessary, as his angst was understood, and his faith in his troops undermined.

St.Clair, as hurt as Knocke by the revelations, tackled De Walle head on.

"So how do you intend to do this, Sir?"

Knocke answered in the Frenchman's stead.

"That is not our concern for now, Celestin. We may not wish to know. So long as our operational efficiency is not affected, Georges."

De Walle nodded back and ventured a suggestion.

"I think it is high time that the Legion was withdrawn from frontline service and given the opportunity to rest. Given the latest deployment of our Allies, I think that High Command would agree to give their finest soldiers a break, eh?"

"Agreed. Now, to Weiss."

De Valois rose slowly.

"I have an idea of how we can turn this to our advantage, Sir, but it will take fast work."

The three men listened to her hastily hatched plan and, despite their objections to the part she chose to play, saw opportunity raise its head.

The plan was agreed.

Anne-Marie de Valois decided on a simple approach. No suspicious adjustment to her make-up or clothing, deciding, quite rightly, that the looks the swine Weiss had shot her so often were enough indication that he desired her.

Time was of the essence, in as much as she needed to buy as much as possible, whilst a convincing alternative folder containing fake information on the Spectrum plans was acquired.

If the misleading folder and the bullets could be replaced without Weiss' knowledge, then an opportunity to mislead the Soviets would exist.

The senior Deus officer knew that such maskirovka already existed, a subterfuge prepared and constructed for when or if an opportunity knocked.

De Walle was already on the phone, establishing what could be done in the time available.

Anne-Marie de Valois paused outside the bedroom.

Such acts as she was prepared to commit herself to now had previously been unthinkable, but her new experience of the sacrifices that others were prepared to make made her more amenable to the idea of using all her womanly charms for the common cause.

Had she walked into his quarters naked she would have not got any more reaction from Weiss.

The man was clearly extremely ill and in a place where her distraction plan was not needed.

She called for the doctor and sat with the German until he arrived.

"According to the Doctor, he probably has a severe chest onfection, but there's a suspicion of something more serious and life-threatening."

She delivered the information matter-of-factly, and it was received in a way that indicated that neither of the listeners cared.

Knocke, tired after a full day spent organising Camerone's withdrawal, had turned in some time beforehand, but De Walle and St.Clair had waited for Anne-Marie's report.

They also waited for the arrival of a file, product of De Walle's enquiries, one to satisfy their hatching of a false information scam on Weiss, one that outlined a deception, a maskirovka, a subterfuge, part of the planning of Spectrum, which was now to be delivered into the enemy's hands...

...always providing that the 'enemy' in the equation recovered.

The Camerone and Tannenberg withdrew over the next two days, moving back into a second line position, permitting two Spanish units to take over their former lines.

On 12th December 1945, the deserted headquarters, for some reason, left unused by the relieving Spanish troops, caught fire.

Much of the building was damaged, certainly enough to prevent its use as a headquarters, or to offer decent shelter in the prevalent weather conditions.

1854 hrs, Tuesday, 21st January 1946, Former Headquarters of 'Camerone', Gougenheim, Alsace.

Against doctor's orders, Weiss had managed to get himself out of the new medical facility at Luneville.

The Legion transport officer proved to be made of sterner stuff than the Medical Officer who had vainly tried to keep Weiss on the ward.

The TO insisted that his valuable jeep would go with a driver and that was that, leaving Weiss no choice but to acquiesce or create a scene that might cause him some problems.

In truth, he was still weak and welcomed the journey without the effort of driving, although he didn't welcome the additional company of the driver, although the driving skills exhibited drew his grudging respect, as the jeep was expertly propelled through snow and ice.

At least the man had the common sense to stay quiet, allowing Weiss to close his eyes and allow his mind to drift to the possibilities.

He had heard of the fire whilst in his sick bed, but hoped that something salvageable would be left for his cause to use against the Allied scum.

Just before seven in the evening, the jeep pulled up outside the darkened shell of the old Legion Headquarters and the driver tapped the sleeping Weiss' leg.

"We're here, Sir."

Orienting himself quickly, Weiss checked the torch's light against the palm of his hand and pulled the side panel back, allowing the snow to float in and melt in the slightly warmer interior air.

"Keep the engine running. I won't be long. I just hope my gear survived the fire."

It was his excuse for making the journey.

Entering the freezing building, he made his way towards his room, checking the integrity of the charred stairs as he went.

They creaked but held firm, permitting him to gain the landing in good time.

He barely cast a glance at the door of the room where he had terminated two lives, intent on recovering his possessions as soon as possible.

His room was badly affected by the fire, and to his horror, part of the floor had burned through.

The wardrobe had come apart, and therefore the nail was lost.

Opening his penknife, he prised at the charred board, fearing the worst.

"Scheisse!"

The folder was there, but damaged, although not as much as it could have been, given the severity of the fire that had embraced it.

Edges were black and brown, pages were wrinkled and stained by the water that had saved its contents from fire. He slid it inside an innocuous paper bag and followed it with the rest of the contents of his cache.

The suddenly flickering of the torch encouraged his haste, and he was back in the jeep within three minutes, the warm interior in contrast to the gathering cold of yet another European winter night.

The sound of the jeep's engine faded to nothing before the watcher allowed himself some small movement, his frozen and aching limbs reminding him of their disgust at over an hour and a half of immobility. Laid out on the floor above, and with a line of sight through a fire ravaged ceiling, De Walle's man had seen all he needed to see.

0310 hrs, Wednesday, 22nd January 1946, the Cemetery, La Petite Pierre, Alsace.

They had found two more dead Soviet soldiers the previous evening, concealed by displaced earth and the constant stream of snow, until once again exposed to the air by the spades of a working party.

It had been too cold for either cadaver to decompose, so the torture of each man's death was clear to see upon the corpses, the end clearly wrought by exposure to the high-explosives and shrapnel of grenades.

Both were buried in a shell hole and earth from the freshly dug foxholes used to cover them over, the frozen soil itself only loosened and shifted by yet more grenades, sunk in hard-worked holes in solid earth mass.

Pedro Oscales had been too young to march with the blue-shirted fascists of the Azul on their mission to rid the world of communism, but now he bore his country's uniform proudly in what some in his homeland were calling the Second Crusade.

Ensign, or Alférez Oscales, akin to 2nd Lieutenant in rank, had overseen the final repositioning of his platoon, the order to adjust 3rd Company's positions closer to the shattered village of la Petite Pierre universally greeted with anguish by the Spanish soldiery, who had reluctantly turned out of their comparatively warm positions into the freezing cold air.

The final works had only been completed two hours beforehand, but the men had made themselves at home in quick order, and stoves warmed the hastily constructed bunkers in which they sheltered.

Oscales moved through his lines seeking out the men of his command, laughing with them, sharing a coffee or a cigarette, the energy of youth and the enthusiasm of his cause keeping him going when other officers had already retreated to their own bunks for the night.

He took his leave of Sargento Velasquez and his section, receiving a grunt of satisfaction from the old veteran as he closed one eye to receive a light for his cigarette, maintaining his night vision.

Cupping the glowing end, Oscales drew the warm smoke into his lungs and felt the chill of his surroundings momentarily expelled, although, in truth, the knowledge of what had happened in this small Alsatian village meant that his god-fearing men believed that the chills would never go away, even in the height of summer.

A different chill visited itself upon him, one born of fear and sudden awareness, as the snow gently flowed across his vision and the weak waning moon provided a sudden and unexpected insight into the area that his platoon had vacated the day beforehand.

At first the words froze in his throat, the prospect of action taking his ability to speak as it knotted his throat.

He tried again.

Nothing but a meaningless squeak.

He fumbled for his sidearm and pointed the Astra 600 in the general direction of the white ants that were swarming in his direction.

Three shots loosened his nervous vocal chords.

"Alarma! Alarma Ombres!"

He fired off the remaining five 9mm parabellum bullets before moving to reload.

Around him, the Spanish positions came to life as his soldiers burst from their bunkers to repel the Soviet assault.

It was too late, and had been long before Oscales had spotted the swarms of white-clad Soviet soldiers.

The outlying posts were filled with blood already icing, spilt from throats slit from ear to ear.

Men rushing to their positions were cut down in the communications trenches; yet others perished as satchel charges were thrown inside their shelters.

One MG34 stuttered into life, putting four enemy soldiers down before a grenade took the life of the three men manning the weapon, and ended the sum total of the resistance offered by Oscales' platoon.

Still fumbling with a new magazine, the young ensign found his voice at the last, if only to scream as an entrenching tool swept down from the snowy night, cleaving deep into the join between neck and shoulder.

And then he was silent once more.

0413 hrs, Wednesday, 22nd January 1946, Headquarters, 16th US Armored Brigade, Fénétrange, France.

Edwin Greiner was not a man given to either panic or exaggeration.

None the less, his arrival in Pierce's quarters unannounced at stupid o'clock in the morning bore all the hallmarks of a man suffering from both, at least to the until recently fast-asleep commander of the 16th US Armored Brigade.

Still waking up, Pierce shook his head dramatically, interrupting the flow of words.

"Whoa Ed, for Christ's sake, whoa there."

Suffering from neither panic nor exaggeration, Greiner realised he had made a mistake trying to lay everything on his commander before he was suitably awake and got out of bed.

As ordered, coffee arrived and Pierce consumed the full measure before he focussed on his CoS.

Swinging his legs out and dropping his bare feet to the cold wooden floor, Pierce prepared himself.

Holding out his mug for a refill, the General snapped fully awake.

"Now, what about the Spanish?"

Four minutes before Greiner had burst in on Pierce, the duty officer had similarly roused the CoS, providing him with an urgent order, straight from De Lattre himself.

The contents of that order fell before Pierce's gaze, causing him to splutter in alarm.

"What the goddamned hell? Intel said nothing was happening… going to happen either. Overrun he says," he angled the paper towards Greiner by way of confirmation.

Then the mind of a General kicked in.

"Ok, get the people up. Get the staff in the office ten minutes ago. Get movement warning orders out to the commands. Have someone liaise with 2nd Infantry and Group Lorraine on anticipated operational boundaries."

He finished up his second mug full.

"And make sure we got plenty of this to hand."

"I'm on it,"

And Greiner was gone.

106

Pierce stared at the message again, almost hoping he had read it wrong.

'Spanish 22nd Infantry Division overrun by Red Army units of unknown type and strength. 16th Armored is ordered to immediately advance and hold the Gungweiler – Siewiller – Vescheim line, maintaining the road communications to the north and south. US 2nd Infantry Division will be on northern flank, Group Lorraine on the southern flank. 16th now under command of Lorraine, effective immediately. De Lattre.'

He had read it correctly the first time.

'Goddamned shit.'

A few minutes later, Pierce was stood before his staff organising the emergency forward movement of his Brigade, to block God knew what enemy force from doing God knew whatever it was that they intended.

Fig# 125 - Town of Drulingen, 22nd January 1946.

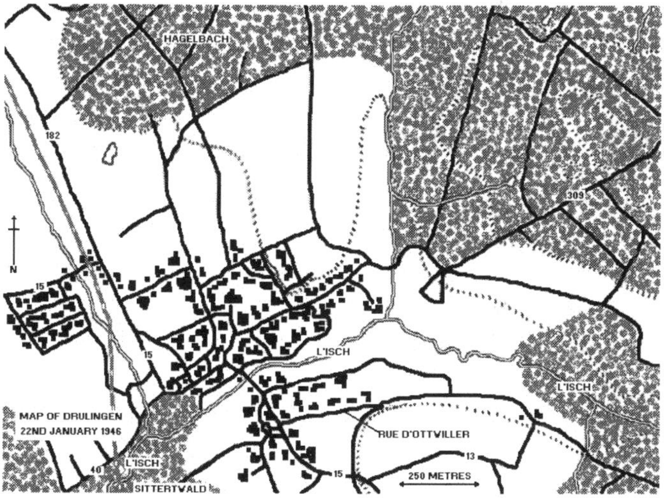

0418 hrs, Wednesday, 22nd January 1946, Drulingen, France.

"Not even remotely funny, Al."

The commander of B Company rolled over under his blankets, seeking further sleep.

"Not joking, Lukas. The commies are coming. Get your ass outta bed. Move it soldier!"

By rights, Gesualdo shouldn't be here, his injuries not yet healed, but he was, hobbling around the guest house which represented the headquarters for B, D, and F Companies, 2nd Ranger Battalion, licking their wounds in the small French village of Drulingen, Bas-Rhin, France.

As senior officer, the newly-promoted Captain Barkmann suddenly found himself in command of three battered companies of Rangers, clearly now sat in harm's way.

"Ok, ok, ok. Rouse the boys. Officers group in five. Senior NCO's to do the rounds and get us firmed up a-sap."

Both men paused as the sound of distant rumbling reached their ears.

Actually, not so distant rumbling.

The two friends exchanged looks, knowing that the day ahead would bring new horrors.

The meeting had broken up quite quickly once the order to hold had been received.

Whilst the instruction itself was precise, there was scant little information on what was coming down the roads and tracks leading from the woods to the East, although the constant use of star shells and parachute flares indicated that whatever it was, it was coming closer.

Establishing contact with the rest of the Ranger Battalion positioned north at Bettwiller and establishing the boundaries at the Hagelbach, Barkmann had made his dispositions as best he could, pushing his forward positions up to cover the line of the L'Isch watercourse, a small frozen stream that ran east from Drulingen, before splitting north and south-east on the edge of the woods.

Two wayward 3" AT guns on their way as replacements for the 16th Armored, whose lost crews had spent the night with the Rangers, found themselves under new management and tasked with defending the approaches to Drulingen, watching Routes 309 and 13.

No contact had yet been made with any friendly unit to the south, so a small patrol was sent south-east in three jeeps with the express need for information.

Barkmann pushed D Company out to Route 13 and had them dig in on a curved line from the edge of the Sittertwald to the junction of Routes 13 and 15, and on to Rue Ottwiller.

B Company took over at that point and sat astride Route 309, all the way to just short of the engineers of B/254th Combat

Engineer Battalion, with whom, he entrusted the defence of the Hagelbach and any approach down Route 15/182.

F Company formed in the village, split into four groups. One fortified the eastern edge of Drulingen, a second did the same to cover the south-eastern approach up Route 15.

The remaining two groups were fully mobile and held in reserve, ready to be committed to where they were needed at a moment's notice.

The defence was also boosted, although somewhat worryingly, by the speedy arrival of Spanish troops withdrawing at speed down the 309.

A fully-equipped Spanish mortar company was welcome, although they seemed less than content to remain in Drulingen. Some of Gesualdo's men moved in alongside them for 'support', as the US officer tactfully put it, although his men understood that they were there to stop the spooked soldiers from running further back.

Immediately on their heels was a headquarters group from a Spanish infantry unit. It was so intent on self-preservation that there was no chance of stopping their flight without the use of force.

The four vehicles sped away into the distance, carrying the Spanish commanders to safety and abandoning their men to their fate.

Fig# 126 – Allied forces at Drulingen.

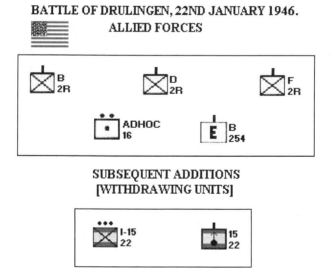

BATTLE OF DRULINGEN, 22ND JANUARY 1946.
ALLIED FORCES

SUBSEQUENT ADDITIONS
[WITHDRAWING UNITS]

Barkmann moved forward to B Company lines and scanned the terrain with his binoculars, after sending up a magnesium flare to add his own illumination to the eerie battlefield.

Immediately his gaze fell upon a group of infantry, clearly struggling under the burden of wounded men, moving back as swiftly as they could whilst other smaller groups fell back, fired, fell back, all the time providing cover for their comrades.

Walter Ford, B Company's senior surviving NCO, heard the whistle and looked around, seeing his company commander trying to attract his attention.

Barkmann's hand gestures were easily understood and Ford quickly detailed every other man to move forward and assist the retiring wounded as best they could.

These Spanish soldiers were clearly made of sterner stuff, their retreat conducted on a swift organised fashion.

As the Rangers of B Company leapt forward in an instant, led by their First Sergeant, unwelcome flares rose into the sky.

0502 hrs, Wednesday, 22nd January 1946, Drulingen, France.

Fig# 127 - Drulingen - positions and assaults.

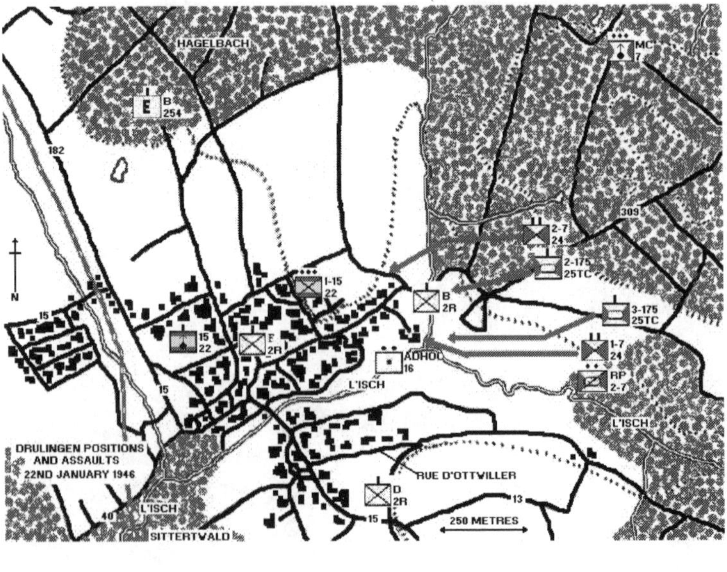

"Enemy infantry just appeared to our front, Comrade Leytenant. The swine must be dug in up there."

"Halt!"

The BA64, moving forward with the advancing infantry, slid to a halt immediately, allowing Junior Lieutenant Sukolov to survey the ground.

That which his driver had spoken of leapt into view through his lenses.

He saw men moving forward to help the hard-pressed Spaniards.

'Amerikanski!'

Wishing to convey his calmness and professionalism to the driver, Sukolov slowly took hold of the radio and made his calculations.

"Shall I move back, Comrade Leytenant?"

The nervousness in the driver's voice was apparent, his own combat experience only slightly more than that of his commander, for whom this battle would be his first time under fire.

Casualties in the Soviet reconnaissance units were always extreme, but this conflict had brought them to a new level.

Not deigning to give the man a response, Sukolov spoke into the radio, establishing contact with the Major commanding his battalion.

After the preliminaries were exchanged, he got down to business.

"Enemy troops in probable company strength minimum, occupying dug-in positions east of Drulingen, set to west of water line. Request anti-infantry fire mission, Gorod-Five-Two over."

0504 hrs, Wednesday, 22nd January 1946, Drulingen, France.

Illumination rounds burst in the sky above.

Barkmann swept the ground in front of him, his binoculars suddenly feeling very heavy.

His ears suddenly exploded with noise.

"Jesus!"

Too late, Barkmann slapped his hands to his ears as the nearby 3" AT gun sent its version of death hurtling across the battlefield.

The crew may have been new to the battlefield, but missing such an easy target was more than they could manage, and the Ranger officer heard their cheers, marking the death of something with a red star on.

Turning back, he could see Soviet infantry now apparent on the edge of the woods and ordered covering fire for his and the Spanish troops still struggling back with an increasing number of injured men.

One of the Rangers' two 50.cal heavy MGs lashed out, and Barkmann could see the deadly bullets ripping men apart, forcing the advancing soldiers to drop into cover.

Garands and .30cals added their own chorus, the Ranger line erupting and then quickly quietening again, as targets became scarce.

In it all, Lukas Barkmann heard the distinctive sound of a Springfield rifle as his sniper, Corporal Irlam, engaged specific targets.

Irlam was generally considered to be one of B Company's greatest assets, despite the fact that everyone in the unit considered him to be totally mad.

His skill with the Springfield was legendary, bringing him regular awards and prizes in Army shooting competitions and, at least at first, earning his comrades many dollars in side wagers against over-confident opponents.

However, his weapon of choice was the dirk, a small Scottish blade.

The one he fussed over on a daily basis had been given to him by his father many years beforehand, and it was kept sharp and deadly, for there was nothing that Irlam liked more than to slide it into some defenceless body without warning.

In times of peace, Irlam might well have found himself in an institution, slated as a psychopath, but in times of war such men are useful, and so he found himself a decorated veteran of the Rangers' war, and one of 2nd Rangers top soldiers.

The Springfield spoke again, sending another son of Russia to his maker.

Just to the right, an enemy vehicle burned.

"Gorod-five-two come in, over."
Static.
"Gorod-five-two come in. Report, over."
Static.
"Blyad!"
The Major in charge knew that Sukulov would never report again.

A recent arrival himself, he tried to work out what was happening, consulted the map, noting the markers suggesting where his point observer had been at that moment and working out where the enemy were.

He tapped the map and nodded to himself.

'You will not have died in vain, Ilya Mikhailovich!'

He ordered the artillery to fire on the point under his grubby fingers.

Fig# 128 – Soviet forces at Drulingen

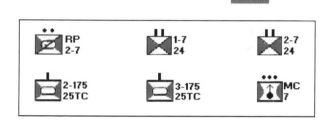

BATTLE OF DRULINGEN, 22ND JANUARY 1946.
SOVIET FORCES

The Spanish troops were all now within the Rangers' lines and Lukas Barkmann was busy sorting them out as best he could.

To their credit, the survivors were still up for the fight.

Ford had a little Spanish language to play with, and two of the Rangers had more than a little Mexican in their blood, so between the four of them they were able to get the battered Spanish soldiers sorted.

The wounded were taken back to the aid station, set up towards the rear of Drulingen.

Detailing his two Mexican-Spanish speakers as escorts, Barkmann organised the remaining forty-one men into a reserve group, and sent them back into the village to lick their wounds in the Protestant presbytery on the Rue Durstel.

No sooner had they been sent on their way than Soviet artillery shells started falling on and around B Company positions.

To the Rangers' front, the Soviet infantry had melted away, going to ground whilst their artillery and mortars worked on the defenders, and whilst their support gathered itself.

Barkmann, back at his command post, radioed his commander with a situation report.

0513 hrs, Wednesday, 22nd January 1946, Headquarters, 16th US Armored Brigade, Fénétrange, France.

Greiner read the message slip and checked off the details against the situation map.

"General, we have enemy contact reports from Ranger units here... and here..." he touched Bettwiller, then Drulingen.

The position of the 16th showed the advance units still short of the target hold line.

"Infantry and light artillery fire only at the moment."

Pierce consumed his fifth coffee in quiet thought.

"2nd Infantry and Lorraine?"

"Not a squeak from 2nd, but Lorraine are receiving incoming artillery and have had light contact around Eschbourg."

Indicating the location of that clash, Greiner waited.

"Anything more from the Spanish?"

"Nothing of use, General. They are still piecing together a better picture. From what we have so far, it seems they have broken open on Routes 9 and 178, here at Petit Pierre... and also on the 919 here at Tieffenbach."

Pierce accepted yet another refill as he thought aloud.

"So the deepest move we have yet is against the Rangers front there at Drulingen. Is that because the Spanish folded easily on that line, or is that the centre of this attack, Ed?"

Greiner knew enough to know that Pierce had his own idea already.

"My gut tells me that they want to cut the route north-south. At Drulingen... well... they pretty much already got it sown up, seems to me. They will want to expand that some. I'm thinking two-pronged, Drulingen and Bettwiller, which takes out the railroad too, Sir."

Pierce frowned.

"Nothing more expansive, Ed?"

Greiner shook his head emphatically.

"I don't see it at the moment. Intel gives them limited resources as it is, certainly nothing has suggested any sort of major attack. My money is on a local op with limited scope for a specific purpose. Someone wants to remind the bosses that he's about and on the ball."

"How do you make that read?"

Greiner accepted the challenge.

"It reeks of a limited op run with assets to hand. No air force support. Yes, we know they are crippled, but if it was significant, then they'd have put some air up. The artillery sounds like divisional at best. Traditionally, they line the goddamn guns up wheel to wheel for full ops, whole divisions worth. Our recon has been excellent, the flights go out relatively unchallenged at the moment, so we pretty sure they haven't moved anything new into the area, plus we've wrecked their infrastructure so bad they'd find it difficult anyway."

"Not hedging your bets, Ed?"

Pierce's smile was genuine, for he knew his CoS always told it how it was.

"I get the big bucks to make you look good, Sir."

"OK then. So, looks like we have some options here. Weather?"

"Seaweed watchers reckon -15°, no snow, clear day all round."

"Air?"

"All we want, and then some."

Pierce finished the coffee and placed the mug down with an air of finality and decisiveness.

"I think we bring them on in outta the woods, get the bastards in one place... and turn air on 'em."

The two officers leant on the map table, eyes drawn to Drulingen and Bettwiller.

"OK, we pull the Rangers back, once we have a secure perimeter here..." Pierce drew a rough pencil line up the 1061.

"Draw the commies on and then wipe the bastards out. Let Lorraine and 2nd be the rocks on our flanks as we feign a withdrawal to this line and bingo. Then we roll them back, all the way to the start line."

Greiner stood.

"I'll cut some orders immediately, Sir."

0525 hrs, Wednesday, 22nd January 1946, Drulingen, France.

In Drulingen, the pressure was mounting, as the artillery fire intensified.

"Al, orders from above. We gotta hold for another hour and then bug out as fast as we can to Weyer."

"OK. Should we start moving some of the wounded back now, Lukas?"

"Good idea. Use any of the vehicles, 'cept the mobile reserve force ones. Get the wounded evac'd and that'll be less for us to worry about when the time comes."

Another 76.2mm HE shell landed close enough to shower the men with snow and earth.

"You get the feeling they're going to push us soon?"

"Sure as shit... they ain't here to admire the view, Lukas."

Gesualdo's grin was infectious.

"Get the wounded out a-sap then, Al."

The 3" AT rapped out a shell, again causing ears to be assaulted by the sound.

"Goddammit!"

Barkmann saw, rather than heard, the replying shell, a supersonic streak of metal move across his vision, just missing the AT gun.

Both Ranger officers looked at the enemy lines and saw that the battle had changed.

"Fuck! Get 'em the hell outta here now, Al!"

Gesualdo was up and running in an instant, turning his back on the solid metal shapes that had materialised on the 319 to their front.

Barkmann grabbed the radio.

0533 hrs, Wednesday, 22nd January 1946, Headquarters, 16th US Armored Brigade, Fénétrange, France.

"Tanks?"

"Yessir... at least company strength by the reports."

"Not good, not good. Can they pull out now?"

"Might just have them overrun as they try, less'n we can interfere. Too early for air, so artillery?"

"I'll scare them up what I can, Ed. Get something going for ground back up and give the commander permission to withdraw back as soon as he sees fit. Warn up the flank units on that score too."

Leaving Greiner to his work, Pierce sought out Hamlett, the bespectacled artillery commander.

116

"Barksdale, what have you got set up ready that can help us here?"

Colonel Barksdale Hamlett Jr produced a sheet of paper from his folder and checked, more for confirmation than anything.

"396th is online and ready to go, General."

105mm Howitzers could have a very negative effect on tanks, so Pierce was more than happy.

"Get them dialled in to support the Rangers at Drulingen, fast as you can, Barks."

0529 hrs, Wednesday, 22nd January 1946, Drulingen, France.

No sooner had Barkmann finished his exchange with headquarters than the 396th came on air, offering up their fire support.

Spreading a map across his knees, the Ranger Captain jotted the coordinates down and relayed them to the waiting artillery.

Leaving the airwaves silent for a moment, Barkmann moved up to the edge of his position and waited for the incoming shell.

Disappointingly, it arrived in the woods behind the advancing tanks and infantry.

They seemed an awful lot closer now and so Barkmann made the call for full fire.

"Drop three hundred and fire for effect, Boxer-six, over."

A lifetime later, or at least that was how it seemed, the landscape around the advancing Soviet elements erupted in high-explosive, immediately yielding two huge secondary explosions, as shells struck home on thin top armour.

Barkmann shouted at his nearest soldiers.

"Pour it into 'em, boys!"

The Soviet infantry of 24th Rifle Division started running as fast as they could, savvy enough to understand that it would be much safer the nearer they were to the capitalist positions.

Veteran tankers from the 25th Tank Corps started to speed in all directions, keen to avoid the rain of death, but also conscious of the presence of the anti-tank guns that had so far claimed two of their number.

One T-34/85, some five hundred yards to the Rangers' front, drew in behind a pile of explosively turned snow, the commander leaning over to consult with the infantry huddled in the flimsy cover.

As Barkmann watched, he saw the man's neck disintegrate and then heard the crack of the Springfield, as Irlam neatly put a round into the tank officer.

The roar of the 3", followed immediately by whooping from the crew, indicated more success for the gunners. Off to the right, another T-34 spilt black smoke over the field as its crew made off to the rear, helped along by fire from the Rangers.

The whooping stopped in an instant of blinding light as a 76.2mm artillery shell dropped millimetre perfect onto the breech block of the 3" weapon, where it exploded with full force.

The gun and its crew disintegrated in a micro-second, as explosive power ripped the metal and flesh apart, scattering deadly fragments in all directions.

The 3" shell that the loader had been holding fell with a heavy thud, point first, into Barkmann's position, coming to rest in the ground, upright, and roughly six inches from his right hand.

'Oh shit!'

It remained dormant.

Something wet clung to his face and formed oily, bloody teardrops as it dripped downwards.

Other bits of men and weapon fell to earth all around him and his nearest positions, and not all missed other targets.

Irlam was struck by, of all things, a pencil, the wood shaft sticking out of the side of his neck like a medieval arrow sans feathers.

A Ranger Corporal, bringing forward more .50cal ammo, was struck in the midriff by the fast moving nearside tyre assembly, which folded him neatly in half and propelled his dead body many yards away. The corpse came to rest in the side of a small snow drift, leaving only a set of hands and a set of feet protruding, either side of the shredded rubber tyre.

Two other Rangers, relocating with a .30cal, were directly struck by whirling pieces of gun, both fatally.

A Soviet shell fragment punched through the chest of a Ranger rifleman stood next to Barkmann, killing the man instantly.

The .50cal fell silent in horror as the loader coughed out his life, his throat and upper chest destroyed by something very solid moving at speed. His gunner did what he could, pulling away at the offending object, unconsciously registering the shape of a Colt 1911A, packing the wound and administering morphine before he accepted that his friend had stopped clinging to life.

Barkmann shook his head, trying to clear the mist that descended after the explosion. Since Hattmatt, he seemed more prone to such things and now was not the time.

From his own position, Barkmann was powerless to do anything but shout.

"Get that goddamned ma deuce back into action, now!"

In the time that the .50cal had been silent, the wave of enemy had covered many yards.

It stuttered back into life as the dead loader and stunned gunner were pushed aside by Ford.

To the right of the weapon, Barkmann saw movement and realised that the enemy were closer than he imagined.

A surge of enemy soldiery issued from behind a low snowy hump, bearing down on the .50cal position.

There was no time.

Shouldering his Garand, Barkmann worked the line, dropping the enemy into the snow from left to right.

The clip pinged out of the weapon as he emptied it into the running group.

He had put six on target, missing two.

That left five enemy soldiers.

"Ford, to your right! To your right!"

The .50cal blotted out his voice, and the Sergeant and gunner-now-loader continued, oblivious to their approaching doom.

'Oh shit!'

He stood and yelled.

"Yaaaaaahhhhh!"

Before he knew what he was doing, Barkmann was up and out of his position, screaming at the top of his voice, and charging towards the five surviving enemy.

The combination of the death of their comrades, and the blood red and gun oil black-faced lunatic closing in on them was more than enough to make them forget everything in favour of sheer survival.

They fled, just as Barkmann ran out of shouting power.

He dropped in beside Ford, gasping for air, and charged his Garand.

A Soviet shell exploded behind the trench and a small piece of metal pinged off the top of his helmet.

"More ammo," shouted Ford, masking a grunt from his companion.

The former gunner slid into the bottom of the position, coming to rest in a growing pool of blood, his sightless eyes not betraying the momentary agony he had felt as shrapnel had ripped into the back of his head.

The .50cal rattled again as the Ranger Captain dashed out to recover two ammo boxes from where the hapless Corporal had his high-speed encounter with the AT gun tyre.

He prepped the box ready, but Ford ceased, leaving twelve rounds hanging at the end of the belt.

"They're bugging out, Captain. All of 'em."

Barkmann took a look to confirm Ford's statement before slapping his NCO on the shoulder.

"Good job, Sergeant, good job. Now I need a radio."

He bolted back to his position and moved the artillery strike zone back into the woods, just to help the retreating Russians along.

He returned to observe his handiwork.

An extremely agitated Gesualdo arrived shortly afterwards.

"What the hell do you think you were fucking doing, you mad bastard?"

"What?"

Ford turned, unaware of his Captain's stupid heroics.

"We saw it all! Charging like a mad dog, five onto one. Are you some sort of fucking idiot?"

Barkmann was taken aback by the ferocity of his friend's words and said the first thing that came into his mind.

"I didn't have time to reload."

Gesualdo's mouth dropped open.

"You'd no fucking ammo in your rifle?"

"I'd fired it all when they went for Ford's MG."

"I saw. You put six of them down... and then you charged them... five of them... with no fucking ammo in your gun!"

"No choice, so leave it be, Al."

"You're a fucking idi..."

"Leave it be, Al."

Gesualdo wanted to say more, but another arriving Soviet shell marked the end of the exchange.

"Right, now we're gonna bug out. Wounded all out, Al?"

"We've got more now, but the others are all tucked up behind the 16th's boys about a thousand yards back."

"OK. Let's pull in everybody to Drulingen and then send 'em straight up the road. F Company and our Spanish allies will be rear-guard. I'll stay with them and bring 'em out."

Both men left their thoughts unspoken, although the vision of the torn corpse of the F Company commander came to both in an instant.

"As soon as possible, I'll drop 'B' back through 'em and Ford can take 'em out. The rest of the details of evac, I'll leave to you, ok?"

"That's a roger, Lukas."

"Let's do it."

0601 hrs, Wednesday, 22nd January 1946, Drulingen, France.

The evacuation had gone smoothly at first, with B Company already on their way to safety, followed by the engineers and the Spanish mortar unit.

At 0601 things changed.

"Jesus! That's big shit!"

Second Lieutenant Wallace Mallender, F Company's only surviving officer, spat the dust from his mouth, as a huge explosion brought down part of the ceiling and blew plaster from the walls.

Barkmann could only agree.

"Sure as shit isn't seventy-six mil!"

More huge shells followed, targeted on the village and its approaches, each explosion releasing more dust and plaster, as well as shaking the nerves of every man present.

Through the detritus of the explosions, the Ranger Captain saw danger approaching.

"Here they come! We can't pull back now or we'll be cut to pieces. We gotta hold!"

Defensive fire was already lashing out at the approaching tanks and infantry, and Barkmann could see men dying before his eyes.

"Wally, get on the horn and get our arty back online. Tell 'em we can't withdraw now, so we're gonna hold."

Not waiting for a reply, Barkmann sprinted as fast as he could, and headed for the buildings that held the Spanish contingent.

He arrived at the back door just as men started to emerge.

"Captain, are we glad to see you. The whole fucking Russian Army's coming down the road. We gotta get outta here."

The young Spanish-speaking Ranger was clearly petrified.

"No we can't, Carrera. We'll be overrun on the move. We have to hold 'em here. Get these boys back to their posts right now. Tell 'em what you need to tell 'em, but get 'em back on the line."

To Carreras's surprise, the Spanish infantrymen moved quickly back into the position and readied themselves.

Barkmann moved on to the next building, throwing himself into the snow on three occasions, as 203mm shells came near enough to worry about.

The rattle of small arms betrayed the closeness of the enemy formation, the distinctive PPSh sounds seeming almost on top of him now.

And then they were there, surrounding a position occupied by a group of Spaniards, throwing grenades in and firing bursts through windows and doors.

Barkmann almost laughed as a Soviet grenade entered one window and immediately was thrown out of the adjacent one, bursting amongst the attackers and sending men flying.

Other Soviet grenades were not ejected, and the screams of the injured and dying Spanish reached his ears.

The Garand started its deadly work, taking out a small party forming for an assault at the rear door.

"Move over, boss!"

Two Rangers flopped down beside him and a BAR was got to work, its heavy bullets smashing into the men grouped on the near face of the building.

"Good work boys. Keep it up."

Discharging the last two bullets in his clip, he reloaded the Garand and moved off to the left, satisfied that the Spanish would hold.

As he was halfway across the road, a wall disintegrated as a T-34 smashed through it at speed.

The hull machine-gun lashed out and he felt the numbing impact of a bullet, then another, as the gunner found his range.

The Garand went flying from his grasp, as the second piece of metal clipped his left wrist and jarred the weapon free.

With a superhuman effort he launched himself over a shallow wall and narrowly missed the two men sheltering there.

"Keep yer head down, Cap'n."

He turned and his eyes opened in fear as he saw the exhaust end of an M9A1 bazooka, just inches from his face.

Rolling away, he missed the moment of firing.

The back flash rolled over him and he felt and smelt his hair singe.

The roar of an explosion betrayed the accuracy of the shot, but the team did not celebrate. Successful bazooka teams left celebration to later times, when they were safe. The smoke trail of a shell was a betrayal of their position, and teams always relocated if they wanted to survive.

"Move it, Sir, quick as you can!"

The three men ran through the garden and into an open doorway.

The gunner dropped to his knee and the loader slotted home another rocket.

"Good work, boys. Is the bastard dead?"

"Reckon so, Captain. But there's more coming."

Flexing his left hand, Barkmann decided that no real damage had been done, although the blood continued to drip from the entry and exit holes.

"Keep at it boys. We're going to have to stay put so knock the bastards out. Good luck."

Pausing to pull out his Colt automatic, the Ranger Captain moved off to the front of the house, barrelling straight into a Soviet officer running the other way.

They bounced off each other and both men went down. Behind the Russian, more men followed on at speed.

Lashing out with the Colt, Barkmann struck the enemy officer in the right ear, bringing an immediate flow of blood and taking him out of the fight.

Bringing the pistol round, he fired into the face of the nearest Russian, missing with the first two rounds but putting the third through the bridge of the man's nose.

He dropped to the floorboards like a rag doll, bringing down the man behind him.

Two shots put down the third in line, the screams instantaneous as the soldier's right shoulder was virtually dismantled by the progress of two .45 slugs.

The next man threw himself to one side as the Colt spat again, each bullet missing its target until the gun stayed open on an empty magazine.

"Shit!"

Beyond the first threshold, more Soviets arrived at the front door.

"Head down!"

The bazooka shell tore through the air and struck the front door frame adjacent to an enquiring head.

Whilst designed for killing tanks, the HEAT rocket of a bazooka was also quite adept at killing soft targets. The combination of explosive force combined with hi-speed wood and brick pieces devastated the gathering assault force.

Barkmann went to reload his pistol, but the wounds and the recent impact of his left arm on the floor had left him with reduced movement in the limb, slowing him up.

Behind him the Bazooka team reloaded.

In front of him, one man emerged from where he had thrown himself and charged.

Instinct alone preserved the Ranger officer, as he twisted out of the way of the bayonet, which plunged between through his armpit area and into the floor below.

Lashing out with his feet, he tripped the rifleman up, causing him to lose his grip on the Mosin.

Quickly recovering, the Soviet soldier threw himself on top of the Ranger and his hands found Barkmann's throat.

More Soviet soldiers arrived and a grenade wobbled past the struggling pair, seeking out the bazooka team in the rear room.

A scream spoke volumes, and three men moved forward, leaving their comrade to throttle the life from the Amerikanski.

The light sound of an M-1 Carbine betrayed the presence of fight in the Bazooka crew, and the three dropped back, one of them bleeding from a leg wound.

Behind them, Barkmann was fighting for his life. Desperately trying to knee his opponent, he found himself unable to make contact, or do anything to loosen the strong grip that the man had on his throat.

The Soviet assault party sent another grenade into the rear room, and followed up quickly, leaving the two combatants alone once more.

The Carbine spoke again, albeit briefly.

Summoning up all his strength, and despite the pain in his wounded arm, Barkmann grabbed the man's face with his left hand, twisting on the nose and lips as he sought a hold.

Shaking his head rapidly, the Soviet soldier easily dislodged the weak attack.

Stars started to explode before the Ranger officer's eyes as the end approached.

With everything last ounce of energy he possessed, Barkmann dug his right hand fingernails into the hands around his throat and rammed his left hand upwards.

The pain in his left arm was incredible, but he drove it up and into the Russian's face as hard as he could.

The scream was awful.

The grip around his throat relaxed.

In horror, Barkmann realised that he could only see half his index finger. The rest had entered the Russian's eye socket and was into the vital matter beyond.

Grasping his face in his hands, the Soviet soldier staggered away, squealing like a pig in an abattoir, blood and other fluids running down his face.

Recovering his breath, Barkmann hauled himself to his feet. The Mosin was still stuck in the floorboards so he pulled it free and finished the job, ramming the blade deep into the hideously wounded man's chest and ending his pain.

Withdrawing the blade, he finished off the unconscious officer with a thrust to the back of the neck before discarding the rifle and selecting a PPSh dropped by another of his victims.

Grabbing two spare magazines, he continued to breathe heavily, his throat bruised and sore.

In the back room he found the Bazooka team still alive but not long for this world, so severely wounded that the Soviet soldiers hadn't spared them another thought.

Both died within seconds of each other.

Shouldering the bazooka, Barkmann grabbed the spare rounds container and moved off, the pain of his injuries obscured by the imperatives of survival.

0643 hrs, Wednesday, 22nd January 1946, Headquarters, 16th US Armored Brigade, Fénétrange, France.

"We'll have air over the field as soon as it's light enough, General. Meantime, the arty's doing all it can. The Rangers are holding."

Pierce knew that his boys were dying out in the snow, holding a piece of real estate that was pretty much worthless, just buying time for his plan to come together.

Such is the lot of a General.

"2nd and Lorraine ready to go, Ed?"

"Lorraine is for sure, General. Garbled report from the 2nd may mean that they've got trouble of their own with commie tanks... trying to firm that up right now. The Legion boys are coming in the southern flank with armour, so reckon we'll still be good to go as 2nd was pretty much just the anvil."

"OK, Ed, just make sure we do everything we can for those Ranger boys."

Behind them the radio crackled into life as Boxer-Six reported in.

125

The command post fell silent as there was a collective holding of breath.

The metallic tones could not hide the weariness in the man's voice, nor could the mechanical precise military words conceal the greater human story.

The message concluded and all eyes turned expectantly to Pierce.

"Tell them well done and to get the hell outta there right now!"

0647 hrs, Wednesday, 22nd January 1946, Drulingen, France.

"Roger. Boxer-six, out."

Barkmann let the handset fall from his hand and he searched in his pocket for a cigarette, which effort was thwarted by the violent shakes that now afflicted him constantly.

"We're pulling out. Now, we're pulling out now. Pass the order."

The men of F Company that had stood with him in the last few minutes moved off, calling to their comrades, and spreading the word.

The Spanish NCO and his four companions remained, their eyes moving cautiously around the area, unable to quite believe that the enemy had withdrawn.

Leaning forward, the Corporal extracted Barkmann's cigarettes and stuck one in the shocked man's mouth, lighting it with an extravagant flourish of his petrol lighter.

"Thanks. Have one yourselves."

The Spaniard didn't understand the words but interpreted the tone correctly, passing them through his men.

The artillery had stopped, both sides seemingly spent.

In the distance, the sounds of retreating diesel engines marked the final disappearance of the surviving Soviet armour, leaving the faint sobs of the wounded to combine with unexpected sounds of bird song and the inexorable sounds of fire.

The Ranger Captain had killed the last T-34 thirty yards from where he now stood, the small hole in the side of the turret betraying a perfect strike.

Smoke rose lazily from the vehicle, as well as from the singed uniforms of the men who had tried to escape from it, still lying where they had been shot down by unsympathetic Allied soldiers.

F Company had taken murderous casualties, fifty-two men dead or soon to be so.

The Spaniards had been whittled down to seven effectives, and few of the wounded expected to see midday.

But they had held, and the hundreds of dead Soviets on the field was testament to their resilience, as well as the skill of the artillery support.

The Soviet tank company, actually the surviving vehicles from two companies, had been savaged, leaving fifteen of their vehicles on the field, three personally removed by the Ranger Captain who was now considered certifiably mad by all concerned.

In the very forward positions something moved.

Pushing the heavy weight off his chest, First Sergeant Ford levered himself upright against the wall of trench. Shoving the dead Russian away, he automatically sought and found his Thompson and checked the magazine.

"Will you keep quiet? I'm concentrating."

Ford did a double take, only just realising that the dead body alongside him wasn't actually dead, but was curled up with a Springfield and evil intent.

"Dirk?"

"That's me. Now, can it, Sergeant. I'm working."

Carefully sliding to the front of the trench, Ford raised his head.

To their front, he estimated at least five hundred yards, was a senior Soviet officer, ranting and brandishing a pistol at anyone he could make eye contact with.

"Think he wants 'em to go again, Sergeant."

"I think he might at that, Dirk."

The officer's pistol flashed and the man he had been addressing collapsed to the floor.

"Shit, he's got a bug up his ass for sure. Maybe I should let him kill them off for us, eh?"

Ford shook his head.

"I think not. Can't risk him getting them all fired up."

Irlam, not inconvenienced by the pencil sticking out of his neck, clicked the sight twice and settled his breathing.

"Cowards! You're all fucking cowards! Now, get ready to advance or I'll shoot the fucking lot of you!"

Lieutenant Colonel Stromov was known as a martinet, but shooting his own men was new ground.

A second soldier crumpled as he put a heavy bullet into him.

"Cowards! We're nearly through! You ran away and we were nearly through!"

He waved the heavy Nagant revolver around, singling out men, who automatically shied away.

"Prepare to attack, you bastard cowards! You're all women... fucking cowardly women!"

"You fucking attack, you prick."

The Colonel swivelled to the source of the voice, facing a bloodied young Sergeant.

"What did you say to me?"

"I said, you fucking attack, you useless prick. We pushed twice whilst you sat in your fucking hole and drank fucking tea, so don't call us fucking cowards, you prick!"

No matter what words the young NCO used, Stromov could only see the SVT-40 the boy was pointing directly at his chest.

"Turn your rifle aside, Serzhant, or I'll shoot you down like the cowardly dog you are."

"You've killed enough today, you fucking asshole."

"You **will** turn your weapon and you **will** prepare to attack, Serzhant."

"No... no, I **will** not."

Lieutenant Colonel Stromov's finger tightened on the trigger.

Serzhant Igorov's finger tightened on the trigger.

Lieutenant Colonel Stromov's blood splattered Igorov, as a .30-06 bullet made its inexorable way through his brain from ear to ear.

The lifeless body flopped into the snow, the officer's eyes wide open in surprise at both his untimely death and the defiance of his men.

The soldiers withdrew into the woods, some pausing only to spit upon the cooling corpse of their regimental commander.

"Nice shot. Damn nice shot."

"Thanks, Sarge."

Ford checked that his eyes hadn't deceived him and let out a low whistle.

"Doesn't that hurt?"

"Hurts like hell, Sarge."

Ford inspected the protruding pencil, screwing his face up at the unusual injury.

"Don't know where the fuck that is in relation to your artery, Dirk, but I sure as shit ain't pulling it out."

Irlam looked over the NCO's shoulder, his eyes suddenly full of concentration.

"Shh."

Ford brought up his Thompson, ready to fire, as his ears caught a nearby slithering sound.

A soft voice caught his attention.

"Rangers?"

Ford relaxed, recognising the source of the challenge.

"Here, Captain. In the trench."

"Coming in."

Unceremoniously arriving on top of Ford, Barkmann rolled into the trench.

"Jeez, First Sergeant, I thought I'd lost you."

Barkmann slapped the sniper on the shoulder and then screwed his face up.

"Ouch. You been fighting the Apache or something, Corporal?"

"It's a pencil, Captain."

The Ranger officer took a closer look.

"Oh lordy, so it is."

Ford's look was enough to bring him back to business.

"Anyway, we're bugging out, so let's get moving, boys."

By agreement between General Pierce and Général de Division Leroy-Bessette, commander of Group Lorraine, the border between the two commands was adjusted to Metting, where the left flank of Tannenberg butted up to the right flank of Pierce's 16th Armored.

In the two hours or so since the Rangers had retreated from Drulingen, the Red Army had renewed its assaults elsewhere, and been stopped dead a mile north-east of Weyer, as well as on the outskirts of Gungwiller.

The arrival of Allied air forces had been instrumental in ravaging the attacking Soviet units before the waiting soldiers of the 16th US Armored and 2nd US Infantry smashed the advancing tanks and infantry in thirty minutes of intense bloody action.

Fig# 129 - Junction between 16th US Armored Division and Group Lorraine, 22nd January 1946.

The original plan had been adapted, having, as often was the case, not survived first contact, and now it fell to Command

Group Lorraine to make the first big strides in regaining the lost ground.

With a firm base at Hangviller, elements of Lorraine's Tannenberg and Sevastopol units would sweep the field, with the immediate goal of restoring la Petite Pierre and Petersbach to Allied control. Subsequently, 2nd US Infantry would recover Tieffenbach, Diemeringen, and Lorentzen.

The lead elements of Tannenberg were already rolling through Schoenbourg and Eschbourg when the first reports arrived, suggesting that a large force of tanks and infantry was approaching Hangviller, seemingly intent on turning Tannenberg's flank.

Fig# 130 - Hangviller - Allied defensive positions.

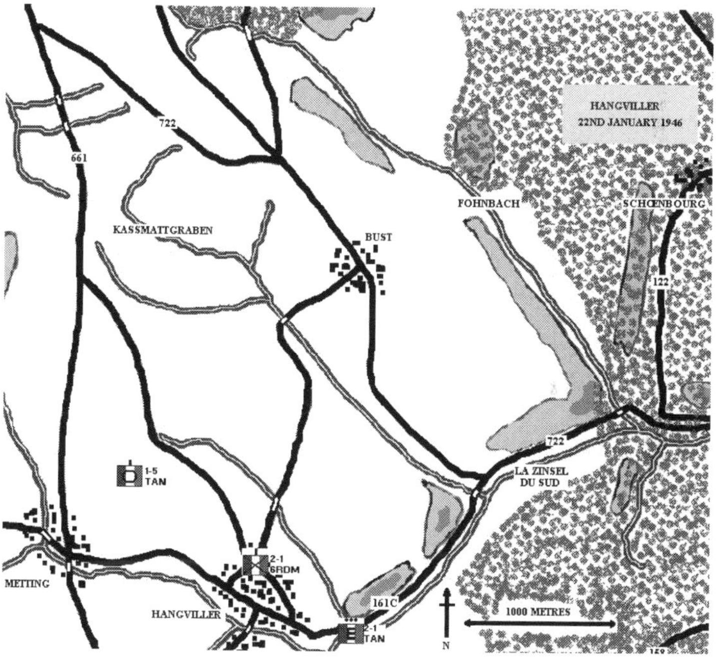

0900 hrs, Wednesday, 22nd January 1946, Hangviller, France.

The prehistoric growling of the Maybach engines was interrupted.

"On."

"Wait."

131

Silence... broken only by the low-key whirr of the electric traverse as the gunner kept track of his target.

"Wait."

Silence... the low sound of orders on the radio net, as the force commander held his men in check.

Across the defensive line, professional soldiers, tried on the harshest fields of man's endeavour, settled behind their machine-guns, in their tanks, and around their Paks.

They waited, trusting the judgement of their officer.

It was called fire discipline.

The tank's gunner could easily have fired and dispatched his target, but the unit commander hadn't yet given the order, so the gun remained silent, locked on to its prey until the moment came.

"Wait."

To their front, a line of Soviet tanks and lend-lease universal carriers advanced inexorably towards Hangviller, the tanks firing as they came, more for self-encouragement than for any expectation of hitting a target.

"Wait," Köster repeated, also more for his own benefit than that of Caporal Jarome, the gunner.

"Wait," hull machine gunner Private Wintzinger heard as he chewed his lip in anticipation.

Fig# 131 – Allied Forces at Hangviller.

BATTLE OF HANGVILER, 22ND JANUARY 1946.

ALLIED FORCES

SUBSEQUENT ADDITIONS

The order to fire combined with the roar of the 88mm, as an armour-piercing shell went down range.

"Hit."

A hit was not necessarily a kill, so Köster waited for a moment before making a decision.

"Hit it again."

'Lohengrin' was a tank that worked like a well-oiled machine, and its crew served it like they were simple extensions of the whole.

Jarome put another shell into the target, and they were rewarded with a spectacular explosion that dispatched pieces of tank in all directions, the turret dramatically bouncing off one of the universal carriers as it cartwheeled across the ground.

"Target, right five."

"On."

The 88mm spoke again, sending more death towards the attacking force.

Schultz, the loader, sweated as he hoisted the heavy shells into the breech, one after the other, rhythmically working, adjusting his position occasionally as he took shells from different stowage points.

Fig# 132 – Soviet Forces at Hangviller.

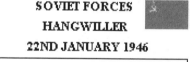

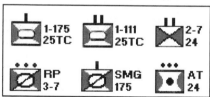

"Load HE next. Gunner, engage the infantry vehicles. Target left two."

Schultz slid the AP round back in place and grabbed for high-explosives instead.

"On."

The heavy cannon spat its shell and a universal carrier disappeared in a ball of flame; detritus, obviously mainly body parts, flew in all directions.

The small personnel carriers were not the swiftest of beasts and the five tanks of 1st Kompagnie, 5th Legion Régiment de Chars D'Assaut, picked them off with ease as they split, desperate to find some sort of cover.

Fig#133 – Soviet assault on Hangviller.

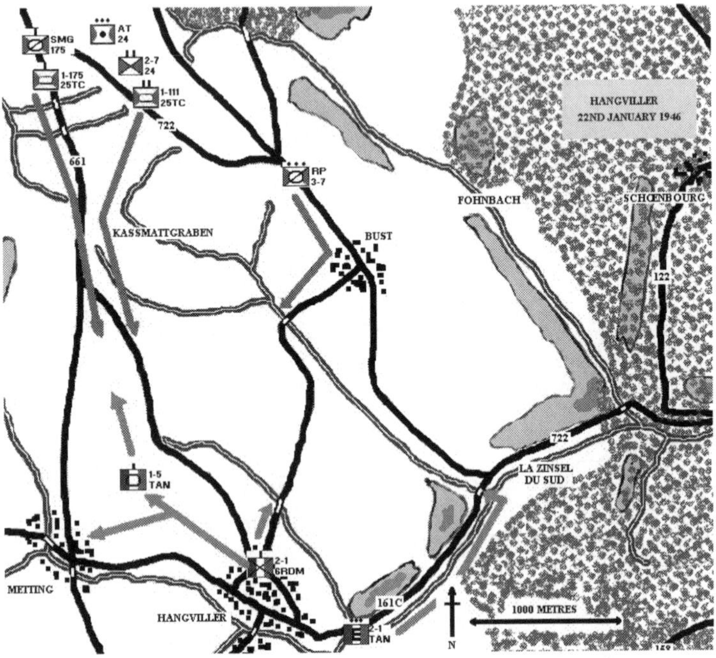

Courageously, some drivers slowed their charges to permit the infantry to dismount and seek their own place of preservation or, in one or two instances, to charge forward with blind courage, holding an anti-tank weapon or mine, intent on distracting the Legion gunners.

Wintzinger's machine-gun started to hammer out and Köster watched fascinated as a group of five Red Army soldiers was literally carved apart by streams of bullets.

"Target, left, two."

The carrier they had sprung from came apart as Jarome put another round bang on target.

Soviet artillery started to land in and around the Tannenberg defensive positions and quickly started to yield casualties amongst the supporting Legionnaire infantry.

134

Köster heard the order immediately, the experienced company commander reacting as would be expected.

"Panzer marsch! Formation Anton!"

His own orders stuck in his throat as he inhaled a piece of paint flake, dislodged by a near explosion.

He coughed it clear and pressed the throat microphone.

"Driver advance... formation Anton... watch out for infantry close up."

As the only Tiger in the company, 'Lohengrin' was the centre tank. Formation Anton required the Tiger to lead in the centre position, moving ahead of the flanking Panzer IV's, who would move outwards, leaving roughly seventy metres between vehicles.

Behind the advancing tanks, the guns of the Legion infantry fell silent as the two platoons displaced.

Machine-gun bullets pattered off the Tiger's armour, ineffective at anything except identifying the location of the firers, and Wintzinger took down each in turn.

The carriers, or what was left of them, were desperately trying to quit the field in the face of the advancing tanks. Again, brave men slowed their vehicles to permit knots of infantry to board their mobile illusion of safety.

"Target...right, three."

The 88mm remained silent.

"You got him, Hans?"

A soft hum was the only reply, and it was a full five seconds before the main gun hammered backwards in its mount.

"Just letting them all get aboard, Oberscharfuhrer."

The target vehicle was in flames, so much so that Köster was unable to see if any of the men that had been clambering aboard had survived.

And then something moved in the flames, a something that had once been a son or a father, but was now in pieces and dying in the most excruciating way.

The main gun was still on target, and Jarome gave a squirt from the co-axial to still the suffering form permanently.

A warning shout from the driver, Meier, cut off halfway through as something smashed into the glacis plate.

"Say again!"

"Anti-tank gun... three hundred and fifty metres...dead ahead, tank moving left."

In truth, Meier had already swung the Tiger to the left, angling the armour for maximum effect, at the moment the 76.2mm

135

Zis-3 fired. The simple act had saved them all as the Soviet weapon was capable enough at that range.

Wintzinger sprayed the location with MG rounds but the Soviet gunners held fast to their task, and the AT gun spoke again.

Another hit, and this time 'Lohengrin' was hurt.

The solid shot struck the front of the vehicle on the corner of the lower hull and angled off into the offside drive sprocket.

None of the crew needed to be told that the metallic sound that assailed them was the track separating and unravelling.

Jarome's shot went high and wide as the Tiger stuttered and slewed before Meier caught the unexpected motion.

The hull MG plucked one member of the Soviet crew from his position as the man leant outwards to properly observe the damage to the enemy leviathan.

The gun commander, seeing the loader fall, stooped down to pick up the dropped shell, cursing the dead boy for his stupidity and the delay it would cause.

Jarome fired again, and again he missed the target, as a heavy artillery shell rocked the fifty-six tons of disabled tank.

The 88mm shell struck the Red Army gun commander in the lower throat, transforming the upper part of his body into flying mincemeat in a micro-second, but with insufficient contact to cause the shell to explode, or even interrupt its journey to somewhere many metres beyond.

The AT gun remained unloaded as the crew abandoned it, most of them carrying some piece of their gun commander on their skin or clothing as they ran screaming from the field.

Wintzinger and Jarome, firing short bursts, mopped them up in short order, the latter's weapon falling silent as he reached for more ammunition.

"Infantry! Close in! Driver, slew left!"

Meier acted instantly, the tank surging on one track and slewing to the left side.

"Scheisse!"

Wintzinger swore as his machine-gun remained silent, the instant manoeuvre having sent the new ammo bag flying from his grasp.

Meier took one look across the tank and acted without a second thought, pushing up on his hatch with one hand as he went for his holster with the other.

Three Soviet soldiers were closing in on the Tiger, two of whom carried large circular mines of a type all too familiar to the Legion's German tankers.

The Walther P-38 took down the leading figure, as two bullets smashed the wind from his lungs and sent him rolling in the snow.

The second figure, free from the encumbrance of a Teller mine, sent a burst at Meier, off-target, but close enough to cause the driver to flinch and miss his shots in turn.

Last in line, the other mine-equipped soldier leapt sideways and disappeared from sight.

"Missed two... and the bastards are close in, near side!"

"Commander out!"

Köster acted on instinct, snatching the MP-40 in the same series of movements that drove him out of the cupola and rolling onto the rear engine compartment.

Behind him, a hand emerged from the turret and drew the hatch closed.

An observer might have found the act harsh, but standing orders and self-preservation dictated that hatches would be clipped down if infantry swarmed near the tank.

Unable to see either of the two Russians, Köster dropped off the rear of 'Lohengrin', where he found one immediately, lying underneath the tank, cradling the teller mine in his arms.

The MP-40 rattled and Köster scrabbled under the Tiger to drag the mine clear.

In an instant his world transformed from the whiteness of snow to the whiteness of a close detonation, as something unforgiving struck the side of the angled tank.

The force of the explosion threw his head hard against the rearmost steel road wheel and he was momentarily stunned.

Above him, a fire had started in the Tiger's engine compartment.

Inside 'Lohengrin', Meier took command, ordering the others to sit tight and fight the tank as best they could.

Pulling himself out of the driver's hatch, he moved at record speed, helped by the searching pings of bullets as Soviet infantry took more than a healthy interest in his actions.

Rolling behind a small drift of snow, Meier took in the scene, swiftly appreciating the danger of the untackled fire.

The turret was moving slowly, electrical traverse having been lost, its weight only shifted by the hand traverse mechanism. None the less, Jarome sought out the aggressor that had wounded them so badly.

The Tiger shuddered as the main gun launched another shell downrange.

Meier couldn't see the end result, but the fact that the turret turned to seek other targets was a clear statement that, whatever it had been, it was now dead.

In his peripheral vision, he could see one of the Panzer IV's smoking, its gun barrel at the sort of angle that indicated severe damage. His hearing picked up the crack of the other 75mm's at work.

Failed by both those senses up close, it was the odour of his attacker that granted him the micro-second that saved his life.

He turned, just as the PPSh came lashing down on him, missing his head and smashing into his shoulder.

The brutal snap of his collar bone and his scream of agony as sharp bones pushed out through soft flesh were heard inside 'Lohengrin', even above the sounds of battle that overtook the inside of a tank in combat.

Rolling away as best he could, Meier's eyes filled with tears of pain, making his vision go misty and imprecise, making his survival less likely as the Soviet soldier attacked again.

The Walther spoke, missing by a country mile, and the PPSh, redirected, smashed into Meier's right hand, accompanied by more sounds of breaking bone.

Again Meier screamed in pain.

Lying prone in the snow, his right side battered and broken, he lashed out with his foot and caught the attacker on the left leg, the heavy boot perfectly connecting with the Soviet soldier's kneecap.

This time, the howls of pain were not Meier's.

The Russian rolled sideways, his fingers searching for a round magazine to fit in his weapon, determined to gun down the SS bastard who had wrecked his knee.

Meier hadn't realised the sub-machine gun had no magazine, and quickly scrabbled left-handed for his dropped Walther.

It was a simple race, with life as the prize and death for the runner-up.

The Russian won as the big magazine slid into place and he levelled the PPSh.

Meier knew he had lost, even as his fingers found the cold metal of his pistol.

The sub-machine gun rattled and Meier screamed in pure fear.

He screamed again as the riddled corpse of the dead Russian soldier dropped onto his legs.

A grinning Köster flopped in beside his driver and swapped the now empty MP-40 for the enemy weapon.

"Stop squealing like a fucking girl!"

Shock rolled over Meier instantly, his limbs shaking, his lips trembling, his bladder control lost.

"Scheisse, Klaus!"

He hadn't appreciated how bad his friend had been hurt.

Instinctively, Köster looked towards 'Lohengrin' for support and immediately saw the gentle waft of smoke rising from the rear.

"Keep your head down, Klaus. Just going to put the fire out. I'll be right back!"

Meier never heard a word of it, his mind fuddled with the excruciating pain of his injuries.

Köster moved gingerly onto the rear of the tank and rapped out a pattern of three and three on the circular hatch. It opened and a pistol was stuck in his face, behind which was the earnest face of Schultz.

"Klaus is wounded. Engine compartment's on fire. Get Erwin to hit the auto extinguisher system, but I'm also tackling it."

The growing smoke caused Koster to cough violently.

"You three have to sit tight and cover or we'll lose our tank. Kapische?"

"I'll leave the hatch unpinned, Oberscharfuhrer."

Köster opened the large rear turret bin and fished out two tetrachloride extinguishers, one in the ambush colour the Tiger had once been painted in, the other a gaudy red, plus a pair of dirty asbestos gloves

The auto extinguisher system had been fired and the effect was immediate, allowing him to pull up the offside grilles, albeit gingerly, as they were extremely hot.

A few bullets pinged off 'Lohengrin's' armour, those responsible immediately drawing angry fire from the machine-gunners, both in the Tiger and the advancing Panzer IV's.

The fire had reduced to nothing more than oily smoke, but Köster waited to ensure it was no longer an issue before returning to Meier's side.

Suddenly the whole situation changed as something extremely large landed fifty metres to the Tiger's front, sending up a veritable fountain of earth and snow.

'Scheisse!'

Not only Köster had that particular thought, as the Soviets redoubled their efforts to push south, and threw in their 203mm artillery against the plum stationary target of the crippled Tiger.

From his position on the rear hull, Rudi Köster could see a wave of Soviet armour advancing again, moving out to the left and right, avoiding the central area where 'Lohengrin' sat.

Another Panzer IV fireballed as a total of four shots struck home in as many seconds, leaving no chance for the crew to draw another breath before they were immersed in flames.

"Achtung! Tanks to both flanks!"

The turret moved lazily, intent on engaging those to the right, where both right flank Panzer IV's had been knocked out.

An 88mm shell flashed downrange, glancing off the side of the lead T-34s turret as a 203mm landed nearer still and rocked the crippled Legion tank.

Grabbing two pouches of ammo from the turret bin, Köster rapped three and three and pulled open the hatch.

The shockwave of a solid shell hitting the mantlet lent additional weight to the hatch, carrying it to the point where it struck the hull, but with Köster's fourth finger in between the two pieces of unyielding metal.

He screamed, so much so that the faces of both Jarome and Schultz jostled for position at the hatch to find out what had happened.

"Ahh, Fuck!"

The smashed finger hung by the thinnest of morsels, the bone turned to dust by the heavy impact. The little finger, whilst it had escaped being trapped, lay at a ninety degree angle to normal, the main joint dislocated by the force of the impact.

As Köster held his ruined hand, the Tiger took another hit, which again flew off harmlessly.

The 88mm spoke again.

The target did not burn, but the only man that emerged hobbled away, leaving a trail of red in the driven snow.

Wintzinger's machine-gun rattled, and his voice screamed an urgent warning.

Rolling to the nearside of the turret, Köster snatched up the MP-40 and fired into the men running directly at 'Lohengrin'.

The moment was so intense that the pain caused by the recoil of the weapon was subdued by the imperative of survival.

A combination of his and Wintzinger's efforts bowled the enemy group over, leaving half of them writhing and moaning on the ground, clutching at ruined bodies.

Köster reached for one of the pouches, intent on reloading, forgetful in the heat of the moment.

His loose finger hung on the rough canvas and the movement of his arm was sufficient to cause the final piece of attachment to snap, which in turn caused his hand to slip, and he caught the dislocation on the end of a magazine.

He screamed.

This time only Schultz stuck his enquiring head out.

Jarome shouted in anger.

"Get out of the fucking way, you idiot!"

Schultz shifted quickly, permitting the gunner to get his shot away.

The secondary explosion was impressive as whatever it was disintegrated in an instant.

Rolling off the tank, Köster dropped into the snow just as another of the large-calibre artillery shells came close, some of the snow and earth falling on him and the comatose Meier, now leaking blood from a head wound.

The situation was spiralling out of control, as the enemy attack moved forward, slowly but surely pressing down upon 'Lohengrin' and the two surviving Panzer IV's.

Even as he watched, both remaining tanks started to back up, keeping their front to the enemy, firing as they went.

"That settles that then! Come on, Klaus"

Köster, conscious of the advancing enemy infantry, slipped the sling of his MP-40 over his neck and dragged the inert form of his driver towards the rear of the Tiger.

Risking exposing his head, he clambered on the track and shouted at the still-open hatch.

"Hans! Max!"

A solid shot sped past the turret, missing the Tiger by the smallest of margins.

Jarome's face appeared.

"What?"

"The IV's are pulling back. Klaus is out cold. Time to go. Get them out, Hans!"

There was nothing else to say.

Grabbing for Meier's armpits, Köster found himself with company, as two legionnaires flopped down behind 'Lohengrin'.

One, a French officer, spoke rapidly.

"Sergent, you've been ordered back. Abandon the tank immediately. Any more wounded?"

"Just him, Sir."

"Quick about it then."

Between the two of them, the French Lieutenant and Köster got Meier on the back of the young legionnaire and the man took off with an impressive turn of speed.

Fig# 134 – Legion reinforcements at Hangviller.

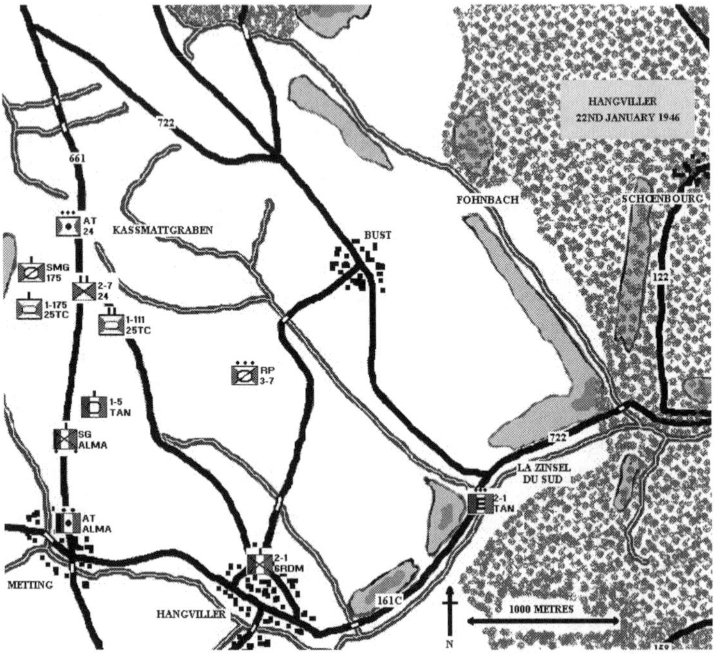

A clang of metal announced another direct strike on 'Lohengrin', and the roar of pain that came from within indicated more hardship for the crew.

Wintzinger arrived, clutching his side, where a patch of red was growing rapidly.

He waved away the enquiring hands as the Frenchmen and Köster sought to explore the fresh wound.

A scrabbling on the deck above them distracted them as Schultz dropped over the side, nearly landing on Wintzinger, his hands raw and blistered from the effect of some previously unsuspected fire.

The Tiger rocked as Jarome fired off a final round, before exiting the rear hatch and joining them.

"Shit, I need to wreck her some more!"

"She's burning anyway, Oberscharfuhrer," Schultz's simple statement accounting for the burns on his hands.

The French Lieutenant waved his own hand theatrically.

"Non! Leave her. We will be back later."

It was no time to argue, but none of them could imagine being back any time soon.

"Maintenant, allez mon braves!"

The group took off at the run, or at least the best they could do with their disadvantages.

"Head for the right of that farm building! Ouff!"

A bullet thumped into the Frenchman's thigh, sending his leg flying out in front of him, causing a stumble and fall.

Jarome leant down and hauled hard on the officer's belt, barely missing a stride, as the two made a decent attempt at a three-legged race world record, chivvied along by more small arms fire from the advancing Soviet infantry.

The front runners threw themselves over a snow heap and down besides the small derelict barn that had been their first target, only to find it occupied by a determined group of legionnaires, armed to the teeth and looking extremely confident.

Köster rose up to assist his gunner, just in time to watch as a 203mm shell landed adjacent to 'Lohengrin'.

Fifty-six tons of tank rose diagonally into the air, turning slightly as it went, before landing upside down nearly twenty metres away from its starting point.

It was a painful moment for the ex-SS tank commander, as much as the loss of a good comrade in battle.

As Jarome and the Frenchman dropped into cover, Köster wrenched his eyes away from the sight of his Tiger with its trackless wheels facing the sky.

The sound that assailed his ears was like an express train without brakes, the 'whatever it was' moving at supersonic speed through the cold winter air.

"What the fuck is that?"

Whatever it was, it was clearly the signal the infantry had been waiting for, and they pushed up to the edge of the snow and started pouring fire at the advancing enemy.

Above the tearing fire of an MG42, the Tiger crew could hear more express trains, more huge explosions, and memories started to work.

Köster looked at his rescuers more closely.

"You're not Tannenberg, are you?"

The Lieutenant, grimacing as Jarome tied his leg up tight, converted his pained expression into a knowing smile.

"Non, Sergent. We are special group from Alma."

Suddenly it all became clear as the memory synchronised with the evidence of his ears.

"Those are Pak44s," he said to no-one in particular, "128mm anti-tank guns," he said to the Frenchman specifically.

"Oui."

The Lieutenant dipped into his pocket and produced Gitanes for himself and the tankers whilst, on the battlefield behind them, the three 128mm PAKs destroyed the survivors of a Soviet tank battalion, helped by the arrival of Escuadrón 205 of the Mexican Air Force, recently kitted out with A-36A Apache ground attack aircraft, configured as dive-bombers.

The Apache, basically a modified Mustang, had been withdrawn in 1944, but the needs of the present war meant that many older types were being pressed into service once more.

The Mexicans enjoyed their second offensive operation of the day, their five-hundred pound bombs proving the final straw, as the assault withered and failed in the storm that they and the Legion created.

Whilst hundreds of Soviet soldiers had been killed and wounded, the SS Legionnaires had also suffered, as first Tannenberg and then Alma resisted the advance.

The latter's special unit lost sixty men, and one of the valuable Pak44s.

1st Kompagnie, 5th Legion Régiment de Chars Spéciale, 2nd Legion Division 'Tannenberg' simply ceased to exist.

The limited Soviet operation was, ultimately, a total failure and, by the late evening of Wednesday 22nd, the Allied line had been restored, all the way back to La Petite Pierre.

When it was all over, no land had been won, no land had been lost, but the fighting had cost nearly four thousand lives.

1101 hrs, Friday 24th January, Ward 22, US 130th Station Hospital, Chiseldon, England.

Major Jocelyn Presley had always known that this one was special. Regardless of the medals a man wore, there was no guarantee that the mind could cope with the damaged body. In fact, coping with severe injury as well as her charge had done, took a special type of courage, and a special type of man.

She was still sad though, for all of John Ramsey's incredible approach to his injuries, and his capacity to endure pain and hardship, the motivation was not to enjoy his life to the full, but to find a way of being useful to his country again.

On the bed were Ramsey's case and other belongings, ready to be taken away by the driver who was coming to get him.

Ramsey himself was moving round the small ward, shaking hands and patting shoulders, taking his leave of men in a similar position to himself, men who had shared the ups and downs of rehabilitation and recuperation on an amputee ward.

Jocelyn Presley watched as her newly promoted Black Watch Lieutenant Colonel took his leave of Manuel Peralta, the young Argentinian Lieutenant, transformed by a Soviet artillery shell from a young and vital boy of twenty into a triple amputee before he even saw an enemy soldier. Ramsey rotated on one foot, not quite as balanced as normal, but well enough that only she noticed, and they shared an insider's look.

Behind her, the rhythmic sound of approaching feet indicated a man of military bearing and she turned to see Ramsey's driver giving her charge the once-over.

"Och, now, ain't ye a sight fae sore eyes."

The two men exchanged silent grins that told Presley that they shared more than the same uniform, and that these two were brothers in arms who had sweated and bled on the same ground.

"Ah, McEwan... Sergeant McEwan I see now, is it?"

"Aye, that it is, Sah. Yer replacement understood ma quality."

Whilst not intended to wound, the words struck home. McEwan was not here to take him back to his unit, but to take him back to visit the reforming battalion, before taking him onto London and the necessary rounds of interviews and meetings that Ramsey hoped would secure him something of interest that contributed to the war effort.

McEwan, aware that his words had hurt, but without the verbal skills to undo the damage, made do with grabbing Ramsey's luggage.

For an English gentleman, what happened next was probably somewhat unseemly, but for an American nurse, who had seen a suffering man rally and fight his way forward, it was completely natural.

She broke from the embrace she had sponsored and kissed his cheek.

"You take care of yourself, John Ramsey. And I will know. Your wife's invited me to visit your home when my duties allow, so I'll be checking up on you."

That wasn't a huge surprise in itself, as Ramsey was aware that the two women had formed a bond, almost an alliance, brought together by the care they both had and gave, in their different ways.

"I shall look forward to it, Florence."

She playfully tapped his arm.

"That's Major Presley to you, soldier."

Strangely, he found himself growing emotional and knew he needed to go quickly.

But he could not stop himself from taking her hand.

"Thank you. Really... thank you, Doc Levens, Doc Gambaccini, all the nurses, but you most of all. Thank you."

She wanted to reply, but couldn't find the words, so just smiled as Ramsey grabbed his canes and sped from the ward as quickly as his prosthetic legs would carry him.

1157 hrs, Saturday 25th January, L'Eglise Saint-Hippolyte, Thonon-les-Bains, France.

Saint Hippolytes, named for a Roman soldier martyred in the 3rd Century AD, was one of those places that you had to go and see if you were nearby.

Famous as the oldest church in the area, it had been erected in the 14th Century and, over time, had become one of the finest examples of a baroque church, resplendent with superb internal detailing, frescos, and a world-renowned Italian-styled stucco crypt.

Those who visited moved around quietly, keeping themselves to themselves and taking in the marvellous surroundings, rather than noticing those who also visited, which was why it had been deemed suitable for what was to follow.

Thonon les Bains had another great charm for two of the people who converged on the crypt that morning, in as much as it was close to Saint-Gingolph, a town half in France and half in Switzerland, and a well-known point where the real world and the world of espionage had their borders well and truly muddied.

The woman, closer to sixty than she cared for, was the wife of a senior Red Cross member. Both her husband and she

146

possessed impeccable credentials for their work with that organisation, and had a notorious and well-established interest in Baroque architecture. She had arrived over two hours beforehand, mixing her main business with pleasure, as she moved quietly around, sketching and photographing, even setting up her easel and canvas to add more touches to her on-going work recording the interior of the Catholic church.

She was a frequent and well-known visitor to St Hippolytes, which made her presence unremarkable in every way, except that she was a former and clandestine associate of one Helen Radó, the wife of Alexander Radó, an important GRU agent in Switzerland, presently awaiting trial in the USSR for anti-Soviet intelligence operations.

Whilst generally unremarkable, Serena di Mattino worked for both the GRU and NKVD, passing on information gleaned from her Red Cross activities, as well as, when the matter was considered vitally important and there was no other choice, acting as a field agent.

Her duties today were vitally important, and there simply was no other choice.

A young priest had stopped to chat with her, seeking some small input on the wonders around him, and proving very attentive to her history lesson on the church and the baroque style in general.

When he left, Di Mattino returned to her labours and found herself lost in it all once more, until she became aware of another presence.

She looked up and smiled at the man admiring her painting, quickly turning back to complete a few more strokes around the pulpit, deliberately reducing some of the shadowing.

"You have talent, Madame. A gift from God, some might say."

The man was clearly an Allied officer, a Captain in full Legion uniform. His unsteady gait spoke of unseen injury and most casual observers had assumed that he was recuperating from wounds sustained in the defence of La Belle France.

In truth, he was recovering from a severe illness, taking in the clean air during constitutional walks along the shores of Lake Geneva.

In truth, he was here, now, at the allotted hour, to pass on vital information.

Di Mattino rested her paintbrush and leant back to admire her changes.

"A gift from God? I think that may be so, but the training my father paid for will have helped I think, Captain."

Code phrases successfully exchanged, the tension, such as it was, disappeared.

"Please sit and rest yourself. You look worn out, Captain."

To casual observers, the two were discussing the painting, gesticulating at the church interior, then examining the art work in turn.

Such observers would also have seen the legion officer open his own small portfolio, showing off pencil sketches and some charcoal work, drawing approving nods and clucks from his lady friend.

Even a suspicious observer would probably have missed the exchange when it took place, blatantly, openly, in full view, but hidden by appearing to be something other than it was.

They both stood and shook hands.

The Legion officer saluted and slowly moved off, leaving Serena di Mattino to continue her art work long into the afternoon, although the presence of that which she now carried within her own portfolio grew and grew as the time dragged on.

But, she always stayed until five, and she wasn't going to break her field craft today, even for such important intelligence.

Sitting just inside a small shorefront Bistro, the Legion Captain looked out over Lake Geneva, sipping his Asbach, happy to be relieved of his burden.

The waiter responded to his summons, and more Asbach filled the glass.

Weiss, surprised that he needed the strong brandy, took a healthy sip and started to feel more relaxed.

The waiter retreated, watching his customer carefully, not only so that he could be as attentive as possible, but also because he was Deux's man.

Outside the church, the young priest was deep in conversation with two nuns, although all three were more than aware of the fact that Serena di Mattino had packed up her kit and was on her way home, for all three were also Deuxieme Bureau, as was the balding man reading a novel, two tables from where Weiss was sitting, and the two walkers who bracketed the Swiss woman on her way to the bus stop, and who knew for a fact that she now carried the plans that supposedly outlined Operation Spectrum.

148

The idea that a war can be won by standing on the defensive and waiting for the enemy to attack is a dangerous fallacy, which owes its inception to the desire to evade the price of victory.

Douglas Haig

Chapter 131 – THE LULL

February 1946, Europe.

At the time, it was described as a lull. Historians writing about the war later described the period of January, through to mid-March 1946, as a respite, an enforced break, and, in territorial terms, nothing of note changed hands.

But to those who froze and struggled to survive, it was anything but.

To those who flew, day in, day out, the war went on in its normal savage way, but with the extra complications of extreme temperatures and the very worst conditions.

The Soviet incursion that was driven back by the 2nd US Infantry and Legion Corps D'Assaut was the last large ground action on the European front, as the continuing winter combined with logistical problems, low morale, and growing non-combat casualties, creating a general malaise that affected both sides of No Man's Land.

The lull; a time when the armies stood quietly apart and exchanged artillery.

The respite; a time when the air forces of both sides did what they could to keep the enemy on the back foot, the Allies with far more success than the Red Air Force could ever have hoped to achieve.

The enforced break; a time when the dying stopped?

Far from it.

2054 hrs, Sunday, 3rd February , Der Brankenwald, one and a half kilometres south-east of Hollenbeck, Germany.

The group had shrunk considerably since the heady days of its early successes, when the enemy was less organized, the targets more numerous, and the cold was a thing of the future.

150

Now, Kommando Bucholz was virtually on its last legs, out of supplies, nearly out of ammunition, with only hope and iron will sustaining them, and the former was fading fast.

At one time, the Kommando had risen to a strength of fifty-two men. The first casualties were all caused by enemy action, but, since the snows came, winter had extracted its price from their ranks, as well as the constant NKVD patrols, leaving only nine men alive.

Their base at Ekelmoor had served them well until it had been discovered, and its loss, and that of nineteen men, had set the Kommando on a downward spiral. Offensive action was almost impossible as they were constantly hounded from position to position by the pursuing Soviet security forces, unable to get any supplies, unable to rest, and unable to respond effectively.

An attempted ambush had cost the Kommando another dozen men, without any notable improvement in their condition.

Lieutenant Staunton, late of the Carleton and Yorks, had succumbed to wounds that morning, two weeks after the mine had taken his right foot and ravaged his body with shrapnel.

In the end, it was a merciful release, as their limited medical supplies had not lasted as long as the ravaged young Canadian.

Now 'Bucholz' had nothing but the nine men; no food, no supplies, only the nine men and the weapons they carried.

Soviet policy in the area had been harshly implemented, and numerous farms that could have given them shelter and food now lay black, where the occupiers had burned them to the ground. The Soviets moved whole families into 'holding areas' and collected foodstuffs into more easily defended locations, effectively cutting off their civilian support.

The survivors had found refuge in a derelict hut in the Brakenwald, a modest forested area surrounded by boggy moorland. It was a double-edged sword for them, the awful conditions keeping the enemy at bay whilst providing them with little let up from the harsh temperatures, save the dubious comfort of the ramshackle building, whose holes were too numerous to plug with snow.

Unable to light a fire, the survivors huddled together under blankets and greatcoats, gathering their strength for the evening's foray.

Driven by hunger and cold, they had decided that the small Soviet supply dump at Hollenbeck would receive a visit.

It was not wise, neither was it well thought through, their desperation driving them to make decisions based on survival, not military reasoning.

Unfortunately, their desperation was anticipated, and their arrival was expected.

2054 hrs, Sunday, 3rd February Three hundred metres south-east of the Soviet supply base, Hollenbeck, Germany.

Having rubbed his stump back into life and re-attached the prosthetic limb, Schultz and Irma settled into position, the lovingly cared-for Mosin sniper's rifle cold against his cheek.

Admittedly, without night sights, Irma would be of limited value, but Schultz also had the flare pistol to hand, ready to send up illumination if there was a problem, illumination that would bring the superb weapon into play.

The rest of the Kommando were implementing the hastily-agreed plan, with four men moving up on each side of the Oberdorf, the long road they intended to use to close on the depot quickly, using the hedgerows as cover.

MacMichaels, the Canadian Seaforths' Sergeant, led the assault group, moving ahead of the second support group by thirty metres. Its commander, ex-Hauptmann Müller, once of the GrossDeutschland Division, drove his weary men on, knowing in his mind that the raid might prove to be a risk too far, but that necessity and survival held sway in his decision making.

Up ahead, the Soviet facility, set in the field adjacent to the junction of Oberdorf and Stahlmannskamp, displayed little by way of life, and what little movement there was betrayed sentries struggling to stay warm, rather than on high alert.

At the main entrance, a Soviet soldier was stamping his feet and slamming his arms against his sides, desperate to maintain blood flow whilst he did his stint outside, whereas his two comrades tucked themselves up in the guard post, complete with stove and extra blankets.

Across the Oberdorf, a line of lorries were parked in a wired-off area, backs towards the main gate, almost ready to reverse in and load up at a moment's notice.

The two open guard towers showed no presence, the sentries clearly skulking below the woodwork and staying out of the icy wind.

That same wind was cutting through the clothing of Kommando Bucholz, bringing already debilitated men to the edge of their tolerance and capacity to endure.

Corporal Forbes, another of the ex-POW Canadians, grabbed Müller's arm as the German amputee's false leg slid away on the ice, threatening to send him flying.

"Steady on, boss. I got ya."

"Danke, Forbes."

The effort of movement left neither of them capable of more words.

Fifty metres from the wire, MacMichaels signaled the groups to ground, allowing himself a few moments to take in the base and the challenges it might pose.

A curtain fluffed at one window in the facility, a building MacMichaels immediately assumed to be a barracks.

Despite his cover, the Sergeant shrank back as two Soviet soldiers padded round the inside of the barbed wire, moving as quickly as they could in the circumstances, clearly wishing to be back inside in the warm.

He watched and congratulated himself when they both disappeared into the suspected 'barracks', which building subsequently disgorged another two men to take over the perimeter patrol.

Müller's unit had swung left, approaching the south-west corner of the supply dump, keeping their attention firmly fixed on the front gate and the nearby tower.

MacMichaels nodded to the man adjacent to him, who slipped his rifle over his shoulder and extracted the wire cutters that would get them inside the facility.

Using his fingers to indicate his chosen point of entry, the Canadian settled behind his PPSh, watching and covering the US engineer as he slid forward over the virgin snow.

The quiet magnified the explosion.

The detonation was followed by screams of extreme pain.

Followed by a moment's silence.

The US Engineer had lost half his face, all of his left arm, and his body had a hundred holes, all leaking blood, fluid that was no longer pumped around his body as the heart was already motionless.

"Mines!"

Both towers came alive and muzzle flashes illuminated the men that had been concealed behind its wooden sides. Both of

MacMichaels' other men were hit immediately, their reactions dulled by hunger and exhaustion.

The PPSh leapt in his hands, and the Sergeant was rewarded with a reduction in fire from the nearest tower.

A flare rose and cast its illumination over the scene.

Müller shouted his men into a firing position and they too engaged the suddenly wide-awake defensive force.

None of them noticed the soldiers bailing out of the parked lorries until the bullets started to impact.

Forbes turned and got off one shot before the top of his head flew off, a round from an SVT auto-rifle striking him in the forehead at the same time as two from the gate guard's PPd took him in the side of the temple, splashing red and grey matter all over Müller.

A rifle bullet slammed into Müller's false leg, sending the wooden limb flying; another struck him in the lower stomach, bringing red-hot agony in immeasurable quantities.

One Soviet soldier dropped from the tower, a single rifle bullet in his brain, as Schultz joined in.

MacMichaels rose, firing first at the lorries, then at the tower, his body blossoming in spectacular red flowers as bullets struck home and he was knocked to his knees.

His screams were more of anger than pain, and the PPSh continued to pluck the life from some of his targets.

In the tower, one Soviet soldier took careful aim and put a single bullet through the Canadian's throat, dropping him to the snow in a microsecond.

There was only one more shot, and that was fired three hundred metres away, from a distance of two metres.

The Kommandos' bodies, there were six in total, were laid out by the side of the road. The US engineer having been recovered in stages, and pieces, as the attempt to drag his body out of the minefield set off another mine, wreaking more ignominy on the dead man.

MacMichaels had also come in for extra attention, a number of soldiers who had lost friends to his firing using their rifle butts and boots to take a little extra revenge on the corpse.

That left three men, wounded, bound, and near death, clad only in the thinnest of tunics and trousers, their greatcoats and blankets stripped from them by their captors.

Müller, his stomach wound frozen, was closest to death. His German Army uniform tunic, with its accompanying medals, had earned him a few blows.

Schultz's Ritterkreuz had been snatched from him and a bayonet wound in the thigh added to the hole in his shoulder gained when the small detachment that had been trailing 'Bucholz' came upon him. More than one of the Russian security troops had given him a punch, as no-one soldier liked a sniper, and his GrossDeutschland armband, as usual, was mistaken for that of an SS man.

Willis, a British latecomer to the Kommando, was unconscious, his skull fractured by the rifle bullet that had creased his head and laid him out.

The Soviet ambush force commander, an NKVD Major, decided that the prisoners had no use for him and ordered them to be tied to the barbed wire fence.

Detailing two men to guard the Kommando soldiers, he decided to accept the offer of a drink with the supply officer, and both strolled off to sample the delights of the local brandy.

It was 2136.

By 2139, the last survivors of Kommando Bucholz had frozen to death.

Treachery returns.

Old Irish saying.

Chapter 132 – THE RETURN

Makarenko did not sleep, although he had expected to, as aircraft held no fears for him that he could not conquer with ease, and he was very, very tired.

After a succession of medical supervisions, combined with interviews that were more often unsubtle interrogations, the NKVD and GRU officers had concluded that he had displayed supreme courage and military skill in the course of his mission and subsequent evasion.

Attitudes changed immediately, and he found himself feted as a hero for his survival and subsequent rejoining of the Army, an attitude that progressed to the very top and resulted in his summons to Moscow for a very public demonstration of the Motherland's joy at his survival, by way of the presentation of the Hero Award from the hands of the General Secretary himself.

A number of senior officers shared the same flight back to Vnukovo, and none of them slept either.

A few were also summoned to the presence of the General Secretary to receive awards for their prowess on the battlefield or in command of their formations. For the most part, their excitement kept them awake.

Others, similarly summoned, understood that a wholly different fate awaited them, for reasons ranging from abject failure to simply bad luck, and they remained awake through fear.

The reason that Ivan Alekseevich Makarenko, Major General of Paratroops, did not sleep would have surprised many of his former interrogators.

It was neither excitement, nor fear.

It was the faces of those who had died, faces that came to him with his eyes shut or open.

'Piotr Erasov, my second in command and friend. Dead.
Ilya Rispan, old experienced officer and friend. Dead.
Stefka Kolybareva, Doctor. Prisoner at best. At worst...
Egon Nakhimov, superb and loyal NCO. Probably no
more.

156

Alexey Nikitin, sniper and model soldier. Most likely frozen to death in the High Vosges.'

He felt the anger build, as the anger always built when their faces visited him, reminding him of his promise.

'All those young boys I took to Haut-Kœnigsbourg... betrayed like so many others.'

Quickly recovering himself, Makarenko looked around to see if anyone had noticed external signs of his innermost thoughts.

No-one was paying any attention to the quiet paratrooper.

'No more betrayal, Comrades.'

The faces faded away and sleep came in an instant, not to be broken until the aircraft approached Vnukovo, and Makarenko's day of destiny.

0701 hrs, Wednesday, 6th February 1946, GRU Commander's office, Western Europe Headquarters, the Mühlberg, Germany.

Nazarbayeva was at her desk early, a deliberate decision to guarantee her time to read through the final reports on the Haut-Kœnigsbourg operation. A very personal matter for the Nazarbayev family, as it cost them the life of one of their precious sons. She studied the reports in her own time, sipping a morning tea, before embarking on the main business of the day; the thorough examination of a fire-damaged folder recently arrived from one of the GRUs agent

She had read much of the Haut-Kœnigsbourg file previously, shavings of information gleaned from sources on the other side of the frontline, and good quality information from their contacts in the Red Cross.

The file now boasted the most complete account yet available, that of the recently returned commanding officer of Zilant-4, Ivan Alekseevich Makarenko.

His recall of those hours was excellent and detailed, and Tatiana quickly found the sections that dealt with the death of her child, finding some strange comfort in the words of the Paratroop commander, as he described the actions of her son, Vladimir, on the lead up to and then the assault on the chateau proper.

Closing up the report where it started into Makarenko leading the survivors off into the High Vosges, she finished the second slice of rye bread and downed the last of her tea.

Unusually for her, breakfast had not satisfied her hunger and so she rose to cut two more rough slices of bread, grab more butter, and refill her mug, before reseating herself.

Opening the folder again, she found herself on a page recording one of the GRU interviews with the General.

'Tiger tanks?'

The GRU interviewing officer had calmly suggested that Makarenko's small force could have contributed something to prevent the defeat at Barr during the disastrous Alsace campaign.

Tatiana smiled.

Makarenko had, equally calmly, suggested that the interviewing colonel had 'his head up his ass.'

She thumbed through, seeking the abridged NKVD report, containing their interpretation of the same event, finding it with ease.

Their wording had initially been very different by far, not suggestions, just bold statements of cowardice and of deliberately avoiding enemy contact, but, eventually, they had accepted the statements put to them, and the Barr matter had been dropped.

Wiping her buttery fingers on a cloth, Nazarbayeva moved quickly forward, scanning the pages, noting the repetition, the standard NKVD attempts to wear down a suspect.

'Suspect? The man is a hero of the Motherland and they've shown him no respect!'

The final sections dealt with his escape through enemy lines, Makarenko's personal account tailoring with that of the Shtrafbat commander in almost every detail.

The last two documents covered the award of the Hero of the Soviet Union, and the travel arrangements to get him to Moscow for the presentation.

She frowned.

'Today?'

Chewing the last piece of bread, Tatiana tidied up the folder, ready to return it to the filing clerk.

As her mind worked on arranging some meeting between her and Makarenko, certain notations on the file sleeve called out to her, unconsciously at first, but growing stronger, until they broke through her thought pattern and became foremost in her mind.

On the outer sleeve were a number of cross-reference sets, indicating other reports that had contributed to the totality of the main folder.

Perhaps she had missed seeing that number as she flicked through previously?

Perhaps it was in the later section that she had quickly skimmed?

The cross-reference set itself was wholly memorable, five of the same number and two of the same letter, which was what had drawn her attention in the first place.

'55555CC.'

She was still searching the folder when her aide arrived in the office.

"Good morning, Comrade General Mayor."

Preoccupied with her search, the normal pleasantries escaped the GRU general.

"This report is incomplete, Poboshkin. Two cross-referenced reports are not here."

The Lieutenant Colonel leant around the desk as his commander pointed out the two omissions.

"55555CC and 55579MA are not here."

Poboshkin was on the phone to the filing section within seconds and the order for the missing files was received by the Senior Filing Officer, who immediately understood that the rest of his career's course depended on the swift execution of the instructions he received.

"My apologies, Andrey Ivanovich. Good morning to you."

To further reinforce her contrition, Nazarbayeva poured the last of the samovar's contents into two mugs and passed one to her man.

A knock on the door heralded the arrival of one of the NCO clerks, complete with a folder.

"Comrade PodPolkovnik. The Mayor is still searching for one of the files, but directed that this one be brought to you immediately."

The file changed hands and the young Corporal saluted, moving away at the highest available walking speed, namely just under a run.

"55579MA, Comrade General."

Nazarbayeva consumed the short report avidly, the Army doctor's findings on Makarenko's condition using all the standard medical terminology such people always used to stress their own education and importance, although two sections speculating on his better than expected overall physical condition drew a second reading.

Consulting the documents prepared by GRU and NKVD physicians, such observations were notable by their absence.

"These two reports are dated 1st January and 3rd January respectively."

159

Poboshkin nodded by way of agreement.

"Neither speak of his better than anticipated physical condition."

"This one, however, dated the 25th December, carried out by a frontline doctor, shortly after Makarenko returned to our lines, reflects surprise at the General's remarkably healthy condition."

"Different standards, Comrade General?"

Nazarbayeva set the folder down gently and grabbed the sides of her desk.

"Or did the two doctors on the 1st and 3rd see a man who they expected to be that fit, or did they just not put two and two together, Comrade?"

The knocking interrupted the analysis.

The same corporal stood there holding 55555CC.

Saluting, his retreat was this time more leisurely and controlled.

Nazarbayeva sipped at the last dregs of her tea as she examined a three page report from an area agent, combining local gossip and acquired information on a modest and relatively unimportant area of the Alsace and Vosges Mountains, the latter location being the reason it had been cross-referenced in the first place.

She stopped, carefully placing the mug to one side, sliding the new report across to leave room for the main folder to be opened and for an examination of Makarenko's interrogations to take place.

Her eyes flitted between the two documents, as she searched one section, then another, always seeking corroboration but finding none.

Makarenko had not mentioned Natzwiller.

Pushing 55555CC and the main file towards Poboshkin, she sat back, calculating the possibilities, waiting for her aide to come up with his own thoughts.

"Govno!"

Poboshkin suddenly remembered where he was.

"Apologies, Comrade Mayor General. This report is low-level of course, but should have been properly cross-referenced. The number indicates that the recipient identified a possible link, so clearly the absence is a procedural error."

He shook his head slowly, the enormity of putting the two pieces of information side by side not lost on him.

"That's for the future, of course, Comrade PodPolkovnik. For now, unless you can tell me that we have any other paratrooper

160

Mayor Generals missing, then I can only assume that the man seen at Natzwiller on December 3rd was Makarenko."

Nazarbayeva did not wait for a reply, immediately leaning across to the telephone and grabbing the receiver.

"Get me Marshall Beria immediately."

0852 hrs, Wednesday, 6th February 1946, Office of the NKVD Deputy Chairman, Lyubyanka, Moscow.

"Deputy Chairman."

"Good morning, Comrade Kaganovich. Mayor General Nazarbayeva of GRU speaking. I've been diverted to you as Marshal Beria is uncontactable."

"Comrade Nazarbayeva, good morning. Comrade Marshal Beria is with the General Secretary this morning, making medal presentations and receiving ambassadors. Can I help?"

"You must, Comrade Kaganovich. I have reason to believe that one of the medal recipients may not be what he seems. There are some inconsistencies in reports that have only just come to light. I believe that he must be detained until we can be satisfied that he is a good and faithful servant of the Motherland."

As much a man of action as his Chairman, Kaganovich started writing notes, flicking his fingers to get the attention of the NKVD Colonel sat opposite.

"Mayor General, you say... ah. Yes, I know the man."

The junior NKVD officer lifted the other telephone as the senior man scribbled his large letter notes and instructions, nodding by way of confirmation of his understanding.

"Put me through to the Kremlin Guard commander immediately."

The information coming from Nazarbayeva's office in Germany hit the jotting pad, and was immediately relayed to the suddenly attentive Kremlin Guard commander.

"Yes, Comrade, I'll act immediately. The presentations are due to start at nine. Yes, I'll ring you back with any news."

The NKVD officers finished their calls simultaneously, and both men's eyes strayed to the large wooden wall clock, whose monotonous ticking advanced the hands inexorably towards nine o'clock.

Five seconds later, the deputy chairman's office was empty, echoing to the receding shouts of worried men calling soldiers about them.

Unusually, Stalin had arrived late, held up by the latest production figures from the Ploesti refineries, figures that did nothing to improve his temper. The Allies continued to bomb the site mercilessly, and it now contributed little more than a dribble to the Soviet war effort.

Avoiding the normal pleasantries, the General Secretary strode into the magnificent vaulted room, constructed in a different age, when the need to impress visitors of the Czar's greatness was translated into opulence of epic proportions. The magnificent white stone walls, gold leaf, superbly ornate floor and stunning chandeliers created an impression on anyone exposed to the hall's delights.

Taking station in front of the NKVD leader, Stalin whispered an aside, whilst nodding in recognition at members of the gathering lining the long walk that each recipient would have to undertake to get their piece of metal.

"Let's get this over with then, Lavrentiy. The standard crowd of heroes and villains, I assume?"

Beria leant forward, his hand automatically masking his mouth.

"Not quite, Comrade General Secretary. Our first man is one we had not expected to see again. It was considered appropriate that, given his feats, he should receive the award from your hands. I was not informed until this morning."

Leaning backwards, the Soviet dictator risked a quick look at his man.

"Go on."

"Makarenko."

Recovering his poise, Stalin pursed his lips.

"And this has happened how?"

"I will know within the hour, Comrade General Secretary."

Stalin's terse reply was lost as the military band struck up the national anthem, and the dignitaries and guests set about their singing with great gusto, the harmonics of the great hall adding to the sense of patriotism and occasion.

As usual in these managed presentations, the master of ceremonies announced each recipient in turn, and they were marched in at the bottom end of the hall, their parade step repeated back off the walls, even though they were required to march up a central protective strip, set in place to prevent damage to the inlaid floor.

Protocol demanded that medals were awarded by level of award and then by rank, so today's first hero was a Major General of Soviet Paratroops.

Once in position in front of the presentation party, today consisting of the entire GKO, the recipient was subjected to an account of his worthy actions, as the assembly was apprised of the official citation and, more often when there were visiting dignitaries that needed to be further impressed, first-hand accounts of the winning of the award.

Both Stalin and Beria examined the man stood a precise six metres in front of them, the man they had sent to what they had thought was certain death all those months ago.

For his part, Makarenko stood ramrod straight, and his eyes never left those of the man he had come to kill.

The account of the Chateau assault and subsequent adventures culminated with the return through Soviet lines and, as was customary, the assembly clapped their hands in appreciation of the soldier's efforts.

An NKVD Major moved forward, cradling a cushion on which sat the Hero of the Soviet Union award, ready for the General Secretary to pin the medal high on the paratrooper's left chest.

The newly created hero marched forward, in perfect step with the two flanking guardsmen.

Doors flew open and armed men flooded into the room.

Chaos.

Shouts.

Screams.

Warnings.

Makarenko produced the concealed 4.25mm Lilliput pistol and took swift aim.

"For all those boys you've murdered!"

Gunfire erupted, the staccato sounds amplified by the great hall.

The cushion-carrying Major's shoulder took the bullet intended for Stalin, the one hastily aimed at Beria missed the gaping Marshal by feet and clipped Bulganin's ear on its way to despoiling the decorative wall behind.

The guns of the Kremlin Guards put seventeen bullets into the would-be assassin, and three into the personal secretary of the Bulgarian Ambassador, who just happened to be in the line of fire.

Both men were dead before their bodies hit the floor.

More Kremlin Guards flooded the room, ushering the GKO to safety and arresting the entire audience for questioning.

163

Safely tucked away in one of the former private chambers, the men of the GKO caught their breath and tried to regain their wits.

Tea arrived swiftly, hot and sweet, and each man was fussed over by the Kremlin's medical staff, all under close supervision of a number of earnest looking guards.

Kaganovich arrived, coinciding with the Guard commander's initial personal report to the General Secretary.

"The security team that should have ensured no weapons were carried are all in custody, awaiting rigid interrogation, Comrade General Secretary."

Stalin's face remained impassive. Their fate was already sealed, regardless of their culpability.

"The traitor is dead."

"His family. All of them. Associates... everyone... round them up."

No reply was necessary, as everyone present knew that the process would have already begun.

"The Bulgarian diplomat is also dead, but the ambassador understands no intent on our part."

Stalin took another sip of his strong tea and offered no comment.

"An Armenian Colonel present to receive his own hero award has been found in possession of a cut-throat razor, so he's on his way to the Lyubyanka."

"Details, details. How did you know what was about to happen, Comrade Polkovnik?"

"I received a warning call from Comrade Polkovnik General Kaganovich, Comrade General Secretary."

Kaganovich was able to assist a little, but only in pointing at Nazarbayeva as the originator of the warning.

Beria interjected, taking over the running from Stalin.

"GRU General Nazarbayeva rang you?"

"Yes, Comrade Marshal. Just in time, so it seems. Any later and I fear things would have been very different."

Beria's eyes were fixed on something distant.

"She rang you... just... in... time."

Kaganovich didn't fully understand, but Stalin, whose adult life was built upon a foundation of mistrust and treachery, most certainly did.

"Lavrentiy, order Mayor General Nazarbayeva back to Moscow so she can present her report… personally."

Now everyone in the room understood, in the context of 'just in time', exactly what that could mean for the GRU officer.

"Continue, Comrade Kaganovich."

0937 hrs, Wednesday, 6th February 1946, GRU Briefing room, Western Europe Headquarters, the Mühlberg, Germany.

Once Nazarbayeva was satisfied that she had done all she could do about Makarenko, she immersed herself in the business of the day, and chaired the meeting that would start to unravel the singed folder passed on from Agent Amethyst in Alsace.

A team had been assembled to interpret what was written, and to try and work out what was missing, in order to put together a full version that could then be judged on its merits. Recent events had demonstrated that the Allies could be just as effective with their maskirovka as the Soviets believed themselves to be.

The work was no more than ten minutes old before the door burst open and a familiar, yet unwelcome face arrived.

NKVD Leytenant General Seraphim Dustov strode in, backed with the authority of Stalin's direct order, and flanked by two NKVD soldiers with PPDs.

None of the GRU personnel moved a muscle and a sudden tension filled the room.

"Comrade Leytenant General Dustov? To what do I owe this unexpected pleasure?"

For all her astuteness in the world of military intelligence, Nazarbayeva was still very much a novice in the political side of matters, and had genuinely no idea as to why Dustov had presented himself.

"Comrade Nazarbayeva, I possess orders for you, direct from the Secretary General, orders that I am required to pass in person, and then assist you in fully discharging."

Poboshkin accepted the document and, at a simple nod from Nazarbayeva, opened and read it.

The atmosphere in the room was extremely charged and the tension increased during the silent examination. More than one hand felt for a holster to reassure the wearer as to the presence of a pistol, and the response of the two NKVD soldiers, easing their sub-machine guns, was automatic.

"Comrade General, this order requires you to hand over to your deputy and return to Moscow immediately, in order to explain the events that culminated in this morning's assassination attempt."

He held out the message form to Nazarbayeva, who ran a cursory eye over it.

She, as had Poboshkin, noted the absence of the word 'arrest'.

"Right. Comrade Poboshkin, please assemble the full file on Makarenko ready for me to take to Moscow. Comrade Orlov," she nodded at her 2IC, "Will continue to run this group and bring the Amethyst file to order, ready for my return. Good day."

The room leapt to attention as Tatiana Nazarbayeva strode out, closely followed by the NKVD escort.

By 1100 hrs, she was airborne.

1203 hrs, Wednesday, 6th February 1946, Bois Neuf, Moselle, France.

Knocke stayed silent, but his eyes narrowed as he took in the sight.

The other tank commanders offered no comments.

Braun was less inclined to silence.

"What the hell is that?"

Beveren conceded the floor to the man in the greasy overalls.

Ex-SS Hauptsturmfuhrer Walter Fiedler wiped his hands with an ever-present piece of cotton waste and gestured to the vehicle that was rapidly approaching. With the genuine enthusiasm common to engineers of all nations, he gleefully set about informing the assembly

"Kameraden, let me introduce the Wolf, a marriage between the Panther and Panzer IV. Simple enough, once the turret ring installation has been welded in place. Tests show her to be nearly ten kilometres an hour faster than the Panther, and we have shoehorned an extra eleven rounds into the hull."

The new tank, Panzer IV turret on a Panther hull, slowed and changed direction, presenting a side view to the assembled group.

The addition of mesh side armour, or Schürzen, added to proof against weapons like the bazooka or panzerfaust, gave the assembly a business-like look.

166

"We have eight of these so far, Kameraden, and my little helpers tell me there are more Panther hulls on the way yet. It is serviceable Panther turrets that we lack, hence this conversion."

A number of the officers and NCOs approached the Wolf and looked it over with professional, experienced eyes.

Knocke could read Fiedler's excitement.

"What else do you have for us, Hauptsturmfuhrer?"

"Sir, the orders were quite clear. Get as many vehicles up and running as possible, maximising firepower at all times. My unit decided that we'd do things as simply as possible. Excuse me."

Fiedler waved his arms at the man posted on the corner, who in turn waved forward the next vehicle.

Actually, vehicles.

What, at first, appeared to be a standard 251 half-track, rounded the bend.

The Puma turret was soon recognisable, as was the new armoured structure on the rear compartment.

"We call this one the Antilope, Sir. Initially, we had an issue with top heavy weight, but cut down the additional plate so it's manageable now."

Again, the vehicle was graced with a full set of protective mesh screens.

"How many?"

"Five, Sir."

The second 251, its own screens hung with freshly-cut vegetation, sported a deadly looking weapon, instantly recognisable as the potent 88mm KwK43.

"Don't know why we didn't have these when we were fighting the bastards the first time round, Kameraden. Surprisingly easy to shift over from a Nashorne. We have four of these, we call them Hundchen, and I think we may be able to manage another one in time, Sir."

The marriage looked extremely deadly.

Knocke kept his feet on the ground.

"How much ammunition, Hauptsturmfuhrer?"

Appreciating the instincts of his senior officer, Fiedler could only concede with grace.

"That's its Achilles heel, Sir. At the moment, we can only safely store fifteen rounds internally."

That made a difference, but Fiedler hadn't finished yet.

"However, Sir, we think that by adapting some American jeep trailers, we can store another twenty or so to be towed behind."

That would make a difference in combat, but would bring its own problems with manoeuvrability.

"Anything else for us, Hauptsturmfuhrer?"

"We're still working on a combination mount for the 251, Sir. Nebelwerfer hull mount from the Maultier, with additional six wurframen 40 carried, just to up the capability of the support elements."

"Sounds interesting, Fiedler. Still working on it?"

"Yes, Sir. We have four suitable vehicles lined up but the traversing gear is proving a problem on the prototype. Nothing we won't solve, Sir."

"Excellent work, Hauptsturmfuhrer. Pass on our congratulations and thanks to your crews…"

Knocke stopped, understanding that there was more to come.

"Sir, we've managed to get five Panthers roadworthy and combat ready. They are ready for your crews to take now. We also acquired some extra vehicles, similarly ready for you to take now."

The Workshop officer waved at the corner man, who was clearly waiting for this moment.

The roar of something powerful became apparent, as did the cloud of smoke from the twenty-three litre gasoline engine that propelled the Porsche-turreted Tiger II into view.

Three others, all Henschell versions, followed behind, and, at the end of the procession, were the vehicles that Fiedler was clearly the most proud of.

It was Captaine Felix Jorgensen, the ex-Frundsberg Panzerjager officer, who noticed first.

"What've you done with that JagdPanther?"

Part of his voice betrayed his disgust that the fine lines of the Panther-based tank destroyer had been messed with, whilst part of his voice recorded the new armament the vehicle carried.

"That, Felix, is the Einhorn, complete with a 128mm. We salvaged the guns from some JagdTigers. We had to increase the space because of the breech and recoil. The speed has dropped a little, but not much. We've managed to get forty-one rounds on board her too."

The Unicorn looked positively deadly.

"Just the one?"

"Three more nearly ready, Felix."

Knocke interrupted the bonhomie.

"Hauptsturmfuhrer, you have a complete list of vehicles that are ready to hand over to us?"

"Apologies, Brigadefuhrer."

Fielder removed the top two sheets from his folder and handed them to Knocke.

"Top sheet is what is ready to go now. The second sheet indicates everything that we can put together with the resources we presently possess, Sir."

Knocke was impressed.

1607 hrs, Wednesday, 6th February 1946, la Mairie, Troisfontaines Moselle, France.

They were all impressed.

The leaders of the command groups had gathered at the temporary headquarters of Leroy-Bessette's 'Lorraine', something they did when circumstances permitted, thus avoiding the interference of headquarters, in the person of Molyneux.

Lavalle asked a very sensible question.

"Training issues, Général?"

Knocke had given this some thought on the short journey from the workshop site.

"Next to nothing over standard familiarisation for most of these vehicles, Sir. My men have used all of it before, just not in these combinations. However, I suspect there'll be handling issues with the 251 conversions, and I think some driver training'll be required. There will be issues with the Aardvark and Hyena, if only because the guns are unfamiliar. Hopefully, General Pierce can provide us with some training officers for a short while?"

Pierce nodded and scribbled a quick note.

"I shall send some of my boys over a-sap, Ernst. I assume training will be done near the workshop site?"

A number of eyes fell on the wall map, seeking a suitable spot nearby.

Demarais found it immediately.

"Here."

A piece of open ground in between large woods to the west of Arzwiller looked perfect.

Lavalle leant forward for a closer examination and grunted in satisfaction.

"We are agreed then?"

The assembled senior officers softly chorused approval and then moved on to the delicate subject of who would secure which vehicles.

1700 hrs, Wednesday, 6th February 1946, Office of the General Secretary, the Kremlin, Moscow.

Immaculate in her dress uniform, save for her cap, Nazarbayeva stood at attention in front of the heavy wooden desk separating her from Stalin.

Flanking the General Secretary were a bandaged Bulganin and, more surprisingly, Molotov. The ever-present Beria sat to one side, working studiously on his glasses.

Whilst Stalin studied a document in total silence, seemingly oblivious to the GRU officer's presence, the others studied her intently, Beria immediately noting that the holster flap was unclipped, deliberately left so by the security detail that would have searched Nazarbayeva thoroughly, removing her side arm and cap as a precaution against repeats of today's debacle.

Stalin, in studied fashion, set down the report and filled his pipe slowly, allowing the tension to build.

Running a match down the antique wood, he gently puffed away, drawing the flame into the rich tobacco and filling the room with its aroma.

He deigned to notice the new arrival.

"So, Comrade Nazarbayeva, it seems that I am in your debt for raising the alarm today."

His eyes burned into her, in a way she had previously neither experienced nor witnessed, a piercing gaze that carried enquiry and malice in equal quantities.

Unexpectedly, it was Molotov that spoke next.

"Comrade General, the Motherland is grateful for your efforts today, but there are some questions that need answering so that we may understand how the situation developed as it did."

"Comrade Minister, I am relieved that I was in time to prevent harm coming to any person."

Bulganin coughed.

She produced the file from under her arm.

"If I may, Comrade General Secretary?"

Stalin nodded.

Slipping from her rigid position, Nazarbayeva opened the folder and delivered her honest assessment of how matters had transpired, leaving nothing out.

Molotov tapped his finger on the desk by way of interruption.

"So you are telling us that this traitor was interviewed by our medical services, and GRU and NKVD interrogators, and there was no warning of this treacherous intent? Nothing?"

Now Nazarbayeva understood why Molotov was taking the lead. Beria was as much in the doghouse as she was.

"What the reports indicate is that we were faced with a hero returning to the Motherland, after months of incredible resistance behind enemy lines."

Lining up the evidence on the polished top, she touched each in turn as she summarised.

"Army doctor shortly after he made contact with the Shtrafbat."

Her hand moved on.

"GRU medical examination report... NKVD medical examination report... summary of NKVD debriefing."

Touching the thickest of the files, she concluded.

"GRU debriefing, conducted over three days."

She stood back.

Almost as a discard comment, Nazarbayeva regretted the absence of the full NKVD interrogation report.

"Comrade General Secretary, each report, in isolation, brings with it no criticism, no suspicion. The initial medical report states that the General was in surprisingly good medical condition considering. Subsequent reports make no such observations. The GRU debriefing is thorough and there are no gaps. I've not had the opportunity to see the full NKVD debrief file on Makarenko."

Bulganin's soft comment was very informative.

"Neither have we, as the fucking file's disappeared."

Instinctively, every eye switched to Beria, to witness him squirm in discomfort.

In the immediate aftermath of the assassination attempt, Beria had pointed the finger very heavily at the shortcomings and last moment intervention of the GRU officer. The absence of the complete NKVD file on Makarenko quickly ensured that the hunter became hunted. In the NKVD headquarters, men had already been arrested for their part in its inexplicable absence.

Nazarbayeva coughed nervously, understanding that she was about to admit shortcomings in her own department.

"However, Comrade General Secretary, the GRU report was absent an associated file that had been identified as being relevant, and which should have been fully analysed. It would undoubtedly have raised some doubts over the veracity of

171

Makarenko's story. My office uncovered this just in time, for which I am extremely grateful."

Her intent was to portray her real relief at interfering with Makarenko's plans, but the others in the room saw only an officer expressing relief that an error was uncovered in time to save their head.

Molotov again took the lead.

"So how was it that you came upon this shocking dereliction today, eh? … and in such a timely fashion, eh? Almost out of time, eh, Comrade General?"

The normally even voice of the diplomat was very much replaced by the strident tones of a communist party high official in full pursuit of helpless prey, his sudden change in mood taking Nazarbayeva by surprise.

"And you rang Comrade Beria. Why not Comrade Kaganovich, who would be better placed to act, having no part to play in the day's ceremonies?

"Comrade Minister?"

"The reports you bring to show us are old, and yet today you take an interest in them?"

"I arrived at my desk early, so that I could examine the GRU file before my day staff arrived, Comrade Minister. I rang Marshal Beria in the first instance, and was passed through to his Deputy as the Marshal was absent. That was clearly a mistake on my part, although I did not know that Comrade Beria was involved in the ceremonies."

"How very convenient, Comrade General, don't you think? More like you are part of the disease spread by the traitor Pekunin, and you panicked yourself into making an earlier call, rather than one just after the deed had been done, as you obviously intended, eh?"

The look Nazarbayeva gave Molotov would have melted marble, and each of the three men at the desk saw it, and each made his own interpretation of its meaning.

Whichever of the three interpreted her look as defiance and anger had their view confirmed by the hard edge to her voice.

"Comrade Minister, the GRU files on Makarenko contained specific information on an operation from 6th August 1945, in which my son was killed. As a mother, I was seeking information on the death of my child, Vladimir. As it was a personal matter, I went to my office early, in order not to interfere with my schedule. The file would not normally have come to my attention, but for my personal interest."

Her gaze switched to Stalin, whose own expression remained totally neutral in the face of the GRU officer's angry delivery.

"Had it not been for that personal interest, I fear the discrepancy would not have been revealed until it was too late. Comrade General Secretary, I give thanks that you were preserved and are unharmed. I also accept a shortcoming by my department in interpretation. I do not accept any accusations regarding any complicity in this event, or doubting my loyalty to the state or party!"

Bulganin went to speak but Stalin's right hand shot out, silencing him with a single curt gesture.

Another match made its noisy journey down the desk and the pipe burst back into life.

The silence was broken solely by the steady puffing, as the General Secretary held the gaze of the woman in front of him.

She saw his eyes suddenly soften as his inner voices whispered in his ear.

'Balls of steel, this Tatiana. You've always said so!'

An unexpected laugh made everyone look at the dictator.

"Comrade Molotov asks only questions that need to be asked, Comrade General."

He indicated the spread of files before continuing.

"There have been errors here, by your department... and others... and we'll soon know the full story. Comrades Molotov and Bulganin will be heading an enquiry, with which you'll cooperate fully."

"Of course, Comrade General Secretary."

"Comrade Nazarbayeva, you are a good and loyal servant of the Motherland and the Party, of that I have no doubt, and again, I thank you for your intervention."

He placed the pipe on the desk and waved a fatherly finger at his GRU commander.

"But you must understand how this could look," he softened further, "Both for you and Marshall Beria."

She nodded as the anger and resentment faded into nothingness.

"You, the woman and mother, have sacrificed two sons in this war... I know this. Such a woman is not a traitor. Such a mother would not turn her back on what her children died for. I know this too."

He looked at both Bulganin and Molotov before continuing.

"Just cooperate with the enquiry, Comrade Nazarbayeva. Comrade Bulganin's office will be in contact before you leave."

"Yes, Comrade General Secretary. For my part, I will order a review of any similar cases to Makarenko's."

"We have already taken steps to ensure no repeats. Thank you, Comrade General, you may go."

The door closed before another word was spoken.

"None the less, Lavrentiy, have her monitored day and night."

There are no extraordinary men, just extraordinary circumstances that ordinary men are forced to deal with.

Adm. William F Halsey Jr USN.

Chapter 133 – THE PROTOTYPE

<u>1104 hrs, Saturday, 9th February 1946, on board S-22, off the coast of Sweden.</u>

It was only after the attack that the Captain had worked out the aircraft was a Saab17 of the Swedish Air Force.

They had instantly known that the aircraft was not benevolent, given the total absence of friendlies in the Baltic skies.

S-22 had just surfaced, forced up by an electrical problem that knocked out its motors. Well aware that he was fifteen kilometres off the Swedish coast, east of Simrishamn, Captain 3rd Rank Jabulov harried his engineering crew mercilessly, whilst ordering more defensive firepower to the bridge.

Without the time or ability to dive, S-22, a Stalinec class submarine of the Baltic Fleet, fired a few shots with her 45mm cannon and hand-held MGs, whilst manoeuvring on diesel power to avoid the falling bombs.

Whilst all four missed, the shock damage was considerable, as leaks were compounded by crew injuries, all set against a backdrop of frequent electrical outages.

Someone, it was suspected one of the MGs, had knocked the Saab down, and its fiery cartwheel into the sea was greeted with a number of relieved cheers.

With diesels hammering at full power, S-22 drove herself away on the surface.

Jabulov, a lifetime spent in Baltic waters, sought out a place where he could hide his stricken vessel from prying eyes whilst repairs were made.

He found what he was looking for in the Christianso group, and, ordering full speed on a course of 134 degrees, he returned to the job of 'encouraging' his crew to get S-22 back in shape to dive.

The men had come from different units, some on transfer, some plucked from hospitals where they were recuperating from wounds sustained in the awfulness that was the lot of the aircrew of the Red Air Force.

The first arrivals had been delivered by truck, picked up from the nearby railway station; men recently discharged from hospital in the main.

Next came three B-25J Mitchell bombers, the last survivors of the now disbanded 890th Bomber Aviation Regiment, touching down in short order on the main runway. The normal complement of eighteen men was swollen to thirty-four, as the three US lend-lease aircraft disgorged flight crew who had no aircraft of their own.

Over the next two days, more aircrew arrived, not only for the newly formed 901st Independent Special Aviation Regiment, but for other special formations based in and around the military airfield that also served as the test field for the Stakhanovo Flight Research Institute.

Presently unemployed, a large number of the 901st's personnel had been attracted to the strange noises of an unknown aircraft type that made its way to the end of the main runway.

Despite the cold, over twenty men stood and speculated over the nature of the unknown machine.

Newly promoted Lieutenant-Colonel Sacha Istomin, Hero of the Soviet Union, only recently considered fit enough to return to flying duties, watched from the relative warmth of the control tower.

The glass-walled structure, normally staffed by a six man shift, was stuffed to the brim with over twenty additional personnel, all, with the exception of Istomin, present to witness the first full test flight of the newly modified MIG-9.

The tower commander, an ageing Captain, was clearly perturbed by the presence of so many high-ranking personages, including GKO member Georgy Malenkov, present in his role as head of aircraft production.

The senior radio operator requested permission for a flight of aircraft to land.

"No, no, no. Wave them off. Send them to an alternate airfield."

The Serzhant operator talked into his mouthpiece, his voice growing in volume as the sound of the MIG-9's reverse engineered BMW 003 turbojets built up, ready for take-off.

"Comrade Kapitan, Mangusta-Seven-One states he is ordered to land specifically at this field."

No one noticed the slight reaction from Malenkov.

"Ordered? I have no flight plan logged for a Mangusta flight? Tell him to maintain holding pattern," he consulted the vertical map, partially obscured by increasingly excited bodies, "Four, pattern four, over Bronnitsy."

"Sir."

The operator relayed the order as the female operator alongside him burst into life.

"Comrade Kapitan, Zvezdnyy-One requests permission for take-off."

A nervous sound rose from the watchers, but was cut short by the commander's voice.

"Wait, Comrade Yefreytor. Comrade Serzhant, confirm the Mangusta flight has been waved off?"

"Yes, Comrade Kapitan. Set on station four, over Bronnitsy, crusing floor ten thousand."

He thought for a moment.

"Make the floor twelve thousand, Comrade Serzhant."

The MIG was to remain below ten thousand for its test, but he considered it prudent to make the change.

"Comrade Yefreytor, inform Zvezdnyy-One of aircraft at twelve thousand, bearing 178 at ten kilometres. Advise him he is now clear for take-off."

Djorov released the brakes and felt the immediate surge as the MIG moved forward, pushing him back into his seat.

Everything felt right; the whole aircraft just seemed ready and anxious to perform for the high-ranking officials gathered to witness a full flight test.

The wheels left the concrete runway and Djorov brought the MIG's tricycle undercarriage up, all the time marvelling at the differences between this time and the last time he had flown it. Those watching on the ground were in awe of its sharp climb and high speed.

Levelling out at nine thousand five hundred feet, Djorov noted a slight flutter and his eyes flicked across the gauges in search of any issues.

There were none, the flutter went, and he commenced a gentle dive and turn. As his confidence grew Djorov started extra manoeuvres, gently at first, then more pronounced.

In the tower, and on the ground, hands pointed out the returning aircraft and were then clapped to ears as the MIG-9 swept down the runway at one hundred feet, the twin turbojets roaring under four-fifths power.

Djorov simultaneously pulled the nose up and advanced the throttles, making the fighter aircraft rise like a rocket.

Istomin's mouth fell open in wonder.

'That's impressive!'

For the next twenty minutes, Zvezdnyy-One performed a series of manoeuvres for the onlookers, all without problems.

The climax of the display was to be an actual firing of the weapons in a ground attack, a worn out T-26 having been set on the edge of the airfield to provide a serious target.

The MIG-9 was designed, primarily, as a bomber interceptor, which resulted in it carrying an armament suitable for knocking heavy bombers down with a handful of hits.

In this instance, Djorov brought the full power of one 57mm and two 23mm cannons to bear on the dilapidated old tank.

He missed spectacularly, churning up the grass nearly two hundred metres beyond the target.

Adjusting his speed, Djorov brought the MIG round in a long and gentle turn, bleeding off height until he was barely one hundred and fifty feet above the ground.

The T26 disappeared as all three weapons spat their shells accurately.

The spectators on the ground were noisily impressed, and more than one senior officer or Mikoyan engineer looked smug beyond measure.

However, the tower staff now had other problems, the tower Kapitan having to shout to make himself heard over the sounds of joy.

"Silence in the tower!"

A few eyes swung in his direction, mainly men unused to being on the end of such treatment.

"Say again, Serzhant."

The senior operator repeated his warning.

"Mangusta-seven-one has an emergency and must land. Twin engine failures. The aircraft is inbound already, Comrade Kapitan."

Pointing at the female corporal, the Captain reeled off some quick instructions.

"Tell Zvezdnyy-One to discontinue the display, take a bearing 90, circle at point 2, Arinino. Make height eight thousand and await further instructions."

He listened as the order was relayed to Djorov and then turned his attention back to the Mangusta aircraft.

"Tell him he is clear for landing, Comrade Serzhant."

Procedure dictated that the crash crews would be prepared immediately an emergency was inbound, and their sirens were now added to the sound of the departing turbojets and the growing hubbub of disquiet amongst the tower's occupants.

The Captain moved through some of those who now served no purpose but to get in the way, making his way to a side window, where he brought his binoculars up.

There was Mangusta-seven-one, both its port side engines clearly feathered.

Whilst part of him took in the details of the problem, another part of him was questioning what exactly he was looking at.

He moved back into the heart of the tower, listening as his Serzhant talked the large aircraft through its final approach.

Suddenly aware of an adjacent presence, he look up, straight into the angry eyes of Georgy Malenkov.

"Comrade Kapitan, make sure you get it down in one piece. We only have three of these."

Being addressed directly by a member of the GKO was not a commonplace occurrence, but he retained enough presence of mind to keep his mind on the job in hand.

"Report, Comrade Serzhant."

"Sir, twelve hundred metres out, pilot reports no handling issues at this time. Emergency crews in position at points one and four."

The extra personnel in the tower now crowded the viewing area for a different purpose, willing the stricken aircraft to land safely. Some, for whom its future was a matter of certain knowledge, knew that more than just one aircraft and a handful of aircrew were at stake.

All around Ramenskoye, those who had gathered as spectators for the MIG-9 test, now had the opportunity to watch something equally dramatic.

One common thought hit many minds.

179

'What the fuck is that?'

Most recognised that the aircraft was in US markings

Very few observers recognised Mangusta-seven-one for what it was, namely a Boeing B-29 Superfortress.

Malenkov was furious, at least internally so.

Even as Mangusta-seven-one, named Ramp Tramp by its former owners, touched down safely, he wondered about the organisation that had brought so many people to Ramenskoye on the same day that a vital ingredient of the Soviet Union's plans for 1946 was supposed to arrive in relative secrecy.

What made him even more furious was the fact that he rather thought he had made the error himself, and, as befitted a survivor in the political arena, he had already worked out who would take the blame for the matter should it became necessary.

Two more B-29s landed without incident, named Ding How and General H H Arnold Special, all three aircraft being immediately shepherded to a remote part of Ramenskoye's north-eastern perimeter.

Granted permission to return, Djorov couldn't fail to spot the three large aircraft taxiing slowly to their concealed positions.

He had seen such beasts once before, killed one in fact, but their presence here, at Ramenskoye, was unexpected.

Later, when he and his new friend Istomin met up, they consumed a great deal of vodka whilst discussing the merits of the MIG-9 and the purpose of three long-range heavy bombers in US markings.

Their discussions on the latter could not have been further from the truth.

1903 hrs, Saturday, 9th February 1946, on board S-22, Østerskær Island, Denmark.

The submarine had made the journey entirely on the surface, and in daylight, or what counted for daylight in February on the Baltic.

The lookouts suffered badly, their nerves frayed by the sight of a simple seagull or a sudden patch of white in the swelling sea, and they were changed round frequently, such was the tension and strain on the damaged submarine's crew.

Darkness had come far slower than they desired, but its arrival had brought some relief, if only in the minds of some, as

Allied maritime aircraft, more often than not, possessed radar capable of seeking them out on the darkest of nights.

But they were lucky, and Jabulov conned S-22 into the quiet bay he had chosen, where he was confident he could disguise his vessel and buy time to effect repairs.

Bringing S-22 into the small bay, he dropped anchor close by on its western edge, set an armed watch on deck, and took the opportunity to get his first sleep in nearly forty hours.

His sleep was interrupted by an urgent summons to the bridge as the dawn sun started to make its presence known.

Never a man to take being woken lightly, an irritable Jabulov arrived on the bridge.

"Well, Comrade Michmann Farenkov?"

"Comrade Kapitan."

The Petty Officer merely pointed northwards down the line of the submarine.

Jabulov followed the line of the finger down the submarine, across the water, all the way to the heap of tangled silver metal that had once been an aircraft.

Submarine commanders are not noted for their hesitancy or indecision.

"Comrade Michmann, I have the bridge. You are relieved. Organise a six man boat party, armed, including yourself and me. Order the Starshy Leytenant to report to me immediately."

The Petty Officer sped away as Jabulov swept his binoculars over the metal heap once more, this time spotting the telltale white star of America... and a man.

The rubber dinghy had no sooner grounded than the party was up and moving, fanning out as they headed straight for the destroyed aircraft, weapons at the ready.

The man seemed transfixed by their arrival, almost in shock.

One of the ratings spoke English, and the Michmann directed him forward as had been agreed.

Relaxing his posture, the young sailor strode steadily up towards the bearded man, who seemed to suddenly understand that salvation was at hand.

He whooped, making the Soviet sailors grip their weapons harder, and then started to bounce around like a mad man, laughing and screaming in joy.

The English-speaking rating tried to engage the man in conversation, but it was one-sided, the man's relief at being rescued taking over completely.

Food and drink calmed him down a little, and they all started to relax.

Leaving the Michmann to supervise outside, Jabulov and another sailor made a tentative entry into the wrecked B-29, once known as Jenni Lee.

There were dead men, some intact, in almost ordered repose, others in pieces, and in positions of extremis. One corpse, in the cockpit, impaled on a metal strut and held aloft like a crucifixion, was particularly horrible. The cold weather had done much to maintain the integrity of the bodies, so there was no putrefaction or significant decay, preserving the horrors of their end for all to see.

Picking their way through the fuselage, Jabulov directed the rating to take photographs of things he considered important enough to need preserving.

He stuck his head outside for a moment, ordering the Michmann to take the survivor back to the submarine, and bring more men back.

Over the next few hours, as work progressed on board S-22, a party of sailors worked their way over the whole crash site, dismantling items under the direction of Jabulov, and photographing larger items. The Navigation Officer had been recruited into the party to take measurements of items that could not be removed.

As the aviation fuel had long since evaporated, Jabulov sought the comfort of the fuselage to enjoy a cigarette out of the growing wind.

"Comrade Kapitan?"

Jabulov held out his pack of cigarettes.

"Thank you, Comrade Kapitan. This object. Do you want it measured? It seems to have no place here."

Lighting both their cigarettes, Jabulov looked at the metal structure his Junior Lieutenant was referring to.

He had walked through this part before, but didn't remember the large round construction.

The younger officer understood what his commander was thinking.

"It was covered up with parachute silk and some aluminium panelling, Comrade Kapitan."

Jabulov said nothing as he stared intently at the object, but his reaction startled the Navigator.

"Comrade Kapitan?"

"It's a bomb."

"What?"

"I said it's a bomb. A very big one, an unusual one for sure, but none the less a bomb."

The Michmann arrived to make his report, but halted, sensing that all was not well with the two officers.

The Navigation Officer was as white as a sheet, and Jabulov seemed totally distracted by the large round thing in the floor of the aircraft.

Jabulov nodded at him.

"Comrade Michmann, direct the photographer to take numerous shots of this object," he indicted the pumpkin bomb, "And do make sure he is careful. It's an unexploded bomb."

Michmann Farenkov drained of colour, and he quickly moved away to find the photographer.

The Navigation officer, under Jabulov's direct supervision, made some drawings and measurements of both the bomb and the damaged framework that it had been held in.

Every single piece of paper was removed from the aircraft; maps through to chocolate bar wrappers.

The bearded man had survived initially on crew rations, but evidence of his fishing prowess was everywhere in and around the shelter he had created for himself against the rocks, where part of the B-29's wing assembly had come to rest, creating a windproof and water tight cocoon for the sole survivor of the crash. Stuffed full of silk parachutes, life jackets and items of clothing, the modest sized area had proven sufficient to protect the survivor from the awfulness of the winter outside.

The embers of a fire still glowed in a bespoke metal fireplace set against the bare rock at the far end of the space, and Jabulov could quite imagine how comfortable the man had been.

Finding a kit bag amongst the items bulking out the bed area, the Soviet officer gathered up the array of handguns, eleven in all, laid out neatly on a natural shelf in the rock.

A notebook, newspaper, and small briefcase also caught his eye, and all followed the handguns into the kit bag.

Emerging from the hide, Jabulov encountered the Navigation Officer.

"Comrade Kapitan, we have completed photography and dimensional drawing work. The cameraman reports that he has seven frames available for overall site pictures, with your permission?"

With a look at his watch, he assessed the situation.

'11.20. Must be nearly done with the repairs by now surely?'

"Very well, Comrade Mladshy Leytenant. Have him take his last photographs and let's get the shore party assembled. We've done all we can do here."

Every piece of intelligence and every sailor was back aboard S-22 by 1155, by which time Jabulov received some positive news on his vessel's recovery.

At 1210, he dropped the submarine below the surface in a controlled vertical dive to the floor below, choosing to remain in the bay during the day to permit further repairs to take place on the submarine's electrical system in the relative safety offered by the island.

S-22 surfaced in the dark to top up her batteries and, as Sunday night moved into Monday morning, the silent boat headed out into the Baltic and dropped below the waves.

2159 hrs, Monday, 11th February 1946, Temporary Office of the Deputy Chief, Deuxieme Bureau, Heming, France.

De Walle was contemplating the short journey from his desk to the cot bed he had ordered placed in his sumptuous office, when the door rattled with urgent knocking.

"Come in!"

He didn't mean to shout in anger, but it had been a long day.

He regretted it even more when De Valois came in, clearly a woman on a mission.

"Apologies, Anne-Marie; it's been one hell of a day."

She shrugged as only the French can shrug, expressing her full opinion on the matter.

Suddenly De Walle became confused.

"I thought you were going to Reims to see the girls today?"

She shook her head.

"Last minute change of plan. We go early tomorrow, back on Saturday evening."

"C'est la Guerre, eh?"

De Walle's smile faded instantly, as he saw his top female officer was agitated by the matter.

"No, it's the cursed Legion taking priority as always."

It was a touchy subject for Anne-Marie, for reasons known only to very, very few people.

"Anyway Mon Général, this message just came in from our British Allies. It's marked for your attention. It's been decoded already."

She passed the sealed message envelope.

De Walle read the contents three times before he passed it to her.

"Read it… aloud if you please, Anne-Marie."

His hands supported his chin as she recited the simple message.

"Troy has not fallen. Ulysees is dead."

The silence continued for some time, as both reflected on the now dead Soviet Paratrooper General Makarenko, who had been so incensed at the conduct of his own leadership and the results amongst his precious soldiers, that he had willingly agreed to try and assassinate Stalin.

The unsanctioned plan had been concocted by De Walle, who enlisted the help of British Intelligence.

No one else knew, and now, no-one else would ever know.

"He was a fine man, Mon Général."

"Indeed he was. Now, Anne-Marie, enjoy your days away, and give both of them a hug from Uncle Georges."

As De Valois closed the door, the message was already burning in the fireplace, and a line drawn under the whole episode.

Surrendering to the cot bed, sleep came eventually to the Deux officer, an uneasy sleep filled with memories of a brave man and his part in his death.

0218 hrs, Tuesday, 12th February 1946, astride Route 58, one kilometre east of Ascheburg, Germany.

Since August the previous year, battlefield promotions had become the norm, so that competent NCOs could fill the gaps left by the increasing number of dead and wounded amongst the junior grade officers in the frontline units.

Before winter brought a slowing down in the tempo of combat, life expectancy for a fresh 2nd Lieutenant was, with black humour, measured in cigarette packets. A pack a day was the standard, and the soldiers started to name their young officers 'five packs' or similar, according to their expected survivability.

Promoting competent Sergeants brought about a reduction in losses, and the onset of winter gave each unit time to bed in its new soldiers and replacement NCOs.

The last eight months had been particularly hard on the 84th US Infantry Division.

The unit sustained one of the first major losses amongst the US formations, when the 335th RCT, built around the infantry regiment of the same number, succumbed to heavy Soviet attacks around Uelzen. In three days of heavy fighting, the whole RCT was destroyed, leaving the 84th woefully undermanned.

As autumn had turned to winter, the division found respite after being relieved, and used the opportunity to reinforce, taking on new personnel, some released prisoners of war, as well as absorbing remnants from other units since disbanded due to casualties.

Restored to full strength, the 84th found itself back in the line, the most southerly of Simpson's 9th US Army troops, their right flank anchored at Ascheberg, against the northern flank of the 266th Infanterie Division, one of the newly established units of the German Republic.

Their 3rd Batallion, 899th Grenadiere Regiment neatly butted up to 1st Battalion, 335th US Infantry Regiment, the three hundred metre gap between the forces being heavily mined and under constant surveillance.

Charlie Company, 355th, was preparing a raid on the Soviet positions opposite.

A group of ten men had assembled, faces blackened, camouflaged in white, and kit stripped back to basics and tied down tight.

The Staff Sergeant in charge of the raiding party double-checked each man's gear personally, pulling at webbing, ensuring no rattles from loose kit.

2nd Lieutenant Hässler took another slug of his coffee, draining the mug. Grabbing the pot, he topped up again and offered a refill to the German officer who had been assigned to his unit as liaison with the 899th.

Oberleutnant Baron Werner Von Scharf-Falkenberg was the stereotypical German officer.

Smart, almost elegant, and precisely two metres tall, his genuine good looks were enhanced, rather than despoiled, by the scarred forehead, courtesy of being caught up in the Battle of Saint-Marcel on 18th June 1944.

The other legacy of that bloody day was less obvious, only manifesting itself slightly when he ran, this left leg now being slightly shorter than his right, courtesy of a shrapnel injury.

Accepting the coffee, he produced his cigarette holder, lit up, and continued his close examination of the raiding party.

"Ready to go, Lootenant."

Staff Sergeant Rosenberg, his battered face sufficiently recovered to permit him proper speech, grinned at his old running mate.

"OK Rosie. Just get out there, do the job, get back, no dramas."

"Calm yourself; don't have a plotz in front of our guest, Lootenant."

No matter what, the Baron couldn't get used to these informal exchanges between the two men, what with one being an officer and the other an NCO.

"OK, boys. Stay safe and bring the bacon back home."

Rosenberg grimaced, as he always did when Hässler played the bacon card.

"Same old shtick, and you used to be such a mentsh too!"

Everyone, save the Baron, shared an easy laugh.

Hässler slapped his old friend on the shoulder and moved to conduct him out of the bunker.

"Oberleutnant Scharf?"

Pausing to flick up his hood, Scharf slipped the MP-40 from his shoulder and followed.

An explosion, not close, broke the silence, and the whispered chatter of the raiding party stopped instantly.

Another explosion followed, then two almost simultaneously, punctuated by a burst of machine gun fire.

Flares rose skywards, their magnesium light revealing nothing in front of the US positions.

"Minefield. With me."

Hässler led off at the double, following the trench line, occasionally having to avoid a sleepy soldier moving to his duty station.

A firefight was developing at the southernmost point of his position. A quick look allowed him to immediately understand what was happening.

The Red Army had had a similar idea, and their own raiding party had entered the minefield, with a view to circumventing the defence and coming up behind Hässler's position.

187

Until one of their lead men stepped on a mine and sent himself into the afterlife.

The larger party, Hässler could see at least forty men moving his way, was under fire from both his and the German positions opposite. The potential problem was immediately apparent.

"Oberleutnant, two green flares now. Danke."

Within seconds, the two flares added their own colour to the surreal montage, the German defensive fire dropping away instantly, in line with the pre-arranged signal.

A .30cal machine gun was spitting fury at the Soviets, who were caught between dropping into cover and moving back to the relative safety of their own positions.

A DP chattered in the snow and the American gunner was thrown back from his weapon, screaming in pain, clutching desperately at the destroyed bloody mess that had once been his left shoulder.

The loader moved across and the .30 roared into life again.

"Medic! Medic!"

Almost immediately, the loader was struck, this time fatally, as bullets chewed his face to pieces.

A group of Russians had decided on a third option, and were almost on top of the position.

Bringing his Garand up, Hässler pulled the trigger, without response.

'Fucking misfire!'

The leading enemy soldier threw himself over the trench parapet, colliding with the US officer and sending both into a disorderly pile of arms and legs, falling on top of the wounded machine-gunner.

His screams added to the animal-like snarls as the two men struggled for a handhold.

Other Russians leapt in.

Some fell in, riddled with bullets; others dropped onto the snow short of their objective.

Rosenberg sensed rather than saw the danger, and flung himself aside as he shouted.

"Grenade!"

The charge went off, adding four more men to the growing total of wounded.

A Soviet officer, his own white all-in-one stained heavily with blood, dispatched two of the wounded with his PPd before

Scharf, his immaculate appearance ravaged by the intense combat, dropped him with a burst from his SMG.

By now, Hässler had gained the ascendency, both his hands choking the life from his weakened opponent, the man's own efforts being solely concentrated on trying to prise the iron grip from his throat.

He failed, and Hässler relaxed his grip as a new flare burst and revealed inert and glassy eyes.

Dragging the dead Russian off the machine-gunner, he checked the man quickly and discovered he was still alive.

"Medic!"

Out of breath, he looked around for his Garand. Grabbing the weapon, he had no time to check the misfire before a Soviet soldier appeared in the trench.

The soldier lunged forward with his Mosin rifle, trying to drive the bayonet through Hässler's stomach.

Lurching to one side, Hässler parried the thrust with the Garand, deflecting the line of the blade, before allowing the man's momentum to bring him onto a short swing of the rifle butt.

The blow demolished teeth and bone, as the butt plate easily won the contest between metal and flesh.

Dropping onto his knees, the Soviet soldier clutched at his ruined face. Hässler, his eyes performing a quick check to make sure he was not immediately threatened, performed another short arm jab with the Garand, this time from behind, crashing the butt into the rear of the soldier's skull.

Death was instantaneous.

A quick look revealed nothing immediately wrong with the Garand, but he decided against attending to it now, preferring to rely on his automatic pistol.

A scrabbling sound made him swivel and point the Colt, but his reactions held firm, preventing him from shooting one of his own medics... just.

"Fuck!"

"Jeez Lootenant!"

There was no more to be said.

Leaving the man to tend to the machine-gunner, Hässler risked a quick look over the parapet. Although only one flare provided any light, fizzing away as it reached the end of its life.

There was no movement.

He then became aware that there were no sounds of fighting from within his positions.

189

Deciding to remain and cover the medic while he worked, Hässler alternated between looking over the silent snows in front of the position, to checking the sounds of movement further down the trench line.

"Herr Leutnant Hässler?"

"Here."

Scharf stuck his head round the trench wall, his MP-40 held ready for any eventuality.

"Alles klar?"

Hässler nodded and relaxed.

"Alles klar, Herr Oberleutnant."

Scharf unwound from his crouched position and moved into the gun position.

Two of Rosenberg's party followed him in, assisting the medic to evacuate the wounded gunner.

When the party had moved out of the position, two more men entered to take over the .30cal, leaving Hässler and Scharf free to move back.

Rosenberg was crouched at the junction of the trench and platoon HQ bunker.

"Shalom, shalom. Thought they'd done for you for a moment."

Hässler shrugged in a manner that let his friend know that things had been tight.

"Report, Rosie."

"We're clean. No more bad guys in our positions. Including your two .30cal boys, eight casualties."

Rosenberg's unspoken enquiry brought an immediate response.

"Plus one dead, one wounded, bad."

Rosenberg nodded.

"OK, that makes it six dead, four wounded. All the bad guys are down. Four are prisoners, but two of those ain't gonna make it. That will make nine of them down in our positions, who knows how many out there."

Nodding his head towards the mined area, he wiped at his face, removing some irritating dirt from his cheeks.

"We're secure and the raiding party's spread out here to keep the numbers up. The reserve moved up, of course, and is being held back at the bowl."

He referred to an area just behind the platoon HQ, where a small spinney, set in a round depression, provided excellent cover for the back-up, should they be needed.

190

"Thanks Rosie. You stay here and keep this lot tight. I'm going to report this and have a chat with our prisoners."

He slapped his old friend on the arm.

"Good effort, Sergeant, We'll make a soldier of you yet."

"Feh! Same old shtick. You wouldn't know a good soldier if you saw one."

The two parted to the sound of laughter.

Scharf had sustained a wound, although for the life of him, he had no idea how or when.

It looked like a bullet graze to the medic who cleaned the shallow scrape in the German officer's side.

Stripped to the waist, Scharf was exactly the same shade of white as the wounded Russian who was similarly undressed, his own shoulder wound already dressed by the medic.

Using the little Russian language at his disposal, Scharf attempted to interrogate the Soviet NCO, but fell short of understanding anything of value in the conversation.

However, the cameo presented Hässler with a great deal of information on the enemy opposite his position.

Scharf was solidly built, muscular and well proportioned, a fact emphasised by the complete opposite presentation of the Soviet soldier.

His ribs were apparent, his muscles less pronounced, and generally, the man's physique seemed to have suffered great deprivations.

Calling a guard to take the man away, Hässler lit two cigarettes, passing one to Scharf as he redressed.

"So?"

Scharf took a deep draw on the Chesterfield.

"Remarkable, Herr Leutnant. The man's from a guard unit. They get the best of everything in the Red Army."

Hässler hadn't known that, and the simple fact made the discovery more important.

Drawing deeply on his cigarette, his eyes bored into those of the German.

"And yet?"

Scharf nodded his understanding.

"And yet they are starving."

Hassler stood abruptly.

191

"Skinny as fuck. This I gotta phone in, Herr Oberleutnant."

The communication caused a ripple effect all the way to Bradley's desk, where it arrived, annotated by the various officers across whose bows it had travelled, complete with the latest intelligence reports on Red Army logistics.

It all made tantalising reading.

'Munitions over food? Surely not?'

Bradley mused on the why's and wherefore's.

He dialled in a number.

"This report on the starving commie soldier. Get it all firmed up and revaluate our reports on Soviet logistics. On my desk by 1500 sharp. I want this to be with SHAEF today."

Putting the phone down on his Intelligence chief, Bradley suddenly felt a lightness spread in his body, a feeling that something had changed, something positive for the Allied cause, a something that would help them down the road to victory.

The phone was in his hand again. He could not overcome the feeling of elation and needed to share it quickly.

Waiting whilst he was connected, he closed his eyes in prayer, which was interrupted by the voice in his ear.

"Ike. Brad here. I'm going to get a report to you by this evening, but I want to share the bare bones with you now."

The report kick started a drive in re-examining Soviet logistics. Some days later, the only conclusion that could be reached was that, simply put, the Red machine was breaking down.

Constant air attacks, partisan raids, losses in support personnel and equipment, damage to infrastructure, all combined to support the notion that the Red Army was slowly being paralysed.

0859 hrs, 12th February 1946, the Mühlberg, Nordhausen, Germany.

The three men were protesting their innocence, their cries ranging from hysterical sobs to controlled pleas for mercy, but mercy was not to be found in the frozen clearing that morning.

Nazarbayeva had attended to watch the NKVD soldiers pay for their murder of Anna Lubova, the medic who had nursed her back to life from the awful virus that afflicted her last year.

The three transport guards had attacked and raped Lubova, and inflicted awful injuries on the woman, resulting in her death on 4th February.

When the GRU officer had heard of the matter, she took a personal interest in ensuring that the perpetrators did not escape justice.

That interest brought her to the Mühlberg on a bitterly cold morning to witness the culmination of her participation in the investigation.

"Fire!"

A dozen rifles spoke at once, and the protestations of innocence stopped in a heartbeat.

The officer commanding the firing squad marched smartly forward, discharging his pistol once at each man's head.

As the doctor moved in to confirm death, Nazarbayeva recalled the telephone call with Beria, the threats and the anger at her direct interference.

She had resisted the NKVD Marshal's insistence at leaving the matter to NKVD internal discipline procedures, instead ensuring the men were processed through an Army court, one where she expected a fair trial to be accompanied by a fair sentence.

As the bodies were cut down, she could see the friendly face of Nurse Lubova, and unconsciously nodded at her memory, hoping that the dead woman could somehow see justice being done.

The vision was quickly replaced with one of malevolence, as Beria's features filled her mind... snarling... threatening... dangerous...

The galleries are full of critics. They play no ball. They fight no fights. They make no mistakes because they attempt nothing. Down in the arena are the doers. They make mistakes because they try many things. The man who makes no mistakes lacks boldness and the spirit of adventure. He is the one who never tries anything. He is the break in the wheel of progress. And yet it cannot be truly said he makes no mistakes, because his biggest mistake is the very fact that he tries nothing, does nothing, except criticize those who do things.

Gen. David M. Shoup, USMC

Chapter 134 – THE CIRCUS

1000 hrs, Friday, 22nd February 1946, Chateau de Versailles, France.

With a sense of dramatic, De Gaulle had personally selected the War Drawing room as the location of the meeting between the heads of the Allied Powers.

Once known as the King's Cabinet, the large room contained celebrations of Louis XIV's military prowess.

The centre of the ornate room was occupied by a huge solid table, providing sufficient space for all the representatives of the Allied powers to be comfortably seated.

Behind each prime position, two or three chairs were provided for advisors, depending on the size of the military contingent.

The head of the table, behind which stood a number of concealed maps, was set aside for the Supreme Allied Commander and his immediate staff. Eisenhower was already seated, drawing heavily on his cigarette as he eavesdropped the British Prime Minister's conversation with Von Papen, present in his role as German Chancellor.

Tedder and Bedell-Smith juggled with a few papers, setting matters in final order before the presentation began.

A few of those present were unfamiliar to him, although most were household names.

Feeling the approach of an invisible energy field, Eisenhower yanked himself from his solitude and stood as President Harry S. Truman swept into the room, quickly extinguishing his cigarette, before earning a disapproving look from his political master. Shaking hands and exchanging pleasantries as he circulated the room, Truman still moved swiftly to his position opposite Churchill, both men sitting close to Eisenhower, as befitted their status.

Pausing only to shake de Gaulle's hand, then Eisenhowers', President Truman slipped easily into the embroidered upholstery of the gilded seat and looked expectantly around him, acknowledging Churchill with a friendly smile.

"Winston."

"Harry."

Such was the relationship between the two.

Truman had arrived in England three days before, spending his time at Chequers, as the two leaders decided on their joint approach to the proposed military plans for the months ahead.

In full agreement, they now sat either side of their chosen commander, ready for the presentation to begin.

Eisenhower stood and cleared his throat.

"Sirs," the simple address had been agreed beforehand, if only to save time, as well as not challenging Ike's memory, "Welcome."

The muttered replies lasted a few seconds, giving Eisenhower the opportunity to sip at his water.

"Most of you have forces already committed to operations in Europe, and specifically within Operation Spectrum."

He moved to one side, where a map outlining Spectrum thus far was marked out, indicating how the Allied forces had taken the initiative.

Using the map as an aid, he gave a quick résumé of the portions of Spectrum to date, commencing with the successful but costly French-led Spectrum-Black diversion, during which De Gaulle adopted the smuggest of smug expressions.

Keeping specifics to a minimum, Eisenhower shifted through the ground and air phases, up to where weather and Soviet resistance terminated operations.

Taking a sip of water, he moved into summing up the present situation.

"Overall, air operations, and in a limited way, ground operations, in line with the basic needs of Spectrum, have been maintained throughout the winter period, and we've taken the opportunity offered by the lull, to reinforce units, stockpile assets, and compile as much intelligence as possible on the enemy we face."

Another sip eased his drying throat.

"In short, their Air Force is all but negated, and has a limited defensive capability, with almost no offensive power whatsoever. We control the skies, gentlemen, although we cannot permit ourselves to be complacent in that regard."

Sounds of agreement gave him a moment's pause.

"Their Navy hurt us badly at the start of the war, but is now pretty much confined to its ports and coastal waters, both in the Arctic and Baltic areas. Occasional excursions have been detected and successfully prosecuted."

"However, their ground forces still represent a huge threat, albeit that we finally stopped their advance in December."

Ike nodded to Colonel Hood who, with assistance from Anne-Marie Foster, uncovered a large map of Europe, showing the dispositions of the two mighty armies, down to Corps level, from Murmansk to the southern borders of the USSR.

Giving the assembly a moment to digest the presentation, Eisenhower fought his desire for tobacco.

Truman was a non-smoker and didn't care for the habit being exercised around him, although he tolerated Churchill's 'Romeo y Julieta' Cuban cigars with good grace.

"A word of caution. These indicators are not indicators of unit size, and some of our units are below full strength, as are numerous Soviet formations."

In addition to the front line forces and reserves, there were two definite clusters of corps markers on the Allied side of the divide, neither in the front line, and the more astute politicians noted their presence with understanding.

Eisenhower then slipped into his briefing with more care, as most of the precise fact was not for the ears of all those present.

Talking in generalities, and waving his hand in indistinct movements, he talked through the intent to take the fight to the Russians as soon as the winter had receded.

Occasionally, Ike stopped to focus on one national group or another, first singling out President Camacho of Mexico for thanks at the arrival of the Mexican Battle group, presently billeted around Nice, getting itself ready for integration into the Allied forces.

Similarly, the Argentine Foreign Minister, Juan Isaac Cooke, received plaudits for the newly committed ground force his nation had supplied.

Whilst the presence of some of these national formations was a political exercise, and the difficulties of integrating them into the fighting forces would undoubtedly outweigh their usefulness, any and all commitments from the Allied nations was to be applauded and 'talked up'.

Eisenhower fielded a few general questions from the floor, delighting Nereu de Oliveira Ramos, the Brazilian Vice-president, with assurances that his military contingent would be handed an important part in the coming offensive.

The presentation concluded on cue, and the politicians rose, the air filled with noises of self-congratulation, before they all moved off to partake of a hearty lunch.

1430 hrs, Friday, 22nd February 1946, Chateau de Versailles, France.

Back in the War Drawing room once more, Eisenhower now faced a much smaller audience.

After lunch, the heads of state had been driven away to observe a parade at the local St Cyr Military Academy, where contingents of every national force would march past.

That left ten men to be fully briefed on the coming Allied operations; men who all understood the need for, and requirements of, utmost secrecy.

The table had been reduced in size, permitting the ten men to sit side by side and facing Eisenhower and his team.

Nearest the entrance sat the French.

De Gaulle had intended to place himself centrally, but had been outmanoeuvred by the early arrival of Churchill and Truman.

Sat with General de L'Armee Alphonse Juin, Chief of Staff of the French Army, he failed to hide his annoyance.

Adjacent to him was the Chief of the Imperial General Staff, Field Marshall Viscount Sir Allan Brooke, himself a fluent French speaker, positioned so as to both communicate with the French leader, as well as overhear anything of note that he and his CoS should discuss.

Churchill was next, sat alongside Truman, far enough apart to give each man personal space, but close enough to allow a modest lean to bring an ear closer to the whisperer's lips.

General of the Army George C. Marshall sat next to Von Papen, engaging in light conversation with the assistance of the interpreter, Major Golding.

Speer was poring over a folder, checking and double-checking figures on production.

The final pair were speaking softly in Spanish, as General Muñoz Grandes answered a few direct questions from Francisco Paulino Hermenegildo Teódulo Franco y Bahamonde, the caudillo of Spain, more commonly known as Generalissimo Franco.

On signal, Hood and Foster removed the largest cover, to sounds of surprise and loud intakes of breath.

The arrows were numerous and bit deep into Soviet-held territory.

Ike revelled in the audacious plan that was set before his political masters.

"Sirs, what you see before you is the general concept for the last phases of Spectrum."

He turned to the map and finally found use for his pointer.

"Violet," he tapped a few of the numerous markers across the length and breadth of enemy territory, "The dismantling of Soviet support infrastructure across Europe, interdiction, and expanded heavy bomber missions to reduce Soviet production and resupply capability."

The pointer flicked to Holland.

"White. The establishment of a FUSAG style decoy, known as SAAG for Second Allied Army group, intended to pin the enemy 1st Baltic Front in place here," he indicated the Northern German Plain."

"Indigo. The invasion of Northern Poland by sea, in order to support the planned revolt by the armed forces of Poland."

He paused, taken in by the grandeur of the next phase.

"Orange. The general rolling back of the Red Army to the positions occupied in August 1945, and beyond."

The very scale of Orange was breathtaking.

Eisenhower was presenting the plan for ratification by those present, as their national forces would be playing the biggest parts in the months to come, and the five national leaders present represented the five largest contingents of land troops in the Allied Armies, with the exception of the Poles, who had been excluded from the presentation solely because no-one from the 1st Polish Army had been available to attend.

De Gaulle, always pressing for a bigger French role, was well satisfied with the assignments for his formations, although noted the relocation that would need to be undertaken to bring his forces in between the German Army and that of the United States.

Neither Churchill nor Alanbrooke bothered to feign surprise, both already knowing most of what the basic presentation held.

Truman and Marshall similarly held their peace.

Franco stared in wonderment at the scale of Allied expectation, his own forces being handed some clearly crucial missions in the plan.

Von Papen and Speer had known the bare bones of it all, but to see the centre ground dedicated to the new German Republican Army, was something else entirely, and both men were moved by the onerous tasks allotted to their troops.

Not the least of which was illustrated by a single black arrow, a symbol of the potential third stage of the advance, which took the German Army to Berlin.

Eisenhower's reasoning had been quite simple, but he kept it to himself in the present company.

Firstly, the Germans would most likely fight harder for their own capital. Secondly, it would be a bloodbath of biblical proportions, one to be avoided by the British, French, and American Armies.

Colonel Hood distributed ten numbered copies of a document to the assembled listeners, and then Eisenhower swung into his presentation proper.

Norway was first, where the forces in country were British, German, and Norwegian.

There had been much deliberation over the possibilities of opening another area of operations by attacking the USSR through Norway, one Churchill was particularly supportive of, the idea of which had received a cool welcome in both Oslo and Stockholm.

Using the additional strain on logistics as an excuse, further development of the concept was put on hold, if only to assuage the fears of their Scandanavian friends

Eisenhower's pointer found 'White'.

"SAAG. This formation comprises no forces of note at this time, although we intend to fill it out when reinforcements become available. Running it as a FUSAG operation, we intend to use it to pin the Soviet 1st Baltic Front in place. From our intelligence sources, it seems that the Soviets have taken the bait."

He took a deep breath.

"Orange and Indigo are mutually supporting sections of the plan."

Using the pointer, he swept the length of the front line from north to south.

"British, Commonwealth, and Free forces will assault on a relatively narrow front, in order to focus power and drive deep into Soviet-held Germany, specifically targeting the 1st Baltic, which will receive a considerable amount of attention from our strike and bomber forces and, for that matter, naval forces, who will support from close inshore where possible. We intend to push this large Soviet grouping into tight pockets where our aircraft can maximise the effect of their strikes, but also remembering that the intent is to breakthrough to the Indigo perimeter."

Von Papen spoke rapidly to Goldstein, causing Eisenhower to stop.

"Sir, the Chancellor asks if the name 'Pantomime' is now finished?"

"Apologies. Pantomime refers to the ground operations subsequent to Indigo, which is the amphibious phase."

Von Papen seemed satisfied, so Ike continued.

"Here, the German Army will launch a two pronged offensive, the initial intent of which is to relieve pressure on the Ruhr. These two assaults will be aimed at... Berlin... and Dresden"

Eisenhower paused for no other reason than a muscle twinge, but the delay allowed the others present to conjure up the sights and sounds of horror that would accompany any clash in the German capital.

"The French Army will drive on Prague, again on a relatively narrow front."

"US forces will attempt an encircling of Soviet forces in south-west Germany," the pointer described circular motions north of Switzerland, "Intending on sealing the enemy forces by taking Munich by south and north-west assaults."

"More German and Austrian forces will drive eastwards, securing the Danube at Vienna."

Last tap on the map highlighted a difficult area, and one that had caused some division amongst the planners.

"North-east Italy will see no great action on our part. Messages from Tito are unclear, but the Yugoslav commitment has remained at the volunteer level first spoken of. Our forces will be under strict orders not to violate Yugoslavian territory or air space."

Ike realised he had raced through his last statement, so paused to allow Goldstein to interpret.

"In any case, we will be reducing the British, Commonwealth and Free forces in Northern Italy, whilst we assess the feasibility of the operation suggested by the Prime Minister."

Churchill had come up with another idea of hurting the Soviet Union and Eisenhower could only admit that it had some merits, although previous looks at the general concept had ensured rejection because of a lack of assets.

None the less, a mission had been sent to establish whether such an operation was possible, and the mission, led by Lieutenant General Sir Frederick E Morgan, was due back from Tehran within the week.

"Spectrum is a far-reaching plan with many facets, and it will need to be revised as we go along, but the general principles are sound."

Placing the pointer on the table in studied fashion, Eisenhower tugged his tunic into place.

"Sirs, this winter has been hard on both sides, but we think harder on the enemy. Our Air Forces have destroyed huge quantities of their supplies, laid waste their infrastructure, disrupted their own recuperation, whereas, our own forces have been able to build-up and strengthen. We are more powerful as an Allied Army than ever we were before, and we have the materiel behind us to go all the way with Spectrum, whereas recent intelligence suggests that the average Red Army soldier in the frontline is starving, literally."

Eisenhower coughed nervously.

"This will not come cheap, by any means, but with air superiority and speed of attack, we can prevail and….."

Eisenhower ceded to the man who had raised his hand.

"General Eisenhower, whilst your plan seems to have merit, and I understand the advantages of speed of attack, the American public saw huge numbers of their boys die in the first few months of this awful war, in larger numbers than in the previous conflict too. I know that our allies all face the same public outcry on casualties. What happens when the telegrams start flooding into post boxes, come the start of this?"

The question was purely rhetorical, the moment orchestrated, and Truman exchanged glances with Churchill, before continuing.

"I'll tell you what will happen. There'll be an outcry; mothers from Maine to Missouri will grieve for lost sons, and in numbers we've not yet experienced."

Churchill stood, gathering himself, looking at the powerful men around him.

"Gentlemen, some while ago we came together as Allies, attacked and betrayed, united by communist treachery. At that time, in those dark hours, we resolved to resist with all our might, and we set out our goals for this present conflict. They were simple and morally sound. They have not changed; no, for indeed, they cannot change. But perhaps now, here, I think we can all see the awful spectre that is the potential bloody price of our commitment."

Grasping his lapel in time honoured fashion, Churchill spoke with real passion.

"I would that no more sons of our nations died in this abomination, but that is beyond our control."

201

"We must end this war, as quickly as possible, staying true to our morals, for the good of all nations, for we cannot let this, any of this, stand."

Looking at Truman, the old campaigner, gathered himself.

"If I may borrow some words from a fine and noble man, who once held me at great disadvantage*," those who knew exactly to whom Winston referred smiled involuntarily, "He said…you cannot escape the responsibility of tomorrow, by evading it today."

He left the quote from Abraham Lincoln to be absorbed in silence.

Gesturing at the map, Churchill waved his free hand over its lines and arrows.

"Regardless of whether this plan is approved, or the next, or the next, there will be a devil's bill of monumental proportions, and we must prepare our people for it, as well as ensure that they understand how much worse it could be if we did nothing."

For some reason, all eyes swivelled to Von Papen.

Surprised by the attention, the elderly politician took a moment to compose himself.

Gesturing Goldstein closer, he whispered into the Major's ear.

"Gentlemen, when Germany entered into this relationship, most of its lands were already under the Communist boot. Since then, more has been taken from us, and in that time many young men have bled and died."

Goldstein leant close in once more.

"Germany cannot be Germany without a plan such as Spectrum, and so Germany accepts that, for it to become whole again, there is a price to pay… and don't think for one moment that we do not understand what losses **that**," he punched out the word as his finger fired out at the capital of his country, "Will represent for the fathers and mothers of Germany."

The US President looked at both de Gaulle and Franco in turn, seeking a sign that they wanted their input, but neither man was particularly forthcoming, each looking to the other to speak first, which was, in itself, unusual for both men.

After some awkwardness, De Gaulle eventually spoke.

"France stands ready, and the French people, who have already suffered so much, will shoulder their part of the burden. We are committed."

Eyes turned to Franco, who spoke simply, accompanying his words with typical Spanish shrugs and hand gestures.

"Communism cannot prevail. Spain was committed to that cause from the outset. We have always known the high price of opposing it. I see no reason for change here."

Truman, lips pursed as he digested the words of the others, beckoned Eisenhower forward.

"General, please proceed with the details."

Eisenhower moved sideways, giving the floor to Bedell-Smith and Tedder, who would impart the details to the political leadership.

[*Churchill was referring to his famous encounter with Lincoln's ghost during a stay in the White House. He exited his bathtub and, without clothing, walked into the nearby bedroom, only to find Lincoln leaning on the mantelpiece. The encounter was much to Churchill's embarrassment, and according to the British PM's account, Winston only managed to say "Good evening, Mr. President. You seem to have me at a disadvantage," before Lincoln apparently vanished, probably as discomfited as his living counterpart. Source Wikipedia and an article by Esther Inglis-Arkell 'When Churchill met Lincoln. Naked' at http://io9.com/5852898/when-churchill-met-lincoln-naked.]

2030 hrs, Friday, 22nd February 1946, Chateau de Versailles, France.

That evening, the heads of state ate a hearty dinner, satisfied that the plan they had endorsed would bring about a swift conclusion to the war, placing the USSR in a position where it would have to negotiate a peace.

Peace.

Many a glass was raised to it, and many a throat was whetted with expensive French wine in its name.

There was even talk, as ever, of bringing everyone home by Christmas.

Speer smiled his way through the toasts and conversation, his mind turning over one simple thought.

'Scheisse verdamnt!'

The aftermath of that fateful day was quite marked.

Across the length and breadth of Allied-held Europe, orders arrived discreetly, preparing senior officers for what was to come.

Supply officers received their instructions, and the expectations of their masters started to cause them headache after headache, long before they commenced their work.

The clandestine agencies went to work with a will, exploiting the false ideas fed to the Soviets, building on the SAAG operation to distract, and preparing new subterfuges with which to confuse and distract their enemies.

Even outside Europe, ripples of new activity made themselves known, as air and naval bases throughout the Mediterranean, Persia and into Asia received quiet orders.

The air war, Spectrum-Green, was ramped up yet another notch, as day and night, the heavy bombers roamed the skies virtually unopposed.

Occasionally there were errors, when a fighter escort missed its rendezvous, leaving the big aircraft vulnerable, but they were few and far between.

Finland formally and noisily protested as RAF bombers regularly violated her airspace. Curiously, the experienced Finnish pilots, flying ME109 night fighters, never seemed to intercept the Allied intruders, so nothing was done to stop the stream of Halifax, Lincoln, and Lancaster aircraft as they flew to Murmansk, Archangelsk, and all points north of Leningrad.

Red, the naval elements of Spectrum, became more aggressive and the Soviet Baltic Fleet, such as it was after months of attrition, was reduced to a shadow by constant air and sea action, even though part of it was still frozen in by the solid ice of the north Baltic.

Every day, Group Captain Stagg appeared with the latest predictions, constantly disappointing planners by offering no definite hope for the future, no potential break in the winter conditions that so constrained both sides.

The air war intensified further, as the first standard B-29's and B-32's arrived in France and Holland, soon to start taking the war further into the Soviet Union itself.

Southampton saw the arrival of the new Essex class carrier Kearsarge, its decks crowded with aircraft securely wrapped up as a defence against the violence of the Atlantic weather. Curious eyes watched as the unfamiliar types were stripped of their covers and unloaded by crane. More of the same type emerged from the hangar below, until over sixty of the propeller-less aircraft were disembarked onto barges and taken up the River Itchen to HMS Raven, the RNAS shore station, where the arrival of the Shooting

Stars caused little fuss, the arrival of two dozen Sea Vampires having already stolen the show.

On land, new equipment arrived in growing numbers. Many M-10's had been withdrawn to undergo a programme of up gunning to 90mm or 17pdr, depending on what was available, as well as receiving additional armour protection.

The M-26, and a lesser number of hurriedly produced Super Pershings, arrived in Rotterdam, being immediately absorbed into the growing US forces.

Shermans, Jacksons, half-tracks and artillery pieces rolled off transport ships or were craned onto transporters in nearly every port in Allied Europe.

In the UK, production of the venerable Churchill tank gave way to an intense run of Black Prince vehicles, designed solely to consume as many Churchill parts as possible, before British factories started to produce Comets and Centurions to equip British and Commonwealth armoured divisions.

The first Panther tanks rolled off factory assembly lines, some only a few miles away from Soviet positions around the Ruhr. At the same time, French factories started to produce the ST44 and MG42, few at first, but in increasing numbers as techniques were improved and more capacity came online.

POWs, debilitated by captivity, were now, for the most part, fully recovered, providing an experienced pool from which rienforcements were drawn for both replenishment and for new units.

The Allied war machine was growing; growing in numbers, in capability, in strength, and perhaps most importantly, in confidence.

0939 hrs, Friday 1st March 1946, Headquarters of 3rd Red Banner Central European Front, Hotel Stephanie, Baden-Baden, Germany.

"I repeat, Comrade Marshal, I haven't received anything like that."

"Balls and fucking nonsense, Rokossovsky, balls and fucking nonsense."

Konev stuck out an imperious hand and an aide slipped a report into it instantly.

Reading aloud, the bald-headed commander of the Soviet Army in Europe, alternated between the report and burning holes in Marshal Rokossovsky with his red-hot gaze.

"Since 2nd January, you have been sent, three hundred and seventy-two tanks of varying kinds, including thirty IS-IIIs."

He slapped the paper with the back of his fingers.

"Four hundred and ninety-eight artillery pieces... one hundred and ninety-seven anti-tank guns... five hundred and forty mortars, Comrade."

Holding the report close to the red-faced Polish officer, Konev tapped an entry with the tip of his finger.

"One and a half million artillery and mortar shells, Comrade."

Almost apoplectic with rage, Rokossovsky waited whilst his deputy, Petrovich, passed him a piece of paper unbidden.

"Perhaps you would care to compare the two, Comrade Marshal?"

Konev snatched the list and held the two pieces of paper side by side, looking from one to the other, his brow creasing as the comparisons struck home.

"Eighty-six tanks? Only eighty-six fucking tanks?"

Trubnikov, the 3rd's Chief of Staff, responded angrily.

"Comrade Marshal, this information was communicated to your headquarters. All of this fucking fiasco was communicated to your headquarters."

"Comrade General Trubnikov, to lose one of the Rodina's tanks is unforgiveable, to lose nearly three hundred makes **you** meat for the fucking firing squad!"

Rokossovsky leapt to his feet.

"There'll be no need for firing squads here today!"

Konev held his tongue as Rokossovsky went face to face.

"The tanks are not lost. The artillery's not lost. None of it's lost. It's out there, lying in mangled fucking heaps where the enemy have bombed it to pieces. We have no air cover worthy of the name, so it gets destroyed before it ever gets near us."

Moving to Petrovich's side, he held out a hand.

"Damage reports please, Comrade."

The sheaf of papers was produced in seconds.

"Here."

He read each in turn, passing the report to a seething Konev.

"Karlsruhe... sixty-one tanks destroyed in one raid."

The next virtually flew from his hand to Konev.

"Waghäusel... two hundred and twenty thousand artillery shells in one raid."

The Polish Marshal waited whilst Konev read the report of the huge explosion at Waghäusel, one that had also claimed nearly a thousand lives.

"Outside Leingarten... here we got lucky and shot down two of the bastards! Not before we lost eighty artillery and thirty-two anti-tank guns."

He ruffled the paperwork noisily.

"Here... and here... and here... the same story day in, day out. They turn up, our anti-aircraft gunners fire what they have, which is sometimes enough to kill one or two of them, and then the enemy destroys our forces with impunity."

Konev stared angrily.

"Your headquarters has been sent all this information, Comrade Marshal."

Rokossovsky calmed down in an instant.

"My losses behind the lines have probably exceeded by combat losses by twenty to one these last few months."

Konev took his cue from the calmer voice and reduced his aggressive tone.

"What have you done to reduce the impact of their temporary superiority, Comrade Marshal?"

The Pole could not help but smile at the word 'temporary'.

"Ammunition has been taken from trains and reduced to much smaller loads, loads suitable for carrying by animal, or on soldier's backs. That's reduced munition losses to minimal levels, but it's hard on both men and animals."

Konev nodded.

"Losses in heavy equipment have been reduced, although not without cost in my fuel reserve, as we move large portions off transport, shifting them mainly by night when the enemy's less effective with ground attack work."

Konev's mind started to think about the other forces under his command.

'Is this scenario repeated through all my units?'

Silently, the Red Army commander sifted through the remaining papers, seeing the tragedy of 3rd Red Banner Front repeated time and time again.

As ever, in these last few months, the main problem was an absence of air cover for his units and logistics.

He handed back the sheaf of papers without further comment.

An uncomfortable silence descended on the room, Konev distracted by thoughts, the others aware that he could explode at any moment.

Trubnikov gestured at a staff captain, who immediately went to work with an incredibly large and ornate silver samovar, producing tea for all the senior officers.

Rokossovsky proferred one to Konev, which broke him from his reverie, bringing him back to his professional self in an instant.

"Comrade Marshal, I appreciate your difficulties, and I'll do what I can. Now… show me your offensive planning for when this freeze is over."

Taking responsibility on himself, Rokossovsky used the situation map to detail his planned offensive.

Konev's face became thunderously dark again.

"Is that it? Is that fucking it? You have a huge war machine at your disposal and you offer me that as an offensive?"

Rokossovsky sighed the sigh of a man about to repeat himself.

"Comrade Marshal Konev, it's true I've a huge force but it's crippled by the weather… by lack of food… by low munitions," he counted each point off on his fingers, "restricted fuel… by the absence of air cover… a hostile population…"

Konev's mouth hung open slightly.

"As a result, the men are demoralised and have low morale. Unless I can have reinforcements, resupply, time to rest my men… and an assurance of air support for daylight combat at least, then I can see little to be gained by launching 3rd Red Banner into a pointless assault that'll undoubtedly fail."

"Comrade Marshal, I think you should think this through very carefully, or you may be summoned to Moscow to account for this traitorous inactivity!"

Petrovich came to attention.

"Comrade Marshal Konev, with respect, sir, Comrade Marshal Rokossovsky is correct and acting in the best interests of the Rodina."

Konev almost turned blue.

"Acting in the best interests of the Rodina? Since when is it in the best interests of the Rodina to disobey fucking orders, Comrade General!"

Trubnikov took a step forward, and Konev's hand automatically went to his holster.

"Comrade Marshal Konev, it is clearly in the best interests of the Rodina not to sacrifice one of her finest armies in a pointless gesture, based on dated ideas and combat against a different enemy. Better we should keep that army intact and await the time when our glorious scientists and academicians can bring forth equipment suitable for the sons and daughters of Mother Russia to use their superior skill and national fervour to win the day."

Both Rokossovsky and Petrovich stared at their comrade, his diatribe being about four times longer than either of them had ever heard him speak before.

Plus, it was undoubtedly a load of political bollocks.

None the less, Konev, the words burning through his anger, could see the logic, although he doubted the occupants of the Kremlin would do so in a month of Sundays.

Part of him wanted to replace the entire frontal staff and stick the Polish bastard up against the wall, but he stayed his hand, or more correctly, his thoughts caused him concern and he knew he had questions to ask elsewhere first.

After the normal pep talk and encouragement to do more, Konev and his following swept off on the next leg of their tour of frontal headquarters, where he asked the questions raised by his meeting with 3rd Red Banner.

By Monday 4th March, Konev had his answer, and it was worse than the reports of the previous months had suggested, or he feared, following his conversation with Rokossovsky. On paper, he controlled the largest field force ever committed by his country. But, in reality, the army was a shadow of its former self, from the 1st Baltic to 1st Alpine, its capabilities worn down by air strikes and the severe winter, by hunger and low morale, all set against a backdrop of a shortage of pretty much everything from helmets to howitzers.

A major spring offensive, such as envisioned by Moscow, could only end in disaster.

Zhukov, appraised by telephone, could only agree.

Behind the Allied lines, units manoeuvred, rested, trained, or stood watch in the front lines, as planners moved their pieces around the board of war.

An increase in temperature, accompanied by brighter weather, offered the Allied Armies maximum advantage, as their ground forces went about their business with relative impunity, whilst the Red Army did what it could under a perpetual umbrella of airborne hostility.

None the less, the Soviet supply units performed heroics, often at great cost, whilst the engineers did all they could to maintain the infrastructure. Much of their work was destroyed within minutes of its erection, but some often remained long enough for something to get through.

In the Motherland, the factories and training camps churned out battle-ready weapons and trained men in impressive numbers.

Spring was coming, and with it would come combat on a scale not yet seen, and when the great devourer, the machine called War, would be insatiable.

Success depends upon previous preparation, and without such preparation there is sure to be failure.

Confucius

Chapter 135 - THE PREPARATIONS

Hodges and Eisenhower were enjoying a coffee together in relaxed circumstances.

Elsewhere in the building, staff officers were working constantly to put meat on the bones of their orders, and to jockey the Allied Armies into position for when, given the right circumstances, the order would be given and the advance begin.

The previous day, both men had been witness to a demonstration of some of the latest technology of war, from improved radar to jet fighter aircraft.

Everything seemed to be going in the right direction for them, except one thing, and that was beyond their control.

Ike responded to the knock.

"Come in."

"Sir, Group Captain Stagg to see you."

"Show him in, Anne-Marie."

Hodges sat upright in his chair, setting his mug on the table.

Eisenhower grabbed for his cigarettes and had one alight before the RAF Meteorologist strode into the room, his gait announcing the nature of his news.

"Good morning James. You look fit to burst; good news, I hope?"

"Good morning, Sir. General Bradley."

He thrust a folder forward insistently.

"The latest reports garnered from our met stations. That's the collated version from which we make our predictions."

Eisenhower perused the graphs and maps swiftly.

"Tell me what I'm looking at here?"

Standing by Eisenhower's side, Stagg swept his finger across the map of Europe as he spoke.

"What this is telling us is that winter is over and that, by the end of next week, the thaw should be well set, Sir."

211

Bradley piped up.

"Temperatures?"

"Hard to say, General Bradley, but within two weeks we could see a mean of 10° to 12° in the zone of operations, except the Baltic and Scandinavia, which should still be in thaw none the less."

"Ice?"

Much depended on Stagg's answer.

"All gone in the area of intended operation, Sir."

Eisenhower held the folder up.

"And this is kosher? 100%, James?"

Stagg eased his collar.

"Nothing is 100% in meteorology, Sir. But I am giving you my best estimation of the weather to come, based on all information to hand."

Ike nodded. Stagg had been the man who had advised him to go for 6th June 1944, despite the atrocious weather in the English Channel. He had trusted him then…

'I'll trust you now, James.'

"OK. I'll wait 'til tomorrow. If there's no significant change in your predictions, then I'll look to initiate Spectrum on…"

Eisenhower looked at the small calendar on the table, one advertising some men's outfitters in nearby Trappes.

Bradley looked down the numbers and satisfied himself as to the prospective date.

"26th March, Brad?"

"As you say, Ike. That gives us time."

"26th March it is then. As always, I'm relying on you, James."

"Sir."

The dapper RAF officer swept from the room, intent on checking and rechecking his findings.

"So, do we give the boys the heads up today?"

Eisenhower considered the suggestion, quickly shaking his head.

"Nope. Let them carry on as normal today. They will know soon enough, Brad."

Both men returned to their coffee, different thoughts now occupying their minds.

1122 hrs, Tuesday 5th March 1946, Wittensee, Bünsdorf, Germany.

CSM Charles looked at his tank with great pride.

The Centurion had been the sole survivor of the six Mk I vehicles given to the Guards Division, before hostilities commenced.

Now she stood amongst the rest of 2nd Battalion, Grenadier Guards, one of two units in the Guards Division fully equipped with the new vehicle.

'Lady Godiva' was the sole Mk I, the unit having received the first production models of the more heavily armoured Mk II version.

It was wholly obvious that, despite her battle damage, her crew maintained the tank in the best fighting condition, the smell of fresh oil and grease hanging in the chilled air.

What troubled Charles was the apparent absence of any crew members.

Hopping up onto the glacis plate, the driver's position was found to be empty. Further investigation established that the fighting compartment was also unoccupied.

Low whistling caught Charles' attention and he spotted his driver, Trooper Wild, wandering in his direction.

"Laz, where's the rest of the lads?"

"Sarnt. Pats and Beefy are o'er by Ordnance, playin' wit tha new toys. 'Parently, the 'onourable Lieutenant Percival thinks," he coughed, setting his throat up to mimic the high-born British officer, "That one's idea is a truly spiffing wheeze, don't you know."

Charles caught his laugh just in time, not wishing to undermine the squeaky clean young 'Rupert', although part of his amusement was at Lazarus Wild's Salford-accented attempt at a plummy public school voice.

"What you doing anyway?"

Wild profferred the grease guns he was holding.

"I were toppin' thems off at maint'nance. Fancy a brew?"

Charles nodded, sensing there was something else to hear.

"What you hiding, Laz?"

"Err…you might wanna stay clear of ol' Pansy forra while."

Charles frowned in suspicion, knowing that WO2 Flowers of the Maintenance Section was a constant target for light-hearted abuse by the tankers of his company.

"And why might I want to do that?"

"Seems he's missin' a shitload of ball-bearings, and he seems to think yer name's written all o'er the 'einous deed."

The NCO's eyes narrowed.

"And why the fuck would he think that?"

Wild shrugged.

213

"Beats me, Sarnt… although…"

"Out with it, you bastard!"

"Well, you writ the chit."

Charles' blank face drew Wild into indiscretion.

"Ball bearings, Sarnt. You signed a chit for some, 'member?"

"Yes, I remember. One box, ball-bearing, ½-inch, for the use of. And?"

"'Parently, Pansy had a shitload delivered t'other day, and now he don't 'ave 'em no more, and yer name is in't frame… err… so I'm told, any road."

The penny dropped.

"Who altered the chit?"

"Pardon Sarnt?"

"You fucking heard me. Which one of you tossers changed the chit. Ten? One 'undred, was it?"

Wild was spared further questions by the arrival of C Squadron's commander, trailed by an extremely red-faced Flowers.

The Squadron commander had resisted Flowers' call for immediate punishment for the perpetrators of the crime, returning the seventy-two unopened packs they had recovered from the Ordnance, which helped smooth his ruffled feathers.

He was further calmed by an invitation to watch the results of Patterson's labours.

'Lady Godiva' had been moved up to the water's edge, some one hundred yards from a moored rowing boat that had clearly seen better days.

Stood on the back of the turret, Charles accepted the nod from C Squadron's Captain and leant forward.

"OK Pats. When you're ready, and I hope for your fucking sake that this works."

The main gun effortlessly moved to line up with the wooden boat.

In the breech lay a special round, universally dubbed a 'Patterson's Peril', although, in truth, the senior ordnance NCO was as much to blame as Charles' gunner.

The 17-pdr spat its contents in the direction of the rowing boat.

The results were staggering.

The boat disappeared in an instant froth of savaged water, as the 'Peril' discharged its contents of thirty-six ½-inch ball-bearings like a shotgun.

Of the boat, there was no recognisable evidence left, only a few pieces of wood floating on the disturbed waters of the Rammsee.

'Fucking hell' seemed to be the consensus of opinion from those present, although 2nd Lieutenant Percival, the Rupert, managed a very convincing 'I say'.

Captain White grinned from ear to ear.

"Sarnt, good show. Tell Patterson he can make some more, say, three per tank, but he must be careful with Flowers, clear?"

"Crystal, Sir."

In fact, Flowers proved invaluable in the process, and, acting to conserve his valuable stocks of ball-bearings, found large amounts of nuts, bolts, and scrap metal, which made for a more suitable shotgun shell, the irregular shapes causing the cone to widen more.

The new shotgun shells were issued out at three per vehicle, and Ordnance held a number of spares, should they be required.

1442 hrs, Tuesday 5th March 1946, Headquarters, 1st Guards Mechanised Rifle Division, Torgelow, Germany.

All four men saluted formally.

"Comrade Polkovnik, a pleasure as always."

Deniken gestured his friend towards a comfy chair, as he dropped back into his own.

Yarishlov gingerly eased himself into the chair.

"Problems, Arkady?"

The tank Colonel shrugged.

"A bit of old age… although, to be honest, I did jar my back a little jumping off my tank. I'll be fine soon enough."

Lisov, the 1st Guards Division's second in command, returned to study the contents of the stacks of paperwork on his desk, his ability to speak greatly limited by the bandaging around his savaged face. A British ground attack aircraft had almost done for him the previous day when he was visiting 1st Baltic's headquarters at Lauenberg, shrapnel from its rockets opening up both his cheeks and claiming three teeth.

The smell of fine American coffee filled the room and, soon enough, some arrived for the four men.

Kriks, Yarishlov's right-hand man, produced a small flask, freshening each man's mug with something non-regulation.

The four drank in silence, although Lisov's discomfort was clear as the hot liquid made itself known inside his mouth.

Deniken relaxed into his padded chair.

"So, Arkady, are you here to discuss the training programme?"

Placing his empty mug on the desk, Yarishlov looked a little wretched.

"Yes, I am."

"Excellent. I heard that your new tanks arrived, so I anticipated this and..."

"I can't do any training with your men, Vladimir, at least not mobile training, which sort of defeats the object."

Kriks poured more coffee, lacing each mug again.

"Thank you. Look, it's a total fucking balls up, simple as that."

Yarishlov was clearly extremely angered by events.

"I have my new tanks, but I don't have fuel. Or rather, I do have fuel, but I'm forbidden to use it for training purposes."

Yarishlov's unit, the recently redesignated 7th Guards Tank Assault Brigade, had been gifted sixty-four T-54 tanks, fresh from the factory, tanks with which the guardsmen of Deniken's division needed to train.

The new tank formation had also been allocated its own constituent SPAT unit, which meant that nine of the extremely potent ISU-122's were under Yarishlov's direct command as well, making 7th Guards the most powerful formations of its type in the Red Army.

"Shit."

There was no disagreement.

Deniken pondered the issue.

"Can you get fuel from somewhere?"

"Vladimir, I can most certainly scrape up some, increase my returns on natural wastage, hide some expenditure in my reports, but nothing like the amount I would need to run meaningful training with your boys."

The infantryman shook his head in disgust.

"I can occupy my boys with more training on the SKS rifle. We'll still do what we can with you statically, so at least the troops can see the new animals up close... but proper training is not an option for now."

Deniken exhaled slowly.

"So, we get specific orders about how our two units must train to fight tight, and in full cooperation, but we don't get the means to fulfil our orders. Marvellous..." he raised his coffee in salute at some unknown imbecile, "Absolutely fucking marvellous."

"At least we won't have the Allies to worry about, save their aircraft of course. You've seen the reports?"

Deniken rummaged for his copy of the latest assessments.

"Weather clearing slowly, temperatures coming up, will take time to recover, et cetera. You think that the Allies are as hampered as we are, Arkady... as our commanders say they are?"

Yarishlov belly laughed, startling Lisov.

"I don't doubt that our comrades from the glorious Intelligence services are wholly correct in their assumptions."

They all laughed.

"You mean, not a hope in hell eh?"

"That's about right, Vladimir. I think intel has it badly wrong and that the Allies have been tucked up nice and warm, just waiting for this opportunity. They'll be along shortly, don't doubt it."

In truth, GRU and NKVD reports were often inconclusive, sometimes claimed that the Allied Armies were crippled by the cold, but occasionally suggested that the Allies had been able to gather themselves and reinforce heavily during the cold months.

Some reports from agents spoke of previously unknown units in French ports or camped outside Italian towns.

It was the Soviet hierarchy that decided to suppress the fears of its agencies, possibly in order not to cause alarm amongst their army commanders, or possibly to mask their own shortcomings.

1102 hrs, Wednesday 6th March 1946, Disembarkation point 1192, east of Rullstorf, Germany.

The small spur ran off the main line and into the woods east of Rullstorf. Shrouded by the canopies of the surrounding trees, DP 1192, a simple double spur off the main line into the woods, was ideal for smaller trains to drop their cargoes, especially as the larger stations drew constant unwelcome attention.

The contents of the two twelve wagon trains were destined for the 6th Guards Independent Breakthrough Tank Regiment, now attached directly to the 1st Baltic Front.

Three of the quickly thrown together ZSU-37-2s, self-propelled AA guns, designed to stay with moving armoured formations, and nine of the latest model IS-IIIs, sat patiently waiting their turn, whilst the first train to arrive yielded up its cargo.

Eight IS-IIs were already idling on the nearby road, waiting on two more of their number, and the two IS-III command tanks, still on board.

His own tank was one of only three survivors from the last battles of the 6th Regiment, but Senior Lieutenant Stelmakh had left it in Scharnebeck. Instead, Corporal Stepanov had procured one of the unit's GAZ cars to drive his young officer to the disembarkation point, where he was tasked with marrying crews and new vehicles.

The men had arrived two weeks before the vehicles, so he had found time to get to know most of them, making his job easier.

Summoning each NCO by name, he was able to detail crews easily to tanks, and the whole process moved swiftly enough to please his watching commander.

The men of the 6th were all briefed on the necessity of remaining in cover, and to be especially mindful of discovery from the air.

Unfortunately for Stelmakh, the units disembarking the previous day had been less adept at keeping their presence secret, attracting the scrutiny of an RAF photo-interpreter, who decided that her instinct was enough to suggest the existence of a worthwhile target in the woods near Rullstorf.

Twelve Mitchell Mk IIIs of the newly fledged 320 Squadron, Marine Luchtvaart Dienst, the Dutch Naval Aviation Service, were sent to turn the small area in matchwood.

Flying in tight formation at twelve thousand feet, the drone of engines from the B-25s announced their arrival just before the whistling of falling bombs.

Thirty-six thousand pounds of high-explosive landed in an area of roughly one and a half square kilometres, transforming the quiet woods into a mass of flailing timber, metal and flesh.

Stelmakh was picked up and thrown through the air, crashing back to ground, before rolling up against a concrete plinth, part of the unloading ramp.

His commander, a Major newly arrived from a quiet post on the Iranian border, disappeared in a red soup, as a large piece of tree trunk flew at high speed through the space he occupied.

Despite the splinters of wood sticking in his left arm, Stelmakh raised himself up, calling to Stepanov, who was scrabbling on all fours, firstly in one direction, and then in another, as explosion after explosion disoriented him.

A bomb exploded in Stelmakh's direct line of sight, presenting him with the awfulness of a dozen men being blown apart and scattered like chaff in the wind.

"Stepanov!"

Finally the confused man heard the voice and raised himself up.

"Stepanov! Here man, here!"

Another bomb exploded, scattering earth and other less savoury detritus over Stepanov, forcing him to drop to the ground again.

A piece of something hard clipped Stelmakh's forehead, breaking the skin. The small wound bled ferociously, immediately flooding his left eye with blood.

Using his good hand, he wiped as much away as he could.

"Stepanov! Come on... move!"

Pushing himself up, the driver sprinted the last few yards, dropping next to the concrete plinth, facing his officer.

Both men were panting hard, effort and shock causing them to seek oxygen in abundance.

A huge explosion sent a shockwave through both men, and their heads turned automatically.

There was only time for one loud, intense, petrified scream, before the smashed hulk of an IS-II landed squarely on top of them.

The Dutch Mitchell Squadron was one of only two intercepted by Soviet fighters that day. Its intended escort of Spitfires XVIe's from 322 [Dutch] Squadron failed to be on station due to a navigational error, leaving the La-7s of the 147th Guards Fighter Regiment, recently released from duty with 106th Air Division at Leningrad, to knock a pair from the sky with their first pass.

Frantic calls for help brought 322 Squadron to the right place, but the low-altitude configured Spitfires were not quick enough to stop another three Mitchells spiralling to earth.

The La-7s flew back to base in good order, having achieved a rare air victory.

On the ground, the newly arrived armour had been badly knocked around, both IS-III command tanks and five of the battle tanks destroyed. Four of the IS-IIs and one of the ZSUs had also been lost. The greater problem was finding troops to marry with the surviving vehicles, some of which would need major repair before being capable of combat, as casualties amongst the waiting crews had been extreme.

The very nature of the attack ensured that there were very few wounded, and those that were injured tended to be severely so.

Given the likelihood of a further attack, the site was quickly scoured for survivors.

The plinth had saved them, that and the fact that the tank had come down top first.

Even though the concrete had split under the blow of forty-five tons of metal, it had still held the crushing weight up above the ground, sufficiently to form a safe pocket in which Stelmakh and Stepanov had survived.

The unconscious men were pulled out from under the tank and whisked away to the nearby field hospital, which had prepared to receive many casualties, but was presented with only five men on which to work.

At the same time as the Lavochkin fighters were savaging the Dutch Mitchells, another air combat took place, this time over the icy waters of the Baltic.

Three Saab-21s of the Swedish Air Force were directed onto a radar contact that had announced itself on screen, seemingly coming from the direction of Latvia.

Had the Swedes been privy to the goings-on in the Soviet fighter bases in and around Riga, then they would have known that Russian fighter regiments had responded to the intruder, engaged it, but failed to shoot it down.

The Mosquito Mk XXXIV photo-reconnaissance aircraft was both unusually low and unusually slow and, as it was nowhere near its normal ceiling and speed, the brand new Saab's intercepted it easily.

The Mosquito lowered its undercarriage, a sign of surrender and that it would comply with instructions from the covering fighter aircraft.

The Fighter controller at Visby indicated that the now identified British aircraft should be forced to land at the Bunge Airbase, which was no surprise to the flight-commander, it being the normal choice for intercepted aircraft.

None the less, he followed his instructions, confirming details to the controller as the Mosquito fell in behind him and his wingmen sat on either quarter, ready to act if any sign of resistance showed in the British plane.

Beside the controller, an army Major stubbed out his cigarette and lifted the telephone, seeking an immediate connection.

In seconds, the man heard a familiar voice.

"Överste, the plane is inbound to you now…wait please."

He asked a silent question of the controller.

"Ten."

"Ten minutes, Överste. Yes, sir."

The Major replaced the receiver and stood, tugging his uniform into place.

"Do I need to remind you of your obligations, Löjtnant?"

They had been made very clear already.

"No sir. You were never here."

"Good day, Löjtnant."

"Sir."

It paid to do what Military Intelligence ordered, so he elected to forget the whole occurrence as quickly as he could.

At Bunge airfield, the Överste stared at the silent handset, just for a second, before slotting it back into the holder.

"Ten minutes."

Then Törget and Lingstrom sat in silence, waiting patiently, conscious of the dangers of the path they were following, but ready to play their part.

2042 hrs, Thursday, 7th March 1946, Den Gyldene Freden, Österlånggatan 51, Stockholm, Sweden.

'The Golden Peace' restaurant had opened two hundred and thirty-four years previously, and was the oldest establishment of its kind in the Swedish capital. Its cuisine and surroundings were legendary, making it far and away one of the most popular places to eat out, and it was always packed.

Some regular customers, such as the Swedish Lieutenant Colonel of Military Intelligence, did not need reservations, the staff understanding that it would be in their best interests to be as accommodating as possible.

It also suited Boris Lingstrom for another purpose, as it was a contact point for passing on information to his Soviet 'masters'.

As usual, the members of the Swedish Academy were at dinner, doing whatever they did to decide their Nobel prizes, although Lingstrom couldn't understand why they were discussing things so far in advance of December's award ceremonies.

None the less, it was all good cover for what he needed to do, and the waiter was a true professional.

Poring over the wine list, Lingstrom sought the man's advice and, as normal, he allied a suitable wine to the officer's choice of dinner, using certain key words to indicate that there was nothing to pass over.

The wine came and a modicum was poured, Lingstrom using the opportunity to comment on its wonderful flavour, repeating himself as he waxed lyrical, clandestinely informing his contact that he had vital information to pass on.

Dinner was excellent, as usual, and the wine complimented it perfectly, as expected.

As was Lingstrom's habit, he handed the waiter a healthy five krona tip, folded, but easy discernible as currency.

It contained information that would cause a storm in Mother Russia.

Friday, 8th March 1946, 1843 hrs, GRU Commander's office, Western Europe Headquarters, the Mühlberg, Germany.

Poboshkin knocked on the door of his commander's office and, when he heard the invitation, quickly stuck his head round, his face openly painted with question after question regarding the events of the last half-hour.

Nazarbayeva beckoned him in, her own face clearly showing puzzlement.

"So, Comrade General, is everything alright?"

"Do you know, Andrey... for once in my life, I don't know."

That, of itself, was enough to cause Poboshkin some concern.

"Shall I order some more tea, Comrade General."

Nazarbayeva thought for a briefest of moments.

"Perhaps you might ask Mayor Rufin for the loan of the contents of his bottom drawer."

It was one of the office's worst kept secrets that Rufin, a competent man whose only vice was a liking for alcohol in large quantities, had a stash of bottles in his desk drawers.

In seconds, Poboshkin returned with a bottle and two glasses.

Pouring good sized measures, he waited for his commander to speak.

She lifted the clear liquid to eye level, raising an eyebrow at the amount her aide had poured.

He shrugged.

"I thought you might need it, Comrade. Your health."

They both sunk the raspberry schnapps in one, gasping as the fire of it assaulted mouth and throat alike.

Nazarbayeva held her glass out, smiling and trying not to choke at the same time.

The refilled glass sat in front of her as she started to openly analyse what had just happened.

"So... the deputy of the NKVD, no less, flies all the way to Germany, ostensibly to protest at my interference in an NKVD investigation into the murder of an Army nurse, which protest takes less than two minutes and was... or at least, I think it was... just going through the motions... like he wanted no part in it."

Poboshkin sipped his schnapps in silence.

"Then I am thanked... no, personally thanked for propelling him into a favourable position during Makarenko's failed attempt on the life of the General Secretary... which has apparently hugely increased his standing in Moscow."

The glass in Poboshkin's hand would remain empty until Nazarbayeva finished her own, something she seemed disinclined to do as she continued.

"And to finish up, we indulge in small talk about family, our own personal views on the war and certain members of the hierarchy."

She sensed rather than heard Poboshkin's sharp intake of breath.

"Calm yourself, calm yourself. I'm hardly likely to be indiscreet in front of a senior member of the NKVD, Andrey, so why was he so... open... err... so indiscreet in front of me?"

To his great relief, Nazarbayeva emptied her glass in one, giving him an opportunity to refill both.

"So, what is your first feeling, Comrade General? Was does your instinct say?"

She laughed softly.

"My instincts tell me never to trust a Chekist bastard with anything."

He shared her amusement.

"But… for some reason… I don't know what or why… I think we have gained a useful friend in circles that normally don't have our best interests at heart."

The glasses clinked together, but before the contents could be downed, a shrilling telephone brought them back to the mundane realities of intelligence matters.

0840 hrs, Saturday, 9th March 1946, Castello di Susans, Majano, Italy.

The Soviet artillery had been pounding the whole front line for nearly an hour, and Haines was mighty sick of it.
Over four kilometres off to his right, a battle royal already raged for control of the important Height 352, Monte Buia.

All the bridges on the River Ledra were down, which meant that the fights for Heights 352 and 265 would be independent battles, the Ledra isolating each from the other.

B Squadron's tanks were arranged defensively on the slopes surrounding Castello di Susans, a thirteenth century bastion set on Height 265, the mix of 17pdr and 76mm tanks there to provide cover for the infantry to their front, in the absence of defensive anti-tank guns.
More to the point, behind the frontline enemy infantry positions, air reconnaissance had spotted numerous Soviet armoured vehicles, suggesting that a large tank force was in the area.

The Ledra ran across the British position, its waters still obscured by a covering of ice. None the less, British engineers had placed a number of bridges across the river, and the preservation of these was a priority, the Rifle Brigade's forward positions being on the far bank.

The new 'Biffo's Bus' was an M4A2[76]W, all but still in its wrappers, so new was it.

Trooper Clair had spent the previous day tinkering with the General Motors' diesels, teasing them into top performance.
Everything had been checked and double checked, fuel and ammunition topped of, and 'The Bus' had been moved up to the dominating heights that surrounded the Castello.

Fig# 135 - Overview of Majano, Susans and Rivoli, Italy.

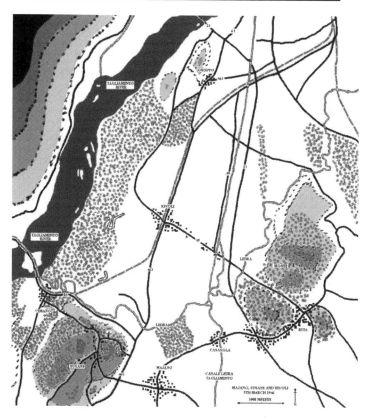

Patterson had been particularly delighted by the availability of HVAP rounds, and secured a dozen of the high penetration rounds.

Haines, now Acting Major in command of 'B' Squadron, 16th/5th Lancers, was fed up with being bounced around in his tank by near misses.

"If those bastards don't stop soon, I'm off down there to bash a few fucking heads together."

The comment was aimed at no-one in particular, except possibly the commander of the Soviet artillery lashing the hill and infantry positions.

16th/5th had received reinforcements after being hammered at Arnoldstein the previous November, and had just returned to the front as the start of a thaw seemed to be starting interest in fighting again. The presence of Soviet armour in Osoppo had meant that his Squadron was advanced to the front line positions in case Chuikov launched an attack, using the wide Tagliamento River as a secure right flank.

The thaw, combined with deliberately applied high-explosive, had reduced the integrity of the ice that had covered the wide river since the freeze began.

Even with the Soviet practice of artillery relocation, a total change thrust upon them by both the success of enemy counter-battery fire and the sovereignty of the air held by the Allied Air Forces, the barrage seemed to grow in intensity.

Fig# 136 – Allied Forces at Majano.

BATTLE OF MAJANO, 9TH MARCH 1946
ALLIED FORCES

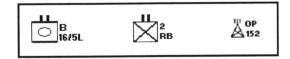

As if to reinforce Haines' suspicions, the first rockets arrived, a Guards Mortar Regiment depositing hundreds of 132mm Katyusha rounds all over the area.

"That settles it. They ain't doing this for fun. Look sharp. They'll be coming directly."

He keyed his mike, broadcasting on the squadron net.

"Cassino-six to all Cassino call signs. Eyes open and keep it tight. Expect to see them any time now. Call it in when you see them. Fire on my order and make every shot count. Out."

The artillery officer from the supporting 152nd RA spotted something from his higher position in one of the square towers of Castello di Susans, and 25pdr shells screamed overhead on their way towards the Soviet positions, in response to his calls for support.

"Cassino-two, Cassino-six, contacts, two thousand five hundred yards, coming down Route 463 like a bat out of hell, over."

"Cassino-six. Roger."

Haines lifted himself out of the warm turret and brought his binoculars to bear. The lead Soviet element was easy to find.

'Struth! He ain't kidding!'

"Cassino-six, all Cassino call signs. Enemy attack in progress. Tanks and infantry on Route 463, coming in fast. Watch your front. Stand by to engage. Out."

Fig# 137 – Soviet Forces at Majano.

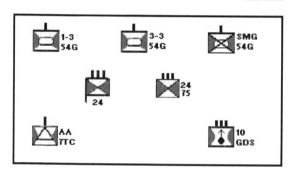

BATTLE OF MAJANO, 9TH MARCH 1946
SOVIET FORCES

Through the binoculars, Haines witnessed the assault formations deploy, the tanks forming line and the infantry vehicles surging ahead, closing down on the foremost British positions.

He quickly debated his next order.

"Cassino-six, all Cassino call signs. Engage the transports first, repeat, engage the transports first. Stand by…"

Most of the Soviet vehicles were American in origin, either lend-lease or captured since the new war started, carrying a dozen or so soldiers in each.

On the slope, a Soviet artillery shell found a target, and pieces of Sherman cartwheeled in all directions.

Haines grimaced, wondering who it was, but without the luxury of time to find out.

Familiar with the distances involved, he waited patiently, ignoring the final flurry of Soviet artillery.

The lead vehicles surged through the remains of the village of Rivoli, where a week of fighting had reduced its buildings to nothing but piles of rubble.

Focusing on the few tree stumps that marked the start of his fire zone, Haines patiently waited, controlling his breathing, judging the moment.

"FIRE!"

16th/5th had been brought up to full strength and now, including the four HQ vehicles, consisted of twenty vehicles in four troops, each of four tanks.

Even the two close support howitzer tanks joined in the first volley, and hi-speed metal flew from the hillside.

Thirteen of the shells fired found a target, although three struck the same vehicle, clearly selected because of its proliferation of aerials.

The M3A1 scout car, lagging behind the first wave, disintegrated in an instant, removing the lead infantry battalion's commander and his staff from the equation in a permanent fashion.

Two of the vehicles burst into flames, incinerating both the already dead and severely wounded who could not escape the ruined tracks.

The others disgorged some of their contents, disoriented and wounded men desperately seeking cover from the machine-guns that chattered as the infantrymen of 2nd Btn, The Rifle Brigade, joined the fight.

A second volley took out another three of the jinking vehicles, all of them turning to funeral pyres in the blink of an eye.

Soviet infantry on foot flooded out from Rivoli, a tidal wave of men desperate to get close to the British positions.

'Fucking hell, but there's a lot of the bastards!'

Haines dropped back inside the tank and spoke rapidly to the air-liaison officer. Satisfied that the man, an unknown quantity recently allocated to the Rifle Brigade unit, was on the job, he turned to fighting his tank.

"Gunner?"

"Target command tank, range fifteen hundred, on."

"FIRE!"

The AP shell missed by a whisker and the enemy command tank, whatever it was, moved in behind some vegetation, disappearing from sight.

Most of the tanks now closing rapidly on the infantry positions were T-34s, and the Lancers had started to take them on, trying to keep the tanks away from the infantry.

A large squat tank with a rounded frying pan-like turret emerged from the British artillery zone.

"Fucking hell! Target, tank, left four, range sixteen hundred, aitch-vap."

The turret traverse hummed briefly as Trooper Cooke, the new gunner, found the IS-III.

"On!"

"FIRE!"

It was a superb shot but totally wasted, as the Stalin tank's armour deflected the shell without any noticeable damage.

"Again!"

0905 hrs, Saturday, 9th March 1946, Rivoli, Italy.

"Try again."

Even as Kozlov gave the order, he knew that the man commanding his motorised battalion would not answer, and that his was one of the vehicles burning on the battlefield in front of him.

24th Rifle Regiment had been handed a double edged sword, firstly being chosen for full reinforcement, following its excellent performance in the Italian campaign, which then meant that it was selected personally by Marshal Chuikov to lead this attack, intended to flank Allied forces in Udine.

The normal exhortations, even promising Guards' status with the inevitable success, made little impression on Colonel Kozlov, newly-fledged hero of the Soviet Union.

"No reply, Comrade Polkovnik."

Acting quickly, Kozlov waved to his second in command, bringing the man sprinting forward.

"Comrade Polkovnik?"

"Ivan, first battalion is leaderless. You need to get up there and push them forward," both men dropped lower automatically as two British shells bracketed Kozlov's position, "Stay with the plan and get them through to the heights. Clear?"

"As you order, Comrade."

Lieutenant Colonel Koranin was not a man for small talk, so was swiftly on his feet, calling his own group around him.

His GAZ jeep soon sped forward.

Kozlov watched the man surge forward into the frenzy of activity to his front before slapping the radio officer on the shoulder.

"Contact Second and Third… tell then to push on faster. I want those bridges intact."

"Yes, Comrade Polkovnik."

Fig# 138 - Soviet assault on Majano and Castello di Susans.

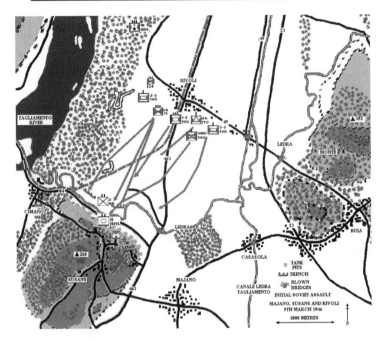

0909 hrs, Saturday, 9th March 1946, Castello di Susans, Majano, Italy.

Three Shermans were destroyed, including that of the RSM and one of the troop commanders.

Nine T-34s added their metal to the growing toll of scrap, and one of the IS-IIIs was burning fiercely, victim of an artillery shell.

The situation had become critical, as Soviet soldiers reached the Rifle Brigade positions in places, and close quarter fighting ensued.

The Lancers had their own problems, as a second surge of tanks came into view and enemy troops bailed out of their vehicles, having driven straight through the infantry positions and across the engineer bridges.

One look revealed a terrible new threat.

"Cassino-six, all Cassino call signs, infantry action front, enemy anti-tank weapons."

He had spotted at least four panzerfausts amongst the Soviet soldiers and immediately witnessed the use of one on a Firefly that was relocating to a new firing position.

The tank's hatches were thrown open and three surviving crew men flung themselves out, only to be mown down by PPSh's.

"Stumpy, move back to our first position, quickly."

The Sherman backed and angled before surging forward, moving down and across to their first firing position.

The hull MG immediately chattered, sending a stream of bullets in the direction of another Sherman that was overrun with enemy infantry.

There was a deafening clang and the tank filled with the smell of singed electrics and tortured metal, but still it moved forward.

"Everyone ok?"

The crew, stunned by the direct hit, eventually shouted back variations on 'I'm fine'.

Haines started checking for damage.

"Intercom's out."

Automatically, Haines checked the main radio.

It was also dead, and suggested itself as the main source of the electrical burning smell.

"Main radio is out. Anything else?"

Cooke shouted.

"Electric traverse out, Manual ok."

Everything else seemed fine and the tank slotted back into its first position.

"Fuck! Infantry, coax traverse left, quickly!"

The turret slewed as the handle was spun, bringing the .30cal coax to bear.

A group of infantry were bearing down on 'Biffo's Bus', intent on getting in panzerfaust range.

The coax stuttered and immediately died.

"Jam!"

Cooke was correct but incorrect, in as much as, the hit on the turret had bent the coax barrel, meaning that the first shots stayed in the barrel, jamming it with metal and rendering it totally useless.

"Shit! Commander out!"

Haines grabbed the Thompson sub-machine gun and two extra magazines, and was up and out of the turret before anyone could ask.

Rolling off the hull, Haines brought the weapon up and dropped the first Russian in his tracks.

A panzerfaust struck the earth in front of the tank, causing the officer to stagger to his left and drop to the ground.

Raising himself to his knees, he pulled the trigger again.

Nothing.

'Fuck'.

He cocked the weapon and repeated the process, this time cutting down the man who was nearly on top of him. The running man was virtually decapitated by the heavy bullets, and flopped lifelessly to the snow.

The Thompson stopped firing, only because the magazine was empty, something Haines failed to register.

A grenade dropped beside him.

Picking it up, he threw it away and ducked.

Meanwhile, more Russians were closing on the tank's right side, unseen, hoping to get close enough to use grenades.

Another grenade arrived, but too far away to grab, so Haines threw himself towards the safety of the 'bus'.

This time he collected a piece of shrapnel, the hot metal slicing across his left elbow, just clipping the bone.

Ducking behind the back of his tank, Biffo found himself looking straight at the three men moving in on his tank, unseen until now.

The Thompson stayed silent, empty of bullets.

Realizing the problem, Haines fumbled for a new magazine. However, fighting with tanks was more his speciality; swapping magazines in the face of imminent enemy contact was not, and he dropped the full magazine into the snow at his feet.

"URRAH!"

The first Russian was on top of him, a bayonet thrusting at Biffo's stomach.

"FUCK OFF!"

The tank officer swung the Thompson so hard that he broke the wooden stock across the soldier's forehead, staving the man's skull in.

Throwing the pieces of submachine gun at the next man, Haines grabbed for his service revolver, only to find an empty holster.

The nearest Russian worked the bolt of his rifle and fired on the move, putting a bullet through the fleshy part of Haines' left arm.

Turning to escape, Haines found the way barred by more Russians from the original tank hunting party.

The first man missed his swing, as Haines ducked under the rifle butt. A rock hard fist connected with the soldier, sending him sprawling back into the man behind him.

Haines screamed as weapons burst into life and bullets spanged off the Sherman's rear armour.

A ricochet hit him in the meat of his left buttock with such force as to take his legs out from under him, but that was his only other wound.

The majority of the bullets struck their intended targets, cutting the two groups of Russians down.

Haines looked up to see the Artillery Liaison officer and his three men running down, the young Lieutenant pausing only to finish off a screaming enemy soldier with a short burst.

He flopped in beside Haines.

"Thanks."

That was all the tank officer could manage at the moment.

"Sorry old chap. Cut that a bit fine but I had to sort the support out before I could help. You've picked up a Blighty one, by the look of you."

It was an easy mistake to make, the combination of blood from his wounds and that sprayed from others had transformed Biffo into a red blob.

"I'm fine. Just a couple of nicks. My radio's out, so what's occurring, Lieutenant?"

"Air's delayed, Major, but we seem to be holding just fine, and, once the Brylcreams get here, we can send Uncle Joe's boys packing."

"Give me a hand, Giles"

Haines offered up his good arm, and the artillery officer assisted him to his feet.

"Thanks again, and we'll talk after this is over. Now, keep at it."

Herbert Giles, nineteen today, saluted and bolted back to the OP in the Castello's North-East tower.

0910 hrs, Saturday, 9th March 1946, Rivoli, Italy.

'Good, he's got them up to the tanks.'

Moving his focus, Kozlov was less satisfied with the progress of the other two battalions.

Clearly, they had made the enemy trench positions in a few places, but it was plain to see that large numbers of men had gone to ground, neither pushing forward nor engaging, just keen to hug Mother Earth and stay alive.

"Tell Second and Third to get moving. Get the fucking bridges... now!"

The radio officer chattered away urgently, relaying the Regimental Commander's orders.

"Comrade Polkovnik, no reply from Second Battalion. Third Battalion reports commander killed, his second in Command has taken over and is pushing into the enemy line."

Kozlov swivelled to look around him.

"Where's the anti-aircraft support. Get them on the radio now!"

Two ZSU-37s, a precious commodity only recently allocated to the 7th Tank Corps, were actually already closed up in support. Kozlov had missed them in amongst the smoke and explosions.

The need to contact the flak commander disappeared, as the Gaz-mounted quad Maxims came into view, spreading out to cover the battlefield.

"Comrade Polkovnik, the flak commander reports being in position."

Kozlov grumbled to himself.

'Late, and I'll give you a kick up the fucking ass when this is done.'

Returning to concentrate on his infantry, he found himself unable to locate any of the First Battalion, but the sight of two of the enemy tanks burning told him that they were still there and fighting.

His own tank support, now under less fire from the enemy AFVs, had closed up and was working well in support of the infantry.

He swore he could see small groups of enemy soldiers falling back over the Ledra.

Before he could radio the question, it was answered, as his eyes confirmed the enemy retreat.

'Perfect'.

"Order Mayor Golin to attack. Plan A."

Plan 'A' was simple; straight up Route 463 to the summit, but a Royal Engineers officer had already negated it by dropping the main road bridge with the twist of an electrical exploder.

Plan 'B' came into being immediately; a surge over the eastern engineer bridges and up the nearest track to the castle.

Major Golin's force was modest in size, but all mobile, with vehicles acquired from anywhere and everywhere. The soldiers were from the tank brigade's SMG unit and anti-tank riflemen from one of his own AT platoons, and the plan was to deliver them straight into the Castello di Susans, wresting the dominant feature from the Allies and forcing them to withdraw.

"Your order for Plan 'B' has been acknowledged, Comrade Polkovnik."

Turning to watch the exploitation unit advance, his view was interrupted by white light, as a newly positioned Bofors gun started chuntering, sending 40mm shells into the sky.

'Govno!'

The tell-tale sounds of attacking aircraft reached his ears in an instant.

"Tell all stations, enemy aircraft warning. Quickly man!"

Perhaps, he mused, it was unnecessary, but some in the vehicles might not hear until too late. And for someone it was already too late, as one of the attacking tanks came apart in a vicious explosion.

Rocket after rocket came streaking in, as the Allied aircraft conducted a line attack, sweeping across the battlefield, virtually parallel to, but north of, Route 84, starting on the left flank of his assault, discharging their weapons and turning out over the Tagliamento, before coming round again in a seemingly endless wheeling motion.

His AA weapons filled the sky with tracers, and three of the enemy were cut down in as many minutes as the light weapons had their chances optimized by the low-level attack pattern.

Not without their own losses, as tanks and infantry paid the price in blood and tears.

Kozlov now realized that the British withdrawal had been planned, performed to get the infantry south of the Leda, and to put distance between the two forces to avoid friendly casualties.

The simple radio message reporting the death of his second in command and friend, Koranin, was sidelined for later and quieter moment, and he kept his grief to himself.

One of Golin's vehicles jinked to avoid a hail of rockets, successfully avoiding a direct hit. The power of the explosions still claimed it, flipping the light lorry over onto its side and crushing most of the men clinging to the sides of the rear compartment. Only a few emerged, stunned, shocked, into a hail of Bren and Vickers bullets.

'They're across the river! Yes! We're going to do it! We're going to fucking do it!'

His AA vehicles started taking hits, as the enemy armour switched its focus in an effort to take the heat off the fliers.

0921 hrs, Saturday, 9th March 1946, Castello di Susans, Majano, Italy.

No sooner had Haines returned to the tank than he was forced to quit it again. 'Biffo's Bus' was now burning steadily, a Soviet tank round having crossed the battlefield from Haines' left flank and carved into the engine compartment.

They had all escaped, only the tank officer carrying any injury, and took refuge in an alternate position belonging to another tank.

Mortar shells, aimed at the recently displaced Rifle Brigade, started to arrive amongst the Lancers' tanks, making life uncomfortable for the crew, as lumps of metal and frozen earth flew in all directions.

"Stumpy, I'm off to find a radio and get this fuck up sorted out. You get the boys up to the castle, ok?"

Stumpy Clair knew better than to argue, and took the proffered Thompson, his nose turning up at the shattered wood stock.

Haines took a tight hold on his revolver, judged the fall of mortar shells and, at the right moment, slapped his driver's shoulder, sending the group on their way.

Once happy with his crew's progress, Biffo Haines tensed himself for the rush to the nearest Lancer tank, some two hundred yards to his right, and slightly downhill.

His attention was consumed by the sound of aero engines, and his aircraft recognition skills were brought into play, as a swarm of Bristol Beaufighters bore down in line formation, discharging rockets along the advancing Soviet forces.

He watched as tanks were hit and infantrymen were scattered, knocking the momentum out of the Soviet advance in seconds. Although cheered by the timely intervention, his heart also sank as enemy AA weapons knocked two of the leading British aircraft out of the sky.

604 Squadron RAF had been disbanded in April 1945, but had been brought back into the Allied inventory and sent to Italy, where it was married up with Beaufighters not required by the USAAF.

They were, in the main, experienced men, but the presence of numerous AA weapons took them by surprise, and a third Beau was clawed from the air, flipping over and ploughing into the ground in a cartwheeling ball of fire.

Pulling himself up on the tank, he rapped his revolver on the metal three times.

"It's Biffo. Don't shit yourselves. Need the radio and quick."

The tank commander's head emerged, one eye closed by swelling from an impact with something unforgiving inside the tank.

"Sir, warm day. Squadron net I assume?"

Haines, struggling with the leads, just grunted.

Sergeant Brian Timms was a veteran, recently returned to the Lancers. Handing his radio headset to Haines, he ducked down into the tank and changed channels.

Biffo stuck his head inside before sending any messages.

"Hit the AA stuff. They're murdering the Brylcreams!"

The turret shifted slightly in response, and Haines ducked down to avoid the blast as the 76mm sent a Quad AA lorry to Valhalla.

"Cassino-six, all Cassino call-signs. First and second sections, concentrate on the flak, repeat, concentrate on the flak. Cassino-Six out."

Taking a moment to assess the battlefield, Haines saw a problem.

'Oh for fuck's sake!'

"Sergeant Timms, switch to the arty channel now!"

A grimy hand sprung from the hatch, the thumbs up clear in its meaning.

"Calliope-Two-Six, Cassino-Six, over."

"Go ahead Cassino-Six, Calliope-Two-Six, over."

"Calliope-Two-Six, enemy mobile force is over the river, cutting round to our right. Stop the…"

A force not unlike a speeding train threw Haines from the tank, as a mortar shell landed mere feet away, tossing him nearly twenty yards and into a shallow depression, occupied only by several dead Soviet soldiers.

He still retained part of the headset into which, in his confused state, he continued to speak.

The destruction of Timms' tank brought him back to reality, as virtually simultaneous strikes penetrated the Easy Eight.

The gunner and loader emerged, blackened and raw. The driver's hatch popped up and hands, surrounded by flame, tried to lever the screaming man of the inferno.

The gunner, eyes wide and staring, jumped from the tank and ran screaming, his nerve gone, broken by the destruction and horrors created inside the tank.

Although wounded and in great pain, Reed, the loader, reached down into the commander's hatch and pulled on something barely recognizable as a man.

Haines shook himself back into reality and moved forward, and was immediately forced back onto the cold ground as more mortar shells arrived.

As he rose again, Reed had got the hideously wounded Timms half out of the hatch, a task made easier by the Sergeant's lack of arms, removed by the second shell, but made more difficult by the flames that licked around the NCO and ate away at clothing and flesh in equal measure.

The screams were awful, every movement an agony for both men.

Timms' screams were silenced in a brilliant flash of orange, as the tank brewed, incinerating the Sergeant in an instant, and converting Reed into a fireball whose agony was manifested in the most awful, most ear-piercing squeals imaginable.

A horrified Haines reached for his revolver but found nothing. He was unarmed again.

Reed's screams burned into his very soul, and the tank officer could do nothing to put the poor man out of his misery.

He remembered the dead Russians, and flung himself back, seeking a weapon.

A Soviet mortar shell dropped next to Reed and obliterated the awful sight before Haines' hand closed around a DP-28.

Flopping back into the depression, Haines gathered himself, becoming aware of the British artillery landing nearby, clearly now redirected, which then reminded him of the change in direction made by the enemy mobile force.

He moved up to the edge and saw hell coming straight at him.

The British artillery had claimed some of the enemy vehicles, but the rest had changed direction again, seemingly intent on running over his position on the way to the Castello.

Retaining enough presence of mind to grab the metal box which clearly held spare ammo for the weapon, and then fumbling with its unfamiliar grip, Haines took aim and pulled the trigger, the light machine-gun answering his command by spitting bullets at the lead vehicle.

Considering it was his first effort with the DP, he was surprised to see his bullets strike home, the men in the lorry cab disappearing behind splintered glass that went red in places.

Above the cab, a man with the same weapon fired back, but lacked the stability offered by the snow and earth around Haines, missing by some distance.

The lorry came to a halt and then started to roll back down the slope, causing others behind to manoeuvre out of its way.

Haines was too busy engaging other targets to notice it roll over, flinging out those who had not jumped or who were already dead.

An American jeep outpaced the remaining vehicles, intent on moving to the tank officer's left. Biffo pulled the LMG round, all the time chasing the little vehicle with bullets, but not hitting.

In an instant, the jeep exploded, hit by one of the last Soviet mortar shells fired, and the six man crew were scattered to all points in pieces no larger than a shoebox.

Moving the DP back to his front, Haines engaged the nearest vehicle or at least for two bullets worth, as the circular pannier gave up its final rounds.

He made a split second judgement, deciding that the unfamiliar reload would take too long, as the enemy vehicle disgorged seven angry men.

He looked around him, immediately spotting the grenade in one dead man's hand.

It looked similar to one's he had used, so Haines pulled the pin and sent the deadly charge downhill.

The Russians went to ground as soon as they saw the F1 fragmentation grenade coming and, as Haines had thrown it too soon, took no damage at all when it exploded.

Haines understood what he had done. A bag around the dead man's body surrendered more grenades.

Again, the seven soldiers dropped as another grenade came their way, and rose again once it had exploded, only to be cut down by the second grenade they had not witnessed thrown.

Three were put down hard and didn't rise again.

The other four, all wounded, closed on the depression.

Haines looked around for more means by which to defend himself, his mind finding time to remind him of the 16th/5th's motto.

'Aut cursu, aut cominus armis'

Acting Major Biffo Haines MC found time to laugh out loud.

239

'Either in the charge, or hand-to-hand'.

His hand closed around the only weapon he could find.

0925 hrs, Saturday, 9th March 1946, Rivoli, Italy.

Colonel Kozlov gripped his binoculars tightly, knowing Golin's switch to attack into the enemy left flank was a bad move.

'Leave the bastards... go around them... for the god's sake go around them!'

"Radio Mayor Golin immediately. Tell him to go around their flank. He must go around."

He winced as yet another of his AA trucks was destroyed, the successful Beaufighter clawing its way back into the sky, leaving a stream of black and grey in its wake.

His focus returned to Golin's force, so he missed the explosion high above the battlefield, as the injured RAF aircraft surrendered to its damage.

British artillery started to beat the zone ahead of the mobile force, causing it to switch direction yet again.

Kozlov was momentarily happy, realising that his command was now back aiming straight at the Castello again, then suddenly realised there was a problem.

"Call 10th Mortars. Tell them to ceasefire immediately."

"Yes, Comrade Polkovnik."

He would worry about where to direct their fire next once he was satisfied that Golin's force was no longer at risk from friendly fire.

One of the vehicles disappeared in an explosion and he knew what he had feared had happened, but such things were more than common in war, and he had done what he could.

Another of the vehicles seemed to be rolling backwards down the slope, until it jammed a wheel, slipped sideways and rolled the rest of the way.

"Go on, Golin! Push on man, push on!"

Somewhere to the mobile group's front, there was some resistance, and a grenade put down some of his men before the rest swept over the enemy position.

Happy that Golin would now make his ground, Kozlov concentrated elsewhere, and discovered that, whilst he had been watching the hill, he had lost the battle in the valley.

His men and vehicles were in retreat, pursued by bullets from the Rifle Brigade and harassed by repeated strafing runs from the RAF heavy fighters. Although each had spent its rockets, each

240

Beaufighter was equipped with murderous firepower, with six .303 Brownings in the wings, and four 20mm Hispano in the nose.

One such aircraft had circled for a fourth strafing run, turned over the Tagliamento River and lazily described an arc as it came back round to do a further east to west attack.

One of the Quad Maxim lorries took it by surprise, causing the pilot to throw his aircraft to the right and out of the approaching tracer stream.

His approach ruined, the angry pilot spotted an alternate target, dropped his nose, and thumbed his triggers.

0930 hrs, Saturday, 9th March 1946, Castello di Susans, Majano, Italy.

The first man over the edge of the depression was probably more scared than Haines, the youngster's eyes wide open in fear as he made to plunge his bayonet into the tank officer.

He missed.

Biffo swung the entrenching tool and connected with brutal and terminal force, penetrating the boy's skull from eye socket to ear and points beyond.

The still running cadaver crashed into Haines, the impact ramming the hard metal of the rifle directly into his wounded left arm.

Haines bellowed with pain.

The next three Russians arrived together and virtually clattered into Haines, the four bodies falling to the bottom of the depression in a disorganised snarling heap.

Two of the soldiers were also mere boys, and at least one had soiled himself in fear, the stench of faeces overpowering to the four men.

Haines lashed out with the spade, one young soldier deflecting the blow with his arm. The sound of the bone snapping was incredibly loud, more so than any other on the battlefield at that moment, before the boy's screams drowned out everything else.

The Soviet officer, a veteran of many a tight skirmish, found Haines lying on his pistol hand, so tried to use his free hand to gouge Biffo's eyes from his head.

Haines felt a grubby finger against his lips and took the opportunity to bite it as hard as he could.

More screams of pain followed, before Haines rolled over and drove his head into the officer's face.

241

Both men squealed, the Russian as his nose was broken and blood spurted everywhere, Haines as he did similar damage to his own nose.

Spitting the severed fingertip into the face of the bloodied Russian, Biffo pulled the man's face towards him and got his head butt perfect the second time.

The officer was out for the count.

Wiry hands closed round the tanker's neck, pulling him backwards, as the last intact Russian soldier tried to throttle him.

Whimpers and curses indicated that the other child soldier was trying to extricate himself from under the pair of combatants.

Haines found himself unable to break the tight grip around his neck, no matter how he struggled.

The other Russian, tears streaming down his face, his broken arm limp and useless, held a small knife in his good hand and rammed it into Haines' stomach.

White-hot pain gave Haines strength and he broke Russian fingers as he prised the hands from his throat.

The assailant dropped away howling with pain.

Squealing with fear, the one-armed boy pulled out the blade and it rammed home again.

The pain was unbelievable.

Lashing out with his right hand, Biffo caught the boy on his broken arm, taking him out of the fight with a white blur of extreme pain. Again, the young soldier lost control of bowel and bladder.

The knife still lodged in his stomach, Haines struggled to his feet and planted a kick in the side of the would-be strangler's head.

Whatever he did, it was permanent and quick, and lifeless eyes stared up at the sky.

Picking up the entrenching tool, Haines dropped to his knees and brought the heavy weapon down on the wailing Soviet soldier with shattered fingers.

When Stumpy and Killer found him three minutes later, he was still chopping away at what remained of the Russian's head.

0925 hrs, Saturday, 9th March 1946, Rivoli, Italy.

20mm cannon shells are very unforgiving things but, remarkably, Kozlov was still alive, at least by the basic definition of life.

His injuries were extreme and the two medics were unsure where to start. Electing to work separately, one placed a tourniquet over the stump of his left leg, stopping the blood loss, whilst the other tried to reassemble his face, carefully tying the shattered jaw in place after ensuring that eyes and nose were in their normal positions, not that the wounded officer would ever see again.

Penetrations to his stomach and chest were bandaged, although the piece of metal protruding from his back was padded and left in place, given its perilous position.

They had no pain relief, and so Kozlov suffered indescribable tortures as he was taken from the battlefield.

Around the desperate scene, soldiers of his unit flooded back in disarray, bloodied and disoriented, the only thought in their minds being to reach a place of safety.

Across the valley, and on the hillside, the fighting had stopped.

The aircraft had gone, the only mementoes of their presence being four burning pyres faintly resembling once proud aircraft.

The artillery and mortars of both sides had ceased fire, permitting small groups of men to recover wounded although, in the main, they only found the dead.

Never one to miss an opportunity, 6th Armoured Division's commander, Major General Sir Horatius Murray, sent a request for a hasty bombing attack on Gemona, anticipating that it would be where the fleeing enemy would congregate.

He was absolutely correct, and USAAF B-26 Marauders from 17th Bomb Group's 95th and 432nd Bomber Squadrons killed and injured many men who had escaped the inferno at Majano, as well as more from the 75th Rifle Division moving up to take over from the savaged frontline units. However, the killing of over five hundred Italian civilians did nothing for Allied relations with the 'neutral' Government in Rome.

Chuikov's insistence on some offensive action had resulted in no gain of ground, and the loss of his 75th Rifle Division and irreplaceable tank and AA assets from 7th Tank Corps.

Whilst the 16th/5th had been manhandled, the Rifle Brigade bloodied, and the RAF fighters handed a beating, the casualty ratio was 10:1 in the Allies' favour, and that was before the Marauders visited themselves upon Gemona.

Chuikov declined to order any more such excursions.

"The lady doth protest too much, methinks"

William Shakespeare.

Chapter 136 – THE DECEIVERS

1554 hrs, Tuesday, 12th March 1946, the Billiard House, Hameau de la Reine, Versailles, France.

The impressive Billiard House, built as part of the Marie-Antoinette estate, was sufficiently removed from the busier parts of SHAEF Headquarters complex as to be perfect for the extremely clandestine work of the disarmingly named 'Joint Committee on Identification and Interment Procedures', the cover used by the group manipulating information to mislead the Soviet intelligence apparatus regarding Allied intentions in 1946.

The central document to which they worked was as secret as they came. It was known, tongue in cheek, as the Ash file, and was an exact copy of the file presently receiving the undivided attention of Soviet Military intelligence, as passed to them by a Soviet agent in the Foreign Legion forces.

This was supplemented by the recent Mosquito internment by Sweden, which directed more misinformation into Soviet hands, and, again originating from the Baltic, Swedish protests regarding increased Allied submarine activity in the Gulf of Bothnia.

The RAF liaison officer reported back on successful reconnaissance trips over Northern Russia and the Baltic States, designed to further convince the enemy as to their intentions in the Baltic and Arctic Ocean.

'J-Cip', as it became known, was also responsible for clandestinely recruiting Finnish, Estonian, Latvian and Lithuanian speakers and giving them secret courses in military radio procedure and terminology, which secret courses were subsequently deliberately revealed to known Soviet agents in the UK.

It was also the group to which Rossiter had, on Donovan's explicit order, revealed the Achilles/Thetis file. Whilst the collective whistle had been well and truly whetted, the decision was made not to use of the head of GRU West's son for now, giving them more time to develop something of true worth.

As the latest D-Day, Tuesday 26th March, approached, the group became anxious to ensure that all that could be done, had been done.

SAAG, noisily announcing its growing readiness to move, was monitored by Soviet eavesdroppers and a picture of an all-arms army, ready to take to the water, was established by both GRU and NKVD listeners.

Some reserve Soviet formations were moved up tighter to 1st Baltic Front, as Allied units in Northern Holland became noticeably more active, supporting the notion of an imminent assault from the Low Countries through the North German plain.

In Northern Norway, Allied patrolling increased, suggesting that combat was imminent in Scandinavia.

A Soviet reconnaissance flight, sent as an act of desperation, achieved the unachievable, and took photos of Harstad, confirming an agent's report on a large assembly of military transports, all of which rode tight to the load line, indicating each carried its full share of the manpower and hardware required for an invasion.

Each had been painted to reflect a fully laden vessel, a masterstroke of subterfuge beyond the detection ability of the Soviet Naval Aviation photo interpreters at Severomorsk.

Permitting the Soviet Yak-4 aircraft to escape from Norwegian air space grated on the Spitfire pilots of 331 Squadron, RNoAF, but orders were orders, and it miraculously survived their attack.

Building up a picture of Allied intents, Soviet reinforcements moved to Kirkenes, sparking a brief but intense exchange with Finnish forces, north of Lake Radjejavri, when Soviet units accidentally crossed the national boundaries.

All of it was the work of 'J-Cip', but still they were not satisfied.

Major General Kenneth Strong, chairing 'J-Cip' called for a final statement from each man present before calling for a show of hands to the latest proposal. His US counterpart, Major General Harold R. Bull, agreed with USMC Colonel Rossiter, resisting any attempts to bring more people into the committee, preferring to seek opinion and advice without exposing the workings of 'J-Cip', thus avoiding the inherent risk of more people knowing its real role.

De Walle and Gehlen both thought it an excellent idea, provided any potential new member was already screened to the highest level, and came from a section of the intelligence services.

Colonel Kazimierz Iranek-Osmecki, the Polish presence in 'J-Cip', was simple in his approach.

"Nie!"

Dalziel, annoyed by the Polish officer's curtness, voted for further inclusions with the security codicils.

Horst Pflug-Hartnung, Oberst and Intelligence Officer advising the German and Austrian leadership, followed suit.

Last to go was Brigadier Tiltman of GC&CS, their cipher and cryptanalysis specialist.

"So long as the buggers don't flap their lips, why not?"

The vote was agreed without the need for Strong's input.

0917 hrs, Thursday, 14th March 1946, Map room, GRU Western Europe Headquarters, the Mühlberg, Germany.

The cigarette smoke hung heavily in the air, reflecting not only the number smoked, but also the length of time that the group had been working.

Nazarbayeva had called a break, to permit bladders to be emptied and lunch to be taken on board.

It turned into a working lunch for the dedicated team of GRU officers, working on divining Allied intentions.

Munching on bread and pickles, the GRU General whispered to her aide, less informally than normal as they were not alone.

"So what are we missing here, Comrade PodPolkovnik?"

"Something totally conclusive... something unequivocal, Comrade General. Something else..."

He shrugged and bit deeply into a baked potato.

Turning to the chalkboard, she read the notations aloud, growing in volume, drawing everybody's attention back to the work in hand.

"Enemy transport vessels confirmed in Norwegian ports, probably in Northern English ports too."

"This Second Allied Army Group is very active, not just new units either, and all suggestions lead to some sort of reinforcement move to Holland."

Poboshkin waved his half-eaten potato at the entry.

"Our forces have already reacted to that, reinforcing Bagramyan's Front."

She nodded.

One of the Major's added his comment.

246

"But we only have names of units, Comrade General. There is nothing on composition, and we know the Allies pulled a similar maskirovka to confuse the Germans in '44. We cannot guarantee this SAAG is what it seems."

Nazarbayeva encouraged free speaking within this group, so her best minds always seemed to have something to say. With no standing on ceremony or fear of punishment, outspoken opinion was the healthy norm.

"So, Norway. The transports were laden. What are they carrying? Not a fictitious army surely?"

Poboshkin narrowed his eyes.

"Actually, Comrade General, we have not seen the original photos. The report is a written report from Naval Intelligence and the photos are copies. Perhaps we should get the originals?"

"Yes, we should. Comrade Kapitan?"

The young Lieutenant rose immediately and left the room to order the originals sent to the Mühlberg.

The discussion continued.

"These language specialists... Latvian... Lithuanian... Estonian..."

"And we've the reports of Norwegian officers being integrated into all enemy units in Norway, Comrade General."

"Also, Comrade General," Guvarin, the bald and scarred Kapitan, quickly searched for a report, locating it easily, "Radio intercepts on units in Northern England report Norwegian in use by some stations."

Silence.

"Why would they do that?"

Nazarbayeva aimed the question at no-one in particular.

"Testing their systems, Comrade General? They were in code, but the accents were unmistakeable."

She nodded at Guvarin's suggestion.

"To mislead us?"

Poboshkin pursed his lips and continued.

"Using the language... well, they know we monitor their radio network... and the messages, whilst in some sort of code, were identifiable as Norwegian. It stinks, Comrade General."

Pinkerova, the young Lieutenant, returned clutching a new report, but she decided not to interrupt the debate in progress.

Nazarbayeva stood in front of the board, tapping the Norwegian photo recon entry.

"How many other flights have been successful, Comrade Major?"

She turned to Poboshkin, encouraging him into a quick response.

"This is the only set of up to date photos that we've received from Naval command, that I know for sure. Comrade Mayor Ergotin?"

Ilya Ergotin checked the file that recorded photographic intelligence and quoted directly.

"Comrades, we have received three other sets of photographs from successful aerial reconnaissance missions on the north-west coast of Norway... Narvik and Harstad on 30th November, Tromso on 3rd December, and Hammerfest and Alta on 13th December."

That stunned everyone into disbelieving silence, broken by a softly spoken Nazarbayeva.

"So, no photos since 13th December, and now we are presented with some taken on 12th March? Three months?"

She approached Ergotin's position.

"Tell me, Comrade, how many missions did Navy fly between December 13th and March 12th?"

"I do not have that information, Comrade General, but I'll get it immediately.

He was gone before the echo of his words had subsided.

Poboshkin noticed the waiting Pinkerova and beckoned her forward, extending a hand to receive the report she was so desperate to share. He encouraged her to speak.

"Comrade Polkovnik, the originals will be sent to us as soon as possible. I have asked them to include the pilot's report on the mission as well. I quickly jotted down some pertinent remarks from it."

Poboshkin scanned the short list and offered it to his commander.

It took only a moment for her to reach a conclusion.

"Clear skies with no cloud over enemy territory or the target... attempted enemy interception, by Spitfires, failed due to poor pilot skills... enemy anti-aircraft fire ineffective... no damage sustained..."

She gripped the paper tightly.

"Good work, Comrade Pinkerova. Comrades," she called the room's occupants to focus on her, "I want a reason, any reason, real reason, a fact, not a suggestion or assumption, but a reason to believe that the intended point of the Allied attack is the northern border of Norway and the Kola."

No-one said anything.

"Anything at all... give me one single fact that supports the notion, Comrades?"

"The photos of Harstad, Comrade General?"

Captain Guvarin became the focus of attention.

"And what do they show exactly, Comrade?"

"Laden vessels at anchor in the harbour, Comrade General."

She nodded vigorously, looking around the room.

"One thing, Comrades, just one thing, and even that may not be what we think, eh? Now look at what we worry about."

She counted them off on her fingers.

"Norwegian spoken on radios they know we listen to."

"No photo recon for three months and then we get some perfect shots."

"Enemy aircraft and AA totally ineffective, so much so that our..."

The door burst open, admitting a red-faced Ergotin.

She stopped talking immediately.

He passed her a report and stood back.

Poboshkin couldn't help himself.

"Well?"

"Nine, Comrade PodPolkovnik."

"Nine?"

"Yes, Comrade PodPolkovnik, and all unsuccessful."

"And the pilot's reports. What do they have to say, Comrade Kapitan. Cloud, engine trouble, what?"

Nazarbayeva passed Poboshkin the report and focussed on Ergotin's reply.

"There are no pilot's reports, Comrade Polkovnik. All aircraft failed to return."

As bombshells went, it was huge.

Nazarbayeva sat against the edge of the desk and eased the tension in her neck with a quick probe of her fingers.

"Who now feels that a Norwegian-Kola operation is probable?"

After a few seconds silence, Poboshkin ventured an opinion.

"Maskirovka, Comrade General. Has to be."

She and most in the room nodded in agreement.

"Maskirovka indeed. However," she turned to Ergotin, "I want your section to maintain focus on Norway operations and come to me with anything, anything at all, that might make us rethink this opinion, Comrade Kapitan Ergotin."

"Now, the Baltic, Comrades."

The analysis went on late into the night and the group did not seek rest until three in the morning, leaving Nazarbayeva sat with Poboshkin, gazing at the board for some moment of inspiration.

"So, after all that, we have reasons to believe that any of the Baltic States could be the target. We can discount Finland. There is nothing to suggest Poland as a possibility, not even a possible maskirovka, which, in itself we find worrying. We cannot even state for sure that the SAAG exists and that the threat to Bagramyan's forces is real."

There was something on his mind, and it showed.

"Go on, Andrey, spit it out."

"Your new found friendship with Colonel General Kaganovich…"

"Go on."

"Perhaps you could take advantage of it and find out what the NKVD knows about all of this, Comrade General?"

Nazarbayev feigned horror at the idea.

"What? Share with the Chekists?"

"We're supposed to be on the same side, after all."

"I will think on it, Andrey."

Her voice trailed off into a tired low tone.

Poboshkin ventured to state the obvious.

"Perhaps we'll see matters more clearly after a good sleep, Comrade General?"

"Very possibly."

She laughed and yawned, all in one distorted action.

"You are dismissed, Comrade. Sleep well."

He took his leave with a less than impressive salute.

Ten minutes later, the night duty officer found his commander fast asleep, and covered her over with a greatcoat.

Espionage, for the most part, involves finding a person who knows something, or has something that you can induce them secretly to give to you. That almost always involves a betrayal of trust.

Aldrich Ames

Chapter 137 – THE COUNTDOWN

1600 hrs, Friday 15th March 1946, Meeting Room 3, The Kremlin, Moscow.

The opportunity to test her new relationship with the NKVD deputy came sooner than she expected, as Nazarbayeva was woken at seven-thirty by a messenger with orders for her to report to Moscow, where she would be required to deliver an intelligence assessment on Allied Spring intentions.

To her surprise, Beria was absent, apparently away inspecting a new facility near Stalingrad.

Kaganovich was there in his stead, complete with all the NKVD files regarding potential Allied operations.

His remit was broader, and so reports of possible Allied activity in Iran and the southern borders were new to the GRU General. Neither was she aware of the assessments regarding potential seaborne invasion of Siberia. Both of these were substantiated by reports from her peers in the Southern and Pacific GRU commands.

Projections for Europe were less clear although, inexplicably, Kaganovich could supply perfect copies of the original Norwegian recon photographs.

The Soviet system and, in particular, the traditional rivalry between GRU and NKVD, was sometimes less than helpful to the Motherland.

On the matter of Norway, the two seemed to reach agreement, and swift access to extra information on both sides reinforced the reasoning behind the advice to treat any Norwegian operation as maskirovka.

Stalin grunted as the two gave their conclusion, understanding that the two Intelligence Officers had an ability to work together, something traditionally absent between GRU and NKVD officers. He wasn't sure that he liked it, as divide and conquer had been his life-long way of working.

251

Nazarbayeva delivered her assessment of the Baltic first, and understood the GKO's frustration with her recommendations which, basically, amounted to 'cater for everything until more information comes to hand'.

Kaganovich could add little to the assessment, save some reports from agents in Poland that suggested increased friction and factionalisation between the two Polish Armies. Stalin directed immediate exploration of any divide between the leaderships of the Polish units.

However, Kaganovich did bring something very interesting to the table; the photographs and written report of Captain Jabulov of submarine S-22.

The photos did the rounds of the table, and drew some admiring words on their quality, as well as excited chatter on the content.

Kaganovich became aware that the photos were not getting back to him, the pile in front of Georgy Malenkov growing by the second.

The Minister responsible for Aircraft Production suddenly leapt into action, sweeping up every one of the photos and moving around to Stalin's side, all in one easy motion.

Encouraging the General Secretary to move out of earshot, a hurried discussion took place, laced with frequent finger pointing at two particular photographs.

Judging by the Minister's face, the conversation clearly went against him.

Both men resumed their positions at the conference table, Malenkov tight-lipped and clearly perturbed.

The General Secretary felt the need to push his man into action.

"Tell them."

Malenkov reluctantly dropped the two pictures to one side, tapping them both to draw the other's attention to the content.

"This is a large explosive bomb; in its own right it is impressive but it is also built to resemble, in every way, another and different special kind of bomb."

Heads craned, assessing the size against the objects photographed with the 'thing' to establish scale.

"Needless to say, Comrades, this matter is of the utmost secrecy, but we are working on a weapon of immense power that also more than resembles this… err… conventional bomb."

That was, perhaps unsurprising, given that their agents had provided them with considerable information of the Fat Man bomb.

The existence of an Atomic weapons programme was news to a few of those present, who had never seen any of the reports from GRU and NKVD agents within the Manhattan Project.

Most of those in the room knew that Malenkov also wore the hat of Head of Research and Production for the Soviet Atomic Energy Programme.

Stalin took the lead.

"So it seems that our enemies are practising with their normal bombs before they use the improved ones, Comrades. Our agents have reported nothing?"

His eyes alternated between Kaganovich and Kuznetsov, NKVD and GRU commanders, seeking verification of his claim, or additional information if available.

Kuznetsov, recently returned from a long bout of ill-health, took the plunge.

"If I may speak freely in front of our Comrades, Comrade General Secretary?"

Stalin respected and liked the relatively young GRU Colonel General, and took the point fully.

"Comrades, nothing that is spoken of in this room may be spoken of outside of it. There are no exceptions."

His eyes swept the assembly for any sign of dissent.

"Continue, Comrade Polkovnik General."

"Comrade General Secretary, according to our current information, the Amerikanski are still some way from producing a viable type-2 device, their last attempted test also resulted in failure."

Nazarbayeva paid full attention to the world that was slowly exposed to her, although she shuddered naturally when specifics about field agents were mentioned..

"Between us, the NKVD and GRU have seven agents well-placed within the innermost workings of their programme, and we have had reports regarding all sorts of problems, from basic geometry to advanced physics. All of which have set back the Amerikanski programme."

Pausing whilst Stalin fired up his pipe, Kuznetsov took the opportunity to fire an apologetic look at his European Commander, whose face, he felt, indicated her unhappiness at being excluded from everything in the first place.

He had no idea that Nazarbayeva been part of a briefing on the Atomic programme before, and therefore had worked out the existence of the full project.

None the less, the detail being laid bare now was all new to her.

Stalin's cough brought him back to the matter in hand.

"These photos, made available to us by the diligence of our Naval comrades, clearly indicate that the Amerikanski intend to deliver this weapon by air, and using this type of aircraft. This confirms what we suspected from their intended Japanese use."

He silently offered Kaganovich an opportunity to take up the baton, and the NKVD officer took the opportunity, nodding to the GRU Commander.

"We must both contact our agents, and confirm the time scale to which the enemy project is working, Comrades. From memory, the last date suggested was November of this year, and that was without the additional problems that they have obviously experienced with the latest failure."

He pulled himself upright, addressing himself to Malenkov.

"This appears to be a race between them and us. Can the Comrade Minister tell us where we stand with our own development?"

Malenkov looked at Stalin, pleading with his eyes, hoping not to have his hand forced. He received no succour from his superior.

"Our own project is expected to yield a viable weapon by September…"

A noise escaped many lips, as the thought that the Motherland would possess a super weapon before the enemy gave voice to cries of pride and relief.

"No, Comrades, no… not this September. We estimate September 1947."

Relief turned to despair in a half-second, as minds did the simple maths.

"Continue, Comrade."

Malenkov looked at his leader with incredulity.

"Comrade General Secretary, I must protest."

"Continue, Comrade. Tell them a little about Project Raduga."

"But w…"

"We did, and now I decide that we will share something to warm the hearts of our comrades. Continue, Comrade."

"Perhaps it should wait until Polkovnik General Vannikov can be here to deliver a fuller briefing, Comrade General Secretary?"

There was no humour present in Stalin's reply.

"Perhaps I should find a new Head of Research and Production for our Atomic Programme?"

The message was received.

"By our orders, Comrade General Vannikov, in conjunction with Comrade Admiral Isakov, and scientist from the Motherland and other friendly nations, has been working on an alternate weapon, harnessing some of the same properties but with less complications."

He made his stand.

"The Amerikanski project has suffered another reverse with their latest failure, and that will almost certainly mean a delay of months for them. I am afraid that I cannot reveal the precise nature of the Raduga weapons, but I can tell you that we anticipate that they will be ready for use by February next year, which should be well in advance of any Amerikanski system."

'Enough, Iosef?'

It seemed so, as Stalin leant back in his chair, puffing away on his pipe, happy that the ensemble now felt more positive about the future.

Nazarbayeva, a previous recipient of a limited Raduga File, now understood that the GRU Commander, Kuznetsov, had no idea of the existence of Raduga, something she considered bizarre, given his foreknowledge of the Atomic weapon programme.

1843 hrs, Friday 15th March 1946, Scientist's residential block, Los Alamos, New Mexico.

Of those seven agents, five were already identified and turned by the FBI. One had chosen a dramatic way out, and his 'suicide' had deeply affected those working with him at Oak Ridge.

At first, the powers-that-be had wondered if that was finally the extent of the penetration, until a wisp of something not quite right emerged from New Mexico.

A wisp had become a sniff; a sniff had become a scent. More assets were moved to Los Alamos, and pretty soon a scent became a trail.

That trail, after weeks of exhaustive checking and rechecking, led Colonel Da Silva to the door he now knocked on.

The bespectacled young man who opened the door seemed unfazed by the uniformed presence at his threshold.

"Good evening, Colonel. May I help you?"

"I rather think you can, Mister Fuchs. May we come in?"

The last agent of the Rosenberg ring was in the bag.

1912 hrs, Friday 15th March 1946, Office of the NKVD Deputy Chairman, Lyubyanka, Moscow.

Having paid a visit to the office of the GRU Commander, Nazarbayeva still had time to accept Kaganovich's offer of a private meeting.

Ordinarily, she might have excused herself, but her impressions of the NKVD Deputy had been positive, so she decided to see how far matters might progress.

Her arrival had been silent and unspectacular, and she was ushered into Kaganovich's office, where she found the Colonel General sat expectantly at a table filled with the makings of a decent dinner.

"Comrade Nazarbayeva, so good of you to delay your flight."

He offered his hand, something that took Nazarbayeva aback and gave him the advantage, albeit momentarily.

She took his lead with the informality.

"Comrade Kaganovich, thank you for the invitation."

Beckoning her towards a seat, he reseated himself and surveyed the spread.

"I know that you haven't eaten, and won't have the chance before you fly back to the front, so I took the liberty of organising dinner whilst we talk."

He leaned across the table, filling her glass with a clear liquid.

"I understand that you have acquired a taste for Raspberry Schnapps, Comrade Nazarbayeva. This is the finest I could find at short notice."

They raised their glasses and drank together.

"Za zdorovje!"

It was excellent, and seared her throat on the way down. His knowledge on her recent drinking habits was impressive; worryingly so.

He read her mind.

"Don't worry about Poboshkin. He's not one of mine. He's your man through and through."

Pouring another schnapps, he indicated the plates of food.

"Please, Comrade, help yourself. Time is wasting."

As she filled her plate with cold cuts and salad, Nazarbayeva's mind was working overtime.

"If you must know, Rufin is my man… and I mean, my man, not anyone else's. He is intensely loyal to you… and always speaks of you in glowing terms."

He slipped a pickled onion into his mouth and choked a little as the sharp vinegar bit his throat.

"I would be pleased if you didn't reassign him… more looked on him as a less obtrusive means to communicate with me, should the need arise."

Nazarbayeva froze.

"Comrade General, I am a loyal member of the party and committed to our leadership, and I will do nothing to compromise that!"

He held up his hands in protest.

"Tatiana Sergievna, you misunderstand. I make no such improper suggestion."

He took a slug of the schnapps.

"The animosity between you and Marshal Beria is well known. To be honest, GRU General Kuznetsov has little working relationship with either Comrade Beria or myself, and I rather suspect that he lives on borrowed time in his position"

The former was a matter of certain knowledge to Nazarbayeva. The latter, that her boss was under threat, was unwelcome news.

"You and I have been given an opportunity to overcome a problem that has plagued the Rodina for years."

Nazarbayeva knew he was talking about the relationship between the two agencies, and the fact that the party leadership seemed to keep the pot of mutual distrust constantly stirred.

"I believe that, between us, we can serve the Motherland far better by communicating without fear or suspicion."

Whilst this was music to Nazarbayeva's ears, the very suspicion that she would love to overcome raised thoughts in her head; thoughts of traps, subterfuge… and treason.

She chewed slowly on a piece of chicken, giving herself time to think before replying.

"I agree. It can only benefit the Motherland if we communicate and share our knowledge, Comrade General."

"Please, call me Ilya Borissovich."

"I cannot do that, Comrade General."

He understood, as her rise to Major General's rank had been nothing short of meteoric, and the familiarity between senior officers was something she had not yet acquired.

"Between us we can improve the Motherland's understanding of our enemies, purely by sharing and talking, without the standard defensiveness and posturing."

She could only agree, and found her last suspicions about Kaganovich dissolving.

Picking up her schnapps, Nazarbayeva committed herself to a new relationship with the NKVD, in the person of Kaganovich, a relationship formed for the benefit of the Motherland and the leadership.

"Za zdorovje!"

The NKVD General smiled and swallowed his pickled egg before joining Tatiana in the toast.

"Za zdorovje!"

He toasted his new relationship with the GRU General, a relationship formed for the benefit of the Motherland… and himself.

"Now, we simply must find a way to make our leadership acknowledge the new threat from the Germans."

1737 hrs, Friday 15th March 1946, House of Madame Fleriot, La Vigie, Nogent L'Abbesse, near Reims, France.

The children were enjoying some quality time with their father in the garden room, which gave Anne-Marie the first real opportunity to discuss matters with her Aunt Armande.

The house itself was set in extensive woodland, which offered both privacy and security, the factors that had made Anne-Marie suggest it as an appropriate place to house the girls.

Aunt Armande had never experienced the pleasures of motherhood, her new husband and only love had been lost forever in the mires of the Western Front in 1918, and she was delighted to look after them.

That delight had turned to love, a love that was wholly returned, making the arrangement a total success.

That they had very quickly formed a bond with Anne-Marie, and vice-versa, was also a reason.

Ignoring the knocking that summoned the butler, both women settled to enjoy the hot chocolate, the timing and consumption of which had become a family habit, leastways in Armande Fleriot's house.

"You seem very happy, chérie."

258

"We have stopped them, and soon we will start rolling them back."

Mme Fleriot snorted.

"That is not what I meant and you know it, Ami."

Which Anne-Marie could only acknowledge with a smile.

A brief knock and the butler admitted himself, his face showing signs of indignant distress.

"Madame, there is an Army officer here with a message for your guests. He refuses to give it to me, stating he must hand it over in person."

Clearly, the struggle for supremacy in the hall had been short but bitter, and the butler had been defeated.

"Then please ask him to come through, Jerome."

"As you please, Madame."

Within seconds, a Legion dispatch rider entered the room and came to attention in front of Mme Fleriot.

"My apologies for the interruption, Madame, but I was instructed to hand these orders over in person."

"I understand totally, Caporal. Please do carry on."

The Legionnaire turned to De Valois and saluted, noting how wonderful she looked out of uniform.

"They are for the Général, mon Capitan."

He showed her the sealed envelope.

"I will take them on his behalf."

"Non… I cannot, Mon Capitan. I was ord…"

"I understand your orders, Caporal, but the Général is with his children right now and, if these are what I think they are, then we should give him every moment we can, don't you agree?"

Stories of De Valois' beauty abounded in Legion circles, whereas her capacity to intimidate was a lot less well known.

Her suddenly piercing eyes carried a clear message to the Caporal.

"I will take the orders, Caporal."

It was a statement that brooked no argument whatsoever.

"Thank you, Caporal."

Tearing the letter open, it took Anne-Marie twenty seconds to read the contents.

"I understand these orders, Caporal."

"And you will give them to the Général immediately, Capitan?"

"I will inform the Général as soon as I can, Caporal."

"Thank you, Capitan."

A swift salute, followed by another nod to Mme Fleriot, and the motorcyclist went to depart.

"Caporal, perhaps you might ask Jerome to find you some food and drink from the kitchen, before you go back out."

"Thank you, Madame."

"I heard a bike outside. Have we got visitors, Ami?"

Anne-Marie passed over the orders.

"Verdamnt."

"I agree. Tonight?"

He thought for a moment.

"Has to be. The girls and I had plans for you tomorrow too, Ami."

He had quickly taken to using the abbreviated form of her name.

"They'll keep, Chéri. Now, we'd best tell them… and get packed straight away."

Greta and Magda were both heartbroken.

1011 hrs, Saturday 16th March 1946, Headquarters, Legion Corps D'Assaut, La Mairie, D'Essey les Nancy, France.

Molyneux cut St.Clair a cutting look.

"You're late."

He knew Molyneux well enough not to even bother speaking about the Sherman tank that ran into his staff car; the Frenchman simply kept his lips sealed.

"Now that Général de Brigade St.Clair has finally bothered to show up, we can progress."

Receiving a small box from Plummer, Molyneux tossed it carelessly to the new arrival.

"It seems someone deems your actions in Alsace worthy of some record. De Lattre asks me to present you with that."

St.Clair opened the box to find a Croix de Guerre with palm inside.

Molyneux intended the slight, but the rest of those present gave him no opportunity to progress, noisily congratulating the French commander of Alma on his award.

"Yes, yes, enough of that."

Standing up, Molyneux pulled his tight jacket into position and took a position of parade ease.

"Colonel Plummer has orders for all of you."

260

The CoS moved forward and handed out the sealed envelopes, pausing to noisily congratulate St.Clair as he moved through the assembled commanders of the Legion Corps.

Unperturbed, the rhino-skinned Molyneux kept talking.

"Most of you have disengaged with the enemy now, and your units are in secondary or rear-line positions recuperating, so your orders should be easy enough to discharge, even for you."

He turned to the recently promoted Major-General Pierce.

"As for you, Général Pierce. Your unit is being returned to the US Army. As of now, you are no longer under my direct command. Bon chance."

Whilst most in the room understood that Molyneux was an ass of the first order, his virtual dismissal of Pierce was inexplicable, given the part that his 16th Armored had played in the Legion's battles.

"Well, open your orders then!"

Envelopes rustled, tore, and surrendered up written instructions.

"Mein Gott!"

"Mon Dieu!"

"Merde!"

"Scheisse!"

The senior French officers of the Legion Corps, and even Pierce, gravitated towards the wall map, fingers searching out the stated locations, whereas Knocke and Bittrich knew only too well.

"Stop acting like a rabble and listen to me."

They dragged themselves away from the map and formed a semi-circle around their commander's desk, Molyneux having taken to his comfortable chair again.

"Général Beveren, Austerlitz will be able to disengage on Monday. Colonel Haefali's brigade will be the last to entrain, as he will not be relieved until Wednesday."

"Sir."

"Général Lavalle, Normandie will form the vanguard when we move forward."

"Sir."

Molyneux looked down his nose at the commander of Group Normandie.

"Oui, Mon Général, if you please."

Lavalle kept silent just long enough to express his contempt.

"Of course, Sir. Oui, Mon Général."

It was one of the pointless exchanges that they had all become used to.

Plummer coughed, drawing Molyneux's attention to another matter.

"Yes, I know."

Unhappy at the interruption, the Corps Commander took a studied sip of his tea before continuing.

"The latest wave of reinforcements from Sassy will be redirected to meet up with you in your new positions. Given the recent problems with spying, I hold each of your responsible for the men under your command."

Finishing the last of his tea, he waved a dismissive hand.

"Now, get back to your units and discharge your orders, and I will not tolerate any delays," he looked directly at St.Clair, "Or lateness."

"What a prick."

Knocke kept his response minimal.

"I can only agree, General."

Others murmured their agreement with Pierce's opinion of Molyneux.

Far from being dismissive of Pierce and his men, the veteran SS and French officers had come to understand what a fine fighting force the man had constructed out of a savaged and beaten unit. The 16th US Armored Brigade was a formation that would do its job, and do it damned well.

Knocke spoke for all of them.

"We will miss you and your men, General Pierce."

Pierce smiled at a man who had once been his enemy.

"And we'll miss fighting alongside you and yours, General Knocke."

The US Officer looked at the assembly.

"We'll miss all of you. It's been a privilege to be part of this command."

The group responded with similar comments.

Knocke held up his hand.

"Before our illustrious leader decides to have another fit, I suggest that we get on with the job in hand."

They all laughed.

"General Pierce, it has been an honour, Sir."

Pierce grasped the proffered hand.

"That it has, General Knocke."

262

Each one in turn shook the American's hand and exchanged soldier's farewells, until only Lavalle remained.

"Whilst I remember it, General, you hang on to my boys until you're up to speed on the vehicles and weapons, then send 'em on back."

Even in the heat of the moment, Pierce had remembered the training group he had sent to the Legion to help familiarise them with US equipment.

"Thank you, Général, I'll get them back to you as soon as possible."

Taking Pierce's hand, Lavalle's French emotions nearly got the better of him, for he had come to rely on and trust the gruff US General.

"It has been a privilege to command you in battle, my friend, and I hope you and your men will, someday soon, return home to the peace you deserve."

Pierce smiled, understanding Lavalle's difficulty.

"So do I, General, and I hope that for both of us... for all of us."

They came to attention and snapped off immaculate salutes, Lavalle letting Pierce leave the building first.

They would never meet again, and Lavalle and Pierce would find 'peace' in very different ways.

The Legion Corps D'Assaut was moving north, like most of the French Army in Europe.

They were to be the left flank of de Lattre's First French Army, directly on the right flank of the German Republican Army...

...in the Ardennes.

1521 hrs, Saturday 16th March 1946, Headquarters, 501st Parachute Infantry Regiment, 101st US Airborne Division, St-Hilaire le Grand, France.

"Colonel! Skata! Will you wake up, for the love of God!"

The Airborne Division had been brought up to strength with transferees and newly qualified paratroopers, and the leadership of the 101st had reported that the unit would be at its absolute peak when called into action again. The 501st Regiment had been training all day and night, and the exhausted troopers had taken to their beds, not to be roused before the mess hall was ready to receive them for dinner.

At least, that was the order issued by Colonel Marion Crisp, which order was now well and truly broken by the insistent shaking of his Greek-American executive officer, Major Constantine Galkin.

"What the f… where's the goddamned fire, Con?"

Taking a respectful step backwards, Galkin allowed his commander to compose himself.

"Sorry, Chief, but I couldn't let ya sleep."

Wiping the muck from his eyes, Crisp sat up, and gestured towards the ever-present pot.

"Coffee."

Crisp was never a morning person, not that it was actually morning; he always valued his sleep.

Galkin poured two mugs and passed one to the slowly surfacing Crisp.

Downing the scalding liquid and willing himself into consciousness, Crisp flipped himself vertical and let his feet touch the cold floor.

"Fire away, Con."

"General's orders. Senior Officer's meeting at headquarters at 1700 hours."

Crisp groaned as he looked at his watch, now realising that he was being parted from his bed after less than three hours of sleep.

"OK, fair enough. Any clues on why?"

"We're on."

Crisp's mind was suddenly alert and fully concentrated.

"Say again?"

"Orders came through. They've handed us a bitch and… leastways from what my spies tell me… it's a bitch we get to ride in ten days' time."

Crisp did the maths quickly

'Ten days… err… today's the 16th… Saturday… so we're talking Tuesday 26th March.'

"That ain't a whole heap of time, now is it!"

Galkin finished his coffee.

"Guess that's why the General's getting everything sorted straight away. I'll have your driver ready for 1600."

Conscious that his commander had not appreciated his nakedness, Galkin beat a hasty retreat.

"I'll leave you to it, Colonel."

Running his fingers through matted hair, Crisp took a few deep breaths.

'Shit!'

The 101st was going back to war again.

1526 hrs, Saturday 16th March 1946, Ward 22, US 130th Station Hospital, Chiseldon, England.

Major Jocelyn Presley was less than happy with the discovery.

A large number of personal effects had accumulated in the loft space above the sluice.

The Sergeant and Corporal who had started placing them in the roof space did so for the right reasons, but simply forgot to tell anyone of their actions. She was satisfied that there was no dishonest intent on their part.

Having tracked down those responsible and halted the activity, she was now faced with sorting through the effects and ensuring their proper distribution.

After taking a break and recharging her caffeine levels, Presley returned to her cataloging and labeling.

Moving a bundled greatcoat, she found a small canvas duffle bag with a card label attached.

'Ramsey.'

She remembered the British officer fondly, and immediately reminded herself to take his wife up on the offer of afternoon tea.

Removing the contents of the bag, nothing of huge significance met her eye.

A garish tassled hat with red and white squares on was first to fall under her eye. Presley would not have known a Glengarry bonnet by name, but she set it aside, secretly admiring the traditional Scottish headgear. Following quickly came a brown corduroy flat hat, which she greeted with less enthusiasm, a lighter, a pristine copy of Ronald Syme's 'The Roman Revolution', and a uniform jacket that gave the impression of having been through a hedge backwards.

Intending to wash the jacket, Presley pulled it out and unfolded it, immediately understanding that Ramsey had been wearing it at the time of his last battle.

Normally, she might have discarded it, but the impressive row of ribbons stayed her hand, and she decided to go through with washing.

The blood and mud stains were all quite dry, and in any case, Major Jocelyn Presley was no stranger to the products of violence, so she fished about in the pockets without concern.

Pulling a few scraps of paper out, she laid the jacket aside, ready for the wash.

The first note was an official order, the one that moved Ramsay's unit to Barnstorf for that awful October bloodbath.

Second, and tricky to unfold, was some sort of poem, obviously something the British Major had been working on.

Third seemed to be a relatively straightforward hand written note.

Except it wasn't.

Ten minutes later, Presley handed it to the camp intelligence officer, who also couldn't read it.

It was not until nearly an hour later that they found a Corporal Potin on Ward 13 who had sufficient language skills to decipher the note.

"Jeez, yeah. Ain't read any of this stuff since ma Grand-pappy got out his old newspapers from the first war."

"So?"

Presley was impatient.

"Yes, Ma'am. It's Cyrillic."

He scanned it quickly, turning it over and whistling as he reached the end.

"Guy first named's a Major Ramsey. It's about a fight at a place called Barnstorf. Man who signed it is a Commie Colonel called Yarishlov."

"So what does it say!"

Alexey Gregorevich Potin, whose family had come to America to avoid the Revolution, read the text word for word.

He finished to the sort of silence that seems oppressive.

The camp IO spoke first.

"Wowee… now, ain't that something."

1530 hrs, Saturday 16th March 1946, the Billiard House, Hameau de la Reine, Versailles, France.

Major General Kenneth Strong, in the chair, called the meeting to order.

"Ladies and Gentlemen, thank you all for coming, and a particular thank you to our three new members who have responded at such short notice."

Whilst each of the people sat around the table was known, if only by name, Strong went through an introductory process.

"Dudley, author of the Cascade operation and head of 'A' Force."

Brigadier Dudley Clarke's credentials were impressive. Cascade had been the operation to alter the German perception of the North African order of battle, and had been wholly successful in convincing the enemy of the existence of many divisions that were solely recorded on paper. 'A' Force was the prime deception unit on the previous Italian Front. Dudley had been involved in some of 'J-Cip's work already, but had been brought in to provide first-hand critique and advice.

"Jane from MI5."

Second to be introduced, and with less of a flourish, was Jane Archer, former head of MI5's Soviet Intelligence Department, and brought in for her understanding of the Soviet psyche.

One look at her was sufficient to understand that the woman was all business and could stand her ground.

Again, with the lack of information due to those from the shady world of intelligence, Strong introduced the final arrival.

"And lastly, Harold. Most of you know Harold from MI6 Counter-Intelligence."

Nods of recognition acknowledged the new member.

Additional copies of the 'Ash' file were passed around and the group go down to the business of fooling the Soviet Union as to Allied intentions.

The meeting broke up later than expected, the new arrivals having been able to provide some excellent insight into Soviet thinking, as well as offering a few tweaks to the disinformation programme that would run throughout the summer.

As they strode from the Billiard House, dispersing to their various destinations, Major General Harold R. Bull waited to pull two people aside.

"Mrs Archer, can you spare me a minute?"

She went to take leave of her companion but Bull continued.

"Both of you please."

Bull produced two tan folders from his briefcase.

"Needless to say these are top secret. We've not yet acted on their contents, so perhaps you could have a look and have some ideas ready for the next 'J-Cip' meeting?"

267

Jane Archer noted the cover, with its impressive markings denoting the highest security requirements, alongside the file's two names.

"Mother and son, General Bull?"

Archer was well up on her Greek Mythology, as was her companion, who followed up Jane Archer's comment.

"So we have an Achilles to worry about?"

Bull laughed.

"No, Mr Philby."

"Please do call me Kim."

"No, Kim, it's Thetis that's more our concern."

Dropping into the back of the US Army staff car he had been assigned, Kim Philby struggled to maintain his composure, believing, rightly as it happened, that the driver was an intelligence operative. The knowledge that he was now aware of a great deception being inflicted upon the Soviet Union nibbled constantly at his composure, as did the concern that he would be in time to prevent the damage it could inflict.

With a fifteen minute drive to his quarters ahead, he decided to read the Achilles/Thetis file as a light distraction.

It proved anything but.

1318 hrs, Sunday, 17th March 1946, Bickenholtz area, France.

Their mission was to go wherever the Legion training detachment went, and bring them safe back to the 16th when they had finished the job.

The small unit could have waited it out in the warmth and comfort of their barracks, but that wasn't the way their senior NCO did things.

So 2nd Special Platoon, 16th Armored Military Police Battalion, found themselves secreted in the countryside outside of Bickenholtz, carrying out a practice anti-partisan surveillance and interception mission, all at the behest of First Sergeant James Hanebury, which experienced NCO, moving between apoplectic and incredulous, was about to visit himself upon the squad commanded by a man who was about as unfit to be a soldier as Hanebury had ever encountered.

"What in the name of the Almighty do you think you're doing, Sergeant Smith?"

The rotund NCO almost jumped out of his skin, so unaware had he been of the approach of his nemesis.

"Top, we've set up an OP here, and we're logging movement through the area, as ordered."

Hanebury gathered himself.

"As ordered? Look at this position! It's fucking useless... no height... no cover worth a fucking damn... and you're set up watching one side. Where's your security? Where's your rear cover eh? Goddamnit Smith, but I fucking walked up on you and your sorry bunch and none of you had a snowball's that I was here!"

Hanebury's eyes bored into the hapless Smith, burning deeply but, as usual, failing to find anything capable of absorbing the lesson.

"This position is shit. Find another."

The experienced First Sergeant looked around, assessing the area, seeking a suitable point to set up and observe from.

There were three choices immediately apparent.

Smith had summoned Corporal Buzzy to his side, a man that Hanebury considered to be equally as useless.

"I'll be back directly. Get it fucking sorted by the time I return, Sergeant."

Smith waited for the grizzled Non-Com to get out of earshot before shaking his head and spitting into the mud.

"Sargeant fucking Lucifer the Perfect says we gotta move to a better position. Where d'yer figure, Buzz?"

Transferred in from a Maintenance section, the new MP was as clueless as his squad leader.

"The old church there?"

He pointed to the far distance, just west of Bickenholtz.

"Too far, I reckon. How about the trees there. Looks like plenty of brush too... and we got a good field of vision."

Buzzy checked his map against the place Smith was pointing at.

"Yeah, I reckon that'll do. Plus, no way for old Lucifer to sneak up on us."

In the distance they could hear the sounds of Hanebury chewing someone's ass.

"That fucker should've joined the fucking infantry if he wanted to play general."

The imminent return checked their conversation.

"Well, Sergeant?"

"We've sorted a good position. You wanna check it out, Top?"

Hanebury held up his hands.

"Nope. Just get your squad settled in, call me up on the radio, and I'll come back and make sure you've got things properly sorted. OK, now let's move, Sergeant."

"Hey, Phelps."

"Sarge?"

Phelps forced his eyes open.

"You still got those special radio parts tucked away?"

"Sure have, Sarge."

"Get 'em fitted a-sap will ya. Want to be outta touch with old Lucifer for a while."

Phelps grinned.

"I'm on it, Sarge."

Smith, although pretty much a waste of space, was not without some cunning, and he had ordered the defective radio parts kept for occasions when he wanted autonomy and peace.

The subterfuge had fooled Hanebury once before, and he figured it would do so again.

Within minutes, both radios were disabled.

Hanebury, back at his own position, accepted the piping hot coffee from his driver, Collier.

"From your face, I'd reckon that Snuffy ain't flavour of the week eh, Top?"

Smith's nickname was not intended to be complimentary

"Typical Smith set up. Total SNAFU, Corporal. He's sorting it out now... I hope."

Hanebury took the approach of putting all his crap in one pot, which was why the expectations of Smith's squad were pretty much non-existent.

Smiling to himself, and without the slightest hint of humour, Hanebury wondered which of the possibles he had spotted would become Smith's chosen location.

"What's the odds on him getting it right second time 'round, Top?"

Hanebury grinned the grin used by senior NCO's the world over; the simple expression that announced hell was coming.

"I ain't taking bets, Lou."

In any case, for totally different reasons, all bets were off.

"Shit, what was that?"

"Just a mangy old dog, Sarge."

"It dead?"

"You fucking betcha it's dead."

The unfortunate beast had decided to run out of its cover and engage the new arrivals in play.

Smith was trying to remember if such an incident was reportable, and whether Old Lucifer would want a ream of paper on the matter. His thought process was suddenly interrupted as he realised how close he was getting to the copse.

"Whoa up there, cowboys!"

The convoy of three vehicles that transported Smith's squad ground to a halt as ordered.

Using his binoculars, Smith surveyed the small copse, noting the ramshackle wooden house for the first time.

Shouting across to the Dodge, Smith passed on the good news to his friend.

"Hey Buzz. Good call eh? Even got us some shelter."

Smith dithered, as was his normal approach to military matters. Eventually, he made up his mind.

"Right, just in case the old bastard's watching, I'm gonna do this proper. OK… Buzz, move your vehicle to the right there and oversee with the .50cal. I'll move left and do the same..."

He looked around and saw a slovenly soldier chewing gum like it was the finest beef steak.

"Hey Idiot, Purple Heart opportunity! Oi, Hartnagel…," the unpopular private pretended not to hear his Squad leader, "Hartnagel, you work shy piece of shit!"

"What?"

Hartnagel was simply the most disliked person in the MP battalion, bar none. His ability to avoid any sort of work was only equalled by his genuinely nasty nature and untrustworthiness.

"Get down the track and check out that stand of trees."

Hartnagel snorted his disgust.

"Bike's playing up, Sergeant."

"Then fucking walk for all I care. Move your ass."

Muttering obscenities, Hartnagel gunned the motorbike and moved off towards the copse, the Dodge 4x4 and jeep moving to either side.

271

Hanebury did not believe in travelling light when it came to weaponry.

He ensured his vehicles were kitted out with anything and everything he could lay his hands on.

The Dodge had a .50cal pedestal mount, and an MG42 jury rigged for the front seat passenger to have a whale of a time with, in the right circumstances. A special housing held a bazooka and two panzerfausts, and four grenade stations inside the vehicle held three deadly missiles each.

The jeep was only slightly less of a handful, with its own .50cal pedestal, and a .30cal mounted in place of the MG42. The jeep also carried three satchel charges. Hanebury had seen action at the Bulge, and understood the definite advantage of having a lot of firepower and high-explosive to hand.

The squad leader's vehicles also benefitted from long leather holsters bolted to the doorposts, in which lay silent but deadly Winchester M-12 pump-action shotguns, two per vehicle.

Whilst the MPs traditionally wore white helmets, each man had a combat grade helmet issued as well. 'Snowdrops' they may be but, as Hanebury was want to put it, 'anyone who messes with us better be prepared for a goddamned world of hurt, and the biggest butt fuck of their short life.'

The only problem with the theory was that this particular portion of their world of hurt was in the hands of the less than competent Smith.

"Quiet."

The whispered command had an immediate effect and silence took over again.

The officer continued, his eyes never leaving the approaching enemy.

"Just one man, but the others are fanning out either side. Ten men in total. No shooting."

Elite troops are always the same; minimum orders required, maximum violence when needed.

Captain Yulian Akinfeev relayed orders to his two senior NCOs with well-practised hand signals.

Serzhant Vetochkin slung his PPd over his shoulder and unsheathed the Finnish Puukko knife that he carried for the close and silent work so often required of the elite reconnaissance platoons of the Red Army. Dropping to his belly, he silently crawled out through the hole in the side wall.

Starshy Serzhant Urusov slipped upstairs to the small window, and settled behind his Mosin sniper rifle.

The remaining members of 322nd Guards Reconnaissance Platoon remained hidden.

Hartnagel hadn't lied completely, because the bike was having problems; starting problems, which was why he left the engine running as he slipped off to investigate the building.

Perhaps if he had switched it off then the telltale smell of Soviet tobacco might have warned him, but petrol exhaust fumes masked all of that. Perhaps the small sound made by Vetochkin's PPd snagging on a branch might have warned him, but engine sounds exceeded the softer sounds of his approaching death.

Vetochkin waited until the enemy soldier was out of sight before acting.

He grabbed the MP's mouth, kicked his legs away, and dropped him to the ground. The razor sharp Puukko opened Hartnagel's throat, everything done in one swift and easy motion, and in such a way as to avoid getting too much red liquid on the man's uniform. Dragging the corpse back by its feet, in order to clear the puddle of blood, Vetochkin stripped the tunic and helmet from Hartnagel.

Other men crawled silently through the vegetation, unseen, but he knew they were there.

He slipped into the tunic but quickly gave up trying to button it up. Hartnagel's wiry frame required smaller clothing than the muscular Russian could comfortably wear.

Watching Akinfeev closely, he waited until he received the signal.

When it came, he carelessly stepped into view, maintaining enough cover to make him seem familiar to the Americans, and yet indistinct, using the uniform and helmet to appear to be Hartnagel waving them forward.

Both vehicles moved forward, and those observing saw signs of relaxation.

Moving into column, Smith's jeep arrived first. The Squad commander stepped out immediately, keen to see how much comfort he could expect from his new surroundings. He suspected 'Lucifer' would leave them to stew for the evening, before introducing himself at some sort of stupid o'clock.

Opening the door, his nostrils received the first of two indications that he was not alone, that being the sort of smell associated with unwashed men gathered together in a confined space, closely followed by the second, more urgent indication, namely the business end of a pistol stopping a few inches in front of his face.

His eyes fixed on the deadly black circle, although he was aware of the sounds of silent killing behind him, as the rest of his squad was liquidated.

All except Pfc Fazzell.

The Dodge had disgorged its crew, save for Fazzell, who swung his Browning HMG from side to side, horsing around by exaggerating the actions of covering his comrades, and so missing the immediate signs of danger.

Too late, he saw what the shadows were trying to hide.

As those around him were swiftly slaughtered, the street-wise kid from New York watched in horror, his capacity to act temporarily removed by the awfulness before his eyes.

He pulled the trigger and was greeted with the silence normally associated with an uncocked heavy weapon.

Urusov, having cleared the misfired round that had granted Fazzell a short extension of life, put a shot through the young soldier's left eye, blowing the back of his head off and sending his helmet flying.

The MP squad, all save Smith, had been slaughtered.

"Goddamned mother-fucking sonofabitch! I will personally chew him a new fucking asshole. Fire discipline, my ass! Get him on the horn!"

The sound of the shot had carried through the quiet and found its way to the ears of First Sergeant James Hanebury, and 'Lucifer' was distinctly unhappy.

Pfc Shufeldt spoke into the radio a number of times, but was unsuccessful.

"Nothing doing, Top. He's either not receiving or he's ignoring me."

Hanebury heard but said nothing, not wanting to take his anger out on any of his own boys.

He turned to the nearest man.

"Rodger?"

His 2IC, Staff Sergeant Rodger Stradley thought for a second.

"Definitely north of us, Top. No doubting that."

Hanebury grabbed the map and laid it on the bonnet of his Dodge.

"The idiot was set up here first time. Reckon he'd three choices on an alternate. Here... here... and here."

"That's the one then, Top."

The first two choices were off to the north-west and west.

"OK. We do this as a drill, and by the numbers. Advance to contact. We'll treat Smith and his bunch as the enemy, so everything from here on in is Indian country."

Arthur Nave, an Oklahoma cowboy and driver of Hanebury's HQ vehicle, went to do a classic Indian brave war cry.

"Don't even think about it, Corporal, or yours'll be the first scalp taken."

Nave grinned and continued checking his weapons.

"Rodger, I want your element to move out here and gain position on this raised ground. Set up over watch and report in. Leave your .50 to cover from there... base of fire... then, when ordered, come in from the north-west, and fast."

Stradley nodded his understanding

"I'm going to move up the '46 here, acting as decoy... that should grab Snuffy's attention... that'll allow you to get good position, hopefully unseen."

He tapped the map on the junction of Route 46 and a small track.

"I'll drop off my M-8 here to cover, and also watch out for anyone bugging out to the west. The rest of my unit'll come in 'cross country, directly north here, so we can be seen by your fire base."

It was a simple plan, as the best often were.

"For a dollar, I'd chuck a few sixtys on his useless head, but I don't need the goddamned paperwork."

Hanebury referred to the 60mm mortar that his unit also sported, acquired from a Legion unit during a feisty game of vingt-et-un. The twelve rounds of ammo had come as a goodwill gesture.

"Synchronise... on my mark 1350... three, two, one, mark. Get your boys moving... I shall move off at 1400, so you let me know when you're in position and ready."

1350 hrs, Sunday, 17th March 1946, the copse, nine hundred metres north of Bickenholtz, France.

"So, what does he say, Comrade Izmaylov."

275

"Comrade Kapitan, I'm not sure of everything he said. Perhaps my English isn't as good as I thought. However, he's a policeman... they're all policemen... and they're doing training in the area, part of a larger, platoon sized group, spread out around Bickenholtz."

The enemy vehicles had already yielded a number of white MP helmets, so the story held true thus far, although the Soviet troopers were also incredulous at the hardware the vehicles carried.

"Not combat soldiers then. Good. Anything else?"

"No other units in the stationed in the area, just the French traffic that's passing through, heading north in the main."

"French? I thought they were Germ... Fuck! We've been watching that group of SS bastards moving."

Akinfeev grabbed his chin, his eyes suddenly staring and fired up.

"This we have to make known immediately."

He turned to the boyish radio operator.

"How's the radio, Comrade Radin?"

"No good, Comrade Kapitan. Burned out totally."

"Go and see what you can scrounge from the enemy vehicles. They must have a radio. We'll use theirs if you can't repair ours."

Corporal Radin was gone in the blink of an eye. Akinfeev had been hampered by a lack of communications since the radio had developed a terminal fault the previous week. Now that he had something major to report, he decided to return to his own lines if he couldn't get a message through.

"Anything else?"

Izmaylov's disgust was evident.

"The man needs new trousers, Comrade Kapitan. I hardly scratched him before he evacuated himself and talked his head off."

"Well, we won't take him with us anyway. Bind him, gag him, give him a tap on the head. We're going to move away in any case."

"Yes, Comrade Kapitan."

Vetochkin offered one of the newly looted American cigarettes to his commander and Urusov.

Lighting up, the Captain shared his thoughts.

"Those SS bastards've been at the centre of things for the Capitalists, and you can bet that wherever they're going, there's going to be a problem of our commanders. We have to report this immediately, comrades."

"So we're going home, Comrade Kapitan?"

"If the radio can't be repaired then yes, Comrade Serzhant, and as quick as we can, and we should thank our Amerikanski friends, who've provided us with the means to do most of it in comfort and style."

Radin returned.

"Comrade Kapitan, there is nothing I can use for repair. Parts are different. Both of their radios are useless too. I can do nothing, Comrade Kapitan."

"Both their radios are broken?"

"Yes, Comrade Kapitan."

His opinion of the worth of these 'policemen' sunk lower.

Drawing in the rich tobacco smoke, Akinfeev outlined his plan.

1401 hrs, Sunday, 17th March 1946, Rue D'Eglise, Bickenholtz, France.

Hanebury's jeep led the way, bouncing over the uneven ground, followed by the M-8 Greyhound, then the Dodge 4x4, the final vehicle in line being the Horch 1A that had somehow fallen into their hands in Prague the previous year.

Meeting up with the Rue Principale, the column turned right and slowly headed north, whilst Stradely's unit moved around to the east, using the reverse slope of the three hundred metre ridge to hide behind.

His unit was moving too fast, so Hanebury changed plans, waving the column to come to a halt. He also saw an error on his part and determined to reposition the Greyhound closer to the copse.

Standing up, he examined the area, fully expecting to see Smith and his squad, or at least part of it.

Unusually, there was nothing to see, which made him wonder if the position assessment had been correct.

He quickly examined the other possible positions and was greeted by the same nothingness.

'Shit. Has he actually learned to conceal himself and his boys at last?'

"OK, Cowboy, move it up nice and slow."

Hanebury decided to pull an extra on his men, and was given an opportunity almost immediately.

"Whoa!"

The jeep shuddered to an immediate halt.

"Suspected mined road ahead!"

He waved and gesticulated, the vehicles behind understanding what was required, as they swiftly responded, moving off to the either side, in case of ambush.

"Reek, you have the detail."

With every weapon manned and ready, the MP group watched as Rickard moved forward to examine the area Hanebury found suspicious.

He carefully moved up to the area and inspected the body, satisfied that whatever it was, probably a dog, was dead.

Removing his bayonet, he gently probed the surrounding area until he satisfied himself that there was nothing more destructive present. Dragging the bloody corpse to one side, he trotted back to the waiting jeep.

"Fresh kill that, Top. Crushed under the wheels of something heavy I reckon."

"Uh-huh."

Such a response was unusual, and they all looked at Hanebury, who was clearly riveted by the view through his binoculars.

"What the fuck?"

Their attention turned to the copse that was consuming their leader.

The rear of a US Army Dodge was now apparent.

"Reek, use your sight. Check out that vehicle."

Rickard grabbed his Springfield rifle and brought it up, using the sights to examine the Dodge.

"What the fuck?"

He thought quickly.

"From the dog, Top?"

"I thought that too, but that's on the back of the vehicle."

Minds worked in silence, until Rickard noted something else.

"Top, look off to the left, next to that little bush. See it?"

"Nope, nothi… shit."

A US helmet lay upright, motionless, but full of warning.

Hanebury stretched carelessly and turned to Rickard.

"Laugh it off, Reek, just for the benefit of the audience, ok?"

Rickard relaxed too.

Hanebury flopped back into his seat.

"Radio."

He held out his hand and the handset was pressed into it immediately.

"Pennsylvania-Six to Pennsylvania-Six-Two over."

"Six, receiving loud and clear, over."

"Six-two, remember the last item we discussed with the Captain before we took up this assignment, over."

"Six, I do, over."

"Six-two, execute immediately, over."

"Six, roger, executing. Out."

Hanebury, keeping his eyes firmly on the copse, gave the radio operator an instruction and the set was retuned to the required frequency.

"Pennsylvania-Six to Pennsylvania-six-two, receiving, over."

"Six, receiving you loud and clear. What gives, over?"

With a sense of the dramatic, Hanebury could not resist the opportunity to repeat history.

"Six-two, this is no drill, I repeat, this is no drill. I believe we may have enemy in the position, that's why I changed frequency. It's possible that Six-four was been taken out. Change of plan follows, over."

The smoothness of the frequency change and the adaptability of the soldiers were testimony to the leadership and training of the unit.

Grabbing his map, Hanebury made his adjustments whilst Rickard attracted the attention of the other vehicle commanders, pulling them all in towards the command vehicle.

"They've stopped to examine that dog. They seem terrified that it's a mine or something."

Akinfeev's opinion of these toy soldiers could sink no lower.

Another of the cigarettes was lubricating his throat with sweet smoke as he watched the useless Amerikanski go about their business.

"Seems they've decided that the dog is no threat, Comrades."

His men laughed dutifully.

His smile turned to a stoney face as he watched further.

"Comrade Serzhant, what do you see?"

Urusov, stretched out on the rickety floor above his Captain's head, whispered back.

"I think they've seen the vehicle, Comrade Kapitan. One of them has a sniper scope; he's looking now, as well as the officer."

Both men saw the Americans laugh and relax.

"If the Amerikanski were all like these, we'd be in Paris by now!"

His amusement was short-lived, as something changed in the group he was observing, men from each vehicle who had casually assembled, clearly now less than comfortable with what their officer was telling them.

However, he already considered these men to have demonstrated themselves as worthless, and his pride in his own unit did the rest.

The group broke up, moving urgently to their various stations, another warning sign that Akinfeev chose to ignore.

And then things changed very quickly.

The Greyhound moved in behind a low wall further up the Rue Principale, clearly taking up a position of overwatch, backed up by the Horch and its crew. Parking their vehicle in a small depression, the four men set up two .30cals, one on either side of the armoured car, and piled some other useful kit close at hand, just in case.

Hanebury and the Dodge crashed off to the east and dropped down into the depression, masking themselves from anyone in the copse.

To the east, Stradley's firebase was established and the rest of his squad was moving as fast as they could to get north of the copse unseen.

"Trouble. The armoured car's moved to cover us, with one vehicle in support, and the other two vehicles have gone. Moving round to our left I should say."

Starshy Serzhant Vetochkin stood and waited for his orders.

"Take two of the panzerfaust, the 34, and three men. Set up on the edge of the trees to our left here. I don't want anything coming up out of the low ground there and into our flank. Clear, Comrade Starshy Serzhant?"

"Yes, Comrade Kapitan."

Clicking his fingers at the nearest three men, Vetochkin assigned the weapons and led his small group away.

"Comrade Yefreytor."

Radin crawled over to his commander's side.

"Same as Comrade Vetochkin. Take three men, two of the panzerfaust and the DP. Cover the north side of the copse. Clear?"

"Clear, Comrade Kapitan."

The group were quickly on their way.

"What's the armoured car doing?"

Sergeant Urusov leant over, looking straight down at his Captain's face.

"Holding steady, Comrade Kapitan. They've set up machine-guns either side of it. These Amerikanski seem to know what they're doing."

The unpalatable thought had occurred to Akinfeev.

Another quickly took its place.

"Comrade Izmaylov, a moment."

Even though Izmaylov was only a private, Akinfeev had always felt comfortable around the highly educated university professor who had volunteered for the Red Army on the day the green toads had invaded the Motherland.

They had shared many conversations about the higher things in life, without any distinction of rank.

"Comrade Izmaylov, something tells me we will not get out of this scrape."

Akinfeev leant across to the useless radio set and pulled out a spare map and the code book.

Marking the movements of the infamous SS units on the map, he folded it and surrendered both the map and code book to the former professor.

"I want you to find a place out there in the copse, away from the building... a place you can hide and not be found, Comrade. I order you not to take part in this battle. You must evade what is coming and report this information to our commanders at the earliest opportunity. Do I need to repeat those orders, Comrade?"

"No, Comrade Kapitan, you do not."

All business, Izmaylov secured the documents before bringing himself to parade attention, saluting formally.

Akinfeev returned the salute and, in a typical display of Soviet comradeship, hugged his man, knowing that he had saved his life with the mission.

That Izmaylov was his friend was a given, but he had selected him for the other qualities that made Rodion Eduardevich Izmaylov the most complete and ruthless soldier he had ever met.

The man was a born survivor and, if anyone could bring back the crucial report, it would be Izmaylov.

By the time he had finished the thought process, he was looking into empty air, as the professor easily slipped away and out through the hole.

The radio crackled urgently.

"Pennsylvania-Six to Pennsylvania-six-two, go ahead, over."

"Six-two to six, we see signs of movement on eastern and northern edges, just set back from the tree line. Infantry only, but certainly not ours, six-two over."

"Six to Six-two, what weaponry, over?"

"Six-two to six, unsure at this time, over."

"Six, roger. Out."

He raised the Greyhound commander, and was none the wiser when that conversation finished.

A decision was quickly made.

"Pennsylvania Six-Two from Pennsylvania-Six over."

"Six, go ahead, six-two over."

"Six-two, hold on your secondary line and deploy the sixty. Do not fire until I am taken under fire myself. Clear? Six over."

"Six from six-two. Understood. Three minutes, six-two over."

1423 hrs, Sunday, 17th March 1946, base of fire position, east of the copse, Bickenholtz, France.

No matter what the plan was, as with most things military, the enemy tended to do things that messed things up.

Hanebury waited for the set up of the 60mm mortar.

To the north, Staff Sergeant Stradley chivvied his men along, trying to get it properly sighted in as short a time as possible.

The M-8 Greyhound crew and their companions waited for signs of anything worth a bullet.

The 60 was setup and Hanebury acted, moving his unit forward and up the concealing slope.

In the base of fire position, Corporal Gardiner used his liberated German binoculars to watch the tree line.

A pink object sprang into view, needing a focus adjustment to interpret as a face... and a...

"Jesus H! Hit the fucking tree line now!"

The .50 immediately spat its heavy bullets in the direction of the copse, the gunner adjusting his fire, walking the stream of metal into the undergrowth.

'Not close enough!'

Gardiner shouldered his Garand and pulled the trigger until the metal clip sprang clear.

Whatever it had been that the enemy soldier had been holding, and it sure looked like a panzerfaust at the time, was now held by bloodied and dead hands.

Other weapons sprang to life around the edge of the copse, themselves starting a chain reaction from the encircling force.

The mortar's first shell missed by a hundred feet, but the adjustment was good, and the rest went on the money.

Hanebury quickly spent every round from the 42 and swapped it for his M-1 carbine, then changed his mind, and grabbed for one of the Winchesters.

The .50cal behind him was deafening, but he enjoyed the effect it was having upon the small wood.

A small smokey trail marked a panzerfaust shot, but it went near nothing of consequence and served only to draw attention from the firebase.

Coordinating with Stradley, Hanebury moved forward, the two forces arriving at the treeline together, Stradley to the north, Hanebury to the south.

Both NCOs shouted the normal warnings about possible friendlies ahead.

The firebase ceased pouring shells into the site, but remained active, watching over the battlefield.

The distinctive sound of .30's betrayed a Soviet attempt to move west. The attempt failed.

Nave was left with the vehicles and the rest spread out. Moving into the tree line.

A groaning off to Hanebury's right drew attention, not the desired sort, as Rickard put three .45s into the wounded man.

He slipped the Colt back into his waistband and took a firm hold on the BAR again.

A flash of movement made him involuntarily scream.

The impact was heavy, but not enough to disturb his balance.

Continuing the scream of fear into one of intimidation, he swivelled and fired the BAR at whatever it was that had thrown the knife.

Vetochkin had lost his left arm above the elbow, courtesy of .50cal rounds fired from the firebase.

He had also taken a bullet in the right ankle, as one of Gardiner's shots deflected and painfully wrecked the joint.

He had thrown the Puukko at the nearest American, knew he had hit him, and still had time to be incredulous that the man turned quickly and fired.

Rickard, having smashed the Russian's body to pieces with heavy rounds at close range, pulled the Finnish knife from the stock of his BAR, knowing how close he had come to death.

Hanebury gave him a moment.

"Reek, check 'em over for intel… then close up when you've done."

'Lucifer' plunged on as an explosion marked some sort of action to the north.

Ahead he could see the shape of some sort of building and…

"Cover!"

The NCO shouted as he threw himself off to one side, the rest of his small group following suit.

With hand signals, he passed on information, and rose slightly to check again with his own eyes.

On first sight, he had seen two enemy soldiers, waiting behind a machine-gun.

From behind the small tree stump, his second view revealed two American bodies and a severed bough.

Relief flooded over him, followed by other, more bestial thoughts.

The corpses were identifiable as Buzzy and Hartnagel.

'They may have been useless bastards, but they were my fucking useless bastards.'

"Covering fire!"

Garands and carbines threw bullets at the building as Lucifer visited himself upon the enemy.

On the north side of the copse, things had gone a little worse. One of Stradley's men was face down in the mud, his life taken by a burst of SMG fire.

Stradley's jeep was burning gently, a panzerfaust having destroyed it only twenty yards short of the tree line.

The only casualty of that strike, Stradley himself, nursed a bloody boot that presently disguised the rough amputation of two toes by shrapnel.

None the less, he pushed his group forward.

Bullets swept through the wooden sides of the building, more than one striking soft flesh within.

A scream made Akinfeev look up, just in time for the first surge of arterial blood from Urusov's shattered thighs to wash over his face.

His NCO died before his eyes, the large arteries spilling his lifeblood in seconds.

Akinfeev resembled the stuff of nightmares, his face and upper body bathed in blood and human detritus.

He screamed, clawing at his hair and face, desperately trying to remove the horrors found there.

Screaming again, he unnerved the few men left in the building as he ripped off his tunic and used the destroyed garment to wipe himself.

One man rose to leave.

"Stay here and defend this position!"

"The battle is lost, Comrade Kapitan, we should save ourselves."

The unhinged officer grabbed for his pistol, intent on shooting the mutineer, until Lucifer entered the room.

As Hanebury moved up, slipping from cover to cover, he became more and more angry, finding another of Smith's men here, two more there.

The support fire slackened and then stopped, conscious that their leader was almost on top of the building.

Some moved forward to support him, but the First Sergeant kicked open the door and swiftly moved inside.

When the American Army had first brought the pump action shotgun to war in Europe, their First World War adversaries, the Imperial German Army, had declared the weapon illegal and threatened to execute any man carrying such a weapon, so devastating was it in the fine art of trench clearing.

In the right hands, the 12-gauge Winchester was also the most perfect weapon for removing any hostile intent in a room.

Lucifer had the hands for the job, and the Winchester blew the intended mutineer off his feet and spread parts of him over the already stressed Akinfeev.

The Soviet officer went into rapid meltdown.

Hanebury's reflexes made him swivel and pump in one easy fluid movement, directing a stream of shot into the three men who started moving to attack him. Each went down and stayed down.

Hanebury brought the weapon back round, but the strap momentarily caught on the muzzle of a propped rifle, which gave Akinfeev time.

The unhinged officer brought his pistol up but, before he could fire, an explosion unbalanced him, buying Hanebury the extra half-scond he needed.

The Winchester deposited its contents in Akinfeev's exposed left side, stripping away flesh, and flaying the stomach and hip area.

Thrown against the wooden wall, Akinfeev somehow retained enough understanding to raise his pistol towards Hanebury, even as his innards started to spill from the horrendous wound.

Akinfeev had no strength, and the pistol sagged away.

His mad eyes, fired with pain and hatred, looked at his killer, and saw only death therein.

Lucifer put the last 12 gauge in the middle of the Russain's chest, and brought instant end to the man's suffering.

Dispassionately examining the horrendous wounds on his victims, Hanebury slid more shells into the Winchester.

Hearing a small whimper, Hanebury dropped behind a table and brought the Winchester up ready. Curled up in the corner was Smith, his own emotional breakdown in its advanced stages.

Relaxing, Lucifer noted the approach of two of his men.

"What the fuck happened to you, Rodger?"

His 2IC stumbled in, clearly in pain.

"Someone put a faust on my vehicle, Top. Seems I left a little bit behind when I bailed out."

"Let's get that seen to. Medic! Medic!"

Stradley tossed his head in the direction of the gibbering wreck in the corner.

"What's with the laughing boy there, Top?"

"Guess he just couldn't cut it, Rodger. Medic! Medic!"

They actually didn't have a medic, but Sergeant Ringold knew his way around battle wounds, so to him fell the task of reassembling Stradley's foot.

"Right, let's get this area secured a-sap. Call the Greyhound team in closer. Leave the firebase for now. C'mon, let's move it, boys!"

Gradually, the MP unit made sense of the scene and recovered the bodies, friend and foe alike.

Those of their unit were laid out and covered, ready to be transported back to civilisation.

Those of the enemy were simply laid out, with all the horrors visited upon them on display.

Nave walked up, having repositioned the command jeep, chewing on a Hershey bar as he inspected the Soviet corpses.

"Jeez, Top. I take it these here are your handiwork?"

Hanebury shrugged, the Winchester sat nestled in the crook of his arm.

"Damn but that thing can fuck up your whole day and then some!"

There was no arguing with that.

Corporal Collier strolled up and mimed taking a chomp out of Nave's Hershey.

"Get ye the fuck!" shouted Nave, his Arizona accent doing its best with the Scottish expression they had frequently been exposed to when camped alongside a Highland regiment in England.

None the less, he extended the bar and Collier nibbled a portion off.

"Top, second sweep is complete. Area is secure. We have eighteen bad guys here, all dead."

"Nineteen."

Both Hanebury and Collier looked at Nave in puzzlement.

"Eighteen," Collier corrected, sure of his figures.

"Come down here a 'ways."

A few yards down the track, Nave stopped and pointed upwards.

"Now, I don't know exactly what that is, but I'm guessing it isn't a fucking bird."

It certainly wasn't, but it was the very devil to get down.

Eventually, the limbless torso was nudged out of the branches and fell into the undergrowth below.

Hanebury searched the pockets for intel before allowing the body to be piled with the others.

He examined the two items quickly and decided he would look at the map and booklet properly later. For now, he just wanted to get his unit secured and the whole affair reported.

1021 hrs, Monday, 18th March 1946, The Kremlin, Moscow, Russia.

Nazarbayeva was quite thankful that she had arrived early for the meeting, as she and a number of other senior officers were presently queuing to get into the building where the meeting was to be held.

Since the failed attempt by Makarenko, security had been tightened up, and no weapons of any kind were permitted within the main buildings, except those carried by the Kremlin Guards and authorised NKVD troops.

Having already been searched twice, Nazarbayeva was now in a line of some fifteen senior ranks, waiting to be sent through the latest acquisition intended to protect the lives of the General Secretary and his entourage.

A large but extremely effective Geffchen & Richter metal detector, stripped from a factory in Leipzig, obstructed the main stairs at ground floor level, leaving no alternative for anyone wishing to go upstairs but to walk through it.

It was a slow process, as there was seemingly no-one without something metal that set off the device, from belt buckles to watches to pens. Those attending had already been warned not to wear their awards, so it was a curiously unadorned group of generals and admirals that waited patiently for their turn.

Zhukov, leading the queue, removed his watch and belt, before stepping through to a relieving silence.

Accepting both back on the other side, he nodded at one or two in the queue and moved off, having 'reassembled' himself.

Marshal Hovhannes Bagramyan ceased his animated conversation with his frontal aviation commander, Major General Buianskiy, and followed next, as behind him the growing queue become a virtual who's who of Soviet military talent.

By the time Nazarbayeva got to the device, most of those waiting understood what would and what wouldn't set the damn thing off, and most already held belts, pens, drinking flasks and a plethora of personal artefacts ready for open inspection.

Nazarbayeva passed through.

'Meeeeeeeeep.'

She searched her pockets again, but immediately understood what the issue was.

"My left boot, Comrade Mayor."

She slipped the boot off and, in one deft movement, flicked it to the feet of the NKVD officer. A number of those present took the opportunity to inspect her left foot, or rather, the absence of it, an injury she had suffered whilst fighting in the Crimea.

Steadying herself on the metal detector, she hobbled back round and through.

The Geffchen & Richter detector remained silent.

Picking up her boot, the NKVD Major in charge of the process slipped his hand inside, immediately finding the L-shaped metal support that helped Nazarbayeva to walk properly. He quickly looked the boot over inside and out.

"Comrade General."

He held the boot out to the GRU officer, who took it, dropped it to the floor, and had her 'foot' inside it in the blink of an eye.

Moving on, Nazarbayeva found herself much in demand, as both Bagramyan and Zhukov descended on her for the very latest information.

1100 hrs, Monday, 18th March 1946, The Kremlin, Moscow, Russia.

Everyone who was anyone in the upper echelons of the command apparatus seemed to be present to hear the delivery of the GKO approved plan for the coming months.

Whilst not totally on board with all its details, Zhukov had managed to steer Stalin and his committee away from some of the more disastrous ideas.

After receiving the most up-to-date information from the various intelligence agencies, projected figures for reinforcements and manufacturing output, expectations on oil production and personnel training, Zhukov started to paint a picture of a Red Army still capable of winning the present conflict, albeit with much more difficulty than had been presented to the same assembly before the tanks had started rolling westwards again.

To a man, and woman, the listeners were sceptical on the promises given about air cover, and how the struggling Red Air Force would start to combat Allied supremacy in the air and provide an umbrella under which the army could operate effectively. Much was expected of the new generation of aircraft, and a speeded up training programme for flight crew.

Novikov, commander of the Air Force, started quoting figures for available aircraft that resembled pre-war levels, and boasted of new types of jet aircraft that would soon be knocking Allied piston-engine craft from the skies.

His hands, like those of Zhukov and others, were tied, and he either went with the GKO plan exhibiting confidence and enthusiasm, or he would be counting trees in Siberia at the very best.

The master plan involved a great deal of maskirovka, as was to be expected, with formations demonstrating their hostile intent on the Norwegian border and Iran.

The upcoming insurrection in Greece would be provided with as much materiel support as possible, ensuring a further diversion of Allied resources.

Soviet forces working alongside the Japanese would be encouraged to be more active, something that Vasilevsky had railed against until his position was almost untenable.

Yugoslavia's position had been clarified by a secret trip, undertaken by Molotov himself, and it was Yugoslavia herself that would offer most of the support to the Greek Communists.

However, whilst volunteers would continue to serve with the Red Army, there would be no change in Tito's stance, meaning that Yugoslavian borders would be heavily policed and any violations would not be tolerated.

NKVD and GRU reports were careful to state what was known and what was surmised, and both drew conclusions that enemy eyes were mainly focussed on the Baltic States, although evidence of an intensification of the bomber offensive across the whole of Europe was clear.

Stalin, knowing that she would not be able to stop herself, asked Nazarbayeva what she thought was planned.

"Comrade General Secretary, all the evidence and suspicion would point towards Northern Norway and the Baltic States for some sort of military offensive operations, although the former can only be limited in size and nature. There are other clues that simply don't fit into the whole but, our comrades in the NKVD agree, the best interpretation of all the intelligence we have received is that there will be an invasion of the Baltic States. When, we don't know, but there are no indicators to suggest that any action is imminent."

Admiral Isakov chipped in with his contribution, assuring the ensemble that the coasts of the three states, as well as higher up the Gulf of Bothnia, and the Polish coast, had all been extensively mined, and that his small but veteran fleet was ready to resist any invaders.

A question on the state of the Finns drew Molotov into the discussion.

"The Finns are and will remain neutral, to all intents and purposes. They have reiterated their stance to us, and the Allies, and Admiral Isakov can confirm, have further mined their coastline to protect from any incursion. Comrades, Finland is neutral for now."

Then it was the turn of the Swedes, and Nazarbayeva was invited to speak.

"Comrade General Secretary, the Swedes appear to have been very active in protecting their borders, and there have been confirmed sinkings of Allied vessels, and shootings down of aircraft. It would certainly seem that the Swedish intend to remain neutral."

Stalin had noticed something in her words but let it go, just for the moment.

Zhukov sought more information from Beria.

"Comrade Marshal, apart from Norway and the Baltic, we expect ground attacks, accompanied by increased air activity, throughout Europe. We have not yet identified a specific axis of attack."

Rummaging in his briefcase, Beria produced a document and handed it to Stalin, immediately following with a copy to Zhukov.

His eyes engaged momentarily with Nazarbayeva. He smiled briefly and carried on.

"These are the units identified as likely to lead any major Allied attacks. We have good locations on all of them, and they are well spread around the continent. There does appear to be some new concentration of Amerikanski units in France and Alsace, to the north of Switzerland. The similar grouping of prime British units on the North German plain is to be expected of course."

Placing the paper on the table, he removed his glasses and started to polish them.

"Information on the Second Allied Army Group is limited, but some veteran formations we thought destroyed have surfaced within its order of battle. Neither the GRU, nor ourselves, can expand the present knowledge at this time."

Beria publically advertised his penetration of GRU organisation, much to Nazarbayeva's annoyance, and Stalin's amusement.

291

"The reforming German Army is another matter, and we have identified new forces in Holland, Southern France and the Italian Alps. Reports state that they are equipped from captured weapon stocks, therefore both NKVD and GRU believe we should treat these reformed units in the same way as before we marched into Berlin."

Nazarbayeva took advantage of Beria's intake of breath to get her own comment in.

"Comrade General Secretary, whilst Comrade Beria is, in general, correct, GRU believes that these reformed units may pose a bigger problem than previously."

Beria's look cut through the air, and Nazarbayeva met it with soft eyes that concealed the hardness she was feeling for the NKVD Chairman.

"There is no evidence for such a suggestion, and remember how hard the green bastards fought in any case."

The conversation had suddenly become private in a room full of people, something everyone realised and decided not to interrupt, even Stalin.

"It seems a simple deduction to me, Comrade Marshal."

"How so, Nazarbayeva? I think you reach too far. They fought for their homeland, and did so tooth and nail. We lost thousands of our soldiers in those last weeks... thousands!"

Nazarbayeva waited patiently as the NKVD boss's voice rose in volume to make his point.

She waited for the echo of his last words to die away before continuing.

"Between us and the Allies, the German was on his knees, both militarily and industrially. They were spent physically and yet, as you observe, made our Army pay a rich price for the victories all the way to Berlin, Comrade Marshal."

She looked around, suddenly aware that those around the two sparring intelligence officers had moved imperceptibly away, creating an area of isolation.

"This new force will be differ..."

"Rubbish! They will be the same old Germanski. Tough but beatable."

He waved a hand to dismiss further comment from Nazarbayeva and turned to Stalin, expecting the General Secretary to move the conversation forward.

Stalin merely waited silently, almost inviting Nazarbayeva to continue, which she did with an air of authority that cut through Beria's self-assurance in an instant.

"No, they will not be the same old Germanski, Comrade Marshal. These Germanski are well equipped, have had time to recover their fitness, and are now supported by the mightiest logistical machine in the history of war. They have had a wave of reinforcements, soldiers captured at a time when their quality was better than the old men and boys that manned the barricades in Konigsberg and Berlin."

Beria was white with fury at being so publically challenged, but felt impotent in the face of Nazarbayeva's words.

"We will not just be fighting them either, Comrade Marshal, but also their new Allies... our old Allies... and whilst some of them are of limited value, none of our military commanders here will tell you anything but that we should not underestimate any of them."

There was a low mumble from the Front Commanders and the few present who had commanded Armies in the recent combat, a mumble that left no doubts as to the truth behind her words.

"These Germans will be the very worst sort. Fit, competent, well armed, well supported, and well-motivated, Comrade Marshal, and we cannot... must not underestimate them."

Stalin decided to rescue his man.

"I don't believe that Comrade Beria was dismissing them, Comrade General. Whilst your interpretation is sound, both of your views have merit. Now, let's continue."

Nazarbayeva, in line with her discussions with the NKVD Deputy, pushed harder.

"Comrade General Secretary, I view it as absolutely essential that we consider these new German divisions as a considerable threat and..."

"Enough!"

Everyone jumped at the punched words.

"Enough."

Although he spoke softer the second time, the Soviet leader's eyes burned into the GRU General's head.

"Your views are noted, Comrade."

Stalin left no room for manoeuvre and invited Beria to continue.

Nazarbayeva looked around the room, seeking some sort of support and found none.

She stared at Zhukov, who was examining some paperwork with exaggerated intent.

Unable to help himself, the balding Marshal made eye contact with Nazarbayeva, who recognised a microsecond of resignation before he looked away again.

Beria finished and others took up the reins, offering their own facts and figures for the pot.

And so it went on, until a loud rapping brought every sound to an end.

Stalin, momentarily staring in disgust at his broken pipe, discarded it without another thought and gently rubbed the table where he had struck it repeatedly, and with a little too much strength.

"Enough. We can continue to guess at Capitalist intents until the snows come again. Let us focus on what we intend to do to them. Comrade Marshals, outline Operation Uragan."

Zhukov, Konev and Novikov came together in front of a concealed map. The commanders of the 1st Baltic and 1st Red Banner, Bagramyan and Malinovsky, moved to the left side, ready to provide specifics on their own forces' roles. Opposite them, Marshals Rokossovsky and Yeremenko were similarly ready to provide deeper insight into their operations.

When the cover was removed, Europe sprang into view, a Europe covered with arrows of different colours and thicknesses, all of which ran east to west.

Uragan had two main parts. The first was designed to sweep through Northern Europe, splitting the Allied armies away from the coast and their main capacity to reinforce and resupply.

The second was in Central Europe, and was designed to pull in as much of the Allied army as possible, defeating it closer to hand, rather than extending their own tenuous lines of supply even further,

Zhukov outlined the major offensive that would break the Allied forces in a war of attrition.

The basics were short and impressive, but before he went further into the plan he ceded the floor to Bulganin.

In an address that was enthusiastically endorsed by both Beria and Molotov, Bulganin explained how a war of attrition could only inevitable end in Soviet victory, as heavy casualties and losses, supported by political agitation in the home countries of their enemies, would break the political will of the notoriously fickle administrations in the so-called democracies. By destroying any public support for the continuation of a war that would, by the time the agitators had done their job, be seen as trying to rescue the former Nazi Germany from paying its rightful dues, the discontinuation of hostilities would be inevitable, especially if the Soviet Union confirmed no threat to the British Empire, the United States or any nation of significance that could stand in the way of a ceasefire.

Then, once peace had settled across Europe, other ways would be found to develop the Communist dream.

As political plans went, it was simple and achievable, and depended on nothing more than the Red Army's capacity to inflict heavy casualties upon the Allies and, as only a worrying few thought, the Red Army's capacity to absorb further huge punishment.

Novikov was enthusiastic over the role of the Air Force, and how a concentration of available assets over the spearhead formations would give the ground troops a protective umbrella under which to work.

Weather would be good for low-level operations across Europe for the foreseeable future of the attack, the forecasters predicting a summer as warm and dry as the previous winter had been cold and wet.

The briefing went on, with impressive lists of air and ground forces committed.

By the time the meeting concluded, minds were reeling with the amount of information, and most were also buoyed by the thought that victory was still achievable.

And they now had a time and date to work to, the moment when the Red Army would roll forward in earnest once more.

0800 hrs, Thursday, 28th March 1946.

2200 hrs, Tuesday, 19th March 1946, Old Town Square, Torun, Poland.

Feeling very much invigorated by the last glass of vodka, Lieutenant Colonel Wyachaski of the 1st Polish Army spotted the statue of Copernicus, the landmark he relied on to find the nondescript cellar, especially when he had consumed slightly more than his limit.

A small sign was the only indication that anything of value was to found at the bottom of some steps.

'Greim's'

Descending the stairs immediately opposite the modest statue, Wyachaski was greeted with by a warm and inviting atmosphere, in which soft music and aromatic tobaccos played a pleasant part, but not as much as the lovely ladies who were prepared to share a drink and, occasionally, more with the right man.

After kissing the proprietress on both cheeks, he was ushered to his normal booth and a bottle of vodka arrived, all without words or gestures.

He poured himself a full glass and, pausing only to acknowledge the raised glass of a faintly familiar Artillery Colonel across the room, he poured the fiery liquid down his throat in one easy movement.

Taking in his surroundings with the apparent effort of a man already closely acquainted with the contents of a bottle, Wyachaski used all his field craft to discover what was behind the warning that the owner had given him.

There it was, no field craft needed, the open presence of two GRU officers causing his heart to skip momentarily.

Both men seemed more interested in the cellar's occupants than the drinks in front of them, and alarm bells began to ring in the intelligence officer's ear.

He picked up his hat, flicking carefully at some imaginary piece of dust in the studied manner of a man under the influence, before placing it back on the table.

Only an experienced field agent would have realised that the badge now faced towards the steps, rather than towards the hat's owner.

Karin Greim, eponymous owner of the establishment, noted the signal meant to caution the arriving contact and ensure she would steer him away from Wyachaski as soon as he arrived.

She now played her own part and whispered to her trusted business partner, Luistikaite.

Renata Gabriele Luistikaite passed herself off as a Lithuanian national, although she had been brought up in England since the age of three. A five foot ten inch svelte blonde, men were drawn to her obvious charms like moths to a candle, something that had proved useful in the past year since the two women had escaped detection by the NKVD and GRU agents set to find them. Luistikaite had been a very fortunate survivor of the ill-fated Operation Freston insertions, but now formed a solid team with Greim.

Karin Greim was Polish by birth, and her recruitment into the Abwehr had come about when her Uncle and both her brothers were confirmed as victims to the Soviet slaughter in the Katyn Woods. Hidden beneath her obvious charms was the cold heart of a killer who would like nothing more than to wipe out the entire

Soviet nation with whatever weapon came to hand, and she was skilled with most.

Luistikaite held an honorary commission in the Women's Auxiliary Air Force, whereas, although without any rank per se, Greim, a consummate spy, was universally known as the Captain.

Not that anyone there really looked upon them as anything more than very attractive women.

Renata grabbed a bottle of their finest vodka and glided across the room, grabbing the undivided attention of the two GRU officers as she moved. Grabbing the attention of the majority of men and women in the room would be truer, such was her presence.

Greim used the moment to run her hand over the 9mm Viz35 pistol that was concealed in a shaped recess under the bar top.

Comforted, she continued to wipe glasses as she watched the GRU officers.

The two men rose, inviting Renata to sit, which in itself was reassuring that they were there for pleasure, rather than business. The trio were joined by 'Greim's' youngest employee, and the four of them became engrossed in themselves.

Whilst many eyes were on Luistikaite's backless red dress and the legs that trailed invitingly out from supersize slits, two pairs were totally focussed on her actions. More specifically, they waited to see the colour of the cigarette holder she extracted from her evening bag.

'White'.

Wyachaski and Greim relaxed imperceptibly, deliberately avoiding any eye contact.

Carelessly, the Polish Intelligence officer knocked his vodka, spilling it across the table.

Cursing, he stepped back to avoid the small flow of liquid, grabbing his hat to save it any indignity.

Greim hurried over and wiped the table down, replacing the glass with a clean one.

The moment passed and Wyachaski settled himself back down to enjoy another drink, his polished silver hat badge reflecting some candlelight into his eyes.

An occasional glance at Renata and the teenager revealed a relaxed group, and the absence of any warning indicators spread that relaxation further.

Clearly there was a downpour outside, as the Polish officer who tumbled in deposited water everywhere he moved.

"Podpulkownik, how lovely to see you again."

Greim took the new arrival's sodden overcoat from him and pointed to where the Signals Officer should sit.

The other occupant of the comfy booth rose and extended his hand.

"Wyachaski. You are well?"

"Zajac, and no, I'm fucking soaked."

Exchange complete, the two relaxed into the comfy seating and enjoyed a quiet drink.

Zajac noticed the two GRU officers and silently interrogated his contact, receiving no sign of alarm in response.

Leaning forward, Zajac produced a cigarette packet and offered it to Wyachaski.

It contained only one.

Indicating that his colleague should take it, Zajac produced another packet and extracted one for himself.

The two men settled into quiet conversation about the forthcoming military exercises being run by 2nd Polish Army.

Greim busied herself with providing another bottle of vodka and then cleared the table of its rubbish.

Back at the bar, the cigarette packet went into the bin as if it was nothing of importance; it would keep for later.

Wyachaski had waited to drop his bombshell.

"My friend, it's no exercise."

Zajac choked so hard that many faces swivelled to watch his impending demise.

The GRU officers were quickly distracted by Renata's joke about the 'lightweight' drinking capacity of army officers, and returned to their ogling and flirting.

"No exercise?"

Pouring another drink, Wyachaski laughed loudly and slapped his comrade on the shoulder.

He drew close to Zajac's ear and whispered.

"The Russians are planning an attack and gearing Świerczewski's 2nd up for a small part. 1st isn't trusted."

Zajac nodded openly, as if in receipt of a personal secret of great import, which he was.

He slapped Wyachaski's shoulder and, in turn, laughed.

"There's more."

"I'm sure there is."

He poured another drink for the both and raised his glass in a toast.

"To the end of the war."

Wyachaski could only share the sentiment.

"To the end of the war."

Something in the intelligence officer's tone gave Zajac a moment's pause and he guessed what was about to be passed on.

'The date...it's been decided... at last!'

"Go on..."

"I have a verbal message for you to take back to Zygmunt."

Zygmunt Berling was the commander of the Polish 1st Army.

"Go on."

"Pantomime twenty-six."

The monumental importance of this message was not wasted on the signals officer, but he said nothing, controlling his excitement.

Wyachaski continued.

"On the 25th, BBC Radio for Occupied Europe will do the normal messages after the Nine o'clock news... the anthems of all occupied states are played at the end of that, yes?"

He received a nod of understanding.

"Normally our anthem is played by an orchestra. Confirmation will be our anthem sung by a male voice choir. Cancellation if a women's choir, clear?"

"Clear."

There was little more to be said.

The two shared another drink, paid their dues, and went their separate ways.

Zajac, the officer who had travelled to Versailles to speak with Eisenhower, returned to his staff car, whose driver waited irritably and ushered him in swiftly, closing the door with a flourish.

The vehicle sped off to the temporary site that had been selected for the upcoming exercise.

'Not an exercise', he reminded himself.

He could not sleep, and his mind simply chewed over everything he knew until the vehicle pulled up outside the barracks in Chermice.

The last of the clientele left and the teenager locked up before going about the nightly business of cleaning the floor, supported by the other girls, each with their own task.

The GRU officers had been the last to leave, keen to prolong the evening, but a firm approach from all concerned managed to persuade them to leave, but not before promises for further evenings had been asked for and made.

Renata and Karen did their normal cashing up, which required them to lock the office door for security purposes.

The cigarette packet lay to one side, as they moved into the cashing up. It was always agreed that no messages would be processed until they had done at least half the proper work.

As they counted and made notes, the tension mounted.

A major question had been asked of their network, one they had consistently failed to answer.

The Polish-Soviet forces planned to move to one of a number of hidden locations in time of war.

The upcoming exercises would, apparently, use the intended headquarters site, to ensure that it was up and ready in the event of a real situation arising.

Despite discovering the five locations that had been set aside by the Red Army, even to the extent of building huts and concrete structures in areas they had no intention of using, the spy network, and therefore their masters in Allied Europe, were none the wiser

Until now.

Greim set aside her notepad as Renata double-checked the door.

The well-thumbed copy of Alexander Wat's '*Bezrobotny Lucyfer*' appeared from its place in the small bookshelf.

Handing the book across to her boss, Luistikaite fitted a cigarette into her holder and drew deeply.

Using page, line, and word numbers, Greim quickly deciphered the eight letter message.

Showing the product of her efforts to Renata, the thin piece of paper was crumpled and dropped into the ashtray, where a match sent it into oblivion.

Greim finished up the cashing process as Luistikaite composed her own message, after which they said their 'good nights'.

Luistikaite arrived home at Flat 3, 2 Franciskánska, pausing only to thank the Peruvian diplomat at Flat 1 for feeding her cat yet again. She passed him a few zlotys to pay for the food and went away to her bed, determined to enjoy two days off work, and now happy that the vital information would find its way to the Peruvian Consulate on Ulica Wschodnia, and from there onto the Allied spymasters. Soon they would know the location of the joint battle headquarters of the Soviet command and 2nd Polish Army forces.

Cierpice.

2200 hrs, Friday, 22nd March 1946, 15th Transportstaffel, Avno Airbase, Denmark.

The tired Colonel was just about ready to turn in when the knock on the door presaged a huge change in his immediate plans.

The Oberstleutnant, the Luftwaffe base commander entered, stepping to one side in deference to the man behind him.

"Herr General."

Confused but calm, he saluted the new arrival, despite the man's lack of uniform.

"This is most unexpected, Herr General. Please, may I offer you coffee?"

He nodded at the base commander, his eyes seeking information with which to work out the events ahead.

None was forthcoming.

Finishing his telephone call, he responded to the General's small talk until the coffee had arrived and the orderly had departed.

Gehlen leant forward and deposited a folder in front of him.

"Cierpice, Standartenfuh... apologies, Herr Oberst."

Skorzeny was still getting used to the idea himself.

"Cierpice."

It was just a word... a statement.

"Could have been worse, of course, but Cierpice will do."

Skorzeny unlocked his desk drawer and pulled out a number of folders, selected the one marked 'Four-Cierpice' and passed it to the head of Germany's Intelligence service.

The folder contained the operational plan that had been developed should the headquarters be located in Cierpice.

"I need to get my second in command in here, with your permission?"

A few minutes later Oberstleutnant Otto-Harald Mors entered the room, immaculate as ever, despite having been on duty all day.

"It's Cierpice, Harald."

The base commander was an ex-Fallschirmjager condemned to ride a desk after suffering horrendous wounds during the battle against the Essex Regiment on Crucifix Hill, Monte Casino. He was in charge of the JU-52 transports allocated to the task of supporting Skorzeny's Storch Battalion, so named for the aircraft that had flown him to fame after Mussolini's rescue.

Cierpice meant an easier logistical problem for him and his men.

Gehlen asked the simple question.

"Can it be done, Oberst?"

"Well, it's no Gran Sasso, that's for sure. Much depends on our Polish Allies, of course."

"The elements are all available," he checked the list off on his fingers as he went, "We have good ground close by... friendly troops who can assist and cover... confirmation that the targets are on this location... good information available on the site... excellent aerial photographs..."

He looked at his second in command, the Fallschirmjager officer who had planned the Gran Sasso raid three years beforehand.

"Our major issue is, as always, fuel. Cierpice also has a particular issue in that the landing zone is shared with the pick-up zone... could cause problems. Anything to add, Otto?"

Mors shrugged his shoulders.

"As always, the unexpected could interfere with everything... but, now we know that four is the location, we can work on the plan even further... develop it... make sure we cover every eventuality... but, as the Oberst says, fuel... and much will depend on our Polish support."

Gehlen nodded his head in understanding and posed a question.

"Any problems with our Polish Allies? Your liaison officer is efficient?"

The two Storch Battalion officers laughed out loud, taking Gehlen by surprise.

"Apologies, Herr General. Maior Romaniuk is, to all intents and purposes, a complete lunatic... a fanatic...," Mors grinned from ear to ear as Skorzeny's accurate description flowed into Gehlen's ears, causing obvious concern, "And to be frank, he worries all of us."

Gehlen couldn't help himself.

"So you need a replacement immediately, I can get..."

Skorzeny held up his hands, stopping the head of German Intelligence in his tracks.

"Oh no, Herr General. Not at all. Romaniuk may be mad, but he's the most complete and efficient officer I've ever met. He hates us Germans with a passion, but he hates the Russian more. Everything he does, he does totally and fully... no lack of commitment... yes, he's a mad dog, but I can tell you now...he knows his job to the smallest detail and... as some are want to say...," Skorzeny ceded the punchline to his second in command.

Mors laughed as he repeated the much spoken phrase.

"The men would follow him into hell, if only to see him kick the Devil's ass!"

Before Gehlen could comment further, a knock on the door broke the moment.

"Come in!"

Skorzeny suspected he knew who would open the door before the face of his Operations Officer came into view, followed by the excited visage of the recently discussed Polish Paratroop Major.

Both men saluted their commander, and then, after Skorzeny's introduction, saluted the civilian, who suddenly became all-important.

Skorzeny slid the folder over to Mors, who passed on the good news.

Von Berlepsch and Romaniuk immediately searched their memories, discarding all the planning for the other sites and focussing on the Cierpice assault.

It was Romaniuk that commented first.

"So, much depends on my countrymen then, Pulkownik."

As Gehlen boarded the Bristol Buckingham transport, he felt confident that Skorzeny would pull of the operation.

Like most of the Allied officers in the know, he would have preferred to visit Cierpice with a squadron of heavy bombers, but the niceties of their new relationship with the Polish Army meant that they had to accede to their request to avoid unnecessary bloodshed.

Which provided the glory-hungry Skorzeny with the ideal opportunity to employ his highly trained Storch Battalion in an attempt to capture, without shedding blood, the entire staff of the Polish 2nd Army.

303

The intention for the associated Soviet command personnel was somewhat less benevolent.

2258 hrs, Saturday, 23rd March 1946, Task Force X-3, the North Sea.

The Captain examined the approaching aircraft with a professional interest, actually, more than partially to satisfy himself that they were friendly and not about to slip a torpedo into him or his charges.

His binoculars moved across the vessels that were his responsibility; eight were placed under his protection. Eight transports, loaded to the gunwales with men and materiel, assigned to him for safe delivery to a beach in the Baltic.

Commander Hamilton Ffoulkes shot a quick look back at the flight of Seafires that was presently undertaking the combat air patrol over his group and W-5, a larger convoy of mainly ammunition and supplies sailing some six miles further east.

HMS Charity had been to the Baltic once before, during the operations designed to destroy Soviet air power in the area, so Ffoulkes was free of any illusions about what might lie ahead.

'Lots of ships, not a lot of sea room,' was a thought shared by most of the naval personnel who headed for the passages through the Skaggerak, Kattegat, and Øresund that would take the armada to its point of delivery... on the north shore of Poland.

Somewhere ahead, on the island of Saltholm, an exhausted Soviet observation party surrendered without a fight, as British Royal Marine commandoes surrounded their hiding place.

Acting under rigid orders, the silent Brits executed their prisoners, and any trace of a Soviet existence on the island was removed.

As the Marines went about their grisly work, dark shapes moved unobserved through the silent waters between Denmark and Sweden, German and British minesweepers preparing the way for the larger vessels to come.

0009 hrs, Sunday, 24th March 1946, Red Army Senior Officers Dacha, Moscow, USSR.

Zhukov was shaken awake, itself an act that implied the utmost urgency.

"Blyad! A moment, man. For the motherland's sake, give me a moment!"

The light was on, burning into sleep-heavy eyes, but he could still see the telephone being held out for his use.

"Apologies, Comrade Marshal, but Comrade Marshal Beria said it was an emergency."

The name helped to bring Zhukov more into the land of the living, and he snatched the phone from the Staff Major, indicating his expectation for some tea.

"Comrade Marshal, I hope this is not an exercise."

"Marshal Zhukov, I have just received reliable intelligence that tells me that the Allies will not be landing in the Baltic States, or Norway, but that they will invade Poland in the near future; a seaborne landing on the north shore. The General Secretary felt that you should be appraised immediately."

Zhukov swung his feet out of bed, the cold floor now the least of his problems.

"Reliable, totally reliable, Comrade Marshal?"

"Yes. Comrade Stalin has convened a meeting of the GKO for 0200hrs."

"I understand. Now, I have work to do. I will see you later, Comrade Marshal."

Zhukov exchanged the handset for the hot tea that the Major returned with.

"Wake up the staff. Send alert warnings to the Front commanders in the Baltic, Norway, and Northern Germany, warning of possible enemy activity, including the definite possibility of seaborne assault."

He had quickly decided to over-mobilise, rather than leave some areas unnotified and risk a disaster, especially if Allied maskirovka was at work.

0022 hrs, Sunday, 24th March 1946, GRU Commander's office, Western Europe Headquarters, the Mühlberg, Germany.

Across Europe, Soviet senior officers were being rudely awoken, and Nazarbayeva was not spared, as the overnight duty officer, Major Repin, woke her.

"What is it, Comrade," sounding more awake than she felt.

"Comrade General, warning orders have gone out to North Germany, the Baltic States, Norway, and Poland, anticipating an allied seaborne invasion. Fronts have been alerted to make their dispositions accordingly."

Now she was awake, and leapt from the bed in just her shirt and the light trousers she had taken to wearing when sleeping in her office.

"Get the staff awake and in the headquarters immediately. I want this looked at... get them to go through everything for the Baltic and North Cape again... everything..."

Nazarbayeva turned away, expecting immediate compliance with her orders, but turned back as Repin stood his ground.

"Comrade General, before that I received another call from Moscow. The caller told me to tell you to concentrate on Poland, and that he anticipated the landing within the week."

Repin was an NKVD agent, initially placed in the GRU to report back, which now was known to her. She had accepted Ilya Borissovich's request to keep him in place as a means of easy communication, and it actually wasn't that difficult to come to terms with as he was efficient in everything he did.

NKVD Major General Ilya Kuznetsov had sent her a message, giving her time to act and save her reputation, for as sure as night follows day, heads would roll if the Allies invaded without a hint of a warning from the agencies of the USSR.

"Thank you, Comrade Mayor. Now, get them out of bed."

Already her mind was seeking information on Poland, recalling assets in place and any information collated already.

"We've missed something", she announced to the grim face in the mirror.

0903 hrs, Sunday, 24rd March 1946, Headquarters of 1st Guards Mechanised Rifle Division, Jatznick, Germany.

Colonel Lisov received the message with no little excitement, tinged with real anger that the training had not been available to refine the newly renamed 1st Guards Mechanised Rifle Division into the extreme war machine that it could become.

He walked smartly through to his commander's office and entered, the open door policy now set in stone as Deniken's management style developed.

"Comrade Polkovnik, we have new orders."

Lisov placed the document on the desk in front of Deniken, carefully avoiding the map he had been examining.

"Give me the rough details, Comrade."

Having been up until the small hours working up a battle drill with Yarishlov, Deniken had not long been out of bed and was stood shaving at a stand in the corner.

"We are to entrain, commencing at 2100 hrs tomorrow night, using the loading facility at Torgelow. Command will provide us with sufficient trains and flatcars to transport the entire division to... and I quote... a location close to the enemy."

Deniken started.

"Say what?"

"That's what it says, Comrade."

"They're not telling us where we're going? What sort of fucking piggery is that? How can I plan with that sort of decision?"

"I'm sure they have their reasons, Comrade."

Deniken waved his razor to emphasise his point.

"Personally, I become less sure each time we get one of these orders, and sometimes I wonder who makes the bastard things up."

At the moment, 1st Guards Mechanised Rifle Division was withdrawn from 16th Guards Rifle Corps and placed under the command of STAVKA and, apparently, also within the jurisdiction of the headquarters of Red Banner Forces of Soviet Europe.

On more than one occasion, the problems associated with that dual command had surfaced to challenge the staff officers of the division.

1230 hrs, Monday, 25th March 1946, OSS safe house, Thompson's Farm, Doddinghurst Road, Shenfield, UK.

Lunch was a simple affair, but tasty. Moreover, the prisoner appreciated that, for a change, the soup was hot and the bread was fresh.

The real prize had been a glass of milk, which was a first in his present surroundings. The new gaoler who gave it to him insisted that it was now part of his feeding routine, so perhaps his treatment would improve even further.

Not that it had been bad since he had been taken, all those weeks ago.

Stretching after his satisfying lunch, he gazed out of his window, the view still impressive despite the iron bars that made his room a cell.

He smiled as a middle-aged couple drove down the nearby track in the battered old Morris in which they did whatever they did, regular as clockwork every week. The car ground through the mud and slush, turning off into the woods for some moments of intimacy. He had seen them many times before, and often mused on their 'romance'.

However, today he felt tired and decided that his bed would receive a visit ahead of schedule.

Leonard Brown had waited patiently until the prisoner was snoring gently.

Slipping into the room, he left everything just as it was, except the empty glass, which he removed and wrapped in a cloth.

Downstairs, he quickly washed the glass, removing all traces of the barbiturate that had been contained in the milk, and placed it back with its five companions, careful not to step on the body of the actual gaoler.

For skilled hands, it had been the work of a moment to break the young man's neck as he turned to answer the phone.

As he had lowered the body down, he congratulated himself on the masterful piece of distraction and timing.

Now he needed to act quickly, in order to discharge his instructions.

Rearranging the corpse to give a passable imitation of someone who had fallen accidentally, he grabbed the paraffin stove and laid it down, working dead fingers around the carrying handle to complete the 'story' he hoped would be swallowed by those who came later.

The reservoir in the heater would normally hold about a third of a gallon, but Brown decided not to stint on the accelerant, so poured the entire amount around the heater, through the kitchen, and to the bottom of the stairs.

The fumes were overpowering and he felt light-headed almost immediately.

Quickly moving to the back door. Brown took a few deep breaths of good cold air before moving back into the kitchen and igniting the candle on the kitchen table.

He pushed the metal holder off and moved away as fast as he could, the satisfying whoof of an instant fire speeding him into fresh air.

Brown did not dally, and was cycling away long before the flames gained the first floor.

"I'm cumming, babe!"

The two lovers moaned through their orgasms, she with her arms wrapped around the driver's seat in front, he with his arms wrapped around her.

As her senses recovered, quicker than her still moaning man, the woman became aware of something out of the ordinary.

"What's that?"

He, suddenly alert, for fear of discovery, listened intently, whereas his lover was sniffing the air.

"There's summat on fire somewhere. I can smell it."

He could too.

Both rearranged their clothes to mask their recent activity, and he drove the car out of the wood.

The source of the smell was immediately apparent.

"Fucking hell! It's the farmhouse!"

Thompson's Farm was a sea of yellow and orange, and all the firemen in the world could not have saved the building.

As the couple drove back down the track to the main road, it was consumed before their eyes.

By the time the Fire Brigade arrived, the roof had already collapsed into the first floor.

A cyclist came up, dismounted, and stood with the couple. The three shared cigarettes as they watched firemen extinguish the blaze and take out what could only be bodies, the two covered shapes dealt with in a manner of respect by the crews.

The Essex Constabulary were also there, so before they could take start taking statements from anyone who might have seen the fire, the three decided, each for their own reasons, to make themselves scarce.

Leonard Brown slipped off his cycle clips and fluffed his trouser bottoms back into shape.

Abandoning the bike in an alley next to Shenfield Railway station, he slipped behind the wheel of his Hillman Minx saloon and set out to leave a chalk mark on an entranceway to Southwark Cathedral, which would signal success to his controller.

In turn, the controller would report back to his NKVD master, confirming that the kill order had been obeyed.

The message would then end up in front of Marshal Beria, part-author of the kill order, who would, when circumstances permitted, confirm to the other part-author that his instructions had been carried out to the letter.

Stalin, when told, grunted in satisfaction that the risk of blackmail against the GRU General Tatiana Nazarbayeva had been removed.

He spared no further thought for her son, Captain-Lieutenant Ilya Yurievich Nazarbayev, murdered on his order.

The NKVD boss, wallowing in his continuing revenge upon Nazarbayeva, did not communicate to her the news of the death of her child, understanding that to do so would undoubtedly reveal his part in the young man's death.

Instead, he said nothing, and no-one else was privy.

A silence that was to cost the Red Navy dearly in the weeks to come.

It was a simple matter of codes, and of Glenlara.

In the London headquarters of OSS, the news from Essex was badly received, despite the first reports suggesting that it was nothing more than a horrible accident.

The Achilles/Thetis file was as dead as the man it detailed, and it was set aside, pending the report on the fire and any other final inclusions.

1602 hrs, Monday, 25th March 1946, Temporary Headquarters, Camerone Division, Schleiden, Germany.

De Walle had personally handed Knocke the unpalatable report from Gehlen's intelligence service the previous evening.

Orders were issued, bringing one of the five men to the divisional headquarters for 1600 hrs on the 25th.

Ulrich Weiss had been known to them, and had been closely watched from the time he had been detected.

Weiss came to attention in front of Knocke's desk and saluted.

"Standartenfuhrer, reporting as ordered."

Knocke looked up from his position and his eyes burned straight through the Soviet agent. Weiss immediately knew that he was lost.

"Personally, you disgust me, Weiss. If it were down to me I'd have you shot immediately. But... others seem to think that you can be of use to us, rather than being placed in front of a firing squad."

For a second, the desperate man thought about the pistol at his side, for either assassinating Knocke, or shooting his way out of the building, or both.

The realist in him understood he would no more than twitch before he would be dead, shot down by one of the officers behind him.

He was not mistaken.

His arrest was swift and silent, and he was taken away to see if he could contribute positively to the Allied war effort before paying his dues to both comrades and country.

Wilhelm Baumer, a sergent-chef in Camerone's supply unit, was caught trying to leave his post, some sixth sense telling him that his time was up.

Otto Hirsch, a new arrival from Sassy assigned to the Stug Kompagnie, resisted arrest and was shot down without compunction.

In the Legion hospital, Capitan Dr Gottfried Pfeffer protested his innocence, but was taken away all the same.

De Walle, ill at ease at the last of Gehlen's discoveries, personally arrested Commandant Guy Parras at the headquarters of Camerone's artillery regiment, removing the highest placed of Gehlen's detections, and a man who De Walle felt was a personal embarrassment and a stain on the honour of the Legion.

Parras' discovery had, by Gehlen's own admission, been a very lucky break; a Frenchman netted in a sweep of German personnel.

Elsewhere in the Legion Corps, others, whose dubious behaviour and associations had brought them to the attention of Gehlen's service, were closely monitored.

1722 hrs, Monday, 25th March 1946, GRU Western Europe Headquarters, the Mühlberg, Germany.

'Pantomime 26?'

Lieutenant Pinkerova read the low-level report from a member of the Peruvian Consulate regarding a recent communication made by one of the senior staff. Using his access to the diplomatic bag, the agent had examined the letter and recorded its contents.

The report had been clerked into the GRU headquarters the previous evening, so was already twenty hours old.

Taking the report, she made the short journey to Poboshkin's office, via the filing desk where she asked for and received the file on 'Pantomime'. On arrival, she placed both in front of Lieutenant Colonel Poboshkin.

After a short explanation, Poboshkin opened the file and started to sift through its contents.

Previously, GRU and NKVD had discovered the scent of something called Pantomime, but the specific operation was unknown to them; despite the considerable amount of paperwork the file contained, there were no facts and precious little but whispers and innuendo to go on. It was a very unsatisfactory file in so many respects, except for three entries which, in the light of recent events, caught Poboshkin's eye immediately.

Poboshkin started, the jerky movement pronounced enough to make Pinkerova recoil automatically.

He screwed his eyes up and re-read the different sheets, laying each out side by side.

"What do you see, Comrade Leytenant?"

Pinkerova was considered bright by those who worked with her, and Poboshkin was just using her brain to confirm his own thinking.

Her eyes flitted back and forth, taking in the minutiae, discarding some things, filing others, until she had her moment of realisation.

"Poland."

"Yes... obviously," he said with some humour.

"This one is from a naval source, isn't it?"

"Yes, Comrade."

"The dates... these reports all come from the last two weeks... significant I think, Comrade PodPolkovnik."

"I agree."

She frowned.

"It's not that simple, is it? The 26th... Poland?"

The knock on the door broke their concentration.

A young clerk nervously entered, bearing a message sheet.

"Comrade PodPolkovnik, I wanted to file this new message, but I'm told you're holding the Pantomime file? Perhaps you wish to see it now?"

"Thank you, Comrade Serzhant. From what source?"

The girl explained that the report originated from one of the members of the GRU openly placed within the 1st Polish Army.

The man, a sergeant in the Army motor pool, had overheard a conversation between two unknown Polish senior officers.

312

Hidden beneath the car he was working on, the two had been oblivious to his presence, speaking in soft whispers that had barely carried to him.

The Sergeant was careful to say what he heard and what he might have heard, but he was certain about the words that stood out in his report.

He felt the hair on his neck stand on end.

Leytenant Pinkerova, sharing the document, experienced the same sensation.

There is was, in black and white, the same phrase.

'Pantomime 26.'

"That's it then. They're coming tomorrow! Thank you Comrade Serzhant. Leytenant, find Comrade General Nazarbayeva and brief her. Tell her I'm informing Army command and I'll bring the file as soon as possible. Quickly now, there's not a moment to lose."

The office emptied rapidly, leaving Poboshkin holding the phone.

"Get me Marshal Konev immediately."

1735 hrs, Monday, 25th March 1946, GRU Commander's office, Western Europe Headquarters, the Mühlberg, Germany.

"That's precisely what my aide passed on to Marshal Konev, Comrade Marshal."

Nazarbayeva listened as Zhukov shouted at his staff, the sudden burst of sound causing her to recoil from the handset.

As she waited for the flow of orders to halt, she beckoned Poboshkin closer.

"Get this copied immediately and get yourself on a plane to Moscow. I'll sort that immediately. I want the GKO to see the raw data... Yes, Comrade Marshal, I'm still here."

She listened for a few moments and replaced the receiver, Zhukov ending the conversation without the normal pleasantries.

A very tired Repin stood waiting for instructions and quickly received some, as Nazarbayeva had been simultaneously composing a written order.

"Tell our mutual friend, then get a team over to this address and get the Peruvian shaken down quickly. Wring him for everything he knows... and get it done quickly. We've no time to lose."

Repin took the order and left as Nazarbayeva turned her attention back to her Aide.

"As quick as you can, Andrey. The Army is alerted but I think that STAVKA will need more persuasion. Good luck, Comrade."

She pressed the phone to her ear once more and hit the exchange button.

"Commander, Nordhausen Airfield please."

1802 hrs, Monday 25th March 1946, office of the Chairman of the NKVD, Moscow, USSR.

Beria was spitting as his excitement and anger powered the rate of words as well as the volume.

"Where's the main document? Has it arrived yet?"

Danilov, Beria's personal secretary, shrugged his shoulders.

"According to that document," he pointed at Philby's covering report on Spectrum, "The item was dispatched on the normal BOAC Stockholm run. It should be here, but it isn't, Comrade Marshal."

Philby had been thorough and copied out the main points of the document and describing the deceptions therein, sending all in a sealed file, complete with film of every page, on the normal communications route.

Beria had taken delivery of Philby's warning that morning but, apart from alerting Senior NKVD commanders in the whole Baltic arena, not just Poland, had done nothing but seek out the main file details that had been sent by the BOAC route.

Whilst he suspected enemy maskirovka at work and, naturally wished to avoid any more embarrassment to his agency, warning his own forces was prudent, as well as deniable if the information was some sort of enemy ruse.

"Find that fucking document, now!"

Danilov departed at high speed, determined to find the missing information.

The phone rang behind him.

"Beria."

The NKVD Marshal's angry voice immediately took on a softer tone.

"Yes, Comrade General Secretary."

No-one was there to witness the foul look that covered his features.

"Has she now?"

314

He looked at Philby's preliminary report, almost taunting him, now that corroborative evidence seemed to have surfaced.

He took the plunge.

"Indeed, Comrade General Secretary. I'd just finished confirming that exact same piece of information. I've already placed NKVD units integrated with the Polish army on high alert and was about to call you and…"

Beria glanced at the large Tsarist mirror and sneered at his own reflection.

"I will be there, Comrade General Secretary, and I will bring my file on the matte…"

After Stalin's final words, Beria was left staring at a silent handset.

"A GRU briefing… a fucking GRU briefing is it?…"

He threw the receiver at the mirror, which flew away, dragging the master unit behind it.

Both clattered to the floor.

He shouted at the top of his voice.

"Danilov! Get me that fucking file!"

The file in question was presently on its way back to England on a BOAC Mosquito courier aircraft, where it would be picked up, at Per Tørget's insistence, by Sam Rossiter himself.

It would not take long for Tørget's reasons to become abundantly clear.

Nazarbayeva's phonecall from GRU West Headquarters sent a GRU team to the door of Flat 1, 2 Franciskánska, Torun, where men with little time for niceties had a deep and meaningful discussion with the male occupant.

Eleven minutes after their arrival, the Peruvian diplomat, dripping blood from a swift beating, started to write out remembered details from messages that he had been involved with passing. He had, after the blow that broke two ribs, surrendered his contact, which resulted in a swift telephone call to the GRU office requesting reinforcements.

She lifted the needle off the record, and the sounds of the Viennese waltz died away as the urgent knocking was repeated.

The door knocks of policemen are the same the world over, and Renata Luistikaite recognised the imperative sound for what it was.

The Walther in her purse was too far away, for she knew that impatient men would kick down the door in seconds.

Smiling, she tried to click open the largest charm on her bracelet, but the hollow piece of silver containing her 'pill' refused to budge and her smile changed to a look of near panic.

As the door gave way, she made a desperate lunge for the window.

GRU Senior Lieutenant Vestulin kicked the scantily clad body in frustration.

"You fucking bitch!"

The rest of the team were already turning over the flat, searching for something incriminating, although they all knew that with the simple act of trying to kill herself, Renata Luistikaite had shown herself for what she was. The problem was that she was no use dead.

He kicked her again, so hard that she rolled onto her back.

She moaned unexpectedly, the blood spilling from her neck where Vestulin's bullet had caught her in mid-run.

"Mudaks! Fyodor! She's ali... Blyad! Come and look at this bitch!"

His friend and colleague, a Junior Lieutenant, took one look at the revealed features and spoke the words that had formed in Vestulin's mind.

"Greim's... she's the sexy bitch from Greim's."

"Interrogation might be fun... if she makes it. Now, get an ambulance before she bleeds out."

Fifteen minutes later, the world was a different place for Vestulin.

His friend and two of his men were lying dead on the floor of Greims, whilst he tried to prioritise his wounds, choosing to stem the bleeding from his shattered forearm, rather than attempt to do anything with the knee that had been ravaged by the last bullet the woman had fired.

All four were victims to Karen Greim's skill with a handgun. The 9mm Viz35 lay next to the wounded woman, her blonde hair soaked with crimson blood where one of his bullets had clipped her scalp.

Her blouse had been ripped open by one of the GRU NCO's who was trying to stop the bleeding from her ruined shoulder and upper chest, exposing her soft flesh.

Despite the pain, Vestulin found himself admiring the form of the badly wounded spy.

Still conscious, Greim looked first at the man trying to save her life, and then at Vestulin.

He did not anticipate her laughter.

The sound died away, leaving only the smile and blood running slowly from the side of the mouth, a mouth that twisted into a sneer of hatred.

"Too late, you Russian bastard. You're too fucking late."

'So, you confirm it... it is today.'

Vestulin stared into the defiant eyes.

"Get me to a phone, now!"

2004 hrs, Sunday, 24rd March 1946, Rail bridgehead at Torgelow, Germany.

Deniken had briefed the assembled unit commanders in silence, save for the odd gasp that accompanied the order to move the other way to that expected, namely into Poland.

Fortunately, they had an abundance of suitable maps, acquired for future training exercises, and now they would prove invaluable in combat.

A few quick questions established that no one had any first-hand knowledge of the area, the division not having been near the area during the German war.

Now that the division might be advancing to close on enemy positions entailed a change in the logistics, and the leading echelon was changed to be more infantry heavy, in order to secure the railhead at Köslin.

There had also been another decision made, which Deniken now shared with the rest of his officer group.

"Here... at Naugard... there's a Polish fuel dump. I want it seized for our use, clear?"

317

Fuel was a thorny issue for every mechanised unit and, even though seemingly a favourite of those in command, the 1st GMRD was no different in having a low supply.

Nodding at one of his regimental commanders, Deniken outlined his plan.

"Comrade Antinin, I want one of your companies dropped off at Naugard. Secure the station and the surrounding area. I want to make sure we can get that fuel to Köslin."

Lieutenant Colonel Mikhail Antinin mentally assigned one of his units to the task and nodded his understanding.

"I want the rest of the 167th to get on the road now, but take only what can move fast and move now. The rest will take its place on the railway according to the shipping schedule. Seize that fuel dump... intact... and without violence."

They all knew that might prove to be difficult.

"Make our Polish Allies understand that it's needed by our vehicles as a matter of utmost urgency, Comrade."

His tone hardened perceptibly

"But we must have that fuel, regardless, so if they hinder you, you may act as you see fit to discharge my order."

Antinin was a no-nonsense officer who had survived the German War. He was also wise enough to know that Deniken had handed him a hot potato, but he accepted his commander's apologetic look with good grace.

Deniken returned to the major issue as he saw it.

"I don't like running across the front of a potential enemy position on a train, and that's a fact, but orders are orders and I hope we can get through to Köslin before any attack... and still under cover of night."

All agreed with that. Whilst the 1st Guards had only been lightly affected, stories of the maulings received by other units at the hands of Allied air power abounded and required no embellishment.

"Comrade Yarishlov, will you be able to get your tanks off whilst we still have darkness on our side?"

Yarishlov had already worked out the implications of distance, time, and the new order of movement.

"Comrade Deniken, my tanks and support vehicles are now more towards the end of the column, which means we may be running it tight. I've no idea what facilities there are at Köslin, but I'm prepared to drive my tanks straight off the trucks if it will get them in cover by daylight, and to hell with the railway timetable!"

Faces split with smiles, knowing full well that Yarishlov saw his tanks as the priority at all times.

318

"Right, Comrades. New order of march. Get your units sorted and get them moving onto the rolling stock immediately. If we can go sooner, then we'll do so. This whole thing stinks of panic, and I want to make sure we survive whatever's ahead. Good luck to you all, Comrades."

2201 hrs, Monday, 25th March 1946, 1002nd Mixed Air Regiment, Pütnitz-Damgarten airbase, Germany.

"Then get it fucking fixed, for the fuck's sake! It'll fly tonight or I'll shoot you myself."

Starshina Jurgen Helmutevich Förster was an ex-Luftwaffe volunteer serving with the Red Air Force.

Product of a German father, a Spartacist who fell in the strife of the early twenties, and a Russian mother, he was a life-long communist and had made himself available once he had been released from Swiss captivity.

His ME-110 had crashed in Switzerland in early 1941 and he had been interned, spending the bulk of the war kicking his heels whilst both his nations knocked hell out of each other on the Eastern Front.

At first, such volunteers were treated with scepticism, but the awful casualties inflicted on the Red Air Force gave 'the powers that be' an imperative they had not previously had, and so experienced flyers with 'acceptable' political credentials were integrated into the Soviet air regiments, mostly placed together under robust supervision, just in case. Most often, Luftwaffe volunteers were matched with captured aircraft, which was how Förster came to be assigned to fly a German night-fighter that night. He had been selected to convert to and master the He-219A7 'Uhu' night fighter, a late-war aircraft that had great potential but had been produced in too small a number to make a difference.

The other 219 and four of the unit's Bf-110g night-fighters were already on their way to the picquet line, part of the Red Air Force's attempts to make a decent challenge to the Allied bombers who owned the night skies.

Only, much to Förster's upset, his aircraft was going nowhere, as its starboard engine simply refused to turn over.

His first operational flight had brought three Allied aircraft under his guns, but he returned without a kill and counting himself lucky to have escaped the enemy night-fighters that swarmed over him in an instant.

319

He had promised himself that this time would be different.

But for now, there was no 'next time', and the crew decided to stretch their legs.

The aircrew climbed out of the Heinkel, eased their backs, then sat on the bench that the mechanics used when waiting to receive the aircraft after a mission. Förster sat in angry silence, smoking his pipe and stroking the tethered dog, a Dalmatian that was his pride and joy. Hans Braun, his radar operator, was sufficiently aware of his pilot's mood as to not indulge in the normal pre-mission small talk.

The senior mechanic was soon back with a face that betrayed the stupidity of it all.

"Comrade Starshina, we have located the issue. A disconnected wire on the starter circuit. I am sorry."

Whilst they were the same rank, the ground crew NCO knew he was decidedly in the shit for this omission, and much would depend on how the pilot handled matters from now on.

Förster was calmer now.

"That's not acceptable, Iosef, and you know it. I hope you chew the useless bastard out who fucked up."

Horolov nodded, although he would need no encouragement.

"You write this up as you see fit... I'll just report the event, not the cause. But, I want the connections checked... all connections... and I want your assurance on that before I take-off. Understood, Comrade?"

Förster was actually being more than fair, and Horolov accepted immediately, turning and shouting at his ground crew, determined to harangue them into a good job, and beyond that point, until he discovered which bastard had let him down.

At 2253 hrs, nearly an hour behind schedule, Förster's Uhu disappeared into the black sky, seen off by a relieved and angry Starshina Horolov, who then turned on the hapless Corporal who had been responsible for the simple error.

By the time he was finished, the newly created Private felt himself lucky to be alive, all despite having, unwittingly, done his Motherland a huge service.

I have learned to hate all traitors, and there is no disease that I spit on more than treachery.

Aeschylus

[Author's note. Of necessity, this chapter deals with one specific set of events, and is out of synchronisation with those chapters that have gone before. My apologies.]

Chapter 138 – THE REVELATION

After escaping the loss of Hamburg, Krystal Uhlmann-Schalburg, sister to Uhlmann of the Legion, had continued her work with British Intelligence.

After some combined work on a project with other secretive agencies, the sister of one of the Legion's best German officers was spotted and headhunted by SOE.

In December 1945, Krystal became a fully-fledged WAAF sergeant, a uniformed cover for her membership of the Special Operations Executive.

She moved quickly through the various courses and disciplines, on her way to becoming a field agent.

1002 hrs, Friday, 22nd March, The Thatched Barn, Borehamwood, England.

The building had started life as a den of iniquity, where the famous could meet the opposite sex and have a sense of security, away from the prying eyes of press and public.

The venture had not lasted long, and ownership passed to Billy Butlin, who intended it to be his first hotel.

However, the German War, in the shape of SOE, transformed it once again, this time into Station XV, the section dealing with such diverse matters as camouflage, codes, clothing, booby-traps, and bombs.

Krystal Uhlmann-Schalburg, now known as Christine Mann, arrived with three other female agents, mainly to be fitted out with suitable attire for their upcoming missions, as well as to become acquainted with some of the devices and secret equipment produced at 'The Barn'.

Normally, a group of four girls, pretty ones too, would have meant that they had the undivided attention of the Station chief, James Elder Wills.

But not today.

Their visit coincided with SOE's latest attempts to calm the ruffled feathers of MI6, which organisation often viewed the other with a distrust bordering on hatred.

A visit had been organised, so that a senior member of MI6 could do the rounds of various SOE establishments and develop a greater understanding of how the organisation worked and, more importantly to SOE's leader, Sir Colin Gubbins, appreciate that it was not a threat and could be an important ally organisation in the fight against communism.

His opposite number in MI6, Sir Stewart Menzies, was also army, and the two found a cordial solution as to which one of Menzies' men would receive the red carpet treatment.

The man selected was actually a former member of SOE, serving as a propaganda expert at the Beaulieu station, which made him eminently acceptable to Gubbins. His commitment to MI6 and diligence made him acceptable to Menzies.

J. Elder Wills greeted the important visitor personally, renewing a passing acquaintance from the other's short period in SOE.

"Good morning, Harold, So nice to see you again."

They shook hands and moved quickly inside out of the rain and wind.

"Good morning, James. Nice to see you again too. Please, do call me Kim."

After a warming cup of tea and the exchange of a few memories, Wills took his guest on the grand tour.

Their mentor, known only as Jasper, herded the girls out of the way, as word of the approach of the Station Chief reached his ears.

"Come on, my lovelies. We don't want to get under the Director's feet, today of all days.

Wills was known as the director because of his work as a film art director and his excellent movie connections, connections that he had exploited to attract over half the men who worked at the Barn, using their stage art skills to good effect for the war effort.

Lucinda, the plainest of the group, exercised her female curiosity.

"Why not today of all days, Jasper?"

"Top dog from another organisation has come to nose around. Can't have him exposed to you horrible lot, can we? What would he think of us if he saw you raggedy bunch, eh?"

Jasper received four playful taps from the girls, but they moved away all the same, but not fast enough to avoid seeing the pair arrive to view the selection of hollow false tree trunk storage containers.

Jasper quickly leant around Christine, pushing the door shut.

"Come on now, girl. Quit gawking and let's get down to the canteen for an early lunch."

Lunch was a humorous and noisy affair, so much so that the three women and one man laughing loudly and making the noise failed to notice that one of their number was not fully joining in.

She was racking her brain, trying to put a name to a face.

1945 hrs, Friday, 22nd March 1946, SOE Headquarters, 64 Baker Street, London, England.

Christine Mann stepped into the office in response to the gruff invitation.

"Ah, Sergeant Mann, isn't it? Do sit down now."

The occupant's hands appeared from behind a desk that, whilst unquestionably organized with military precision, was full to overflowing with paperwork, ushering her to a large chair that had undoubtedly seen better days.

"I hear you're doing rather well. A natural, so the gossip says, what?"

"Thank you, Sir."

"So, what brings you into my den at this unearthly hour?"

Gubbins stood dramatically.

"Where are my manners? My abject apologies, Sergeant Mann. May I offer you tea?" he gestured towards the fine bone china teapot.

"No, thank you, sir."

Topping up his own cup, the head of SOE returned to his seat, carefully sliding two sets of files to one side to permit him a better view of the woman in front of him.

"Fire away then, Sergeant."

"Sir, it may be nothing, but I think that it is quite important."

Sir Colin Gubbins occasionally pursed his lips, steepled his fingers, or sipped his tea, but generally remained silent as 'Christine Mann' went through the story of a chance encounter in Wandsbeck, Hamburg, during June 1945. She had been walking with one of the MI6 officers, prepared to act as interpreter for a clandestine meeting with a German 'businessman', when the Captain had spotted something strange going on between another member of MI6 and a known Soviet NKVD officer.

She described how the Intelligence Officer had quickly moved into the shadows, dragging her with him.

They had both observed an animated verbal exchange between the two, during which the Russian had appeared to take the lead, almost, as her British companion stated at the time, like a man giving orders to a subordinate.

The NKVD officer had the last word and left abruptly, leaving the other man to walk away, passing the place where Christine and her companion had hidden.

She emphasized to a curious Gubbins how she had had the clearest view of the man's face.

His curiosity grew when she identified the man as the same one she had seen in the 'Thatched Barn' during her recent visit there.

"And this was reported at the time, of course."

It wasn't a question.

"Captain Chivers did write a report. He didn't include me in it as my presence might have brought on some... err... awkward questions for him... it was not an official meeting we attended, you see."

"I understand fully, Sergeant. Who was the MI6 officer you saw today...err... and in Hamburg?"

"A man called Philby, Sir."

Alarm bells went off inside Gubbins' head.

"Please, do go on."

"Captain Chivers died two days later."

Gubbins' eyes narrowed.

"Who was the NKVD officer?"

"I can't remember the name I'm afraid, but Herbert, sorry, Captain Chivers, was very agitated and he recognized him immediately."

Gubbins left it at that for now.

"Please continue."

"Pleske, the businessman, was never seen again, Sir."

"Obviously, the report would have named the NKVD man, but did the report name this Pleske, do you know?"

The head of SOE's interest had been greatly aroused.

"No, Sir, Chivers told me he'd just said something like a local Wandsbeck black-marketeer... but Pleske was not the only such 'businessman' to disappear at that time. In fact, the Military Police were running around for weeks afterwards, as bodies turned up all over Hamburg, all of them Wandsbeck men with a reputation as 'suppliers'."

Mann waited for a response from across the desk.

"So, let me see what it is that you think. Chivers' report was seen by someone, who then took steps to protect something of value, which would seem to be either the NKVD officer or Philby. Chivers and anyone who fitted the description of 'black-marketeer' was quietly done away with... how did Chivers die?"

"Fell under a Hamburg tram in front of a hundred witnesses, Sir."

"Fell."

"Yes, Sir."

"Fell?"

He knew she had something more to say on the matter.

"Chivers was extremely fit, very sure on his feet. I didn't think about it at the time... I was upset... he was a lovely man, married with three strong boys... but now, my mind wonders, Sir."

"Quite."

Gubbins checked the clock and found the result agreeable, moving quickly to the decanter and pouring two modest whiskies.

Mann accepted hers with the nod of her head.

"The thing is, if, let's just say if... if the NKVD were prepared to purge Wandsbeck of all the black-marketeers, that is no small matter, and would only be done to protect something extremely valuable.

"Yes, Sir."

"The NKVD officer possibly..."

"Chicky...Chacky..."

His brain analysed her attempts to summon the name and immediately married them to a name indelibly engraved on his own.

"Ivan?"

"Yes, Sir... Ivan Chicky..."

"Ivan Chichayev?"

"That's the name, Sir."

"Colonel Ivan Andreyevich Chichayev... also known as Vadim..."

He downed the whisky in one and stood, offering Mann his hand.

"You were absolutely right to bring this to me, Mann. Now, I must ask you not to speak of this again. I'll investigate this as a matter of urgency, and I will discuss what I find with you. But I think the very fact that you know these things places your life at risk."

Gubbins opened a small notebook, made a swift entry and ripped out the page.

"Gather a few things and go to that address now. When you get there, ask to see Mr Campbell Stuart. Use my name as you see fit. When you see him, tell him that I said 'cloche'. Clear, Sergeant?"

"Sir."

"Mr Stuart will look after you and keep you safe. You will respond to no instructions or orders that do not contain the code word... err... Herbert. Is that clear, Sergeant Mann?"

"Yes, Sir."

Closing the door as quickly as he could, Gubbins strode purposefully to his desk.

The phone was instantly in his hands.

"Ah, Turner, get me the director of MI6 please."

Sir Stewart was not in his office and the duty officer was not prepared to divulge the present location of his boss to someone who not might be what he said he was.

Gubbins dialled a number from memory.

"The Guards Club. Good evening, how may I be of assistance?"

"Good evening, Squires."

"Sir Colin, good evening. How may I help, Sir?"

"Is Sir Stewart there this evening by chance?"

"Yes, he most certainly is, Sir. I've just seen him pass by. Please wait, Sir."

Squires moved as quickly as his disabled leg permitted, intercepting Menzies and bringing him to the phone.

"Menzies."

"Colin here. My apologies for hunting you down, Stewart. I've just received some information that I need to share with you, and you'll want to hear it now. Where's convenient?"

Menzies would have liked to say the Guards Club, but it was extremely busy that evening so it simply wouldn't do.

"Your office suit, Colin?"

"I will be waiting for you, Stewart. Come straight up. I will have the duty officer informed."

No further words were spoken, at least not until Sir Stewart was sat in the chair recently occupied by Christine Mann, armed with a large scotch and an impatient ear.

Gubbins spoke at length without interruption.

"Damn and blast, but I hope you're not right, Colin. I mean to say, the implications of… well, damn and blast it, man."

"Quite."

Menzies downed the remainder of his scotch in one.

Standing, he extended his hand to the SOE chief.

"Thank you for bringing this to me. I can do nothing tonight, not without raising suspicion. I'll check Chivers' report discreetly, and see what Philby's contact report has to say about our mutual friend Vadim."

"I'll leave it with you, Stewart."

"Thank you, Colin, thank you for your discretion too. I'll keep you informed."

They shook hands in genuine friendship, something they both appreciated and understood as a difference to the normal indifference and thinly veiled suspicion.

1312 hrs, Saturday, 23rd March 1946, MI6 Headquarters, 54 Broadway, London.

Fenton was part of the furniture as far as everyone who ever visited MI6 records was concerned. Rumours abounded as to his past and how he had come to be entrusted with the written history of the intelligence organization, but no one really knew anything about him, except that he was somewhat mad and also could find a specific file in the dark with a blindfold on.

Whilst his clerks could spend from five minutes to five hours locating a requested file, Fenton could just stroll down the lines of shelves, pause briefly, and return with the correct file every time, with or without the file code, originating officer, department prefix, often with nothing more than a rough date or a probable geographic location.

Black magic, some called it.

Both clerks recognized their latest caller and started to bluster.

"Calm down, I'm not here on an inspection. I just want to see this old fool."

Fenton didn't bother to look up from his desk.

"Just 'cos you're the boss now doesn't mean that I've to stand for your insults, you know. I have my pride, Captain, Sir."

The two clerks winced in anticipation of an explosion of voices, but Fenton was already rising to shake the hand of his former commanding officer.

"Lawrence, you old rogue."

The two shook hands and patted shoulders, exchanging greetings like men who had shared extreme perils in each other's company, as they had during the Great War.

"Right you two… hop it. Give the Captain and I the chance to catch up on tittle-tattle."

The two needed no further invitation to escape the presence of the MI6 director.

Waiting until he was sure they had gone, former Battery Sergeant Major Lawrence Fenton was suddenly all business.

"I assume I did the right thing, because this isn't a social call is it, Captain?"

"Correct, as ever, Sarnt-Major. Something to stay just betwixt thee and me."

"Tea, Sir?"

"Most certainly, Sarnt-Major."

A second cup had been consumed and still Menzies had not seen a single item of paperwork.

"Look, Lawrence, I don't doubt your skills, but I believe that at least one report was filed on the 12th by Captain Chivers, and I know all our records were removed from Hamburg in safety, and I know they were brought here intact. It must be here."

"Sir, respectfully, it isn't here."

"They cannot both have gone missing."

"Unlikely I know, Sir, but I will know soon enough."

Fenton strode off and disappeared out of sight.

"Early June 1945, you say, Sir?"

"Yes."

Fenton returned with a number of leather bound books.

Menzies frowned.

"They're not reports, they're…"

"… logbooks. Yes, Sir, logbooks. We'll soon know."

Fenton ran a finger up and down the logged in documents, firstly looking at the filing officer names.

"Here you are. Chivers... 8th June... report on a communist engineer officer he interviewed... follow up on the 10th..."

Fenton looked at the details and leapt off to get the files.

"Here they are," he announced triumphantly, holding two standard report folders in his hand.

They took a cursory look at the contents, both hoping to find that which they sought simply mis-filed.

"Right, so we know he did his paperwork diligently..."

"It must be here!"

Fenton was away again, but this time returned without the triumph.

"No, it's not there. It's definitely not there. Now, the 'event'," Menzies had not told him everything, "Took place on the 11th June as far as you know, and he fell in front of the tram on the 14th. You assumed the report was filed on the 12th earliest and you were probably spot on."

Menzies nodded.

"One moment, Sir."

The file master returned with another red leather bound tome.

"You're a genius, Lawrence."

He had the visitor log for the Hamburg section.

"Yes and no, Sir."

Menzies understood immediately.

The page for the day in question had been removed.

"Well that in itself proves that something isn't right here."

"Most certainly. Right then, Lawrence, can you get me all the filed contact reports for the 12th please."

Within eight minutes, the files were present.

"These are kept in the annexe, hence the wait."

Fenton leafed through them.

"What are you looking for, Sir?"

"Name of filing officer."

"Ingram... Barton... god, I remember that idiot... Bridges... Cox... and Scotford."

"Is that it, Sarnt-Major?"

"Yes, Sir, just five that day. Nothing looks out of the ordinary, except it seems that blithering idiot Barton could actually write."

Fenton had always suffered fools badly, but Menzies didn't inquire further.

"And the log for contact reports?"

329

With barely concealed smugness, Fenton leant across to the pile of logbooks he had retrieved previously, sliding the correct log book out.

'Black magic!'

Consulting the appropriate page, the ex-BSM announced the names.

"10:02 Ingram, 10:04 Cox, 10:09 Scotford... Barton at 10:32... 12:33 Bridges. At 12:58, we have Chivers. That is all, Sir."

'Oh my God!'

Menzies stood.

"I won't leave it so long next time, Lawrence, I promise. Thank you for your help, old friend."

"My pleasure as always, Captain, and mum's the word."

"Quite."

1201 hrs, Sunday, 24th March 1946, MI6 Headquarters, 54 Broadway, London, UK.

He had asked his opposite number in SOE to pop round, in order to fill him in on the latest developments.

Having done so, the head of MI6 was interrupted by the arrival of a large brown envelope, containing information that he had requested especially for this meeting.

Making his apologies, the envelope was opened and the contents scrutinized.

His visitor waited patiently, sipping an extremely pleasant sherry.

Major General Sir Stewart Graham Menzies read through the list carefully, the third time he had done so since the document had arrived on his desk.

It was uncomfortable reading, no matter how many times his eyes passed over it.

"Dear God."

Suddenly remembering the other man in the room, he passed the document across, something he would never have dreamed of doing only a week previously.

"Sorry, Colin. This is a list of Philby's commitments and involvements, and this," he indicated the considerably larger document he had not yet read, "Is his roster and itinerary since 1st February."

The head of SOE flashed his eyes over the single page summary that screamed nothing but trouble for the Allied cause.

"J-Cip? He's part of J-Cip? How on earth did that happen?"

"I've no idea, Colin, but that could spell disaster for all our intended operations. We need to have a chat with him right now. If he's talked, then we will find out and warn our leaders that we could be walking into an unmitigated disaster!"

"Either way, we need to have a word in the ear of someone at SHAEF."

"Indeed. I'll have a quick chat with Kenneth Strong and let him know that there may be a problem."

Both men stood, knowing that delay was not in anyone's best interests.

"Thank you for the sherry, Stewart. I'll leave you to it, but do let me know if I can help further."

"Thank you, Colin. I will do."

Showing the SOE head to the door, Stewart Menzies voiced both their concerns.

"Let us pray that we can avoid a disaster."

1557 hrs, Sunday, 24th March 1946, 7 Leinster Mews, Bayswater, London, UK.

Kim Philby sat at the desk, smoking calmly, his face betraying some amusement at his predicament, or perhaps a confidence in his cause, or in his understanding that the British played by gentlemen's rules, or perhaps mere bravado.

The hidden observers couldn't decide which.

The door opened and the main players entered to start a process that, once he saw who confronted him, he had little doubt, would end up not going well for him.

The hidden observers watched his bravado waver.

Sat opposite him were MI6's main hatchet man and his sidekick, men with a reputation for being quite ruthless in pursuit of the truth.

"Right then, Philby. For now, I've no sodding interest in your political motivation. No interest in the whys and wherefores of what you've done, so save us all any political justification tosh to excuse your treachery."

Philby gave nothing away, but was disappointed, as he had been practising the defence of his personal convictions since he had been dragged out of his office and driven off to God knew where some time beforehand.

"I think it's fair to say that you and I both know that you are in the shit up to your fucking neck. And talking of your neck, we already have enough to slip a noose round it and send you to Hades."

Schofield and Tester, MI6's men to call on when 'wet work' was the order of the day, stayed silent to let the former's words burrow home.

The two had been selected very deliberately, Menzies believing that Philby's knowledge of their reputation would give the proceedings a head start.

In this assumption, he was wholly correct.

Philby was dragged swiftly from his thought process, as Tester cracked his knuckles noisily.

Behind the two-way mirror, Menzies smiled at the theatrical but effective move.

Schofield leant forward.

"So, Philby," he spat the name out like it was poisonous, "I want to know what you have passed on to your Communist bosses, and we will start with your involvement with J-Cip."

Philby smiled.

"Sorry, can't tell you. It's Top Secret."

In a blur, Tester moved forward and planted a hard slap directly on the traitor's left ear.

The pain was excruciating, as the shock wave did damage internally.

Philby yelped and started to shed tears, as much from the shock of being struck as from the pain.

"You can't do that, you bastards. We don't do that!"

Schofield laughed.

It wasn't a pleasant laugh and would have graced a Hammer horror villain's repertoire.

"You useless piece of shit! No one cares about you. Understand, you fuck? No-one cares about you at all? Your only chance to see the fucking sun again is to sing like a fucking canary on heat."

He sat back, lit two cigarettes, and passed one to his companion.

"Now, before my agricultural friend decides to hit you hard, I suggest that you tell me what you've passed to your masters."

"This isn't right. You can't do this. Ask Sir Stewart. Ask him. He won't stand for this abhorrence!"

Leaving his observation point, Sir Stewart Menzies entered the interrogation room as if by magic. Schofield and Tester leapt to attention.

"Ah, Philby."

"Sir Stewart. Help me please. This is all a mistake and I can explain everythi…"

"No mistake, you traitorous swine. None at all. You'll answer each and every question these men ask you. That's all that you need to think about right now."

"But Sir Stewart, this is wrong, so wrong. Now you've seen this, you have to stop it…please!"

Menzies leant forward, his nose almost touching Philby's, the malevolence in his eyes telling the traitor everything he needed to know about his future, should he not talk.

Menzies words reinforced his inner screams.

"Who do you think ordered this, you treacherous scum?"

He let the words sink in and watched as Philby's eyes betrayed him.

"Listen to me, you worthless piece of shit. You are here because I want you here. Talk and you will live. Hold anything back and my two men here will have no qualms in introducing you to death in a variety of awful ways, and, for the record, they will be acting under my orders."

Without a further word, the head of MI6 exited the room, climbed the basement stairs and departed from the MI6 safe house, knowing that his men would get all that was needed.

Tester cracked another few fingers and chuckled audibly.

Schofield hawked and spat a gobbet of phlegm straight in Philby's face.

Philby fell apart.

1616 hrs, Monday, 25th March 1946, 12th US Army Group Headquarters, Arlon, Belgium.

"Good God man! You tell us this now? Now?"

This was an Eisenhower that Bradley had seen once before, but was an all-new experience to Sir Kenneth Strong.

"It was felt that… I felt that I needed to know exactly what had happened before I brought this to you, Sir."

Eisenhower lit another cigarette in his anger, the one he had let at the start of Strong's report still smoking away by his right hand.

"So we could be compromised across the board, Sir Kenneth?"

"Yes we could, Sir, but I take another view."

Eisenhower and Bradley exchanged glances, and it was Bradley that gave voice to their feelings.

"And how do you get to this view, Sir Kenneth?"

"The wretch Philby was incorporated into J-Cip group on March 16th. We've examined his official business and involvements, and there are no cross-overs with anything that could bring him good information on Spectrum or Pantomime, not until the J-Cip involvement."

The two American officers remained silent and impassive.

"That involvement presented him with a disinformation folder containing the efforts being made to mislead our Soviet enemy. Now, much may be extracted from that, but it would be without proof. Furthermore, we have seen some enemy responses which would indicate that our operation with the French was successful in planting the false file in such a way as they have taken it as fact and moved some forces accordingly.

Bradley poured himself another coffee, his face reflecting the thunderous turmoil inside.

"The very latest photo recon missions show no response that could be interpreted as inconsistent with the enemy's full belief in 'Ash', and certainly nothing that might make us think that our real intentions have been compromised."

"Nothing?"

"Absolutely nothing at all, Sir."

Bradley took a swig and set the mug down slightly harder than he intended, sending some over the table.

"So... are you seriously asking me to risk my army in an attack that may be compromised by some English spy who was given a complete Ash file, who passed that on to his masters, who may remain fooled by it and some other French file... or may not... on the basis that there doesn't seem to be any movement of enemy forces that would be appropriate to a compromised Rainbow Plan?"

Ike doubted he had heard that many words from Bradley in one go in his entire time with the man.

"General Bradley, what I am saying is that it is my firm belief that Spectrum is not compromised, and there is evidence to support that. We have every asset in place, hours and hours of planning have brought us to this point, and I can find nothing firm by way of evidence that would make me advise the abandonment of tomorrow's attacks."

"Nothing?"

"Nothing, Sir."

Bradley looked at his commander, expecting Eisenhower to take up the reins, but all he saw was a man intent on silent thought.

"Thank you, Sir Kenneth. Let me think on this for a while."

Alone with Bradley, Eisenhower alternated between cigarettes and coffee as he read and reread the intelligence reports, particularly the list of Philby's activities and the confession that Schofield and Tester had extracted.

There was nothing, no clue as to which course of action he should follow.

He turned to Bradley.

"Well Brad, what's your take on this?"

The commander of US Twelfth Army Group had his answer prepared.

"It's a risk. It's always a risk, but someone has seen fit to pose us a question. Put simply, the risk would appear greater now than it was, but is that sufficient to make us abandon months of planning and to possibly lose the initiative again?"

Eisenhower nodded, inviting his main General on.

"When you made the decision to send our troops ashore at Normandy, the risk was great, but different. Here it isn't the weather, but the enemy possibly having knowledge of our plans. We are told that probably isn't a problem, but we cannot be sure."

Bradley waked over to the huge map, with its notations and markings, the Allies dormant forces displayed for both men to see.

"You presently control the largest Army in history, men from a hundred countries in their thousands… tanks, aircraft, ships, everything in an abundance that we have never dreamed of."

He finished waving his hands over the silent markers and turned back to his friend.

"We must go. I see no alternative, Ike. If we don't then what do we do? I say we trust Sir Kenneth's judgement."

Eisenhower smiled.

"That is the decision I have reached, Brad."

The two shook hands.

"Now, best you get back to your own outfit. If there are any issues, you'll be the first to know."

Bradley snorted and turned towards the map again, pointing without drama.

"Actually, Sir, I think that they will be the first to know."

Both men's eyes fell on the Baltic and North Poland.

"Then let us pray that I am right, Brad. Good luck to you."

Half an hour later, news of the recovery and return of Philby's file was delivered by a relieved Rossiter to a decidedly more relieved Eisenhower.

When the Marine left, Ike took a moment to offer silent thanks by way of a prayer to his maker, before moving to the telephone to pass on the good news.

Tomorrow, and for the rest of our lives, we can study history. Today, we will have a chance to write it.

Major General Kazimierz Glabisz,
Officer commanding 4th Polish Infantry division.
Extract from his written address to the men of his division,
26th March 1946.

Chapter 139 - THE LANDINGS

<u>0028 hrs, Tuesday, 26th March 1946, the night skies over
Northern Europe.</u>

The skies of Europe may well have been dark, but they were alive with aircraft of all sorts, as heavy and medium bombers proceeded on their missions to drop high-explosive, night-fighters swarmed to protect their charges or move off independently to hunt alone in the night, and transports carried their vulnerable cargoes, ready to deposit men and equipment in enemy territory as part of the master plan.

Across Soviet-held Europe, phones were ringing either spreading the alert that had come from headquarters, or reporting more damage and destruction to vital infrastructure and assets in the Soviet rear.

The only Allied night-fighters not airborne that chilly night were those unfit to fly, or for whom there was no crew available, as the Allied Air commanders deployed every last asset available.

The Soviet defence response was cut to pieces in the early stages, as groups of American, British and German killers destroyed everything that came their way, for very little loss.

One DRL crew, flying the advanced JU-388J hunter-killer and tasked with protecting the transports, rounded on a flight of Soviet Bf110g's, sending three spinning to the invisible earth below in under eight minutes.

Its five companions from 12th NachtJagdstaffel destroyed two more ex-Luftwaffe aircraft, although the sole Soviet-manned He-219A7 killed two of the German Republic's aircraft before it caught fire and exploded in mid-air.

Elsewhere, exchanges were much more favourable to the Allies, with at least three Allied pilots making ace in just one flight.

The Europe-wide warning initiated by Moscow had the effect of encouraging Air Regiment commanders to send up anything and everything they had, which resulted in a rolling uncoordinated response by the Soviet Air regiments.

In less than an hour, the Soviet night fighter force suffered over sixty percent casualties.

By the time the dawn rose, there were many bases where mechanics and ground crew waited in vain, if only for a single aircraft.

The Allied air forces had delivered a tremendous blow, and Soviet night aviation would never recover, although Starshina Jurgen Helmutevich Förster was yet to find glory and a deserved and unique award.

It was actually the fault of the pilots from the 12th NachtJagdstaffel, who inadvertently strayed away from their assigned area in pursuit of some contacts to the south, opening up a gap between them and the aircraft of the 23rd NachtJagdstaffel.

The gap was small and invisible to the naked eye. The Major in charge of the 12th realised their position and moved part of his squadron back to cover the area. Although unconcerned, he reported the matter to control but, when questioned, was happy to vouch that nothing had broken the cordon.

He was wrong.

"Yes, Comrade Starshina."

"Will you knock it off with the Russian crap, you idiot."

"Zu befehl, Herr StabsFeldwebel."

"One day, Hans, one day I'll turn thing thing upside down so you fall out, after I've taken a shit in your parachute!"

Forster's laughter died away as he detected only a hummed response from his radar operator.

The man was concentrating.

Hans Braun let the radar repeat its first visual announcement before informing his pilot.

"Achtung! Radar shows numerous contacts ahead... straight ahead, working on height now..."

"Numbers, Hans?"

Silence.

"Anything else. Give me something. Man?"

"Jurgen, the screen can't cope. There are at least thirty definite contacts... seems like they're almost travelling in tandem... range three miles... height... scheisse!... fourteen thousand!"

Jurgen Förster pulled gently up on the stick, bringing the advanced night fighter up and above the rapidly approaching stream of aircraft.

A quick radio report notified their base of the approaching problem. On the direct orders of the vector commander, a harassed Air Force Colonel, the operator did not tell them that they were on their own.

Ever a problem for night fighters, friendly flak started to burst around the approaching enemy formation.

In this instance it provided him with the means to identify the aircraft now passing underneath his Heinkel.

"They're transports and gliders... look... that's why they registered in tandem... they're being towed, Hans."

He banked the aircraft to permit Braun to see clearly.

"Escort?"

"I've been looking. Nothing obvious... the streams seem regular... nothing outside…"

"I'm attacking, rear first... vector me in on the end of the central stream."

"Course... 225... maintain height."

The fox moved silently closer to the chickens.

The aircraft in question, RAF-manned C-47s, were transporting the Polish Parachute Brigade and elements of the British 1st Air-Landing Brigade to their paradrop and glider landing zones in and around Köslin, Poland.

In the centre of the stream, a bright flash marked the direct hit of a flak shell. Those who could see through nearby windows, watched in morbid fascination as the C-47 fireballed and turned slowly over, heading straight as a javelin towards the ground and dragging its Hadrian glider down with it.

The two disappeared into the darkness and no-one observed the fireball as they smashed into the soil of Pomerania below.

Förster was conscious of the death of the aircraft ahead of him, but concentrated more on the steer he was receiving from Braun.

He had decided on attacking with his Schräge Musik in the first instance.

The two 20mm MG-FF's, the original 30mm Mk108 cannons having been removed because of their shorter range, were set to fire upwards out of the He219, at between 65 to 70 degrees, depending on the crew's wishes.

Braun talked the 219 into its approach before Förster took over for the final sighting of the weapons.

"Firing!"

The proximity of the weapons to Braun's position made the warning much more than a courtesy.

As with all uses of the Schrage Musik, the attacking aircraft had to be able to get out from underneath its target quickly, as 20mm explosive cannon shells tended to affect the target's aerodynamic efficiency quite dramatically.

Above them, the C-47's left wing detached, its engine still pouring out power, the two parts folding inwards and starting the inexorable drop.

This time the glider crew managed to detach the tow, so only the transport went down.

Braun, always methodical in combat, commenced steering the fighter towards its next target.

Three Allied transports and two more gliders were shot down in short order. Not having realised that they were under attack by a night-fighter, a common problem with interpreting the attacks as ground fire, the transports had not called for support until a bursting flak shell had granted an alert co-pilot a swift glimpse of the servant of the Grim Reaper at work in their midst.

The two transport squadrons yelled out for help and their calls were swiftly answered, as RAF controllers vectored in the two Luftwaffe Geschwader and an experienced Mosquito flight that had been held circling, ready for any problems.

None the less, there was still time for Förster and Braun to slip underneath a final C-47 and pump the last handful of shells into its vulnerable belly.

Förster, in a typical move of bravado, pulled the Heinkel closer to the belly of the nearest glider, flying in its 'shadow' less than sixty feet from its wooden fuselage.

The performance of the radar fell off as a result, but Braun was engaged in trying to reload the two cannon, so Mark 1 eyeball was the most efficient warning in the interim.

It produced a result almost immediately, a defective exhaust system on a nearby aircraft revealed that there was something sharing the sky with them.

'That looks like... a 110...'

"Hans, we have an enemy fighter... bearing 80... how long?"

"Three."

Reloading the two cannons wasn't easy on the ground, let alone in the air. More often than not, aircrew didn't carry spare magazines, but Förster and Braun had decided otherwise.

'What the... two more... they look like... Mosquitos...'

"Scheisse... Hans... there's more... sure I saw at least two more trailing the first. Speed up, man."

"Two."

"You've got to hurry up, Hans."

The sound of activity behind him grew, as Braun struggled to clip home the final magazine.

Off to his right, the night became day as one of the Mosquitos pumped Hispano cannon shells into its target, with dramatic effect.

The two faint shapes veered off into the night as the burning Messerschmitt plunged to earth.

"Done!"

Förster and Braun had no idea of the screaming and shouting on the Allied radio circuit as a long-standing Luftwaffe night fighter ace was hacked to pieces by friendly RAF planes.

The Allied controller, realising his terrible mistake, called off the two Luftwaffe units, leaving the flight of Mosquitos to deal with the threat to the Polish Paratroopers.

"The bastards have hacked down one of our lads!"

Which was the way it seemed of course, but the kill gave both men impetus to perform.

The Heinkel 219's nose rose, and Förster used his forward firing weapons to lash out at another C-47, before peeling off to the left, intent on getting some sort of radar picture of the night sky before continuing with his destruction of the transports.

As the night-fighters continued their dance, there was little but the sound of wind racing through holes in the fuselage aboard C-47 F for Freddie.

Förster's burst had raked the belly of the aircraft and turned the insides into a charnel house.

Unforgiving 20mm shells had chewed through flesh and bone, transforming trained paratroopers into unidentifiable lumps of meat in a microsecond.

The flight crew fared little better, although the co-pilot retained his hold on life, despite the loss of his left arm and being blinded.

At the very rear of the fuselage, Flight Sergeant Terry Walker was in a state of shock.

Pieces of his passengers were everywhere, although much of the contents of the cabin was white silk, the small pieces of shredded parachute whipped by the airflow into something resembling a snowstorm.

His mind started to regain control of itself, and rational thought commenced.

Running his hands over his own body, Walker managed to work out that he was untouched which, giving the storm that had visited itself upon the aircraft, was a total miracle.

He got up and picked his way forward, not bothering to check for any signs of life, as there was little left that could have even been expected to be alive.

Opening the cockpit door, the horror continued.

The pilot resembled beef mince from the waist up, the navigator and radio operator being somewhat more intact, although still unrecognisable.

Grieves, the co-pilot, was making some deep animal noise, as his body struggled against the wounds, his instincts to try and fly the surprisingly responsive aircraft.

The smell of smoke made itself known to Walker, although Grieves was too far withdrawn into his world of pain to bother with the sense of smell.

"Skipper... we're fucked... "

Grieves interrupted him.

"Who's that?"

"It's Terry, Skipper."

"Terry, I can't see... can't do anything 'cept hold it straight and level... get 'em out... no idea where we are but get 'em out. Not sure how...," he coughed producing a heavy gobbet of blood from an injury unseen.

"I don't know how long we've got... so get 'em out now!"

Walker put his hand on his co-pilot's shoulder.

"Forget me, Terry. I'm fucked anyway. Just get 'em out safely... then out with yourself."

The extent of Grieves' wounds convinced Walker.

"Good luck, Skipper."

Moving back through the fuselage, Walker separated a Thompson and some ammo from something that bore a faint resemblance to the British liaison officer he had been talking to a few minutes beforehand.

Pausing for one final look at the human abattoir, he launched himself out into the blackness.

Eight minutes later, F for Freddie and its tragic load found a resting place in the soil of Pomerania, perhaps serving a greater purpose in death than it did in life.

0047 hrs, 26th March 1946, seven kilometres north-west of Naugard, Pomerania.

"Govno! Brake! Brake!"

Captain Ursha of the 167th Guards Rifles was riding in the locomotive, enjoying the warmth generated by the boiler's fire, when the world in front of the train went from black to yellow in an instant.

His warning was unnecessary, as the residual fire illuminated the fact that the track had been destroyed by the impact of the aircraft.

The driver had reacted swiftly and the screech of metal was already piercing and uncomfortable. Reversing the wheels' direction gave slightly more purchase, but Ursha knew they would not stop in time.

The TY2 locomotive almost made it, but ran into the section where the rails parted, smashing sleepers and carving lines in the ground underneath.

The fireman screamed as the engine canted wildly to the left, his body catapulted into one of the protruding brass control wheels, leaving him bleeding and scared.

The lean increased as the engine started to take the downbank leading to the adjacent road.

Some subterranean object proved a momentary obstruction, and the shudder was sufficient to loosen Ursha's grip and he dangled precariously from the side entranceway, his left arm flailing in an effort to grab something solid.

The TY2 came to a reluctant halt, canted over to more than 45°. The driver fought his way back to the controls and did what needed to be done, all the time conscious of his bleeding companion.

Dangling from the side of the engine, Ursha looked beneath his feet and realised that he was no more than three feet from the road, so let go and dropped onto the hard surface, the snap of his ankle lost in the shouts and orders as officers and NCOs took command of the situation.

Lying on the cold road, Ursha composed himself and accepted the pain, as he brought his heart rate down and made an appreciation of the situation, taking in the surroundings, illuminated by numerous fires of what was definitely a crashed aircraft.

Along the length of the train, soldiers were deploying in a professional manner, and Ursha felt his chest swell with pride, as his boys responded well to the unexpected disaster.

Second in command of the 3rd Battalion, 167th Guards Rifle Regiment, Panteilmon Ursha had seen many battles in the German War and survived without a scratch.

His war ended as eighty-four tonnes of locomotive lost its battle to stay upright and rolled onto its side, settling flat on the road, despite the modest resistance offered by a human body.

The Major in charge of the 3rd Battalion contacted those units following on, informing them that the railway was blocked, and to detrain at Naugard.

1st Guards Mechanised Rifle Division would not make its destination at Köslin where, even as the Major spoke into his radio, Polish paratroopers and glider troops were making a difficult night landing on zones prepared, marked, and illuminated by expectant members of the First Polish Army.

The downside for the attacking forces was that the 1st Guards, not part of any Allied planning, would now all be centred around Naugard.

0204 hrs, Tuesday, 26th March 1946, Drop Zone around Konnegen, Poland.

The red light shone in Crisp's face as he was buffeted by the air racing past the door.

Checks complete, the stick of paratroopers from the 101st US Airborne Division stood ready to jump, a scene repeated throughout the sky over Pomerania, as the Allied forces prepared to take the fight to the enemy.

Closing his eyes, Lieutenant Colonel Marion Crisp, commander of the 501st Parachute Infantry Regiment, sought to confirm his relationship with his God.

'Dear God, keep me safe, keep me alive, so that I may go home. Lord, look after m...'

He launched himself out into the dark instinctively, the slap from the dispatcher sufficient to interrupt his thoughts.

Beneath the stream of transports, soldiers of the Polish Army had turned night into day, using anything and everything that came to hand to bathe the ground in light.

Elsewhere, landing zones had been set up to accept the gliders that would bring the heavier support weapons of the division, as well as the glider infantry elements.

Everything was going according to plan, which in itself was new to Crisp.

His experience of war was similar to the old adage that no plan survives the first engagement.

'Maybe this will be different.'

He considered that proposition as he floated to the ground.

'Yeah, fucking right it will be.'

Lieutenant Colonel Marion J Crisp was the first man of his regiment to touch down in the fields surrounding Konnegen, twenty-three miles northwest of Naugard.

Part of the 101st, including Crisp's Regiment, were committed to defending the eastern edge of the Stettin Lagoon and the banks of the Dziwna River, prioritising the capture and retention of the bridges at Wollin.

The other part, the larger part, was assigned to the areas around Gollnow, from Schwente and Fürstenflagge in the west, Czarna Łaka and Rurzyca in the south, and Buddendorf to the east, all used as drop zones, the latter less than three kilometres southwest of Naugard.

The German 2nd Fallschirmjager Division, not fully formed but stacked with experienced paratroopers, landed in and around Bärwalde.

The three Allied airborne groupings were assigned to support the initial cordon organised by the 1st Polish Army, a cordon to ensure that the men and vehicles approaching the northern coast would land with a minimum of trouble.

0149 hrs, Tuesday, 26th March 1946, two kilometres north-east of Cierpice, Poland.

Out of twenty-one DFS-230 gliders, two had been totally wrecked on landing, and a further one had been destroyed in flight.

Only one man of those carried on the three, out of a total of thirty men, including the pilots, was saved.

His glider had skidded across the landing zone and into the cold waters of the Vistula. A group of Polish soldiers had thrown themselves into the fast flowing river, only for two of them to get into difficulties and be carried away into the night.

The sole German survivor was taken from the water, unconscious and out of the fight to come.

The landing ground was quickly cleared of gliders and those who had sustained injury were taken to a facility already established by the Poles, who had prepared the landing zone according to requirements originating from Skorzeny.

The JU-52's circled until the signal to commence was received, each making a steady approach and landing, careful to touch down sweetly, given that each was carrying fuel drums to get them all home.

The transport aircraft were carefully shepherded to positions off the grass strip, one coming perilously close to dropping a wheel into the Nieszawski Kanal, earning the pilot a black mark from his staffel commander. They were parked up where refuelling could be safely conducted, ready to evacuate the members of the 'Storch' Battalion, and, for that matter, anyone else they could lay their hands on.

Impressed with Polish efficiency, some of the Luftwaffe pilots watched as the illuminated strip spread further south, as the efficient Poles marked out a longer landing strip.

All the JU-52's had engines off now, so the approaching deep droning was clear to everyone, and more than a few who were not in the know raised their heads to view whatever it was that was approaching.

The Messerschmitt-323v16, more commonly known as the Gigant, had left friendly territory before the JU-52s, because of its slow speed.

Its personal fighter escort circled, watching carefully for possible enemy interference.

The huge six-engine aircraft came in on its approach and made a perfect landing, although the length of runway only proved sufficient by about twenty metres.

The prototype 323 had somehow escaped Allied attention in the German War, and was the last Gigant flying. This was probably its last mission, as there were no definite plans to take it home, and it was not to be left for the enemy.

The pilot turned the lumbering giant and positioned it facing back the way it had come, just in case circumstances permitted a return.

The nose opened up and ramps were positioned by the crew, permitting two vehicles to surge out and across the grass.

Both were Schwimmwagens, amphibious cars, and were equally kitted out with extra machine-guns and radios. The rearmost one stopped immediately as men handled a bespoke four-wheeled trailer, manufactured to Skorzeny's own design, up behind the waiting vehicle, where it was attached.

It contained a Maxson mount, kindly donated by 548th AAA Battalion of the 102nd US Infantry Division, along with enough ammunition to test the carrying capacity of the Gigant.

It was affectionately known as the Porcupine.

The unusual combination drove off at speed, pairing up with the first schwimmwagen and heading off to support the advance elements of 'Storch'.

0252 hrs, Tuesday, 26th March 1946, Joint Command Headquarters, Cierpice, Poland.

Skorzeny was unhappy, the schedule already lagging behind, as the four kilometres from the landing zone took a greater toll on his men than he had anticipated.

Despite splitting into three forces and using all three crossing points available, the modest Nieszawski had slowed them up more than expected.

As promised, the Polish soldiers had kept the occupants of Wielka Nieszawska indoors, so none saw part of the assault group steal around the small hamlet.

First Lieutenant Baron Georg Freiherr von Berlepsch, 'Storch's' Operations officer, another veteran of the Gran Sasso operation, waved his men out into stealthy deployments, as his group

347

drifted through the woods and invested the area around the main operations centre.

Fig# 139 - Cierpice 26th March 1946 - Storch Assault.

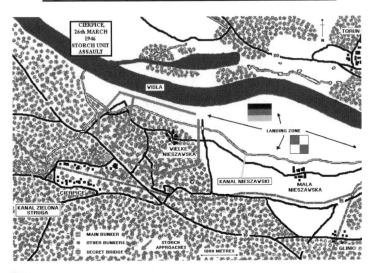

Other groups, with different priorities, glided through the modest light cast by a reluctant moon, the trees rustling in the modest breeze, adding to the surreal effect of camouflaged uniforms creeping gently through their moving shadow.

As the force waited for the newly decided time line of 0300 to arrive, they made the most of the extra few minutes and identified every target.

The concrete structure, covered with earth and trees, was almost devoid of any openings, save a few doors for access, and, to the watchers, it stood silent and inviting.

At 0300, the distinctive call of a Hoopoe did not seem out of place to any of the patrolling enemy soldiers, although the origin of the sound was a Polish Major who did not have their best intentions at heart.

At Romaniuk's signal, men rose from concealed positions and claimed lives in silence, knives mainly accounting for the wandering sentries.

Others fell as silenced weapons clacked and spat deadly metal, or taut wire bit into yielding throats.

In less than ten seconds, over thirty men had died and the way to the headquarters buildings was open.

348

Fig# 140 - Alternate Command Post, Cierpice, Poland.

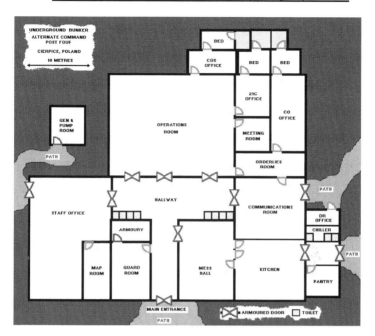

There was no need for further orders as Mors led the prime assault force forward, the gangly Major Romaniuk by his side, dressed as a Polish Lieutenant General, ready to shout orders at his countrymen inside.

Even though Skorzeny had some Polish blood running in his veins, his language skills would not measure up, so Romaniuk bore the full responsibility of talking his countrymen into not responding with force.

He was immediately brought into action, as a gaunt-looking Colonel in Polish uniform stepped outside for some fresh air.

"We're friends... we're friends... don't resist!"

'*Man shouting something... German soldiers...*' the confused man grabbed for his pistol.

"Don't shoot, Pulkownik!"

As the weapon emerged from its holster, a knife took the man in the throat.

He sagged against the wall and gently slid down it, before dropping face first onto the concrete.

"Damnit!"

349

Orders were to keep the Polish contingent alive at all costs, but the Colonel had appeared not to make the passive choice, so the German who had thrown the knife had acted correctly.

Both Mors and Romaniuk stood back to let the five man silent penetration group move forward.

Two men with silenced pistols, one with a silenced Sten gun, and two equipped with PPSh weapons, just in case stealth became a secondary issue.

The two SMG men opened the double doors and the rest moved forward, with Romaniuk and Mors close behind.

The next man they encountered was a Soviet orderly and both pistols took him down in an instant.

The rough diagram that they had received from 1st Polish Army sources had allowed them to plan their assault, and the well-oiled machine went to work.

Covered by a second group, the 'silent' group took out the guardroom first, safe in the knowledge that no Polish soldiers would be inside.

Both occupants went down quickly and without resistance.

Elsewhere, another group, similarly equipped, entered the dispatch rider's office and disposed of the sleeping Soviet motorcyclist they found there.

The final group slipped into the outside hall leading to the kitchen, where, according to their planning, a more difficult issue waited.

Pausing to quickly check the chillers, pantry, and toilets, the killers concentrated on the kitchen door.

They burst in, only to find the room empty, not full of a mix of Polish and Soviet staff busy making coffees and snacks for hungry generals and their staff.

The Oberfeldwebel leading the team considered the empty room with an element of relief.

'All the better for making things easier.'

The team moved forward, ahead of schedule.

Beyond lay the mess, which, it was professionally considered, could be a difficult clearance.

On his mark, the group would use all three doors to gain entrance, weapons ready to cut down anyone in the wrong uniform.

They waited.

'0303...'

There were now four teams inside the headquarters, waiting for the next deadline which would bring them to the phase where silence was no longer necessary.

Mors and Romaniuk waited with a reinforced group brought up by Skorzeny, ready to go for the Operations room.

The senior NCO, a Hauptfeldwebel who had once landed at Eben Emael, held his group ready outside the Staff Office doors.

On the other side of the building, an Unteroffizier stood with his hand on the door of the Communications room, one eye on his watch, waiting for the seconds to tick away to 0303…

0303 hrs, Tuesday, 26th March 1946, Joint Command Headquarters, Cierpice, Poland.

The second hand ticked into the vertical on a number of closely observed wristwatches, stimulating a burst of frantic activity.

All assault groups moved in.

The mess room was empty, save some basic furniture and the occasional discarded plate or mug.

"Scheisse!"

There were five petrified men in the staff office. Three, all in Soviet uniform, were gunned down in silence, the two Poles spared, but kept covered under the muzzles of sub-machine guns.

The radio and communications room yielded four soldiers, their gaunt white faces full of fear as the Unteroffizier's group charged in.

Apart from noticing their dirty nails and lack of personal hygiene, the NCO immediately spotted that the radios were either not working or not switched on.

Skorzeny's group crashed through into the ops room, fanning out quickly to allow the maximum men to get in as possible.

A dozen faces looked back at them, faces ravaged by sheer terror.

Every man's instincts squealed in protest at the scene, and each man saw his own issues… his own reason to distrust what was in front of him, whether it was the thin hands, or the thin faces, the smell of poor hygiene, or the obvious sores.

Whether the man was in a Soviet or Polish uniform was suddenly irrelevant, as they were clearly not what they … what they were supposed to have been.

Skorzeny pointed at Romaniuk.

"You've got one minute. Find out what the fuck's going on here."

351

The Polish Major moved forward to engage one of the Polish 'officers' in conversation.

They did not understand him.

Meanwhile, Skorzeny had moved back through the doors and met up with his NCOs, after ordering a search of the bodies, living and dead.

As he received their reports, understanding exactly what each meant, the results of his search order became known.

"Nothing?"

"No, Herr Oberst. There are weapons but no ammunition... we cannot find the key for the armoury, but none of these men or their casualties have capable weapons.

Romaniuk emerged, his face bright red with anger.

"They're all Jews... kitted out with uniforms and told to wait here while an exercise was run tonight. If they did what they were told... played the game properly... then they'd get a decent meal tomorrow."

Skorzeny nodded.

It was a trap and he had led the Storch Battalion right into it.

"We move back to the drop zone now... at the run... forget the evacuation plan... we go as a group... get the men assembled in the radio room... pass me that..."

He took hold of the SCR-536 radio and spoke rapidly to the relay station at the mid-point between the landing zone and himself.

Tossing it back to the man detailed to carry it, Skorzeny moved off to lead his men out of whatever it was he had led them into.

The woods erupted after they had advanced no more than two hundred metres, the Unteroffizier being the first of the Storch Battalion's dead as he was riddled with bullets from a DP-28.

All was confusion as flares cast their light through the trees.

Others soon joined him in death, as the ambush poured fire into the group of one hundred and twenty-five men, deadly metal lashing them from both sides and from the rear.

Von Berlepsch, towards the rear of the group, dropped off a security group, including an MG34, to watch for anything coming up from behind. He then organised a group of twenty

Fallschirmjager to swing off to the right in an attempt to turn the flank of their ambushers.

They charged forward blindly and almost immediately started taking fire.

A bullet tugged at Von Berlepsch's jacket and had passed far into the trees behind before he realised it had also journeyed through his flesh. The side of his stomach started to leak blood and he felt himself weaken.

Suddenly the wound became secondary, and his MP-40 rattled as he instinctively shot the moving shadows in front of him.

Both Russians went down and stayed down.

He shouted and gestured to the remaining men of his group.

"Move right! Move right!"

The running group swung right, avoiding any more direct contact.

"Now, left!"

Desultory fire chopped down two of the running paratroopers, but the remainder were quickly falling upon enemy soldiers who had been more intent on killing those to their front than watching their rear.

A Soviet platoon was butchered in short order, although another three men were down.

One, a long-service Corporal, had been slashed in the crotch by a desperate flail with a sharpened spade, and his screams were awful, penetrating the night and overriding most of the weapons fire.

Von Berlepsch organised a carrying party as the trapped elements of 'Storch' responded to his Handie-Talkie call to the area he had opened up.

Skorzeny slapped his shoulder in thanks and congratulations, not realising that his Operations officer had taken a bullet.

The First Lieutenant yelped as the vibrations reached his broken rib.

"Can you still fight, Georg?"

A nod was all Skorzeny needed, and all he received.

"Take your men forward to the staging point. Watch out for the Porcupine, Georg. When you find it, make a firing line facing this way. We will fill into it. We have to discourage these bastards from following us. Klar?"

For some minutes now, the MG34 team stationed at the rear had sounded extremely busy.

"How many back there?"

"Six, Herr Oberst."

Skorzeny gestured at his man.

"Get moving. I'll make sure your boys pull back."

Von Berlepsch was away immediately, calling his group to him.

Mors arrived, his face bleeding from a score of cuts.

He held out a smashed radio.

"Fucking bullets hit it and I got peppered. Saved my life."

The handie-talkie was just so much scrap.

Skorzeny filled Mors in on the plan and directed him to recover the rear-guard, moving them back steadily until set-up on the Porcupine.

The two parted, and Skorzeny took the main body to the east, aware that the firefight behind them had grown in intensity.

Mors found the rear-guard under pressure and unable to disengage. Two men were wounded, one of whom was unable to walk unaided.

The relieving group was waved left and right, and found themselves immediately under fire from the pursuing Soviet infantry.

To their immediate rear, the good citizens of Wielke Niesakszka cowered under their blankets.

Catching the attention of one of his men, Mors used his fingers to get the man to concentrate wider, as it would only be a matter of time before they tried to outflank.

A solid lump fell to ground with a thud and the group around the MG34 hugged the damp earth.

The grenade exploded, sending deadly fragments in all directions.

None of the group near the device was hit.

However, one small piece struck the HauptFeldwebel in the back of the neck, passing inexorably through his spinal cord and coming to rest in the temporal lobe.

His body stayed upright for a second, before dropping like a rag doll on to forest floor, the NCO's eyes wide open in indignation.

Three more grenades were thrown, each as deadly, reducing Mors' force and, in the case of the last grenade to arrive, silencing the machine gun.

Shouting wildly, the Soviets charged forward and overran the rear-guard.

Up front, Skorzeny, who had hidden a chest infection from the Medical Officer, was struggling to keep up with the bulk of his men.

Stopping occasionally, under the pretext of encouraging stragglers, he found himself at the very rear, accompanied solely by his self-appointed personal bodyguard, a Viennese paratrooper called Odelrich, formerly of the SS-Fallschirm Batallion 600, who had first served with the Colonel during the Battle of the Bulge.

Skorzeny set his hands on his knees, drawing in cold air, all the time listening as the firefight behind intensified and then stopped altogether.

"Either they're on the run or they're down, Standartenfuhrer. Either way, we've got to move on now."

Odelrich moved to support his commander, but Skorzeny waved him away.

Taking one deep breath, he leapt forward in pursuit of his men.

Behind him, Mors and two of his men found themselves in the hands of angry Soviet NKVD soldiers.

Von Berlepsch had arranged his force according to Skorzeny's order, flanking the waiting Porcupine.

The first members of the main body arrived and were sent off to positions either side, further widening the defensive line on the kanal.

He had detailed a senior Corporal to count off the men as they arrived.

"How many, Stabsgefreiter?"

"Eighty-seven, Herr Oberleutnant, not including either the Oberst or Maior Mors."

"Scheisse!"

"Rescue party, Herr Oberleutnant?"

"Pull one man in four…quickly… have them assemble at the porcupine. I need to brief Bancke."

The Stabsgefreiter ran off, pulling men from their defensive positions and sending them after Von Berlepsch, who was in animated conversation with the slightly mad Feldwebel Bancke, the commander of Skorzeny's secret weapon.

The need for a rescue party disappeared with the arrival of Odelrich and Storch's leader.

Von Berlepsch explained the situation but before Skorzeny could offer up orders, a wave of infantry appeared in the weird light, moving in between the straight trunks of the trees, closing on the Fallschirmjager line.

"Bancke! Feuer!"

The gunner needed no second invitation and the Maxson mount burst into life, accompanied by the lesser instruments of death in the supporting line.

At a rate of two thousand rounds per minute, the quadruple mount started to alter the landscape, as the occasional tree was sawn through by a steady stream of bullets.

The loaders stood ready to replace empty ammo panniers with full ones, hoping to keep the time the weapon as silent to a minimum, although the gunner was always aware of overheating the barrels.

All of Skorzeny's men had seen the Porcupine in practice and drill, but not in battle, and being used on human beings.

NKVD soldiers literally flew apart or were cut in half, and the attack quickly lost steam and went to ground, although that didn't stop the killing, as bursts fired into the woods caught men following up in the second and third echelons.

"Achtung!"

Skorzeny shouted, getting the attention of the men nearest to him.

He pulled his 'jack in the box' from his pocket and waved it around, showing those that saw him what he wanted.

The order went along the line quickly and the British designed mini-mines were quickly positioned, on the banks as well as around the crossing points.

Consisting of half a pound of explosive and a friction trigger, the simple wooden bomb had a three metre length of thin cord attached to the upright, which was, in turn, attached to something immovable.

The non-standard mine, the brainchild of a British Sergeant of the Royal Engineers who had been 'adopted' by Skorzeny's unit, was armed simply by raising the wooden arm and pushing it into position in the slot, which then solely required the upright piece to be pulled for the friction igniter to do its work.

Each man in the main force element of 'Storch' carried one, which meant that Skorzeny's order resulted in sixty-eight 'Jacks' being planted.

Using hand signals, Skorzeny ordered the line to fall back at speed, using the Porcupine to dissuade the pursuing enemy.

His soldiers responded instantly, rising up and moving back towards the landing strip.

Skorzeny moved back to Bancke and made sure he understood what was required.

"Feldwebel, you must stay here until we signal. Alright for ammo?"

"For sure, Herr Oberst, I have another five panniers for each gun."

"That should be enough. Now, hold the bastards off. I'll send up the two reds and you get yourself and your men back immediately. Is she prepared?"

Skorzeny anticipated the answer, as Bancke knew his job, but he still wanted to know that the porcupine would not fall into enemy hands.

"She won't be recognisable, Herr Oberst."

"You may have noticed... no Polish officers... it was a trap, so expect them to be here in numbers. Look after your men and yourself... and get back on the aircraft when I signal."

"Zu befehl, Herr Oberst."

Two minutes and two thousand rounds later, Bancke looked into the sky as the star shells burst.

'Green and red?'

"Keep firing, menschen!"

Green and Red was not Skorzeny's signal to fall back.

The signal originated from NKVD Colonel Volkov, commander of the force that lay in hiding around the landing zone.

Mortars sent their bombs skywards, intent on bringing destruction to the parked JU-52s.

They couldn't miss.

Heavy machine guns opened up, cutting down the Polish security force, men on the landing field, and those running from the woods towards the illusion of safety that their aircraft represented.

From north and south came light armour, T70s and T80s of the 4th NKVD Rifle Division, supported by lorried infantry.

Mobile flak units covered the take-off points, creating a hell from which there seemed no escape.

357

Skorzeny, his chest infection suddenly forgotten, urged his men onwards.

Remembering the Porcupine, the Colonel stopped and selected the two star shells, sending them into the sky one after the other.

Satisfied that the signal had been seen, he turned back to the immediate problem.

Fig# 141 - Cierpice 26th March 1946 - NKVD ambush.

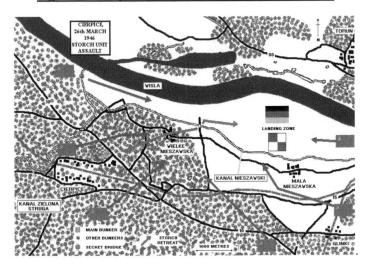

One JU-52 was speeding down the grass runway, following the instruction to evacuate the ground crew if there was a threat to the landing zone.

The starboard engine was clearly misfiring before it clawed its way into the air, not that it mattered, as 37mm shells chewed the wing off and the aircraft flipped over and smashed into the ground.

The whole landing field looked a disaster movie.

Skorzeny, moving as fast as his weakening state permitted, ran straight into an exploding mortar shell, which sent him flying back the way he had come.

The excruciating pain prevented him from any feeling of satisfaction as the 'Jack-in-the-box' charges started to claim lives amongst the pursuing soldiers.

Skorzeny could neither move nor feel either arm, which in the case of the left arm was not surprising, given that it was some ten feet away.

At least six fragments had perforated his stomach, but he couldn't regain enough control of his right arm to allow him to press his hand to the awful wounds to help dull the pain.

His face, once proudly bearing a duelling scar, was now devoid of a mouth and half a chin, as metal fragments had carried soft tissue and teeth away in an instant.

Skorzeny screamed with the agony of it all, as best as his ruined mouth would permit.

Beside him, his bodyguard, Odelrich, moaning in pain whilst knelt in a prayer position, face rammed into the mud, his only wound the very obvious gaping hole in his lower back.

Skorzeny's pain lessened and he became quite calm and focussed.

From his sitting position, he watched as the Soviet tanks rounded on the Gigant and other transports, flaying them with machine-gun fire and 45mm shells.

In short order, the last surviving Gigant was nothing more than a large bonfire, effectively blocking the centre of the runway.

Skorzeny saw the two schwimmwagens bound past, heading for a knot of Fallschirmjager. A handful of lucky men scrambled aboard before the vehicles leapt away again, driving hell for leather towards the Vistula.

The cold started to invade Skorzeny's innards and, had he retained enough understanding of his wounds, the approach of his death by blood loss would have been apparent.

However, Skorzeny saw only surrendering men of his command being exterminated by the jubilant NKVD troopers.

Odelrich moaned and flopped to one side, his legs useless and uncontrollable.

Gritting his teeth, he levered himself on his elbows, covering the few feet to his commander at great expense to his fading reserves of strength.

He visually assessed the injuries to his CO. Odelrich's experience of battlefield wounds told him all he needed to know, and his horrified look similarly enlightened Skorzeny.

Shouting disturbed them, and both men could see the approaching NKVD soldiers.

Trying to form words with his ruined mouth took Skorzeny to superhuman effort, but he managed.

"Together, old friend?"

"Ja, Standartenfuhrer."

Odelrich fumbled for one of his M-39 grenades, the pain of the movement causing him to groan and curse.

The bodyguard unscrewed the cap and took hold of the cord.

Tears of pain streaked Skorzeny's face as he worked his painful jaw one more time.

"Hals-und beinbruch, Kamerad."

Odelrich coughed up a gobbet of blood and spat it to one side.

"Hals-und beinbruch, Standartenfuhrer... it has been a privilege to serve with you."

He pulled the cord.

Four seconds later, both were dead.

When the Gigant had exploded, Von Berlepsch had been on his way to it, hoping to evacuate with the motorised team.

Instead, he sought cover as the huge aircraft spread itself in all directions.

Both schwimmwagens drew close and he risked a swift wave, counting himself fortunate to be noticed against the backdrop of destruction.

Bullets zipped through the air, and three men with the Lieutenant went down in as many seconds.

"Come on man!"

Bancke shouted at his officer, indicating the back seat, from where a wild-eyed Romaniuk and another Storch man were firing at anything in range.

Von Berlepsch threw himself on board, ramming into the Polish Major so hard that he winded the man and knocked the G-43 automatic rifle from his hands.

Any sound the man made was lost in the animal scream from the Fallschirmjager officer, as his broken rib sliced at internal tissue with increasing success.

The schwimmwagen leapt forward, almost bowled over by an adjacent bursting shell.

The second vehicle was not as lucky, and a 45mm HE shell exploded against the driver's door, killing all six men clinging to it.

Containing only the dead, the shattered vehicle rolled over and over, disintegrating as it went.

Behind the escaping group, the NKVD troopers closed in, accepting surrenders and executing wounded, until the survivors consisted of twenty-eight 'Storch' troopers, four Polish soldiers, and thirteen Luftwaffe personnel.

As Bancke's driver slowed to enter the water, the pursuing tanks fired their last shells, none of which came close.

"Propeller!"

Bancke, familiar with the vehicle's workings, ran to the back and fixed the propeller in placed, folding it down from its normal travelling position. When in the 'water' position, the propeller axle came in contact with a drive in the back of the schwimmwagen's bodywork.

With the extra man aboard, the driver took it carefully, and the 'swimming car' entered the water at low speed.

By turning the steering wheel, the vehicle used its front tyres as rudders, and the overloaded car went with the flow of the Vistula, heading northwards to the Baltic.

The last sounds of battle split the night, as jubilant NKVD troops executed all but the sole officer from amongst the survivors.

The officer's interrogation, under the direct supervision of Colonel Volkhov, was thorough. For the young Leutnant, it would be a long painful night, but a short life.

The opening engagement of Pantomime had been an unmitigated disaster.

0500 hrs, Tuesday, 26th March 1946, Kolberg, Pomerania.

The highest point in the ravaged town of Kolberg was the old water tower, which made it the place that the local NKVD commander had commandeered for his personal observation post

"I swear I saw something, Comrade Polkovnik."

All five men had binoculars pressed to their faces, using the modest light of the stars and moon to search out to sea.

NKVD Colonel Ilya Bakhatin spoke arrogantly to his Polish superior officer.

"Are your soldiers ready, Comrade Mayor General Kieniewicz."

The General, commander of the 4th Polish Infantry division, answered positively, although he suspected that the NKVD bastard meant something entirely.

By now, Soviet officers and NCOs attached to units within 1st Polish Army, should have been either taken prisoner or

361

met a silent end, the choice wholly theirs, dependant on their reaction to the impending change.

Colonel Bakhatin of the 4th Polish Infantry's integral NKVD battalion was Kieniewicz's responsibility, one he had been relishing.

Removing the binoculars from his face, the Polish General took a step back and nodded to the waiting men.

A few rapid sounding steps drew Bakhatin's attention, but he had no time to turn before a rough hand clamped over his mouth and a cruel blade punched deep into his vitals.

The Polish General spoke softly in the dying man's ear.

"Die, you Russian piece of shit. Your war is now lost."

The Polish general whispered to himself.

'So, now it starts.'

He viewed the bodies of the six slaughtered NKVD soldiers with disinterest.

"If you please, Chorąży."

The Warrant Officer had been ready for the order since the contingent had arrived on the roof of the water tower and, in short order, he had three flares floating in the breeze, red-white-red, the signal that the liberation of their homeland was about to start.

The 101st Airborne had landed in the right place, and most of the reduced size division was moving according to orders, although some notable contingents were missing.

Colonel Chappuis, commander of the 502nd, had disappeared, along with every man from his aircraft; divisional command feared the worst.

Bud Harper, Colonel of the 327th Glider Infantry, had recently returned to active duty following a broken foot. That foot and the attached leg were now the subject of debate, as doctors in the casualty clearing station fought to save the damaged limb, following Harper's glider crash.

Overall, the new and leaner 101st had come off pretty well, with less than a hundred men killed or injured in the drop.

Evidence suggested eight aircraft lost on the flight, which meant that the division was still effective and able to do what it was supposed to do.

That could not be said of the Polish Parachute Brigade to the north-east, who had suffered under the night-fighters and flak, losing a number of valuable aircraft and gliders.

Part of the unit, nearly three companies in total, jumped over unfriendly forces, receiving ground fire from Soviet NKVD troops and members of Polish 2nd Army. The latter had no idea of the identity of their attackers as they had not been involved in the Polish deception.

Polish soldiers of the 36th Regiment, 8th Infantry Division, slaughtered over two hundred paratroopers of the Polish Parachute Brigade.

0600 hrs, Tuesday, 26th March 1946, Factory Rinat, Chaiky, Kiev, Ukraine.

On the 26th March 1946, the British Broadcasting Corporation began its new BBC Russian Service, broadcasting short wave radio programming toward the Soviet Union.

The initial item was a news programme, describing the war as the Allies saw it, and impressing upon the Soviet people the inevitable conclusion.

The concept had initially been part-propaganda tool, part genuine wish to share unembellished news.

The announcements that followed the news also served a third purpose, as an item regarding a new Government policy towards the Nationalist movement in the Ukraine reached waiting ears.

Those ears that only needed to hear the six key words to initiate a revolt within the USSR, bringing the Ukrainian people into more direct opposition with those that they saw as occupiers and oppressors.

The radio in a small factory office in Chaiky, Kiev, struggled to stay on frequency as the announcer went through his script.

"Therefore, in the matter of a sovereign Ukraine…"

"…His Majesty's Government is increasingly adamant…"

"…That the matter should be incorporated in any agreements on the political restructuring of the post-war Soviet State."

Shouts of joy and encouragement rang out, the coded message for action quite clearly received, and the armed group moved off to visit itself upon the nearby Soviet airbase.

In scores of places across the vast Ukraine, men and women slipped out into the early morning cold to hit pre-selected targets, intent on damaging as much of the Soviet war machine as possible, before slipping away to recover and repeat the process the following night.

And, for that matter, repeat it every night necessary until the Soviet Union no longer held sway over their country.

The Ukrainian Uprising had begun.

0602 hrs, Tuesday, 26th March 1946, Beach Zulu, Kolberg, Pomerania.

High and low tides were not a problem for the approaching seaborne forces, as the Baltic had no significant tidal range.

The major issue had always been ice, and for weeks, reconnaissance aircraft had been studying the sea ice, and other aircraft had visited particular areas with bombs or napalm, just to assist the thawing process.

Allied planning made sure that the alternate areas in the Baltic States and Norway also received attention.

Last observations had confirmed that ice would not inhibit the landing forces. However, its continued presence in the North, and in the Gulf of Bothnia, would not help any Soviet response, not that the Red Navy had much capacity to interdict the large Allied Naval forces committed to the enterprise.

As per the Allied request, the friendly Polish forces had set out coloured markers in lines of three, designed to steer incoming landing craft into the correct beach areas.

Lessons learned off the coast of Normandy could be applied, but landing on friendly territory, with the cooperation of forces in situ, made the whole operation much smoother.

The chugging of the approaching landing craft made many a Polish soldier tighten his grip on his weapon, until the familiar tones of Polish voices raised in excitement relaxed them.

Soldiers of the 8th Brigade, 4th Free Polish Infantry Division, supported by tanks from the 14th Lancers of the 16th Polish Armoured Brigade, led the first wave. Heavily laden soldiers ran down the grounded ramps, through the chilly waters of the Baltic, buoyed by their return to their native land.

The organised beach deployment rapidly descended into happy chaos, as soldiers in different uniforms, united by a common language and nationality, embraced each other in celebration.

Officers and NCOs barked orders, trying to separate the two forces and gain some sort of order, but the Poles had been subjugated for far too long for such an historical moment to pass quickly.

It was 0630 before the first organised units from either group made their way off the beach and inland, leaving room for the next wave to land behind them.

0833 hrs, Tuesday, 26th March 1946, ten kilometres east of Bärwalde, Poland.

A number of the assembled orders group showed the signs of their stiff encounter with the NKVD unit that had tried to force its way up Route 11.

2nd Fallschirmjager's 7th Regiment had been tasked with blocking any movement by Soviet forces, and had arrived at Route 11 just in time to engage a large force of NKVD troops.

A hasty attack had cut the road and a blocking force was set in place to hold any further Soviet attempts to advance.

Two such efforts had been made, and made with great force, the final attempt only being stopped by a swiftly organised counter-attack, led by Major Kurt Schuster, formerly of FallschirmBatallion Perlmann, heroes of the defence of Hamburg.

The Perlman soldiers had been absorbed into the 7th Regiment, serving as its third battalion.

Perlmann now commanded the regiment, or what was left of it, as the NKVD assaults had badly savaged his jager platoons. His temporary aid stations were overflowing and already creaking under the pressure of work created by two hours of hideous battle.

A brief radio conversation took place with the headquarters of the commanding General, Wladyslaw Bortnowski, Lieutenant General of the Polish Liberation Army Group.

The Group had been created on the shores of the Baltic and consisted of friendly units of the 1st Polish Army, the specially constituted Polish Tenth Army, whose units were still coming ashore, and the 1st Allied Airborne Corps, whose paratrooper and glider elements had landed throughout Northern Poland.

By the time Perlmann handed back the radio handset he understood that, although help would soon be at hand for the Fallschirmjager, things were not all going the Allies way, and that there was still the potential for abject failure.

History shows that there are no invincible armies.

Joseph Stalin

Chapter 140 - THE BEGINNING

0844 hrs, Tuesday, 26th March 1946, Europe.

From the Baltic to the Adriatic, eyes watched, waiting, as innumerable second hands swept round circular dials, bringing Europe inexorably to renewed conflict on a huge scale.

Five Allied Army Groups were ready to move forward and take the fight the Red Army, ready to start the long road back to the Polish border... and beyond.

At 0845 precisely, the Spectrum plans required huge artillery forces to commence a short sharp bombardment of enemy defences.

Along the Allied lines, thousands of gun commanders gave orders that triggered their weapons and launched metal into the cold air. The artillerymen worked hard, oblivious to the damage caused when their contributions arrived on target; they just concentrated on serving their gun.

Allied reconnaissance had been excellent, or so it seemed, and many Soviet positions had been discovered and slated for destruction.

The artillery was superbly handled and accurate, and many a Soviet soldier died without truly understanding that the war had suddenly gone 'hot' again.

The Allied plan was simple.

Hit hard, hit fast, and give the Soviet High Command as much to think about as possible.

In the south, planning deliberately took any Allied offensive action away from the Yugoslavians, mainly to prevent any unfortunate accident that could pull the large Yugoslav Army into the war on Stalin's side.

Whilst not quite a general attack, the expectation was for a number of penetrations in the Red Army lines, all of which would be exploited to the maximum degree.

Part of the planning was to remove Soviet troops from the borders of Switzerland and, in the doing, relieve the position of US XXXIII Corps.

Both British 15th Army Group and US 6th Army Group both had parts to play in that, before a wide advance aimed at allowing the 6th to gain Munchen and south-west Czechoslovakia, maintaining contact with the 12th and 15th either side, whilst the 15th moved parallel to the south of them, and into Austria.

US 12th Army Group had Prague as its primary objective, although the attached French Army had Dresden as its goal.

The German Republican Army, full of veteran soldiers despite its infancy, had been handed the prize, although all knew it would be a bittersweet experience.

Berlin would cost many lives.

British 21st Army Group was tasked to bash its way along the northern coast, relief of the Polish bridgehead as its priority.

In general terms, Allied planning catered for occupation of all lands up to the west bank of the Oder River, but Eisenhower and his generals, and even the politicians, were realistic enough to know that it was unlikely that Operation Spectrum would take them that far.

Their greatest advantages lay in logistics and air power, the former incredibly complex machine coiled ready to bring the requirements of war from around the globe to Allied ports in Europe, and then distribute them swiftly and efficiently to the formations at the sharp end of combat.

The latter machine, the air force, had been hammering the Red Army across Europe for weeks, and the 26th March offered up opportunities for greater destruction, as available targets multiplied with the expected Soviet ground response and the decimated Red Air Force rose to meet the inexorable swarms.

Time alone would tell how a battle-ready, well-supplied, well-equipped, and well-motivated Allied Army would perform against a savaged but still more numerical Red Army, bolstered by some new technological advances and inspired by an implacable political regime.

0909 hrs, Tuesday, 26th March 1946, Operation Heracles-I, above Nordhausen, Germany.

By all definitions, this portion of the Heracles missions was a total milk run.

Whatever flak there had been had missed by a country mile, surprisingly less effective than Soviet AA had started to become in recent months.

There had been a brief suggestion of intercepting fighters, but defensive aircraft had moved in and, apart from two bright but short-lived flashes at distance, and a drawling American voice announcing two bogies down, there had been nothing to really suggest their presence.

The eight Lancasters of the RAF's 9 Squadron lined up their target perfectly. Elsewhere, the rest of 9 Squadron and other specially trained RAF and RAAF Lancaster squadrons approached their own objectives, one of the ten goals of the Heracles missions, the priority targets being spread over the length and breadth of Europe.

Behind each leading group came larger groups, carrying conventional HE and incendiary loads.

There were more behind them too.

The Master Bomb-Aimer was conscious of the responsibility on his shoulders.

"Steady... steady..."

Through the small formation, anticipation was growing, especially with the bomb-aimers, to whom fell the responsibility of ensuring that their single bombs hit right on the money.

"Steady... steady..."

Visibility was perfect, not a cloud and excellent early morning light by which to aim with the utmost precision.

9 and 617 Squadrons were two of the RAF's finest, although it was the modifications to their Avro Lancasters that gave them their roles within 'Heracles'.

The plan was ruthlessly simple.

Nordhausen had been visited in the German War, with some success, but not as hard and in such a short time as was about to happen.

"Steady... steady... stea... bomb gone!"

No-one really needed telling, as the release of the twelve thousand pound Tallboy bomb could not go unnoticed, the lightened Lancaster springing upwards instantly.

The eight Lancasters were flying in two diamonds, incredibly close, with one diamond tucked in behind and slightly above the other with little room to spare. Within ten seconds, each aircraft had deposited their cargo into the air above Nordhausen; above the headquarters of the Red Banner Forces of Soviet Europe.

Six Tallboy bombs led the way, three each on a specific point.

Already in the air behind them came two Grand Slam bombs, twenty-thousand pounds of Torpex D1 explosive, intent on finishing the work started by the six Tallboys.

The follow-on attack might experience some difficulties with the aftermath of so many large explosions. Planning and practice meant that the big bombs were all aimed and laid before the target was obscured by the debris thrown up by the rapid detonation of one hundred and sixteen thousand pounds of high-explosive doing what it does best in an intended target area of less than six football pitches.

Between 0904 and 0922, aircraft from 9 Sqdn, 115 Sqdn, 617 Sqdn, and 460 Sqdn RAAF visited ten separate targets, identified as 'Heracles I to X', placing over a half of the Allied stock of tallboys and two-thirds of the Grand Slams on their targets; over a million pounds of high-explosive, all dropped with a single purpose.

To cut the heads off the Hydra.

Author's note on the remaining chapters of Sacrifice.

Most readers with any knowledge of World War Three will know the general outcome of the final operations of Spectrum, and will therefore appreciate how long and complex this section of combat and political history would be to both read and write.

I have decided to follow certain of the key personnel from both sides, who served within areas specific to Allied Army Groups, as well as on the home fronts, or reflect famous engagements, through to the conclusion of 'Spectrum'. I hope I can write well enough to give a flavour of how those dreadful days passed for the soldiers, sailors, and airmen of both sides.

Despite the fact that isolating fronts risks missing some of the times where the effects of a single operation spread further into surrounding formations, I can see no alternative to avoid this history becoming cumbersome.

I hope you will agree.

Freedom is never free.

Author Unknown

Chapter 141 - THE FIFTEENTH

<u>0958 hrs, Tuesday, 26th March 1946, the grounds of Schloss
Maria Loretto, Klagenfurt, Austria.</u>

He had no idea how long he had been unconscious for,
except that it had been long enough for his headquarters to be
destroyed.

Shaking his head to clear his vision, he listened without
hearing to the man on the other end of the phone.

"Speak up! I can't fucking hear you!"

Another bomb exploded and the blast wave hit the small
bunker that he used to sleep in, a decision that had undoubtedly
preserved the life of the commander of 1st Alpine Front.

The blast threw more dust into the air, forcing Chuikov
further under the table, clutching the telephone box to his chest.

"No, I didn't hear you, Comrade."

The urgent voice repeated its enquiry, only louder.

"At this time, I can only fucking guess, but if they're
working me over, then it'd be a fucking fair assessment, old friend!"

More bombs, further away this time, rocked the concrete
structure that had saved his life more than once since the first Allied
aircraft appeared overhead just after 9 o'clock.

"No...no... nothing. My men are working to get it all
connected... no... radio room took a direct hit from something
huge...yes...yes, I'll wait..."

At the other end, Zhukov was receiving a report from
another source, so Chuikov took the opportunity to light a cigarette,
although his preference would have been to knock back a vodka...
or two.

"Hello, yes, I'm still here... what... really?"

Zhukov relayed the report of an attack on 1st Southern's
Headquarters, whilst Chuikov worked his jaw in an effort to improve
his hearing.

"Is Yeremenko ok?"

Chuikov grimaced and spat, waving his arm at the waiting
Lieutenant General, whose blood was steadily dripping onto the

Marshal's boots. The exhausted man lowered himself onto the ground, careful to avoid any sharp debris.

Chuikov tossed his cigarettes to his Chief of Staff and probed him with his eyes as he listened, and received a small shake of the head.

A near miss shook the whole structure, causing concrete to spall off the roof and drop on and around the pair.

"Hello... hello..."

Chuikov placed the receiver on the box and set the combination down on the floor.

"Telephone's fucked too now."

The two senior officers drew on their cigarettes.

"Well, Alex?"

Lieutenant General Bogoliubov pulled out a cloth and bound his badly gashed hand.

"Whatever they were that the bastards dropped in the first attack... well... they were huge. We've lost our complete radio facility and all the staff... one bomb, dead centre, now just a huge hole surrounded by a pile of rubble and dead... burning too... the schloss is flattened... motor pool's the same," he grimaced as he pulled the temporary dressing tight, knowing that something was still lodged within the wound.

"As far as I can see the headquarters is totally gone... smoke and flame... everything. I've organized efforts to firefight and rescue but... well... the whole duty group..." both ducked instinctively as the rain of bombs continued.

Something was burning close by and the smoke started to trouble both men.

"The whole duty group is probably gone, including Colonel General Tsvetayev."

Shouts and cheers outside marked a success against the medium bombers that were undertaking the third attack in the space of an hour.

Another close one, probably the closest yet to Chuikov's battered senses, shook the whole structure, and only the keenest ear would have managed to separate the sound of the explosion and a piece of heavy metal striking the side of the sleeping accommodation.

"So, all fucking communications are down," he kicked out at the useless telephone, "I've lost half my fucking staff, my fucking second in command... any good news, Comrade?"

"None that comes immediately to mind, Comrade Marshal."

Outside there was a silence of sorts.

No bombs.

No firing.

The occasional whimper of a hideously wounded man.

"So, what do we have?"

"Mess hall is still standing. Re-establish there and get ourselves sorted out quickly?"

Chuikov shook his head.

"I think not. Find me an alternate place, nothing fancy, a chair in the fucking woods'll do, a radio and a phone," he looked around him, "But I'll not do business here again."

Chuikov climbed out from under the table and dusted himself down, only then realizing that his left thumbnail was blacker than a lump of Siberian coal.

Shouts from outside seemed to indicate that the enemy attack was over.

"Right, Alex. Let's get this fucking mess sorted."

Things for Chuikov were much worse than he had first imagined.

The whimpering drew his attention to an awful sight.

A quadruple Maxim mount, the source of the metallic thump against the bunker wall, had pinned its mangled gunner to the blood splattered concrete.

What was moaning was not really recognizable as a human being.

Chuikov fumbled with his holster but the wreck gave up its last breath on cue.

The commander of the 1st Alpine Front looked around him.

The first thing he really noticed was the absence of trees. The Chateau was a decoy, his actual headquarters buried in the adjacent woods, camouflaged by real trees and netting and, as he thought, undetectable.

The results of the efforts of Allied photographic interpreters lay all around him.

Nearly two thirds of his headquarters staff had been obliterated in the first attack, the huge bombs taking out a large number of those off-duty as well as in the headquarters bunker.

Only two platoons of his security detail remained, shocked and stunned by the loss of so many of their comrades.

His radio equipment had all gone; nothing was salvageable, or at least, they couldn't even try until the flames were extinguished.

Telephone communications were out, the bomb that had cut his call with Zhukov taking out the telephone exchange with an inch perfect arrival.

He suddenly had a thought.

'Zhukov? Why Zhukov, not Konev?'

The few wounded were being spirited away, bearing injuries of the hideous nature that accompanies the application of high-explosive to the human body.

As Chuikov walked around the site, he recognized bits and pieces, lumps and slivers of things that had once been the sons and daughters of Mother Russia.

'This is fucking worse than the Mamayev.'

Coming from the Victor of Stalingrad, who had stood and held at the Mamayev Kurgan, that was an admission indeed.

He was not alone, for every Front command, and some Army commands, had received visits from the Allied air forces and, in truth, some of them were much worse off than 1st Alpine.

Impatience was a Chuikov trait that was not always a vice, and he had travelled to the headquarters of 4th Guards Cavalry Corps, on occasion dodging the roaming Allied ground attack aircraft by the skin of his teeth.

The only vehicle he had found capable of immediate use was the trophy Zundapp motorcycle combination that had been the plaything of the now dead Front Political officer.

His arrival at the unattacked headquarters deep in the Schlieflinger Wald was greeted with no amusement, the soldiers all aware that something terrible was in progress.

Chuikov arrived in the office of the Corps commander unannounced.

Lieutenant General Fedor Kamkov sprang to his feet, still holding the telephone that had been denying all his attempts to speak to the man who was now in front of him.

"Comrade Marshal, what's going on?"

Chuikov took a few minutes to fill him in on the details, such as he knew.

A few minutes later, 4th Guards' headquarters started to put out contacts to other units, trying to establish a picture for Chuikov.

By the time that Chuikov had established an element of control, the Allies had ruptured his lines in at least two places.

Once Bogoliubov had got some sort of effective headquarters put together, the 1st Alpine commander issued some final instructions to Kamkov and mounted the Zundapp for the brief ride back to Klagenfurt.

1058 hrs, Friday, 29th March 1946, St Ruprecht district, Klagenfurt, Austria.

1st Alpine's headquarters was now spread through a number of buildings in a section of St Ruprecht in the southern suburbs of Klagenfurt.

The previous day had seen the destruction of acres of woodland around Krumpendorf and Viktring, as Allied bombers sought out the command structure.

Front signal troops had worked miracles establishing a means of communications that half measured up to the one that had suffered at the opening of the Allied offensive.

Chuikov was taking advantage of his new freedom by shouting down the phone at Zhumachenko, the harassed commander of 40th Army, one of the formations that had taken the biggest hits.

"I don't give a fuck, General. You are not authorized to withdraw, not now, not later, not tomorrow. Is that clear?"

He clicked his fingers, summoning a map.

Running his dirty fingers over the creased paper, he confirmed his thoughts.

"Now listen to me, Comrade Zhumachenko. You will hold the line from… Tolmezzo across to… what does that say?"

Bogoliubov strained his eyes.

"Moggio di Sotto…"

"Moggio di Sotto… and above all, you and the Yugoslavians will hold Tarvisio, clear? What do you have there at the moment?"

He spat to one side as an unsatisfactory answer was delivered.

"No, no, no, that's not enough. Put more there and do it fucking quickly, man!"

Lighting a cigarette, the Marshal relaxed back into a rocking chair.

"Look, Comrade. The capitalists've caught us by surprise, by there's no chance of them breaking us, provided your army sits fucking tight and holds. I'm getting 7th Tanks and 4th Cavalry to dig in hard in the Gail valley, and you'll provide the time for that. I wish you good luck, Comrade."

Terminating the call, Chuikov waited whilst his CoS received a written report, expecting it to be more bad news.

He was clearly right as Bogoliubov rummaged for another map.

"Comrade Marshal, 7th Guards Army has a big problem."

He held out the written report but Chuikov declined to take it.

"Show me."

"Here… at Vipiteno… 53rd Rifle Division is uncontactable and here… at Imst… 28th Tanks have come under direct fire… in a rear line position."

"Get me Shumilov immediately."

The signals officer got to work immediately whilst Bogoliubov proffered the signal again.

"Report originates from Quartermaster Mayor General Alexandrov of 7th's rear services."

"What have we got to spare?"

"27th Army of course, but you want to save that for counterattacking still."

"Only if we have something else we can send, Comrade."

Examining the unit roster, Bogoliubov married names with places, and found some assets.

"163rd Rifle Division is resting here at Telfs."

"Good, good… more."

"115th Guards Anti-tank Artillery Regiment is here," he sought out the location and placed his finger on it, "At Nassereith, complete with a Shtrafbat."

"Excellent, get them moving immediately, place them under the command of 28th Tanks. I know the man and he'll do the job. Tell the 28th what's coming and that he is to hold his ground at all costs."

The signals officer held out a radio handset.

"Comrade Colonel General Shumilov, Comrade Marshal."

Chuikov took the handset swiftly.

"Comrade General…"

Showing unusual patience, Chuikov gave the man some licence to vent his anguish, waiting until the man had fired out his report and expected plea for air cover and reinforcements.

"Mikhail Stepanovich, you know you can whistle for air cover, but I'm working on your problem right now. 28th Tanks has reported as engaged at Imst. I've sent 115th Guards Anti-tank and what's left of the 163rd Rifle to bolster that position. What you've just told me fits that scenario... wait."

The map lay open in front of him and the Marshal did some swift calculations.

"I'll authorize an adjustment to the line based on Imst to Vipiteno, which you must retake immediately. Clear?"

Chuikov's eyes flashed in fury.

"I don't give a fuck! You'll damn well do it or I'll find someone with the balls to do it and you'll be counting fucking trees!"

Chuikov took a sip of his tea as he listened to Shumilov's angry retort, knowing that he had wound the competent man into coiled spring with his words.

"Good, Mikhail Stepanovich. Now, above all, you will hang onto 1st Southern and 26th Army. No gaps that the bastards can slip through. Your priorities are to protect Innsbruck and the routes to the north into Germany. Do you understand your orders, Comrade General?"

"Fine. Now, put someone on who can fill my staff in on your dispositions please. Good luck, Comrade."

Handing the phone to an aide, Chuikov stood and looked at the situation map, knowing that it was already outdated.

Author's note - The Heracles Missions

Allied Commanders had decided that, in conjunction with the main assaults of Spectrum, precision bombing missions would be dispatched to take out the headquarters of the Soviet Fronts and other priority formations.

The limiting factors were the availability of properly trained aircrew, a similar issue with suitably modified aircraft, and limited stocks of the devices that were to be employed; namely the Tallboy and Grand Slam super bombs.

Planners decided on ten missions in total, which left some of both types of bomb in reserve for priority missions in support of the objectives of Spectrum.

Below are the now accepted results of the Heracles missions.

Heracles I - HQ, Red Banner Armies of Soviet Europe.

Smashed, rendered ineffective, heavy casualties amongst Frontal command staff, and with Marshal Konev killed. The command group needed to be completely re-established. Zhukov took command from distance in the interim.

Heracles II - HQ, 1st Polar Front.

Heavily damaged, rendered ineffective but command fully restored within three days. Alexandrovich was amongst the wounded, and he succumbed to his wounds on 2nd April.

Heracles III - HQ, 1st Karelian Front.

Smashed, rendered ineffective, with heavy casualties amongst Frontal staff. Govorov was badly wounded.

Heracles IV - HQ, 1st Baltic Front.

Missed its objective completely. Allied intelligence was misled, and an alternate command position was bombed instead. This was, perhaps, the biggest failure of the Heracles Missions.

Heracles V - HQ, 1st RB Central European Front.

Command facility totally destroyed, with heavy casualties to Frontal staff, but, due to Malinovsky's organisation and alternate deployments, with only slight disruption to command ability.

Heracles VI - HQ, 2nd RB Central European Front.

Heavy damage and rendered ineffective for four days. Heavy casualties to Frontal command staff. Petrov, temporary commander, was amongst the dead.

Heracles VII - HQ, 3rd RB Central European Front.

Light damage inflicted overall, but severe damage specifically to communications. Restored to full working ability within four days.

Heracles VIII - HQ, 1st Southern European Front.

Smashed and rendered totally ineffective. However, 1st SEF had a mirror facility set up to train replacement personnel. This was swiftly organised to take over control, resulting in less than 24 hours disruption. Yeremenko was slightly wounded and continued without a break.

Heracles IX - HQ, 1st Alpine Front.

Severely damaged and rendered ineffective. Heavy casualties to Frontal staff. Chuikov was slightly wounded and remained in command.

Heracles X - HQ, 1st Balkan Front.

Modest damage and casualties, including Tolbukhin wounded, albeit lightly.

Six RAF and one RAAF aircraft were lost, with four of those from one mission, that being Heracles X.

Debate on the effectiveness of these missions continues to this day, and it is certain that the failure to inflict any damage on 1st Baltic counts greatly against Heracles.

However, the prime target was obliterated, including the commander of the Soviet Armies, Konev, and success also came in the killing or incapacitating three more Front commanders. It should be noted that two of those were against targets that were engaged purely to maintain the illusion of threat to Northern areas.

Had the Allies been more successful in removing the true talent of the Red Army, such as Malinovsky, Bagramyan and Yeremenko, then perhaps history would trumpet the Heracles Missions as a success.

For now, we must be content with reading the opinions and arguments of historians, and form our own opinions as best we can.

It is my opinion that Heracles did a little to change the initial resistance offered by the Red Army, but achieved little, if anything, in the long run.

1008 hrs, Monday, 1st April 1946, the Kremlin, Moscow.

The mood was sombre, despite the threatening eyes of the General Secretary rounding on anyone who seemed in the slightest bit defeated.

"We have been in situations like this before and we have triumphed each and every time, Comrades."

More than one person in the room understood the vital differences this time around, although clearly not the man who really needed to do so.

"Now, we have a mess to deal with. Comrade Zhukov."

Standing at a much-changed military situation map, the Marshal, white and shaky, briefed the listening GKO on the strategic situation.

"The Allied armies and air forces have launched heavy attacks that appear to be aimed at these major objectives."

"Munich."

"Prague."

"Berlin."

He paused before tapping the map for a fourth time.

"Poland."

"In Italy and Austria, Marshal Chuikov has slowed their advance and is confident that he can stop further major incursions. Here the Allies have been clever, and have tried to avoid combat in any areas where the Yugoslav Army is drawn in on our side. We have tried to provoke such a thing but have not yet succeeded. Perhaps Comrade Molotov may be able to provide us with happier news on our Yugoslavian comrades' future commitment?"

Eyes swivelled to the Foreign Minister, who shifted uneasily under the heavy scrutiny.

"Comrades, I can report that further attempts to persuade Comrade Tito to our side have been fruitless… in fact, my report indicates no sense of shift in his position, although we are told that another brigade of their soldiers has volunteered to fight for the cause."

One brigade wasn't going to make a huge difference, but it was the best thing that Molotov could offer.

Stalin spoke through puffs on his favourite pipe.

"So, the great communist… will not join the great struggle against… capitalism… not join the great cause… and sweep Europe clean of fascists forever… why not?"

Molotov eased his collar like a silent movie star.

"Because he says he will not ally himself with the losing side and risk communism's extinction, Comrade General Secretary."

There was a silence, broken only by the sound of an angry man sucking on a pipe.

With a calm he did not feel, Stalin pointed at Zhukov.

"When we've defeated the capitalists, you'll present me with a plan to knock that treacherous piece of shit off his perch, Comrade Marshal. Now, continue."

Still in the early stages of the heart attack that would hospitalize him for some weeks, Zhukov struggled on.

"Every front has suffered heavy casualties, every rear echelon has been savaged by their air attacks."

He turned to the map.

"However, here, under Marshal Bagramyan, we've inflicted great losses on the enemy, mainly British. The incursion into Poland has been halted, their attempts to link up with the bridgehead have been stopped dead at Wismar, although the southern flank is threatened by the advance of the new German Army cutting upwards and trying to join up with a British thrust down from Denmark. Marshal Bagramyan is confident he can extricate his forces, and I have given him permission to withdraw this group," he indicated the armies between Bremen and Bielefeld.

Stalin remained silent, unexpectedly.

379

"The Polish excursion has been further reinforced but it would seem unlikely that more assets will arrive. It is contained for now and we will be strong enough to reduce it very soon."

"The Poles?"

Beria had wanted to let his NKVD divisions loose but, unusually, Stalin had stayed his hand.

"Some remained loyal. Although it is certain that some were involved in the Allied landings and airborne operations. Fortunately, we stripped a lot of their assets to bolster our own forces in Europe, so most of their units are under equipped, although the Allies may well have supplied the traitors with arms themselves."

Zhukov steadied himself and more people started to notice his colour.

"Once the loyal Poles can be disengaged, we will reorganize them and move them to an area away from their countrymen. Comrade Marshal Beria's force can then operate in the full knowledge that they will be dealing with only traitors."

Zhukov took a deep breath.

"The bridgehead is contained at this time."

Stalin relit his pipe and gesticulated at the map.

"So, Comrade Marshal, we have pretty markings that show us that the Allies have made advances. It was to be expected, of course."

No-one would have dared voice such an expectation a week previously, but the General Secretary operated under different rules.

"Where is the danger, Comrade Marshal? Where is the threat here? They are grinding to a halt in the North and South. The Germans are moving but will run out of steam soon enough. The Amerikanski have been bloodied on the Rhine and Mosel. So where is our biggest issue eh?"

Zhukov, head swimming, easily tapped the board, the shot like sound causing more than one to flinch.

"Here, Comrade General Secretary. Here is our biggest problem."

Eyes focused on markings that suggested a US Army Group.

Stalin snorted.

"The Amerikanski?"

"One Amerikanski called Patton, Comrades. He was sat here, with his entire Army… a huge army… waiting for the right moment to move forward and exploit a breakthrough."

Zhukov felt really faint but stuck to his task.

"This morning he got his breakthrough here... between Mainz and Koblenz."

Actually, Patton had found his opening on the 27th but, perhaps unsurprisingly, Soviet intelligence was overwhelmed and such omissions were commonplace.

Zhukov collapsed, clutching his chest, his pain evident.

The doctor was called and the Marshal was taken away.

All the time, Stalin's eyes remained fixed on the map, taking in the smallest details.

'Mainz.'

'Koblenz.'

His eyes moved eastwards.

'Frankfurt.'

And further on.

'Nuremberg.'

And further o...

Stalin shook himself out of the process.

'Enough! You've defeated worse than this bunch of Amerikanski and lapdog British before, so enough! The Red Army will be victorious, so enough, enough, enough!'

Zhukov's departure had added to the growing list of dead and incapacitated Soviet Marshals, and Stalin's pot of reliable and competent senior officers was shrinking daily.

The briefing continued, as Nazarbayeva and Beria brought new intelligence to the attention of the GKO.

1209 hrs, Friday, 5th April 1946, Headquarters of 1st Alpine Front, Stainach, Austria.

Chuikov's latest headquarters exceeded his, by now, limited expectations.

Located on the one thousand metre long, heavily wooded Sallaberg, a mass that rose to nine hundred metres above sea level, his latest headquarters seemed ideal and undetectable.

He reminded himself that such thoughts had sprung up in his mind when he settled into St. Ruprecht and Teufelberg, yet the Allied air forces had discovered them.

Settling into a soldier's lunch, he recounted the morning briefing and his response to the overnight changes.

Although he was still going backwards, Chuikov was immensely proud of his soldiers and how they had responded to the

Allied attacks, above all the constant air attacks, to which there seemed little answer.

His plea for more AA assets had been sent, and resent, but none arrived and, he suspected, neither would they.

The map showed further losses, but also reflected some more favourable positioning, much of it based around his ability to create a new reserve, now that Tolbukhin's forces had come into the line between Yugoslavia and the edge of 1st Alpine's units.

Aggressive, Chuikov had lashed out at the Allied spearheads and, on a number of occasions, bloodied them to a standstill, albeit a temporary one.

Supplies were a constant problem but he was coping.

Bogoliubov limped in, his calf injury causing him great pain, which was only to be expected given that the triangular piece of house brick had removed a significant portion of the muscle on its way through his trousers.

He rejected orders to rest, orders which Chuikov had only half-heartedly given, in full expectation of his CoS's refusal to comply.

The map reflected a week of hard fighting that had simply not gone his way.

Innsbruck was invested and would surely soon fall, despite the additional resources he had placed under Shumilov's command.

However, the wily general had held the line, buckling but not breaking, bending back but still hanging on to the friendly forces either side of him. He had sent 7th Guards Army a newly arrived heavy tank regiment to help firm up their defences.

4th Guards Army had lost its commander that very day, the man falling victim to nothing more sinister than a car accident.

Chuikov remembered the old veteran with fondness, recalling the Hitler-like moustache he had insisted on sporting as *'he'd had it all his life, and long before that hound came on the scene'.*

He raised his mug in a silent toast and went back to his review.

'Bloody terrain!'

The Alps was certainly not ideal terrain, although the defence was assisted greatly. Valleys ran in all directions, in between peaks of great height, some impassable, others with small paths that determined men could traverse and use to get behind defences.

That had happened a few times, not the least of which was the damn Poles, who had got behind his boys at Panzendorf and cost him large numbers of guns and AA weapons as they ran amok in the rear echelon. Only a costly attack by nearby battalions of the 3rd Guards Airborne Division had opened the way, permitting the retreating units of 21st Guards Rifle Corps to escape.

His boys had also given the Germans a damn good thrashing at St Martin and Bruneck, where 31st Guards Rifle Corps and 1322nd Anti-Tank Artillery Regiment had held the green bastards at bay, leaving their bloodied corpses strewn across the landscape.

Chuikov still husbanded the 27th Army, hoping above hope that he would have a suitable opportunity to inflict a great defeat on the enemy. As yet, none had materialized, and, in any case, the hostile skies would always pose a problem to such an enterprise.

A call from Derevianko, the new commander of 4th Guards Army, disturbed his thought processes, but the news was welcome.

Part of the 31st Guards Rifle Corps had successfully counter-attacked at Anterselva di Sotto, forcing the German 18th Infantry Division to flee back to Rasun.

'Good news at last!'

There was very little of it in the days to come.

1238 hrs, Friday, 12th April 1946, Headquarters of 1st Alpine Front, Stainach, Austria.

Chuikov held the boy as he died.

Although a man by definition, he had been the youngest and bravest soldier in the 3rd Guards Airborne Division, which fact had brought him here, to his commander, to receive an award for his bravery.

Now he lay legless and with his chest penetrated in a dozen places, victim of the airborne curse that plagued the Red Army incessantly.

"Easy lad, easy now."

One cough, one spurt of crimson fluid, and life's journey ended for the young soldier.

Chuikov's own wound hurt like hell, and he plucked at the wooden splinter protruding from his ankle.

It refused to budge and brought excruciating pain as a reward for his attempts.

Chuikov looked up into the now empty sky and silently cursed the enemy aircraft whose engine sounds were nearly faded away to nothing.

Bogoliubov limped up, an apparition in red and black.

He coughed a reply to Chuikov's unspoken close examination.

"Not mine, Comrade Marshal. I'll get the doctor for you, but I think we need to move house again."

"Help me up, man"

Assisting the unsteady Marshal to his feet brought on another bout of coughing.

"Just dust I think…"

The two limped away in unison, supporting each other, seeking to bring order to the chaos around them.

1109 hrs, Wednesday, 17th April 1946, Headquarters of 1st Alpine Front, Klaus an der Phyrnbahn, Austria.

Fortunately, the weather was warmer now, as the new headquarters to which they had just relocated, was generally bereft of cover.

Some tarpaulins had been erected, even some wooden sheds 'stolen' from gardens in nearby villages and placed around to serve as bedrooms for a select few. Even the Mamayev had more facilities, Chuikov confided in his staff.

His ankle had developed an infection, despite the close ministrations of the senior doctors, and his hobble was now as pronounced and genuine as the pain that came with each step.

Sitting on a brightly coloured chair, recently liberated from an Austrian gasthaus, Chuikov rested his foot on a lump of timber specially placed there for the purpose.

The map on his lap showed the present situation, or at least the one in place before they had set off to the new location.

It had been a hard few days, and he had lost some fine units from the order of battle.

3rd Guards Airborne Division had been slaughtered in the hopeless defence of Lienz, where heavy bombers, medium bombers, and ground attack aircraft had mercilessly cut the veteran paratroopers down in their hundreds.

28th Tank Brigade had simply vanished, one moment under concerted attack, and then simply not there.

7th Tank Corps had taken a huge hit on the Gail River at Arnoldstein, but had held together in the retreat to Villach.

384

40th Army was a skeleton of units, bereft of serious artillery and low on ammunition.

The presence of Tolbukhin's forces had allowed them to pass through the front lines and head back to a recovery area where they could lick their wounds and gather what few supplies were to be had.

26th Army was on its third commander since the Allied offensive had commenced.

'Their air power is destroying us!'

One ray of hope that morning had been the news that Zhukov would soon be back at his desk, and with his return came more hope that the Red Army could find a way to stem the Allied flow.

Although made of stern stuff, Chuikov automatically cringed as the roar of aero engines approached, although there was no point running. The slit trenches were still being dug and were now filled with the men who had been wielding the spades.

Incredibly, there was cheering, as, through the green canopy, a diagonal line of five Soviet fighters flew past. Making a rough calculation, the Marshal estimated that the friendly aircraft were heading towards the desperate affair developing at Obervellach.

'Obervellach'.

1st Alpine's CoS dropped onto the camping stool beside his commander.

"Message from Derevianko. Good news, Comrade Marshal. The enemy attack on Obervellach has been stopped in its tracks. He reports hundreds of enemy dead. More to follow when he has better information."

Fishing in his pocket, Bogoliubov held out a small flask.

"Makes the water drinkable, Comrade Marshal."

Grinning, Chiukov took a hefty swig, nearly choking on the contents.

"What in the name of the great steppes is that?"

"That is Austrian Blue Gin, and it's as smooth a drink as you will taste, Comrade Marshal."

"Tastes like fucking aviation spirit to me!"

The two roared with laughter, drawing attention from all quarters, as laughter was a rare thing in those heavy days.

"If I was trawling for whores, then it would be my drink of choice, Comrade. However, I'm an officer of the Red Army. Get me a fucking vodka or I'll have you shot for trying to poison me."

Bogoliubov raised an admonishing finger, and produced another flask, a glass one, clearly containing a darker fluid.

"Perhaps this is more to your taste?"

It took two snorts to satisfy the Marshal's taste buds.

"Blyad! That's more like it."

"Stroh rum, and it is quite plentiful so I'm told."

They clinked flasks and downed more fiery liquid.

Another group of aircraft flew overhead, but this time higher, leaving contrails in the sky, flying north-east.

Followed by another group... and yet another... until the sky was filled with dots and white lines.

"Someone's going to cop it."

That someone was Bratislava, its bridges, infrastructure, occupying Bulgarian units and, of course, the civilian population.

1301 hrs, Friday, 19th April 1946, headquarters of British Fifteenth Army Group.

Leese finished reading the report as Alexander poured another tea.

The Eighth Army commander read a virtual mirror of his own report, citing heavy casualties, higher than expected consumption of the stocks of war, fatigue, battle weariness, call it what you would, but it seemed that the US Twentieth Army was running out of steam, like Leese's Eighth Army, and the German pair sat between the two.

"So Oliver, what do you think of that, eh? All in the same boat. What?"

"Seems so, Sir. But if we're tired, they must be tired. We know they've less supplies and were in poorer shape at the start of this show. The evidence of that has been spread before us as we've advanced."

He sipped the delicate china cup.

"Granted, they fight like the very devil. Damn good soldiers, these Russians, but surely we can give it one more go. The blighters are close to breaking, I know they are, Sir."

Leese had been brought back from the Far East to command the Eighth, his old Army, when McCreery had been handed the 21st.

He had the advantage of being a good friend of his commander, which gave him latitude when in private.

"Personally, I think we have gone about as far as we can, Oliver."

"Don't think we've reached the boundary quite yet, Sir. My lads have got at least one more good shove in them. Give me two days and I'll have them fully booted and spurred for another crack at the Bolshevik hordes."

"Opinion noted, Oliver, and as ever, you're irrepressible."

They drank the rest of their tea in silence.

Reese understood that Alexander was coming to a decision.

"Well quite", he announced, placing his cup and saucer on the small table, "It would be rude not to, I think."

Reese stood.

"I will tell Eisenhower that we have one good shove left, and that we will go on the 22nd. That gives you an extra day to get the full war paint on, Oliver."

Reese gathered himself and threw the Field Marshal the kind of salute that only a Guards Officer can deliver.

"Thank you, Sir. I will have a plan to you by tomorrow evening, if that's acceptable?"

"Most acceptable. Thank you, Oliver. Charles, will you see the General out please."

1101 hrs, Monday, 22nd April 1946, Headquarters of 1st Alpine Front, Klaus an der Phyrnbahn, Austria.

Chuikov listened impassively as the latest reports were translated onto the situation map.

The few days grace afforded by not being discovered had provided enough time to construct a rough shelter for the main headquarters staff, and the long map took centre place on the rear wall.

What he saw was not good, amounting to an attack virtually all along his defensive line, including a stunning developing air and ground attack against his previous lightly troubled Yugoslavian volunteer forces.

Garbled reports from one contact suggested that the 21st Serbian Division had collapsed entirely.

A good portion of his limited reserve was already en route to back up the Yugoslavians, and the Marshal was within a few minutes of finally committing the 27th Army, the formation he had preserved for a chance to strike back.

Tolbukhin's situation was slightly different, as the Allies continued to avoid activity adjacent to the Yugoslavian border. Whereas, at the other end of his line, the 1st Southern European

Front reported nothing out of the ordinary, just the steady constant attacks that had been the stuff of every day since the sun had risen on the 26th.

He did what he could, with scanty resources, ordering this movement, that spoiling attack, an adjustment here, a tactical withdrawal there, but, annoyingly for Chuikov, he had no assets with which to cause mischief.

The initiative seemed to be well and truly in the enemy's hands.

23rd April 1946, Area of operations for the British Fifteenth Army Group, Austria and Italy.

The initiative appeared to be lost.

The 'good shove', as Alexander had put it, failed spectacularly and became the stuff of huge debate for historians in the decades after WW3 ended.

Polish III Corps had advanced down a narrow route, the 3rd Mountain Division flanking the central core of 2nd Polish Armoured Division at Kremsbrücke, had run into thick minefields in the Heitzelsbergerwald and Maisswald. Combined with a heavy Soviet infantry presence and a large deployment of rockets and artillery, both divisions had suffered heavily.

That the Soviet artillery and Katyusha units suffered badly in counter-battery fire was of scant comfort to those who had been on the receiving end of their efforts.

Despite three assaults, the Poles could make no further progress.

The post-mortems started almost immediately, the narrow pass and single road echoing dissections of the Market-Garden Operations of Horrocks' XXX Corps; they still continue to this day.

Whoever was to blame for the debacle in which three and a half thousand Polish soldiers were killed or wounded, the result was indisputable.

Fifteenth Army Group had run out of steam.

1009 hrs, Tuesday, 23nd April 1946, Headquarters of 1st Alpine Front, Klaus an der Phyrnbahn, Austria.

"Check again."

Chuikov took a pull on a glass of water, the uncharacteristic choice of drink symptomatic of an extremely strange morning in 1st Alpine Headquarters.

Bogoliubov directed the communications officer to the task and, as he listened to the exchanges, mentally ticked off each Senior Command contacted.

The reply was the same from each, although sometimes couched in suspicion, sometimes in surprise, but always with noticeable relief.

"Nothing, Comrade Marshal."

"Nothing at all?"

"Nothing."

"Well, I may have to take up bible bashing after all... fucking hell."

Chuikov grabbed his chin and worked it, feeling the stubble under his fingertips, his piggy eyes devouring the information on the map, which was, to all intents and purposes, exactly the same as it had been the previous evening.

'The bastards are up to something.'

"Get me Marshal Vasilevsky!"

Author's note - Following the disappearance of Marshal Konev, assumed killed in the bombing attack on Nordhausen, Vassilevsky had been immediately selected as commander in chief of the Red Banner Forces of Soviet Europe, handing over command of the increasingly impotent Eastern Forces to his deputy.

Many saw Vassilevsky's appointment as an incredible snub to Zhukov.

Stalin undoubtedly put Vasilevsky in place as he considered the man competent, yet malleable to pressure.

Marshal Zhukov's personal diary makes it clear he saw the move as a good thing for the Red Army and Mother Russia, his personal negative feelings about Konev being reasonably well known in higher circles.

Zhukov's relationship with the new commander was very good, both viewing the other as an excellent field commander and adept strategist.

Once Zhukov returned to work, their cordial professional relationship would be tested over the coming months but would, undoubtedly, make a positive impact on Red Army performance during their period of command.

I no more believe in God, the Devil, or Heaven than I do in mermaids and fairies. However, Hell's another matter. It exists; it's a very real place. I know 'cause I've been there.

Lukas J. Barkmann, Major, US Rangers.

Chapter 142 - THE SIXTH

0758 hrs hrs, Tuesday, 26th March 1946, Toul-Rosières, France.

The young and enthusiastic war correspondent, only recently arrived in France, hopped from foot to foot in excitement, watching the USAAF P-51s rise into the air.

Three squadrons, one after the other, a total of sixty-three aircraft, took a long time to get airborne, but the spectacle engrossed the reporter for its full duration.

"How long before they're back, Hank?"

The MP Corporal assigned to 'keep the goddamn limey reporter outta the goddamn way' actually had no idea but plumped for two hours.

"Time to get a cup of tea then."

The two sauntered off to the mess hut where the reporter's hunt for tea proved fruitless, and coffee became a substitute.

Rapidly consuming a plate of eggs, fried potato, and fried ham, he set up his typewriter and set to work on his first report 'from the front'.

The journalistic reports of John Thornton-Smith, War Correspondent for the Daily Sketch newspaper.

With the United States Army Air Force, somewhere in Eastern France, 8:42am, 26th March 1946.

Dear Reader,

Today is the first day of the grand new offensive, aimed at kicking the Communist hordes back to whence they came, something we have all been waiting for ever since their dastardly betrayal last August.

You will all be thrilled to learn that our soldiers, airmen, and sailors are all keen

390

to press on with the job, and to carry the fight back to the enemy, and they speak of nothing but victory and getting the job done.

At the time of writing, I am sat waiting for a group of young Americans to return from their first combat of the day, the whole three squadrons having leapt into the crisp morning air and sped off to do battle with the enemy, before returning home to prepare for another joust later in the day.

Around me, the airfield is a hive of activity, even though there are few aircraft left to tend. The ground crews are taking no rest, preparing the fuel, bombs, and bullets to be loaded on the returned aircraft, to quickly make them ready for the next show.

I spoke to an experienced Captain, a leader of men, with many kills under his belt already.

He spoke of his pride in his boys and the way they had handled everything that this war had thrown their way.

A quiet, unassuming man, his pilots obviously worship him. I can only call him Jim, but many of you will have read his name during the previous unpleasantness.

Jim is a man of few words, but before he climbed into the gleaming aircraft, he asked me to send his love and best wishes to his family back home, especially his wife Martha, and his two sons, James and Richard.

His steed is a modern, state of the art fighter, and he has promised me a closer look once A-GQ returns.

How I envy him and his men the freedom of the skies and the wondrous experience that must be the carefree nature of flying.

How wonderful it must be to return from lashing the enemy, and to exchange yarns on the day's events.

I will share some of those stories with you in due course, but, for now, you all back home can rest assured that our finest are doing their best and that it is only a matter of time.

John Thornton-Smith
(Correspondent)

With the United States Army Air Force, somewhere in Eastern France, 9:13am, 26th March 1946.

The aircraft are returning and excited ground crews celebrate when they recognize their own man and machine taxiing into the bays where each aircraft is worked on.

Two fire engines almost seem to twitch nervously on the perimeter road, although all the aircraft so far landed seem to have had an easy ride and to be without any marks of distress.

And yet, as I type, one aircraft comes into view, its presence marked more firmly by the smoke it trails behind it.

The damaged fighter bumps down hard, both fire engines in hot pursuit, keen to get to grips with any fire that might endanger man and machine.

The aircraft slips off the runway onto the marshy ground and is brought to a swift stop by the cloying grip of the mud that surrounds this base.

The firemen are all over the aircraft and the pilot is removed. He is taken to the arrived ambulance to be whisked away to the doctor for a check-up

Beside me, Jack, a USAAF cook, compares numbers with his pal, Ray.

The numbers do not tally and it appears that some aircraft have not returned.

That is not unusual, for even though the Allies have mastery of the air, losses are inevitable and, sadly, there is occasionally loss of life, which can affect those in a tight-knit Squadron such as this.

Let us hope that our brave fliers have landed elsewhere or managed to take to a parachute.

Now I must away, in order to share in the sense of fun that must accompany these men returning from their labours against the foe. I shall report back with some of their stories of missions accomplished and great deeds performed.

John Thornton-Smith
(Correspondent)

[Author's note – On the 26th March, 354th Fighter Group flew 178 sorties out of the airbase at Toul-Rosières, France. The group lost a total of seventeen aircraft that day, and twelve pilots were killed over their targets, with two severely injured, including the pilot whose landing was watched by JTS, namely the 355th Fighter Regiment's Captain James Z. Steele Jr, pilot of GQ-A. He had flown with the RAF Eagle Squadron in the Battle of Britain and was a highly experienced flier with eighteen and a half kills. After-combat reports all agreed that Steele's aircraft was struck by ground fire as he led his section in a ground attack role on Soviet armoured and motorised forces at Imbsheim, Germany. He died in the ambulance, succumbing to his wounds.]

With the United States Army, somewhere in Eastern France, 11:13am, 28th March 1946.

Dear Reader,

Unfortunately my time with the brave US air force pilots was cut short, so I never had the chance to look over AC-Q, or to hear the yarns of aerial combat as the pilots boasted of their successes.

I promise to return as soon as circumstances permit.

Now, I find myself with the Army Command, observing the machine that moves our glorious soldiery around the landscape of Europe, sending extra men to trouble spots, directing fast-moving reserves to exploit holes riven in the front lines of our

393

dastardly foe, and that organizes the whole war with the ease of a game of chess.

Whilst the great General himself organizes the movement of his huge army, I have been extremely fortunate to have been shown around by one of his senior staff, who I can only call Colonel Arnold.

He has explained the complexities of warfare on this scale, as best as this reporter can understand, and it seems that our forces have planned and planned for this huge battle, and that all is going precisely as anticipated.

Colonel Arnold tells me that there have been some casualties, but less than predicted, which can only be a good thing, and supports the view that this is going well and easier than expected.

The loss of any soldier is a tragedy, of course, but back home, you can rest assured that your fathers and brothers, husbands and sons, are in the best possible hands and as safe as can be.

The offensive goes on and, with the special permission of the commanding general, I will be permitted to go further forward tomorrow, and visit a Division Headquarters where I can get experience of real fighting at first hand.

To me, this is yet another indication of the ease and success of our efforts against the enemy of free Europe.

The best indication of all is the confidence of the officers and men moving around me, their serious faces showing dedication and great intent in their work, betraying their total commitment to the success of this great crusade.

The General himself, who I cannot name, works with great energy and care, his ebullient manner and outgoing nature both clearly advantages in the management of his war machine and the men who serve it.

Before I finish this report, I must speak of what now flies over this headquarters. My companion estimates some seven hundred aircraft, of all types, passing over our heads, carrying the war forward.

Such numbers will not, cannot be denied.

We must all give thanks for our leaders' planning and the strength of our armies.

Perhaps our boys really will all be home for Christmas.

John Thornton-Smith
(Correspondent)

[Author's note – On the 28th March, US Seventh Army logs show the presence of John Thornton-Smith, and also show that he was placed under the care of Lieutenant Colonel Arnold H. White. A note from White's personal diary betrays a certain dislike of the young reporter, based around his innocence and enthusiasm for war. According to that diary entry, it was Patch's deliberate decision to send JTS forward, where he might get some experience to be able to understand what war was actually about. My profound thanks to the family of Brigadier-General Arnold H. White.]

With the Allied Army, somewhere in Eastern France, 3:17pm, 29th March 1946.

Dear Reader,

Today I am privileged to be able to speak with soldiers from across the ocean.

Not from our dear Allies, the Americans or Canadians, but from new Allied states.

I write of the South Americans.

All around me are excited men and officers, assembling for a briefing on the present state of affairs at the front. None of these men know, but today may bring their call to action, as all their units have, so far, acted as a reserve, and lain awaiting the call to summon them to glory.

My guide for the day, a South African Captain called Johannes, walks with me amongst

395

the excited jabbering common to the races of that wonderful continent.

Amongst them are voices from Rio de Janeiro, Montevideo, Buenos Aires, Asunción, Havana, and Mexico City.

Smart and well armed, these soldiers from so far away are ready to fight and play their part in the great journey that is being undertaken, and, to a man, they pray that it will take them all the way to Moscow and beyond.

Most of these men could not have dreamed of being here a year ago, and you can see their pride and fervour.

They display their weapons with pride and, despite their relaxed manner, exhibit an energy I have rarely seen amongst the common soldiery.

Their very real joy when friendly aircraft fly overhead brings on spontaneous displays of emotion, manifesting itself in shouting, prayers to God and, when the excitement is too much, the firing of weapons into the air, something their officers move quickly to discourage.

You cannot fault the ardour of these men, and their wish to get to grips with the enemy.

It is my fondest hope that I will have an opportunity to observe these wonderful soldiers experience their first taste of battle, when, I am convinced, they will take the battle to the Communists with great elan.

John Thornton-Smith
(Correspondent)

Further to my submission, the briefing did not bring forth the news that these brave soldiers were waiting for, and they are yet to remain in our reserve, waiting for the moment that they are set loose.

Whilst their disappointment was evident, they resumed their duties with joy in their hearts.

The atmosphere around me is one of noisy anticipation, and I suspect that the campfires will be surrounded by laughter and song well into the night.

For my part, I will miss it, as I move forward again.

[Author's note – On the 29th March, JTS was visiting the forces of SAFFEC, the South American grouping that was kept in reserve during the early days of the attack. I discovered that his guide, Captain Johannes de Wilhout, acting as a liaison between 6th SA Armoured and the SAFFEC headquarters, was killed in an accidental discharge incident two days later. His room mate, Major Fidel Castro, was also wounded.]

With the United States Army, somewhere in Eastern France, 11:13am, 30th March 1946.

Dear Reader,

Having taken my leave of the wonderful South Americans and my gracious South African host yesterday evening, my excitement knew no bounds this morning, as I arrived at the battle headquarters of a division at the cutting edge of our glorious advance into enemy held territory.

The sound of gunfire reached my ears, heavy gunfire that continued without let up, as nearby friendly artillery units persistently poured their shells into the enemy hordes.

How marvellous it was to listen to the wondrous instrument of war that our leaders have created, the constant crack and rumbling of heavy weapons a fitting backdrop to the critical decisions being made within the command tent in front of me.

Today, my escort was Major William, an experienced front line soldier with more medals on his chest than I have seen in a lifetime.

A man of few words, his grunts of agreement and occasional shakes of the head answered all my questions, as we observed the divisional commander responding to whatever problem was brought before him.

Muddy men came and went, some with information, others to take away orders.

This was where the business of war was done, and where the link between the commanding general and the man in the trench lay, translating the orders into commands that the Lieutenants and Sergeants could understand.

Occasionally something would happen, an unexpected event, a problem, but the commanding officer of the division would calmly consult with his closest advisors.

Once, our planned move forward was halted, even as orderlies and officers worked to strike down tables and phones. A small enemy counter-attack gave the command group a different priority.

It proved to be no great issue, and the command group relocated some hours later.

The weather played a part today, as torrential rain curtailed some of the carefully laid assault plans and played a merry dance with our expected air support.

Again, I found myself given permission to go even further forward, and I am so excited that I will be given the opportunity to smell the smoke of battle first hand.

All the better to tell you, dear reader, what the war really is like for the men who carry the rifles and drive the tanks that are pushing the hated enemy back into their lair.

John Thornton-Smith
(Correspondent)

[Author's note – On the 30th March, JTS was known to be at the headquarters of the 66th US Infantry Division. Whilst I can find no official record of his presence (many of the 66th's files were lost subsequently), I managed to get a word of mouth report from Sergeant Hank P Watermayne, a senior NCO with the unit. According to his report, Major Guillame J Rousseau, who was JTS's escort, could barely speak to someone he considered an idiotic child. It was Rousseau who secured permission for JTS to go forward to the 264th Regiment, possibly to rid himself of a troublesome duty. As an extra, the reason that the headquarters did not relocate was because of a violent Soviet counter-attack that, according to the divisional history, very nearly split the 262nd Regiment in half. The counter-attack that was, according to JTS, no great issue, was the single-greatest loss of life to the 262nd Regiment in a single combat, as five hundred and thirty-seven men became casualties in the two hour struggle against a strong counter-attack, out of which three hundred and two men permanently fell. The 66th Division had experienced a catastrophic day once before when, on Christmas Eve 1944, the troop ship Leopoldville, carrying members of the division to Cherbourg, was sunk by a torpedo. This sinking, only a few miles off the French coast, resulted in the loss of seven hundred and sixty-two men.]

With the United States Army, somewhere in Eastern France, 12:33am, 1st April 1946.

Dear Reader,
Today I am privileged to be with a Regimental Command group in a fighting American division.

This group of young GIs has been in Europe since December last year, and have been constantly embroiled in the heaviest fighting against the former German enemy.

Now, allied with those same soldiers, they push forward against a common foe.

My escort for today hails from St Petersberg, but not the former city in the Russian Empire, but the city in Florida, USA, a place where cold and wet conditions such as we have today are rare, and sun is the norm.

Lieutenant Joe is new to the war, a recent arrival to the division, one of many sent up to fill the gaps that inevitably come with high-level combat.

Tomorrow I will travel with him to the frontline, and for that I cannot wait.

Today, I am struck by the energetic movement of everyone in this headquarters, the shouted orders responded to in an instant, the whole affair organized and dedicated to doing the best for the boys up front.

The Colonel in charge looks tired and worn out, but that is not how he conducts himself. Whilst the war may well have left its mark upon this veteran officer, he is on top of his job, shepherding his men like a father does his children.

A small convoy passes the headquarters tent, carrying food and ammunition forward, and I am tempted to climb aboard one of these huge lorries.

Unfortunately, we have to leave the headquarters whilst a situation is dealt with, but that gives me the opportunity to type this report whilst sampling the delights of the regimental mess.

Hopefully, there will be more to report later.

John Thornton-Smith
(Correspondent)

The great American General Robert Lee is quoted as saying that it is just as well that war is terrible or man would grow too fond of it.

Perhaps, today, I have seen something of what he meant.

This place, which I cannot name, has seen the footsteps of war on at least one other occasion and, as Joe and I walk amongst the shattered houses, we come across a field where high-explosive has done its work.

A pit where enemy bodies had been buried has been opened by explosive force, and the poor dead have had further ignominy visited upon them.

It is a terrible sight, and the odours that accompany it are sufficient to turn the strongest stomach.

Further on, we find a graves unit removing some glorious American dead from their temporary graves, probably men who fell in the battle that has recently rolled through this corner of France.

I admit, the sight of the still bodies, riven by weapons of war, is as awful as can be, and we must thank the Lord that so few of our men have fallen in this noble cause.

We do not dwell to gawk at the dead, offering them more respect by retreating.

I pray that they will be the last mortified souls that I see, but I fear that will not be the case.

John Thornton-Smith
(Correspondent)

[Author's note. The location on the day that JTS visited was Hattmatt. I know that the graves that he witnessed being dug up were casualties from the previous winter's fighting. US Graves Registration records support this, although the entries are, in fairness, none too legible.

Clearly, the Soviet bodies were from the Ranger assault and were probably uncovered by the violent barrage launched by the 66th's artillery elements. The 66th's records of the 264th's attack on Hattmatt speak of little fighting, recording one KIA and four WIA before the Soviet forces gave way. Of note is the fact that shortly after the 264th RCT's headquarters moved on, five members of the 3060th US Quartermaster Graves Registration Company were killed by a booby trap hidden in the bodies of the 2nd US Ranger slain months before, almost certainly installed by the Soviet forces who subsequently retook the village.

Clearly, his recollection of the words of Robert E. Lee was inaccurate, but the spirit of what the old General meant was still carried through in JTS's words.]

With the United States Army, somewhere in Eastern France, 12:33am, 2nd April 1946.

Dear Reader,

Today I am with the brave men in the front line and, perhaps, this is where all of us who wish to bring to you the events and happenings of this war should be.

I have seen efficiency and calm behind the lines, where Generals and Colonels organise their staffs and bring together plans to send their men forward and destroy the enemy forces.

Here is where those orders come, to be translated in actions and deeds.

I am sorry to report that my companion, Lieutenant Joe, has been slightly wounded and forced to return for some medical assistance. His first day in combat brings a wound that he may bear with honour and regale his grandchildren about in the years of his dotage. I hope he returns soon.

So, for now, I am placed under the care of a senior NCO, a man called Ron, who hails from Washington State, USA.

Occasionally, the experienced NCO, a man with twenty-eight years of soldiering under his belt, will grab me and drag me down, citing the possibility that the enemy may see me, but I am confident that the men around me can take care of themselves, and certainly cope with any threat the enemy might offer.

Under Sgt Ron's supervision, I move through the trench lines so recently held by the enemy, finding squads of GIs going about the business of war in stoic fashion.

We reach a larger bunker, one that probably once held the Russian commander, one that still shows traces of its former occupancy. The red flag has been left in place, but with certain additions written on it by soldiers with wit that I simply cannot pass on to the reader for fear of offence.

But we cannot blame them for their words, however immoral they maybe.

Now we can take a break and I seize the opportunity to eat some of the food that these boys consume on a daily basis. Coffee is plentisome and the men, although obviously seeing me as an outsider, answer my questions when they hear them above the racket of guns outsi

---

Oh, my dear reader,

I now find myself inside the very vestiges of hell.

The enemy has struck back at use with their dastardly artillery.

Some of the wonderful men that I spoke with have fallen, claimed by the dice of war, purely for being in the wrong place at the wrong time.

As the shells swept over us, we could hear the cries of the wounded, cries to which the brave stretcher bearers responded.

Both those valiant men lie amongst those who have made the ultimate sacrifice in this war against the aggression of Communism.

Giorgio, an Italian-American who spoke of little else but a future in professional baseball, has departed in the ambulance that took away four of our wounded souls.

They lied to him, assuring him that he would be well. He has lost a leg, and the knowledge of that would have struck him as mortal a blow as the enemy metal that has deprived him of his career.

My escort, Sergeant Ron, has disappeared, and my comrades fear the worst for their rock, as they call him.

Before I came on this personal mission, I can only confess to how little I understood of the cost of war, and the loss of these few men has made a deep impression upon me. I cannot begin to imagine how deeply it will

affect those who have sweated and bled beside them, only now to find them gone forever.
John Thornton-Smith
(Correspondent)

[Author's note. The unit that JTS joined was Baker Company, 264th US Infantry Regiment. The Divisional history indicates that the 1st Battalion, of which Baker was a part, had seen some ferocious fighting in the first days of combat, during which over two-thirds of its leadership was killed or wounded. That makes me wonder greatly as to why JTS was sent to them, and especially given the plans for their use during the upcoming renewed assaults.

2nd Lieutenant Joseph S. Warner never returned to the front line, as he developed complications and died a month after his injury was sustained. According to witness testimony, his time actually in the front line amounted to no more than twenty-five minutes.

First Sergeant Ronald F. Gregson disappeared in the artillery strike that JTS speaks of. It is known that he left the safety of the dugout before the medics, but nothing is known of his actions or demise.

According to the battle-diary of First Battalion, the enemy artillery barrage lasted for no more than seven minutes, during which time Baker Company lost eighteen men WIA and eleven KIA. Three men were MIA, including Gregson, who had fought with the 42nd Division in the Great War,

The Heavy Weapons Company lost six WIA and five KIA.

Replacements were with the company within twenty-four hours.]

With the United States Army, somewhere in Eastern France, 12:33am, 5th April 1946.

Dear Reader,

Today I am to closely observe an attack, as the men of this company push forward to take a vital position, in preparation for a larger attack on a nearby town.

Around us are the wrecks and marks of previous combat.

Of particular note is a ruined tank, besides which are set five graves.

A German tank for sure, so it is a relic of the previous war, but none the less poignant to this reporter's eye.

The marks on the tank reveal how it met its end, two holes, once bright, now rusted, betray how the vehicle was knocked out.

Clearly the men inside would have had no chance.

Enemies or not, I find myself feeling sympathy for them, and for their families.

My concept of war seems to be changing as I see more of the loss and horror it brings.

It is difficult to find glory besides these five graves, or those I walked past some days ago.

There seems little glory in the screams of wounded men, or in the endless silence of the dead.

I have experienced loss, the departure of men with whom I have spent a few minutes, so how must it be for these soldiers, who see their friends and comrades taken from them so regularly?

I pray to God that these men will be preserved today, and yet, as I walk amongst them as they prepare, I wonder to myself whose voice will be heard no more, whose heart will be stilled, whose family will wait in vain?

I hope my prayers are listened to.

John Thornton-Smith
(Correspondent)

Dear Reader,

It is my duty, my awful duty to speak of the events that fell before my eye as these brave men went about the business of war.

I am now more convinced than ever as to the bestiality of it all, and ask what we achieve by sending our young men into circumstances that can only be described as hell on earth.

My prayers have fallen away, clearly unheard, at least I hope that is the case, not that they were unheeded.

The company was magnificent, moving forward on foot towards the objective; a piece of raised ground that dominates an important road junction.

Accompanied by another unit on our left flank, the men pushed forward hard until the enemy mortars started to drop amongst them.

Men that I had just shared coffee with fell in front of my eyes, never to rise again.

The company commander, wounded by a metal fragment, called his own support down upon the hill, and within seconds the high-explosive started to change the landscape towards which our troops again advanced.

More shells landed amongst the advancing waves and I saw grievous work done amongst the other supporting unit.

Again, the advance halted whilst more support was organised.

Within minutes it arrived, in the shape of seven aircraft. I did not recognise the type, nor the markings, but they were friendly and attacked the Soviet-held hill immediately.

I am told that they used something called napalm.

Whatever it was, the sight of its effect will live with me forever.

The whole hill was enveloped in roaring flame as, one after the other, the Allied aircraft dropped their deadly cargo.

After a second pass, the enemy mortars stopped their fire, and there was nothing by way of resistance from the smoking hill top.

Our men swept up and over the location, intent on pushing past the feature. The remaining units of the First Battalion, plus extra support, followed up quickly to secure the position and prepare for any counter-attack.

I went with them and found that, whatever I had thought about the weapon in use, the effects upon the occupying enemy were catastrophic.

It was the sweet smell, carried on the gentle breeze, which first assailed me.

I little understood its nature until I was confronted by my first corpse, charred black and shrunk to the size of a dwarf, the grotesquely smoking skull gaping wide displaying what can only have been the extremes of suffering.

This truly awful sight paled into insignificance as I moved further up the hill, where the numbers of shrunken black pygmies grew until, just the other side of the summit, I found the most awful tableau of man's suffering I think it is possible to see.

A wide trench, clearly the place where the enemy assembled their wounded, was filled with bodies, all ravaged by the excesses of fire. A score? Thirty? I have no idea how many men had been there when our air force struck. Whatever the number, they were all now permanently together in death, the horribly burned bodies welded and melted together by the deadly napalm.

Hell could not look as appalling as the aftermath of our attack on that hill.

It is my fondest hope that I never witness a napalm attack again for as long as I live.

The bodies scattered around the hill top, and the few, so very few who screamed their way through hideous wounds, were the enemy, and in combat our men must use every advantage of technology available to them.

But perhaps there are limits to the advances, and I use that word advisedly, that we should permit upon the field of combat.

407

I confess, I looked back on the route our soldiers had advanced and saw, with tears in my eyes, silent shapes that marked a fallen friend. More would have fallen taking this windswept charred piece of France had it not been for the air attack.

Yet perhaps, dear reader, you should wonder and judge if we can consider our humanity intact and our morals sound when we bring such awfulness to the field of combat.

John Thornton-Smith
(Correspondent)

[Author's note. The Panzer IV, whose crew was buried alongside the destroyed vehicle, belonged to the Alma Division, Legion Corps D'Assaut, and they fell in the move towards Brumath the previous year.

The units that JTS observed making the attack were Baker and Charlie Companies, 264th US Infantry Regiment. The height, Hill 846, can be found five hundred metres north of Minversheim, although all traces of the incident have been erased by time.

Both companies lost six men KIA, with Baker sustaining six WIA, and Charlie eighteen WIA and one MIA.

There were two napalm attacks carried out in that vicinity during the time frame, and it appears most likely that the responsible aircraft were the Thunderbolts of Escuadrón 203, Fuerza Aérea Mexicana (Mexican Air Force).

Soviet records are sketchy and I cannot be certain sure, but it would seem likely that the defenders of Hill 846 were a Shtrafbat, greatly reduced by heavy fighting, supported by a mortar company, probably from one of 90th Rifle Corps reserve units.

None of the hideously wounded Soviet soldiers lived out the day, and there are no known survivors.

Replacements were with Baker Company before night fell.

They would need every man for the challenge ahead.]

With the United States Army, somewhere in Eastern France, 12:33am, 6th April, 1946.

Dear Reader,

Today, the men of this proud unit, are assembling for a full-scale attack on a tough enemy position.

I cannot tell you where it is, but I can say that we are about to tread ground that is already riven by battles past, recent battles that have left the gruesome trophies of destruction as far as the eye can see.

Without a doubt, I can feel the difference in the air today; the atmosphere is steeped in anxiety and foreboding.

I took the opportunity to speak with a young 2nd Lieutenant called Richard, who has told me of his dread about the coming attack, both for himself, and for the men under his command.

And yet, he goes about the business of leadership, moving amongst his soldiers providing calm inspiration and reassurance.

I find myself asking how men can do such things?

When the time comes, none of these young Americans will hide, or run, or baulk from the challenge.

They will all rise up together and charge together, and possibly they will die together.

Perhaps that is the greatest privilege of the profession of arms; that special togetherness that inspires and drives men to great deeds for no other reason than their comradeship?

Of course, some fight for country and ideals: it was ever thus.

But it is now my feeling that most fight more for the man beside them, and that is something that those of us who have no experience of such matters, will never really fully understand.

That manifests itself in front of me, as comrade laughs with comrade as they check weapons and kit, ready for the attack.

The time draws near so I will stop my report now, and conclude it when we have done what we have to do this day.

John Thornton-Smith
(Correspondent)

Dear Reader,

So much has happened since last I put words to this paper.

Much of it is beyond my limited capacity to explain or even to understand.

We are back where we started, those of us that survived the hail of metal that greeted the charge.

I watched as these brave men pushed on, as our artillery and mortars swept the objective, and as our troops entered the village.

I watched as enemy rockets and artillery smashed what left of the pretty buildings, and a counter-attack pushed our men back towards this position.

The enemy counter-attack pressed on through the villages and, with tanks in support, the wave of enemy dashed itself upon these positions.

One dead Russian lies four feet from my typewriter as I make this report, shot down my own hand.

I picked up a fallen soldier's handgun and killed the man without a qualm.

I cannot believe I acted, and still my hands shake at the thought.

I am not proud of what I did, nor do I celebrate. I did so out of self-preservation and, perhaps just a little, out of the comradeship I have experienced amongst these American GIs.

The bravery of our troops in their assault was not unlike the bravery I witnessed in the counter-attack that pressed us so close. The only differences really being the directions they charged and the uniforms worn.

Richard, my officer friend, has been taken to the rear, grievously wounded.

He led his men forward and then back, only to fall in defence of our start position. I can only wish him well, but I fear the worst for this brave soldier.

Around me there are gaps, holes left by the absence of comrades who have been struck down in an action that has covered nearly two miles and yet has gained no ground.

The losses, however, are very real and, if it were not for the anti-tank gunners who so bravely stuck to their posts, the enemy tanks might well have overrun us.

Before I sat down to write this report, I sought out some familiar faces. Some I found, others were conspicuous by their absence.

I did not feel able to ask the survivors as to the whereabouts of the missing.

There is something about these men, something I have noticed before, but never quite as strongly as I do now.

It is in their eyes, a look that speaks of faraway places and not of the present, either in time or location.

An unblinking stare that holds no joy, no fear, no love, no hate; it holds nothing but the emptiness that combat brings.

The men sat around me, silently smoking, have it.

The NCOs moving round, organising the men, have it.

The officers, trying to bring order out of the chaos, have it.

The corpses, American and Russian alike, have it.

But, at least for the dead, the horrors of war are over.

The survivors must continue to have the experience until war's end.

The European theatre it is called, suggesting a well-orchestrated and rehearsed public presentation with given processes and endings, fit for public consumption, where the ending brings a satisfactory and entertaining climax, drawing applause from all who witness it.

Of course, nothing could be further from the truth.

When I first came to the European theatre, I saw, naively of course, a great crusade against the belligerent forces of Bolshevism.

The closer I have come to the front, I have gained greater understanding of this violent process that we so readily resort to, often in preference to sitting down and resolving our differences with negotiations and goodwill; the process we call War.

Admittedly, we did not start this war, but then, neither did most of the people who stand on the other side of No Man's land.

Wars are started, most often, by those who sit in comfort and beat their breasts at some perceived slight or aggression, before issuing a rallying call and dispatching the youth of the day to do their dirty work for them, whilst they remain in safety and comfort many miles from danger.

Perhaps, when those who decide to go to war are the ones who stand in the front line of an army, then we may see less dying and more trying.

I am convinced that those who have died, or are returning home broken, would agree.

Perhaps, when this ghastly mess is over, we can begin to have a world where war is seen for the abhorrence it is; no glory, no honour, no wondrous adventure, just a gutter affair in which we visit awfulness upon men who could so easily be our brothers and, with whom, in the main, we have no disagreement or dislike.

We can but pray.

John Thornton-Smith
(Correspondent)

[Author's note. The attack was carried out on the village of Rottelsheim, and was part of the major assault upon Brumath and its environs. 264th US Infantry Regiment was tasked with taking the route through Rottelsheim, in order to prevent reinforcements moving south. The Soviets had anticipated this move and sent extra forces, units that bolstered the defence to the extent that the rest of the 264th's units failed to make their objectives.

1st Battalion made Rottelsheim, possibly due to the late arrival of the Soviet bolstering force, which force then counter-attacked and pushed the GIs all the way back to the 1st Battalion's start line.

The Soviet forces involved belonged to the 15th Mechanised Corps, the unit mainly credited with arriving on the field at Brumath in time to halt the US offensive.

I have been unable to establish which units comprised the original defenders of Rottelsheim, so don't want to confuse the situation by taking an uninformed guess.

The after-action report of 1st Battalion, 264th Regiment, reveals horrendous losses which, when combined with the strains of the previously days of combat, were to make the unit combat-ineffective and in need of withdrawal.

The Battalion lost exactly one hundred men KIA, one hundred and seventeen WIA, and six men MIA. The six MIA were located during road widening works to the north of Rottelsheim during the summer of 2005. It appears likely that they had been captured and executed.

Soviet casualties are estimated at three-hundred plus.

2nd Lieutenant Richard G Flores lost both his right leg and right arm during the defence of their positions. He survived the war.

An investigation was launched as to why expected air support did not arrive, and the blame was placed on an air-controller who, without the necessary authority, sent the supporting unit elsewhere.]

Dear Reader,

The day has brought no renewed fighting.

It seems both sides have battered each other into a stupor and now pause for breath.

We are to be relieved, news that brought surprisingly little reaction amongst the men here.

Everywhere I go, there is a low hubbub of whispered conversations, but there is nothing of the banter and exchanges that filled the hours before yesterday's attack.

Soon we will be gone from this place, so perhaps there is no surprise that, when the big NCO calls for volunteers for a patrol, there are none.

Men are ordered to the duty, and they grumble, but still rise and prepare to go out into No Man's Land once more.

The pistol that I picked up yesterday is now mine to keep, complete with an old leather holster tossed to me by the same NCO who has permitted me to accompany the small patrol. A sign of acceptance from the men who I have come to think of as friends?

I will compose my last front line report upon my return.

John Thornton-Smith
(Correspondent)

Dear Reader,

Our patrol has returned, but not without incident, and strange incident at that.

As suspected, the Soviet forces have pulled back a little and confine themselves to the village, leaving the outlying areas free of their presence.

We proceeded on orders, and moved quietly around, checking buildings and natural defensive points, all so that we can hand over to our relief and arm them with the best knowledge available.

Near the end of our patrol, three ragged men alarmed us as they emerged from a ruined set of buildings, shouting, their hands raised to indicate no weapons.

My veterans hit the ground and the trio were challenged by Sergeant Bill, the mission commander.

Beckoning them forward, the three ragged men closed on our patrol, details becoming clearer the closer they came.

Beside me, I heard a muttered oath as a long-service corporal saw things he recognised and, I am certain, never expected to see again.

Sergeant Bill rose to meet the three and found that one had sufficient English to make himself understood. As the conversation continued, the sight of SS uniforms made many a trigger finger itchy.

In short order, Sergeant Bill organised an escort for two of the men, whilst the one who spoke English took his leave. It seemed an emotional goodbye, but Bill soon cut it short.

We returned to the front positions and our new arrivals were taken away.

Just over an hour later, I now find myself having to pack away my typewriter, as the relief company has arrived and we can make our way back to an area where we can be safe and sleep will not be interrupted.

My war is run, and I only hope that I never again experience anything that it has to offer. The sights and sounds that have assailed me these last few days will stay with me for all my days.

There is no glory in death, of that I am convinced.

From this day forward, I will concentrate on enjoying everything life has to offer, come what may.

                          John Thornton-Smith
                          (Correspondent)

[Author's note. The failed assault on Brumath marked the high-water mark of the attacks in that area, although elsewhere, some successes were still realized. The presence of forces dedicated to the Soviet's own plans of attack undoubtedly meant that US 6th Army had a harder time than some others.

The relieving unit was from the 263rd Regiment, who were in turn replaced three days later, allowing the entire 66th to recuperate behind the lines.

Perhaps the strangest part of the last day's activities was the surrender of the two men who emerged from the shattered Buildings.

According to the report submitted by Sergeant William J Brown, the two ex-SS men were apparently members of the Foreign Legion who had been left behind during the previous battles.

The senior officer, whilst dressed in German combat gear, certainly bore insignia and rank markings that could have been French in origin, but it was the presence of German gallantry medals alongside a Silver Star that most drew his eye.

Without a German speaker in the unit, Brown could not get further information, but he ensured the two were properly treated and sent back to the rear echelon.

The officer in question was eventually identified as Rolf Uhlmann.]

With the United States Army, somewhere in Eastern France, 12:33am, 11th April, 1946.

Dear Reader,
I had expected some immediate relief from the horrors of war, but they have not been forthcoming, rather the memories have become clearer and more horrible with the passing of time.

My dreams have become nightmares, and my nights have become broken by visions of men now dead, or dismembered, or missing.

I awake from my tortured sleep imagining the sights and smells of battle and its aftermath.

How must it be for those who have experienced the hardships and violence of combat for so much longer than I?

Around me, the voices have returned but the stares are still there.

I have seen men throw themselves to the ground in fear when a bin is dropped, men who have experienced the heights of hardship in the presence of the enemy cowed by a simple sharp noise.

A Corporal, much respected by his men, wet himself in terror when a salute was fired over a fallen soldier's grave.

Three of our comrades have not stayed with us, their tears and broken minds ensuring that they are taken to a place where they can be better repaired and cared for.

We are told to expect at least eight days more in this camp, where the US Army has tried to lay on every convenience and entertainment to help these weary boys recover.

Talk is that our part of the offensive is to be halted, and our successes held, whilst other units elsewhere take up the running.

There are no cheers at the news, for we all know that the Russian is not yet beaten, and there will be great hardship ahead.

My time with these fighting men is done, and I will be leaving them to their rest and recuperation first thing tomorrow.

I will miss them all, and I thank them for their companionship and acceptance.

Let us hope and pray that this hideous game called war is soon ended and these young men made safe again by its absence.

On your behalf, dear reader, I wish them well and that they will all soon be back

across the Atlantic and safe in the bosom of
their loved ones.
    My future path is now clearer.
    Rather than report on the horrors of
war, I will now dedicate my life to working
against the whole futile process that throws
our young men against each other, for I never
wish to experience, nor would wish the
generations ahead to experience, this
pointless bestial charnel house again.
                 John Thornton-Smith
                 (Correspondent)

[Author's note. JTS left the rest camp at Saverne, in company with two men from other units. The three were never seen again, and their disappearance is a mystery to this day. There was some partisan activity behind the lines, but communist attacks were ineffective, as well as few and far between, as the groups were progressively culled by effective 'behind the lines' policing.

One rumour that surfaced is that a vehicle was possibly seen crashing into the Saar near Imling. There is no evidence that this was ever followed up, or indeed, happened.

In July 1996, a street market stall in Maastricht offered for sale a battered old Corona typewriter in its case.

The purchaser discovered all of Thornton-Smith's correspondence within the case pocket. The Dutch national donated both the typewriter and letters to the 'Het Persmuseum' in Amsterdam, Holland, where they can be viewed today.

My thanks to the museum's director and staff for granting me access and permission to copy the originals exactly. I should state that neither machine nor paperwork showed any signs of water damage.]

12th to 20th April 1946, Area of operations for the US Sixth Army Group, Germany.

Lieutenant General Patch continued to drive his Seventh Army units forward, successfully linking up with British Fifteenth Army Group early on in the attack.

Brumath fell on the 13th April, after bitter fighting that saw the 76th US Infantry Division shattered, and CCB of 9th US Armored badly mauled.

The loss of Brumath brought about a small concertina effect, resulting in an American surge that took units to the shores of the Rhine at Erstein, Goldscheuer, Kehl, and Rheinmunster, and provided a valuable, but small, bridgehead across the important watercourse, centred around Rheinau.

General Patch pushed both the 9th US Infantry and 9th US Armored at the bridgehead, and they successfully held against severe counter-attacks between the 15th and 18th March, when the Soviets admitted defeat and reformed their line some distance back.

The 66th US Infantry Division, positioned in and around Wissenbourg and Lauterbourg threw back a large assault on 17th March. The Soviet infantry and tanks attacked from first light to sunset, suffering huge losses, but rendering the 66th combat-ineffective for some time to come.

A relieving assault by an adhoc task force from US XV Corps eventually turned the northern flank of the Soviet forces, causing them to quit the field.

On 20th April, two major US thrusts were finally halted. The southern attack took the tanks and infantry of US IV Corps to the outskirts of Memmingen, where 1st US Armored Division and 3rd US Infantry Division ground to a halt in the face of fanatical Soviet resistance.

The northern attack, in tandem with units of US 12th Army Group, came up 10 miles short of Sinsheim before intricate Soviet defences halted the attempts of a reinforced US XV Corps, resulting in the 6th Argentinian Division and 2nd Uruguayan Infantry Brigade being withdrawn from front-line service after sustaining heavy casualties in two days of cruel fighting.

Seconded from SAFFEC, both formations fought hard and well, ensuring that SAFFEC would be given more responsibility by Allied generals, and full respect by its previous dubious enemy.

After looking at his options, Lieutenant General Jacob Devers contacted Eisenhower, informing him that the 6th Army Group could go no further.

The person who says it cannot be done should not interrupt the person who is doing it.

Chinese proverb

Chapter 143 - THE FIRST

1558 hrs hrs, Tuesday, 26th March 1946, Ahlen, Germany.

The main attack had rolled through Hamm like a hot knife through butter, the Soviet defence, such as it was, swept aside in a burst of artillery and a rapid advance of panzers and panzer-grenadieres.

The weight of the German I Korps' attack had been applied by the 1st Panzer-Grenadiere Division, which lay in front of Beckum, held up by a ferocious defence.

I Corps command ordered 1st Panzer-Grenadiere to orient towards the left flank, where the division again started to make progress, although not without some danger, as the rear was left exposed to a Soviet held position at Ahlen.

To counter this problem, a Kampfgruppe, mainly drawn from the 266th Infanterie Division, was sent forward to encircle and reduce the enemy pocket.

Fig# 142 – Kampfgruppe Bremer.

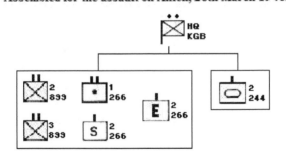

Kampfgruppe Bremer
266th Infanterie Division
Assembled for the assault on Ahlen, 26th March 1946.

Oberleutnant Baron Werner Von Scharf-Falkenberg watched as the 105mm leFH howitzers peddled their trade, dropping shells in and around the enemy positions in front of Ahlen.

Enemy counter-fire was ineffective, a handful of casualties being caused by mortar fire before the guns were shifted and the threat silenced.

Bringing his binoculars to his eyes again, a fourth examination of his line of attack brought no additional information or relief; the difficulties were obvious.

His battalion's advance would generally be centred on Route 671, with two watercourses to traverse before the unit could deploy into Ahlen proper.

Each of the battalions had two STUG SP guns attached, with the remaining four held in reserve, along with the Pionieres and both battalion's panzer-jager companies.

The Battalion commander gave the order, and 3rd Battalion moved forward.

Fig# 143 - Town of Ahlen

Von Scarf had been given extra troops from the Machine-Gun Platoon, Battalion supply train, and a short platoon of men leavened from other Battalion units. As he finished organising his force, the sounds of wounded men screaming out their last few seconds on this earth surrounded the assault group.

"Menschen, the mortars will put down smoke to cover this end of the bridge, but we will move to the right...here."

He drew his thoughts in the earth, the leadership craning to see how their commander was going to crack the target.

The previous attack had run into a machine-gun nest and concrete bunker network sat on the edge of the Stadtpark, a solid position that covered the approach to the bridge and dominated Weststrasse.

The first assault had been bloodily repulsed.

"The smoke will be between us and the bunker complex, but we will actually be beyond the killing zone at the end of the bridge, and so should avoid the bastard's fire."

The nodding around him showed that the men approved the plan so far.

"The panzerjager kompagnie is not available, so the two STUGs will move up and cover the bridge, bringing the bunkers under fire, and generally supporting our assault."

He looked up at an old Lieutenant, recently promoted from the ranks.

"Otto, you will keep two platoons here. No-one comes over that bridge and gets on our flank, Klar?"

"Jawohl, Herr Oberleutnant."

The newly promoted Hauptfeldwebel who had filled Otto Pausch's shoes was next.

"Riedler, I want you to take one platoon and sit out here," he stabbed the earth to the right of the assault groups intended position, "To secure our right flank."

By way of explanation, he pointed further off on the right flank.

"At the moment, we still have contact with the left flank of 2nd Batallion, but that may not last. You're there to make sure we have no surprises. Klar?"

"Jawohl, Herr Oberleutnant."

"Right, get your men in order. Two grenades a man minimum, full ammo load. No back packs. Two fausts a platoon, just in case."

He looked at his watch.

"We attack at 1645. Dismissed."

Fig# 144 - Soviet forces in Ahlen

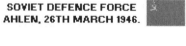

1645 hrs, Tuesday, 26th March 1946, two hundred metres from the Werse River, Ahlen, Germany.

Fig# 145 - Von Scharf's assault on Ahlen bridge.

The werfers threw their smoke shells onto the right spot, concealing the end of the bridge.

"Vorwaerts!"

The assault group leapt forward as the Soviet defences lashed the gathering smoke with hails of bullets and high-explosive.

Pausch's force commenced their own fire, just in case the Russians tried any funny business.

Rielder pushed his platoon out to the right flank immediately, but encountered no problems.

Moving forward in leapfrog bursts, the assault group ate up the ground to the river in short order, with only one casualty sustained, claimed by a stray bullet from the smoke.

Until the two lead men were chopped down, sending the whole group scattering.

"Scheisse!"

Von Scharf drew heavily on the cold air as he rubbed his bruised knee, knowing that some of the bullets had passed dangerously close to him.

"Obergefreiter Grun!"

He got the attention of the NCO lying in the rubble across the pathway.

"Cover fire. I'm going left through that building. Keep the fire up, just enough to keep his head down. Watch for us on target, klar?"

Even though bullets were pinging off the concrete and brick all around them, the NCO understood his task and got his men into position.

Von Scharf called to the men around him.

"Ready, menschen! When Grun starts firing, we go in pairs!"

He chopped a palm in the direction he wanted the group to assault and gave Obergefreiter Grun the nod.

A desultory fire halted the enemy light machine gun and gave its own signal to the waiting assault force.

"Raus!"

The first two soldiers were up and away before the word had died on Von Scarf's lips, the next two before he could give the second command.

In spite of himself, he found a wave of pride surge over him.

"Gute männer!"

Fourth up was himself and the radio operator, and they made the ground floor without issues, although his old leg wound nearly made him lose balance at one crucial stage.

The fifth pair tumbled in, having tripped each other up in the threshold.

The last two men came under fire and one man had his rifle sent flying from his grasp as a bullet clipped his wrist.

Despite the pain, he dropped to the ground and slid back to retrieve the weapon.

"Köhler… Köhler… nein!"

The wounded man understood and hunkered down whilst Von Scharf led the assault forward.

Finding a set of stairs, the officer sent four men along the ground floor, accompanying the other six upwards to where the enemy machine gun was now firing more steadily.

The lead man fired a shot and a lifeless enemy body stumbled over the balustrade, falling onto the ground floor below.

Von Scharf gestured at a soldier with an MP-40, who nodded and pushed past to take the lead.

Another SMG armed NCO split to the left.

A Soviet soldier opened the door directly in front of the man, and took a burst in the chest and neck.

The body was propelled back into the room behind, in which the Unteroffizier glimpsed at least three men.

"Granate!"

He tossed a British-issue Mills bomb inside and turned to cover his face.

The bang and the screams combined in one awful sound.

Bursting in through the door, each of the bodies, moving or not, received attention from the MP-40.

A quick appreciation of the situation told the NCO that this group, complete with a Maxim machine-gun, were set up to shoot up the flank of any assault made directly against the bridge.

He picked up one curious looking weapon and made his way back out into the corridor.

"Herr Oberleutnant. A new one, I think."

"Looks like it, Keller. Hang on to it for intelligence. Try not to cut yourself."

The new weapon had an integral bayonet folded back under the barrel, which left a cutting edge exposed. Intelligence would eventually identify it as an SKS semi-automatic carbine.

Guttural shouts and a burst of fire brought both men back to reality.

"Keller, go and back them up. Send back to me if you need any more."

The Unteroffizier dashed down the stairs in the direction of the growing firefight.

Ahead, the cry of 'Granate' cut through the smoke and dust that was now becoming a problem.

The building shook as one, and then a second grenade exploded.

The tell-tale sound of a PPSh letting rip followed, and brought squeals of pain from some unfortunate along the hall.

Von Scharf moved on.

"Granate!"

Instinctively, the officer threw himself backwards through the open door, understanding that this grenade was incoming.

The door was thrown fully open in the blast and pain speared through his exposed foot as fragments clipped flesh and bone on the way through his boot.

Rolling back over himself, to clear away from the door quickly, Werner Von Scharf narrowly missed being hurt by the second enemy grenade that arrived without warning.

"Grenate!"

A splash of blood was thrown against the open door, marking the passage of metal through unfortunate flesh.

Bringing up his Gewehr-43, Von Scharf instinctively put two bullets into the first shape, the shriek of horror in Russian confirming his suspicion.

A rifle cracked and a second Soviet soldier dropped.

Von Scharf moved to the doorway again and risked a look towards the Soviet end of the corridor.

"Scheisse!"

He shouted instinctively, as fear prompted his survival instincts.

The Gewehr quickly emptied its magazine into the group of enemy that had been moving forward.

Like an automaton, Von Scharf reloaded.

'I'm too exposed... too far forward...'

His thoughts were interrupted by calls from his right.

"Oberleutnant! Stay in cover... stay in cover!"

He needed no second invitation.

The corridor burst into life as an MG34, brought up under Keller's orders, turned most of the doors and walls into matchwood.

"Raus!"

Men swept past Von Scharf's hiding place, men in German uniform with murder in their hearts.

The firefight at the end of the corridor was brief and one-sided.

Keller appeared, grinning with relief that his officer was relatively unharmed.

"The enemy MG?"

"Kaputt, Herr Oberleutnant. Now, the Sani for you I think."

The wound in his foot stung to high heaven so, with the position taken and the competent NCOs in charge, Von Scharf was helped to the medical station.

1744 hrs, Tuesday, 26th March 1946, Werse River Bridge, Ahlen, Germany.

By the time that Von Scharf had returned to lead his men, they had forced the bridge, and Otto Pausch was dead.

Pausch had spotted the opportunity to push across and form a bridgehead, and he was not a man to ignore such gifts when the gods of war presented them.

His orders had taken a good portion of Von Scharf's remaining force over and into a fan shape around the head of the river bridge.

The old Lieutenant was struck down by enemy mortar fire as he organised the defence, one of only eleven casualties sustained in the crossing.

Riedler's platoon had fought a bitter battle on the right flank, when Soviet infantry tried to sneak down the west bank behind the bridge assault force.

One of the STUGs had been sent to bolster his defence, but had thrown a track en route, the sound of hammers and curses betraying the hard work the crew were putting in to get their vehicle back into the fight.

The other STUG was still west of the river, its track shattered by a near miss, but in an excellent position to provide support to the defence, as the burning T-34 amply demonstrated, taken out with a single shot through the hull within a few seconds of its appearance.

The ammunition situation was acceptable, but the units over the bridge could not afford to be profligate, especially as the Soviets had it back under direct fire. The German defenders were troubled by mortars whenever something worth shooting at was seen.

Having risked the dash across the bridge, Von Scharf found that the previous owners had left him a more than acceptable bunker from which to exercise command.

"Glad to see you back, Herr Oberleutnant."

Scharf's pack had already been brought forward, which pleased him no end.

"We've checked the bunker for booby traps, command wires, and demolition charges. Nothing found, Sir."

"Excellent work, Keller, excellent. Now, do we know where their damned OP is?"

"I have an idea, Sir."

He moved to the map the Soviets had left behind in their haste.

"My Russian's a bit rusty but I think that'll be it there."

Von Scharf looked at the map like it was gold dust, which it technically was.

"Mein Gott! This has their full position marked out, man."

"I was going to send it back to battalion, but I thought you'd want a look at it before it went, Sir."

It was an excellent call by the NCO.

"Right, let me get this copied over quickly and we'll set about that nest of vipers very shortly," he tapped the map on a point some two hundred metres away from where he presently stood.

Von Scharf screwed his eyes up, trying to read the legend under the Soviet scrawl, ignoring the growing throbbing in his injured foot.

'St. Bartholomäus.'

He searched his memory.

"Ah yes, the flayed saint."

"Sorry, Sir?"

"St. Bartholomäus was skinned alive."

Keller screwed his face up at the thought.

"Right, get me a runner so this can go back, and then the STUG can fix the bastards. I'll radio the Oberstleutnant."

By the time the runner had arrived, Von Scharf had transferred all he needed to his own map, and the priceless original was quickly sent back to the battalion headquarters.

But all was not well.

Unteroffizier Hermann Keller sensed the tension in the atmosphere as he entered the bunker.

Scharf was seething.

Battalion command had forbidden the destruction of the tower, citing its use for the same purpose under German control as the reason that Von Scarf's infantry would now lose men negating the enemy OP.

However, he had a job to do.

"We'll go to the church with… two platoons, I think."

He added an after-thought.

"Leave Rielder's lot alone. Let them rest."

1814 hrs, Tuesday, 26th March 1946, Werse River Bridge, Ahlen, Germany.

Fig# 146 - Von Scharf's assault on St Bartholomäus.

The two platoons waited as the seconds clicked away.

There was no sophisticated plan of attack, just the standard fire and movement that marked infantry tactics the world over.

Gathered in the houses overlooking Hospitalergasse, there was a twenty-five metre gap, partially rubble and partially undergrowth, before the advancing troops would find cover again.

Once across that piece of open ground, the two platoons would split and proceed to attack the church from either side, although, to save friendly fire casualties, only second platoon would enter the building itself in the first instance.

1814 became 1815, and the ubiquitous whistle sent third platoon scurrying forward by sections.

Beside Von Scharf, his unit's sniper took a shot that presented itself and worked the bolt, searching for a second opportunity.

"Herr Oberleutnant, that's where they sit for sure. I think I just popped an officer in the belfry, and there were other faces too. Heads are down now…"

Von Scharf took his eyes off the advancing platoon as the sniper's briefing cut short.

The Kar98k barked again.

"Heads are now well and truly down. That's another of the schwein with lead poisoning, Herr Oberleutnant."

"Stay here until you hear our grenades, then push up. If safe… only if safe, klar?"

The man hummed his understanding, his eyes firmly glued to the scope.

The whistle sounded on Von Scharf's lips, and first platoon surged forward.

Ahead, small arms fire started to rattle and grow in volume.

Making an instant decision, Von Scharf waved a hand and took his group left, the platoon's commander already ahead and to the right.

The section with him sped up demonstrably, as hot metal started to ping around them.

Behind them, two men of their platoon had gone down, as Russian fire spat from upper windows in front of them.

The lieutenant leading his platoon crashed into the rubble face first, as a bullet passed through his throat.

His men surged, opening wider to create more gaps in their line.

430

Another soldier spun away, his thigh ruined by the passage of a Mosin bullet.

The de facto platoon leader, an experienced Feldwebel, grabbed at a stick grenade as he ran, weaving quickly as he unscrewed the cap and grabbed the cord.

In one easy movement, he lobbed it through the open first floor window, narrowly avoiding the body that was thrown out by the blast.

A landser shot the moaning lump as he ran past.

Inside the building, the defending Soviet soldiers were quickly overtaken by a combination of bullets and bombs.

To save time, Von Scharf detailed one of third platoon's sections to make up the shortfall in first platoon, adding his own group to third platoon.

"Raus!"

The two platoons rushed forward, leaving behind a section to support the machine-guns set up behind as cover.

Von Scharf screamed loudly, partially because his wounded foot cannoned off a lump of brick, and partially because the muzzles of a lorry-mounted twin-DShK swung in his direction.

His brain quickly calculated that he was a dead man, but his heart drove his legs forward and worked his right hand, the index finger pulling the Gewehr-43's trigger in a futile attempt to preserve his life.

The muzzles stayed silent, despite the efforts of the gunner.

The loaders ran as the grey-green tide swept over them.

Eyes wide open in terror, the gunner evacuated both bladder and bowels as one of Scharf's men dragged him from the gunner's position.

"Prisoners, Herr Oberleutnant?"

"Ja…", Scharf took in the surroundings and pointed to a large bomb hole off to one side.

"There… put the boy in there… stand guard and no risks. Alles klar?"

The foul-smelling gunner was pushed along by the muzzle of a rifle, taking refuge in the hole where he was subsequently joined by two more prisoners, each equally young and equally scared.

Keller appeared, his cheek streaked with blood.

"Just a scratch… grenade splinter I think."

He nodded at the prisoners.

"They're just boys, Herr Oberleutnant. All of this lot were just boys… fifteen at best I reckon."

Von Scharf automatically checked his weapon as he spoke, his face altered by a wry smile.

"Then maybe this war'll be over quicker than we thought eh, Keller?"

The low laugh betrayed the NCO's views on such stupid thoughts.

"Right… I'll get this lot organised and we'll attack immediately."

Soviet mortar rounds started to arrive, clearly called in to keep the assault force away from their target.

"Let's move, Keller!"

A dull swooping sound and one German soldier dropped to the ground as his stomach started to spill from his riven belly.

The three Soviet prisoners on whom it had dropped barely resembled human beings.

"Sani!"

The orderly was already on his way to the stricken guard, knowing all he would achieve would be to ease the veteran into the afterlife with morphine.

The mortars' rate of fire increased, which in turn spurred the platoons to greater efforts.

A small firefight developed when an unseen trench, near the base of the tower, burst into life, its five occupants opening fire prematurely and failing to register a single hit on the attackers.

The location was quickly flanked and two grenades silenced resistance.

First platoon swept either side of the church, leaving third to go up the centre and assault the main entrance.

1825 hrs, Tuesday, 26th March 1946, St. Bartholomäus, Ahlen, Germany.

The first pair through the tall rounded double doors had spilt either side, but it hadn't saved either of them, as both PPSh and DP-28 poured fire into the narrow confines of the entrance.

A runner from Keller arrived.

"Herr Ober… leutnant…"

"Catch your breath, kamerad… steady now."

"Sir, Unteroffizier Keller… reports growing numbers of enemy… coming through the marketplace… like a counter-attack is developing…"

Growing sounds of small arms fire supported Keller's view.

"Alarm! Panzer!"

The call came from the AlterHof side of the church grounds, and was quickly followed by the detonation of one of their few panzerfausts.

Von Scharf realised instantly that it was too late to pull back, as Soviet infantry came into view in AlterHof, and yet others emerged from Südenmauer.

The radio operator called urgently, adding to his officer's mental load.

"Sir, headquarters, Oberstleutnant Bremer himself, Sir."

After a moment's hesitation, Von Scharf spoke quickly to Keller's runner.

"Can you make entrance to the church your side there?"

"Yes, Herr Oberleutnant. Windows and a door."

"Tell Keller that we're stuck here. It's up to him to gain entrance... and do it fucking quickly!"

The man was instantly on his way.

"Scharf."

The radio crackled into life and the commander of the Kampfgruppe broke the news of the enemy counter-attack.

"Ah Scharf...it seems we've driven straight into the 513th Motorised Rifle Division's centre. A new division, not on our intelligence sheet. Probably just arrived, as it's not on that map. It has an integral tank battalion, so watch out for tanks, over."

"Already encountered some at the bridge, and now near Bartholomäus church. We're already nearly surrounded by the enemy surge. I'm going to barricade myself inside the church until the attack is beaten back. These new troops, Sir, they're boys and old men, low quality, over."

"That may well be, Scharf, but air reconnaissance reported a column moving up. We've checked it with your map and it's coming from a position marked for a Guards Engineer Brigade, so don't expect children and geriatrics when they arrive, over."

Firing from inside the church revealed that Keller had made an entrance.

Scharf waved one section forward, to try the main entrance again.

"Sir, do we have any air support, over"

"Not yet. It appears that our 1st Panzer-Grenadieres have run into a tank unit and are having a time of it, over."

433

Von Scharf dropped the handset and put two rounds a piece into the pair of Soviet infantrymen who loomed up behind his radio operator.

The funker went white as a sheet but stuck to his radio.

Retrieving the handset, Scharf was eager to get moving.

"Sir, I must sign off, It's getting hot here. I'll contact you once we're in our strongpoint, over."

"Keep your heads down, Scharf. Our artillery took a beating from some counter-fire, but we do have more artillery coming soon, so if you can provide some fire control, it will help. Hals-und beinbrach. Out."

A single bullet whizzed past his ear as he passed the handset back.

"Raus, Schneider."

The radio operator needed no second invitation.

Inside the church, the firing had stopped and Keller was already making it into a fortress.

Fig# 147 - Soviet reinforced forces at Ahlen.

"Then fix the shitty thing, Schneider. It's vital."

The radio had simply decided that enough was enough. Whilst it seemed undamaged, there was no spark of life in it.

Spotting from the tower proved to be a hazardous duty, and one Gefreiter had already been shot dead trying to look around.

The Soviet OP had been disposed of, mainly by the sniper, the remaining two men quickly cut down by the first landser to reach the top of the tower.

Across the way, Von Scharf had spotted his sniper, safely concealed in a gorgeous spot adjacent to the chimney stack in a

434

ruined attic. How he had got there, Scharf had no idea, but it was a perfect place from which to shoot and feel safe from interference.

Three Soviet rushes had faltered around the church, as the heavy structure performed like a fortress for the defenders.

For the last twenty minutes, the Guardsmen Engineers, for that was what they clearly were, had satisfied themselves with containing the bottled-up Germans, whilst the rest of what was probably a reinforced battalion pushed hard against the bridgehead.

Scharf's men at the bridge were having a very hard time, but the STUG was holding the tanks at bay superbly, having added three more to the tally of metal hulks in front of the German line.

Von Scharf found a hole in the stonework and used it to observe enemy preparations for another bridge attack.

His foot was screaming blue murder but he ignored it as best he could.

Looking straight down Kampstrasse, two T-34s were revving up ready to dash forward, and a company of engineers were moving along the road, ready to support them.

The failing light was of little help as his eyes strained at three lorries set well back from the point of attack.

He fumbled for his binoculars.

"Mein Gott!"

Turning back to Schneider, he spoke with a calm he didn't feel.

"Alles klar?"

"Just about to try it again, Herr Oberleutnant. The capacitor seemed to have come adrift a little."

Schneider worked his magic, and the radio burst into life.

"…ive-three come in please!"

"Koenig-five-three receiving, over."

"Scharf! Thank god! Situation report, over."

"Herr Oberstleutnant, we're bottled up, but they can't get us out of here. Sturmgruppe has seven casualties. Ammunition low. Ready to spot for artillery, over."

"Received. The artillery support is online and ready, 32.2, call sign Surfer. Latest assessment is that the entire engineer brigade has moved forward. Surfer's available just for you. Use it to keep them off that fucking bridge or you'll be cut off and we won't be able to get to you. Out."

Consulting the map already laid out on the floor and weighted down with rubble, part of Von Scharf's brain processed target information, whilst part wondered what sort of unit 'Surfer' was.

"Schneider, get Surfer up on 32.2."

He listened as an American accent acknowledged the message.

Passing Schneider the coordinates, Von Scharf decided that the three lorries with the red explosives flags were worth the effort.

A single large-calibre shell arrived, sending pieces of engineers flying in all directions.

"Tell them left two hundred. salvo fire!"

Twenty-three seconds later, twelve M-101 HE shells, each containing just under ninety-five pounds of high-explosive, arrived in and around three lorries carrying roughly two thousand pounds of captured American manufacture TNT demolition charges.

The result was spectacular for onlookers, much less so for anyone within the burst radius of shells and charges.

A substantial part of Kampstrasse and Freiheit disappeared in one monumental surge of energy.

Of the line of waiting engineers, half simply evaporated, half were knocked senseless by the blast.

Von Scharf had thrown himself on the radio with the first flash, understanding what might be about to happen.

Bits of the belfry flew off as the shockwave washed over the church.

"Fucking hell!"

Schneider blinked his eyes free of dust and rammed his fingers in his ears.

"What the hell are they firing?"

Von Scharf grinned.

"Trucks carrying explosives… they hit trucks carrying... a lot of explosives!"

He risked a quick look and saw utter devastation, added to by another salvo landing on the money.

"Tell Surfer to cease fire and await further instructions."

He looked at Schneider and waited for the order to be relayed.

"Mind you, someone should have their arse kicked for putting that lot so near the danger area. They must be desperate to bring the bridge down, but still... dumb move."

The man responsible for the 'dumb' move had been pressured beyond measure by his commanders. Tasked with blowing the bridge at all costs, he had brought up his explosive to reduce the delays involved, as the infantry commander held little hope that the bridge would be retaken and held for long.

436

In any case, the engineer officer had been among the first casualties vapourised by the explosions.

The Soviet infantry commander immediately halted his attack, set his men into some sort of defensive positions, Setting one of his more trusted officers to get the engineers into some sort of order, he sent a message for more explosive, and then turned his eye on the group of Germans in his rear.

"Panzer!"

The T-34 rumbled around the corner of Südstrasse, into the Markt, where it abruptly stopped.

The 85mm gun adjusted slowly and fired an HE shell at the church.

It struck the mid-point underneath a small window on the north-east corner, overlooking the square.

The MG34 and crew were not directly struck, but the blast and spalding stonework destroyed them equally as well.

Scharf pulled the OP group off the roof and down to the next level, away from any windows or openings.

Quickly checking his map, despite the cascade of dust and stone caused by a direct hit on the position he had just vacated, Scharf passed coordinates to his radio man.

"And tell them not to undershoot. Danger close, tell them danger close."

The German officer's plan was simple but dangerous.

Get the artillery dropped to the east of Südstrasse, preventing any reinforcements moving up. If he got lucky and speared the tank, then great, but Scharf couldn't count on it, so made his way to the ground floor to set another plan in motion.

The US artillery was superb, dropping accurately amongst the Soviet infantry who had formed up in the built-up area, east of Südstrasse.

The tank, and another that emerged from the fire zone, remained alive, pounding the church and surroundings with direct fire.

Behind the German front line, the situation was suddenly considered dire, as more Soviet forces than expected were present.

Additional units were requested and approved, creating a growing focal point at Ahlen.

The German command seized the opportunity immediately and turned the reserve of the 1st Panzer-Grenadiere Division back, to head north-west, and into the rear of the Ahlen defences, anticipating the destruction of a good portion of the defenders, as well as relieving the under-pressure infantry division.

Whilst the forces of both sides gathered themselves, the soldiers and civilians in Ahlen continued to suffer under heavy mortar and artillery fire.

2058 hrs, Tuesday, 26th March 1946, Hamelin Jail, Hamelin, Germany.

Having narrowly escaped the destruction that befell his headquarters facility at Barntrup, Malinovsky had, on nothing more than a gut feeling, declined his alternate set-up at Gross Berkel, settling for a swiftly organised additional site at the notorious jail in Hamelin, where, amongst a German civilian population, he felt safer from further Allied air attacks.

Reports of the destructive raid at Gross Berkel reached him as he pondered the recently updated situation.

"What's that swine doing?"

Savvushkin, his second in command, was equally exasperated.

"I don't think the idiot knows to be honest, Comrade Marshal."

They were referring to the newly frocked Major General Inutin, commander of the 4th Motorised Army, one of Stalin's new formations.

"And he's definitely been given the order to withdraw?"

Savvushkin checked his notes.

"On three occasions, Comrade Marshal, and each time acknowledged."

"Fucking swine."

The situation for 4th Motorised Army was nothing short of dire.

Faced with German forces to its front and southern flank, pressed by an American Corps to the north, it would take only a change of axis by the German forces attacking Beckum to seal a good part of the Army in a pocket from which there would be no escape.

"Beckum will hold."

It was not a question.

438

"The reinforcements we sent have stopped the enemy advance in its tracks but..." Savvushkin described a single line from Beckum to Ahlen, "That might be because they have moved to take advantage of Inutin's lack of movement."

'Lack of movement?'

Before the rebuttal sprang to Malinovsky's lips, Savvushkin's eyes betrayed another presence.

"Greetings, Comrade Mayor General."

Malinovsky turned as the round faced NKVD officer strode in with his normal arrogant gait.

"Greetings, Comrade Marshal. How goes the fight against the Capitalist forces today? It seems their Air Force was very lucky earlier?"

Mayor General Vladimir Budarev was the Chief Counter-Intelligence Officer and Commander of the SMERSH Western Front units, and normally to be found at the European Forces HQ.

He had avoided the destruction of the main headquarters at Nordhausen and was now, acting under instructions from Beria, and ultimately Stalin, moving between the various front command centres and ensuring full Soviet enthusiasm for the unyielding defence and subsequent counter-attacks.

Which, in the present military circumstances, made him a very dangerous man indeed.

Without any hint of sarcasm, Budarev made comment on the map notations.

"So, what skilled plan have you devised to push the fascists back, Comrade Marshal?"

The abundance of arrows were unclear in their meaning to a man like Budarev, whose position had been earned on the basis of political reliability and a fanatical obedience of all orders, not military knowledge

"We are recovering 4th Motorised from the Ahlen area, in order to make the enemy overextend himself."

Savvushkin moved his hands rapidly around the markings, whilst Malinovsky kept his amusement firmly hidden.

"So, you are conceding ground to the enemy?"

"Yes, we are retiring under orders, whilst still in contact with the enemy. The Marshal has arranged our remaining anti-aircraft assets to cover the build-up of forces as we compress into this area, before launching a counter-attack aimed at relieving Beckum by retaking Hamm."

Budarev made the noises of a man studying the situation, and both senior officers wondered if he actually believed he was fooling them, or even fooling himself with his ponderings.

"When this is approved, I wish you every success, Comrades. Now, I must report back to the Chairman."

Formally saluting, Budarev disappeared as silently as he had arrived.

Waiting an appropriate time, Malinovsky looked at his 2IC with a quizzical look.

"So, I've ordered my wealth of AA assets to cover a counter-attack against Hamm, have I?"

Savvushkin replied with a deadpan expression.

"Not wholly untrue, Comrade Marshal. A reserve AA regiment has been sent to cover the withdrawal of 4th Mech assets..."

"And Hamm?"

"I suspect that your masterful plan will be overtaken by events."

Malinovsky slapped his man on the shoulder in his normal hearty fashion.

"Quick thinking, Mikhail."

Hands on hips, the commander of the 1st Red Banner Army of Soviet Europe eased the stiffness from his back.

"Right, no more worrying about Budarev. Let's concentrate on saving the 4th and stopping the Allied advance. Give me some alternatives, Comrade."

Within ten minutes, Malinovsky sent the order that relieved Inutin and replaced him with his 2IC. It was accompanied by another that again ordered 4th Motorised to move back to bring the line level with Beckum, especially as the German attack there had been halted so convincingly.

Part of that repositioning required the defenders of Ahlen to stand and die or, more accurately, to attack and keep Allied attention firmly fixed on the small German town.

4th Motorised was to sacrifice one of its units so that the others could escape.

As the young soldiers of the 513rd charged with fanaticism, the rest of 4th Motorised Army, or at least what was left of it, disengaged and fell back, unobserved in the first instance.

Allied artillery and night attack aircraft harried the retreating columns once the withdrawal was detected, but the Soviet air defence commanders had called upon all of their remaining night fighter assets, and the Allied attacks were often spoiled.

And whilst the movement of divisions took place, the danse macabre in Ahlen reached a peak.

2328 hrs, Tuesday, 26th March 1946, St. Bartholomäus, Ahlen, Germany.

Der Totentanz.

A fortunate by-product of the artillery cover was the amount of firelight that spread around the church, illuminating any enemy movement, whilst the fires themselves denied many areas to the gathering Soviet soldiery.

It was added to by the two burning T-34s, which had both been knocked out by direct strikes from Panzerfausts.

Scharf failed to see it as a success, as only one man from the six who had attacked the tanks returned.

The remains of the five others lay in clear view, three ravaged bodies entwined behind a pile of rubble to the left of his vision; to the right the two others, less distinguishable as German soldiers, the effects of HE having spread the two brave men for yards around.

The sani had finished redressing his foot, and Scharf felt the improvement immediately.

It had been over ninety minutes since the enemy had last attacked and, for young boys, Scharf could only admire the effort that drove them to the walls of the church itself and, in one instance, through a window.

The three enemy bodies had been placed to one side and the position reoccupied by the dwindling defenders.

Scharf had started the assault with sixty-eight men, and achieved the church with a group numbering thirty-one.

One section of eleven men from the other platoon group arrived during a lull and brought his strength up to twenty-seven fit or slightly wounded soldiers; the rest lay either dead or severely wounded amongst the church stalls.

One in two men were presently resting as the other kept watch.

It was a rude awakening as Savvushkin's alternative arrived on cue.

"Alarm!"

441

The cries rang out, not only in the church of St Bartholomew, but at the bridgehead, as the commanders of the 513rd Motorised Rifle Division threw their ravaged battalions forward, the sacrificial lambs to cover a swift withdrawal of more valuable units, such as the Guards Engineers.

The defenders cut loose, knocking down the leading attackers, their silhouettes easily picked out against the shifting orange background.

Scores went down, scythed like corn in a field, but there were hundreds more of them.

"Keep it up, menschen!"

Schneider spotted the Soviet stick grenade deflect off the stonework of the small window.

"Grenata!"

He threw himself forward and grabbed the charge, flinging it into the nearby stone recess.

No one even noticed his heroism.

The Soviet pressure was immense and started to tell as weapons flailed at windows, showing where the attackers were close enough to lash out with rifle butt and bayonet.

"Schneider! Don't leave your radio, man!"

Von Scharf scuttled over as bullets pinged around the stonework.

"Tell Surfer... we're being overrun... fire on our location immediately!"

Appreciating the significance of the order, Schneider was immediately on the radio and commenced an exchange with the US artilleryman some ten miles away.

Von Scharf caught only one side of the brief conversation.

"Yes, we're all in the church, over... yes... it's intact, over... right. Thank you, out."

Schneider looked at his officer.

"They are firing now. He said they have VT so keep away from the windows."

Whatever VT was, Scharf decided to take the advice, and immediately got his men to keep their heads down and deal with the enemy outside solely with their few remaining grenades.

Within a few seconds, modified M-101f shells, with proximity fuses, started to arrive around the church.

The M-101f had a fragmentation core instead of the supplementary charge, which made it a great shrapnel killer. Combined with the T-76E1 proximity fuse, the 155mm shell was an airburst with immense killing potential.

The effect upon the massed soldiers of the 513rd Motorised was similar to the simultaneous firing of a hundred shotguns.

Men went down everywhere, including inside the church, as the angle of burst inevitable propelled metal in through the windows and other holes in the structure.

Fanaticism had driven the young Soviet soldiers all the way to stand toe to toe with their enemy; the carnage and inevitability of death in the open herded them into the church, despite dying in their droves.

"Keep it up, Kameraden! They'll break... they'll break!"

For every two or three that went down under an MP-40 burst, one got close enough to grapple with one of Scharf's men, and within seconds, only Schneider and Scharf were not close up and personal with a screaming Russian.

Swinging his Gewehr from side to side, the Oberleutnant selected single targets, where there was no risk of hitting his own men.

In front of him, superior size and build, combined with years of experience, meant that the landser were killing and wounding in great numbers, but occasionally a veteran would go down, allowing more enemy into the fight.

An American shell, its fuse faulty, crashed into the ground in front of the main entrance.

Outside, there was carnage.

In the entranceway, there was carnage.

The shrapnel and pieces of stone pathway continued through the men fighting in the main church, cutting down German and Russian without favour.

Even though he was appalled, Von Scharf seized the moment.

"Fall back, on me! Menschen! Fall back on me!"

Disciplined as ever, the survivors moved quickly back to the corner area, removing the threat of a rear attack.

The Soviet boy soldiers threw themselves forward again, perhaps realising that the end was near for one or other of the two combatants.

Scharf put a bullet through the face of a blonde haired youth. The scream pierced every ear and went on for some time.

Caught as he inserted his last magazine, the Oberleutnant could only parry the thrust of a bayonet.

The momentum carried the enemy soldier forward and Scharf swung the Gewehr, slamming the butt into the left ear and mashing the skull in an instant.

The next attacker received two bullets in the chest.

Schneider was puffing and squealing as he rolled over on top of another boy, one of heavier build and greater strength than most, trying to throttle the life from the Russian.

Wading in quickly, Scharf kicked out, landing hard on the boy's forehead as he squirmed his head from side to side. The stunning blow robbed the Russian of his strength, giving the radio operator time to grab his knife and open up the farm boy's heart.

A sharp pain focussed Schneider.

The bayonet sliced through his side and then ripped the flesh as the weight of the thrust carried the weapon forwards.

Instinctively, he turned and flailed with the blade. He was rewarded with a squeal of agony and felt the heavy bump of flesh contacting his hand.

Not that he cared, but the blade had cut across the man's eyeball, which spilled clear fluid in an instant.

Schneider punched his blade into the soldier's throat, killing the enemy NCO in a heartbeat.

Von Scharf discharged his Gewehr for the last time, the final round missed its immediate target, but hit enemy flesh in the mass behind.

He bought himself a valuable second by throwing the useless weapon at his next assailant, taking up the Mosin dropped by Schneider's nemesis.

The enemy's bayonet thrust rammed hard into the stock and skipped off under Scharf's right elbow.

Using the damaged butt, the Oberleutnant shoved upwards with his right arm, breaking two of the man's fingers as they gripped his rifle, before angling off the Soviet soldier's shoulder without landing a heavy blow.

Another German soldier dispatched the wounded Russian with a butt thrust to the back of the head.

His attention drawn to saving his officer, the man was quickly set on.

Stabbed in the gut by a bayonet, Grun went down and in an instant, he was underneath two boy soldiers, whose combined age was probably less than the veteran Obergefreiter.

Von Scharf moved to help, but was immediately knocked off his feet by two more Russians, ending up in a similar predicament to Grun.

Hands scrabbled at his neck, mouth, and eyes.

The corner of his mouth gave way, splitting towards the right ear in a squirt of blood.

The pain was intense and Von Scharf bellowed.

The split caused the enemy hand to lose purchase. The returning fingers found themselves lodged firmly between Scharf's teeth as he took three digits down to the bone in an instant.

The other Soviet soldier relinquished his hold on the officer's throat, as Schneider slammed his bayonet into the back of the man's skull, scrambling his brains.

A hand came across Von Scharf's vision, hooking its fingers into the screaming boy's nose, moving the head up enough to permit a knife to sever anything of value in the soldier's throat.

Ignoring the hot blood that gushed over him, Scharf pushed away at the dead bodies, trying to regain his feet before another threat arrived.

Keller wiped his knife on the enemy's greatcoat and held a hand out to his officer.

Köhler arrived with the dead sani's pack and started to work on Von Scharf's disfigured face whilst Schneider helped himself to a bandage for his side.

Unteroffizier Keller called his men forward, intent on posting one of the dozen or so survivors on each window, from which the enemy seemed to have melted.

Only two live Russians were in the church, lying amongst their own fallen on the cold floor and moving in the slow and considered fashion of the badly wounded.

The artillery had stopped of its own accord, something that Von Scharf only now appreciated.

2359 hrs, Tuesday, 26th March 1946, St. Bartholomäus, Ahlen, Germany.

Sixteen men remained alive in the end, one of which was still seeing stars; Scarf's other men would never see anything again.

It appeared that grenades had done for the German wounded at some time during the combat, the alcove in which they had been housed showing clear signs of an explosion.

Only Keller had not acquired a new wound, although his helmet and uniform showed signs of his close calls.

Köhler had sustained another wound, a clip on the thigh; nothing serious but enough to make his eyes water when Schneider bumped against him.

Von Scharf sat on one of the intact pews to take Keller's report, his face afire with pain.

His watch had been broken at some time in the hand-to-hand fighting so he 'borrowed' one from Grun's corpse, vowing to see it returned to the dead man's family.

It was midnight.

Keller came to attention in front of him.

Scharf waved him to sit beside him.

"No ceremony now, Unteroffizier. Report."

At least, that was what he intended to say, but he couldn't manage an understandable word.

In any case, Keller made his report.

"The enemy has disappeared completely, Herr Oberleutnant. There is no one between us and Berlin, or back to battalion, as far as I can see anyway."

He coughed violently, probably because of the smoke that invaded every space in sight, then took out his canteen. Scharf refused the proffered container but allowed his NCO a moment to drink.

"The men are keeping watch, and I have the remainder scouring the bodies for ammunition and supplies."

Keller took another swig.

"It seems that I am the only man unwounded. Fourteen men capable of duty, including yourself, Sir."

A final tug on the canteen and then the exhausted Unteroffizier put it away.

"Herr Oberleutnant, we have two Panzerfausts, no grenades, depending on what they find amongst the enemy dead, no machine-gun ammunition, two clips for the MPs, three for your Gewehr, and no more than five rounds per carbine."

Von Scharf nodded his understanding.

'We are finished here...'

He wrote out a swift message for his man to transmit.

Schneider read it back.

"Contact battalion. Tell them we're not in contact and are withdrawing back to the bridge for 00:10. Sixteen survivors, including wounded. Blue smoke as marker."

That got a nod of confirmation from his officer.

The funker got through immediately, and although Oberstleutnant Bremer wanted to speak directly to Von Scharf, Schneider deflected him, knowing that his Oberleutnant couldn't speak.

Raising himself unsteadily, Von Scharf squeezed Keller's shoulder in thanks and moved off around the men. Whilst unable to talk, he enquired with raised brows or a throaty sound, and each man replied wearily, assuring him of their ability to keep fighting.

It didn't take him long to do the rounds.

Taking out his notebook, he wrote a swift instruction, showing it to Keller.

It gave command of the short evacuation to the Unteroffizier.

Accepting the coloured smoke grenade, the Unteroffizier nodded his understanding.

Keller called to the men around him.

"Achtung, menschen!"

He detailed those to take the lead, those to bring the wounded, and those to bring up the rear.

"Alles klar?"

Their voices chorused in understanding.

"Marsch!"

The move back was slow and precise.

Two runners were sent to bring back any survivors from the other group.

They returned empty-handed.

The sniper still sat in his prime position, watching the enemy positions through glassy lifeless eyes. How he had died was not immediately apparent, but he was certainly dead.

The small party pushed on, arriving at the T-junction on Weststrasse, just forty metres short of the bridge.

Keller looked at the exhausted men around him.

"One more hop, Kameraden."

He tossed the smoke grenade ahead and waited until the smoke bathed the street, its blue colour obvious even in the firelight.

"Marsch!"

The survivors moved off and through the smoke, moving as fast as they could, expecting a bullet in the back with every footfall.

No shots were fired, and the leading men emerged to see comrades waving frantically, gesturing at them to speed up.

Man by man, they tumbled into the German positions, where their comrades helped them down the bank to waiting boats, that carried the survivors across the river.

At 0300, a three-pronged assault squeezed the life out of Ahlen and the area around it.

By 0500, apart from a handful of stragglers, 513rd Motorised Rifle Division and a handful of smaller support units had been utterly destroyed, and there seemed to be a hole rent in the Red Army's defences.

The Allies hailed it as a victory, whereas Malinovsky knew it was actually his victory, and that he had preserved 4th Motorised Army to fight another day.

0639 hrs, Saturday, 30th March 1946, III/899th Grenadiere Regiment Rest Area, Gütersloh, Germany.

As in any army at war, there was nothing quite like combat to bring about advancement, and newly-fledged Captain Von Scharf profited from the woundings and deaths of a number of the 266th's hierarchy.

Whilst he retained his company, the new rank gave him seniority, in the event that Battalion headquarters suffered more of the sort of discomfort such as was inflicted upon it at the end of the Battle of Ahlen.

An extremely rare Soviet air attack had opened up a number of vacancies for experienced men.

Von Scharf had declined Bremer's invitation to leave his front line post and join him in Battalion.

His refusal had been met with understanding. Bremer was a quality leader, unlike the oaf Major Hinzig, who was 2IC.

Von Scharf and Hinzig had never seen eye to eye. Von Scharf had been through the latest reports from 3rd Korps headquarters and, in the main, the reading was good, with the exception of the 35th Division's problems south of Oerlinghausen.

A Soviet tank and infantry force had counter-attacked across lands known well to any German tanker; the Sennelager-Paderborn training grounds.

Panzer Brigaden Europa and the 519th Panzerjager Abteilung had quickly slammed the door on the enemy advance, making the lead elements bunch into a rich target for their heavy guns.

The work had been finished by the 13th Sturzkampfstaffel, its dozen JU-87Ds and four HS-129/B3s completing the rout of the large Soviet force.

448

For good measure, the retreating force also received the unwelcome attention of two flights of Tempest V's, decked out with the latest Hispano V cannons and topped off with a pair of two hundred and twenty-seven kilo bombs apiece. The after-battle report made great play of the assistance offered by the French pilots of 3^e Escadron de Chasse, led by the famous Pierre Clostermann.

1st Panzer-Grenadiere Division again took up the advance but floundered on the slopes of the Teutobergerwald's high ground.

Part of the 35th Infanterie Division had been assigned to break the defences to the north, and failed bloodily.

Von Scharf sipped his coffee and re-read the concise report of the 35th's assault.

A knock on the partially ruined door broke his concentration.

"Ah, come in, Unteroffizier. Take a seat, man."

Von Scharf's voice was still not normal, but he had mastered the art of making himself understood, even with the stitches that held his cheek together.

"The men are rested?"

"Another two weeks should see them in top shape, Herr Hauptmann."

"That would be wonderful, of course"

He passed his NCO a coffee.

"Anyway, I think not, Keller. We have orders."

The Regiment had been withdrawn whilst a Kampfgruppe from 35th Infanterie Division had been moved in. The 266th Infanterie had only two line regiments at the commencement of the assault, with a third one being organised, with a view to reinforcing the division by mid-April. Until then, the 266th needed bolstering from time to time, so Corps command had a force based around the 109th Grenadiere Regiment to lead the way.

That force, Kampfgruppe Aldegger, named after its now deceased Colonel, had run into severe difficulty north of Sennelager and Paderborn training area, successfully driving the Soviet defenders out of Sennestadt and Lippereihe, before grinding to a bloody halt on the hills that run north-west to south-east through the Teutobergerwald.

"Oerlinghausen."

Passing the map to Keller, Von Scharf took a careful swig from his coffee.

The experienced NCO looked at the map with disgust.

"Marvellous. When do we go, Herr Hauptmann?"

"I haven't briefed my officers and other NCOs yet! But, as you ask, orders group'll be here in," he checked his new watch, "Nineteen minutes. We move off at 0900."

Keller enjoyed the taste of real coffee and, in savouring the last few dregs, missed his cue to speak.

"Pardon me, Herr Hauptmann."

"Help yourself to a refill, but leave enough for the briefing."

Keller needed no second invitation.

"We've been handed the prize. Our regiment's to take a line from Oerlinghausen to Hill 334... the Tönsberg."

Keller considered the map with this in mind, and quickly offered his considered opinion.

"Scheisse!"

Von Scharf laughed.

"I'll drink to that."

The coffee mugs clashed.

"So there you have it, Kameraden. Order of March has us placed last, which probably means that we'll be regimental reserve."

The inexperienced pair of Lieutenants brightened at the thought, where as those who had already made acquaintance with all that war had to offer did little more than grimace in understanding of the likely butcher's bill.

Von Scharf decided to bring the two new boys down with a bump.

"For those of you that think that's a good thing... it isn't. Understand that means we'll go where it's hardest when our time comes. Klar?"

All eyes were on the new pair as they mumbled their understanding.

"Any questions?"

His briefing had been thorough, so there were none.

The officers all shaped to go but Von Scharf brought them back to him.

"Before you go, kameraden, I have a few formal announcements to make."

His eyes floated around the room, taking in veteran and infant soldier alike.

"It seems that our leaders have streamlined a process that took considerable time in our previous fight."

He delved into his tunic pocket and extracted an official document.

"Following the Battle at Ahlen, I submitted a list of recommendations to Battalion."

He held the document aloft, just to add a touch of drama.

"I received this letter from Feldmarschal Guderian's headquarters less than two hours ago."

Everyone missed the clue in that statement.

Most of the men in the briefing were honoured up to and including the Iron Cross, First class, including a German Cross in Gold for the man reading the list, an addition that had been made by Oberstleutnant Bremer himself.

Words of congratulations floated round as each award was greeted with gusto.

"In addition to that, our soldaten have their own crop of tin. Your recommendations and mine have been accepted en masse, it seems. Twenty-eight awards to the boys in total. Anyway, there's no time now to parade the men formally. Battalion inform me that there will be official presentations when we are next withdrawn. So please pass on my congratulations to those not here, and assure them we'll have our time together and do this all properly when this attack is over."

Unsatisfactory, but they all understood that there was little choice.

Von Scharf's grin widened, and those that knew him well understood he had been a little mischievous.

"Oh... I nearly forgot. It appears that our leadership has seen fit to also honour our comrade... Unteroffizier Keller... with an award."

Keller was not a glory-hunter, although his uniform already sported numerous awards from a grateful nation, up to the First Class Iron Cross. He had not even thought of his absence from the list of those honoured.

Von Scharf moved forward and extended his hand, grasping Keller's firmly and in real comradeship.

"Kameraden, let us congratulate our new Ritterkreuzträger, Unteroffizier Keller."

A cheer went up, and Keller's hand was in great demand.

By the time that the battalion had lorried forward and was set in its positions to the west of Oerlinghausen, a more than passable version of the Knight's Cross had been manufactured by his men and dangled proudly around Keller's neck.

It was a popular award to a popular soldier.

[Author's note - The previous awards procedure had involved any submission for the Knight's Cross having to pass across a large number of desks before it arrived with the highest authority.

The process now, whilst observing the previous values regarding no distinction in rank for recipients, was to be speeded up and could be approved or disapproved at Army level, requiring ratification from the Republican Armies highest-ranking active soldier, namely Guderian himself.

Given that he was extremely busy, the FeldMarschal had delegated the task to a man of great honour and worth, whom he trusted implicitly. Oberst Bernd Freytag von Loringhoven had once been his aide and, in spite of his close association with Hitler in the last days in the Berlin Bunker, was of unimpeachable character.

Only once had Guderian disagreed with Von Loringhoven's recommendations, and that was in approving an award of the Knight's Cross that the Oberst had felt not quite merited.

Unteroffizier Hermann Keller was the 28th recipient of the Knight's Cross of the new German Republic.]

<u>Fig# 148 - Oerlinghausen and the Teutobergerwald, 1st April 1946.</u>

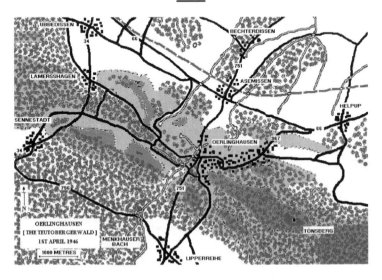

Lieutenant Colonel Bremer cast his eyes over the soaked men who had assembled to receive the Colonel's orders.

The rain hammered down outside, reducing visibility to fifty metres, maybe less.

Much of Lipperreihe had been reduced to rubble, first by the advancing Red Army, and second by the air and artillery forces of the Allied Armies.

The close quarter fighting had been bloody but brief, the Soviet forces quickly pushed back into the Teutobergerwald.

None the less, Colonel Prinz, the regimental commander, had found a reasonably comfortable headquarters in the Gaststätte Dalbker Krug.

"Stillgestanden!"

The men came to full attention as Colonel Lothar Prinz entered the extensive dining room.

"At ease, meine herren."

Prinz had commanded the 899th since before its surrender at Brest in September 1944.

When the new Republican Army had been thrown together, the 266th was reconstituted as was, as much of its soldiery and staff were still intact, albeit ex-POWs.

Although still a two regiment division, it was a different proposition to the static division in Brittany that had been supplemented by numerous 'Ost' units.

"Now, to the point. The attack is postponed."

The silence held a maelstrom of feelings; disappointment, elation, relief, indifference…

"The Luftwaffe simply cannot fulfil their obligations in this foul weather, and the spotters will also have difficulties, obviously."

He turned to the map that held all the vital details of the attack.

"The plan remains almost the same, just a few changes in the order of battle to cater for; the timings will change of course."

He picked up a curtain pole that served as a perfect pointer.

"We'll now not have the Panzer-Grenadiere group from Army reserve. They'll be needed elsewhere."

453

Bremer and Von Scharf caught each other's eye and exchanged silent words.

'Almost the same? A few changes in the order of battle?'

They were not alone in their thoughts.

Prinz knew that his officers were rattled and moved on quickly.

"The plan is now one of central diversion and feint, and our emphasis will fall on the two flank thrusts."

'Scheisse!'

"I have organised three special groups from divisional and regimental troops, fitted out with a lot of transport. They will feint centrally and keep the enemy focussed on Route 751. The STUG's of 244th Abteilung will provide close support, but will be positioned with the special groups to give the centre the appearance of weight."

The plan raised the mood a little, although the reserve unit commanders now knew they would not escape the day ahead.

"Division is going to use the extra time to put more assets on the ground."

He drew their attention to the secondary positions.

"Third Battalion will reorient, purely covering First Battalion's assault. 2nd Pioneer Kompagnie has been allocated some inflatable boats, should the Menkhauser Bach prove an issue," he looked out the window at the downpour, "Especially if this shit continues."

The pointer descended again.

"We have 266 Fusilier Battalion assigned to act as reserve for Second Batallion's assault on the Tönsberg."

At last, some smiles appeared amongst the leadership of 899th Grenadiere Regiment.

"That's it for now, meine herren...moment..."

He beckoned a waiting staff officer forward.

Reading the message, he signed his name and passed the board back.

"So, we now know with whom you're going dance tomorrow. Photos yesterday showed no tanks, and dug-in anti-tank guns are registered by our artillery and on all your maps already."

Turning back to the map, he ran his finger over the Tönsberg and down into the town itself.

"Your old friends are here, Bremer. 1st Guards Engineer Brigade... much reduced by recent events but... still... they're hard men, as you know. Intelligence estimates run between six and eight hundred men."

Shifting to the other side of Route 751, he tapped the heights that guarded the north-western side of the battlefield.

"35th took a prisoner yesterday. That's the report I just received. A new unit's set up here. A 14th Guards Engineer Battalion. Apparently, they've had a hard time of late, so perhaps First and Third will have the easier task tomorrow, especially as intel believes they have only two hundred or so men."

He turned back to his officers.

"Menschen, return to your units. Use this extra time wisely. Check your concentration and assembly points, radio call signs, artillery plans… leave nothing to chance."

The normal chorus of voices told him that they were still worried.

The group dismissed.

The Colonel made his way up into the attic where an observation post had been established.

Hasty waterproofing had just about kept it dry and functioning.

The ageing Artillery Oberwachtmeister sprang to attention but Prinz waved him down to relax, pulling out his binoculars and joining the First World War veteran in surveying the sodden countryside, as best the rain would allow.

Prinz had once been a history teacher by calling, before the war had given him another cause.

He didn't blame his officers for being worried; he was himself.

In another time, the rains had descended on another conquering army, an army that disappeared into history in ignominious defeat.

In 9 AD, the Roman Legions of Publius Quintilius Varus were slaughtered by the Germanic tribes in the Teutobergerwald.

On cue, the rain lessened sufficiently for an indistinct dark outline to become apparent.

Prinz felt a chill of foreboding.

"Quintili Vare, legiones redde!"

"Pardon, Herr Oberst?"

He had not realised that his mouth had given voice to his thoughts.

"Quintili Vare, legiones redde… it's Latin, Oberwachtmeister… a quote from another age. It means…"

"Begging your pardon, Herr Oberst, but it means 'Varus, give me back my legions'."

Prinz looked at the old man with surprise.

455

"That it does, that it does."

The Oberwachmeister smiled at the unspoken enquiry in the Colonel's voice.

"I was a history teacher once, Herr Oberst... in another age."

The rain increased again, masking the shadows of the Teutobergerwald hills, noisily beating down further attempts at conversation, and defeating the puny attempts to waterproof the observation post.

Fig# 149 – Allied Forces at the Teutobergerwald.

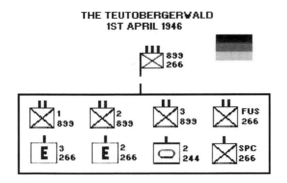

THE TEUTOBERGERWALD
1ST APRIL 1946

2046 hrs, Sunday, 30th March 1946, 14th Guards [Ind] Engineer-Sapper Btn HQ, the Menkebach, Oerlinghausen, Germany.

"So that's that then. They're not coming again today."

"Seems that way, Comrade Polkovnik."

The rain beat down on the canvas tent hidden in the woods on the edge of the small body of water called the Menkebach.

Both men were dry and warm, and the view through the open doorway was, despite the downpour, very easy on the eye, and they could almost have forgotten that there was a war going on around them.

Except for the shell holes, of course.

"Night attack?"

"I doubt it, but we'll cater for it none the less eh, Comrade Polkovnik?"

456

Chekov stretched contentedly, enjoying the extended period of quiet that the rain had afforded.

"Of course, Pavel... but I don't think they'll come. The bastards will save everything up for tomorrow. The Guards' Polkovnik assures me it'll be fine weather from first light, so their aircraft will be up and there'll be hell to pay for the bloody nose we gave the Fascists yesterday."

Pavel Iska, now a Senior Lieutenant and commander of the First Company, had been a major contributor to repelling the German attack.

14th Guards had seen a great deal of action since their first outing at Trendleburg, and very few of the original personnel were left, providing a small hardcore around which the unit had been brought up to strength, ready for the renewed offensive, only to find itself pitchforked into defensive actions against the Fascist assaults.

Chekov, now a full colonel, commanded the survivors, a force of two hundred and two men, led by himself, two other officers, and three senior NCO's.

The commanding Colonel of the 1st Guards Engineers had given him the forty-two surviving men of 1st Battalion's 1st Company, under the command of a 'Hero of the Soviet Union' award-bearing Senior Sergeant.

Whilst small in number, the extra bodies were appreciated.

"So, Pavel, what do you think of our 'Hero'?"

The two men had been through enough together for the junior man to speak freely.

"Personally, I think the man's a prick and a half."

Chekov choked loudly.

"A fine assessment, Starshy Leytenant. And on what evidence do you base this opinion?"

"Way he talks... way he walks... too full of piss and importance... plus... he's an Armenian, isn't he? Untrustworthy carpet-munching fuckers they are too, Comrade."

Iska was a wonderful soldier, but some of his other qualities remained well hidden; qualities such as forbearance, understanding and the avoidance of prejudice.

"Armenian or not, he wears the star, Pavel. Who told you he's Armenian anyway?"

"Balyan... it's an Armenian name."

"Old Yurakin told me the lad said he comes from Stavropol, so you may have it wrong."

457

The junior man hawked and spat out of the open flap, into a noticeably lighter rain.

"Old Yurakin's as deaf as a corpse, so who knows what he heard."

"Set against him, aren't you?"

"Well, Comrade Polkovnik, we'll know soon enough, won't we? Tomorrow, the green toads will come, and they won't make the same mistakes. I say, watch him and his men. I don't trust them and their swaggering ways."

"Bit harsh, Pavel."

Iska rose to take his leave.

"I'm off to check that our gardeners have finished the job. I'll walk the lines and set the night's routine in place. One in three, Comrade Polkovnik?"

One in three men awake at all times and in their defensive positions was the standard way of life since the Allied attacks had begun.

Chekov nodded.

"You mark my words, Comrade, those strutting bastards'll let us down tomorrow. You know what day it is, eh?"

"Yes, I know, Pavel, the first day of April."

"You mark my words, Comrade Polkovnik."

Fig# 150 – Soviet Forces at the Teutobergerwald.

THE TEUTOBERGERWALD
1ST APRIL 1946
SOVIET FORCES

Iska was already out into the wet evening before his Colonel could reply.

Chekov recommenced cleaning his automatic rifle, with half his mind thinking about the worth of the forty-two men led by Starshy Serzhant Ivan Alexeyevich Balyan, Hero of the Soviet Union.

'Is the old dog right?'

458

He worked the bolt smoothly, but oiled it a little more in any case.

'Has Iska seen something I've missed?'

By the time the SVT-40 was in pristine condition, Chekov had decided upon a change in his defences.

0757 hrs, Sunday, 1st April 1946, the Teutobergerwald, Germany.

The 14th had not been idle in defence. The 'gardeners', as Iska had called them, had worked into the small hours to finish preparing the approach route for any enemy attack.

Trees had been cut down, creating a modest killing zone in front of the engineer's defensive positions, the trunks used to create solid bunkers and machine-gun posts.

Chekov had oriented his men on the reverse slope as they waited, expecting some sort of enemy artillery fire to seek out defenders on the western edges of the peaks.

Only listening posts remained exposed, ready to give warning of an enemy attack and bring the defenders forward.

The alterations that Chekov had made were implemented, with half of Balyan's men spread through Third Company's platoons, under the watchful eye of Kapitan Vsevelov, a new arrival, but a competent officer, even in Iska's eyes.

The other half, plus ten men lifted from each of First and Second Company's, formed the sole reserve available to Chekov, and he took it under his personal command, with Balyan as his 2IC.

The Starshy Serzhant was noisily bawling out two of his men over some minor infraction.

Now that Iska had sown the seeds of doubt, Chekov began to see the confident swagger, the self-belief, behaviour he had seen before in men trying to hide their fears and doubts behind a wall of bullshit.

'Engines?'

More than one head turned to the sky.

'Aircraft engines?'

"Take cover!"

Fig# 151 - Oerlinghausen - Soviet Positions.

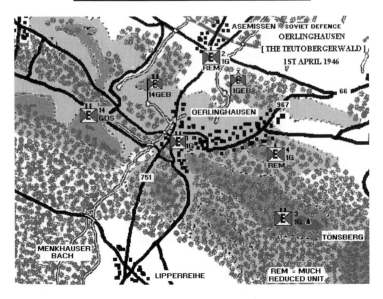

One minute ahead of schedule, the Teutobergerwald Hills were visited by a combination of British and American technology in the hands of men who acquired their skills with the Luftwaffe between '39 and '45, namely the DRL's 3rd Kampfgeschwader.

The 19th Kampfstaffel had been equipped with B-25 Mitchells, twin-engine aircraft considered more suitable for pilots and crews who had once flown Dorniers and Heinkels over London.

Carrying three thousand pounds of high explosives apiece, the eighteen aircraft flew in perfect formation, their precise approach and delivery uninhibited by the modest flak defences.

No matter how many times you saw it, the vision of a ground target being worked over by bombers was always impressive, albeit less so for those closest to the display.

Chekov and his men watched as Hill 334, the Tönsberg, disappeared in flame and smoke, the very ground beneath their feet shuddering in protest at the violation.

Another group of aircraft, set in a wider formation, approached in the same leisurely manner, content that their fighter escort had seen off the handful of Soviet planes that had risen in challenge.

Oerlinghausen suffered a similar fate to the Tönsberg.

Chekov understood what was happening.

460

The enemy were bombing backwards, so the target approach was not obscured by smoke.

The change in wind direction meant that they were bombing to a reversed attack plan, visiting the Tönsberg first, instead of last.

'Fuck!'

"We're next, Comrades. Stay down! Stay down!"

As 19th and 18th Kampfstaffels flew away, 13th Kampfstaffel prepared to rearrange Chekov's defensive positions.

0809 hrs, Sunday, 1st April 1946, III/899th Grenadiere Forward Headquarters, on the Schopkettalweg, Lipperreihe, Germany.

Von Scharf and the other company commanders had assembled on a temporary raised platform, called together by Prinz to observe the effects of the medium bomber's attack.

Through the tree tops of the wood into which they would soon advance, the officers watched high explosive pour down upon the waiting Russians.

Prinz was first to break away from the sight.

"Kameraden. To your men... and yourselves... the very best of luck. Dismissed."

Salutes were exchanged and the officers rushed back to their units, knowing that the DRL had not yet finished mauling the enemy positions.

As the company leaders picked their way forward through the trees, 7th Kampfgruppe's three staffels of Mitchell Bombers arrived, only one minute behind schedule, to work a repeat upon the enemy below, hoping to catch their quarry emerging from cover.

The waiting soldiers of 266th Infanterie Division's assault force heard the noise of explosions and felt the earth complain beneath their feet, the vibrations carrying over that of the enemy artillery fire that had started to arrive in the trees ahead of them.

Hauptmann Von Scharf arrived as Keller was making his men go through the last minute checks associated with infantry assaults.

Webbing, ammo, slings, grenades, close-combat weapons, boots...

"Unteroffizier!"

"Herr Hauptmann?"

"Medal presentation has been sorted for next Wednesday. Once this is over, we'll be relieved and reinforced. The FeldMarschal himself, no less. You should be honoured."

Keller shrugged with indifference. It would have suited him better to have an informal handover from his Company commander, but Division was insisting, as, apparently, were Guderian's staff.

Fig# 152 - German Republican Army assault force - Teutobergerwald, 1st April 1946.

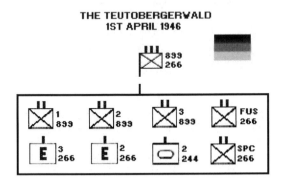

Von Scharf leant in closer.

"Mail's arrived. I left it up at battalion. Best the men stay focussed on this attack."

The two shared a cigarette as the time to advance approached.

His relationship with Keller had altered. He saw the man as more than an extremely competent NCO…

'Now I understand those two Amerikanski.'

He smiled at the thought of the diminutive Jew, Rosenberg, and the German-American officer, Hässler, and then at a man he considered his friend.

"We'll move off soon", he announced.

'Not yet though! One more little surprise for you communist bastards!'

He angled his watch towards the Unteroffizier.

'0825'.

Keller nodded his understanding as the sounds of low flying aircraft suddenly penetrated the nearby artillery explosions.

"Good luck, Herr Hauptmann."

They shook hands as the first of 19th Jagdstaffel's P-38 Lightnings flew low over the Tönsberg defences.

The sound was like nothing the two men had heard before and, even though they had been told what was going to be dropped, the enormity of it suddenly hit home.

Keller, a religious man, crossed himself at what sounded like the opening of the doors of Hades.

Twelve DRL Lightnings deposited over two thousand gallons of napalm, concentrating on the peak and the reverse slope.

Soviet Engineer Guardsmen died by the score, burned to death in an instant.

Others died quick as the intense heat destroyed them, even in cover.

Yet more died as the oxygen was burned away, leaving nothing for the lungs that drew so desperately on the boiling air.

More than one tank crew, secreted on the rear slope, died silently in their boiling metal tombs.

Anti-tank weapons on the ridge, set-up to crossfire on the main road, lay black and burned, surrounded by the charcoal remains of the men that served them.

And then there were those who did not receive the mercy of a swift death.

Men ran around, consumed in fire, screaming and crying, until the flames won the one-sided battle.

Others, hideously burned, lay screaming beside more fortunate silent comrades, their flesh bubbled and spilt, blisters weeping the fluid so necessary for life.

A few, a handful, survived with enough mental faculty to get themselves out of the affected area; some even paused long enough to grab a damaged body and drag it to some sort of safety.

The hillside was on fire; vegetation, bunkers, clothing, leather, flesh, all added their flavoured smoke.

One shattered P-38 had smashed into the ground a few metres short of the Tönsberg, downed by defensive AA fire, the only casualty of all the aircraft in the DRL assault.

It is said that quality troops can stand when others will fall back, and the 14th Engineers were quality troops.

But fire is a great leveller, and it equally held that the flamethrower will take the heart of even the bravest.

Many men of the 14th panicked and started to break.

A few started to move back, walking, sliding, crouching, before breaking into a blind run to safety.

Chekov had to act, and act quickly. He fired in the air.

"Stop! Stop, for fuck's sake, stop!"

The first man went down as the Colonel shot him in the leg.

"You idiots! Stop! Go the other way! The other way! Over the hill top... quick as you can."

One or two men heard and heeded, reversing their intended route, inspiring yet more to follow suit.

But many still plunged down the slope to the illusion of safety ahead.

Gasping for breath, Chekov flung himself into a small hollow on the enemy side of the ridge, just as the 11th Jagdstaffel arrived to finish the job.

The whoosh as the Napalm consumed the air around it was intense, the wind of replacement air sweeping up and over the prone soldiers gathered around their Colonel.

Screams, awful screams, rose above the other sounds of battle, as the immolation on the Tönsberg was repeated.

To the rear, the Soviet mortar positions were swept with 20mm and .50cal, as the German pilots, many of them veteran pilots who once went to war in the ME-110, returned to expend some ammunition on targets of opportunity lying outside the smoking attack area.

The mortars had a hard time of it, as did the few flak positions that exposed themselves to drive the Lightnings off.

At the bottom of the slope, German eyes watched second hands tick into the vertical as 0835 arrived, and with it, the attack.

"Back, Comrades, move back... quickly... make ready... the green toads will be coming!"

Men rose up on his command, barely believing that they had survived, knowing full well that many a comrade had perished in those few minutes.

The internal battle between elation and sadness was writ large on every soldier's face.

The surviving engineers moved quickly back to barely recognisable positions, staffed by barely recognisable human forms, and surrounded by barely recognisable bodies bent by the extremes of temperature and pain.

Around thirty or so men had stayed put, and none had survived.

Radio communication was out.

Telephone cables were out.

Selecting two men as runners, Chekov sent them in either direction to obtain reports from any surviving leadership.

"Comrade Polkovnik."

Balyan saluted with a red raw hand, his uniform still smoking.

"Good to see you, Comrade. Report."

"Thirty-two men under my command. Two light machine guns. Now back in reserve position, Comrade Polkovnik."

Chekov's mouth refused to close.

"How did you manage that, Balyan?"

He turned and pointed at the distant recently constructed bunker containing reserve ammunition.

"On my orders, when the Amerikanski started to drop their bombs, I sent my boys to take cover. I thought the enemy wouldn't know it was there as we only built it two days ago, Comrade Polkovnik."

Chekov toyed with the concept of taking cover in company with the battalion's reserve ammunition and HE stock as he composed his answer.

"Well done, Starshy Serzhant, well done."

The younger man soaked up the praise,

"Now, send twelve of your men to me, all with spare ammunition, and return to your troops. I'll be down when I've sorted this mess out."

Balyan was already moving.

The dozen men were sent to flesh out the frontline, but in no way made up for the losses.

Iska's positions had taken a beating, the HE turning the organised trenches and bunkers into a moonscape, albeit a defendable one.

"Our orders, Comrade Polkovnik?"

"Our orders are to hold, and we'll hold, Pavel. The enemy seem to want this bit of Germany, so we must hold it for as long as possible."

Chekov looked towards the south.

"If the 1st cracks, we're in the shit. Orders or not, if they fold, we'll retreat immediately. We'll still sit on Route 751... so, if we have to run, Asemissen will be the rally point. Clear, Pavel?"

"Asemissen. Understood, Comrade Polkovnik."

Chekov slapped Isla's shoulder.

"Look after yourself, Pavel."

Iska stared after the running shape.

'You too, Gennadi.'

Fig# 153 - Oerlinghausen - Allied assault.

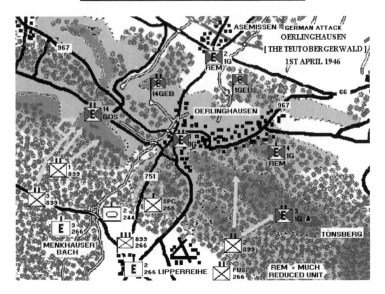

First Battalion had already stepped off, moving through the woods and up the gently rising slope.

No battle formation or line abreast.

Squads moving through the smoke with stealth, using trees as cover, clumps of undergrowth as a base of fire, inexorably moving upwards.

There was no shooting.

Nothing except the fading sounds of agony and terror ahead.

A large explosion broke the calm, closely followed by the screams of the wounded.

A single shattered trunk swept downwards, severed by an explosive charge, triggered by a careless step.

Another man was crushed as the heavy lump of timber crashed to earth.

"Achtung! Trip wires!"

The fruits of the 'gardener's' labours were about to be realised.

Too late the warning, as another crump rang through the woods.

Then two more, as a falling tree set off other charges nearby.

The First Battalion commander urged his men to advance with care, knowing the delay in bringing up the pionieres would allow the Russians too much time.

He yelled at the radioman who relayed the leading company commander's request for engineer support.

"Tell him no! No! No! He must push on quickly and press the enemy before they recover."

First Battalion moved on.

A sharp crack marked the ignition of an anti-personnel mine, the cries of bloodied men marked its efficiency.

More and more mines exploded, occasionally accompanied by the heavier sound of an HE charge, and the resulting fall of a tree.

A few enemy mortars started to lob shells into the area, adding to the growing confusion.

Officers and NCOs tried to regain order and push their men forward, with some success, but some groups floundered, and a few decided to go no further.

Those squads and platoons that carried forward found more mines, and a high proportion of the leadership fell, dead or wounded, victims of the anonymous killers.

The leading grenadiers reached the top and found the small clearing cleared by the defenders.

The gunfire exchange started, as the remaining German leadership worked to find a suitable way to assault across the deadly space.

Two fallen trees suggested the place, and Second Company immediately launched an attack, using the smoke and debris as cover.

The defending engineers had also realised the significance of the fallen trees, and the concentration of firepower they had built up stopped Second Company halfway across.

The radio hummed with exchanges between the mortar companies and the lead element.

Mortar shells started to arrive on the concentration of Russians, causing casualties and a change of thinking.

The defenders spread out more, reducing casualties, but also reducing effectiveness.

First Battalion gathered itself for an assault.

Sounds of air combat drew upward looks from both sides and, to the horror of the Germans, and wonderment of the Soviets, two smoking Shturmoviks appeared, flying down the same line the Mitchells had used a few minutes previously.

467

The FW-190s swarmed around them, but both seemed indestructible, right up to the moment that the rearmost exploded in mid-air, sending pieces flying in all directions.

The lead Ilyushin jiggled out of one attack and dropped two large packages that seem to come apart in mid-air.

The FW-190s, wishing to avoid the burst of whatever had been dropped, pulled away sharply, granting the Shturmovik a moment's grace, which it took advantage of and drove hard for the ground and the route home.

The Ilyushin was a superb ground attack aircraft, but its efficiency and accuracy depended greatly on the skill of the pilot, and this pilot had a great deal else on his mind other than accurate bombing.

He tossed his two AB-250-3 bombs into the woods to the west of the leading German units, completely missing his intended target.

Not that Third Battalion celebrated as the ex-Luftwaffe cluster munitions came apart, each sending one hundred and eighty two-pound bomblets into the woods on and around them.

Many burst above ground level, adding wooden splinters to the terrible metal pieces that flew through the Teutobergerwald.

Others dropped to ground, some exploding on contact, the rest delaying their ignition to catch the unwary, unhinged, or dazed.

More than one disoriented soldier set off a waiting charge as he stumbled around.

Tree charges and mines added to the confusion, some set off by the cluster munitions, others by the feet of frightened men.

Collapsing trees often found more unexploded bomblets, starting the process of killing all over again.

For the men of Third Battalion, it was nothing short of hell on earth.

Eight and Nine Companies came off worst, losing over seventy men between them. Counting the wounded, both companies had been rendered almost combat-ineffective by one single aircraft.

Von Scharf's Seven Company lost only one man slightly wounded.

His men were in awe of the events that unfolded in front of them and, in truth, most were unnerved by the scale of the destruction and death.

The radio crackled into life with demands for a report from Battalion Headquarters.

Scharf did his best to describe what had just happened to Bremer's second wave.

It almost seemed that Bremer was shouting so loud that a radio was superfluous.

"Attack... you must press home the attack! Von Scharf! I make you personally responsible! Attack... take that fucking ridge and push the swine back. That's an order! Att..."

Hauptmann Von Scharf tossed the headset back to Schneider in disgust, understanding that Bremer was losing his mind under the pressure.

'Attack with what, you arse!'

"Unteroffizier Keller!"

Within seconds, the NCO appeared.

"We continue with the attack, Keller," he held his hand up as the objections formed on Keller's lips, "No... a different attack."

Keller looked unconvinced, even though Seven Company was still fighting fit.

"We're going to go round the left flank... move in that direction," he tossed a careless hand to the north, "Two hundred metres should do... and then we go over the hill top and sweep along their line."

Scharf took a swig from his canteen and then offered it up to Keller, who refused.

"A simple move, that's all. The Communists have got to be shattered by the bombing."

Keller shrugged as all NCOs shrug when faced with orders that sound like death sentences, but he knew Von Scharf, and knew the officer would do his best, although it seemed that this time he was offering nothing but a suicide mission.

"Runner!"

A rifleman stepped forward as Von Scharf scribbled on his order pad, repeating his written word to the shocked young grenadier.

"Find Oberleutnant Rieke, Leutnant Grüber, Hauptfeldwebel Riedler...whoever is in charge over there... tell them we'll be moving around the flank now... attacking left to right across their front. Form up what they can and stand ready to come to our support. Secure the right flank. Von Scharf"

He ripped the page off the pad.

"Now... be careful of mines and trip wires. Go!"

The boy scuttled away as fast as his legs could carry him, his eyes glued to the ground on which he stepped.

"Move them out now, Keller."

Seventh Company moved to the left.

It was Iska's company that first engaged the new attack.

A pair of machine guns opened up from the ridge, causing the engineers to dive for cover, distracting them as Von Scharf slid around the flank with the bulk of the Seventh.

However, Iska had a blocking force on the end of his line, just in case the enemy tried such a manoeuvre, and it was this group that spotted the men slinking through the trees.

A DP-28 opened up, bowling over a handful of green clad soldiers.

Keller yelled at his men and they dropped into cover in an instant. Using hand signals, he communicated his plan to the NCOs around him, and the three men prepared their smoke grenades, ready to throw on order.

"Now!"

The four grenades landed, spewing their chemical smoke instantly.

Keller cut the air with his left hand, sending the leading group even wider, a wise precaution, as the defenders commenced putting bullets into the smoke.

Two grenades exploded, the defenders expecting to reap benefits amongst the attacking troops.

No screams greeted the explosions, and Iska immediately understood.

"Right... Tartasky! Your section to cover right... now!"

His hand shot down the path that he wanted Corporal Tartasky's section to cover, only to see dark shapes emerging from the edge of the smoke cloud.

In an instant, Iska snatched out a grenade and primed it, running down the line towards the end of Tartasky's line.

He flung the charge and it exploded in mid-air, some three feet from the face of a German soldier.

Pieces flew from the man, and two more soldiers running nearby, all three dropping to the earth as if poleaxed.

Bringing up his SKS, Iska hastily discharged his magazine as he rushed to the support.

As he leant down to speak to Tartasky, the man's face was obliterated by a pair of bullets, throwing blood and human matter over Iska.

The horrible mess gave Iska a demonic look, and more than one of Tartasky's men shuddered at the sight as he called them to hold the line.

Slipping a ten round charging clip into the carbine, Iska engaged the looming shapes, suddenly realising that the smoke was drifting towards them.

He looked behind him.

"Back... behind that tree trunk, Now! Move!"

He almost threw a couple of reluctant soldiers in the direction of the fallen trunk, grabbing a third by his straps and dragging him along.

As he flopped behind the trunk, the defensive position that the eight men had occupied a moment before exploded as stick grenades arrived.

"Now, Comrades! Kill the fascist bastards!"

The German infantry swept confidently over the position, expecting to have to finish off some wounded, only to be hit by accurate fire from the displaced defenders.

Six went down swiftly, but the others dropped to the floor and started to fight back, scoring hits amongst the defending engineers immediately.

Keller swapped his magazine and let rip for a second time, seeing another defender disappear in a red mist as a reward.

"Now, menschen!"

He rose up and charged the ten metres to the tree trunk, not bothering to see if the rest of his group were with him.

They were.

A man with one of the new weapons shot at him, sending his helmet flying as a round clipped the metal. Another round hit his MP-40, knocking it from his grasp.

Unarmed, he threw himself over the trunk and onto a soldier grappling with reloading a DP-28.

Grabbing the engineer's head, he propelled it into the trunk, driving a branch stub through the soldier's right ear.

Iska used a short arm jab to smash the jaw of a German soldier, driving the butt of his SKS hard into the man's face a second time, just to silence the gurgling screams.

Pausing to quickly unfold the attached bayonet, he suddenly found himself airborne, as a grenade exploded behind him.

Propelled back over the trunk, Iska clattered into two German soldiers.

Recovering the quickest, he snatched off his helmet and used a roundhouse motion to smack it into the head of one of his adversaries.

The other lanced his bayonet across Iska's thigh, causing him to bellow with pain.

He swung the helmet again, missing, unbalancing himself and dropped to the earth.

The German rifleman's satisfaction turned to despair, as two bullets robbed his lungs of air.

Dead before he hit the ground, the Kar98k dropped virtually right at Iska's feet.

Behind him, on the other side of the tree, Keller had snatched up a solid lump of wood and had already succeeded in braining one Russian soldier.

More Germans arrived, the first running straight into a complete fighting lunatic.

Iska worked the bolt, but the weapon jammed, so he drove the bayonet point towards his enemy.

The combination of thrust and the speed of the attacker drove the screaming German soldier up to the muzzle of the rifle, the bayonet protruding from his back by at least four inches.

A German officer pointed at Iska, and immediately he felt the impact of bullets.

Robbed of his strength, he dropped to one knee.

Meanwhile, Keller had taken up a dropped PPSh and used it to sweep the area that a handful of Russians had swarmed from a moment before.

Greeted by wails and screams, he contented himself with emptying the magazine into the undergrowth that clearly contained hidden troops.

A bullet struck his shoulder, sending him flying back against the tree.

German soldiers surged over and round him, as Von Scharf pushed Seventh Company along the Soviet line.

Two men dragged Keller around the tree and into safety, where the Sani started to work on his messy wound.

"Fucking hell, Unterroffizier! You've already got the fucking cross. You after another one?"

Keller's reply was cut short as the medic probed the wound, causing lancing pain.

"Reckon that's your shoulder blade gone. Sit still now."

The medic quickly bandaged the wound and packed it to prevent more bleeding.

He lit a cigarette and stuck it between Keller's lips, then moved to another German soldier, face smashed in by a rifle butt. After a few cursory checks, he pulled open the soldier's tunic and split the tag, taking half so that the man's death could be properly recorded.

"What about him, Sani?"

Keller nodded towards the bleeding Russian officer.

The medical orderly looked at the sitting man, and saw the look of defiance and hatred.

"What about him, Unteroffizier?"

"He's wounded."

"So fucking what? The bastard did for a few of our boys. He can take his chances with the fucking fairies, far as I'm concerned."

Keller started to protest, but a coughing fit wracked his body. He yelped in pain as the grating bones caused mayhem inside.

"For God's sake, Unteroffizier, will you calm down and rest."

The medic pushed one of his few remaining morphine ampoules into Keller's thigh.

Keller started to feel drowsy, imagining whistles and shouts, gunfire and grenades, until merciful darkness ended his pain.

0924 hrs, Sunday, 1st April 1946, the Teutobergerwald, Germany.

Chekov and Balyan, blowing their whistles as hard as the climb would allow, led the small reserve force into the flank of Seventh Company, driving it back on itself with ease.

Only the direct intervention of Von Scharf stopped the German flank from being turned.

The two sides drew back from each other, almost as if by mutual consent, recovering their breath and regaining strength for what would come next.

A runner dropped at Chekov's feet, panting, red faced, the effort of his mission almost too much for the wounded engineer.

"Comrade Polkov... nik... message... from Polkovnik... Nagan..."

Chekov, keeping half an eye in the direction of the enemy, quickly read the order.

"You've got to be fucking joking," he said, to no one in particular.

Showing the order to Balyan, he waited for the younger man's reaction.

"They've got to be fucking joking, really they have, Comrade Polkovnik!"

Turning back to the exhausted man, Chekov gave him his orders.

473

"Can you manage to get back to Polkovnik Nagan?"

The man nodded wearily, especially as the alternative was to stay in this hellhole.

"No time for writing, so tell Polkovnik Nagan, orders received and understood. Off with you, and good luck, Comrade."

The man beat a hasty retreat, much faster than his exhausted condition would have seemed to allow.

The reply would never reach Colonel Nagan of the 1st Guards Mechanised Engineer Sapper Brigade. Not because the messenger failed in his duty, but because the Colonel was already dead by his own hand.

"Right, Starshy Serzhant, get the men ready to move on my order."

"But…"

"No buts, Comrade Balyan, no buts. Orders are orders."

0925 hrs, Sunday, 1st April 1946, the Teutobergerwald, Germany.

Some metres away, Von Scharf listened to the repeated order.

'You've got to be fucking joking!'

"Received, Herr Oberstleutnant, but I think it's a bad idea. Why don't…"

The other set went to transmit, crashing the system.

Von Scharf stopped talking.

"…bey your orders or you'll be relieved. Implement by 0930. Ende."

Von Scharf focussed on the handset he held, his anger directed at the inanimate lump from which this most stupid of orders had come.

Controlling himself, he passed it back to Schneider.

'0930… less than an hour gone… My God.'

Regaining his composure, Von Scharf pointed at the wounded men.

"Sani! Get them away down the hill now. Take whoever you need to help. Get moving now!"

The medic immediately started to organise the evacuation of the wounded.

Scharf could see no officer or NCO of note in sight.

He knew that Rieke and Gruber had both fallen, and Keller was amongst those broken bodies being taken back down the slope.

He checked the magazine in his Gewehr.

Hauptfeldwebel Riedler stumbled into view, his ripped trouser leg exposing blood and dirt on his left calf.

"Are you well, Hauptfeldwebel?"

"Just a few wood splinters in the leg, Herr Hauptmann."

Indicating that they should crouch, Von Scharf listened to Riedler's report.

It was awful listening.

The two companies that had been attacked by the Ilyushin now consisted of eighty-three shattered men, survivors of the two hundred and seventeen soldiers who had led the second wave. In Riedler's opinion, the stunned men were incapable of doing much for the foreseeable future.

"Right, well, we'll combine them into one unit under your command, Hauptfeldwebel."

Riedler nodded and waited for his orders.

"With respect, this is a joke, yes?"

"No, Oskar, I'm afraid it's not. You'll lead," he checked his watch, "And we're late already. Get back to your men and get them moving now. Good luck, and make sure they look out for more mines and trip wires."

Riedler rose and moved off to get the two shattered companies roused and moving.

Two separate orders, born miles apart, but with one shared purpose.

Colonel Gennadi Chekov's orders were to withdraw immediately, and fall back to the new defensive line being established in the farmland to his rear.

Having sacrificed so many of his men, quitting the Teutobergerwald Hills was a hard thing to do, despite the joy of seeing Iska carried off the slopes, wounded, but not so wounded that he couldn't use every swear word in the Russian language.

Chekov was the last man to walk off the hill, pausing for a moment to look back over the dead of both sides, some still obscured by smoke from smouldering items of all shapes and composition.

On the other side of the Teutobergerwald Hills, First Battalion, 899th Grenadier Regiment, had already moved back under orders, forming a defensive line almost back on the start line.

Third Battalion moved back towards them, with Seventh Company providing the rear-guard.

The final casualty fell to an unexploded butterfly bomb, a simple stumble sending the senior NCO on top of the waiting device.

More than one tear was shed as the destroyed body of Hauptfeldwebel Riedler was wrapped in a zeltbahn and taken off the slopes.

On the other side of the valley, the Tönsberg had not fallen either, the situation that resulted becoming a mirror image of the fate of First and Third battalion's, except that the Fusilier battalion escaped heavy casualties.

The unexpected success of another attempt west of Detmold, combined with American successes by the 84th US Infantry Division to the north meant that the Oerlinghausen attack was overtaken by events.

The decision to halt the fighting was made to prevent unnecessary casualties, casualties that had already been suffered long before the order came.

1st Guards Engineers, worn down by days of heavy fighting, could muster less than two short battalions in the field. 14th Guards, under Chekov, was disbanded and merged into the 1st Brigade to bolster the numbers.

It seemed only right that Chekov would step into the shoes left by Nagan's death.

899th Grenadier Regiment started the day with nine companies, and ended it with the equivalent of three and a half.

Hundreds of men from both sides had died in a pointless exchange, disputing a piece of ground that neither occupied at the end of the day.

Such is the way of war.

1703 hrs, Sunday, 1st April 1946, 899th Grenadiere Regiment Headquarters, Gaststatte Dalbker Krug, Lipperreihe, Germany.

Prinz stood beside Johansen, the old Oberwachtmeister, surveying the aftermath of the battle as best he could.

His adjutant arrived with the news.

"Go on, Sauber."

Keeping the binoculars to his eyes, Prinz blanched as the butcher's bill was laid bare.

"Thank you, Hauptmann."

"There is also a message from division, Sir."

Tensing, Prinz merely nodded.

"You are to report to Generalleutnant Spang as soon as possible, Sir."

"Thank you, Sauber."

Still glued to his binoculars, Prinz's eyes were moist as he probed the smoke, hoping to see something there to assuage his pain.

Of course, there was nothing but smoke, trees, and the dead.

The Oberwachmeister understood the Officer's grief.

Prinz turned away, preparing himself to go and 'face the music', as he expected to be blamed for the destruction of his regiment.

He stopped momentarily, a smile crossing his face.

Looking back at the old artilleryman, he spoke softly.

"Quintili Vare…"

"… Legiones redde," the Oberwachmeister completed the quote, throwing up an immaculate salute.

The modern day 'Varus' returned the salute and descended the ladder.

1st April to 17th April 1946, Area of operations for the 1st German Republican Army Group, Germany.

The 266th Infantry Division played no further part in the offensive, being withdrawn to Beckum, where it was rested and reinforced, as well as performed security duties at the Soviet POW camp that had been established there.

German III and X Corps drove hard into the Red Army and achieved a signal victory east of the Teutobergerwald, destroying a number of Soviet infantry and artillery formations, and opening a gap in the defensive line that carried III Corps to the outskirts of Springe, southwest of Hanover.

Marshal Malinovsky responded, allocating everything he had to hand, driving a counter attack into the southern flank of III Corps on 14th April, virtually destroying the 5th Infantry Division, and badly damaging the adjacent X Corps unit from 12th Infantry Division.

German 63rd Army fought its way to the Weser at Beverungen, where it was only halted by destroyed bridges.

An ill-advised amphibious crossing floundered in the face of heavy resistance, and a tragic friendly fire attack by DRL medium bombers, killed or wounded many of the assault pioneers and lead infantry units forming for a second attempt.

On 17th April, CI Corps, with 3rd Fallschirmjager and the 116th Panzer Divisions leading, blundered into a trap outside of Trendleburg, including a massed mission by ground attack aircraft of the Red Air Force, resulting in the loss of 40% of the 'Windhund' Division's precious tanks in three hours of fierce fighting, and over two thousand casualties amongst the paratrooper infantry.

After twenty-five days of constant combat, the DRH was exhausted, and, reluctantly, FeldMarschal Guderian advised Eisenhower of his need to revert to a defensive role until his troops were rested.

C'est magnifique, mais ce n'est pas la guerre. C'est de la folie.
Translation – It is magnificent, but it is not war. It is madness.

Pierre Bosquet, Marshall of France, observing the Charge of the Light Brigade at the Battle of Balaclava, fought against the Russians in 1854.

Chapter 144 – THE TWENTY-FIRST

1600 hrs, Tuesday 26th March 1946, Schafstedt, Germany.

"Gentlemen, gentlemen, thank you for coming."

Colonel Prentiss, the Viscount Kinloss, called his officer's group to order, and then spotted something...

"Good lord, Algie, where did you get that abominable cravat?"

The A Squadron commander rose to his feet in triumph, displaying the blue and red silk Guards Regimental colours for everyone's consumption.

"Sir, I liberated the item from some Coldstream Guards' officer by way of a pistol competition. The honour of the Regiment was at stake... and was preserved in style, I might add, Sir."

Prentiss wrinkled up his nose.

"To be frank, Algie, that is not style and, were I to compete for **that** prize, I suspect my aim would have been somewhat wayward, honour or no."

To a chorus of hoots, Major Algie Woods resumed his seat.

"Now then, gentlemen, let's see how the war's going, shall we?"

He turned to the briefing map and used the thin pointer to highlight the areas he was speaking about, starting with Denmark.

"Our German cousins have started tremendously well, and there are reports of Soviet surrenders in large numbers, and the latest griff suggests that we are already in possession of the Isle of Mon, and half of Falster too."

He moved the pointer.

"Royal Marine Commandos landed here... at Harpelunde, and are being reinforced as we speak."

He flexed the wooden pole between both hands, like a headmaster emphasising a point.

"The Soviet forces on the Danish islands are expected to either surrender or be overcome within the next twenty-four hours."

He let the murmur die down of its own accord.

"Now, here, our pals in the 7th Armoured have broken through the enemy front and are on the outskirts of Bordesholm... ahead of schedule I might add."

He flicked at a hair that had dropped across his eyes.

"Now, the 11th, with the Fifes leading the way, as you know, have bypassed Itzehoe, leaving some of the Rifle Brigade to mop up the blighters who have dug in there. 55th Division have put some men on the road to relieve them immediately. Rifle Brigade will then come back together and get back up to the Fifes."

The annoying hair returned.

"Now, 3rd Tanks," he referred to the 3rd Royal Tank Regiment who, with 2nd Fife and Forfar Yeomanry, joined with Prentiss' 23rd Hussars to complete 29th Armoured Brigade, 11th Armoured Division, "Will move in front of the Fifes to continue the drive at first light, heading, as planned, towards Hamburg."

He drew their attention to a different route.

"This is our new route of advance, gentlemen."

They all strained to understand the map.

"We will move up shortly, moving around Itzehoe, and driving up Route 206 here... all the way to Bimöhlen, cutting the north-south road and, as the General expects, cutting off the retreat of some of Uncle Joe's units that are presently holding up Guards Division's move south down the Reichsbahn."

A number of the men in front of him looked a little wary of such a task.

Not without reason.

Prentiss soothed them immediately.

"Now the General understands this could become a bit dicey, so he's given me command of some extra stuff, which should all come in handy."

He consulted his notebook quickly.

"118 battery from 75th Anti-tank, 1st Cheshires as infantry support, two recce squadrons from 15th/19th Hussars, and first call of some Army Artillery assets."

That removed a few of the worried looks.

"I believe we'll cope with that, don't you think?"

Major Merton, B Squadron's commander half rose from his seat,

"Any air, Sir?"

"Actually, the General specifically said you're not to be involved with the usage of any complicated machinery, especially the likes of warplanes, Freddie."

Raucous laughter drowned out Merton's attempted riposte.

"Seriously gentlemen, we will have first call on air support from our naval brethren who, whilst we eat the mud and dust of European roads, are safely ensconced in their warm boats, just off shore. From what I've heard, they're rather good at their job too, so we should treat them nicely, which," he looked steadfastly at Merton, "Was probably what the General meant regarding your involvement, Freddie."

The knockabout continued for a few minutes, something Prentiss actively encouraged as, in his view, it made for better teamwork.

Checking his watch, he tapped the floor with the butt of his pointer, calling a halt to the exchanges that had suddenly become a good-humoured attack on Emerson, the C Squadron 2IC, whose brother served with the RN on aircraft carriers.

"Gentlemen, gentlemen, listen in now. D Squadron will remain here until the fuel situation is sorted."

A supply of contaminated fuel had been used to fill each of D Squadron's tanks, much to the chagrin of Major Thomas Fanshaw, its commander.

A quick investigation had discovered nothing of note, but security was tightened on all storage facilities.

"I want you back with your boys and set ready to move off on my order. Timing will depend on the arrival of our support elements and," he tapped the map again, "How long it takes the Rifle Brigade to sort out Itzehoe."

He pointed at Woods.

"For your sins and poor taste, A Squadron will lead, Algie."

"My pleasure, Sir," words his face denied, despite the smile.

"Rightho. If there's no more questions, let's get our innings underway."

Itzehoe had fallen by the time Prentiss returned to his tent, or rather, the Soviet defenders withdrew in the face of building pressure.

23rd Hussars and their additions were on the road and passing Itzehoe as the sun started to descend on yet another bloody day.

15th/19th Hussars led the way, backed up by the Cheshire Battalion in its half-tracks.

The decision to push on at night was not an easy one, but melting Soviet resistance emboldened the British.

Expecting to find defences in Kellinghausen, Prentiss urged caution on his recon element, intending to avoid any meaningful engagement until the sun returned.

However, troops approaching Kellinghausen found only relieved German civilians celebrating their liberation. He was persuaded to continue by the enthusiastic 15th/19th Major, setting the railway line at Wrist as the furthest point of advance for the opening day of the Allied offensive.

The railway line at Wrist, running across the front of the advancing Hussars, and set between two watercourses, also coincided with the only Soviet point of resistance on the road to Bimöhlen, an overenthusiastic interpretation of a withdrawal order removing Soviet units from Prentiss' axis of advance.

The lead Staghound armoured car set off a hastily laid mine, drawing defensive fire upon itself, a brief encounter that cost the lives of four of the crew and saw the vehicle provide a flaming beacon by which the Soviets brought the following troops under fire.

After a quick briefing from the Recon commander, and consultation with the last set of reconnaissance photographs, Prentiss was reasonably satisfied that nothing substantive lay ahead.

However, attacking such a position at night was not an undertaking for the faint-hearted, even with some of the new German design twin binoculars, one side normal, the other side infra-red, such as equipped each of his recon vehicles and his command tanks.

His orders on avoiding risk to his valuable heavy tanks were quite explicit, and a night attack into probable infantry positions with the lumbering Black Prince tanks was a risk too far

His orders on achieving Bimöhlen as soon as possible, and no later than midday on the 27th, left little room for manoeuvre.

A quick orders group committed the Cheshires into a hasty attack, supported by the Comets from A Squadron, 15th/19th Hussars, the FOO close by, ready to bring down the artillery, and with the engineers in tow, in case mines should prove a problem.

The engineer commander's comments about the issues of night mine detection were acknowledged, but politely disregarded, as nothing in the venture was without risk, the need to advance reinforced by a curt message from Brigadier Roscoe Harvey, the 29th Armoured Brigade's commander.

The assault moved in carefully, one mine causing two injuries amongst the Cheshire soldiers, but the enemy was gone, using the advantages of night to fall back under orders.

Prentiss Force pushed slowly forward, moving steadily eastwards.

To their north-east, the sky flashed and thundered as the Guards Division put in a night assault.

Fig# 154 - Bimohlen - Prentiss Force

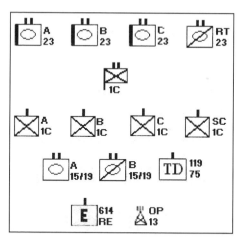

0502 hrs, Wednesday, 27th March 1946, Headquarters of 10th Guards Army, Bad Oldesloe, Germany.

"He did what?"

"He pulled back beyond point dvadtsat' sem'... and we've only just found out, Comrade Polkovnik General."

Mikhail Ilyich Kazakov stroked the ends of his moustache into points which, to his staff, was a tell-tale sign that an explosion was about to occur.

Mishulin, his recently appointed deputy, had circled point twenty-seven, the nondescript number allocated to a position of prime importance, namely Wrist.

"What order was Ibiankii given exactly?"

Mishulin snapped his fingers and a folder was passed over, listing all orders issued by 10th Guards Army command since the enemy had attacked.

"Quite clear. Hold the position around dvadtsat' sem' until further orders."

The folder crashed onto the desk, scattering pencils and unweighted papers in all directions.

"The man's an idiot... worse than that... what, Comrade?"

Mishulin kept a straight face as he delivered his information.

"Ibiankii is uncontactable. Apparently, he went forward to personally supervise the defence of dvadtsat' sem'. His deputy suspects he may have fallen to one of the air attacks."

Kazakov grunted and his mind moved immediately to solving the problem.

"So, we have part of 7th Guards and 17th Anti-tank trapped above, being pressed by this Allied division."

Again, he sensed his CoS had more to say.

"It's just been identified as the British Guards Division, Comrade Polkovnik General."

In Kazakov's mind, that gave it a high status as, in the Red Army, reference the Guards was synonymous with increased combat skill and efficiency.

"So, we have their Guards and 7th Tanks, all coming down one axis, it seems."

Kazakov sat back from the map, his hands selecting a Red Star cigarette that he crimped without looking, his eyes roving the map for a solution.

He tossed the pack to Mishulin, who was less sure about the harsh cigarettes. He carefully squeezed the cardboard tube that held the tobacco wad, flattening the tube in two different places, a necessary procedure for those who wanted to keep their throats intact. Mishulin was a Chesterfield man through and through,

484

although, since they had captured a huge stock of British supplies outside of Lubeck, his preference had been for Craven 'A' cigarettes.

"Cancel the orders to 3rd Guards Mechanised immediately. Tell them to stand their ground and await further instructions."

It was the way Kazakov operated; swift, clipped instructions, delivered unequivocally, and to be instantly obeyed.

He leant over the map, beckoning Mishulin to come closer.

"9th Mechanised Brigade are the nearest. Fuel situation?"

"As of the 0300 report, 9th were fully stocked, ready to move off south-west at 0600, Comrade."

He took a scale ruler and drew a single line, then set the ruler at right angles across it.

"45th Tanks?"

"The 0330 report had them in the process of refuelling. They are still light on ammunition," Mishulin leant across to the stack of papers recently retrieved from the floor and swiftly found the one he needed, "...on average 80% stock per vehicle, across the range of types, Comrade."

"They'll do. Send them a hold order immediately."

Mishulin turned back from the clerk who ran off with the order.

"1823rd Artillery?"

"Not so good, Comrade. 50% ammunition, and their fuel train was attacked by aircraft before they filled up. There is a shortage of 76mm at the moment, which is being worked on. The quartermasters are also trying to get spare fuel to them as soon as possible, but we are..."

Kazakov interrupted.

"We are short, as always."

However, a decision was needed.

"Tell 1823rd to hold immediately."

He swiftly put his thoughts onto the map.

"Right. The Marshal was quite right to order us out of this peninsular, but I'm not going to leave behind the larger part of a Guards Rifle Corps doing it. We'll organise a joint attack, bringing the 7th Guards southwards to here, and sending 9th and 45th Guards up from the south, squeezing the life out of this enemy force, and allowing the 7th to escape."

Mishulin nodded and quickly spoke.

485

"An excellent plan, Comrade General. Should we seek support from Twenty-First Army from the east?"

Kazakov laughed, seeing the unintended humour in his CoS' words.

"I rather suspect old Gusev has too much on his hands at the moment, don't you?"

The map showed the understrength Twenty-first Army being pushed backwards slightly quicker than Marshal Bagramyan's plan dictated.

"Right. Put that into orders my generals can understand and have them execute the assault at 0800. Make sure they know to get in close as they can to avoid problems from their Air Force."

Mishulin scribbled away.

"The elements of 7th Guards will continue on through, the 9th Guards will cover the withdrawal and..." he came down the map a short distance, representing some five kilometres, "...the new line will be held at Kaltenkirchen."

The scribbling stopped and his CoS waited expectantly.

"Get it done then, and accept no excuses. They can all be on time, regardless of the weather or supply. I'm going to phone the Old Armenian fox and tell him what I'm doing."

The staff sprang into action as Mishulin issued the orders, Kazakov moving into his office to converse with Bagramyan, 1st Baltic Front's commander.

By the time that he had finished the call, Kazakov had the agreement of Bagramyan, and unexpected support from Buiansky, the Frontal Aviation officer.

The opportunity to give the British Guards a bloody nose was not going to be wasted.

0745 hrs, Wednesday, 27th March 1946, Field Headquarters of Prentiss Force, Bad Brahmstedt-land, Germany.

"Maybe the buggers aren't so short on ammunition, eh?"

Prentiss addressed the remark to no-one in particular.

Soviet artillery had been striking his positions since about 7am, and had drawn blood in both men and machines.

Prentiss Force was arraigned in a U-shape, the bowl of the U embracing Bimhölen, and with the open end towards where the British had just come from.

486

Fig# 155 - The Battle of the Streams.

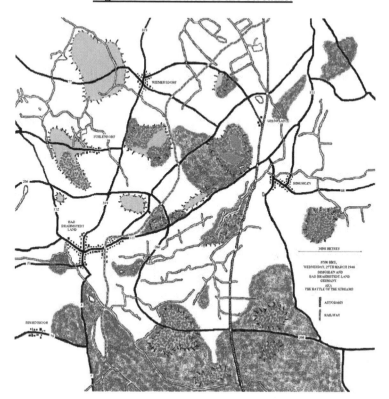

  The northern side started at Fuhlendorf, where part of the Cheshires' support company, plus their 6 Platoon, were situated. Spreading eastwards from there were the **Cheshires' A Company** and the four tank troops of Algie Woods' A Squadron, backed up the H Troop Achilles' of the 75th Anti-tank's 119th Battery.

  In and around Bimhölen, I Troop of the 75th and B Company, 1st **Cheshire Battalion**, sat alongside the Comets of 15th/19th Hussars.

  The southern edge was screened by the Staghounds of the recce squadron, and formed from Merton's B Squadron, C Company of the Cheshires, with some of the Engineers acting as infantry until reinforcements arrived.

  The end of the line terminated at Bad Brahmsted-land, where the 75th's G troop and 23rd Hussars headquarters combined with the company of engineers.

Major Blacker's C Squadron acted as reserve, sitting in the small woods on Bimhölenstrasse, and able to move in any direction.

The FOO positioned himself on the high ground immediately west of the junction of the autobahn and Route 111.

Here, Prentiss also positioned some of his headquarters Crusader AA tanks, using the high ground to extend cover to as much of his formation as possible, not that air attack was very likely, given the state of the enemy's air force.

Fig# 156 - Bimohlen - Prentiss Force initial dispositions.

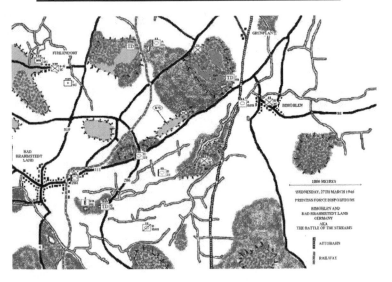

The rest of the regiment's headquarters men and vehicles remained on the eastern outskirts of Bad Brahmstedt-land, a local farm proving ample for Prentiss' needs, the farmer's wife plying the liberators with the fruits of her labours, in both solid and liquid form.

At 0754, the first of the air support promised by Major General Buiansky arrived, unchallenged and keen to make its mark.

The 314th Fighter Bomber Regiment, an under-strength mixture of IL-3 Shturmoviks and Yak-3 modifications, swept over the battlefield, releasing a cocktail of HE, AP, and fragmentation rockets on the northern defences.

Close behind came the remnants of another regiment, the 277th Ground Attack, whose six Il-10s dropped their bombs all over the defenders of Bimhölen.

Above them, Yak-3s of the 4th Guards Fighter Division waited for a challenge that never came.

Encouraged by the absence of enemy aircraft, both attack regiments swept over the battlefield again, intent on knocking out whatever it was that had clawed two of their number from the sky on the first pass.

Two Crusader AA vehicles engaged the lead Shturmovik with their 40mm Bofors, knocking vital lumps off the aircraft, which nose-dived into the roadway adjacent to the Osterau, a small stream.

The next three aircraft shredded the lightly armoured AA vehicles with 23mm cannon shells, causing one to burn spectacularly, the 40mm shells exploding like a Chinese New Year party. The destruction of the nearby FOO was an unknown bonus.

Their flight path took them over the hidden reserve who, faithful to Prentiss' orders, refused the opportunity to fire at the Soviet aircraft.

Not so the remaining AA vehicles around Bad Brahmstedt-land, who plucked one, then a second Shturmovik from the air in under ten seconds.

One of the Yak-3s, a 3K version mounting a 45mm cannon, took a different path, rounding the northern positions and running north to south over Bad Brahmstedt-land, successfully engaging and destroying a Crusader AA before mechanical unreliability cut short its attacks and forced the failing aircraft to fly away.

A third sweep of the battlefield rewarded the Soviet flyers with more kills, as cannon and machine-gun bullets found bodies and vehicles, inflicting casualties on both the anti-tank vehicles and Cheshires, knocking out one of the Achilles.

One Yak-3, a UTI trainer pressed into frontline service, took fatal hits from a Cheshires' Bren gunner, flipping over and burying itself in the earth twenty yards from A Squadron's command tank.

A piece of flying propeller decapitated Algie Woods with the precision of a quality surgeon, sending the head with upper teeth flying away, and leaving his ruined body to drop on to the turret floor, the blood still spurting from the open wound, drenching the gunner and loader in an instant.

The lower jaw, all that was left of Woods' head, seemed to laugh at its unfortunate predicament.

Cheshire infantrymen and Hussar tank crew alike, as much as a hundred and fifty yards away, heard the animal-like screaming from inside "Agincourt".

The attack aircraft departed, leaving behind five of their number.

The Soviet artillery started up once more.

Major Stuart French, the Hussars' 2IC, was white as a sheet.

"Sir, it's Captain Soames, Sir. Major Woods is dead, Sir."

"Good grief, poor Algie. What's A Squadron's report?"

"Three tanks lost, Sir, two more disabled... track damage, being worked on now."

Soames was a new arrival, an unknown quantity, and one that now gave both French and Prentiss a moment's concern.

Prentiss made his decision swiftly.

"Right. I'm going to drop in on Soames... just to make sure he's ok, and see to poor Algie. Gather the reports and radio me if there's anything significant, otherwise I'll be back toodle-pip."

"Yes, Sir."

Prentiss climbed into his Dingo armoured car and moved off to assess A Squadron's abilities, or rather, to see if its de facto commander was capable of running the show.

The enemy artillery seemed to grow in intensity, making Prentiss check his watch.

0820.

The Dingo pulled up near to 'Agincourt', but within the shelter of a stand of three trees, screening it from any observation.

The sight of the Black Prince's crew appalled Prentiss.

Two of them were simply drenched with blood, the other two less so, but all four were clearly in a state of extreme shock.

Standing over them was Captain Soames, whose voice carried over the sounds of bursting shells.

"It's now your tank, Sergeant, so I suggest that you get a grip of yourself and get it back into action. That's a bloody order, man!"

"Ah, Captain Soames, what have we here?"

The immaculate officer sprang to attention and peeled off a parade ground salute, which Prentiss casually returned, his mind already forming an opinion that was not complementary.

"Sir, these men refuse to remove Major Woods from the vehicle and get it back into action. Despite my best efforts they..."

490

"Thank you, Captain. You may return to your command. I will come and see you directly. Where's your vehicle?"

Soames pointed to a well-camouflaged tank in the next stand of trees.

"Very well. Carry on."

Prentiss turned to the four men of 'Agincourt's crew, their faces raised in expectation of a beasting from their CO.

"Sergeant Thorne."

"Yes, Sir?"

"Will you be able to command her if we can get poor old Major Woods' out?"

His voice said yes, his eyes said otherwise.

"Good man."

A distant voice hailed Prentiss and he turned to look, ignoring the object in the grass, hastily but only partially covered with piece of bloody cloth.

The approaching RSM was limping and running in equal measure.

After a splendid salute, RSM Stacey stamped his foot and answered his CO's query.

"Near miss, Sir. Slammed my ankle into one of the stanchions. Nothing to worry about, Sir."

Prentiss beckoned the RSM away from the forlorn tank crew, a nearby shell burst adding urgency to the Colonel's words.

"Most of poor old Woods is still in the tank. I'll need your help, Sarnt-Major."

Divesting themselves of their tunics, Prentiss and Stacey climbed up on the tank, the former disappearing inside the commander's hatch.

'Oh my Lord... oh my Lord...'

None of his crew watched as the hideous body of Major Algernon Woods was hauled out, still containing enough blood and fluid to make it extremely unpleasant for the two handling his corpse.

Stacey laid him on the rear engine covers and grabbed a small tarpaulin from the turret stowage boxes.

Prentiss and he wrapped the still form carefully, before dragging Woods off the tank and placing the cadaver next to a tree.

"Thank you, Sarnt-Major. Most unpleasant. I'll speak to them and get 'Agincourt' back on the run. Keep a close eye on things here, if you please."

491

The message was not lost on Stacey, who threw up a salute and limped back towards his own tank, some five hundred metres away.

"Lads," the vacant faces met his, albeit slowly, "We've moved your boss out of the tank now."

The faces were still blank, but there did seem a slight flicker to Prentiss' eyes.

"I need old Agincourt back in the fight now, y'hear. I know what you've lost, lads, you know I do... but we've got a war to win, and you know that your Major would be spitting feathers if he thought his tank wasn't there when needed, eh?"

The flickers were more pronounced now.

"Come on then, boys. What do you say, eh?"

He waved at his driver, who bounded over from the Dingo.

"Baines will make up your crew. He's done the conversion, so put him where you want, Sergeant Thorne."

Thorne stood slowly, legs shaking and unsteady, but he drove himself up to stand at attention.

"We won't let you or old Splinter down, Sir."

The other three joined him with reassurances.

They moved off towards 'Agincourt', taking the first steps to mount with demonstrable effort.

"It's none too pleasant in there, Baines. Keep an eye on them, Corporal. I'm relying on you now."

"Yes, Sir."

Gingerly, the men of 'Agincourt' returned to their positions, and the tank became a fighting machine once more.

As Prentiss dropped into the Dingo's driver seat, he wondered how effective it would prove.

Slipping the small armoured car into gear, he headed for Soames' tank.

Before he got there, the Soviet Army launched an attack that would bring Prentiss Force to the point of extinction.

0850 hrs, Wednesday, 27th March 1946, Astride Route 111, Germany.

Soames' Black Prince engaged something, Prentiss didn't know what, but soon it seemed that all of 'A' Squadron was firing, supported by the Achilles TDs of the 75th, and heavy machine-guns from the Cheshires.

British mortars added to the resistance, and Prentiss quickly steered away from the position that the mortar platoon was secreted in, not wishing to expose it to fire.

Slipping into cover a reasonable enough distance away, Prentiss pushed himself up out of the driver's seat and pressed his binoculars to his eyes.

Fig# 157 - Bimöhlen - Soviet Northern assaults.

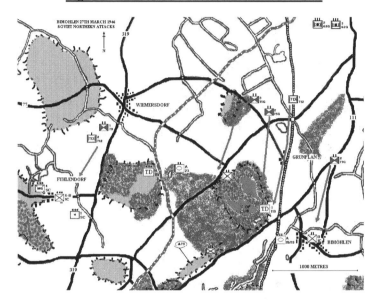

Enemy armour and infantry on foot were swarming out of Wiemersdorf, seemingly intent on overwhelming the defenders of Fuhlendorf before the British could get reorganised.

It was immediately clear to Prentiss that his left flank was already in danger.

A short radio conversation sent his CS Churchill tanks, fitted with 95mm howitzers, and two of the Crusader AA vehicles, to support the defence of Fuhlendorf.

'Damn and blast it. Where's our artillery?'

His eyes blazed, even though numerous Soviet vehicles were now smoking on the field.

Back on the radio, Prentiss switched to the Artillery network and gave precise orders.

He waited until the artillery shells started to arrive before revving the Dingo and returning to his HQ.

493

Once inside the farmhouse, the briefing started.

Prentiss Force was being assaulted at four points; two from the north and another pair of attacks coming from the south.

"FOO?"

"No contact, Sir. Nor from the AA troop stationed nearby. I suspect they've had it."

Prentiss worked the problem.

"Lieutenant Jemeson, take three men from the signals section, maps, radios... drive like blazes and get back on that hillock. You're our FOO until relieved."

Fig# 158 - Bimöhlen - Soviet Southern assaults.

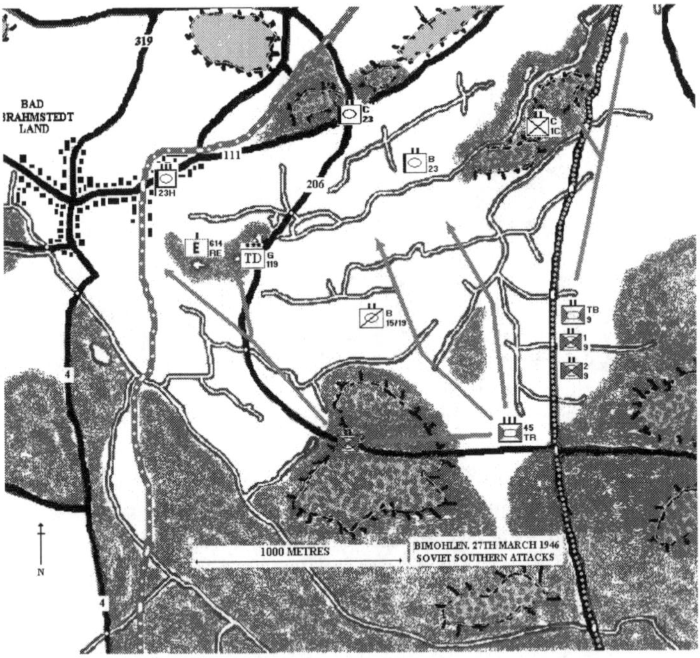

A voice summoned him urgently.

"Sir!", he turned to the signals sergeant, "It's Captain Soames reporting in, Sir."

Quickly moving over to the NCO's position, Prentiss listened in as the newly frocked commander of 'A' Squadron made his brief report.

"Blackberry, over."

494

"Blackberry, this is Apple-five, they're falling back. Fifteen enemy tanks destroyed. Apple has lost four vehicles total, over."

"Roger, Apple. Out."

A shell fell nearby, dropping a lump of plaster from the ceiling, straight onto the map table.

Prentiss swept his hands over it, clearing the dust away.

"Talk to me, Stuart."

"Sir, 'B' Squadron has taken fire from a combined tank and infantry force that moved obliquely across them... seemingly headed for Bimhölen."

French drew a rough pencil line.

"Major Merton stopped the blighters here, and they've fallen back. 'B' has lost three tanks, with two disabled but still in the fight. Also, two of the Stags have been knocked out, Sir."

"Can he hold?"

"Freddie says he's in good shape, Sir."

"Any word from the Cheshires' CO?"

"Light casualties generally, Sir... except Bimhölen, where the Soviets pushed in very close. The Cheshires hung on there by the skin of their teeth so it seems. 15th/19th counter-attacked and knocked the stuffing out of the enemy, who fell back. Only one Comet lost, Sir."

The Hussars' Colonel accepted a mug of steaming hot tea from his batman.

"Thank you, Wrigglesworth."

Others also got their own, allowing Prentiss a few moments to take the full situation in.

"Right, Stuart. I want Cecil to send his 'C' Squadron closer to Bimhölen. Tell him I want them tucked up safe in these woods here," his fingers hovered over the woods near the autobahn immediately west of Bimhölen.

"Send First Platoon of the Recce Troop as well."

Prentiss moved on, seeking additional alternatives, and spotted one immediately.

The Regimental administration troop was backed up in the western end of Bad Brahmstedt-land.

"Right, Stuart. I want to form another infantry reserve right here. Leave one man per vehicle, and get the rest up here immediately...with transport... make sure Sandy knows that I want him in position quickly."

Captain Lysander Chandos Montagu, commanding the Regiment's logistical support troop, was not known for his speed at the best of times, and Prentiss wanted to make sure the man got the message.

"And 'D' Squadron? Anything from Tommy at all?"

"No, Sir."

A young radio operator interrupted.

"Begging your pardon, Sir, but Major Fanshaw has been moving for some time. He apologises but was unable to get through on the radio. The transmission was lost before completion, Sir."

"Get him back as soon as possible and find out his arrival time here."

"Yes, Sir."

Both Prentiss and French stood back from the map.

"Right. So we will get 'D' Squadron at some time, but we don't know when. We still have some armour reserve, and Sandy's boys as infantry for the moment. That'll have to do for now."

He addressed the radio operator curtly, revealing the stresses of command.

"Get me the Brigadier immediately."

Taking the last gulp from his mug, he offered the empty up to the hovering Wrigglesworth.

"We need more infantry, and another FOO... and I think soon. Let me know as soon as Jameson reports in."

The conversation with Brigadier Harvey started with a quick briefing on the situation. Prentiss' plea for reinforcements was cut short by the arrival of a 76mm HE shell.

0939 hrs, Wednesday 27th March, 1945, 23rd Hussars HQ, Bauernhaus Holzbein, Bad Brahmstedt-land, Germany.

"Sir? Sir?"

Nothing.

The 76mm shells, there had been three in total, had not hit directly, but had been close enough to do harsh work amongst the men and equipment of the Hussars' headquarters.

The Holzbein's farmhouse was levelled.

Lysander Montagu's men had already dragged dead from the rubble and laid the distorted bodies out with as much reverence as shattered bone and riven flesh allowed.

Major French, identifiable by his epaulettes only, seemed to have taken the most punishment, the general effect of which had been to virtually rip his limbs from his torso, what attachment remained made the corpse resemble a string puppet of the most ghoulish kind.

496

Next to him lay the totally intact Wrigglesworth, unmarked, save a light covering of dust, but equally dead.

The radiomen were stretched out, completing the line of five bodies so far recovered.

"Sir? Sir?"

Prentiss dragged himself from the edge of the black abyss.

"H-H-Here!"

Pressure grew on his legs as someone stood on top of the debris hiding him from the rescuers.

Something… a door possibly… was pulled away and a draft of cool air hit Prentiss in the face.

"Here he is!"

Hands grabbed at him, bringing comfort by their presence alone, whilst others worked to move the 'something' that made breathing so damn tricky.

The weight came off and he found himself dragged, not into the room in which he had stood a few minutes before, but into an open area topped by a greying sky.

"Sir?"

Prentiss looked up at the portly frame of Captain Montagu.

"Give me a moment… there's a good chap."

The Hussars' commander mentally examined his person, ticking off the list and becoming more incredulous as he neared the end.

'Legs… arms… am I bleeding?… no?… what nothing at all?… jammy blighter… nothing broken…ah! Eyes… bit smudgy but working… Ah… I've a roaring headache… still… miraculous stuff…"

A shell exploded nearby, reaping a harvest amongst the soldiers of Montagu's group. Hot metal brought forth screams of pain, which served to bring Prentiss out of his dreams.

"Sir, the Russians are attacking north… south… everywhere, Sir."

As Prentiss became more aware, he sorted out the sounds of high-velocity guns, machine-guns, mortars, and aircraft engines.

"Get me up, Sandy."

Montagu swept the Sten round to the small of his back and, with another soldier, helped Prentiss to his feet. Their helping hands were then waved away.

Swaying unsteadily, he looked around, sparing a lingering stare for the line of casualties.

"Right. Walk me to my Dingo, will you?"

'Bit shaky old chap... but what do you expect eh?'

"I'll need your man here to drive me, Sandy. I need to get a grip of this situation, or we'll all be rather inconvenienced, I think."

Prentiss mounted the small command vehicle with incredible difficulty, his balance becoming worse, rather than improving.

"Damn and blast."

Prentiss took a look at his new driver and then raised an eyebrow towards Montagu.

"Green, Sir."

"Right, Sandy. Keep an all-round formation, but pay more attention to the river road... Route Four I think it is. You've got Recce and AA back-up. Stay close to your radio."

He held up a radio handset to emphasise his point.

"Good luck old chap. Drive on, Green. Get me to Bimöhlen."

Lysander Montagu stood saluting a cloud of exhaust fumes as Trooper Green gunned the 2.5 litre engine and the small armoured car leapt away, sending Prentiss tumbling backwards into the passenger compartment.

Prentiss arrived at the Cheshires' HQ, set on raised ground between the two main defence lines.

"Blazes, Cam, what happened to you?"

Robin Kreyer, the Cheshires' OC, examined the haggard and blood-streaked cavalry officer, who waved away his enquiry, seeking a map from which to work.

"This current, Robin?"

"Indeed. Tea, Cam?"

"Love one."

"Situation, Robin?"

The Cheshires' Lieutenant Colonel immediately pointed at Bimöhlen.

"Buggers pressed us hard here, but we're sound again."

His finger moved to the west.

"Your tanks arrived in the nick of time, and your vehicles on the ridge drove into the side of the attack, and they've fallen back into Wiemersdorf."

Tea arrived, and Kreyer paused for the smallest moment.

"If you've got anything else to stiffen Fuhlendorf then send it would be my advice, Cam. I can send 11 Platoon that way?"

Major Blastow of the 75th supplied an additional solution.

"My HQ troop is at a loose end. You've still got your squadron as reserve, so shall I take Fuhlendorf, Sir?"

"That should do nicely. 11 Platoon and your HQ troop it is. Now, if you please, Major."

Blastow saluted and sped from the tent, and almost immediately the sound of roaring 6046GM diesels filled the silence, as the four Achilles drivers ensured they were all warmed up and ready to move.

Prentiss returned to the map and examined the southern edge of the battlefield.

"So who the dickens are these blighters then, eh?"

"Damned if I know, Cam! No mention in briefing... no clue from photos... nothing. They've come out of thin air, but they are certainly real.

Fig# 159 - Bimöhlen - Soviet Forces.

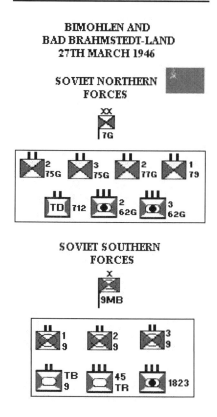

The 'blighters' in question, 9th Guards Mechanised Brigade and 45th Guards Tank Regiment, had simply been undetected, mainly due to their expert camouflage and fire discipline, meaning that the Allied command had committed Prentiss Force into a position where they would be attacked on two sides by forces twice their size.

More pressingly, the 'blighters' in question were already on the move northwards, and in greater numbers than before.

1005 hrs, Wednesday 27th March, 1945, Prentiss Force HQ, Hill 73, Bad Brahmstedt-land, Germany.

The reports started to arrive, as hard-pressed tank and infantry officers relayed news of the approaching hordes.

The immediate impression was that Bimöhlen would hold, but that the north and south would probably be overrun.

Fighting for their survival, the guardsmen of the 7th Guards Rifle Corps threw themselves forward, supported by a handful of SP guns from the 712th AT Battalion. The remaining AT guns and infantry were working some miles to the north, holding back the attempted advance of the Guards and 7th Armoured.

On the southern edge of the battlefield, the Shermans and T-34/85s of the 9th and 45th advanced in waves, the mechanised infantry following close behind, all preceded by superb artillery support from the SU-76s of the 1823rd.

The Cheshires' map reflected the desperate position.

"Right!"

The sharpness of Prentiss' voice indicated that he had made a decision.

"Robin, if we try to do everything, all we will do is nothing... so... I'm abandoning Bimohlen and reinforcing Fuhlendorf."

"But..."

Prentiss held up his hand.

"Bear with me, Robin."

Grabbing a pencil, the Cavalry officer drew a few rough pencil lines, mumbling explanations and expectations as he went.

He had converted the Cheshires' commander long before he finished.

The orders went out immediately and, Prentiss mused as he swigged the cold tea, would be sorted in time to give the Russians a bloody nose.

Part of his decision was already redundant, as he found out, as waves of messages flooded the headquarters.

"Sir, they've pushed our units out of Fuhlendorf."

"Sir, 'A' Squadron close to being overrun. Requesting permission to withdraw."

"Sir, Captain Montagu reports that enemy infantry have infiltrated the southern outskirts of Bad Brahmstedt-land."

"Sir, 'B' Squadron reports losing two more tanks."

"Sir, 'B' Coy Cheshires disengaging. Enemy infantry investing Bimöhlen."

"Sir, 75th 'I' Troop report two vehicles disabled by artillery at..."

"Robin, we're going to circle the wagons. Too late to do anything else. Here."

More pencil marks.

"Right ho, Sir"

Orders to quit Bad Brahmstedt-land and Fuhlendorf were sent, as Prentiss pulled all his forces into a circle roughly twelve hundred metres in diameter, all except for the southern edge, where a different decision was applied.

1015 hrs, Wednesday 27th March, 1945, Prentiss Force HQ, Hill 73, Bad Brahmstedt-land, Germany.

Freddie Merton waited for the 17pdr to send its shell downrange before querying the order.

"Just sit tight and hold the buggers, Freddie."

"Blackberry, roger. Sir, can I..."

Prentiss did the battlefield version of 'hanging up the phone', and the radio went silent, although the squadron net was still full of excited and strained voices reporting enemy kills or hits sustained.

B Squadron's Black Prince tanks had acquitted themselves well, especially against the 76mm Shermans of the Soviet mechanised brigade.

The Soviet commander seemed happy to let the Shermans slug it out, whilst the T-34's manoeuvred and used their 85mm guns to good advantage with angled shots.

Prentiss committed his reserve squadron, sending all but one troop to support B Squadron, his HQ troop, and anything else he could scrape up, understanding that the escaping forces would flow around his positions, trying to gain friendly ground, whereas the

501

southern attack was one that intended to roll over his force and, therefore, presented the greater risk.

"Robin... I'm off to fight my tank. You know the score and can act accordingly. Best of British to you and your men."

What happened next came to be known as 'The Battle of the Streams".

1015 hrs, Wednesday 27th March, 1945, Route 206, Bad Brahmstedt-land, Germany.

The tanks, infantry, and SP guns swept down upon the Soviet infantry and their handful of supporting tanks like avenging angels.

The imposing Black Prince heavy tanks, although slow, moved fast enough to overrun the first infantry units, caught indecisively between advance, retreat, and surrender.

Many Soviet guardsmen raised their arms.

"Sir?"

Houlihan, Prentiss' hull gunner, posed the question through the tank intercom.

"No time... no facilities... sorry."

The 7.92mm BESA mowed the dozen men down, and the scene was repeated elsewhere.

"Gunner, target tank, range seven hundred, left ten degrees."

The 17pdr moved effortlessly.

"No target."

"Damn, target moving left, come left five degrees."

"Identified... on..."

"FIRE!"

The gun sent another AP shell out into the battlefield where it sought out a Sherman tank and burrowed effortlessly into its hull.

Nothing but smoke emerged from the open hatches.

'Kinloss', Prentiss' Black Prince, moved on as others halted, fire and movement, fire and movement, just like an exercise.

"Infantry to front!"

The BESA rattled as Prentiss stuck his head out of the open hatch to assess the threat.

"Faust!"

The Panzerfaust missed him by a foot, even as the firer was cut in half by the tank's machine gun.

502

Unperturbed, Prentiss kept his head out, the better to examine the battlefield.

He had launched his attack down Route 206, intending to hold the small bridge over the Schmalfelder Au, securing his rear, before driving eastwards into the flank of the attacking formation.

As counter-attacks went, it was unexpected and effective, up to a point.

The slowness of the British tanks gave the enemy a chance to orient themselves and the Soviet commander turned a full company of T-34's towards them, as well as sending infantry anti-tank units into the woods on the British right flank.

The Soviet tanks charged forward, keen to close the range and, although unclear on the type of enemy they faced, the experienced Soviet tankers understood that close in was where the T-34 would profit most.

A spent round pinged off the turret hatch, reminding Prentiss of the unhealthy nature of being exposed.

"Blackberry-six, Conference-zero, over."

Cecil Blacker's voice responded.

"Blackberry-six, Conference-zero... halt advance. Hull down and knock 'em out on the run in, over."

"Roger, Blackberry."

As the C Squadron commander passed the order on, Prentiss took control of his own HQ tanks and formed a line.

The enemy mortars and artillery seized on their immobility immediately, a chance he took to knock out more of the enemy tanks.

His gunner was engaging at will, as Prentiss controlled the battle from his exposed position.

The 17pdr whirred left momentarily, before firing, the muzzle flash hiding the end result.

A second shell followed the same path and, whilst the Colonel saw no hit, the shrieks of delight from inside his tank told him of success.

'Bloody headache won't go away.'

He shook his head to clear his eyes and squinted through his binoculars to the woods on his right.

Snatching up the microphone, he contacted the recon commander.

"Roger, Blackberry."

In response to Prentiss' order, three Staghounds moved around the rear of 'C' Squadron and started engaging enemy infantry in the woods.

503

The 17pdr fired again, and Prentiss slammed his head against the hatch.

In anger, he shouted through the hatch.

"Don't forget the bloody warning, Cream!"

Sergeant Cream exchanged glances with the loader, who could only shrug as he slid another round home.

The 'fire' warning had been given as plain as day.

"Blackberry-six, Chester-six...sitrep, over."

The Cheshire's radio operator passed the handset to Lieutenant Colonel Kreyer.

"Chester-six, as you expected. Enemy forces moving down Route seven. We're shooting them up from the flank but they keep on running. Holding elsewhere, but do watch your rear. Still unable to raise our air support, over."

"Blackberry-six, roger."

The tank rocked as a shell exploded adjacent to the rear compartment.

"Fucking hell!"

Briggs, the driver, clutched his forehead where the blast had propelled him against the episcope.

"Just a bit of claret, Bert. Just give it a wipe, lad."

Houlihan even helpfully threw a dirty handkerchief to the young driver.

A shell struck the front of the tank adjacent to Briggs' driving position.

The inside took on a taint of redness for the briefest of moments, but there was no penetration.

Houlihan shouted.

"Find the fucker, Tim! Where's he at?"

"Got him... FIRE!"

Houlihan only spotted the T-34 because it suddenly fireballed.

It had driven up the stream, using the banks to cover its side armour.

As had many more.

"Colonel, they're in the stream beds... the stream beds!"

Prentiss came around.

'What the deuce?'

He had fallen comatose for the briefest of moments.

Dragging himself back to consciousness, he queried the report.

"The bastards are in the streams, Sir, We can hardly see 'em!"

His eyes focussed on the blazing tank so recently killed by Cream.

"Blackberry-six, all units. Enemy tanks using streambeds to move forward under cover. Out."

The Black Prince nearest Prentiss took a hit, a shower of sparks flying from the tank's turret.

The hatches opened, and the driver and hull gunner started to emerge.

The vehicle exploded, sending the turret straight upwards and the driver forwards, minus his legs.

'Oh my God.'

Prentiss fixed momentarily on the horrible image of the burning gunner, trapped by his mangled legs, hanging from the hull hatch, writhing, twisting, screaming...

'Oh my God!'

He spotted the movement close in.

"Gunner! Left ninety, target tank, range thirty metres!"

"Fucking hell!"

An expression shouted by most of the crew.

The gun turned, seemingly taking an age.

"He's spotted us! Smartly now, Cream!"

The gun levelled with the accelerating Soviet tank.

"FIRE!"

The smoke cleared.

"Shit!"

Prentiss felt the heat of the muzzle flash as the 85mm shell bored into the side of 'Kinloss', wiping through both Briggs and Houlihan before ricocheting back, causing both cadavers more indignity.

The hot shell came to rest on what used to be Houlihan's lap, sizzling like a chop on a barbecue.

The loader vomited.

Cream fired again.

Prentiss shook his head to clear his vision, which responded sufficiently to observe the Soviet tank part company with its turret in dramatically spectacular fashion.

"Fire in the tank!"

Higgins, the loader, shouted, in between clearing the vomit from his mouth and adding to it.

Retaining enough presence of mind, he started to extinguish the small fire that had started around the mess that had been Houlihan.

"Load me up! Another tank coming in!"

505

Prentiss dropped inside and grabbed a shell.

"FIRE!"

The shell hit dead on.

The T-34 kept coming.

"What did you load, Sir?"

'Oh bugger it!'

Higgins, fire extinguished, virtually barged his Colonel aside, grabbing an AP shell.

The previous HE shell had wiped a grape of infantry off the T-34, scattering them far and wide, and given the Red Army tank crew the fright of their lives.

Their reply missed the stationary 'Kinloss' by the width of a fly's genitalia.

Cream put the AP shell straight through the turret ring.

The T-34 halted and backed up, its gun slightly canted where the shell had bounced back into the mounting, wrecking it.

Prentiss stuck his head out again, his binoculars in hand.

Bullets twanged off the metal, as infantry in the woods saw an easy target.

They, in turn, were silenced by the armoured cars, who dashed forward, keeping on the move, using their speed as defence.

Again Prentiss tried for a view of the battlefield.

What he saw was staggering in its intensity.

The Soviet armour lay shattered, pillars of smoke and flame indicating where British shells had met Soviet metal.

However, his own tanks also contributed to the scene of desolation. One Black Prince, probably from 'B' Squadron's 3rd Troop, glowed like a brazier, an incandescent red tank standing out in a sea of red blood and red fire.

And still it went on.

Another British tank erupted in fire, the flames dying as quickly as they started.

Aircraft swept overhead, Fleet Air Arm, and rockets flashed, descending somewhere to the north of Bad Brahmstedt-land, where the escaping 7th Guards Rifle Corps flowed around the central core of Cheshires and Hussars.

Soviet artillery stopped almost instantly.

"Right, prepare to move out. Higgins, you'll have to drive."

"Sir, she won't start. Briggsy said, Sir. That close one did something and knocked the engine out. We're on battery power, Sir."

Prentiss had no recollection of the report.

506

He stuck his head out and surveyed the rear of the tank.

Two engine covers were open, testament to the force of the blast.

"Right. Nip out and see what's to be done, there's a good chap. Let me know what's up on the squawk box. Watch out for enemy in the woods."

Higgins pushed himself up through his hatch and disappeared from view, although the sounds of his efforts, couched in colourful language, could still be heard inside.

"Tank target, three hundred."

Prentiss looked and saw the T-34s turret emerge from behind a rise in the land.

"FIRE!"

The shell cut through the earth and grass, emerging in perfect position to strike the gun mantlet.

"Fuck".

Cream watched as the white blob went skywards, the rounded mantlet winning over penetrative power.

Prentiss was conscious of the gunner's eyes on him as he loaded a replacement shell.

The 17pdr fired and the shell arrived as the T-34 lurched into a deeper part of the stream.

The commander in the turret disappeared in sparks as the AP shell struck the base of his cupola and carved its way through his body before deflecting back inside the tank.

A small curl of smoke betrayed the success of the shell, and the tank came gently to a halt, clearly out of the fight.

"Bloody hell!"

Prentiss slotted another shell home, surprised at the fear in Cream's voice.

"Didn't you get him?"

"Sir, you'd better have a gander at this lot... I mean... Jesus..."

Before he could raise his head out of the hatch, Higgins dropped back in, accompanied by the patter of bullets striking the heavy armour.

"Why didn't you use the squawk box, man?"

"It's knackered, just like the engine, Oil everywhere... musta burst all sorts of couplings. In any case, Sir, nearside track's off."

Prentiss continued on up through the hatch and saw that which had frightened Cream.

At least another forty T-34s were committing to the battle, turning off the autobahn and heading towards HQ and B Squadron... or what was left of them.

Another Fleet Air Arm flight went over, again dropping their ordnance north of Bad Brahmstedt-land.

'Can't they see they're needed here!'

Lieutenant Colonel Kreyer had no idea that the Hussars were in such dire straits, the radio links shot to pieces, literally as well as proverbially.

He was controlling his part of the battle with flair, directing the Fleet Air Arm against the forces escaping to his west, where there were fewer assets to interdict them. To his eastern side, the escaping 7th Guards was running across the front of his forces, and his infantrymen and the Hussar tanks were enjoying a turkey shoot, just as Prentiss planned.

Matters were hotter on the northern edge of his position, where cannier Soviet officers were trying to get their men closer to the British positions and move on through the woods, rather than the two exposed flanks.

The Cheshires' 'A' Company had needed stiffening, and Kreyer had sent his last formal reserve, the remainder of 'D' Company, to help 'A' hold.

None of this was known to Prentiss. His overriding priority was now the distinct possibility that his command was going to be overrun by a superior enemy tank force...

"What the deuce..."

Behind the tanks came half-tracks and lorries, of all shapes and sizes, but many familiar to an Allied officer.

Prentiss Force was about to receive the full attention of 9th Guards Mechanised Brigade, as its commander threw in everything to ensure the evacuation of the trapped guardsmen.

There were more tanks to kill than shells in the magazine, a thought that occurred to Prentiss and Cream simultaneously.

"Engage at will, Cream, engage at will. Just keep it up and keep the bastards under pressure."

Prentiss fiddled with his radio, trying to raise someone... anyone...

"Blackberry-six, any station, come in, over..."

Static.

"Electric traverse gone. Using hand traverse."

Cream's report indicated a worsening electrical situation, hardly encouraging for a Colonel desperately in need of a working radio.

Prentiss Force was living on borrowed time.

1111 hrs, Wednesday 27th March, 1945, Route 206, west of Bad Brahmstedt-land, Germany.

Major Thomas Fanshaw had, despite his and his mechanics' best efforts, still not managed to bring his entire Squadron along for the ride.

Six vehicles had fallen out on the forced march, victims still of the dodgy fuel issue, which looked more like a case of sabotage the more the MPs looked at it.

That meant that D Squadron, 23rd Hussars, arrived with eight fully functioning Black Prince tanks, a platoon of infantry seconded from the 4th KSLI, and a Forward Air Support section, whose jeep bounced along behind the lumbering tank of the 'D' Squadron commander.

Fig# 160 - Prentiss Force - Late arrivals

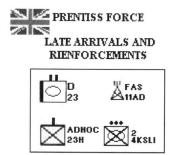

Fanshaw realised that the lack of communication with any of the Hussars stationed to the south was bad news, and had taken six of his tanks along the same route plied by Prentiss an hour or so beforehand.

Held up by some Soviet infantry who blundered into their path, seemingly escaping from Bad Brahmstedt-land, Fanshaw took a moment or two to examine the battlefield ahead.

The number of Black Prince casualties alarmed him infinitely more than the number of dead Soviet tanks. The new force of enemy infantry and tanks brought him down to earth with a bump.

"Damson-six, all Damson. Large enemy force to front. Line abreast and engage at will. Out."

As he concluded the message, he saw the immobile tank of his commander, enemy infantry creeping forward, moving down from the woods.

"Driver, forward, right turn... head for the CO's tank."

The FAS jeep tucked in close, ready to receive the inevitable order.

Fanshaw hesitated to pass it as yet, the battlefield ahead too confused to know just who was who, at least with the certainty required to avoid friendly kills.

Prentiss saw the Hussars' tank approaching and slipped out of the turret, dropping into cover alongside 'Kinloss'.

When Fanshaw's tank had stopped, he ran across the small divide and dropped in behind the Black Prince, releasing the squawk box handset from its mount.

"Tommy, thank the lord you got here on time!"

"I've got eight tanks, an extra platoon of infantry, and a FAS controller. He's in the jeep behind us, Sir."

"Splendid, Tommy. You've radio contact with everyone I assume?"

"No Sir, I've..."

Prentiss ducked as bullets spanged off the rear armour, the two Soviet soldiers who fired quickly dropping back into cover again as a half-track arrived and spilled some KSLI infantrymen, initiating a brief firefight that cost five lives.

"Say again, Tommy."

"I have no contact with anyone on your net, Sir. 'D' Squadron only for some reason."

The sharp sound of tank guns seemed to accelerate in frequency and increase in urgency.

"Tommy, tell whoever you can get hold of... on my command... fire smoke, red smoke, into the enemy positions, leading edge, clear?"

"Crystal, Sir. Red smoke at enemy positions."

"Wait for my order to execute. Out."

Prentiss closed his eyes as the headache washed over him, almost wishing he could scrape the afflicted organ through his eyes.

He focussed on the jeep, its position betrayed by two aerials sticking above the level of the scrape it had dropped into, and made the short dash in safety.

"Flying Officer Rogers, Sir."

"Rogers. Do you have a tentacle link?"

"Yes, Sir, I do."

"On my order, give the coordinates for this location," he put his finger on the F/O's map, "Red smoke, Limejuice... understand... initiate Limejuice."

"Yes, Sir, err, I'm on it right now, Sir."

The pilot officer, young enough to have been a twinkle in his father's eye when Prentiss first took up soldiering, noted a map reference and calmly passed it to the Flight Sergeant next to him for checking.

"That'll do nicely, Sah."

Prentiss touched the young RAF officer's arm.

"Give me a thumbs-up when confirmed."

The radio operator went live on the tentacle net, a two-way system that put the Forward controllers in touch with the Air Support commander attached to 11th Armoured Division.

Passing the details, F/O Rogers gave the map reference, colour, and, for the first time in his short career, initiated a limejuice attack.

Prentiss had already gone and was back at the D Squadron commander's tank, preparing to issue his order, watching the two aerials sway.

A solid shot hit the tank and whooshed away, narrowly missing the half-track that had disgorged the KSLI infantrymen.

The Black Prince rocked back slightly, as the 17pdr sought retribution some six hundred yards down range.

On Rogers' third attempt to be seen, Prentiss noticed the signal and acknowledged it, speaking rapidly into the squawk box.

"Tommy..."

"Yes, Sir."

"I make the wind southerly. Confirm please."

After a moment, Fanshaw agreed.

"Excellent."

It was probably the first bit of luck the Hussars had all day.

"Fire the smoke, Tommy. Just keep it thick enough, nothing fancy. Limejuice inbound."

"Roger, Sir."

Red smoke shells started to burst amongst the leading elements of the renewed attack, and a number of vehicles, tanks and infantry carriers pushed faster, trying to get out of what they assumed was a developing kill zone.

A few surviving tanks from 'B' and 'C' Squadrons joined in, understanding what was needed.

Not one tank fired two smoke shells in a row, as survival meant reverting to solid shot, to kill the enemy forces as they closed in.

1121 hrs, Wednesday 27th March, 1945, Hill 79, adjacent to Route 206, Germany.

Colonel Karpetian screamed.

He screamed at the aircraft that immolated his command.

He screamed at the dead tank regiment commanders for not hearing his warnings.

He screamed at his second in command for no other reason than he was there.

He screamed at himself, inside, knowing that he had committed his men to no avail, and lost them all for nothing.

The codeword 'Limejuice' initiated a rolling air attack, the likes of which he hadn't previously seen.

The newly rejuvenated Allied ground attack force had stacked its aircraft neatly behind the front line, each squadron issued with a target, but each required to delay in the queue, just in case a priority target was called in.

Such was the 'Limejuice' system, which initiated the air controllers vectoring in available formations, sending them to the map coordinates, with strict instructions to attack the 'red'.

Karpetian's order that his own men should fire red on the enemy positions could not be obeyed; there was no red smoke available.

The SU's had fired everything they had as well.

And so Daniil Karpetian could only watch as Thunderbolts, Typhoons, Whirlwinds, and Mustangs ravaged his veteran units.

Prentiss was back inside 'Kinloss', picking targets for Cream to destroy.

The gloomy voice of an exhausted Higgins made itself heard.

"Last AP going in. Only got HE left now, Sir."

'That's bally awkward!'

Prentiss could only make one decision.

"Engage the soft-skinned stuff. Leave the tanks for D."

512

The last AP sped across the wet ground and disappeared into the innards of a T-34 that was pushing itself out of a streambed, exposing its underbelly.

Men emerged, screaming, their clothes burning, their flesh melting.

"Target half-track, three hundred. On.

"FIRE!"

A miss, the jiggling vehicle making it as difficult as possible to get a hit.

Another shell swept across the field, striking the vehicle in its bogies and shredding the track instantly.

Cream's second shell caught the human content as it tried to bail out.

Pieces of body flew in all directions and no-one stirred once the smoke had cleared.

The air attack was growing in intensity, as more assistance was brought in to stop the Soviet counter-attack.

Every weapon that could be brought by the Allied ground attack aircraft was released above the streams of Northern Germany.

Fire... shrapnel... explosions... bullets... rockets... all brought horror and death, as the Soviet mechanised units struggled to either extricate themselves or push forward.

A French piloted Whirlwind, a venerable aircraft dragged out of mothballs to help equip the newly re-established Armee de L'Air, selected a juicy target and lined up its four 20mm Hispano cannon.

The pilot, for too long a prisoner of the hated Boche, shredded the half-track with a short accurate burst and turned away to find another target of opportunity, not hearing Prentiss' cursing, nor the popping off of MG rounds as the KSLI vehicle burnt.

The surviving light infantrymen braved the burning half-track, and desperately tried to recover the driver... and failed.

The last Whirlwind placed its five-hundred pounders very precisely, despite the loss of its port engine.

Two Soviet-manned Shermans and a half-track were turned to scrap metal in an instant.

The French pilot failed to adjust for the loss of weight, and the aircraft tilted, exposing the full profile to a ZSU AA mount.

The airman was dead before the port wing clipped a smoking T-34 and the whole aircraft turned end over end, like an out of control Catherine Wheel, pieces flying off with each earthly contact, until the strain caused the shattered air frame to come apart completely, showering some hiding Soviet infantry with burning aviation fuel.

They ran around like human torches until a merciful bullet struck them down or a fiery death overtook them.

To the eternal credit of the experienced 9th Guards Mechanised, those at the front still tried to press, and closed, in some cases, to zero range with the British tanks.

Those in the killing zone were visited by another wave of Typhoons, seemingly beyond numbers, who discharged rocket after rocket into the disappearing red smoke.

A few British tanks topped up the marker, allowing the airborne killers to continue their assault.

It was a slaughter direct from the days of the Roman Empire, or the Crusades, blood and bodies visible everywhere upon the field.

In 'Kinloss', the turret was turned by hand, and the BESA used to discourage a group of infantry who seemed intent on approaching.

"Cease fire, man!

Cream stopped immediately.

"They're surrendering. They're bloody well surrendering!"

All across the field, dazed and shattered Guardsmen raised their hands in surrender and gradually the guns became silent.

Not so the Typhoons, and an appalled set of British tankers watched as more than one non-combatant was cut down in a strafing run.

Prentiss shouted towards the jeep, hoping to catch Rogers' eye.

A second run had finished before someone noticed him, and understood the signal he was giving.

'Stop the attacks, for the love of god!'

There were no more, the controllers glad to reign back their assets and send them south to a situation developing around Hamburg.

Prentiss took leave of his crew and, sending one of Fanshaw's troopers to bolster 'Kinloss', left the D Squadron commander in charge of the area and commandeered the jeep for his own purposes.

"Drive on, Flight Sergeant. I'll show you the way."

The jeep turned and headed back towards the centre of Prentiss Force, the dead body of F/O Rogers curled up in the back.

514

As the vehicle drove Prentiss away from the centre of fighting, he looked sorrowfully at the evidence of his losses.

His Hussars' Black Prince tanks were everywhere; dead, burned out, punctured, living, the whole range fell before his eyes.

Even then, he really had no idea of the cost that victory had exacted.

Whilst the Southern Defences had been embroiled in their life or death struggle, Lieutenant Colonel Robin Kreyer had ravaged the two groups of the 7th Guards Rifle.

Around Fuhlendorf, the drive south had been totally blunted, and the Guardsmen either surrendered or moved off eastwards to try their luck elsewhere.

Many of that group were swept up in the attacks on the Cheshires' 'A' Company, and the battle on the edge of the woods had, for a little while, hung in the balance.

Timely use of his reinforcements gave Kreyer victory in that area too.

Perhaps the greatest success was on the autobahn side, where the larger part of 7th Guards had tried to escape.

Shot at by tanks, AA guns, SP guns, and infantry, the toiling Soviet escapees suffered hideously from the flanking fire, and many turned back northwards, running into their retreating rearguard, and the leading tanks of the Guards Division.

The final Hussar casualty was A Squadron's First troop leader.

His tank engaged an armoured vehicle to its front, moving south, some distance away, intent on driving down Route 111.

The Black Prince missed; their target didn't, and a 17pdr APDS round punched through the turret, neatly removing the commander's left arm at the elbow.

The radio net was full of excited voices, all of which revealed the truth of the exchange.

The Guards Division had entered the battlefield, and the destruction of the 7th Guards Rifle Corps was complete.

Leading the way came 'C' Squadron, 2nd Battalion, Grenadier Guards.

The Centurion II at the head of the column moved cautiously off the road and crossed the autobahn to where its recent target lay abandoned.

"Laz...Pull in alongside her."

The commander heard the mumbled response but was engaged on other matters already.

Recently promoted CSM Charles checked the surroundings, and saw only friendly pudding bowl helmets amongst the living soldiery, or at least those armed with guns, the others being unarmed and shuffling the walk normal for shocked and dejected prisoners of war.

Behind the tanks, half-tracks fanned out across the ground, disgorging squads of soldiers to help sweep the field clear of any hiding survivors.

"He fired first... stupid... just stupid..."

"Can it, Pats."

The gunner was mortified that he had fired at one of his own.

"I must've killed someone, for crying out loud, Sarnt Major, I must've!"

Charles dropped down into the turret and selected the Thompson sub-machine gun.

"Pats... listen to me. I gave the order, end of. He fired first, end of. He's a Black Prince, and unless I'm very much mistaken, the first bugger you've seen. Certainly the first I've seen. No blame attached to us, no matter what, ok?"

The gunner nodded, but it was plain he didn't see it that way.

"I'm off to take a gander. Stay tight and keep your eyes peeled. Commander out!"

The Black Prince had taken, by Charles' quick estimation, eleven direct hits, and had still been operational.

'Impressive stuff, gotta say.'

He clambered aboard, waving to a passing Cheshire Corporal, herding four dirty and dishevelled Soviets with the point of his bayonet.

A quick look inside the tank filled him with relief, although the blood certainly meant that someone had taken a tap from Patterson's shell.

A Cheshires' Sergeant wandered up and begged a cigarette.

"You the buggers what bagged him, are ye?"

He flipped his petrol lighter, giving first light to Charles.

"Yep. He fired at us, but missed… we didn't. Know what happened to the crew, Sarge?"

"Think the commander lost an 'and or summat. Rest were fine seemed. They took the lad off t'aid post."

Charles looked at the Cheshires' NCO quizzically.

"Cheshire?"

The Sergeant laughed.

"Feck orf. Wiltshire born and bred you."

They shook hands and parted.

Charles dropped back into 'Lady Godiva II' and slapped Patterson on the shoulder.

"Bloody good shot, Pats. Seems you clipped a Rupert on the way, but everyone's alive... and the tank will be back working directly. No great harm done."

Charles wasn't being insensitive to the tank officer who had lost his hand, more realistic about needing his gunner fully on the job.

"OK. Laz, move her on down the road."

The centurion moved not one inch.

"Laz, you dozy bugger. Wake up before I put my size ten up your ass!"

Patterson tapped Charles.

"You're not coming through on my headset, Sarnt Major."

Charles looked and immediately coloured in embarrassment.

He had forgotten to connect himself back up.

Correcting the error, he tried again.

"Lazarus Wild, you northern monkey. Get this tank back on the road."

"Northern monkey, is it? Weren't my fault that t'bloody NCO din set his comms up proper like, were it?"

Charles was hoisted by his own petard, and the chuckles around him confirmed his crew knew it.

"Weekend passes revoked, you bastards."

The Centurion moved back onto the Autobahn, everyone understanding that there would have been no weekend passes for the foreseeable future.

The remnants of Prentiss Force were concentrated in the area round Hill 73. Mostly concealed within the edges of the woods that surrounded both ends of the small ridge.

The 1st Cheshires had suffered dreadfully, with four hundred and eight dead and wounded, over half of the men who had taken to the field.

75th Anti-Tank's Jackson M-36s had done extremely well, losing only three of their number, and claiming an extraordinary number of vehicle kills.

The platoon of the King's Shropshire Light Infantry's 4th Battalion lost eight men dead and three wounded, only one of each to the errant French Whirlwind.

15th/19th Hussars had taken heavy punishment, with seven of their armoured cars knocked out, offset by only two losses amongst the Comets.

23rd Hussars had suffered more than any British cavalry regiment in modern times.

Prentiss had commanded a modern armoured regiment of new battle tanks and experienced personnel, bringing them into harm's way with confidence. Fifty-six Black Prince tanks, virtually the entire number sent to Europe for front line service. They were accompanied by eleven Stuart tanks, ten Crusader AA tanks, and a plethora of support vehicles and personnel.

Of the 23rd's personnel, only one-hundred and ninety-nine were living on the field. Some of the casualties were laid out, some covered, some uncovered, or were screaming amongst the two hundred or so to be found in aid stations set up around Fuhlendorf.

Other Hussars remained within their armoured vehicles, waiting for their recovery by men with a stomach for such things.

The Regiment gathered round, and an unsteady Prentiss climbed on top of his Dingo armoured car.

So many familiar faces were missing.

His eyes sought and failed to find men with whom he had served since Normandy.

Algie Woods...

Stu French...

RSM Stacey...

Old Wrigglesworth...

Others were absent but still alive, their wounds being tended and soon to return. Others, such as Soames and Jemeson, would never return, and might not survive to see another day.

The 23rd Hussars were a seasoned unit, with many hard fights under their belts, but the eyes that looked back at Prentiss had seen the vision of the doors of hell fully opened, inviting them in, pulling them closer and closer to the threshold, until the vision started fade, the doors closed, and silence fell on the battlefield.

Somehow, their gaze seemed focussed on something miles behind him, as if each man was still, in his mind, somewhere else... somewhere awful...

Prentiss jumped.

'Wake up, man!'

He had almost drifted off whilst stood upright.

For some unknown reason, he suddenly felt very weak, not just tired and exhausted, but almost unable to stand.

His mind focussed quickly, and he made a decision.

"Sit down, gentlemen... please do sit down."

As his men sank to the floor, Prentiss sagged and managed to arrange himself on the rear deck without anyone noticing his weakness.

"Lads... have you all had a brew?"

"Is the Pope feckin Catholic, Sah?"

The unforced laughter almost made him well up, so proud was he of the men he commanded.

'Such spirit... brave lads...'

"Well then... let me say that I am proud of each and every one of you... you've done magnificently today... truly you have."

A trooper made an enquiring gesture, and Prentiss nodded.

"Yes, do smoke if you have them, gentlemen."

He paused whilst pockets disgorged the necessary and lungs were filled with the comforting smoke.

"Right then, gentlemen."

He rubbed his left eye to stop the nagging pain, not, as some thought, to hide a tear.

"We've lost some fine friends today... more than we've ever done before... but what we've achieved here today will be remembered long after we have left this land."

He acknowledged the unit's padre shuffling.

"A special church parade will be held at 1800. The padre will find a suitable place to set up. Of course, we must bury our dead, and Captain Montagu has found a lovely spot just down the road there."

Normally, the tankers lost a crew or two in a day's combat, and the logistics of their death were little by way of a challenge. The Battle of the Streams was decidedly otherwise.

"We... together... will carry our comrades from the field... and we... together... will bury them."

Prentiss pushed himself to stand.

The gathered men sensed the change and stood as well, all coming to a position of attention.

"I am so proud to have served with you all. Through from Normandy to this place, the 23rd have brought professionalism and skill to the battlefield. We have also brought comradeship... and in the spirit of that comradeship..." Prentiss snapped into a rigid pose and raised his right hand in the military fashion, "I salute you all."

One hundred and ninety-eight hands returned the salute.

"Right then, gentlemen, let's get busy. All officers, report to me for orders, Parade... dismiss."

The men turned smartly to their right in a standard dismiss, and failed to see Prentiss on the way down, the building pressure of the swelling in his brain overcoming his efforts to remain standing.

He clattered onto the Dingo and rolled off, unconscious.

That he was unconscious was a blessing, as he fell onto a vehicle jack blasted from a Staghound as it passed through the Soviet artillery barrage earlier in the day.

Concealed in the grass, the pointed metal top plate penetrated his back, punching into his thoracic spine at Th8.

Colonel Cedric Arthur Moreton Prentiss, the Viscount Kinloss, would never walk or soldier again, and became the final Hussar casualty of the Battle of the Streams.

[Author's note- The investigation that was initiated regarding CSM Charles' destruction of the Hussar Black Prince exonerated Charles and Patterson, whilst, perhaps understandably, falling short of pointing blame at the Hussar tank commander.

The actions of Prentiss and his force have been the stuff of debate by historians and military minds ever since, and will undoubtedly continue well into our future.

Some have condemned his decision to 'circle the wagons', offering the alternative of withdrawal from the field, leaving the Air Force to pummel the Soviet forces. Others have said he over-extended himself in the first place.

It is undoubtedly the case that the Air Force ground attack formations saved the day, otherwise Prentiss Force would have been wiped out.

I am no expert, but I offer some observations.

He was under direct orders to take and occupy Bimhölen, denying transit to the escaping 7th Guards Rifle Corps and its accompanying units.

The force he took, whilst enhanced by the 75th AT Achilles SPs and the 15th/19th Hussars' Comet tanks, was light one complete Squadron for most of the battle.

His air controller was lost early in the battle, claimed by a Soviet air attack that simply should never have been permitted to get through in the first place.

The location of the 9th Guards Mechanised Brigade was not known, and its arrival on the battlefield was a total surprise. I am unclear as to why a full missing mechanised brigade did not set off alarms with those who planned the attacks, particularly as 3rd Guards Mechanised Corps was identified as being in the area, and known to consist of the three mechanised brigades; 7th, 8th, and 9th, plus the 45th Tanks.

Lastly, it is undoubtedly the case that Prentiss suffered his debilitating head injury during the farmhouse collapse, probably enhancing its effect during the subsequent tank battle. In my humble opinion, that makes his subsequent command performance all the more remarkable.

The battle attracted the attention of the media, and as a result, those who fought there were feted and their names spoken of around dining tables from Wick to Redruth.

The officers and men of 23rd Hussars received a shower of medals, Kreyer's Cheshires featured heavily in the subsequent Gazette announcements too.

DSOs and DCMs were the order of the day for most of the senior commanders and NCOs, and MCs and MMs were commonplace, a total of eighty-one awards placed for a single battle that lasted just over four hours.

Perhaps there are two matters that are surprising, given the allocation of awards.

Captain Lysander Chandos Montagu, the portly support officer who wasn't 'quite the ticket' as far as his fellow officers were concerned, and to whom Prentiss had trusted the ad hoc command, for no other reason than he was all that was available, was a deserving recipient of the Victoria Cross for his personal bravery during the defence of Brahmstedt-land. His superb leadership and command throughout the difficult hours of the Battle of the Streams quickly became the stuff of legend.

The last matter is more surprising.

Colonel Prentiss, destined to spend the rest of his days in a wheelchair, received no recognition for his efforts, perhaps because of the debate over the soundness of his decisions.

In my humble opinion, a travesty occasioned by the need of the military establishment to make ready a scapegoat for a battle that, for some, was seen as a defeat, or at minimum, an unnecessary bloodletting.

23rd Hussars and 1st Cheshires were both withdrawn from the 11th Armoured Division.

A decision was quickly reached, and the Cheshires were reinforced and returned to duty within four weeks.

The 23rd Hussars passed into history, being officially disbanded on 8th April 1946.

27th March to 14th April 1946, British Twenty-First Army Group's advance into Northern Germany.

Twenty-First Army Group pressed, and pressed hard, profiting from an air superiority that was rarely challenged and never overcome.

Soviet units melted away in front of them or, as in the case of Hamburg and some others, stood their ground, permitting the Allied soldiery to flood around them.

McCreery, bold as the young cavalryman he had once been, drove his divisions forward, moving south and to the east, opening up the route out of Denmark.

Known for his planning and attention to detail, McCreery's efforts were often hampered by surprisingly poor intelligence, often as a result of superb maskirovka and camouflage on the part of the Soviet forces.

Despite the Allied mastery of the air, the 1st Baltic, the formation into which the British and Commonwealth troops punched, had clandestinely assembled large numbers of units that had escaped the attention of Allied intelligence.

These units had been intended for the renewed Soviet offensive, but circumstances overtook the Red Army plan, providing Marshal Bagramyan with excellent reserves with which to disrupt the Allied offensive.

Bagramyan was not called the Armenian Fox for the way he looked, but for the way he thought and then created orders to suit.

Initially, Bagramyan was most concerned about hanging on to the neighbouring 1st Red Banner Front, who had their work cut out dealing with the US Corps of the British Army Group and the German Republicans, both of which forces were hurling themselves on top of Malinovsky's men, who in turn had to worry about holding on to 1st Baltic and 2nd Red Banner, whilst carefully watching the mighty US Twelth Army Group battering away to the south.

But out of the chaos, Bagramyan saw an opportunity, one that might, in another age, have earned him a bullet in the back of the neck.

1st Baltic Front gave ground, not easily, rarely without pain and heartache but, none the less, each day, each hour, Soviet soldiers were a few steps nearer to Moscow.

McCreery, pressured by his need to drive to the relief of Polish forces, and encouraged by some success, seeing nothing untoward, pressed his Army commanders hard. In turn, they cascaded the pressure down through Corps to Divisions.

Eventually the pressure came to rest on the young subalterns of shire regiments, or NCO tank commanders in van of the armoured squadron.

"Push hard… push hard and they will crumble!"

"Press forward, keep the enemy in sight, and drive him back to the Volga!"

"Charge on, men, charge on and relieve our valiant Polish allies!"

Such words had their effect and the efforts redoubled, assisted by a magnificent logistics effort from both RASC and RAF commands.

As matters like the unexpected appearance of the 9th Guards Mechanised Brigade become more numerous, 21st Army Group staff began to get twitchy, and McCreery could only agree.

Photo recon flights were increased and some startling discoveries were made, but nothing that appeared that it could not be handled by a change in plans and the application of sufficient force.

Photos were 'appreciated' more than once, cutting down on human error.

Such a process revealed something interesting occurring in and around Waren, Northern Germany.

'Some sort of fixed fortification' was the best guess, and recon flights were stepped up. Similar works were seen to the north and south.

Where the Allies made a clear error, and history has already pointed the finger of blame, was in the area around Wolinow and Ludwigslust, where units waiting for the new offensive had assembled, and were now sat waiting for the right moment to turn the advance of 21st Army Group from a victory into a complete disaster.

Acting under orders, the northern group of Bagramyan's armies fell back slightly faster than the rest, bringing the Allied forces forward quicker there, slowly but surely creating a bulge into the Soviet lines.

The manoeuvre did not go without problems, and Gusev's 21st Army was pressed into the area surrounding the Hemmelsdorfer See, where it was pummelled from land, air, and sea. The Red Army soldiery had not been on the receiving end of 16" naval shells before, and HMS Rodney and her consorts crushed Soviet morale and will to fight more and more with the delivery of each huge shell.

Only a handful of Gusev's men escaped across the water to the Priwall Peninsular, to the illusion of safety in the Soviet positions in Mecklenburg-Pommern.

Escapees and defenders alike swiftly realised that more distance was needed to escape the Rodney's big guns, and the backwards move came close to a rout, before NKVD troops moved up and selected a few ringleaders as examples.

The traditional disposal stopped the rot and Marshal Bagramyan's plan was back on track.

Further west, Canadian First and British Eleventh Armies toiled heavily against stiff opposition, occasionally being held up, sometimes bypassing strongholds.

Whilst the press reported success after success, a shambolic attack at Wunstorf, where the 117th Royal Marine Infantry Brigade was all but destroyed in a Soviet pincer attack, went hardly recorded.

Only the timely intervention of British 8th Armoured Brigade saved the day, although not enough men were salvaged from the debacle to put the 117th back into line. It was subsequently disbanded and its survivors posted to the 116th, bringing it back up to strength as well as adding additional manpower.

The two VCs awarded to Royal Marine NCOs made front page news, as did the 'heroics' of 8th Armoured.

The true and unedited facts of the disaster did not.

It was ever thus.

As his armies got more and more out of position, relative to each other, McCreery ordered the Canadians to redouble their efforts, in order to make more gain on the right flank of British Second Army.

The valiant Canadians pushed even harder, and made more ground, but not enough, and many men were lost in the effort.

New units, held back for fear of revealing Allied plans, started to arrive in Denmark and Holland, although not disembarking in Hamburg, which continued to defy the attempts of British and Canadian troops.

So, whilst the commandoes died in their droves, the Canadians fell in their scores, and the civilians of Hamburg suffered further indignities, Second Army drove the Red Army slowly backwards.

And as they drove the Red Army deeper into Germany, the Fox watched.

The Fox watched, and the Fox waited.

1209 hrs, Sunday, 15th April 1946, 1st Baltic Front Headquarters, Heiligengrabe Abbey, Germany.

Bagramyan sat drinking water and munching on some delicious pork sausage and bread, grudgingly provided by the nuns who were the original occupants of his new headquarters.

His staff worked as he sat contemplating the situation map, his keen eyes taking in the little changes that were recorded as more reports came in from his commanders.

Giving nothing away, he kept his fascination to himself, but nothing could stop his eyes being drawn to Schwerin.

'Nothing... still nothing?'

He selected another sausage and patiently resumed his vigil.

More contacts reports were posted.

'Neubukow...'

He sucked on the spicy sausage, slowly and pensively, almost smoking it like a cigar.

'Jurgenshagen...'

'Dabel...'

Placing the half-consumed sausage on the plate, Bagramyan stepped smartly forward.

Chief of Staff, Vladimir Vasilevich Kurasov, stiffened automatically, and others who knew their boss, tensed themselves, their senses tuned to Bagramyan's every move and word, whilst retaining the outer skin of busy employment.

Bagramyan beckon his CoS closer.

"Contact Gnidin... ask for a situation report please, Comrade."

Kurasov summoned a runner and wrote a swift message.

The man disappeared at speed, watched by his pensive commander.

"Shall we, Comrade?"

Bagramyan strode off after the message holder with his CoS in step behind.

Waving down the men who stood to attention as he entered the communications centre, he listened to part of the exchange.

Kurasov moved in closer, and the operator felt perturbed by his presence.

He placed a steadying hand on her shoulder as he watched the words appear on a message form, her hand trembling slightly as she wrote.

"Confirm... ask him to confirm immediately and contact us back immediately."

"Yes, Comrade Polkovnik General."

Kurasov moved back to Bagramyan's side and spoke out of the corner of his mouth.

"It appears the circumstances now exists, Comrade Marshal. I have taken the liberty of getting a confirmation."

Bagramyan nodded in satisfaction.

Kurasov knew his methods well, and acted instinctively, as his commander would wish.

Six minutes dragged by, but eventually the message came through from Major General Gnidin.

'No contact with enemy forces on my line. Confirmed as of 1222 hrs."

135th Rifle Corps, Gnidin's command, sat policing a west-east position between the Schaalsee and Schwerin.

The British had moved passed him, failed by their lack of knowledge, intent on driving towards their Polish allies.

Bagramyan had gambled that they would do so, and placed 2nd Tank Army and 5th Motorised Army in a position to cut through to the Baltic Sea, stopping the British drive and denying relief to the embattled Poles.

A sudden silence had fallen upon the communications room, the occupants, without exception, focussed on their commander.

The Armenian Marshal nodded to his CoS.

"Now, Vladimir Vasilevich, execute the attack now."

Whilst other men stood watch, the crew of Lady Godiva II stood down for a treat. Their tank was concealed in a hasty scrape in the ground, made large enough to house a crew rest station, and extra space for their guests. All was concealed by a net that had already proved to keep some heat in, as well as protect from air observation.

The whole squadron was positioned on the raised ground in front of Lützow, arranged to defend against attack from the south or south-east.

Fig# 161 - Lützow - Allied Forces.

LUTZOW 15TH APRIL 1946

ALLIED FORCES

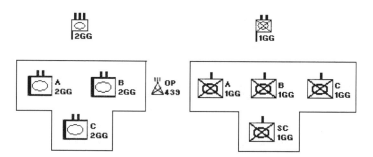

The experienced tank crew had returned their Mark I tank to workshops, and a new Mk II had been issued, something that gave the men mixed feelings, although the extra refinements and thicker armour were most welcome.

But for now, more earthly matters filled their minds.

"Bloody marvellous, Laz... no really... bloody marvellous!"

The words were punctuated by regular spoonfuls and the wiping away of delicious juices.

The crew of the Centurion were downing the finest food they had tasted for some time, courtesy of relieved local German residents and the culinary prowess of their driver, Lazarus Wild.

Fig# 162 - Lutzow - Allied dispositions.

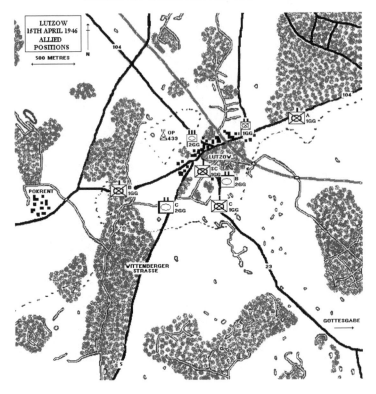

Pork and apple, with potatoes and gravy, backed up with a sweet pastry concoction prepared by the farmer's wife, topped off with a bottle of Becks each, just to wash it all down nicely.

Herr Förster, his wife, and their three children, having no English, could only moan in satisfaction as the delicious pork disappeared at speed.

Laz Wild, beaming with satisfaction, went to the cooking pot and lifted the heavy weight.

"More, Frau Förster?"

The slender woman took a second full portion without a word.

Wild saw his crew exchange envious looks.

"Quit yer possitin now, lads. There's plenny for all."

Herr Forster and the children also received extra portions.

The children were sat on the tank's fender, legs dangling down, the war a million miles away and beyond thought.

The British tank crew laughed.

The family Förster laughed.

Life was good...

A sentry's warning...

Godiva's crew suddenly alert...

A distant heavy crack…

The passage of a tank shell...

Screams... the screams of those who are witnessing true horror...

The tank shell had missed the Centurion, passing down her nearside at a height of about one foot above the fender, casting aside the slight resistance offered by the Förster children's bodies.

Blood and pieces swept through the air, and no-one was spared the awful distribution.

Frau Förster had stopped screaming and now lay unconscious on the cold earth.

Herr Förster was emitting a low animal sound, as he rummaged through the awfulness in vain, seeking something that he could hold and mourn.

Wild and Patterson moved forward, not to the children, but to the parents, knowing where they could best help.

Charles stuck his head over the earthen edge and saw the legions of the enemy approaching .

"Enemy to front! Man the tank!"

Wild and Patterson looked at him like he was a mad man.

"Man the tank!"

"But..."

Charles took a step forward and grabbed Patterson's shoulder, the blood splattered over his face making him seem to be 'not of this world'.

"Pats, there's nothing we can do for them, any of them. Now, let's avenge them. C'mon man, move!"

Wild stood up.

"She's gone, Sarnt-Major, just gone."

The wife and mother had simply expired on the spot.

"Mount up, Laz, c'mon now. We're going to make the bastards pay, so come on!"

The two moved forward, passing the farmer who seemed to have recovered something worth cradling.

Patterson and Beefy were already working on the netting, whilst Roberts, the radio operator, contributed his own warning to the contact reports filling the radio net.

Tossing the last of the net aside, the rest of the crew dropped inside and brought the Centurion up to readiness.

Charles was spoilt for choice when it came to targets.

"Gunner, target tank, range 1300, dead ahead."

"Searching."

Charles ducked inside the tank in response to a tugging on his trouser leg.

Roberts shouted above the noise of battle.

"My intercom's fucked, Sarnt Major. Radio's full of contact reports. Squadron orders are to hold."

Charles nodded.

"Rightho, wingnut. Get your intercom sorted."

"On!"

Charles leant back and gave the order.

The 17pdr sent a shell towards the force that had caught them on the hop.

Fig# 163 - Lützow - Soviet Forces.

LUTZOW 15TH APRIL 1946

SOVIET FORCES

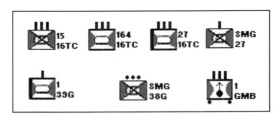

The shot struck the IS-II's offside track, sending it running off the wheels like a dying snake.

"Again!"

530

Enemy artillery now started to drop on the British positions, previously kept quiet to mask the stealthy approach of a tank-heavy formation intent on smashing through to the coast.

Everything from 76mm to 203mm rained down, and some found targets amongst the tanks and vehicles of the 1st and 2nd Battalions Grenadier Guards, recuperating on the British flank.

And then the Katyushas arrived, the rockets streaming down in huge numbers, as the 1st Guards Mortar Brigade applied itself to the task.

One rocket landed close to Lady Godiva II, and administered mercy to the mad Herr Förster, stopping his suicidal attempts to dash his head in on the Centurion's wheels.

Charles, caught between fighting his tank and trying to establish the tactical situation, remained surprisingly calm, even though his attempts to raise his leadership fell on deaf ears.

The British fought back, knocking out enemy T-34s and IS-IIs, cutting down infantry, but not without loss.

The British infantry colonel was carried from the field, shattered by a bursting shell, and Guards' officers rallied their men by example, one that often cost them their well-being.

The artillery FOO did superb work, directing available Corps artillery onto the advancing Soviet force.

The Grenadier's tankers lost heavily, although the ratio of loss to kill was greatly in the Centurion's favour.

It was the artillery and the IS-IIs that proved most capable against the new British tank.

Both Captain White and Lieutenant Percival were already out of the fight, the former smashed with his crew by a 122mm artillery shell that arrived through the turret top plate. The badly injured young subaltern clung to life still, the sole survivor dragged from his destroyed Centurion by brave infantrymen from the Grenadier's Mechanised 1st Battalion.

If Charles did but know it, the opening exchanges had broken the nerve of two young replacement officers, and they and the valuable tanks they commanded were already heading to the rear at speed.

The rest of the leadership of 'C' Squadron were out of action, either wounded or removed from command in a more permanent way.

Which meant that the newly-frocked CSM Andrew Charles commanded what was lef....

"On!"

"Fire!"

Patterson was rapidly becoming the best gunner Charles had ever seen, bar none.

He had just put an APDS round right on the spot, causing the targeted IS-II to lose interest in proceedings.

"Pats, all yours for the while."

That was music to Patterson's ears.

He pressed his forehead to the sight and sought another target, a none too difficult matter in the sea of enemy vehicles and infantry approaching... not approaching....

'What the fuck?'

Patterson did a double take.

'What the...'

"Sarnt-Major... the bastards have stopped..."

Charles was already aware.

"Cease fire. Keep a close eye on them."

He took a quick look at his watch.

'1335... God... is it only twenty minutes since... since...'

He looked around and saw a number of clearly destroyed tanks in a landscape that bore no resemblance to that he had sat down in for lunch.

"Driver... move to alternate two."

"Roger."

The Centurion's engine went quickly from idle to power, and the vehicle slowly edged backwards out of the scrape, heading for the second back-up position they had created when the Grenadiers had arrived the day beforehand.

A burning Centurion exploded, sending a spider's web of smoke lines into the air and across the ground surrounding it. Its surviving crew had long evacuated.

Alternate Two was adjacent to the wood line on raised ground and Wild skilfully dropped down behind the skyline and negotiated the small distance, unobserved, and in good time.

As the Centurion was moving, Charles again tried the radio.

"Alma-Charlie-three to all Alma, report."

By the end of the exchanges, Charles understood that he now commanded six running tanks out of twelve that had been runners before the enemy arrived.

Switching to the regimental net, the CSM made contact with Scipio-six, the Grenadier's commanding officer.

After reporting the state of 'C' Squadron, Charles mainly listened, checking things off on his map, as the radio spewed instructions.

The upshot of it all was that, as ever, 'C' should hold their ground, along with the adjacent 'B' Squadron, buying time for division to establish a meaningful line to the rear. The Colonel had decided against telling Charles that another enemy attack was in progress to the west, which, if successful, would ensure that all their efforts were in vain.

Charles eased the headphones off and wiped his brow.

"We stay and hold... for at least two hours."

The crew knew a death sentence when they heard one, but only Patterson gave voice to his opinion.

"Tell the old man, he can come and take my fucking place."

Patterson's comment was then echoed by the rest of the crew.

"Steady, lads. We've got a job to do for... "

He stuck his head out of the turret in search of the source of the growing engine sounds.

"Aircraft... our brylcreams are taking a hand!"

Relief spread through the tank, and on through the remains of 'B' and 'C' Squadrons, and finally into the mechanised infantry.

Relief faded in an instant as aircraft with red stars appeared overhead, shedding munitions that rained down upon the British positions.

Nothing of note came near Lady Godiva II, the air attack concentrated around Route 104 and the positions to the south-east of Lützow. The enemy approach came in from Renzow, permitting the Soviet aircraft to drop and then make a starboard turn, sending them back to relative safety.

"Beefy, stick your head out and keep an eye on their tanks and infantry."

Beefy Silverside stuck his head out immediately.

Charles observed at least three of 'B' Squadrons tanks take fatal hits in short succession, whilst other bombs and rockets clearly claimed lives amongst the infantry.

He switched back to observing the tanks and infantry that had clearly gathered themselves to await the air strike.

More aero engines swept overhead, as a regiment of ground attack IL-10 Shturmovik followed their older sisters, venerable Il-2s.

However, the calls for assistance from the FOO and 'B' Squadron's commander had not gone unheeded, and aircraft arrived bearing friendly markings.

"What the hell are they, Sarnt-Major?"

The twin-tailed aircraft wore RAF markings and had no propeller.

Charles searched his brain for the air recognition information and quickly pulled the necessary from the depths of his mind.

"Vampires... they're the new jet... bloody Vampires."

Ground fire stopped rising from the defensive positions, as the gunners on the Grenadier's AA tanks realised the risk of hitting their own.

247 Squadron RAF had arrived with eighteen Vampire Mk Is. Although not the ideal aircraft for low altitude interception, they soon knocked five Il-10s out of the sky, each one of the jets mounting four Hispano Mk V cannons, whose 20mm shells tore the vitals out of the Soviet attack aircraft.

Overshooting was clearly a problem, and some Vampires swept past Shturmovik targets without having engaged.

One such failed pass ended in death for a jet pilot, as he inexplicably flew across the front of another Ilyushin, exposing himself to a quick burst that severed one of his tail planes and sent the Vampire straight into the German soil, although the disoriented pilot arrived a micro second before his upside down aircraft, as the ejector seat fired him into the cold damp earth.

The remaining Vampires set about the IL-10s with renewed vigour, attacking more from the flank, using deflection shooting to overcome the high gain speed that was a problem approaching from the rear.

The air battle moved away eastwards, as the Shturmoviks sought ground level and ran back to their own lines.

The Soviet bombardment recommenced, quickly followed by the artillery of the Guards and Corps units.

"Sarnt-Major, the buggers are on the move now."

A quick look confirmed Beefy's warning, but further examination revealed that the angle of their attack had changed, the village of Lützow itself now the focus, rather than the original attempt to circumvent, although some forces still manoeuvred on the flanks.

Charles made a quick decision and levered himself out of the turret.

"You're in charge, Pats. Back in a mo. Commander out."

He dropped to the ground, mentally avoiding the question of what he had just stepped in, and ran to the nearby infantry positions.

Rolling into an old shell hole, he found half a dozen determined looking guardsmen lining the rim.

"Who's in charge, corporal?"

The dirty faced NCO looked around him.

"Guess I am, Sarnt-Major. Our Sergeant copped it, so I'm it. What you need?"

Charles moved up to the rim and lay next to the Corporal.

"Right, as I see it, the Sovs are crossing our front, although still pushing some elements up the flank."

His finger pointed at each in turn.

"I'm going to hammer them from this flank, but I need to have my own flank secure."

The Corporal took a quick look.

"The woods?"

"In one, Corporal."

He grabbed his jaw.

"I'll grab a Bren section and stick them in here. That'll cover your front. My boys and I will tuck in on your right side there, keep any nasties that come from the woods off you. That OK, Sarnt-Major?"

Charles appreciated the man's no-nonsense approach.

"What's your name, Corporal?"

"Barclay, Sarnt-Major."

"Good work, Barclay. Use our squawk box if you need anything."

He slapped the man on the shoulder, took a brief moment to check his route, and then flung himself upwards and ran back to Lady Godiva.

1408 hrs, Sunday, 15th April 1946, 15th Motorised Rifle Brigade forward headquarters, west of Gottesgabe, Germany.

Just prior to the renewed advance of the Soviet forces, a confrontation took place at 15th Motorised's forward headquarters.

"Why did you wait? Now they have a chance to gather themselves!"

The 16th Tank Corps was a relatively new formation, the previous having gone on to glory and Guards status; none the less, it had a leavening of experienced and competent officers to balance the inexperienced majority. One of the latter was now rounding on two of the former.

Colonel Pavelkhin, commander of the 164th Tank Brigade and de facto commander of the attack force, exchanged glances with his fellow commander, Colonel Maslov of the 15th Motorised.

Both men were bristling with indignation.

"Because your orders clearly stated not to advance until the air attack was complete, Comrade Mayor General."

"It's complete... it was complete some time ago... and yet you move out as slow as can be long after our aviators have left the scene. Why's that? Why is that?"

"There was no warning that the attack had finished, Comrade Mayor General. Your order specifically stated an attack by three regiments... three regiments..."

Pavelkhin forced himself back from the abyss his anger was sending him towards.

"There has only been a two regiment attack so far, Comrade Mayor General."

Trufanov, commander of 16th Tank Corps, sent spittle flying in all directions as he ranted.

"Any fucking idiot could see the flyers have had a hard time. Any fucking idiot should have seen that and ordered his men forward immediately but not, it fucking seems, the fucking idiots that command have lumbered me with! I thought you both knew how to soldier!"

Pavelkhin, his face bearing the scars of combat with the enemy, and Maslov, whose chest bore a plethora of valour awards earned since the earliest days of 1941, stood stunned, as rebuke after rebuke washed over them, all in front of their men.

"Right, you pair of useless bastards! I'll do it myself. You're both relieved."

Trufanov rattled out his instructions, sending the 164th Tank, 15th Mechanised, and 27th Guards Heavy Tank Regiment's units back towards the centre, intent on grinding straight over the top of Lützow, regardless of cost, and also dispatched a part of the reformed 39th Guards Heavy Tank Brigade to back them up.

Satisfied with his actions, Trufanov turned and spotted the two Colonels stood to one side.

"Get out, the pair of you. You're no use to me. Consider yourself arrested. Now... go on, get out."

Pavelkhin and Maslov saluted smartly and turned on their heels, dreaming of shooting holes in the General as they marched away.

They sought refuge in a clump of trees, from where they could observe what came next.

Fig# 164 - Lutzow - Soviet attack.

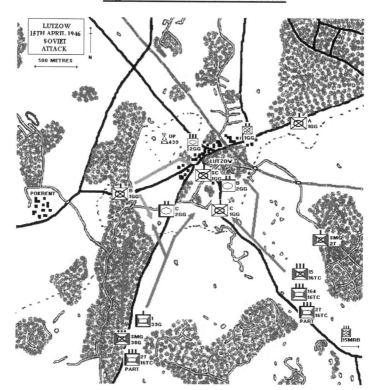

1318 hrs, Sunday, 15th April 1946, Guards Division positions, WittenbergerStrasse, Lützow, Germany.

"Stupid... really stupid..."

Charles was speaking to himself, but the crew understood perfectly.

The enemy advance was moving straight across his position, displaying tender sides to the deadly 17pdr gun.

Charles checked the flank force, and was amazed that it still hadn't moved forward.

A strange sound behind him brought a moment of amusement, as Corporal Barclay marshalled more men and equipment for his private army.

A 6pdr anti-tank gun was pushed into place, the men involved glowing red with the effort.

Nearby, a Vickers MG group was setting up, dragging wood into a rough wall to protect the crew from harm.

The lead elements of the Soviet force started to take fire from the village and environs, less than before admittedly, but still accurate.

Smoke and flame marked British success followed by British success, the Centurions proving equal to the task.

"Pats, steady. No firing yet, come right twelve degrees, range twelve hundred. IS-IIs, and a lot of them."

The turret whirred as Patterson sited the gun.

"Oh bloody hell."

Fifteen tanks, a mix of T-34s and IS-IIs from 27th Guards Heavy Tank Regiment, combined with seventeen IS-IIs and IS-IIIs from First Battalion, 39th Guards Heavy Tank Brigade, were flanking the main Soviet attack, seemingly intent on passing very close to where Lady Godiva II lay.

Charles kept his thoughts to himself this time.

"Unlike that lot, this commander seems to know his business."

The heavy tanks were manoeuvring well, some stopping, some moving forward, one group covering the other as they alternated.

Clinging to each tank was a grape of infantry from the 39th's SMG Company.

Charles stuck his head out and shouted at the passing Barclay.

"Corporal! Your AT gun. No use against the big buggers. Tell them to concentrate on the T-34s. You get the infantry all to yourself. Good luck."

Barclay's reply was lost in the whoosh of passing shells, as some of the advancing tanks engaged the likely looking hump that was the concealed Centurion.

"Are we on?"

"On."

"FIRE!"

Godiva spat venom at the approaching mob and achieved a hit, without penetration. The infantry bailed off the tank at speed, self-preservation lending them wings.

"Target hit. Again."

"On."

"FIRE!"

The tank, jinking to avoid a repetition, took Patterson's shell in the rear drive, knocking the track off and slewing the IS-II, exposing the offside.

"Side shot, Pats. Fire when on."

Pats shouted and sent the solid shot down range.

It punched through the side armour and into the engine, bouncing back through the metal that separated the crew from all the motor paraphernalia.

Two men emerged and the IS-II was out of the fight.

There was no time for celebration, as more targets required their urgent attention.

The 6pdr claimed a kill with its first shot, the whole Soviet crew abandoning their vehicle.

Just to make sure, a second round was applied to the stationary tank, and the smoke left no doubt that it was beyond use.

Soviet artillery, called in by the commander of the 39th, started to drop to the rear of their position.

It was quickly corrected.

The Vickers and its servants simply disappeared; one moment firing at the grapes of infantry, the next a smoking hole that yielded no clues to the whereabouts of either weapon or men.

Shrapnel pattered off the Centurion's armour, giving the tankers an idea of the hell endured by the Guardsmen outside.

"FIRE!"

Patterson placed a single shot perfectly between hull and turret, killing the IS-II and her crew in one hit.

"Shit! Target tank, left two degrees, fire when on!"

'Jesus! It's a three!'

The shell spanged off the turret armour in such a way that both Patterson and Charles doubted the Russians even knew they had been hit.

Another shell hit the tank in its offside, probably one of 'B' Squadron's vehicles making the most of a flank shot.

The IS-III stopped dead, and black smoke blossomed from its ruptured engine compartment.

Its 122mm gun belched flame and the huge shell seemed to come straight down the line of Patterson's sights.

The slightest of pings indicated that the lump of metal had kissed the top of the commander's cupola.

Their unknown saviour in the village completed the job, and the Grenadier's Bren gunner mowed the escaping four man crew down without a moment's hesitation.

539

Scream from Laz Wild was immediately followed by the clang of a solid hit.

"Laz?"

Wild's voice betrayed his fear.

"Came straight at me, that one... nearly shat meself."

"On!"

"FIRE!"

Charles said the word automatically as his mind worked another problem.

The breech of the gun sprang back into the turret as the recoil tried to rip the 17pdr off its mounts.

"Solid kill, Sarnt-Major."

Sneaking a quick look, the recipient of the AP shell was already brewing up dramatically.

The heat, smoke, and fumes were all building up inside Lady Godiva, despite the extractors going full blast and having the commander's hatch open.

Sticking his head further out, Charles tried to clear his stinging eyes to take in the bigger picture.

Whilst the 'private army' had done good work from the flank, the Soviet advance was virtually upon the defensive positions in Lützow itself and, to the east of the shattered village, already through.

'B' Squadron seemed to consist solely of smoking wrecks, although the numbers didn't tally, which meant, to Charles' reckoning, that some had made a fighting withdrawal.

Which brought him nicely to his own dilemma.

'Stick in this position which gives us reasonable cover or move...'

CLANG!

Charles had ducked instinctively as the white blob tore across the ground towards him.

A solid shot had struck the gun mantlet, imitating Thor's Hammer at its most violent.

It failed to penetrate and Patterson was already seeking the perpetrator.

"On!"

"FIRE!"

The Centurion rocked as it sought its revenge.

Charles returned to his mental exercise.

'... or move and attract every shot going...'

"Infantry, close in, right side!"

Charles grabbed two grenades from the ready rack, primed one and stuck his head further out.

Three Soviet soldiers had managed to get close, avoiding Barclay's covering force.

"Grenade!"

The Guards tank commander tossed the fizzing bomb at the small group and ducked.

The sharp crack was accompanied by screams.

A swift look confirmed all three enemy down and out of the fight, although none seemed to have been killed in the blast.

A pair of guardsmen arrived, one to cover the other, whilst the second dragged two of the wounded enemy into the small depression where the other survivor had been propelled.

Charles debated the wiseness of the act of kindness for a second, and then found other things to do.

"There's more! Jesus! Peril, right side… quickly!"

One of the shotgun shells was loaded up and, once the turret had rotated swiftly onto the rush of infantry, discharged to impressive effect.

There was no need for a second shot, only a bag in which to put the pieces of what had been four men.

For Charles, the problems kept on coming.

Two IS-IIIs came round the edge of the wood, their distinctive shapes appearing and disappearing in the gaps between the trees.

"Target tanks, both IIIs, right eleven degrees, Load Sabot."

Patterson moved the turret and his sights filled with the frying pan turret of an IS-III.

He dropped the gun's elevation the smallest amount.

"On!"

"FIRE!"

The APDS round left the gun at high velocity, the sabot split open, leaving the smaller diameter tungsten core to make the short journey alone.

As one piece of the discarded alloy sabot nearly struck one of the wounded Russians, the APDS round went through the IS-IIIs lower hull as if it was made of cardboard.

The small round moved around inside the tank, bouncing off inner surfaces until its power was spent.

Inside, the major workings of the tank were reduced to scrap, and the crew resembled nothing that could be considered to bring to mind anything human.

"On!"

"FIRE!"

A second tungsten dart was launched from Lady Godiva II, and it hit, but the rearmost IS-III had moved perfectly, and the high-speed dart struck the turret side at the worst possible angle.

Charles saw the APDS round disappear into the air.

"Again!"

The massive 122mm gun swung the few inches it needed to bring the Centurion fully into view and both guns fired together.

The APDS round penetrated, but did no damage of note, as it expended itself with a perfect jam in the corner of the bulkhead, having neatly removed the commander's right leg at the knee.

The 122mm shell did not penetrate, but it killed Lady Godiva II just the same.

Ears ringing, eyes streaming, chest tight from the extreme pressure wave, Charles tried to orient himself.

"Jesus Christ!"

He could see sunlight where no sunlight should exist. Through the modest flicker of flames, he understood what had happened.

The turret had been displaced by the force of the strike.

"Abandon tank! Get out, lads!"

He heard all the calls and pushed himself out of the cupola, suddenly aware that his left arm wasn't pulling its weight.

Blood betrayed an injury beneath the sleeve of his overalls.

Patterson pushed himself up and out, coughing and spluttering, followed by a waft of smoke.

Bullets pinged off the armour and a scream from the front indicated that at least one had found a target.

Charles and Patterson both instinctively stopped and turned back, seeking information through the gathering smoke.

"It's Laz... I can see the old bugger... hang on, Sarnt Major...I'll pass 'im down..."

Charles dropped off the side and moved forward, helping Patterson with the semi-conscious driver.

"Taken one on the napper... one in the arm, Sarnt-Major."

Patterson rolled Wild over and into the waiting arms of his tank commander who, ignoring the sudden sharp pain, controlled Wild's drop to the ground.

Grabbing the neck of Wild's overalls, Charles dragged the now comatose driver away from the smoking tank.

Exhausted, he flopped down next to three guardsmen who had come forward to help.

One of them was Barclay.

"You lucky bastard, Sarnt-Major!"

A quick look back at the Centurion confirmed Barclay's observation. The turret, looking decidedly out of shape, had moved backwards and upwards, bursting out of its ring mount.

It was a miracle that no-one had been killed.

Patterson was moving slowly, his uniform smoking, illustrating his close brush with the flames that were now clearly gaining hold in the turret area.

And then...

"Mummy! No, Mummy! Help me!"

Both Patterson and Charles turned to the tank, and were moving before they could think about what was happening.

The pleas turned to screams, turned to animal mewling sounds, turned to screams, to squeals of extreme pain, and back to calls for a mother who couldn't help.

Roberts was still in the front of the tank.

Patterson leapt up on the vehicle with ease; Charles tried and fell off, his left arm failing him.

"Wingnut! Give me your hand!"

Patterson leant down through the smoke and into the compartment below, ignoring the surge of pain that threatened to overcome him.

"Mummy! Oh God, Mummy! It hurts! Ahhhhh!"

"Wingnut, for the love of god, grab my hand!"

The squeal from the trapped man rose to the highest possible pitch and Patterson felt his skin blister as the fire suddenly became a living thing.

"Wingnut!"

Roberts could only hear his own screeching now, and was oblivious to everything except the fire that was consuming him.

"Pats! We can't save him! Come back, Pats!"

Patterson rolled away from the hatch and dropped to the ground, oblivious to the modest flames that were eating the sleeve of his overalls.

Charles beat the flames out with his hands and grabbed the dazed gunner, pulling him away from the burning Centurion.

Both men tumbled into the position where Barclay and his men lay, seemingly asleep, but all equally dead, killed by a mortar shell that had done its work efficiently. Only a little blood on the lips of one of Barclay's men betrayed the possibility of any wounds in the group.

Dragging two of the Soviet soldiers wounded by Charles' grenade, the two guardsmen rescuers arrived, panting with the effort. The third wounded man had expired, and the burning tank had made their refuge unsafe.

They then dragged all the five wounded men into cover and made off, intending to escape with their lives.

A shout from the nearby 6pdr marked another kill, the very last, as the ammunition was all fired off.

The few survivors of Barclay's group disappeared as numerous Soviet tanks, supported by infantry, swept over the position.

An occasional wounded Guardsman received a coup de grace from a Soviet, more intent on pursuit than taking prisoners.

The battle moved on.

2020 hrs, Sunday, 15th April 1946, former Guards Division positions, WittenbergerStrasse, Lützow, Germany.

"Sarnt-Major... psst...Sarnt-Major... Pats... Pats, you fucking lump of lard... wake up... you're alive... wake up..."

Charles was first to surface through the fog, his eyes squinting in the moonlight that now illuminated a quiet battlefield.

"Beefy?"

"One and the same, Sarnt-Major."

Pats groaned, his renewed consciousness bringing about an unwelcome awareness of his raw hand.

Laz stared silently, almost unseeingly, his breathing heavy and pronounced.

The moon made a surge in its efforts, and Beefy turned his nose up.

"Blimey, but if you three ain't been through the wars, ain't you."

Charles tried to bring himself up onto his elbows, but found a solid lump preventing him.

It was one of the Russians.

They were both dead, probably bled out from the numerous wounds caused by the grenade. Both had eyes staring off into space, calm, almost serene, but most certainly dead.

Beefy offered his hand and pulled Charles to his feet. The NCO nearly dropped straight back to the earth, but found some strength from somewhere, and fought his way upright.

544

Beefy nodded towards Lützow.

"The bastards are looting the village and our positions down there. I reckon won't be long before they fetch up here, Sarnt-Major."

Charles nodded, the moonlight providing sufficient illumination to observe the locust-like activities of the Soviet soldiery in the wake of the battle.

A shot rang out.

No one needed to ask the question; all three knew what it was, and it spurred them on.

"Right, we need to get the heck out of here. You wounded, Beefy?"

"Not a scratch..."

A roar of aero engines made the group duck instinctively as a flight of aircraft drove in hard.

Death tumbled out of the night sky, as the intruder-configured Havoc bombers of the RAF's 226 Squadron determined to savage the enemy force that had inflicted such a crushing defeat on the Guards Division, and now threatened the spearhead of British 2nd Army.

"Let's use this diversion. Can you manage Pats?"

Beefy helped pull the gunner to his feet.

"I reckon so, Sarnt-Major."

"I'll bring Laz."

Charles leant down and paused, straightening back up, easing his back.

"Come on, Laz. Ups a daisy now."

He leant down again and pulled the driver upright.

"Before we go, lads."

Charles turned to Lady Godiva II, the Centurion II now totally wrecked and turretless, ravaged by internal explosions and still smoking.

"Atten-shun."

Each man tried, in his own fashion, to salute the wreck and the friend who lay within it.

"Right... move!"

Turning their backs on the airborne destroyers, the party limped away to the north-west, avoiding Route 104, hoping to find friendly forces near Gadebusch.

Behind them, the victorious forces of 1st Baltic pushed northwards, creating a potential disaster for 21st Army Group

545

Gadebusch had fallen quickly, as the skeleton force defending it was taken by surprise, unaware that the Grenadiers to their front had been overwhelmed.

Holdorf was proving more difficult a task, and the 16th Tank Corps had already been thrown back twice.

Trufanov was still ranting at anyone and everyone who came in range, including the two hapless Colonels, who he dragged along, probably just for that purpose.

The losses in the lead formations had been murderous, and the arrival of enemy aircraft delivering bombs over his rear echelon units, did nothing to improve Trufanov's humour, especially as he had personally ordered his fuel train into Lützow an hour beforehand.

Regimental and Battalion commanders were berated, or their deputies received the blast if the original commander had been killed in discharging their orders. Surviving officers were relieved and ordered back to headquarters under arrest, the whole hierarchy of the Tank Corps made unstable through the actions of a man losing his mind under pressure.

The main door of the Rathaus swung open under the guidance of two guards, who admitted a small party without challenge.

Trufanov was in full swing, the Major commanding 37th Separate Engineer Battalion somehow receiving both barrels for something that occurred at Pokrent, a place he and his unit had never been or seen.

The Major stiffened, immediately followed by Pavelkhin and Maslov.

Trufanov was in a world of his own.

"You fucking moron! How can you knock down two bridges? You're relieved. Consider yourself under arrest! When I've sorted this fucking mess out, you'll be lucky to just be counting fucking trees, you useless bastard!"

Trufanov stopped dead, realising that eyes were not on him, but elsewhere, eyes that held knowledge to which he sensed he ought to be privy.

He turned, ready to chastise whichever idiot had ventured within range, and immediately decided to keep his mouth very firmly shut.

546

The new arrival spoke first.

"Good evening, Comrade Mayor General."

Trufanov came to attention and saluted.

"Comrade Leytenant General. I regret that I'd no idea you were coming."

"Indeed, Comrade Trufanov, so it would appear."

The NKVD Lieutenant General was known to only one person in the headquarters by sight, but to everyone by name and reputation.

"I was attending your headquarters on a social call, but now I find something that draws me to duty."

He removed his hat and polished his glasses, the dust from his brush with the night bombers obscuring his vision in the artificial kerosene lighting.

His roving eye caught sight of the young signals officer, but his face remained impassive.

Replacing his glasses, he suddenly seemed to remember something.

"My apologies, Comrade. I am Leytenant General Nikolai Georgievich Khannikov."

Everyone now knew that they were in the presence of the head of the 1st Baltic Front's SMERSH units.

More than one heart pumped at twice the rate when the name fell upon their ears.

"Right then, Comrade Trufanov, what the hell is going on here?"

Trufanov fell to the task of allocating blame with a will, singling out the two Colonels for most of the denouncing, tossing in the names of some dead regimental commanders for good measure, and exonerating himself in the process.

"Well, that's a very sorry state of affairs. What do you two have to say for yourselves?"

"Comrade Leytenant General. It's not as Comrade Trufanov states. He relieved us from duty for some perceived indiscretion prior to the main attack."

Trufanov drew breath but a single raised finger stopped him before he could rant his innocence.

"Continue, Polkovnik."

"Sir, it was his order that sent our units into a killing zone. We were ordered to be silent and placed under arrest, as have a number of capable officers. The General is seeking to blame others for his own issues, and continues to do so now, Comrade Leytenant General."

Trufanov heaved air into his lungs again, and again, the single finger stopped him dead.

"Wait."

Khannikov already had a flavour of what was going on; the sounds of ranting had found him long before he entered the Rathaus.

Despite being NKVD and a member of SMERSH, he was a combat soldier, and his read of the battlefield, even by moonlight, was that something had gone badly wrong.

"So, what am I to do here? I have a General telling me one thing, and two arrested Colonels telling me another. Message logs."

He held out his hand, the imperative quite clear.

The signals Major quickly swept up the necessary paperwork and presented them smartly to the NKVD officer.

"These are all?"

"They are all the records we have, Comrade Leytenant General."

"Stand at ease, Comrade Mayor."

The young man did so, relaxing slightly more than would be expected in the presence of such a dangerous man.

"If I read these, what will I find, Comrade Mayor."

Without a moment's hesitation, Mayor Golubtsov spoke clearly and decisively.

"Comrade Leytenant General, you will find that some messages are not present, as they have been removed. Those messages would entirely support the version of events given by Polkovniks Pavelkhin and Maslov."

Trufanov managed to stutter a few words.

"You too? You traitor... liar..."

Khannikov looked Trufanov in the eye.

"If I have to tell you to be quiet one more time, I will take you outside and neck shoot you myself. Is that clear, Comrade?"

Trufanov could only nod.

"Now, Mayor. Where are these missing records?"

"General Trufanov destroyed them before we moved to this location, Comrade Leytenant General."

"A serious matter, Comrade Mayor."

"Yes, Comrade Leytenant General."

The rest of the headquarters staff, and particularly the communications group, were all studiously avoiding involvement, undertaking the mundane tasks that kept them away from scrutiny.

"Comrade Trufanov. What do you have to say?"

"Liars, all liars! My orders were disobeyed and undermined at every turn. He," the accusatory finger singled out the signals Major, "He has removed the messages that support what I am saying. He's a traitor and an enemy of the state! I demand you arrest him… and them!"

The finger swivelled to the Colonels.

"Thank you, Comrade Mayor General."

The men behind the NKVD officer tensed, holding their weapons slightly tighter, as they knew that the end was in sight.

"Polkovnik?"

"Pavelkhin, Comrade Leytenant General."

"Comrade Pavelkhin, Comrade Maslov. You are reinstated. Resume your commands immediately…"

"They're all ly…"

He turned as rapidly as a cobra striking its prey.

"Shut your fucking mouth!"

Trufanov's protest died as quickly as it started, and was replaced by the icy grip of fear.

"I want this mess sorted out as quickly as possible. Who's in command?"

His hand shot out and slapped Trufanov in the process of speaking.

"I am, Com..."

"Next in seniority?"

16th Tank Corps armour commander stepped forward.

"Polkovnik Abashkin, Comrade Leytenant General."

Abashkin had a steady eye, and the man exuded competence.

"Very well. You have command, on my authority, until you are replaced. Clear, Comrade Polkovnik?"

"Yes, Comrade Leytenant General. If I may?"

Abashkin grabbed a map and went to work, dragging in the engineer Major and the two rehabilitated Colonels.

Khannikov looked at the broken Trufanov with dripping contempt.

"Now, you may speak."

"Comrade, I protest! You take the word of a mere Mayor over mine. That cannot stand, Sir. He's lying."

Khannikov silenced the protests with a raised hand.

"Comrade Mayor Golubtsov is not a liar."

He slapped the officer on the shoulder and smiled benignly, as an uncle would do to a favourite nephew.

Trufanov looked from one to the other, not understanding.

"I have known Vladimir Georgiyevich all of his life, and I have never known him lie to me. Do you know who his father is, Trufanov?"

"No."

"Malenkov. Georgy Malenkov."

Trufanov saw his doom approaching.

Malenkov was a member of the GKO and one of the most powerful men in the Soviet Union.

"Now, do you wish to change anything you've said to me, traitor?"

The Major General collapsed both physically and mentally.

Khannikov stepped back, allowing his men to drag the condemned man outside.

"I bring regards from your father and mother, but it seems you are needed, Vladimir Georgiyevich. I will not stay. Take care and I will come back soon."

"Thank you, Uncle."

The two embraced and kissed as Russian men do, before they stepped back and saluted, in which they were joined by the three colonels.

"Good luck, Comrades."

Khannikov turned on his heel and strode from the room, his departure marked by a single shot from somewhere outside that, in turn, underlined the change of command for 16th Tank Corps.

Everyone stopped talking and looked at the Signals officer with different eyes.

He looked defiantly at them, senior and junior, each in turn.

"Comrade Polkovniks, it makes no difference. I'm here, and under my mother's name. I seek nothing that I haven't earned, and I am not threat."

He moved forward to the table where Abashkin was planning.

"Your orders. Comrade Polkovnik?"

Both Pavelkhin and Maslov leant over the map and slapped the younger man on the shoulder, grinning from ear to ear, before returning to the tactical situation.

The 16th Tank Corps went back to war.

Fig# 165 - Pomeranian names – then and now.

1946	NOW
Berg Dievenow	Dziwnów
Damerow	Dąbrowa Nowogardzka
Eberstein	Wojcieszyn
Farbezin	Wierzbięcin
Grosse Mokratz	Mokrzyca Wielka
Hagen	Recław
Kartzig	Karsk
Klein Mokratz	Mokrzyca Mala
Minten	Miętno
Naugard	Nowogard
Neu Kodram	Kodrąbek
Plötzin	Płocin
Strelowhagen	Strzelowo
Swinemünde	Świnoujście
Treptow an der Rega	Trzebiatów
Wismar	Wyszomierz
Wollchow	Olchowo
Wollin	Wolin

I have fought the good fight, I have finished the race, I have kept the faith.

The Bible, Second Epistle to Timothy, 4:7

Chapter 145 - THE PANTOMIME

<u>0259 hrs, 26th March 1946, Wollin and Hagen, Pomerania.</u>

The paratroopers had come together well, only a handful of men missing from the unit tasked with taking and holding the Dziwna bridges at Wollin and Hagen.

At 0300 precisely, ninety-eight RAF Lancaster bombers visited themselves upon Anklam, intent on disrupting the Soviet rail and road network by bringing down the bridges over the Peene.

Although a precision daylight strike would undoubtedly have been more effective in reducing the existing rubble of Anklam to smaller pieces, their purpose was also one of distraction; a distraction that required split-second timing. The deluge of high explosives and incendiaries, and subsequent inferno, would provide a diversion to draw the attention of any guards at Wollin, as well as an orange sky against which enemy sentries would be illuminated as the 101st troopers advanced.

Officers pumped their fists, sending men forward, as the bomber's display provided the backdrop for silent killing.

Small groups had gone ahead, armed with the tools for deadly close work, with orders to remove the sentries.

Ahead of his headquarters group, First Battalion swept forward. Able Company, closely followed by Charlie Company, moved over the Zamkowa Bridge, dropping off a few squads to wreck any wiring that might be found.

Baker Company moved to the south, ready to provide a base of fire if the lead units got into difficulties.

Battalion headquarters and the support company remained in reserve, ready to move forward and react to any enemy threat.

To the north, Second Battalion had the real prize. It was tasked with taking the rail bridge and adjacent road bridge, creating a secure perimeter, but it was the rail bridge that was all-important.

The road bridge was a recent repair, and Allied planners had been rightly nervous about its ability to take heavy tanks, whereas the rail bridge suffered from no such problems.

Third Battalion provided rear security, setting blocking forces on all approaches to ensure no surprises came from the east.

The 501st was tasked with taking the three bridges, and establishing a bridgehead across the Dzwina into Wollin, holding until relieved.

Taking it was a relative doddle, the small Soviet defensive force gobbled up in a moment, with scarcely a shot fired.

Holding it was an issue that raised its challenges in the light of the new day.

Fig# 166 - Wollin - Initial Allied Forces.

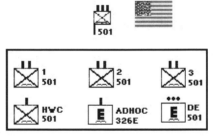

0921 hrs, Tuesday, 26th March 1946, Wollin, Pomerania.

"Well, it's nearly fifty miles from Kolberg to here."

The leadership of the 501st was gathered around the camp table being used as headquarters map table, dining table, and personal equipment store.

Constantine Galkin, Crisp's exec, munched noisily on one of the liberated Polish sausages that had turned up during a search of the decrepit barn that Crisp had selected as his CP.

"According to headquarters, we can't expect to be relieved today, so we gotta sit out whatever the Reds throw at us."

The mumbles were indistinct but confident in nature.

"Intel has nothing else for us, so no update on whether we're facing old men and boys."

The veterans in the assembly understood the gallows humour and remembered the empty assurances of D-Day.

"So probably just as per briefing... adding in those boys," Crisp nodded his head at the ever-present sound of falling mortar rounds, "To the rear-echelon security troops and a handful of regular army infantry and engineer units... nothing special... and nothing we can't handle."

Crisp watched as Galkin finished his feast, and immediately started on consuming another.

"Help yourself to the sausages, boys, if my second in command has left you any."

Modest laughter greeted his attempt to shame Galkin into stopping his gluttony. His effort failed miserably, as the Greek-American simply leant over and swiped two more for later, just in case the assembled officers felt hungry.

Some clearly did, and Crisp decided to join them.

'Damn, that's good.'

"Right, listen in. Our positions are sound... we're up to strength pretty much... we'll hold."

Using the sausage as a pointer, Crisp went over the positions with his officer group.

More stragglers had come in since the 501st swept into Wollin and established itself on a rough curve between Sulomino and Darowice, occupying the high ground between Route 65 and the railway line.

First Battalion sat astride Route 65 and had responsibility for the hill, leaving one company back as a reserve, hidden in the woods at Plötzin.

Second Battalion took the remaining frontage of the arc, with the Regimental Heavy Weapons Company lying back in support of both forward units.

Crisp sent his HQ demolition platoon northwards to Darzowice, with orders to prepare to drop the bridges if threatened, as they were not vital to the Allied plan.

In Wollin and Hagen, the support and medical services established themselves, the former also containing the 501st Regiment's headquarters units.

Third Battalion screened the rear areas, protecting against any unexpected arrival that might threaten Hagen, and provided one company as a reserve, positioned around the west end of the rail bridge.

"Right. Any improvements we can see here?"

Lemuel Pollo, Captain of Engineers, commander of the two platoon group allocated to the 501st, had clearly been itching to contribute.

"Colonel, we took a pile of high-ex off that bridge. My boys can create some nice surprises for Ivan if he gets over ambitious. Sink a few in the road, in natural gathering areas, that sort of thing?"

His voice ended the statement in question mode.

"Don't see any reason why not, Lem. What sort of detonation?"

"All command detonation, Colonel. Nothing fancy, and nothing our boys can tread on by accident."

"Good for me. Present me with a laying plan a-sap. Anyone else?"

Fig# 167 - Wollin - Initial Allied dispositions.

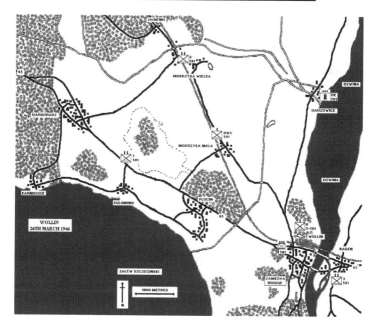

Major Timothy Simpson, the Second Battalion CO, shuffled uneasily before taking the plunge.

"Well, Sir... the terrible twosome've asked me to get permission for a special squad, based around the big rifles we captured."

The lead elements into Hagen had discovered a small repair facility, in which different weapons were undergoing maintenance.

555

Sergeant Major Baldwin and First Sergeant Hawkes, the 'terrible pair' in question, had 'appropriated' six pristine anti-tank rifles, the purpose of which was now laid bare by Simpson's request.

Crisp laughed.

"Well, I didn't make Colonel by taking on impossible missions, so I guess we'll give 'em their head. Keep an eye on them though, Tim."

Baldwin and Hawkes formed a powerbase that most officers avoided like the plague, although both were always suitably respectful to the rank, and positively reverend to their colonel.

"Ok then boys. If there's nothing else, let's get back to our units and pep 'em up. Uncle Joe'll be coming to play real soon; he can't afford not to."

Salutes were exchanged and the officers group split up, each commander returning to his unit as quickly as possible.

Not that they knew it, but 'Uncle Joe' was only ten minutes away.

0954 hrs, Tuesday 26th March 1946, Second Battalion CP, near Klein Mokratz, Pomerania.

The first casualty of the battle was Simpson, and before a shot was fired.

He tripped on a piece of loose carpet and missed a step.

The Major fell down the stairs into the basement that held the command apparatus of the 501st's Second Battalion.

The snap of his left leg was heard like a rifle shot.

His scream of agony came immediately afterwards, the pain compounded as additional damage was done as he tumbled down the remaining few feet, the broken tibia and fibula punched out through his flesh, impaling themselves in the calf muscle of his right leg.

The Battalion Medical officer rushed over, already fumbling for morphine.

Simpson was quickly moved into an unconscious state as a heavy dose of the powerful drug hit his system.

Outside, mortar rounds started to arrive. Although not directly on the CP, they most certainly announced to the occupants that Soviet activity was about to commence.

Organising a stretcher detail, the MO evacuated Simpson to the aid post, where a complicated fracture became tricky surgery under extreme duress, as Red Army artillery joined in and started to fall danger close.

1000 hrs, Tuesday 26th March 1946, Second Battalion front, near Grosse Mokratz, Pomerania.

"URRAH!"

"What the fuck?"

Paratrooper heads rose from cover to establish what the heck was making that noise.

"URRAH!"

"Stand to! Stand to!"

Fig# 168 - Wollin - First and Second Soviet attacks.

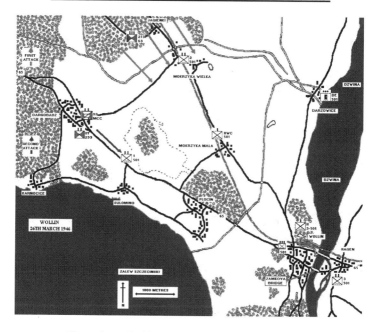

The cries of officers and NCOs went up from along the defensive positions, calling men to expose themselves in air thick with shrapnel from mortars and artillery.

Four lines of infantry were charging forward, weapons held out in front, like a scene from an old Great War newsreel.

Easy Company's Captain was obliterated by a mortar round as he went to give the fire order; his 2IC remained identifiable, although he was equally dead.

557

Dog Company opened fire, prompting the entire Second Battalion to start pouring on the heat.

.30 cal machine-guns, BARs, and Garands lashed out at the advancing NKVD infantry regiment, knocking men over like skittles in a bar.

Now and again, an airborne trooper would wheel away, clutching some wounded part, or drop silently to the earth, never to rise again.

The Soviet mortars still took their toll, but, as the human wave closed, the mortars advanced, for fear of hurting their own.

Montgomery Hawkes, Easy Company's First Sergeant, rallied a group of troopers who were about to be overrun.

"Stay put and hold!"

Hawkes dropped three running enemy with a swift burst from his Thompson,

"Incoming!"

One grenade was clearly thrown well short, but the other was accurate.

Hawkes threw himself to his left, catching the deadly egg, and throwing it back, all in one movement.

It exploded in front of the position, claiming no victims.

'Hot damn!'

"Jesus, Sarge, you should be playing for the Yankees!"

There was no time to celebrate, as the mass of enemy grew ever closer.

The .30cal next to Hawkes stopped, the gunner reeling away as two bullets smashed his shoulder.

The loader was already out of the fight, his life claimed by a mortar fragment moments beforehand.

Hawkes dropped to his belly, unceremoniously pushing the wounded gunner out of the way.

The man's wailing was drowned out by the .30cal resuming its duty.

"Layder, ammo me up!"

The old hand rolled across the side of the position and set to work.

Elsewhere, the attack seemed to be faltering, but, for some reason, the boldest and the bravest all seemed to make for Hawkes' position.

As they got closer, so the NCO's voice became louder and louder, almost attracting enemy soldiers to him.

"Fuck off, you bastards, fuck off!"

The barrel swivelled frantically, with only occasional breaks in the relentless stream of bullets.

Three men made a surge and Hawkes swivelled the weapon, knocking them all down in the blink of an eye.

"I said fuck off!"

"Nearly out, Sarge! One belt after this one!"

Without pausing in his personal crusade, Hawkes directed Layder to find some more.

When the temporary loader returned, the firing had ceased.

There were two bullets left on the belt...

... and the Russians had gone.

Out of the nine hundred and thirty men who comprised the 273rd Regiment of the 63rd NKVD Rifle Division, only three hundred and thirty-two returned to their starting positions intact.

The rest lay upon the field, dead, alive and cowering, or wounded, bleeding, wailing, suffering until death made a judgement.

In the tent that served as the 273rd's HQ, the radio crackled with more orders, the fanatical Divisional Commander ordering another full-frontal attack on the 'weakly armed' paratroopers.

"Stand aside, Hagan."

A single bullet ripped its way through the radio set.

The Lieutenant Colonel, his face like thunder, returned his automatic to his holster.

"Message not received, Comrade Polkovnik!"

NKVD Serzhant Hagan, the now redundant radio operator, stared silently as his commander broke down in tears.

1200 hrs, Tuesday 26th March 1946, Second Battalion front, near Grosse Mokratz, Pomerania.

Crisp had gone forward to see the situation for himself, and, in the case of Second Battalion, to see how the replacement leadership was handling matters.

The Soviets had launched another attack, this time aimed at First Battalion.

Most of the infantry were motorised, ranging from motorcycle to half-track, which made it a more dangerous proposition than the assault on Second Battalion.

It had run in close, and some enemy soldiers had made it into the trenches, before being thrown back out by a surge of two reserve platoons from Plötzin.

The paratroopers' bazookas had proved extremely effective against the infantry vehicles, as well as light tanks that had accompanied the attack, whose rout from the field discouraged the infantry from pressing home the attack just at the moment when pressing might have brought about a breakthrough.

As per the NKVD attack before it, the push by Shtrafbat 299 and elements of the 92nd Motorcycle Battalion withered bloodily, and the survivors fell back.

The Soviet units were in disarray, and it was not until nearly two o'clock that a pair of senior Red Army officers arrived on the field to take charge and organise the disparate units into one coordinated fighting force.

Across No Man's Land, a quick telephone exchange satisfied Colonel Crisp that the situation was again stable.

Ordering one platoon from each of Third Battalion's companies to double westwards to form an additional reserve, Crisp quickly organised his regimental assets.

The recently promoted Captain Desandé now found himself as de facto Battalion commander, and, as Crisp slowly smoked his way through a Chesterfield, he watched the young officer grow into the role.

Hawkes arrived and offered up his own report, the commander of C Company having sent him, hoping that the notorious scrounger could also scare up some more ammunition.

Report complete, Hawkes responded to the gesture from Crisp and sat down.

"First Sergeant."

"Colonel."

"How are you getting along with those rifles you acquired?"

"Well, Sir... the Sergeant Major has them at the moment. We're just waiting your say-so."

'Simpson didn't tell them... of course he didn't.'

"Hell, I need all the firepower I can muster, First Sergeant. Green light from me, just keep me informed."

"Thank you, Sir."

"How are the boys doing?"

Crisp knew he would get the bottom line from the experienced NCO.

"Most of them are just fine, Colonel. Funnily enough, it's the veterans who are itchy."

"How come?"

"They know how these things work, Colonel... how we always end up swinging our balls in the breeze for much longer than the brass say we will."

"Ain't that the truth, First Sergeant."

Hawkes looked at Crisp quizzically, but quickly understood that his Colonel saw himself more as one of the doughs than brass.

"For what it's worth, Hawkes... I truly believe we just have this one day to stand 'fore we're relieved."

He accepted a cigarette and lit it and Hawkes' with one easy motion.

"Keep an eye on things in Second for me, 'kay?"

"Yes, Sir."

Both men rose and donned their helmets, a distant whooping and cheering suddenly apparent.

The noise of engines revving broke through the human noise.

'What the...?'

Grabbing his Garand, Crisp stuck his head out of the bunker entrance.

'Well, I'll be damned!'

Hawkes slid in beside Crisp, trying to get a good view of the arriving jeeps.

A Major dismounted from the leading vehicle, waving the remaining fifteen, some towing trailers, into cover behind a large barn.

Once his unit was tucked out of sight, the Major hopped back in his jeep and rode the remaining yards to the CP.

The glider-infantry officer spotted Crisp and dismounted, showing his experience by not saluting.

Once inside the headquarters, military protocol was satisfied before Crisp took the Major's report.

"Major Field, 327th Glider, Heavy Weapons. General Taylor ordered us over here. Reckoned you need some extra firepower, Sir."

Crisp nodded enthusiastically.

"We sure do, Major. What do you got for us?"

"I've got six vehicle mounted M-20s, and twelve M-18s on tripods, thirty rounds to go with each, plus the crews, Sir."

561

Crisp had just been given the capacity to inflict a whole load of extra hurt on any attacker.

The M-18 was a 57mm recoilless rifle with a capability for firing HEAT, High Explosive, and White Phosphorous.

Its bigger brother, the M-20, had a calibre of 75mm, with the same range of shells.

Captain Louis Desandé, proving that he was on the ball, spread out a map of the 501st's full defensive position before being asked, enabling Crisp and Field to work out how best to utilise the new arrivals.

Field copied details over to his own map. He left to organise his force whilst Crisp was back on the field telephone, apprising the various units of the new support available, call signs, and how to best utilise the new assets.

Desandé accepted the two mugs of coffee with a nod and a smile, waiting for his Colonel to finish before handing his over.

"Yowl! For the love of mike, your hands must be asbestos, Louis."

The Louisiana lawyer grinned.

"Damn, but we needed those RCLs. God must surely be smiling down on us today."

The two engaged in small talk, driven by Crisp, as he tried to understand how his new man was operating.

Satisfied that the Captain was coping, and would cope, and with coffee consumed, Colonel Marion J Crisp took this leave.

It was then that his God smiled down on him once more.

A jeep in the markings of the 1st Polish Corps bounced round the corner, narrowly missing three deploying RCL jeeps, its roof up and proudly displaying the orange panels that were intended to keep friendly vehicles from friendly attack from the air.

The driver, *'clearly a man with a death wish'*, spun the wheel, missing a telegraph pole by a fraction of an inch, before swinging the back end of the vehicle round in some incredibly extravagant handbrake turn, bringing the lend-lease vehicle to rest, sideways on to, and no further than, two foot from a solid stone wall that could have crushed the vehicle and occupants without any difficulty.

Revving the engine to emphasise his point, the driver, a Polish NCO, spoke excitedly and encouraged his passengers to dismount.

The three men, gingerly handling boxes of equipment, stepped down unsteadily, clearly victims of an epic and exciting journey.

No sooner had the last box cleared the back seat than the jeep was rammed into gear and leapt away, accelerating between two of Field's jeeps when such a manoeuvre seemed impossible.

The British personnel, they were clearly British to Crisp's mind, stood in silence, looking at the flying mud as their tormentor disappeared from sight.

The Paratrooper Colonel moved forward to find out what was going on.

The officer looked at him, and looked again in the direction of the disappeared jeep, speaking slowly and with control, his drained white face betraying everything about the journey he and his men had just experienced.

Seemingly unaware of Crisp's rank, solely his presence, the Lieutenant Commander offered up an opinion, accompanying it with a gesture at the departing lunatic.

"You know... after that... I must confess... I'm surprised any of the buggers make it to adulthood at all. Totally bonkers. Never been so frightened in my... good grief... my apologies, Sir."

The naval officer came to attention and peeled off a smart naval salute, which Crisp, his face wearing an expression of solid amusement, acknowledged in total silence.

"Bathwick, Lieutenant Commander, His Majesty's Royal Navy, seconded from HMS Nelson for shore duties, Sir."

"Lieutenant Commander."

"Sir, if you can show me where my men and I can best set up, we'll get ready to help out if the enemy get restless."

He snapped at the rating who nearly dropped one of the boxes.

"Harrington! Steady, Killick. It survived that nightmare. Don't bugger it up now."

"Aye aye, Sir."

"Sorry about that. Sensitive stuff, our equipment, Sir."

"Stuff?"

"Radio equipment, Sir. We'd be bugger all use to you without it, now wouldn't we?"

Crisp felt he was being stupid, but he really had no idea what the clearly crazed Englishman was on about.

"Lieutenant Commander Bathwick. I've no knowledge of your attachment here, or of what you can do for me."

The naval officer smiled knowingly.

"Another balls up. Oh well. Colonel, Sir, I can bring down some fire from our vessels at sea to support your defence here. I'll need to see your maps, tie in with your own radio frequencies, et cetera, et cetera, and," he looked at his watch, "If all goes tickety-boo, I'll have everything online for you within twenty minutes or so."

'Tickety-boo? Are you goddamn kidding me or what?'

"What sort of support you got for me, Lieutenant Commander?"

"Well, Sir, I'm from the Nelson. She's a battleship. That's nine sixteen-inch guns just for starters, and I've got a link to our Fleet Air Arm boys as well," he spared a look for his hapless rating, "Provided that Harrington hasn't buggered it up with his antics."

'Sixteen inch guns. Oh my God.'

Crisp felt like all his Christmases had come at once.

Fig# 169 - Wollin - Rienforced Allied Forces.

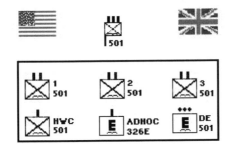

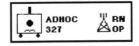

"Lieutenant Commander, I've a piece of high ground that'll suit you just dandy. First Sergeant!"

Hawkes had moved away when the Polish jeep had first approached, and now moved back to his Colonel at the double.

"First Sergeant. Scare up a squad of your boys and help the Lieutenant Commander and his men set up on Point Curahee a-sap."

"Yes, Sir."

Hawkes disappeared in search of hapless victims to help in fulfilling the order.

"You're very welcome, Lieutenant Commander. I'll come up and see you when you're all settled in. Meantime, Captain Desandé there," he pointed at the 2nd Battalion CP, "Will supply you with all unit call-signs and, I daresay, a decent cup of coffee. Ask him to arrange a field telephone for your position. I'll sort a small security section from my headquarters troops. They'll be with you directly. Happy with that, Lieutenant Commander?"

"Absolutely, Sir. Thank you."

"What's your call sign, so I can let my boys know?"

"Hardy-four, Sir."

"Right then, let's shake things up. Uncle Joe's likely to come calling real soon, and I daresay he won't be making the same mistakes again."

Crisp was correct on both counts.

1348 hrs, Tuesday 26th March 1946, HQ of 63rd NKVD Rifle Division, the woods west of Neu Kodram, Pomerania.

At any time, the unexpected arrival of two senior officers in a battle headquarters is not a cause for celebration.

For Bestov, the commander of the 63rd, it was almost the straw that broke the camel's back, as he was totally out of his depth.

The senior of the two newcomers posed a direct question.

Bestov's answer was simply put.

"We're just about to attack again, Comrade Leytenant General."

"Cancel the order to attack immediately, Comrade Polkovnik."

"But, Comrad..."

"Cancel it immediately. All you're doing is throwing away lives in stupid unsupported frontal attacks. Cancel it and we'll do it right."

"But you're Army. My unit is under direct NKVD control. We're not Army assigned, Sir."

"Consider yourself under Army command as of this moment, Comrade Polkovnik."

"No, I will not, Comrade General. You've no authority here and I'll report this unwarranted interference with internal security matters immediately."

Bestov picked up the telephone and sought a connection with the head of NKVD forces in Poland.

Despite the fact that both Generals had their own entourage, neither was shy of undertaking the dirty work themselves.

By unspoken agreement, they moved forward, unbuckling their holsters.

Bestov was still waiting for his connection when the muzzle of a Nagant revolver gained his full attention.

"By the orders of Marshal Bagramyan, commander of 1st Baltic Front, and Marshal Vassilevsky, Commander of the Red Banner Forces of Soviet Europe, I, Leytenant General Aleksandr Kudryashev, am appointed to command the forces surrounding the enemy landing, to create order, using any and all land forces available, and suborning all available men and equipment for the purpose of repelling the invader."

Colonel Bestov stood, eyes wide open, holding a silent handset.

To emphasise his point, Kudryashev placed his thumb on the hammer and pulled back, the click of the hammerlock sounding like a clap of thunder in a totally quiet room.

"To create order... using all land forces available... suborning ALL available men and equipment... which includes you and your men, Comrade Polkovnik."

Bestov's mouth hung open as his mind tried to cope with the enormity of what was happening to him. Suddenly, a thought occurred and threw him a lifeline.

"But... but... but... you have no authority... let me see your authority!"

Kudryashev shrugged but kept the revolver level and steady as a rock.

"The paperwork will come later, Comrade Polkovnik. Now, I've no time for this. Accept my authority or accept arrest. Which will it be?"

"But you have no..."

"Mayor!"

Kudryashev, like many senior officers, had his own personal bodyguard, the Major commanding the small detachment stepped forward, his mere bulk enough to shut Bestov up in an instant.

The PPSh looked like a children's toy in his huge hands, but still had the required effect on those present.

Under the Major's orders, the stunned NKVD officer was bundled away at great speed.

Rybko took the opportunity to theatrically replace his revolver, noisily slapping the flap of his holster shut.

"Anyone else wish to dispute the Leytenant General's right of command?"

There were no takers.

Kudryashev and Rybko, the CoS's of 4th Shock Army and 6th Guards Army respectively, had been attending a pre-attack staff conference at Swinemünde, something that had been cut short by the Allies' own efforts.

Instead of returning westwards to resume their own positions, the two had been headed off by Bagramyan and given the job of sealing up the enemy incursion, before destroying it, although it was more likely that they would both be relieved before then.

But for now, the two had a job to do, and coordinating the efforts of the forces to the west and south of the pocket was their first task.

Whilst by no means ideally situated to control the defence, being at the top end of a long curved defensive line, early arrival and intervention had been thought more crucial to a successful prosecution of the Allied landing.

Complete with a party of signallers, until recently happily languishing in a small training facility nearby, and now, less happily, swept up as Kudryashev's headquarters and communications unit, the Lieutenant General and his new NKVD staff officers went to work. The priority was to contact the units under his command, establishing unit strengths, and acquiring as much information as possible.

Whilst that went on, Rybko planned an attack with the hastily designated Baltic Coastal Army.

2055 hrs, Tuesday 26th March 1946, Second Battalion front, near Grosse Mokratz, Pomerania.

Galkin was doing the rounds, at Crisp's behest, dropping in on frontline units, just to get a feel of the men and their situation.

He had found Hawkes with an inevitable 'liberated substance' on hand, and enjoyed a nip of something warming as the two stared out into the darkness that was No Man's Land.

The wind shifted and brought with something vaguely familiar but, as yet, unidentifiable.

"What's that, First Sergeant?"

The sound was indistinct, but stirred pleasant memories, although there was not enough of it delivered by the stiffening breeze, at least not yet enough to have a moment of full recognition.

"Tell you something for sure, Major. Whatever it is, it ain't good. Get the boys shaken up?"

"Quietly... I'll get on the horn and spread the word."

Major Galkin was in the platoon command post within seconds, and on the field telephone to Second Battalion HQ equally quickly.

"Captain Desandé please, Major Galkin here."

"Lou? Con... there's something happening out in front of your positions. Noise of some sort, Whatever it is, it ain't good news, so I've woken up the frontline. Spread the word, Lou. Pass the stand-to up the line... let the Colonel know I'll be staying here for the while."

As Desandé asked a few pertinent questions, Galkin looked at his watch.

'Just coming up to nine. On the hour... betcha.'

"Yep, Lou... Yep... nope... I'm not taking command... if you need me just holler, but this is your battalion... 'ppreciate that. Lou... yep, you too."

At nine precisely, the culmination of Kudryashev's and Rybko's efforts visited itself upon the troopers of the 101st.

"URRAH!"

"URRAH!"

"URRAH!"

"Here they come!"

A young airborne Sergeant yelled what was probably the most unnecessary warning in the history of warfare.

Rybko had been cunning, for those shouting did not advance, but stayed hidden in cover, solely bringing the defenders up from their holes, ready to repulse the renewed infantry attack.

At two minutes past the hour, Soviet artillery and mortars commenced a barrage that hammered First Battalion's entire position but, for some reason, visited itself selectively on Second Battalion.

Few in Second Battalion noticed, but those that did welcomed the fact that they were spared the deluge, whilst units either side took the full weight of the barrage.

Rybko's plan had been to bring the defenders to readiness and then hit them with artillery, and it reaped rewards, as numerous paratroopers were ravaged by high explosives and shrapnel, their screams adding to the terror of a night that was frequently rent by flashes, and that promised death in many forms.

568

The 'urrahs' continued, although less distinct in the deafening cacophony of repeated explosions.

The explosions also masked the approach of a major asset in Rybko's planning.

He had cut his cloth according to his means, and the NKVD BEPO Nr 319 'Alexsandr Shelepin' had a vital part to play in the destruction of the Capitalist forces to his front.

It was also the reason that parts of Second Battalion, especially those near the railway tracks, had avoided the deluge of shells.

The 'Alexsandr Shelepin' moved forward, and the sound that had been indistinct to Hawkes and Galkin now became recognisable and, in the same moment, the reason for the space in the enemy barrage was clarified and became the shouted word.

"Train! It's a train! They're gonna ride straight through!"

Which was precisely the plan.

Fig# 170 - Soviet Forces surrounding Wollin.

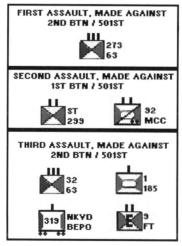

SOVIET FORCES - WOLLIN
26TH MARCH 1946

"Flares!"

A few parachute flares added their steady light to that of the numerous explosions, and the airborne defenders took their first look at a Soviet armoured train.

Allied intelligence had listed such a vehicle as immobilised at Swinemünde. That had been true, but superhuman efforts had removed the destroyed carriages and repaired the track, allowing the NKVD train to form a pivotal part of the attack.

Whilst lacking some of its firepower, the train still possessed enough clout to make a huge difference in the battle ahead, especially if it could get through the paratroopers' defensive line, and deliver its two T50 tanks and eight dismountable SMG squads to create more confusion in the Allied rear.

If the Second Battalion let it through...

Or, more factually, if Second Battalion could stop it.

Fig# 171 - Wollin - Soviet Third Attack.

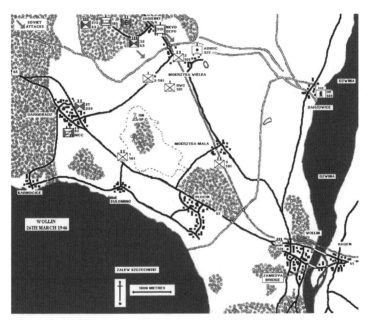

"Bazookas, forward! Stop the fucker before the hut!"

A small platelayer's hut marked the point where the Second Battalion's line crossed the rail line near a small T-junction in the dirt track that led to Jagienki.

Sat back from the front, the AT squad had not received any incoming fire, concealed, as they were, adjacent to the rail line that Soviet artillery and mortar fire was studiously avoiding.

However, the area was being heavily swept by large calibre bullets from covering 12.7mm weapons, and the leading flat car contained a quad Maxim that added to the lethal storm.

The leading bazooka man fell the second he rose, himself and his metal tube holed and out of action, the loader dropping to the ground before he shared the same fate. The second team decided to move their position and crawled across the earth, up to the cess adjacent to the single track.

Their movement was spotted by one of the men manning the quad maxim on the flatbed, and the weapon was redirected effectively.

Both teams were out of action and the slow-moving train was now less than two hundred yards from the hut.

Captain Pollo, his charges set mainly around the road junction, looked on helplessly, his own bazooka team elsewhere on the battlefield.

Montgomery Hawkes, from his own position, determined to grab the serviceable bazooka, and prepped the men around him.

He pushed upwards and out of the small crater and was immediately spun round as two heavy calibre rounds struck him.

The NCO fell on top of the two men following him, the three inextricably entwined rolled to the bottom of the hole, cursing and shouting.

Hawkes steeled himself, expecting death, before realising that, apart from something digging into his thigh, he felt intact.

He laughed, knowing he had been lucky beyond words.

His Thompson was shattered, a round having struck it in the cocking chamber and expending itself without finding his flesh. He cut his finger on the sharp metal as he examined the terminal damage to his pride and joy.

The other strike had hit his left heel and ripped off the entire sole of his jump boot, revealing evidence of a distinctly non-regulation sock.

The 'something' digging in his thigh squealed in protest at the weight of the NCO pushing his face into the soil. Hawkes' pain was caused by the back edge of the trooper's helmet.

The three sorted themselves out, the two giving their NCO looks containing equal amounts of annoyance and incredulity.

"Thanks for the soft landing, guys."

Incredulity moved over to allow a little more room for annoyance.

Hawkes shrugged.

"Sorry... right, let's do it."

He stuck his head over the edge of the crater and saw the train almost on top of his position.

"Shit! No time. Forget it. Grenades out, boys... get 'em in the front cart or we're fucked!"

The three paratroopers primed and took a swift look at their target, immediately launching their deadly charges.

Two missed, one landed dead on target.

In the wagon, the AA gun's NCO commander sacrificed his life by falling on the grenade.

One of the troopers with Hawkes risked a look before the First Sergeant could pull him down.

Bullets emerged from the semi-darkness and removed the top of the man's head, completely and messily, splattering blood and brain matter over the two others.

Hawkes swapped his wrecked Thompson for an M-1 carbine, suppressing his disgust at having to go into battle with the underpowered weapon.

The train was level now, and the AA crew, having seen where the grenades came from, returned the favour, dropping two into the shell hole and on top of the pair of Americans.

"OUT!"

Hawkes, battle-hardened, and with the reactions of a viper, was up and out before the first fuse did its job.

The second trooper, a recent replacement, was caught in the blast and thrown out of the hole.

Stunned, but somehow unwounded, he rose groggily to his knees. A sub-machine gun spat bullets from a shuttered window on the third coach, throwing the now-dead trooper to the ground. He rolled back into the shell hole with all the grace of a rag doll.

Hawkes suddenly found himself exposed and threw himself back into the shell hole on top of the two lifeless bodies.

A sharp crack marked the commitment of Master Sergeant Baldwin and his special AT squad, a heavy PTRD bullet slamming into one of the carriages.

More AT bullets struck, as the rest of the ad hoc unit opened up.

It was difficult to miss the armoured train, and most bullets seemed to penetrate, although none seemed to have any effect.

That was not a view held by those on the receiving end. Inside the different armoured carriages, the heavy bullets did horrible work amongst gun crews and assault personnel, but 'Alexsandr Shelepin' kept coming, and, as the train moved forward, more and more of her weapons were unmasked, bringing greater firepower to bear on either side.

The second armoured carriage mounted an old 76.2mm L/11 T-34 turret, a weapon long replaced in the production halls, but one still good enough to out deal death and destruction in a battle with lightly armed paratroopers.

Baldwin, squinting through the returned darkness, suddenly had his world illuminated, as the T-34 turret sent an HE shell in his direction.

Whilst it missed, it increased the urgency amongst his small command, as earth and stones fell upon them like rain.

Baldwin urgently redirected his gunners.

"Nail that goddamned tank wagon! Hit the wagon, not the turret!"

The six AT rifles were all brought to bear on the wagon and the heavy bullets bit home, converting the insides into a charnel house.

However, the 76.2mm gun refused to stay silent, and coughed another deadly shell in their direction, blotting out two rifles and killing four men in the blink of an eye.

"URRAH!"

"URRAH!"

As planned, once the front line positions were under flanking fire, the 32nd NKVD Regiment launched a frontal assault, supported by a dozen tanks from the 185th Tank Regiment, T-34m43s, sporting the F/34 version of the 76.2mm gun.

In battle, it is often the case that many things happen all at once, and a decisive moment comes and goes without the knowledge of the participants.

Outside Wollin, 2111 hrs on 26th March 1946 was such a moment.

Crisp arrived with his handful of men from Third Battalion, having intuitively understood that everything else was a diversion, and that the attack on Second Battalion was the real deal.

He had also ordered most of Third Battalion to move forwards and form another line, should Second fail to hold.

Desandé had ordered his men to hold the line, whilst he led a small group to try and wreck the tracks ahead of the armoured train.

573

Hawkes decided to stay put, and policed up a dead man's Garand.

Field committed two of his RCL jeeps to stop the train.

But perhaps the most spectacular event was orchestrated by Bathwick.

By the time that he had established contact with HMS Nelson and her cohorts, the armoured train was too close.

Now, another target presented itself, and he made the necessary adjustments.

Whilst he had given the order prior to 2109, the effect of his instructions was delayed until, across the battlefield, second hands swept past 2110...

... by which time, Master Sergeant Baldwin was dead, blown apart by a 76.2mm shell...

... and Captain Desandé was rolling in the dirt, his insides spilling out around him, his stomach riven by a burst of MG fire...

... and Colonel Crisp was clearing the blood from his eyes, the deep wound under his eyebrow caused by a piece of bone from one of the troopers near him. The unfortunate 3rd Battalion man had been hit multiple times, causing his left arm to disintegrate, deluging his companions with fleshy, boney, bloody detritus...

... and First Sergeant Hawkes was scrabbling for more Garand rounds, as Soviet assault troops spilled from the leading crew wagon...

... and Major Field was whooping with joy as his RCLs ripped the leading AA carriage into pieces and caused the front T-34 wagon to come apart as it's ammunition exploded...

... and Captain Pollo tumbled away from the demolition charge he had just set on the rails...

... and nine sixteen-inch shells flung by HMS Nelson arrived, followed by eight fifteen-inch monsters, contributed by HMS Warspite.

0211.

Those who saw their arrival would never be able to adequately describe what they witnessed.

The 32nd NKVD Regiment disappeared in the briefest of moments, the exploding shells providing sufficient illumination for observers to see men, whole and partial, thrown hundreds of feet , propelled at high speed into the air or sideways, reaping more death as bodies smashed into bodies.

The T-34s were wiped out, although only one took a direct strike, the blast waves sufficient to turn over all but one of the vehicles, killing or incapacitating their crews.

The rear AA carriage received the full blast of one of Warspite's shells.

Later, the crew were found in soft repose, but very dead, much the same as those who manned the rearmost tank wagon, whose KV-1 turret remained silent for the rest of the battle.

Warspite was capable of putting out two rounds a minute; Nelson, two every three minutes.

Warspite's secpnd salvo ploughed the same turf as before, killing many of the dazed survivors, but mainly visiting more horrendous injuries upon the fallen.

Nelson's next salvo was misdirected, but landed to the advantage of the airborne troopers, dropping in the woods behind the smashed leading battalions, and finding the remnants of the 273rd NKVD Regiment, the entire 9th [Independent] Flamethrower Battalion and the rest of the T-34 company waiting to move up.

Backpack flamethrower tanks rose like flaming torches, further illuminating the stripped trees, sometimes just the fuel tank, but often complete with its unfortunate operator.

Bathwick was already on the radio, halting further fire from offshore, the task successfully completed in two awful minutes.

2113 hrs, Tuesday 26th March 1946, Second Battalion front, near Grosse Mokratz, Pomerania.

Whilst the battle was technically won, there was fighting left a'plenty, as the armoured train continued to lash out at the paratroopers, despite the fact that Nelson and Warspite had wrecked the track behind them, and Captain Pollo had done the same to the train's front.

More than a few troopers were caught out as they watched the naval display with incredulity, only to expose themselves to bullets from the 'Alexsandr Shelepin'.

Pollo and three of his men tumbled in beside Hawkes, their unexpected arrival nearly costing them their well-being.

The engineer officer checked his men, cursing that two had been felled on the run in, both of them the ones carrying the explosives with which he intended to attack the crew coach, whose metal-shuttered windows spouted bullets in all directions.

Underneath the wagon, survivors from some of the Soviet assault groups had gathered, glad of the top protection.

Pollo ordered covering fire, intending to try and retrieve one of the explosive bags.

He rose and immediately fell back coughing, a pair of SMG rounds smashing through his right lung in an instant.

Hawkes directed one of the engineers to tend the wounded officer, and prepared the rest to cover him whilst he tried the same mission.

The largest of the engineers, an older man who should probably have been at home in front of his fire, shuffled the flamethrower off his back and laid a hand on Hawkes.

"My job, Sarge. No one's a-waiting for me back home, not since both ma boys went to God at Ie Shima."

The older man, showing remarkable agility, was up and out and had dropped beside the first engineer's corpse before any serious fire came his way.

"What's he getting?"

Hawkes popped up and placed two bullets in a crawling NKVD rail soldier, intent on getting closer.

"HE blocks. We still got some of the stuff we lifted from the Commies. Enough to fuck that piece of shit twice over."

The engineer rose and put some of his own bullets on target, knocking two men over as they scrabbled around under the rail cars.

Hawkes recharged his Garand and tried a difficult shot, watching the bullet ping off the metal side next to a shutter.

The shutter opened carefully and Hawkes, exhaled.

The Garand cracked

'Ouch! Whatever that hit'll have a goddamned headache and a half.'

He hadn't needed the modest spray of blood to tell him that his bullet had found a mark.

An AT bullet chewed through the armour, as the last PTRD was brought into action.

Hawkes turned to the old engineer and shouted.

Rising up, the man was halfway through his second step when the world turned white.

Those in the shell hole, protected from the blast, were only stunned.

Other paratroopers nearby were killed and wounded as the canvas bag was hit by bullets and the Soviet explosives surrendered to the laws of nature.

The older man simply disappeared.

Trying to clear his head, Hawkes suddenly found himself experiencing a phenomenon of the battlefield.

The Germans have a word for it; blutrausch, and it has a number of similar interpretations.

A rush of blood.

A lust for blood.

A trance-like state where the one who experiences it goes berserk, embarking, without fear or reason, on a journey of violence and murder until it passes.

Hawkes was that man.

He grabbed the flamethrower pack in his left hand and charged out of the hole.

Bullets split the air all around him, but the Soviets, particularly those under the wagons, were as disoriented and shaken up as Hawkes and his engineer buddies.

Firing the Garand one-handed, the 101st NCO put down three men hard. The charger pinged from the empty rifle, but Hawkes continued onwards.

A panicky NKVD trooper rose up, his hand trembling so much that he couldn't fit the new magazine into his PPSh.

Hawkes rammed the Garand barrel into the petrified man's face, sending him reeling away and squealing at the extreme pain of his wound.

Using a strength lent to him by the 'Blutrausch', Hawkes swung the cylinder in his left hand, staving in the head of an NKVD NCO who was calling on his men to target the devil in their midst.

The webbing caught up in the insensible man's arms as he collapsed.

Hawkes let it go and swapped the Garand around, holding the barrel end, and swinging the rifle like a club.

Another victim fell, head smashed through to the cortex, as the heavy butt cracked the woman's skull like papier-mâché.

Not a sound escaped Hawkes' lips; neither scream, nor grunt, nor yell.

The group under the wagon melted away, turning to run back down the track, leaving two shocked soldiers to hold up their hands in surrender.

As their comrades were cut down by other paratroopers, the two fell victim to Hawkes' lack of reason and temporary suspension of reality.

Both died under the whirling rifle butt, during which frenzied attacks the wood was splintered and damaged beyond recognition, the last two blows inflicting hideous open wounds, as the sharp splintered edges wrought destruction on the man's face.

With no enemy to hand, Hawkes went in search of more. Elsewhere, the train was being knocked apart, as RCLs and bazookas did steady work.

The crew coach, around which Hawkes had done his awful work, still resisted, and the airborne NCO immediately set about dealing with it.

Having prepared his equipment, he scaled the side, clinging on to the metal rungs that normally permitted entry to the main door.

He waited patiently. An occasional bullet pinged off the armour, fired from the enemy's positions by one of the few still mentally capable of that simplest of military tasks.

Those who spoke of what they witnessed post-battle, talked of a blood-soaked Hawkes, his hair cut in the Huron style, making him appear like a bloodthirsty savage of old, clinging to the side of the armoured train, illuminated by the fires and explosions of the battlefield.

The later descriptions of their NCO normally included words like 'mad, 'lunatic, or the universally popular 'the devil.'

The metal shutter on which Hawkes concentrated, started to shift upwards, and he readied himself.

Unknown to Hawkes, the car's officer intended to have a look before surrendering his command.

The shutter moved open just enough and Hawkes lunged.

Everyone inside the armoured wagon knew exactly what it was, and the screams started long before Hawkes pressed the trigger.

In his efforts, the NCO lost his grip and fell from the armoured train.

No matter, one burst, in that confined area, was enough.

The flamethrower hung from the opening by its barrel, now bent beyond use by the weight of Hawkes as he fell. The tank dangled above Hawkes as he shook off the latest indignity of his fall.

Inside, the twenty men and two women were noisily incinerated.

Paratroopers swept forward, and the wounded of both sides were recovered and taken to be either tended or eased into the next life.

No-one went anywhere near Hawkes, who sat on a discarded ammo box, chain smoking whatever he could find, Russian or American, staring at something a thousand miles away

Anyone who came within twenty yards felt threatened, albeit silently.

Moving around the battlefield, Colonel Marion J. Crisp was apprised of Hawkes' state, and immediately moved to help resolve the situation.

Grabbing another box, the paratrooper Colonel took a seat and lit his own cigarette in silence.

Hawkes had no idea he was even there.

This was not the first time that Crisp had seen such an event; he understood the risks of touching the NCO, but did it anyway.

Hawkes struck his hand away.

"Steady, Monty. It's me... you know me... c'mon Monty... take my hand now."

Hawkes looked vacantly at his Colonel.

"Hi Monty. Now then... take my hand 'kay, eh?"

Hawkes stared at Crisp's hand, covered with the Colonel's own blood, then his own hand, cut, bloodied and bruised, almost as if reacquainting himself with a long lost friend.

After some moments, he extended it.

The two hands met and Crisp took a firm but gentle hold.

"I think we might go now, Monty... don't you?"

"Can't."

"You can't? Why can't you come with me, Monty?"

"Haven't been relieved. Must be relieved."

Crisp could only smile.

"First Sergeant Hawkes."

The eyes that looked at Crisp were changing, reflecting the ongoing departure of whatever it was that had transformed the NCO into a berserker.

"Colonel, Sir?"

"First Sergeant Hawkes, you are relieved."

"Did we hold 'em, Colonel?"

Crips nodded, trying not to think of the cost of victory, for, despite everything, that was what it was.

"You held them, First Sergeant."

Hawkes' eyes softened, and Crisp seized the moment.

"I think we should go now, Monty. Stand up."

Still holding hands, the two came to their feet and officer helped NCO from the field.

As soon as was practicable, Crisp made time to visit the position of the Naval support team, for no other reason than to congratulate them on a job well done.

As he neared their position, he became aware of bodies, lots of bodies, mainly clad in the uniform of the enemy, but occasionally those of men from his own command. He even recognised some dead troopers from regimental headquarters, sent up to ride shotgun over the Naval officer and his radio operators.

"Damn."

His voice drew a challenge.

"H-Halt! Who goes th-there?"

He recognised the voice immediately.

"Colonel Marion J Crisp approaching, Lieutenant Commander."

"You m-may approach, C-Colonel."

Bathwick's Lanchester sub-machine gun was a large piece to drag into the field, but it seemed to have proved effective, given the dead enemy surrounding the Naval officer's position.

The Killick, Harrington, was fiddling with his radio, teasing the top performance from it. The other rating was laid out reverently, alongside two of Crisp's men, seemingly fast asleep, but decidedly dead.

Bathwick's hands were shaking like a man with the DTs, the shock debilitating him as sure as any bullet.

There was little purpose to deep conversation whilst the man was so wiped out by his experiences, so Crisp went for easier fare.

"One day, Lieutenant Commander, you must tell me what happened here. I'll bet it's one hell of a story."

Without trying, the Airborne Colonel had managed to see over forty enemy bodies within fifty yards of the positions the Naval OP and his men had held.

A cloud of cigarette smoke from one pile of earth and wood indicated that some of his men were still alive, and he rose to make his way over, maintaining the crouch that veterans use to move around with in the presence of the enemy.

"Thank you, Lieutenant Commander. You made all the difference."

"T-Thank you, Colonel."

As Crisp engaged the survivors of his own Headquarters covering group, the sound of approaching engines drew cries of alarm from along the 501st's lines.

"Stand to!

"Here they come again!"

But the sound grew behind them and, accompanied by great relief, units of the 1st Free Polish Armoured Division arrived.

The same was repeated at other positions on the paratroopers' front, as the well-equipped units of Polish X Corps caught up with the demanding timetable.

101st US Airborne Division had held until relieved.

The 501st suffered 35% casualties during the first day of the landings, the majority of which came from the battered First and Second Battalions. Two hundred and thirteen of their casualties were dead, the same as the regiment lost in the duration of its commitment to the D-Day landings.

It was subsequently estimated that the naval shells from Warspite and Nelson, claimed a minimum of six hundred and fifty Soviet lives in less than two minutes.

But for the naval support, the Soviet night attack would probably have achieved its objectives.

As it was, Kudryashev's and Rybko's initial plans came to nothing.

They would do much better next time.

0304 hrs, Friday, 29th March 1946, shoreline of the Vilm-See, Pomerania.

The hole was constantly filling up with water, the marshy terrain unsuitable for foxholes, but occupying one was far better than being exposed if the Russians lobbed mortar shells in their direction, so the picquet grinned and bore the wetness with stoicism.

A pair of sentries from the Fallschirmbatallion Perlmann, 7th FJR/2nd Fallschirmjager Division, posted to watch for any activity in the lake, sat closely observing the far bank, conscious that something was occurring.

The senior man wasted no time in calling the events in, and soon the readiness squad was deployed either side of them, commanded by an Oberfeldwebel, and with Major Kurt Schuster in tow.

A plume of orange flame leapt into the night sky across the dark waters of the Vilm-See, the largest lake in Pomerania, illuminating furious activity, easily observed despite the thousand metres that separated the two forces.

The sound of an explosion quickly followed, causing many of the Fallschirmjager to tighten their grips on their weapons, whilst understanding that whatever it was, it wasn't directed at them.

581

It was one of the original pair that hissed a warning, focussing the watchers on a new threat, approaching from the island side.

"Hold your fire, menschen," hissed Schuster, immediately moving across the rear of the position to get closer to whatever it was...

"It's a boat, Herr Maior... there... low in the water..."

The sentry held out his arm, pointing down the line of sight.

Snatching up his binoculars, Schuster strained his eyes, trying to work out what was the source of the growing engine noise.

'What the hell?'

Shouting.

"Can you hear that?"

"Yep, Herr Maior. Don't know what he's saying though."

"Weapons ready!"

The paratroopers settled themselves, waiting for the fire order.

Shouting.

"If they're trying to make a sneak attack, then someone should tell them how to do it!"

No-one even sniggered, as minds concentrated on getting the first shot just right.

Shouting.

'What?... what the he...'

"Hold your fire! Hold your fire!"

The tension left many a trigger finger, although more than one veteran looked at officer wondering why.

Shouting... in some unknown tongue... and in German.

"Watch them closely, menschen."

Schuster moved off to one side and flicked his torch, sending three swift bursts of light in the direction of the approaching 'boat'.

"Come this way, whoever you are. I warn you, no tricks."

The schwimmwagen, Schuster recognised it as it reached the shoreline, pushed itself up and out of the water, moving forward slowly until the driver found a place that obscured him and his vehicle from the sight of the Soviets they had left behind.

The occupants were wise enough to stay silent, surrounded as they now were by tough-looking paratroopers.

"You get one chance at this, so make it good."

Even as he spoke, Schuster noted the familiar SS camouflage and what looked like a Polish General's uniform.

582

"Herr Maior, we're all that's left of Battalion Storch, Skorzeny's special raiding group."

"Your ID, Feldwebel."

Bancke collected up the necessary from the four silent men with him, and passed it over to Schuster.

The Polish ID card drew closest examination.

"Skorzeny's raiders eh? Where is the mighty Colonel?"

"Somewhere back there, Herr Maior. Far as we now, he never escaped. We got away after being ambushed by the NKVD, first night of the attacks. Been running ever since."

He pointed across the water.

"And that? A diversion, I assume?"

"Yes, Herr Maior. Couple of our special friction charges were set and all we had to do was hide and wait for someone to set them off."

Handing back the ID cards, Schuster gestured to his men, signalling a relaxation in approach.

"Well, Feldwebel, you're all back in friendly lines now, so welcome to the fuck up that is liberated Poland."

The tension disappeared in an instant.

Beckoning to two troopers, Schuster assigned them to cling to the vehicle and direct the escapees to the aid post, where their obvious wounds and bruises could be attended to.

Taking his leave of the readiness squad's commander, he helped Bancke adjust the rear propeller and found a perch for himself.

1001 hrs, Monday, 1st April 1946, Treptow Palace, PLAG Headquarters, Treptow an der Rega, Pomerania.

Even without an overall organising force controlling Soviet resistance at the commencement of the landings, the Polish Liberation Army Group had been in trouble from the start.

The rapid organisation of Soviet resistance under Kudryashev and Rybko, combined with the excellent defence and subsequent counter-attack that Bagramyan mounted against the British Twenty-First Army Group, meant that it was still in trouble.

During the planning stage, even though the rewards for success were huge, many had considered the Pantomime operation to be too ambitious.

Some had even drawn parallels with Market-Garden, with its paradrops at considerable distance, and the narrowness of the route that the relief force would take.

The doubters were in the minority, and frayed nerves had been soothed by the fact that considerable friendly forces would already be on the ground, in the person of First Polish Army [AWP].

Perhaps, not surprisingly, the invasion element had gone extremely smoothly, the supporting divisions and subsequent logistical support delivered according to timetable, thanks to experience gained in Allied operations against the German enemy.

The Red Air Force had valiantly tried to interfere and, barring one bomb hit on the battleship HMS Warspite, had failed, and done so at further great cost to their dwindling number of men and machines.

Surviving submarines from the Baltic Fleet had also tried, with much more success, torpedoing three Allied warships.

The USS Reno, an Atlanta-class light cruiser specifically on station for her enhanced AA abilities and only recently returned to service following damage sustained against the Japanese in 1945, was again struck and damaged. Only a few minor injuries were sustained, all her guns remained in action throughout the day, and she remained on her battle station.

HMS Saintes, a hastily commissioned Battle class AA destroyer, lost her stern to twin torpedo strikes, and had to be towed back to Kiel. Thirty-seven of her crew were killed in the explosion and the subsequent desperate attempts at damage control.

The AA ship, KMS Thetis, a former Norwegian pre-dreadnought battleship, converted post-1940 Norwegian invasion and taken into German service, succumbed to two torpedoes and settled upright in shallow water, some two hundred yards off Berg Dievenow.

She continued to fire throughout the attack, and for days to come, despite the loss of twenty-seven of her crew.

None of the attacking submarines returned to their home ports, as American, British and German sub-hunter groups proved extremely effective, sending eight to the bottom of the Baltic in as many hours.

One German destroyer, KMS Karl Galster, brought about her own problems by enthusiastically following up a depth charge attack from the Dutch HNLMS Van Galen.

Once the Soviet submarine had been sunk, the Van Galen took the stricken Karl Galster in tow, the blast of the Dutch depth charges under her stern having blown numerous prop seals as well as wrecking the shaft mountings and bending the shafts themselves.

In spite of these relatively minor issues, the Allied fleet poured men and equipment ashore, plus much needed munitions, stocks captured from the Soviets destined for the Poles, whose own supplies had been eroded by demands from the Western Front.

The Polish Liberation Army Group comprised two Armies, the First [AWP] and Tenth.

The former was comprised of the original Polish forces in country and was now stable. Within First Army [AWP], there had been many Soviet officers and men, and the vast majority were handled with care and disarmed without violence, out of deference to comrades who had fought side by side against the German. Although many Russians had already been sent westward to other units to replace battle losses, non-Polish soldiers still accounted for nearly 10% of the strength of First Army [AWP], creating a logistical issue as prisoners by their numbers alone.

Despite the warnings from the intelligence services, some NKVD units had still been unprepared, and many of their soldiers were caught napping by Polish soldiers intent on carving out their country's freedom.

The NKVD divisions that had been placed strategically around Pomerania had been emasculated by silent attacks, the commanders either captured or killed, depending on how much resistance they chose to display. There was no love lost between Pole and NKVD soldier, something that manifested itself clearly, as the slightest hint of dissent or failure to lay down weapons was met with brute force rapidly applied.

140th and 269th NKVD Divisions were dismantled within the first hour, their weapons and equipment going into Polish stocks. More than one group of prisoners was mercilessly chopped down in retribution for NKVD atrocities, past and present.

64th NKVD Division managed to escape with three of its rifle and border regiments intact, the hapless 98th NKVD Border Regiment finding little forgiveness at the hands of their captors.

Thousands of Soviet prisoners filled the combat area, something that was less than desirable for all concerned.

However, plans had been made to evacuate these men in the vessels that delivered supplies, lessening the demands on the logistical chain.

The Second Polish Army [AWP] had been withdrawn under the direct orders of the GKO. It was heavily policed by NKVD units, and most units were either disarmed or, as was the case with 5th Polish Infantry Division [AWP], massacred piecemeal as the various units arrived at pre-ordained rendezvous points, staffed by security troops with a very specific brief.

At first, there had been issues with loyalty, as confused soldiers found it hard to understand who was who, and officers with leanings towards the Soviet regime held sway in most areas of Polish Second Army.

Matters were quickly sorted out, but not without some tragedies, and most of the Polish Second Army moved eastwards and away from the fighting, finding employment in the Ukraine, where civil disorder was rapidly turning into open civil warfare.

Only the 5th Polish Heavy Tank Regiment, 4th Polish Engineer Brigade, and 9th Polish Infantry Division defected en masse to the newly formed Polish Liberation Army Group, where there was understandable scepticism about their loyalty.

One issue that arose was unit numbering, as there were divisions that shared the same title allocated to different corps, hence the labelling AK with every ex-Soviet unit.

Soviet initial efforts had been aimed at destroying the bridgehead but quickly became a task of containment, as lack of resources swiftly became an issue.

The impending presence of the British Twenty-First Army Group caused most of the spare major units that could have been used for counter-attacks to be hived off for defence on the main front, leaving barely sufficient units in place to hold the landing in check.

Soviet command quickly started to pull in more resources, hampered, as ever, by the enemy's command of the air.

From the start, the Allied plan had been obvious.

1-Strike eastwards along the Baltic coast with 21st Army Group.

2-Drop paratroops to secure the bridges and crossing points to allow the new forces to move westwards from the bridgehead.

3-Connect the two, thus posing an unendurable threat to the flank of the entire European force.

4-Reinforce and support the existing Polish forces, creating a whole new and proficient manpower group to cause more problems for the Red Army.

Allied intelligence had failed to locate many of the dedicated assault formations assembled by 1st Baltic, and these had hammered into the British advance, halting it, moving it back, and then stabilising the front, ensuring that the bridgehead would not be relieved.

1st Guards Mechanised Rifle Division, under Deniken's command, had moved and found itself isolated at Naugard, which in itself, upset Allied plans for British XXXIII Corps to attack through Stettin.

The second incarnation of 6th Army was moved swiftly to ensure that any attempt to advance through Swinoujscie, most probably by Polish IX Corps, would die in its infancy.

And so it proved.

The Polish bridgehead became an attritional stalemate, with the occupants too weak to push out, and those surrounding it too weak to crush the resistance.

Bortnovski, low on options, ordered one last effort to get his formations moving, ordering the thorn in his side to be removed by force.

The Naugard attack plan would be completed, regardless of the cost.

The bulk of British 2nd Armoured Division was kept back to exploit the breech.

An assault force of the Azul Division, part of the Guards Battlegroup, the 5th Polish Heavy Tank Regiment [AK], and a German Fallschirmjager battle group were designated for the assault. They would be supported by every artillery and mortar weapon the Polish General could lay his hands on, topped off with air support from the carriers off shore.

Bortnovski completed the planning with a flourish, having added a few smaller specialist units to the assault on Naugard.

Standing erect, he issued his verbal order, confirming the attack.

"Gentlemen, the assault will be preceded by an intense bombardment, commencing at 1230. This will cease at 1300, to be followed by an air attack on the entire Soviet front line position."

The assembled officers knew this, but it was the Polish General's way.

"The assault force will then move in at speed, obliquely, striking at the north of Naugard, with the main force moving around to the south-west and pushing the Soviet forces away from the main route, occupying Wollchow, securing it, before striking into the enemy rear."

"Gentlemen, you have your orders. I wish you luck."

The Polish Lieutenant General threw up a magnificent salute and watched as his officer trooped from the room.

Władysław Bortnowski had been a prisoner of the Germans since commanding the Polish Pomorze Army during the 1939 invasion of his country. He had been liberated in 1945.

As a very senior Polish officer, well-known amongst his soldiery and civilian population alike, Bortnowski probably had no equal, and it was this public image and his obvious skill at arms that propelled him into the position of Commander, PLAG.

A reputation gained in different times against the German Army of 1938 had been tested against a wholly different foe in 1946, and opinions differed on how well the fifty-five year old General was standing the test of time.

1236 hrs, Monday, 1st April 1946, HQ, 7th Guards Tank Assault Brigade, Wollchow, Pomerania.

Yarishlov and Kriks shared a table, although not conventionally.

The former, having alerted his command to stand to, sought refuge under the large and robust piece of furniture to use the field telephone in safety, as the Allied artillery lashed down upon Soviet positions from Wollchow to Eberstein.

The latter was protecting two mugs of coffee, or coffee the way Kriks made it, with something extra that mustn't be contaminated by descending dust.

He could hear Deniken's voice quite clearly.

"No, Arkady, the 23rd report little activity, neither do the 333rd Regiment to our south-west. Seems this is all for us."

Yarishlov digested the information.

"So, what do you want me to do, as it seems likely we're going to get hit?"

"Stay put for now. My own tanks are covering here. Perhaps ready a company to send off immediately to support the defences here, if I scream for more. Meantime, keep your head down and stay safe. I'm sure the Capitalist bastards will give us something to think about soon."

"Just one company?"

"Two would be better, of course."

"It is done."

"If their ground attack... stupid... when their aircraft come, the AA commander has prepared that surprise we discussed. I think we may show them a thing or two, Arkady."

Both chuckled.

"I suspect you're correct, Vladimir."

The Allied ground attack aircraft had been ruling for too long, and today, when they came, they would face a challenge.

"Signing off now. Good luck, Comrade."

"And to you, Comrade."

Yarishlov took the coffee from Kriks, and the two sat in silence to consume the drink.

The tank Colonel spoke to his Senior NCO as he would speak to a friend.

"If someone walks in right now and finds us hiding under a table drinking coffee, we'll have to do some fast talking, Praporschik Kriks!"

An artillery burst gave the NCO a moment to respond.

"I don't envy you, Comrade Polkovnik. I am a lowly soldier, just following orders, whereas you're a Hero of the Soviet Union with a reputation to maintain. Best of luck with that."

He clinked jugs and downed the last of his brew.

"I should have you arrested for insubordination, Praporschik."

Kriks grinned.

"Oh, the stories I could tell. The Chekists would be delighted to confirm their veracity with you, Comrade Polkovnik."

Yarishlov spluttered in his mug.

"I'm away to man my vehicle whilst you organise my detention and interrogation."

With an exaggerated salute, Kriks quit the room, leaving the door wide open.

Yarishlov grinned like a Cheshire cat.

"Bastard NCOs."

He picked up the receiver to make another call, only to find it devoid of sound.

The artillery had cut the line.

With nothing else to do, Yarishlov ordered the line repaired, left the small headquarters, and made his way to his T-54 command tank.

1259 hrs, Monday, 1st April 1946, Naugard, Pomerania.

The previous battles in and around Naugard had been modest affairs, and few of the 7th Guards Tank Assault Brigade's tanks had been involved, the 1st's integral 121st Guards Tank Battalion having been sufficient to see off any enemy armour.

Yarishlov and Deniken had been particularly keen to keep the 7th Guards uncommitted and, more importantly, unappreciated for what it was.

589

Whilst the presence of the new tank was known, the numbers were probably not, and that was a factor in both Soviet Colonel's thinking.

Four had been totally lost, two to accidental internal fires, and one each to enemy ground action against tanks, and to air strike. Seventeen more were mechanically unsound and had been withdrawn to the workshop facility in the woods between Wollchow and Wismar, where the mechanics worked feverishly to get the valuable tanks back into the line.

Losses and breakdowns left the 7th with forty-three intact T-54 battle tanks.

Yarishlov's SPAT company had been sent to bolster Deniken's positions in Naugard, and three of the monster ISU-122's had already succumbed to enemy fire.

Fig# 172 - Naugard - Soviet defensive force.

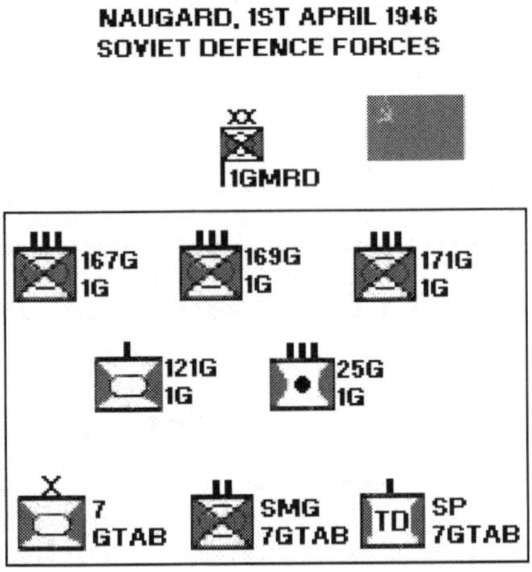

NAUGARD, 1ST APRIL 1946
SOVIET DEFENCE FORCES

The Allied artillery gently melted away to nothing, leaving a surreal quiet over the Red Army positions, occasionally interrupted by a secondary explosion or a scream of pain.

Two minutes later, Barracudas from 814 and 837 Squadrons FAA, configured as dive-bombers, arrived to do their part and swooped down from the sky, dropping their bombs on targets identified by the photo recon interpreters; a possible strongpoint here, a likely anti-tank position there.

Fortunately for them, the Soviet AA commander had configured his defence for the normal low-level runs of Typhoons and the like, but the Soviet flak still brought down one Barracuda II and sent a couple more home trailing smoke.

Whilst the Fleet Air Arm attack planes did their bit, top cover was provided by 802 Squadron FAA, their Seafire L/III's easily repulsing a sally by a handful of Yak-3's, losing only one Seafire downed to four Yaks confirmed.

Once the Barracudas had safely left the area, 802's commander responded to the pleas of his pilots and permitted a single sweep over the target.

As predicted by the Soviet AA commander, the Seafires commenced their run as had others before, sweeping in from west to east and using the road from Schwarzow to Naugard as a guide.

802's first combat loss to enemy aircraft was quickly followed by its first combat loss to ground fire.

The combination of 12.7mm, 25mm, and 37mm fire tore the Squadron Commander's aircraft apart around him, the Seafire splitting open and coming apart in dramatic fashion, leaving the Lieutenant Commander to ride the cockpit and engine into the woods that concealed Yarishlov's tankers.

The next two aircraft were smashed in short order, one flipping over and burying itself in the soft ground next to a road junction, the other pulling upwards in an attempt to evade the deadly fire as the cone of fire slowly enveloped the cockpit until only the wingtips and tail could be seen outside the flaming orange-yellow mass that was bringing a horrible death to the British pilot.

The next aircraft flipped away in a hard port turn, the damage easily discernible as pieces of the wing and control surfaces fell away in its slipstream.

Three more Seafires were knocked out of the air, none of the pilots having the remotest opportunity to escape before the expensive aircraft converted themselves to scrap as they drove hard into the ground.

The remaining Seafires aborted their attack and formed up around the damaged aircraft, determined not to lose another friend on a day when the war had become more than a game.

Offshore, the damaged aircraft waited whilst the remainder of 802 landed on their carrier, the Barracudas having already been recovered and been taken down into the hangar.

HMS Venerable, a Colossus class carrier, recovered her Seafires and then the flight operations officer set about bringing in the damaged bird.

No sooner had he lined up the damaged Seafire, than the weakened wing structure lost more integrity and the resultant displacement was sufficient to spin the aircraft into the water.

Most aircraft could float for enough time to allow the pilot to escape, but this aircraft was keen to rest on the bottom of the Baltic and speared under the water in the blink of an eye.

A wingtip appeared, as the buoyant wing struggled to bring the fighter back up, but it quickly disappeared, taking another of 802's pilots with it.

Back at Naugard, the AA's success was already forgotten as the British attack smashed into the Guards positions.

[HMS Venerable was sold to the Netherlands in 1948 and served as the HNLMS Karel Doorman. She was later sold to Argentina and renamed ARA Veinticinco de Mayo. She was scrapped in 2000.]

1331 hrs, Monday, 1st April 1946, HQ, 1st Guards Mechanised Rifle Division, Farbezin, Pomerania.

Deniken listened to Lisov summarising what was going on, or as best as the man could interpret from the reports of soldiers under pressure.

Fig# 173 - Naugard - Soviet defensive positions.

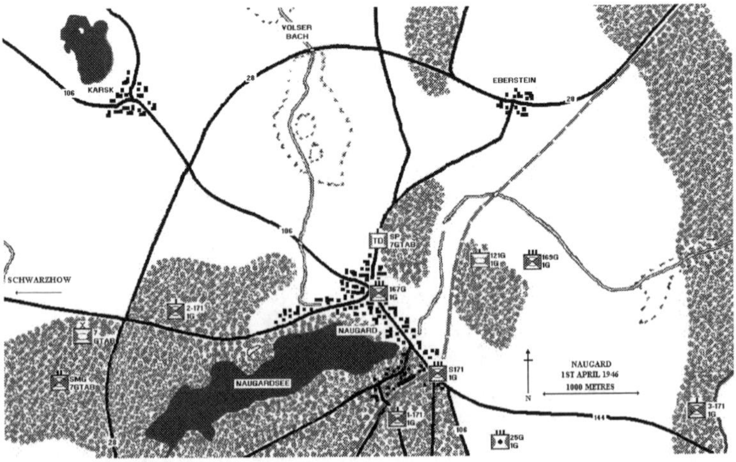

The major combat elements of 1st Guards, Yarishlov's Tank unit aside, were the 167th, 169th and 171st Guards Rifle Regiments, 25th Guards Artillery Regiment, and 121st Guards Tank Battalion, the latter a mixed bag of T-34s, but with Yarishlov's old T44/100 in the HQ unit.

The artillery were well set back, covering all areas.

The 167th and 169th Rifle Regiments were arranged numerically from west to east, with the 167th centred on Naugard itself. The 171st provided the main infantry reserve in Deniken's pocket, the headquarters units and First Battalion lying back from the frontline to the south of Naugard.

2nd/171st sat between Naugard and Yarishlov's tanks, whilst 3rd/171st was on the other side of the defences, in the woods north of Route 144.

Yarishlov's SPs covered the approach from Kartzig, the 121st, less a shock group of six tanks, set up ready should anything approach from Eberstein or Minten.

The fighting to date had claimed many lives and consumed ammunition at alarming rates, forcing Deniken to send roving units into the rear, seeking ammunition and supplies willingly given or, if kind words failed, to appropriate anything that was needed regardless.

The commander of 1st Guards Mechanised intended to keep his unit in the fight for as long as possible, and his orders to hold left no room for personal interpretation.

Now, his 2IC seemed to describe a full frontal assault by Allied forces, aimed directly at Naugard.

Tanks and infantry picked their way steadily forward, angling in towards the town.

Deniken felt confused.

"7th Tanks?"

"Comrade Polkovnik, the enemy attack is angled in as you see, more so than previously for certain. The flank seems a little exposed, an error that I haven't seen from these English before."

'Is it an error... or is it something else...'

Deniken put his thoughts into words and then started to work the problem.

"If it's a mistake, then 7th can move up to the edge of their woods and take them in the flank."

Lisov nodded, accepting the unspoken invitation to continue with the hypothesis.

"If it isn't a mistake, it might be an attempt to get us to push 7th up and expose it to some other sort of attack."

Deniken nodded.

"Air attack? Heavy artillery? Something else?" Lisov countered.

"They have no heavy artillery of note, or they would have used it by now. We're beyond their naval guns so, if it is such a manoeuvre, then it must be aircraft... or it's a big error... either way, you need to decide, Comrade Polkovnik."

Fig# 174 - Naugard - First phase of the Allied Attack.

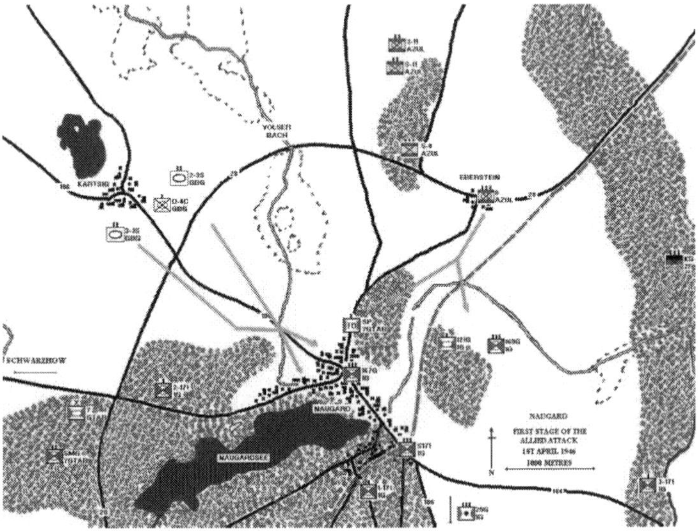

Time and battles wait for no man...

Deniken spoke quickly to the communications officer.

"Confirm with 7th Tanks that they have no direct threat, only the enemy moving across their front to Naugard.

The steady crack of 122mm guns reached their ears, as the ISUs started to engage.

Impatiently, Deniken waited, passing the time by playing with his lighter, his last cigarette consumed when he rose for breakfast.

Lisov leant forward and whispered in a runner's ear, sending the man on a mission of mercy.

"Comrade Polkovnik, 7th Guards report nothing directed at them. Only targets are enemy tanks and infantry moving eastwards towards Naugard."

594

That was the confirmation Deniken needed, and yet, he still hesitated.

'Why do I wait? They're there, ripe for the plucking...'

The runner returned with the opened packet of cigarettes he had found in Lisov's quarters, as directed.

Deniken smiled and scrabbled for a life-saving cigarette.

"Thank you, Comrade Yefreytor, thank you!"

The man stood back, happy to have been praised by his commander.

Deniken leant into Lisov's neck and whispered.

"Can I award a medal for providing me with nicotine?"

With a deadpan expression, Lisov delivered his considered opinion.

"If I write it up, you'll sign anything I put in front of you."

Deniken slapped his 2IC's shoulder, resuming the mental tussle with his tactical problem.

The field telephone announced itself, and an incoming message was taken and quickly passed on.

Lisov moved to the map.

"We have a problem here. Apparently, a Germanski paratrooper unit has pushed into our flank... here. A reinforced battalion is the best guess at the moment."

South-east of Eberstein lay some woods, and the enemy had used them to sneak the Paratroopers in close, a threat that was now moving south to turn the flank.

"They intend to pocket us up."

Lisov pondered the statement as, somewhere on the battlefield, artillery started to drop in increasing volumes.

"Possibly, Comrade Polkovnik, but where is the power here. None of our units report overwhelming force to their front. No-one is screaming for more men and vehicles. This Germanski unit is easily stopped, by committing our reserve immediately."

Deniken absorbed the words and processed the map information.

"Get the reserve battalion and the special tank group together and stop that Germanski force from manoeuvring... Tell them not get committed yet, just to stop the green bastards from moving around... keep the enemy north of the river if possible."

Lisov moved and got the orders passed with professional speed and efficiency.

"Comrade Polkovnik, we are delaying. The 7th's in an ideal position. If you order them to advance now then we have the British on a plate. Even if they are trying to encircle us, that part will come to nothing... end of problem."

Although the sound was no different to any other time the field telephone had rung, this time it somehow oozed urgency, and both Colonels instinctively sensed that the game was about to change.

Fig# 175 - Naugard - Allied Assault forces.

The signaller wrote out the message and passed it to the Communications Officer, who, in turn, passed it to Lisov.

"Govno!"

Deniken knew what it was before Lisov briefed him.

"That artillery? In front of Yarishlov's positions?"

"Yes, Comrade Polkovnik. Heavy calibre rounds from at least fifty guns firing in salvoes."

"And?"

"Enemy force of tanks and motorised infantry in sight, running from Kartzig area, straight at his positions. Looks like they intend to go between the lakes, Comrade Polkovnik."

Deniken remained silent for longer than anyone felt comfortable with, before pouncing on the Communications officer.

"Is the 7th still on the line?"

"Yes, and awaiting orders, Comrade Polkovnik." He moved across the intervening space like a sprinter, taking the handset from the signaller.

"Polkovnik Deniken speaking, who is this?"

"Praporschik Kriks, Comrade Polkovnik. Polkovnik Yarishlov is easing his units up to the wood line and has asked me to get your orders."

"Kriks, tell him that everything else is a feint, a device. Everything rests on his holding. The enemy intend to push us away from the main road. I believe they'll try and mount a full-scale attack down it once we've been pushed aside. We will not be pushed aside. Tell Arkady I'll send what extra I can find, but he must hold and ensure that nothing pushes him away from Route 28."

Kriks repeated the order as, across from Deniken, Lisov tried to understand how his commander had arrived at such a conclusion.

Discussion complete, Deniken moved back to the map.

"Right, Comrade. What can we send to prevent this fucking disaster from happening?"

"Are you sure, Comra..."

"Yes, Comrade Lisov, I'm sure. I'm staking my life on it."

Shells churned up the area where 7th Guards might have been, had they accepted the possibility of making the flank attack.

Six miles to the north, men sweated over the huge 7.2" Mk VI Howitzers, trying to maintain a round every three minutes and, beat it if possible.

Behind the slowly creeping barrage came the spearhead of the Allied attack, the 5th Polish Heavy Tank Regiment [AK] supported by two motorised battalions from the Azul Division's 11th Assault Infantry Regiment, the new designation of the 263rd Regiment from the German War.

The 8th Assault Infantry Regiment formed the greater part of the forces attacking Naugard direct, with the 11th's remaining units forming a sizeable reserve force.

By comparison to the defending Soviet forces, 8th and 11th Assault Infantry Regiments were at full strength, bringing nearly three thousand five hundred men to the field, whereas none of the three regiments in the 1st Guards exceeded a thousand and the 167th Regiment only just crossed the seven hundred mark.

Reports flooded into Deniken's headquarters, detailing the building pressure of the attacks, but still none pleaded to withdraw or sought more men, although resupply of ammunition was a constant theme.

His interpretation, some would call it guess, seemed correct.

Fig# 176 - Naugard - Second phase of Allied assault.

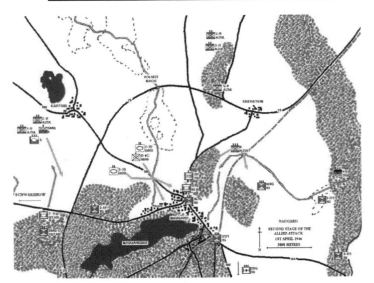

There was no urgency about the Allied thrust; no speedy work, except for the group driving hell for leather at Yarishlov.

He eyed his PPSh, hanging on an old hat stand, and momentarily considered driving out to support his friend on the field of battle, but those days were, for him, now gone.

So he studied the map, absorbed the changes, the new reports, the spoken information, and imagined himself leading soldiers in battle alongside Yarishlov's tanks

He closed his eyes and could imagine the green tanks in the green woods, moving into firing positions...

The green tanks moved forward through the green woods, carefully easing themselves into prime firing positions, their caution aided by the Typhoons now circling the battlefield, waiting patiently for a target of opportunity.

The Allied artillery had stopped, the last shell dropping short of the woods by just under fifty metres. Not dangerous as such, but close enough to leave little silver scars on the nearest tanks, courtesy of shrapnel from the huge shell.

The SMG battalion shook out well behind the T-54s, its role now one solely of covering their armoured comrades' rear, keeping any infantry anti-tank teams from getting in close.

The tactics that were to be used excluded them from sitting tight to the T-54's.

Some medium artillery started to drop in the woods and achieved some success amongst the infantry. Most importantly, amongst the command group, who suffered one direct and two close hits in under two minutes. Men and equipment suffered badly, and a lesser unit might have had problems, but the 7th Guards SMG Battalion was an experienced unit.

As their former commander and half his staff were taken away to the casualty station, the Battalion command shifted effortlessly to a Major who knew his business just as well.

Kriks had passed Deniken's orders and was now in his own tank, three to the left of his commander.

Radio communications still only existed in limited numbers of tanks, and these, reasonably enough, were reserved for unit commanders.

That the Soviet sets were unreliable was a fact of life the Red Army tankers simply accepted with stoicism, unless they were lucky enough to have their set replaced with one 'liberated' from enemy vehicles. Poor radio communications was a fact of life that hamstrung the effectiveness of the Soviet war machine throughout the conflict.

Yarishlov spoke into his microphone softly, his eyes firmly glued to the enemy force, estimating the range.

"Drakon-lider, all commands. Stand by."

There was a certain irony that the first real opposition his unit would face would be tanks born in the same factories as those the 7th rode into battle.

The approaching front of metal consisted of IS-IIs and T-34s, more the former than the latter, which made them renegade Poles, and beneath contempt.

"Drakon-lider, all commands. Tanks to front are Soviet build. You know their weak spots. Stand by."

The IS-IIs made Yarishlov think, their thick armour worrying him into delaying the fire order.

Kriks was humming 'Kalinka' to himself, his nervous energy building up and needing some sort of release.

He had long ago selected his first target, an IS-II virtually at 0° to him, one he had selected according to doctrine, to avoid multiple shots at one target.

His headset spoke and he automatically gave the order.

Yarishlov had sprung the ambush.

The opening volley was spectacular for a number of reasons.

The first reason was that the 100mm gun on the T-54 had excellent hitting and penetrative power, and made short work of the T-34m44s available, only one surviving the initial salvo of AP shells.

The second reason was the incredible sight of numerous white blobs bouncing skywards, as IS-II armour proved its value against 100mm shells.

Yarishlov gave the order.

"Drakon-lider, all tanks, advance! Out."

The T-54s pushed forward immediately, knowing that the woods would soon become an artillery killing zone. Keen to get closer to the IS-IIs, understanding that losses would occur once the Typhoons understood the danger, and accepting them for the safety that proximity to the enemy offered.

The 7th Guards were well trained, despite the limitations of supply, and practised move-stop-fire tactics to increase their hit ratios.

Yarishlov saw an opportunity, as one IS-II swung on a broken track.

"Gunner, target tank at three left, nine hundred, engage."

"Set."

"FIRE!"

As soon as the shell left the barrel, the driver eased the T-54 forward and jinked left and centre, moving forward but changing lines.

Yarishlov slapped his gunner on the shoulder.

"Hit! Well done, Anatoly."

The professional was back in an instant.

"Driver, halt. Gunner, target tank at zero, eight hundred. Engage."

The delay was tangible.

"Set."

"FIRE!"

The last T-34 exploded in a fireball, leaving no doubt about the effectiveness of the round.

"Driver, find me a hull down position."

The driver had already scanned ahead but not seen anything suitable.

He moved the tank forward, angling left.

An opportunity presented itself immediately, and he dropped into a shell hole, shouting a warning as he approached.

The T-54 was swallowed up, the hole bigger than expected, leaving Yarishlov with no vision whatsoever.

"Sorry, Comrade Polkovnik."

"This will have to do," and Yarishlov eased himself up out of the cupola, discovering that if he knelt on the metal roof, propping himself against the DSHK mount, he could see the battlefield reasonably well.

The tactical situation was favourable and he pressed his mike to issue an order to take advantage of it.

"Drakon-Lider, Drakon-odin, come in."

The first battalion commander responded immediately.

"Drakon-odin, move your battalion around to the left, circling the village. The enemy has narrowed his front. You can get at his flank, over."

Dragon-one acknowledged and Yarishlov's first tactical decision was implemented.

He then realised that he had made an error, the sort that could prove fatal on a battlefield policed by aircraft.

His tank had sat still for too long.

A typhoon was already in its death-bringing dive.

'Blyad... no time!'

Instinctively, he dropped into the turret and grabbed the firing handles.

The Typhoon was aimed at a point behind Yarishlov, the pilot allowing for the natural fall of his rockets, which leapt from the rails in pairs, until all eight were in the air.

The heavy machine-gun rattled as Yarishlov put up his own message of defiance, his teeth gritted, but failing to prevent an animal-like sound of concentration and fear escaping.

601

For the crew of the T-54, everything suddenly went brown, as large quantities of earth arrived and covered the vehicle.

The rockets kept arriving, and more earth rained down.

Yarishlov dropped inside the turret, his face bleeding where something sharp had accompanied the earth.

The rockets missed.

Every one of them.

The large explosion that rocked the tank was not a rocket, but the Typhoon. Yarishlov had put five bullets into the most vulnerable piece of the flying machine; its pilot.

The remaining Typhoons flung themselves upon the Guards' tanks, and T-54s died, blown apart by the tank-busters, eager to avenge their comrade.

Yarishlov pushed up at cupola, clearing away the debris and received the fright of his life.

"Gunner, target tank, maximum elevation, 2° right. Twenty yards!"

He had no help in estimating the angle or elevation, just the imperative of the looming shape of an IS-II coming over the edge of the shell hole.

"SET!"

"F..."

The gunner fired on the intake of breath, not waiting for the spoken word.

The 100mm shell entered the floor armour of the IS-II, passing through the driver and smashing into the breech of the main gun, adding pieces of it to the whirling metal that harvested the crew.

The IS-II hung on the edge, seemingly undecided about what to do next. The engine stalled and the tank settled back, electing to stay above ground level.

Yarishlov, his heart almost bursting out of his chest, propelled himself out of the turret and checked the way ahead.

Dropping back in, he gave the order to advance, and the T-54 pulled itself out of the shell hole, passing the now smoking leviathan that had nearly surprised them.

The Poles seemed to be withdrawing or, at the least, had stopped advancing.

Yarishlov's tanks were virtually on top of the enemy, making air attack risky. The British aircraft wisely held off, hoping for a target of opportunity amongst the T-54's.

On two occasions they found such an opportunity, and each attack brought about success for them.

Yarishlov shouted into his radio, encouraging the unit commanders to keep their men in close.

Smoke shells started to burst on the field, accurately laid by Spanish mortar crews, obscuring the Polish and Spanish vehicles as they turned controlled withdrawal into urgent retreat.

Whilst the extra smoke helped obscure them from the circling vultures, so was generally welcomed by the Soviet tank crews, the presence of smoke brought other perils.

A rocket trailed smoke past the command tank's turret side, close enough for Yarishlov to feel the heat of its passing.

Snatching at the DSHK, he chewed up the ground around the bazooka team, forcing them back into cover.

"Gunner, target stone wall, right 6°, fifty, fire when set. Ready on the co-ax for infantry."

The 100m shell sent stone and body parts flying, negating the use for the SGMT co-axial machine gun.

"Drakon-tri to Drakon-lider. Drakon-tri to Drakon-lider, over."

The third battalion commander sounded very excited.

"Drakon-Lider receiving, over."

"Enemy tanks, at least forty, approaching from Damerow, range 2000, type unknown, over."

"Drakon-Lider, received, standby."

Yarishlov conjured up a mental picture of the landscape, whilst a small part worked out if he had fallen for some trap.

Again, he selected First Battalion.

"Drakon-Odin from Drakon-Lider, over."

"Drakon-Odin-Two receiving, over."

Yarishlov grimaced, understanding that a reply from the First Battalion's 2IC could only mean that the veteran Major was out of the fight.

"Drakon-Odin-Two, move your formation to the west and engage the enemy force coming from Damerow. Identify and report soonest. Do not let them turn our flank, over."

The orders were clear and quickly acknowledged.

"SET!"

The gun rocked back and sent another Polish crew to their fiery deaths.

Yarishlov hadn't noticed the IS-II, so engrossed was he in the possibility that he was about to become the prey.

"Infantry left!"

He snatched at the machine-gun handles, too late to stop the world going yellow and red.

Kriks, as he always did, kept half an eye on his commander, and so had a grandstand view of the effects of a bazooka round successfully penetrating the lower hull armour of a T-54 battle tank.

He screamed as he pulled the machine-gun round, screamed as he cut the enemy anti-tank team in half, and screamed as he watched a heat haze grow above the cupola.

No-one had emerged.

"Driver, right, to the Polkovnik's tank, quickly!"

Kriks was up and out of the turret swiftly. In a moment of madness, he took his life in his hands jumping across from his to Yarishlov's tank.

The sounds he heard were of men in extremis.

The heat pushed his face away from the open cupola, but he returned to look inside.

Yarishlov was pulling at the loader, the wounded man squealing with pain as his right leg completed its detachment process, ripping the last vestiges of muscle and sinew as his Colonel got a good hold and pulled upwards.

Whilst the sight itself was appalling, what appalled Kriks the most was that both men were gently burning, their uniforms turning orange and red, their hair melting, their flesh blistering and splitting.

He leant in and grasped the loader's collar, biting deep into his lip as the burning sensation threatened his consciousness.

The loader came out, lighter because he had no legs to speak of.

Kriks' own gunner and loader had joined him and took the stricken man from the Praporschik's painful grasp.

A dull moan focussed Kriks back on the tank, and he looked inside, only to be pushed out of the way by a very badly burned gunner.

A waft of flame followed the wounded man, as the internal fire grabbed a firm hold.

"Arkady! Give me your hand! Arkady! Arkady!"

Yarishlov looked up through blistered eyelids, the pain clearly overtaking him.

His hand felt for that of his NCO's and he was dragged upwards by the force of a man lent extraordinary strength by extraordinary circumstances.

Using his hands to subdue the flames, Kriks shouted at his own crew.

"Get the tank out of here now!"

His driver needed no second invitation and the T-54 pulled off to one side.

Kriks laid the smoking officer on the fender and dropped to the ground, hardly noticing that he de-gloved most of his right hand as he steadied his descent, the cooked skin pulling off with relative ease.

He pulled the unconscious Yarishlov to him and laid him over a shoulder, pausing only to beat out a re-ignition in what was left of the Colonel's uniform.

Urgency gave him more strength, and he ran with his burden, reaching his own tank and the helping hands that took Yarishlov from him and lifted him onto the rear deck.

The legless loader had already died, and the gunner had passed out, his blisters and burns expressing life-giving fluid like a leaking tap.

Yarishlov was badly burned, and Kriks, indeed all of them, had seen such burns before.

They understood that there was no way back from such injuries.

The liquid welled in Kriks' eyes.

He punched the side of the tank, causing his burns to reannounce themselves in horrible fashion.

He screamed, partially in extreme pain, and partially because of a lack of hope.

And then providence took a hand.

An enemy half-track emerged from the smoke, clearly confused, advancing when it should have been retreating.

It braked to a sudden halt and a man in the front stood up, extending his hands in surrender, not realising that the 100mm gun pointed directly at him had no gunner, and that he could simply have driven away.

"Get us over to that enemy vehicle now!"

His gunner repeated the order into the open turret, and the T-54 moved alongside the Spanish ambulance half-track.

The enemy officer, his hands still raised, feared the worst as he was dragged forcibly from his vehicle, his orderlies also ordered out at pistol point.

However, he understood better when he was pushed up onto the tank and confronted with men carrying injuries of the severest nature.

The Doctor shouted at his orderlies, reassuring Kriks with sign language, as stretchers, fluids and other paraphernalia appeared, as if by magic.

Overhead, the Typhoons noted the two vehicles sat side by side, electing patience over the possibility of killing friendly troops.

The Soviet tanks embroiled themselves in the business of killing the British Shermans that had appeared, something which they did extremely easily, and with little loss by way of return.

Occasionally, the Typhoons would drop down and attack, but the smoking battlefield favoured the Russian armour now, obscuring more and more as vehicles died and contributed the products of their fiery demise; there were no more RAF successes and the Typhoons were limited to impotent inactivity until fuel considerations forced them to depart.

The fighting continued, long after it was obvious that the Allied plan, meant to push 1st Guards away from the main road, had failed, and that Naugard and its environs would remain Russian, for another day at least.

Whilst the battle raged, another battle, one to save two badly burned men was fought, and both won and lost.

When the battle petered out and the night staked its claim to the field, the new phenomenon of 'night scavenging' took place, an activity that had started through necessity, units here and there finding what they could, until now, when the activity was officially sanctioned and encouraged by higher command.

Outside Naugard, as with a hundred other locations in Europe, special Soviet groups silently stole into the silent arena seeking anything and everything that could be carried, dragged or hauled back to their own lines.

Vehicles gave up fuel, siphoned from intact tanks, or ammunition, taken from undamaged containers.

The dead bodies of both sides surrendered their unused bullets and grenades, abandoned positions often yielding a fine harvest of heavier weapons and compatible ammunition.

As the practice grew, many an Allied soldier found himself shot at by weapons made in his own land, held in the hand of someone who wasn't.

"So, are we agreed, gentlemen?"

Again, Lieutenant General Bortnowski sought their agreement, some might say complicity, in the message he had prepared for the consumption of McCreery and Eisenhower.

"We can still attack but..." Major General Boruta-Speichowicz, commanding officer of Polish IX Corps, conceded, "As you say, we must retain the ability to respond in force to any unexpected Russian activity."

Bortnowski's eyes fell upon Barker, the commander of British XXXIII Corps. Whilst of equal rank to the Pole, he was not in command, and it did not sit well with him.

"I don't agree and, furthermore, I believe we should continue the pressure. However, you are in command, General."

Next was the Spanish officer, Muñoz-Grandes, released from his liaison duties with SHAEF to command the Spanish I Corps.

"Sir, Twenty-First Army Group is still advancing, so perhaps it is prudent to harbour resources to assist in our relief," Bortnowski nodded in acceptance of the support, too soon, as Grandes had not yet finished, "But it could be equally prudent continue attacking towards our British saviours, Sir."

Barker looked at Grandes.

'Drag up a fence and sit down why don't you.'

Last was Lieutenant General Matthew B. Ridgeway, former commander of the slaughtered 82nd US Airborne Division, and subsequently given the top job with the 1st Allied Airborne Corps.

"General, Sir, I think we should keep up and at 'em. Their losses've been far greater than ours. Our air's solid, our supply's solid, morale's great. Twenty-First's pushing hard and we can help 'em. I say we hold to the east and get everything going west a-sap."

The same proposition that 'Old Iron Tits' had tried to persuade Bortnowski to follow previously.

"Thank you, gentlemen. You may return to your units."

Bortnowski saluted them and waited for his commanders to file out.

He was alone for only a moment, as his CoS entered as agreed.

Passing the unaltered message to the poker-faced officer, Bortnowski felt a moment of relief.

"Send that to 21st and SHAEF immediately."

Much like the Anzio landing before it, the landing in Poland was about to metamorphose from wildcat to stranded whale.

The train, clearly marked with huge red crosses, was ready to make its way back across occupied Europe, carrying a forlorn human cargo of bodies damaged by war.

Kriks, his right arm bandaged to prevent infection seeking out his burns, watched as the stretcher was carefully loaded on board, the dedicated team of three following on with everything that would keep Yarishlov alive until he got to the hospital on Gorodomlya Island, where the task of putting the badly burned man would be taken up by a specialist burns team.

Deniken stood stiffly and shouted an order.

"Soldaty! Fall into ranks!"

Men and women in different uniforms, and of different ranks, all responded immediately, falling into ranks as directed.

"Soldaty! Atten-tion!"

The entire platform was lined with soldiers at the attention as the train sounded its whistle and gently started forward.

" Soldaty! Sal-ute!"

One hundred and thirty seven right hands, one heavily wrapped and painful, responded to the order, offering a salute of respect to a man long past caring about such matters, but for whom the gesture was sincerely meant.

Deniken dismissed the impromptu parade and, with Kriks in tow, disappeared to examine a schnapps bottle.

"Why didn't you go, Praporschik. You should have gone with him, really you should?"

Kriks debated his reply for the briefest of moments but he was comfortable with the able infantryman, rank differences aside, and trusted the judgement of Yarishlov, his commander and friend.

"I didn't go because he asked me not to, Comrade."

Deniken looked at Kriks, his lips forming a question that the NCO pre-empted.

"No... not since his injuries, but before then... before this battle, Comrade."

"Before this battle?"

"Yes... you see, Comrade Polkovnik... Arkady knew he was on borrowed time... we all are really... so many close calls... miraculous escapes... you know..."

608

Deniken nodded, staying silent to encourage Kriks to speak further.

"He suspected his time was approaching and made me swear to stay with you, come what may, Comrade Polkovnik."

Deniken poured two more measures, wishing to loosen any further resolve before he pushed Kriks harder.

"To Arkady."

Kriks nodded and voiced the same toast.

"To Arkady!"

Fiery liquid burned throats, but not enough to stop the conversation.

"Why did he ask that of you?"

"Because... don't be embarrassed, Comrade Polkovnik... but because he said you were the future of our country... you and men like you... that when all this fucking mess was over, you would be needed to build Mother Russia up again."

The words arrived and were absorbed immediately, although the processing of their meaning took a little longer.

Deniken, genuinely confused by what his mind suggested, could only voice its findings.

"You mean that he thought..."

"Yes, Comrade Polkovnik... Arkady Arkadyevich Yarishlov, Polkovnik of Tanks, Hero of the Soviet Union, understood before this last battle. The evidence is clear for any fool to see, he told me. The war's lost... if not today, next month or even next year... the war is lost... and men like you will be needed to repair the damage caused when it's all over."

"And him? Why not him?"

Kriks refilled their glasses.

"He told me that he has a bill to pay, and that he comes from another time. It is Deniken's time now, he said."

Kriks lifted his glass and stood unsteadily.

"Comrade Polkovnik. I give you a toast. To the end of the war and to the start of the peace."

They drank together until the bottle was gone.

There are not enough Indians in the world to defeat the Seventh Cavalry.

George Armstrong Custer.

Chapter 146 - THE TWELTH

Patton listened as the officer finished his briefing on the day's events, and excellent listening the Brigadier General had made too.

The Allied plan to hit the Russians pretty much everywhere seemed to be paying off, with notable successes already in the bag.

Whilst it rankled that he and his Third Army were not totally committed to the opening phase of US Twelfth Army Group's assault, the part set aside for him and his men would bring him opportunity and glory in equal measure.

But first, the way had to be opened by other units of US Twelfth Army Group, attacking specifically from a hinged base, to sweep Soviet forces apart and open a gap through which Patton could charge, preferably with Rhine crossings secure.

An airborne force, a reinforced Regimental Combat Team from the 17th US Airborne Division, was set aside to make a swift drop to secure such a crossing if necessary.

The French 1st Army's Legion Corps kept its left flank securely placed against the German Republican Army, whilst, in the south, the right flank and join with US 6th Army Group was maintained by US XXXVII Corps of US 15th Army.

Thus far, the attacks had met with nothing but success, and all advances were as projected, with the exception of French II Corps, whose lead units had taken a heavy hit at Rheinbach. This was partially from a Soviet counter-attack and partially from a devastating friendly-fire attack by US bombers, who dropped on Rheinbach due to a navigational error. However, despite losses amongst command and infantry units, 2nd French Infantry Division continued to press for their objective; the Rhine at Remagen.

US Third Army was playing a modest part in the opening phase, with its US III Corps nestled between US 9th and 15th

610

Armies, its own target Koblenz, unless the door hinged open before the city was reached.

Patton had his force spread wider than would be considered prudent, but he wanted to make sure he could plunge straight through any gap created, and had faith that his boys would manoeuvre as and when asked, to bring about a deep penetration of the enemy lines.

Not that his units stayed still, constantly moving up behind the lead and reserve echelons, topping off fuel tanks, keeping men and machines in top order, waiting for the moment to charge forward.

1803 hrs, Tuesday, 26th March 1946, US Third Army Headquarters, Hamm, Luxembourg.

The briefing followed the same pattern as before, registering more gains but, this time around, without the repetition of the friendly fire event.

Patton, savouring his pipe, listened as more Allied successes were recited, and then reflected on the situation map.

Combining the two was easy for a man of Patton's calibre.

He looked at familiar ground, earth over which he had already fought, admittedly against a far weaker enemy than that now facing the US units, but one that Patton was confident he could send to hell just the same.

He acknowledged the arrival of a fresh coffee, but never took his eyes off the wall map, eyes that started to narrow at the possibility developing before him.

US 15th Army was making exceptional advances, well beyond projections.

Patton knew the commander well, and could imagine 'Old Gee' pushing his men hard and harder still.

In reality, Lieutenant General Gerow's opposition was melting away quicker than he could pin it down.

What Patton had spotted was the fact that, regardless of the reasons behind it, the Soviet frontline was falling back to settle on the Rhine, clearly intending to use the large obstacle to halt the Allied advance.

Pausing to relight his pipe, he asked for the latest photo recon and intelligence information, specifically for the eastern side of the great river.

611

Although not always accurate, the intelligence and reconnaissance arms did a pretty good job overall, something that Patton acknowledged openly.

He studied the evidence to hand, trying to understand the enemy's mind as best he could.

A large concentration of enemy units was sat across the Rhine, opposite the French and Bill Simpson's Ninth Army.

It made sense, as the shortest route to the Rhine was marked on the situation map by where those two armies were headed.

There were yet more units further south, but less so.

This had been known, but the situation conjured up by Gerow's success in the advance created new possibilities.

The Moselle valley was not ideal by any means, but if 15th Army could shove the enemy back at the same rate then maybe, just maybe, Patton could get the Third across the Rhine before any units of note concentrated on the east bank.

If he could achieve that, then there were many possibilities open to him, something that titillated his soldierly pride and ego in equal measure.

But for now, unusually, Patton decided to wait.

2323 hrs, Tuesday, 26th March 1946, US Third Army Headquarters, Hamm, Luxembourg.

The last briefing before General George Smith Patton took to his cot had come and gone, the whole Allied front having seemed to lift up and move forward, from the Baltic to the Adriatic.

Sharing a last coffee with three of his officers, Patton was in easy mood, knowing that time would soon bring him the opportunity he sought.

His CoS, Brigadier General Hobart Gay, was complaining about the inactivity.

"Well, Hap, be that as it may, if Leonard's Fifteenth keep going as they are, then we'll be busy soon enough."

The other two officers, his G3 and G4, Colonels Halley Maddox and Walter Muller respectively, were still working over the issues that the rapid movement of the Third Army would bring.

"Sir."

One of Patton's personal aides arrived, red faced from his dash from the communications tent.

"Spit it out, Major Stiller."

"There's a break, Sir. Confirmed by Fifteenth Army."

612

Patton stood, energised immediately.

"Where, goddamnit?"

Stiller extended the message sheet, which his commander snatched unceremoniously.

"Map!"

Hobart Gay grabbed his briefcase and laid one out swiftly.

"Where's Zell-Mosel?"

Four pairs of eyes swept the map and then followed the finger that appeared before them, as Major Stiller enlightened them.

"Son-of-a-bitch!"

Patton questioned his aide.

"Major, how firm is this? We need to know before we roll the goddamned parade on this."

"General, I asked for full confirmation and Fifteenth's intentions before I brought you the message."

Patton nodded his approval of his aide's actions.

"Get that confirmation immediately, Major. I want it here right now... and send me the duty signals officer."

Stiller almost flew out of the commander's tent, and was very quickly replaced by a worried looking signals Captain.

The four-star commander was in 'General' mode, and addressed each man individually, starting with Maddox and Muller.

"OK, I want logistics and planning on moving the army to take advantage of this. Hal, Twenty-two Corps's nearest, so get 'em prepped for an immediate movement order. Give them a probable destination so they can get the map work sorted. Then prep the rest. Captain, I have a message for you to send Fifteenth Army headquarters."

The tent suddenly emptied, leaving Patton and the Signals Officer alone, the former scribbling a note whilst the latter felt distinctly uncomfortable being alone with the 'old man'.

"Here, get that off straight away. Any reply comes back to me a-sap."

Patton didn't stop his continuity of thought and action, immediately lifting the telephone and calling for a connection to higher authority.

It took two minutes to speak to the name he asked for, indicating that his commander had already taken to his bed.

"Bradley here. What's going on, George?"

Bradley could almost hear the smile down the phone.

"Brad, we've got the sons-of-bitches split, and we didn't even try hard. They've done the job for us."

"Where we talking, George?"

"On the Moselle. You gotta map to hand?"

"Yep. Fire away."

"Seems like Fifteenth pushed on the join between two units, and they both moved open, creating a gap. Guess the bastards didn't want to be caught in the river bends. Look at Zell-Mosel in the south, Cochem in the north. I'm finding out what Leonard has planned, but it seems to me that, if the gap is that wide, it's a great spot to go. Brad, I know the terrain's not ideal, but we've been here before, and Koblenz is goddamned close."

"Your assets, George?"

"Have the Twenty-second to hand immediately. The logistics people are working on the rest, but I can get my whole outfit online in two days, guaranteed."

"How firm is all this, George?"

"I'm getting the full picture now, but I see no goddamned sense in delaying, so I'm preparing all my boys for a swift move forward."

The delay in Bradley's was minimal, but none the less evident.

"Okay, George, but make sure Leonard is onside with your plans before you move, clear?"

"Sure thing, Brad. Will you prep the airborne boys, just in case I need 'em?"

"Will do. On that one, advise me of likely drop sites a-sap. I'll call this one up to Ike with my endorsement...err..." the pause as Bradley consulted a list was considerable, "I'm assuming you are looking at Plan Delaware or Oregon?"

These were two of the thirteen possible attack options laid out prior to the assault, basic framework plans on which meat and bones could be hung when the actualities of combat were known.

"First thought's Delaware, given the other goings-on, but I ain't committing to anything as yet, Brad."

"Okay, George. Keep me informed. Good luck."

"Thanks. You too, Brad."

Both men replaced the telephone and then picked it back up.

Both men repeated the same message, almost word for word.

"Get me Fifteenth Army, General Gerow, immediately."

Bradley lost the race and made do with the Fifteenth Army's CoS, who confirmed everything Patton had said, and more.

Next call was for Eisenhower, who was enthusiastic beyond words.

614

Bravo Company, 320th Infantry Regiment had point, backed up by a platoon from 35th Mechanised Recon.

The messages had driven them on faster than they would have liked but, maybe, just maybe, the brass knew what they were doing, for nothing got in their way.

Until Alf.

Sat at the narrowest point between two curves of the Moselle River, the smallest of German villages was full of desperate Soviet soldiery, all intent on escaping through a gap less than four hundred metres wide.

Bravo's company commander knew a turkey shoot opportunity when he saw one, and soon afterwards shells from the 127th and 161st Field Artillery Battalions started to claim scores of lives amongst the retreating men.

Charlie Company pushed up level and the two units together herded the enemy into the fire zone.

A radio message shifted the fire of the 127th's 155mm's towards the crossing point at Zell, but the Major commanding understood perfectly that the bridge was needed intact, as did the aircraft that were soon to follow on in.

The escaping Soviets, a mish-mash of supply troops, rear-echelon security forces and escaping frontline stragglers, were pounded into pieces by the relentless accurate fire.

An AOP arrived overhead, taking over direction duties, and moving the fire to the two hundred and fifty metre summit on Barl, as well as the rear slopes on either side, down to the district of Kaimt.

The other infantry company, Able, found the bridge at Reil damaged but passable, and quickly disposed of the small engineer force waiting in vain for orders to blow the Moselle bridge between Kaimt and Zell-Mosel.

Able Company pushed hard, losing their lead half-track to a random mine, and found a vantage point from where they could overlook the main crossing point at Zell, a solid structure that was rapidly becoming crammed with fleeing Russians.

Thoroughly briefed on their mission, A Company's commander contacted the AOP and had fire moved, and then used his own forward air controller to call in the hounds of hell.

The unfamiliar aircraft is US markings swept over Alf, travelling around the height at Barl, using the Moselle to guide their attack.

AD-1 Skyraiders, a new aircraft in the Allied ground attack inventory, had been hurried to the ETO well ahead of proper schedules, their superior abilities recognised at an early stage, although the haste of their deployment led to tragedies early on, with some structural and mechanical failures, something that low-flying tolerates very badly.

The USAAF planners had got their act together, and the Skyraiders were equipped with nothing that could overly damage the bridge.

That would be of little comfort to the fleeing Red Army soldiers.

Fourteen Skyraiders came in, line astern, pumping 20mm cannon shells into the helpless mass struggling on the bridge.

Two twin DSHK mounts, mounted on high ground surrounding the bridge, opened up, solely succeeding in drawing attention to themselves.

The flight leader detailed one aircraft for each, and both positions were obliterated in short order.

The geography of the target was poor on their first run, denying them a proper opportunity to drop ordnance, so the Major leading the squadron took his aircraft round in a lazy circular route. Approaching from the south-east, up the valley that carried Route 194, presenting a length-on target to the deadly aircraft.

The leader dropped his payload beyond the bridge, the mass of soldiers being too easy to miss.

Each M-29 cluster bomb weighed in at a healthy five hundred pounds, and the formidable Skyraider carried ten, which were now descending through the Moselle's morning mist.

Nine hundred bomblets, ranging from five to thirty second fusing, hit the packed masses.

The Major was already pulling up on his stick, rising into the air, and therefore not able to witness the butchery that occurred as his plethora of four-pound charges started to explode.

Behind him, the second in line had placed four napalm bombs on the same spot, immolating hundreds in the blink of an eye.

The second pair dropped the same loads, but nearer the bridge, working back and pulling up before risking any harm from exploding munitions dropped by the lead.

And so it went on, seven attacks in total; cluster bombs followed by napalm, until the final drop was made on the junction of Routes 421 and 194.

Many of the men of Able Company, watching from their vantage point above Zell, watched in horror at the fate of hundreds of men, women, and horses, all destroyed by the efficient killing machines of artillery and aircraft.

The Skyraiders swept back over the scene, but the total devastation yielded nothing worth shooting at.

Not wishing to take ordnance back to base, the Major commanding split his force into two groups, both of which used their remaining weapons on the enemy troops that had avoided the devastation at Zell, killing hundreds more on the roads to Walhausen and Altlay.

After the air attacks and artillery barrages had done their work, 1st/320th pushed on.

Such was the horror of their advance that very few soldiers, from veteran to greenhorn, held their breakfast down, and half-tracks were streaked with vomit as the companies pushed forward towards the bridge.

It got no better when they got there, and the awfulness of that bridge was to haunt many of the 320th's young soldiers until their dying day.

There was no alternative but to drive on through the sticky mass of charred flesh.

There was no chance of anyone having survived the onslaught, and it was not until the lead units reached the fork in the road that truly recognisable pieces of human or animal bodies really started to appear.

As agreed, Bravo Company and the Recon element took the left turn, following Route 421 and heading up the sharp windy hill out of the Moselle Valley.

Charlie Company committed to the right, using Route 194.

Once the units were clear of the killing field, both commanders pulled them over, set out a temporary picquet line, and gave their boys a little time to recover.

Able Company, detailed by the Regimental commander to secure Zell-Mosel and the environs, found themselves unable to avoid the dreadful sights.

Moving through Zell, squads sent to find any enemy stay-behinds found civilians and Soviet soldiers sat together in the numerous flood cellars, shocked, stunned, most clinging to each other with vice-like grips, regardless of whom it was they sought their solace and support from.

The doughboys of A Company treated all equally and, in many ways, they were as shocked and stunned as those who had seen and heard the awfulness at first hand.

One platoon of Able Company secured another route out at Merl, finding only civilians, and Route 199 free of any obstructions or enemy troops.

As each report made its way back to the 320th's commander, he grew more excited, seeing the bigger picture immediately.

His report arrived with the commanding officer of the 35th, Major General Paul W. Baade.

He encouraged the 320th to exploit the gap, opening it wider and pushing ahead, and to the latter task he dispatched the remainder of the 35th Recon, as well as the entire 60th Engineer Battalion.

Whilst not fully appreciating the situation at Zell, he realised enough to send extra hands, so medical units, quartermaster troops, and even the divisional band were ordered forward to help clear the way.

Before he also went himself, having decided to move his headquarters forward, Baade passed his information up the line.

Ernest. N Harmon, commander of US XXII Corps acted immediately, ordering his assets towards the potential opening, and then contacted his own superior.

0939 hrs, Wednesday, 27th March 1946, US Third Army Headquarters, Hamm, Luxembourg.

"Sir, General Harmon."

Patton covered the distance to the telephone like a cheetah in pursuit of a gazelle, almost physically wrestling it from the Communications officer's hand.

"Ernie, George."

It took only a moment for everyone to understand that Harmon was giving Patton just the news he wanted.

"Sonofabitch! What you doing about it, Ernie?"

Patton flicked his fingers at the map table, sending his staff there to wait for him, grabbed the telephone's body and moved to put some geography to Harmon's words.

"Excellent, excellent. Now... first things first... Rheinböllen... get me Rheinböllen, secure it, leave summat to hold it

618

and then... hell for leather, Ernie, hell for goddamned leather, you take your boys all the way to Mainz and get me across the goddamned Rhine."

Patton half-listened to Harmon's objections, open flank, unknown defences, poor roads... but only half-listened, because the Third Army's commander was already looking at what he intended to do next.

"Ernie, will you cut the 'can't do's' and give me Rheinböllen... and when you've done that, on to Mainz. You can do it, and you will do it. Just keep an eye on your right flank and work with Twenty-three Corps to stay secure. Hugh Gaffey will hang on to you, no problem."

Patton twisted a smaller map to face him and studied it whilst he made the hum response to Harmon's continued concerns.

"Listen, Ernie, I'm putting Twenty-one Corps online behind you, and I'm gonna drop the 15th Armored into line too, so you have some real beef back-up. Yes, it's a goddamned logistical nightmare but we'll overcome as always."

Harmon was obviously somewhat soothed by this addition.

"Seventeen Corps will head towards Koblenz. The rest of the Army'll close up, ready to exploit the breakthrough, and I want it to be you, Ernie."

Patton laughed at his Corps Commander's response.

"You and I go back way too far for me to soft-soap you, Ernie. Now, I'm relying on you. Stick to Plan Delaware until I tell you otherwise, clear?"

Patton listened to the rest of Harmon's words, looking at the staff around him, already working out how best to implement the plan he had outlined to Harmon.

He nodded in approval, for no one's benefit but his own.

"Remind me, where's your HQ at? Fit for purpose is it?"

Patton already knew the answer to question number one.

"Excellent. Best you get yourself forward then, cos that will be my HQ this evening, Ernie."

Patton pursed his lips as Harmon told him the Corps HQ was nearly ready to move forward.

"Okay, Ernie. Pass on my thanks to General Baade and his boys and let's get this show on the goddamned road."

He hung up and passed the telephone back to the waiting signaller, who had desperately hung on to the cable to stop Patton losing the connection.

"Right, I can see you're all on the ball here. Get the orders cut and sent for Seventeen, Twenty-one, Twenty-two and 15th Armored... get the rest of the Corps' prepped ready for an immediate move."

Orders issued, Patton stood back and let the staff officers rush off like a firework display rocket bursting.

Repacking his pipe, he silently beckoned to his CoS, Hobart Gay.

Chuckling, he passed on the gist of the exchange.

"Old Gravel was none too pleased 'bout airing his right flank, Hap."

"Can't say that I blame him, General."

Patton nodded at Gay's honesty.

"He won't have anything to worry about. Look at the bigger picture."

Pointing with the stem of his pipe, Patton ticked off the concerns.

"Sixth Army Group are doing just fine... good advances... no issues hanging onto our coat tails."

Another stab towards the map.

"The sonsofbitches are just melting away from us... in fact... all across Europe... look at it all, Hap."

"Yes, I know, General. But are they going 'cos we're shoving, or going according to their plans. I just don't like it... seems too easy... they're too quiet."

Patton laughed again, using up the last of his daily allowance before lunchtime.

"What are you, Hap, some goddamned western movie? Well just so... we're the cavalry and them there red men, the sonsofbitches, are the Indians... and we always win."

There was no arguing with that, so Gay and Patton set about the business of deciding who would go where and, before Hamm's church clock struck six pm, the entire Third Army was on the move eastwards.

Hamm was quiet once more.

1238 hrs, Thursday, 28th March 1946, US Third Army Headquarters, Haserich, Germany.

Patton's humour had evaporated earlier that morning, when his headquarters, on the move forward from Wittlich-land, had been hit by an unexpected Soviet air incursion.

620

Three dead and eight wounded did nothing to calm his anger, and, even though he had blazed away with his .50cal from his Dodge command car, shooting off a belt of ammo had not assuaged his anger, neither had the downing of one of the enemy craft.

The air waves crackled with anger as he tore a strip off the highest ranking USAAF officer he could reach by radio, making the man personally responsible for covering every inch of air over Third Army.

Patton had almost calmed down when the headquarters convoy reached the river bridge at Zell-Mosel.

Despite the ongoing clear-up operation, graves registration and service units had made only modest inroads into the detritus of battle.

Normally unshaken by the sights and aftermath of intense combat, 'Old Blood and Guts' remained remarkably quiet until arriving at the selected headquarters position at Haserich.

Ahead, Third Army's soldiers pressed hard towards the Rhine.

Standing with his hands on his hips, the classic Patton pose, he considered his personal options, which took about two seconds, as part of his mind was already determined to go forward.

"Hap, you're gonna hold the fort here. I'm going on up to Ernie's HQ, just to put a burr under his ass. Be back later."

The statement brooked no argument, not that Gay was going to raise one; he knew his man too well.

Patton was already some distance away, calling the Captain in command of his escort to 'get the men mounted the hell up'.

Within two minutes, Patton's convoy was only noticeable by the faint noise of engines in the distance.

0621 hrs, Monday, 1st April, 1946, US Third Army Headquarters, Rheinböllen, Germany.

George Patton had been awake for over three hours, dragged from his bed by news of Soviet counter-attacks.

The last report arrived, speaking of successful defence and battle lines held... and more besides.

Hobart Gay took the message and moved to his commander, who was contemplating the successes of Harmon's XXII Corps.

Ernest Harmon had already beaten back a number of concerted counterattacks and was following up hard, pushing the

16th Armored Division up alongside the 35th Infantry and pressing the retreating Soviets all the way to the Rhine.

"General..."

His concentration broken, Patton accepted the proffered message form.

"Well I'll be goddamned. Mark it up, Hal."

Patton returned the paper, substituting it for coffee, and watched as his CoS directed the staff to upgrade the situation map, reflecting the unexpected turn of events at Koblenz.

'Sonofagun... damn...'

Small raiding parties had been paradropped, some had even used boats to get upriver, and all had met with startling success.

Every bridge on the Rhine from Neuwied to Koblenz-Horchheim had been primed for blowing, and each was saved by the speedy intervention of the raiding parties.

Only the Metternich Bridge over the Moselle had been destroyed completely, the Pfaffendorfer Bridge in Koblenz proper partially damaged, the recent repairs made by Soviet engineers removed by Soviet high-explosives.

Clearly, the bridge was still capable of supporting the vitals of war, as made clear by the report from US XVII Corps' 4th Armored Division, which indicated that their lead elements were already fighting in the Koblenz districts of Ehrenbreitstein, Horchheim and Pfaffendorfer Höhe, all on the east bank.

Opportunity knocked twice before lunch, as Harmon's boys broke through to the Rhine at Mainz, although heavy resistance prevented them from crossing at the rush.

Patton had already dispatched amphibious assault equipment to broach the huge river at Sankt Goarhausen, and had begged more from SHAEF and US 12th Army Group, most of which was already on the road for Mainz.

It was a good day for the Third.

1714 hrs, Saturday, 13th April 1946, US Third Army Headquarters, Ducal Palace, Wiesbaden, Germany.

The good days had continued, only the odd temporary setback discouraging the ebullient Patton, whose confidence cascaded down to the very point of Third Army.

Wiesbaden's Ducal Palace provided Patton and his staff with a much needed bricks and mortar location where they could wash away the grime of being on the road for nearly two weeks.

The old Music Hall in the Mittelbau provided a suitable venue for the main business of governing a vast army, and it was here that George S. Patton received the news of a bloody defeat.

"Goddamnit! What was the man thinking? That the sonsofbitches would keep on running? Goddamnit!"

Third Army had crossed the Rhine with an ease that beggared belief.

Mainz fell after a short but intense tussle, 35th Infantry and 16th Armored taking a heavy hit but getting the job done.

Koblenz felt a few hammer blows, as Soviet commanders desperately tried to push the XVII Corps back over the Rhine. The counter-attacks all failed but ate up valuable time, allowing the Red Army to re-establish itself in the hills beyond.

The small crossing that Patton manufactured at Sankt Goarhausen became a success beyond his wildest dreams, and he focussed much of his bridging assets there.

Four separate bridges appeared, permitting US III Corps to come up and, with all the spare units Patton could muster, from tank-destroyers to engineers, cross the Rhine and exploit the relative absence of organised Soviet resistance and linking the crossing points at Koblenz and Mainz with incredible speed and efficiency.

Ernest Harmon's XXII Corps had been moved to the flank for a rest on the 8th April, allowing US VI Corps to take up the running for Frankfurt.

The experienced units of VI Corps, 10th US Armored and 45th US Infantry, slugged it out with battle-hardened Soviet units, pushing their way into the western outskirts of Frankfurt by the evening of April 12th.

Meanwhile, Patton organised further excursions.

Hindered by US Sixth Army Group's problems around Heidelberg and Mannheim, even Old Blood and Guts shied away from launching his men around to the south of Frankfurt, which inevitably meant his eyes had turned to the northern route.

He ordered US XXI Corps through the mountains and deep into enemy lines, intent on cutting enemy supply lines through Butzbach and Reichelsheim. He reassigned 15th US Armored Division for some extras clout.

Major General Fairvale, commander of 15th Armored, was the subject of Patton's present tirade.

The inexperienced division, despite having some of the best tanks available to the US Army, had walked into a Soviet trap at Bad Nauheim, one that cost the division heavily, as well as halted the flanking drive in its tracks.

"Goddamnit!"

Contrary to perceptions, Patton rarely fired his Generals, preferring to mould them and educate them in place.

However, in this moment, and given other issues relating to the command of the 15th, he made an executive decision.

"Fairvale gets a rear line job as of now. Who we got to replace him?"

"General Silvester?"

Lindsay McDonald Silvester had been commander of 7th Armored, but had been relieved following perceptions of poor performance in the German War.

His mind processed matters for a moment before he made a swift decision.

"Find Major General Silvester and tell him he's ordered to report to me a-sap."

Thirty-five minutes later, the newly appointed commander of 15th Armored, feeling uplifted by Patton's full confidence in his abilities, was on the road to, as Patton had put it, 'get the goddamned division sorted out and moving east before I put my boot up everyone's ass.'

1117 hrs, Wednesday, 17th April 1946, outskirts of Reiskirchen, Germany.

Colonel Bell was a man on a mission.

Commander of the 359th US Infantry Regiment, he had driven into the front line to resolve an unexpected situation.

His men had been slugging their way forward since taking up the front position for the assault on Giessen and, until this moment, they had done everything he asked.

Until now.

First and Second Battalions had taken a rousting in Giessen, Wettenberg, and Buseck, even with tank support from the 4th Armored's CCB.

Grosse-Buseck had seen a severe reverse, one that cost CCB nearly a quarter of its tanks and armored-infantry, as well as rendering 2/359th virtually combat ineffective.

Raymond E. Bell, pressurised from above, the desire for forward progress cascading down from Patton to every manjack in the field, had pushed through his Third Battalion and part of CCB, in order to rush Reiskichen before the Red Army could settle.

In short, the result was a disaster, although not one he had fully appreciated, as radio communications with his forward units had been all but lost, the messages broken and interrupted, failing or simply not getting through at all.

His lunge forward brought him into the presence of the commander of Love Company, Major William S Towers.

For his sins, Towers had been ordained as temporary commander of 3/359th by the fickle finger of fate, as a devastating combination of artillery and mortar fire left barely a dozen men of the Battalion command structure standing.

"Say that again, Major."

"I won't do it, Colonel. It's suicide, plain and simple."

"You'll do as you're fucking ordered, Major, or I'll have your rank and kick you up front with a rifle."

"You'll do as you wish, Colonel, but I ain't ordering these men into certain death... no way and no how."

Bell's eyes widened in disbelief as the flagrant disregard for rank and authority continued.

Towers maintained his defiance, pointing around the position in all directions.

"Colonel Bell, Sir, we simply don't have a King Company any more. Wiped out pretty much... few survivors fallen in with Item for now. The 7th Armored's boys took a fearful shellacking and they've fallen back. No way they're going to go in again, short of the rest of their division arriving."

He gestured the Colonel forward.

"Look here, Sir. As far as the eye can see... mines... all sorts... not hastily laid either, but real professional job. Engineers have been swatted away whilst trying to get us some fighting room. Round to the right there, more mines, mix of wire obstacles too, all covered by machine-guns."

He moved his arm, taking his Colonel's eyes away from the death trap on the right flank.

"On the left there, see where the tankers got to?" he didn't wait for a reply, plunging on into his plea for common sense, "Line of mines just behind them and then the Reds opened up a can of whoop-ass on them. Anti-tank guns... we couldn't get to them. Armored-infantry tried... well, you can see what happened there, Colonel."

Most of the half-tracks were still smoking.

"Basically, we can sit here and stop them coming back, but we've no power to move forward. Artillery's still got supply issues... the 7th's outta tanks... battalion's shot away command-wise... there's nothing to be done that isn't suicide, Colonel, and the President's entrusted me with these boys so don't think I give two hoots about my career, position and rank, when the alternative is to lead them into a slaughterhouse."

Bell looked Towers straight in the eye.

"Have you done, Major?"

"Yessir."

First Sergeant Micco slithered into the position with a report, but sensed the atmosphere and wisely held his tongue.

Bell spoke, his voice much calmer than it had been previously.

"You're right, Major. No sense it pushing again with no support. I simply didn't understand the situation."

Towers nodded and a line was drawn under the confrontation.

"Now, you've got Third for the foreseeable future. Get them shaken out for defence a-sap. Report to me on your status, casualties, needs... you know the drill. Orders are simple. They shall not pass, Major. Clear?"

"Crystal, Colonel."

The message went from the 359th Regiment to divisional command... to Corps command... to Army command... to Patton.

It was greeted with the normal tirade, but it passed quickly as George S Patton understood its significance.

He held the telephone receiver in his hand, silently waiting for his connection to be made.

A voice growled in his ear.

"Bradley."

"Brad, it's George."

"Morning, George. Please tell me this is a social call."

"'Fraid not, Brad. Bottom line is I'm spent for now. Can't get into Frankfurt unless you let me bomb it, and you won't, so I can't. Been stopped just west of Giessen now, and we just ain't got the power to muscle through any more. Supply problems, high casualties... I have to let the Third recover, Brad."

The man on the other end of the line understood how much that cost the man who prided himself as a charger and a go-getter.

"No shame, George. You've done well, Heck, everyone's done well, but we got it wrong again, didn't we? Across the board, we've lost momentum. The Reds have stopped us. OK, we've gained a lot of ground, but now they've stopped us."

Patton nodded unseen.

"Next time we won't make the mistake of underestimating them... yet again."

The silence was disturbed only by the light crackling of the phone line, as both men contemplated the incredible resilience of the Soviet soldier and the professionalism of the Red Army command.

Each man's face altered, unknown to the other, as thoughts of undiscovered enemy units turning battles invaded their thoughts.

'Why are they so good at hiding stuff?'

"Okay, George. You may discontinue the attacks. Sort your line out as you need, but don't give anything back if you don't absolutely need to. I don't need to tell you to be aggressive where you can be, but nothing fancy."

"Thank you, Brad. I'll have my full report with you soon."

"No shame, George. Look after your boys now."

"Goodbye. Brad."

"George."

The Allied Armies' largest formation had been stopped, albeit after some excellent successes.

Allied efforts would rumble on for a few days, mainly in the south, but, on the 23rd April, Operation Spectrum, in all its guises, was terminated.

There is small risk a general will be regarded with contempt by those he leads, if, whatever he may have to preach, he shows himself best able to perform.

Xenophon

Chapter 147 - THE RAMIFICATIONS

Gathered in the briefing room were the commanders of the Allied Army groups and many other senior officers, mostly those in command of national contingents.

Eisenhower had completed his assessment of Spectrum, praising its overall success, emphasising the heavy blows that had been dealt to all branches of the Soviet military. He accepted the Allied casualty numbers as heavier than expected, conceding that the logistical issues had helped undermine the Allies advance, as well as the Soviet defence.

He made no mention of the avoidance of heavy bombing certain centres of German culture, which had also contributed to the less than full completion of Spectrum.

No-one spoke of it as a defeat, for it simply wasn't.

However, it had not achieved what it had been expected to achieve and, like Patton and Bradley before him, Eisenhower cited the major reasons.

"I underestimated them. Simple as. The Reds are more resilient than I could imagine, even with their physical and military weaknesses, little supply, hostile environment, and our control of the air... they have still held us up long enough for our own logistical tail to wag the dog."

Everyone there understood that the limited gains, limited as far as Spectrum was concerned anyway, could be viewed as a setback for the Allied cause.

In truth, Spectrum had, in all its sections and sub-sections, ground the Red Air Force and Baltic Fleet down to a relative nothingness, permitting an unprecedented freedom of action in the Baltic and in the skies over most of Europe.

Soviet infrastructure had been hammered and hammered again by incessant heavy bomber attacks, hampering the front line efforts.

The Ukrainian uprising seemed to have drawn some combat formations away to help quell the revolt, inspired and provoked by Allied agent-provocateurs, although, in truth, only the timing was provoked, as the Ukrainians needed little pushing into open conflict with their Soviet masters.

This had further destabilised the Red Army, as many of her Ukrainian troops served with mixed loyalties anyway. The effectiveness of some formations was greatly reduced, as desertions and interventions by the NKVD took their toll.

The situation of the Poles was tenuous, their enclave surrounded by growing forces and the British relief stopped dead some distance hence.

Eisenhower was upbeat about the future, and this enthusiasm flowed into everyone present, as he promised that the lessons would be learned the next time, and that more and more reinforcements would be arriving, men and materiel from every Allied nation focussed on destroying the Communist state.

He closed the meeting with encouraging words.

"The Soviets have no more cards to play; they are, in essence, fully committed, almost fully spent."

"Having tapped every source of manpower and brought their industrial base to peak production, they have simply failed to prevent our Allied armies recapturing large areas of Germany, albeit not yet back to where we started in August '45."

There was only one outcome now, he assured them, only one.

"The defeat of the Soviet Union is inevitable."

And with a final flourish, Ike announced his bottom line.

"It is only a matter of time."

1209 hrs, Wednesday, 24h April 1946, Meeting Room 3, the Kremlin, Moscow.

Beria watched his master very closely, waiting for the final sign before the General Secretary exploded.

In reality, he was quite surprised that the man had not already exploded, given the presentation that Vasilevsky and the still weak Zhukov had laid before him.

Beria had seen men manhandled away and shot for much less than what these two Marshals had done.

629

And yet, the General Secretary held his peace...

"...and that, Comrades, is the present military situation. In summary, we have stopped them on all fronts. This has been achieved at great cost in manpower, equipment, and munitions... and by ceding German soil."

Silence greeted Vasilevsky's delivery.

Half because the men, even though they had received daily briefings, were stunned by the enormity of the 'defeat', and half because they dare not say anything before Stalin.

The leader of the USSR sat silently, his face devoid of everything except total anger and fury.

Vasilevsky and Zhukov knew that these men viewed what had happened as an ignominious defeat, whereas they, as military men, understood that the Red Army had achieved miracles, and had, by their own and their generals' efforts, been preserved for another day.

Stalin rose slowly, pushing his chair back and, clasping his hands behind his back, walked around the table until he stood between the two Marshals, his eyes firmly glued to the large map that showed today's positions.

His thoughts would have surprised everyone in the room.

'They have disobeyed our orders... retreated... and yet had they stood... what then... what then...'

He turned to Vasilevsky so quickly that the Marshal almost jumped in surprise.

"And you, Marshal Vasilevsky," he turned to Zhukov at similar speed, "And you, Marshal Zhukov, have both presided over this... this retreat... specifically against the orders of your leaders?"

Zhukov took the lead.

"Yes, Comrade General Secretary."

"Why?"

There was no sense in wrapping it up; both men had agreed beforehand that they would tell it how it was.

"Had we stood and fought, we would now be briefing you on the destruction of our Armies in the west... on that we are both agreed, Comrade General Secretary."

Beria made a distinct noise in anticipation a tirade from Stalin.

There was none forthcoming.

"And what would you suggest now... now that you have done what is done and can't be undone?"

Vasilevsky took up the baton.

"Comrade General Secretary, we must rearm and reinforce. The closer we are to the Motherland, the easier it is to get resources to our troops..." he didn't mean it to sound like that, but it did, and more than one member of the assembled GKO envisaged a suggestion of further retreat to shorten supply lines even more, "...And less chance of interference from enemy air activity or ground attack."

Stalin stroked his moustache into place.

"Go on, Comrade Marshal."

"Swap out some of the units from our southern borders; the Allies are doing nothing there, so replace the quality with units under training, or badly damaged veteran units that can renew themselves away from the European war."

Stalin scoffed immediately.

"That will bring us... what... two-three armies at best. What you need is a million men, not three armies."

He turned to Zhukov.

"I see... you two want more from Manchuria and Siberia. No, no , no, no, no... how many times must we tell you, NO!"

He slapped the map with his bare hand, sending a few pieces of pinned paper dropping to the floor.

"If we take from there, they would be sent to the Ukraine where those bastards are playing up."

"No, Comrade General Secretary, that is not what we suggest."

Stalin's mind was suddenly exactly focused on what they intended."

"NO!"

Exasperated, he turned away.

"Comrade General Secretary," Vasilevsky, the not-so-malleable Vasilevsky, pursued Stalin with his firm words, "If Mother Russia is to survive, then we see no alternative."

Stalin whirled around in an instant, the outburst that Beria anticipated forming on his lips.

But it died there.

Turning back to the table, the General Secretary snatched up his cigarettes and matches, taking a couple of steadying puffs before looking Vasilevsky in the eye.

"Speak."

"At this moment, we have one hundred and eight thousand troops dealing with matters in the Ukraine and Marshal Beria has, what... two hundred thousand NKVD troops deployed also."

Beria conceded the number with the slightest of nods.

"Give the ex-prisoners guns and make them into units. They have skills already, so would need little training. Feed them, clothe them, and send them in against the Ukrainian rebels, which would relieve the NKVD and our Army troops for service nearer the front line."

Stalin's eyes narrowed as he turned to silence a rumble of protest from one corner of the room.

Bulganin, suitably cowed, stopped his discontented mumbling.

"Go on."

"You have told us time and again that these men failed the Motherland. We all agree this... all understand it. But now the Motherland is in need. Marshal Zhukov and I believe that these men should be given an opportunity to prove themselves worthy again," Bulganin's mumblings started once more, "An opportunity of our choosing and one that serves the Motherland best."

Stalin silenced Bulganin with another look and turned back, this time to direct his words to Zhukov.

"So what is it that you two propose?"

"Comrade General Secretary, at this time we have approximately nine hundred thousand men within our borders, men who were once soldiers of the Red Army... trained men. We propose to equip them as best we can, organise them into units that are identifiable as ex-prisoner units, and offer them the chance of redemption by destroying the Ukrainian uprising... quickly and without mercy."

Stalin nodded, understanding the aspects of brutality that would be needed.

"Those units that prove themselves worthy will be reinstated into the Red Army proper, given suitable designation, and allowed to serve again, without any reference to their former dishonour."

Bulganin pushed his chair back and rose.

"Comrade General Secret..."

"Comrade Bulganin... how the fuck can we make a decision on the future of our glorious Motherland with you interrupting all the fucking time?"

Suitable cowed, Bulganin sank back into his chair and decided on dignified silence.

"And those that don't?"

"Those that don't will be employed to sweep our supply lines, in support of the excellent work done by our NKVD comrades, or be drafted to work in factories alongside our workers, producing the means of war, Comrade General Secretary."

Nazarbayeva wondered if she had just watched two excellent officers commit suicide, not that she didn't agree with them, on both their withdrawal and their proposal.

"The last time you made a suggestion regarding these men, matters were stretched beyond what was agreed, and some were employed other than directed, for which we hold you, Marshal Zhukov, directly responsible."

Zhukov wondered why such a strange and worthless statement had come from his leader's mouth, before realising that it was that which hadn't been said that was important, and that a battle was going on inside the General Secretary's mind.

Stalin turned and spoke to the gathering, outlining the proposal with great care, and in a surprising even fashion.

"Comrade Bulganin. Your thoughts?"

"Comrade General Secretary, the treatment of these men as non-citizens is accepted as correct. They have failed the Rodina by their surrender and we cannot trust them again. I see no reason to entrust the safety of our Motherland to those who have already demonstrated their capacity for failure."

Stalin spoke with unusual warmth and softness.

"As ever, your words carry the weight of Party doctrine, and are wise and considered, Comrade. But I must ask you this."

He lit another cigarette before continuing.

"The plan of these two officers calls for the commitment of these men to be made against the rebel Ukrainians, not the Allied armies. They will have no one to surrender to second time around, and in any case, I'm sure Comrade Beria's men will hang on tight to their coat tails, should the situation arise."

Bulganin could understand that.

"If, I stress, if we were to use these men against the rebels, we can observe them... understand if they have redeemed themselves by their actions, long before we would need to trust them again."

Bulganin could see gentle nods around him and decided to drop his resistance.

"As you say, Comrade General Secretary."

Stalin moved around the tables, openly voicing the plan and seeking the thoughts of each and every person.

The political animals who had been around Stalin for many years understood that his seeming agreement could be nothing more than a smoke screen to highlight weakness in Soviet resolve, and all hedged their bets accordingly.

One person in the room was free from such political burdens.

"And you, Comrade General. What do you think?"

Nazarbayeva had not expected to be asked, but answered firmly in any case.

"I agree completely with the proposal put forward by Marshals Zhukov and Vasilevsky. Give them a chance to prove themselves and we lose nothing. If they do carry out their duty to the Motherland satisfactorily, then the Rodina and the Party can only gain. I see no downside to this proposal, Comrade General Secretary."

'Hah! Spoken like a non-politician, my dear Tatiana... like someone who hasn't nailed their colours to this political mast for the last twenty years or so... still...'

"Is there anything else, Comrades?"

Zhukov and Vasilevsky suddenly realised that it was they being addressed.

"No, Comrade General Secretary."

"Then the GKO will debate this issue, and you will be advised in due course."

Within the hour, the Red Army acquired nine hundred thousand more trained troops.

Somewhere, in a grand building in France, faint echoing words suddenly became hollow in meaning, although he who had uttered them did not yet know it.

"The Soviets have no more cards to play; they are, in essence, fully committed, almost fully spent."

"Having tapped every source of manpower and brought their industrial base to peak production, they have simply failed to prevent our Allied armies recapturing large areas of Germany, albeit not yet back to where we started in August '45."

There was only one outcome now, he assured them, *only one.*

"The defeat of the Soviet Union is inevitable."

"It is only a matter of time."

Time brings all things to pass

Aeschylus

I know not with what weapons World War Three will be fought, but World War Four will be fought with sticks and stones.

Albert Einstein

Chapter 148 - THE DEVELOPMENT

0545 hrs, Monday 29th April, 1946, White Sands Bombing Range, New Mexico, USA.

At precisely 0545 hrs, the gadget was detonated.

The beginning of the end?

Glossary

A-36A Apache	Ground attack or dive-bomber version of the P-51 Mustang. Withdrawn in 1944, and returned to combat within RG.
Aardvark	Marriage of a Panzer IV hull with an Achilles turret.
Aitch-vap	Another way of saying HVAP, as in High Velocity Anti Tank.
AK47	Soviet assault rifle, similar to the ST44.
Antilope	Marriage of an SDKFZ 251 half-track with a Puma turret, containing a 50mm gun.
AOP	Aerial Observation Post, such as an Auster Aircraft.
APDS	Armour Piercing - Discarding Sabot.
ARL-44	French heavy tank designed by the CDM during the occupation and produced post-1945. As part of France's desperate attempt to regain a position as a world power. It was an unsatisfactory design.
Asbach	German Brandy.
B-29	US four engine heavy bomber, also known as the Super fortress.
B-32	US four engine heavy bomber, also known as the Dominator.
BA-64	Soviet 4x4 light scout car.

637

BBC Russian Service	The BBC Russian service did indeed commence broadcasting on 26th March 1946.
BEPO	Acronym for a Soviet armoured train - bronyepoyezd.
Black Prince	British tank, based on Churchill components but with a 17-pdr. The project was abandoned as satisfactory vehicles were available, but I have resurrected it for RG, as there were masses of components available.
Blyad	Russian for whore/bitch
BOAC	British Overseas Aircraft Corporation.
Bristol Buckingham	British twin engine bomber more used in liaison and passenger roles.
Brylcreams	Slang term for the Air Force.
C-47	US twin engine transport used for paratroopers or supply.
de Havilland Vampire	British single engine jet aircraft, produced in fighter, night-fighter and carrier versions.
Der Totentanz	Dance of Death / Danse Macabre.
DFS-230	WW2 German glider for up to 9 men [15 for F1 version].
Dingo	British Daimler 4x4 reconnaissance and liaison vehicle.

DRH	Deutsches Republikanischen Heer [Army]
DRK	Deutsches Republikanischen Kriegsmarine [Navy]
DRL	Deutsches Republikanischen Luftwaffe [Air Force]
F80 Shooting Star	US single engine turbojet fighter.
FN	Fabrique National, Belgian arms manufacturer.
FOO	Forward Observation officer
FUSAG	First US Army group, a subterfuge around D-Day, intended to mislead the Germans about the invasion's focal point.
G43 Gewehr	German WW2 7.92mm semi-automatic rifle.
GC&CS	Government code & cypher school, now known as GCHQ, Cheltenham, UK.
Geffchen & Richter	Company that produced the first walk-through metal detectors [mid 1920s].
Gigant	German Messerschmitt 323, motorised version of a heavy gilder, equipped with six engines, and capable of carrying a light tank or other vehicles.
Govno	Soviet expression for shit/bullshit/rubbish

Gran Sasso	September 1943 raid by Fallschirmjager and SS troops to liberate Mussolini from Italian captors.
Grand Slam	British earthquake bomb containing 22000 lbs [10000 kgs] of Torpex D1, equivalent to 6.5 tons of TNT.
Hals-und beinbruch	Literal meaning is 'break a leg', but is always intended as 'good luck'.
He219	German night fighter, also known as the Uhu [Eagle-owl]. First operational military aircraft to have ejector seats. Was greatly feared, but only produced in small numbers.
HEAT	High-explosive, Anti-tank. Shaped charge shells that penetrate using the Monroe effect.
Heracles Missions	So named as Heracles had killed the multi-headed Hydra, the Heracles missions were designed to cut the head off the Red Army by killing the front and overall command structures in Europe.
Hershey Bar	American chocolate bar
Horch 1a	German 4x4 multi-purpose vehicle.
HS-129/B3	German Henschel twin-engine ground attack fighter, known as the Panzerknacker. B3 version was equipped with the 75mm Bordkanone, and was a successful tank killer.

Hundchen	Marriage of an SDKFZ 251 and a Pak43 88mm anti-tank gun. Unsuccessful as it was top heavy.
HVAP	High Velocity, Armour Piercing
Hyena	Panther hull married to an M4A3 or similar turret, mounting a 76mm gun.
Imperia	Belgian automotive factory.
IS-IV	Soviet upgraded version of the IS-III, with increased armour, improved engine, longer chassis, but retaining the 122mm gun.
Jaguar	Panther modification, similar to the Ausf F.
JU-388	German Junkers twin engine multi-role aircraft.
JU-52	German three engine transport aircraft.
JU-87D	German single engine dive-bomber, known as the Stuka.
Killick	RN Leading Seaman
Koorva	Ukrainian word meaning whore.
Lanchester	British copy of the MP28 SMG.
Lilliput Pistol	German semi-auto pistol of 4.25mm calibre. 4.25" long and with a barrel length of 1.75".
M-18 RCL	US recoilless rifle of 57mm diameter.

M-20 RCL	US recoilless rifle of 75mm diameter.
M-29 Cluster bomb	US 500lbs cluster bomb containing ninety 4lbs charges.
M39 grenade	German egg-grenade.
M8 Greyhound	US-manufactured six-wheel armoured car, armed with a 37mm gun.
M9A1 Bazooka	US 57mm diameter rocket AT weapon.
Mamayev Kurgan	Dominant feature in the Battle for Stalingrad. Height 102.2 changed hands a number of times.
Matrose	Soviet seaman
Maxson mount.	A powered gun mount for 4 .50cal heavy machine guns, effective as an AA weapon or for ground use.
Me 323 Gigant	German Messerschmitt 323, motorised version of a heavy gilder, equipped with six engines, and capable of carrying a light tank or other vehicles.
MG-FF	German 20mm auto cannon used by the Luftwaffe.
Oberwachtmeister	Literally, Senior watch master. In German Army, equivalent to Oberfeldwebel.
Operation Cascade	British deception operation mounted in 1942 in the Middle East.

Operation Freston	British mission to Southern Poland in January 1945. Considered a failure as most of its personnel were captured by the Red Army.
Operation Pantomime	Within RG, land operations including and following the coastal invasion of Poland.
Panje Cart	Horse-drawn cart used by the Red Army
Panther Felix	French-produced Panthers with a 17pdr gun.
Panther II	German upgraded Panther, with increased armour and gun mounted.
Project Raduga	Raduga is Russian for Rainbow.
PTRD	Soviet anti-tank rifle firing a 14.5mm round.
Pumpkin Bomb	US conventional HE bomb, built to resemble the 'Fat Man' Plutonium bomb.
Purple Heart	US military award for being wounded or killed in service. It was also awarded for meritorious performance of duty, which reason was subsequently discontinued.
RASC	Royal Army Service Corps
Rheinbote	In German, the Rhine Messenger, a short-range rocket intended for use as artillery, with an effective range of around 100 miles.
RNoAF	Royal Norwegian Air Force

Saab 17	Swedish single engine reconnaissance bomber.
Saab 21	Swedish single engine pusher type fighter/attack aircraft.
SAAG	Second Allied Army Group, a formation created to fool the Soviets about Allied intentions.
SAFFEC	South American Field Forces, European Command.
Schrage Musik	German upward firing auto cannons. Literally 'Jazz', the weapon enabled attacks from underneath target aircraft.
Schwimmwagen	German military car capable of 'swimming'. Powered by a rear mounted propeller and steered by the front wheels.
SCR-536 Handie-Talkie	The original walkie-talkie of early WW2 movie fame.
SGMT	Soviet infantry and tank mounted MG, also known as the SG43 Goryunov, firing a 7.62mm round.
Skata	Greek word for shit.
SKS	Soviet semi-automatic carbine of 7.62mm calibre, complete with integral bayonet.
Skyraider	US single engine ground attack aircraft with high load capacity and excellent loiter time.
SMERSH	Acronym for Spetsyalnye Metody Razoblacheniya Shpyonov, a group of three counter-intelligence agencies. Also known as 'Death to spies.'

SNAFU	Abbreviation for 'Situation normal, all fouled up'. The reader may substitute 'fouled' as he/she sees fit.
Spartacist	A German group of radical socialists, which went on to become the German Communist Party.
SPAT	Self propelled anti-tank.
Springfield Rifle	US .30-06 bolt-action rifle replaced by the Garand.
Staghound	US produced T17E1 armoured car, known as the Staghound in British use. Armed with a 37mm M6 gun, plus 2-3 MGs
STAVKA	Soviet term for the High Command of Soviet Forces. Junior to the GKO.
Super Pershing	US heavy tank mounting the improved T15E1 90mm gun and extra armour protection.
T20E2 Garand	US selective fire version of the Garand, with a 20-round magazine and a recoil checker.
T3 Carbine	US M2/3 Carbine fitted with infra-red siting and a 30 round magazine.
T-54	Soviet MBT armed with a 100mm gun, superior in performance to the 88mm on the Tiger II. Eventually the 54/55 became the most produced tank in history. RG introduces the 54 ahead of schedule.

T-70	Soviet light tank with a two man crew, armed with a 45mm gun.
T-80	Soviet light tank with a three man crew, armed with a 45mm gun.
Tallboy	British earthquake bomb of 12000lbs of Torpex D1 explosive.
Teller Mine	German made AT mine containing 5.5kgs of TNT.
Teutobergerwald	A range of low wooded hills strung between Lower Saxony and Rhine-Westphalia. Once much larger than it is today, legend suggests that it was the location for the loss of Varus and his Legions in 9AD.
TOE	Sometimes known as TO&E, an acronym for table of organisation and equipment.
Torpex	Explosive 50% more powerful than TNT, originally designed as torpedo explosive filler, hence the name.
Vernam's cypher	Named for Gilbert Vernam, the cypher became the basis of the coded one-time pad, believed impossible to crack [if properly random.]
Westland Whirlwind	British twin engine fighter withdrawn from service in 1943. For RG, a handful were reinstated to equip two squadrons in 1946.
Willie Pete	White Phosphorous.

Winchester M-12	US pump action shotgun with an external tube 6 shot magazine. [12, 16, 20, and 28 gauge.]
Winchester M-69	US bolt-action .22 rifle fitted with a suppressor.
Wolf	Marriage of a Panther hull and a Panzer IV turret.
X7 Rottcapschen	German wire-guided AT missile used during WW2. Literally 'Red Riding Hood', the missile apparently enjoyed success against the IS series of heavy tanks.
ZSU-37-2	Soviet SPAA mount on the SU-76 chassis, of twin 37mm guns.
Zundapp	German motorcycle, either single or combination.

Fig# 177 - Rear cover from paperback of 'Sacrifice'.

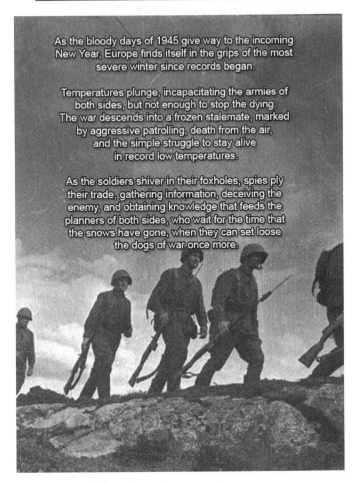

As the bloody days of 1945 give way to the incoming
New Year, Europe finds itself in the grips of the most
severe winter since records began.

Temperatures plunge, incapacitating the armies of
both sides, but not enough to stop the dying.
The war descends into a frozen stalemate, marked
by aggressive patrolling, death from the air,
and the simple struggle to stay alive
in record low temperatures.

As the soldiers shiver in their foxholes, spies ply
their trade, gathering information, deceiving the
enemy, and obtaining knowledge that feeds the
planners of both sides, who wait for the time that
the snows have gone, when they can set loose
the dogs of war once more.

'Initiative' - the story continues.

Read the opening words of 'Initiative' now.

Now I am become death, destroyer of worlds.

Robert Oppenheimer, quoting Krishna, avatar of Vishnu, from the Hindu text, the Bhagavad Gita.

Chapter 149 - THE POWER

1000 hrs, Tuesday 30th April, Frankenberg an der Eder, Germany.

It was the eighty-third anniversary, and the Foreign Legion's most important and significant day of the year.

Camerone Day celebrated the lost battle of Camerone, named for a hacienda in Mexico, where sixty-five legionnaires resisted a force of nearly three thousand Mexican soldiers.

It, above all other battles, created the mystique that surrounded the Legion from that day forward.

The commander, one Captain Jean Danjou, was killed early on in the battle, but his false hand was subsequently found, and became the subject of veneration each Camerone Day, when the icon, the symbol of the Legion's fighting spirit, was paraded in front of ranks of legionnaires.

The honour of holding the icon and marching with it in front of assembled legion units was a singular one, an honour that had once been afforded to the long dead Vernais, tortured to death in front of Brumath.

Normally, the most precious item in the Legion's inventory remained safely within the confines of its headquarters but, as most of the Legion was in the field in Germany, the Camerone Day parade was being held in a large open green space on the north bank of the Eder River.

Every Legion unit found in the French First Army had a representative section present, the main guard being mounted by men of the 1st Régiment Etrangere Infanterie.

The Legion Corps D'Assaut group was led by a proud Lavalle, the mix of ex-SS and long-service Legionnaires blending seamlessly into one group, and into the parade in general.

It had been too much to expect one of the new German contingent to be included in the direct parading of Danjou's hand, but it was a source of celebration and immense pride that Haefali had been honoured with command of the parade, and the singular honour of carrying the sacred relic had been granted to a Marseille-born Legion Caporal-chef from the Alma, and command of the honour guard given to Oscar Durand, Lieutenant in the 1st Régiment de Marche.

There was even a small squad comprising members of the 16th US Armored Division, until recently a solid member of the Legion Corps, their tank being one of two on parade that day, the other vehicle the only noticeable German contribution to proceedings.

The Sherman M4A3E8 led the way, followed closely by the noisier and larger Tiger Ie.

The day beforehand, a Legion tank crew had been assembled at the repair facility and presented with their vehicle, lovingly restored by cannibalism from wrecks found across the battlefields, or by manufacturing those pieces that escaped detection.

Each of the five men wept as Walter Fiedler, the workshops officer, presented them with the repaired heavy tank...

...Lohengrin.

[http://en.wikipedia.org/wiki/Battle_of_Camarón]
[http://en.wikipedia.org/wiki/Jean_Danjou]

1100 hrs, Wednesday, 1st May, 1946, Red Square, Moscow, USSR, and the Oval Office, Washington DC, USA.

Stalin stood upright and proud amongst the political and military leadership of the Soviet Union, as large bodies of troops and vehicles swept past, the traditional 'urrahs launched from thousands of enthusiastic throats.

It was an impressive display, that fact more appreciated by the hierarchy than the multitude of citizens that gathered for the traditional International Workers' Day parade, who saw nothing unexpected about the standard huge display of Soviet military might.

The participants had been stripped from internal commands, men on leave, those recuperating from wounds, anything that could stand or march was on parade.

For the citizenry it was as impressive as ever but, in reality, it was an illusion.

Of course, T-34m46's, with thicker armour and adapted to take the 100mm, T-44's similarly armed, followed by a phalanx of one hundred and twenty IS-III battle tanks, decked out as a Guards formation, all received rapturous receptions, appreciated as clear indicators of Soviet military superiority. Had they not been receiving specifically edited reports of fighting in the frontline, they may have felt differently.

The fly past of Red Air Force regiments was extremely impressive.

The political decision to retain the majority of new and replacement aircraft, depriving the front line units solely to ensure sufficient numbers were on display on May Day, had been heavily contested by the military contingent, but to no avail.

More importantly to the hierarchy, the large numbers of aircraft were there to protect them from any Allied attempt to disrupt the Soviet showpiece.

None the less, the new jets were impressive, although those with experience would have noticed the gaps in formation left by the three that had failed to take off, one drastically so, smashing back into the runway and spreading its experienced Regimental commander across the airfield.

The captured V2s, now in their new Soviet livery, were also impressive, although virtually useless for anything but fooling civilians.

Almost unnoticed, four large football-like shapes, huge bombs carried on Red Air Force vehicles, passed by, their arrival and departure overshadowed by more jets and the very latest in Soviet technological advances; the IS-IV heavy battle tank and ISU-152-Z, once known as Obiekt 704, brought to fruition for the heavy tank and tank destroyer brigades in Europe.

Almost unnoticed, the four mock-up representations of the pumpkin bomb found on the crashed B-29, left the square, immediately being surrounded by a heavily armed contingent of NKVD troops.

Almost unnoticed, but not quite...

As the Marshal climbed the steps to the top of Lenin's Mausoleum, his heart protested, reaching its point of toleration before he reached the top.

Zhukov, panting and eyes screwed up with pain, collapsed heavily.

"So that's that then. We've batted this around for months in anticipation of this moment, and we're still doing it now."

Truman wasn't scolding, just trying to draw a line under matters so they could progress.

The conversations still went on around him.

"Gentlemen, gentlemen... please."

The four other men settled down in silence, looking at the chief executive in anticipation.

"One final word... a sentence or two, no more. George?"

The outsider, George C. Marshall, Chief of Staff of the US Army, spoke in considered fashion.

"The scientists assure us of no consequences globally. It **will** save thousands of American boy's lives. No brainer for me, Sir."

"Thank you. Joseph?"

Acting Secretary of State Joseph Grew was slightly more animated.

"Sir, I support delay. Offer them the Mikado, lessen the terms, and they will fold. Blockade and conventional bombing will stop them. Soviet support is of little consequence to them now."

"Thank you, Joseph. James?"

"I agree with Joseph. We can still come back to this solution, but offer up the Mikado, and I see them collapsing. As stated, Soviet support counts for nothing now... in fact, it might work in our favour."

"How so?"

It was Marshall that posed the question and, surprisingly, it was Truman that answered it.

"They've been raised up, and now they're back down lower than a rattler's belly."

Marshall nodded his understanding.

"Thank you, James."

Forrestal, Secretary of the Navy, settled back into the comfortable couch.

"Henry? This is your baby."

"I'd have it in the air right now, Sir. Yes, the Nips might fold, but then, they might not. They'll fold once the weapon is deployed. Also, as I've said before, the use may be enough to guarantee this world's future."

"Thank you, Henry."

Henry L. Stimson, Secretary of War, even though he had trotted out his position before, wanted to say so much more.

To say that this weapon could make war obsolete, solely by its use, so awful as its use would be, therefore demonstrating that future wars could hold no advantages for aggressors.

He wanted to say that its use would end the Japanese war now; not in a year's time, but now.

He wanted to say that the forces freed up by this act would help defeat the Soviets all the quicker.

He wanted, God, how he wanted to resign and walk away from the pressures of government, his body announcing its displeasure at his continued exposure on almost a daily basis.

Most of all he wanted the whole goddamn war to be over, and that meant using more bombs; lots more.

Thus far, the notion of deploying them on the Soviet Homeland had been avoided, sidestepped, even ignored.

Military minds saw advantages in spades, and almost no problems, but the political considerations were many, from whose air space the bombers would fly over, where the bombers would be based, guarantees from scientists that there would be no repercussions to basic objections on moral grounds.

But Stimson understood that to defeat the Soviets, they would have to demonstrate to them the idiocy of further aggression, and that was best done, at least initially, by exterminating an area of the Japanese home islands.

"Thank you, gentlemen. Give me a moment."

Truman rose and moved to the window, taking in the view across the well-kept grass, noting the gardeners hard at work.

'Not a care in the world.'

He laughed perceptibly, but unintentionally.

'Care to swap?'

Work continued, his offer unheard.

"Gentlemen...I've made my decision. The mission is a go."

653

List of Figures within Sacrifice.

Fig# 1 – Table of comparative ranks. 8

Fig# 117 - Map of Europe 23

Fig# 118 – Explanation of Military Map Symbols 40

Fig# 119 - The Military Map of Europe, March 1946. 41

Fig# 120 – Forces involved at Glenlara, Monday, 1st January, 1946.
.... 48

Fig# 121 – Joint IRA-Soviet Naval Camp, Glenlara, Eire. 50

Fig# 122 – Glenlara Camp, IRA codenames. 56

Fig# 123 – Glenlara Camp, Ukrainian location codes. 58

Fig# 124 – Glenlara, Assault. 60

Fig# 125 - Town of Drulingen, 22nd January 1946. 107

Fig# 126 – Allied forces at Drulingen. 109

Fig# 127 - Drulingen - positions and assaults. 110

Fig# 128 – Soviet forces at Drulingen. 113

Fig# 129 - Junction between 16th US Armored Division and Group
Lorraine, 22nd January 1946. 130

Fig# 130 - Hangviller - Allied defensive positions. 131

Fig# 131 – Allied Forces at Hangviller. 132

Fig# 132 – Soviet Forces at Hangviller. 133

Fig#133 – Soviet assault on Hangviller. 134

Fig# 134 – Legion reinforcements at Hangviller. 142

Fig# 135 - Overview of Majano, Susans and Rivoli, Italy. 225

Fig# 136 – Allied Forces at Majano. 226

Fig# 137 – Soviet Forces at Majano. 227

Fig# 138 - Soviet assault on Majano and Castello di Susans. 230

Fig# 139 - Cierpice 26th March 1946 - Storch Assault. 348

Fig# 140 - Alternate Command Post, Cierpice, Poland. 349

Fig# 141 - Cierpice 26th March 1946 - NKVD ambush. 358

Fig# 142 – Kampfgruppe Bremer. 420

Fig# 143 - Town of Ahlen 421

Fig# 144 - Soviet forces in Ahlen 423

Fig# 145 - Von Scharf's assault on Ahlen bridge. 423

Fig# 146 - Von Scharf's assault on St Bartholomäus. 429

Fig# 147 - Soviet reinforced forces at Ahlen. 434

Fig# 148 - Oerlinghausen and the Teutobergerwald, 1st April 1946.
....452

Fig# 149 – Allied Forces at the Teutobergerwald. 456

Fig# 150 – Soviet Forces at the Teutobergerwald. 458

Fig# 151 - Oerlinghausen - Soviet Positions. 460

Fig# 152 - German Republican Army assault force -
Teutobergerwald, 1st April 1946. 462

Fig# 153 - Oerlinghausen - Allied assault. 466

Fig# 154 - Bimohlen - Prentiss Force 483

Fig# 155 - The Battle of the Streams. 487

Fig# 156 - Bimohlen - Prentiss Force initial dispositions. 488

Fig# 157 - Bimöhlen - Soviet Northern assaults. 493

Fig# 158 - Bimöhlen - Soviet Southern assaults. 494

Fig# 159 - Bimöhlen - Soviet Forces. 499

Fig# 160 - Prentiss Force - Late arrivals 509

Fig# 161 - Lützow - Allied Forces. 527

Fig# 162 - Lutzow - Allied dispositions. 528

Fig# 163 - Lützow - Soviet Forces. 530

Fig# 164 - Lutzow - Soviet attack 537

Fig# 165 - Pomeranian names – then and now. 551

Fig# 166 - Wollin - Initial Allied Forces. 553

Fig# 167 - Wollin - Initial Allied dispositions. 555

Fig# 168 - Wollin - First and Second Soviet attacks. 557

Fig# 169 - Wollin - Rienforced Allied Forces............................. 564

Fig# 170 - Soviet Forces surrounding Wollin. 569

Fig# 171 - Wollin - Soviet Third Attack. 570

Fig# 172 - Naugard - Soviet defensive force................................ 590

Fig# 173 - Naugard - Soviet defensive positions. 592

Fig# 174 - Naugard - First phase of the Allied Attack. 594

Fig# 175 - Naugard - Allied Assault forces................................... 596

Fig# 176 - Naugard - Second phase of Allied assault. 598

Fig# 177 - Rear cover from paperback of 'Sacrifice'.................... 648

Bibliography

Rosignoli, Guido
The Allied Forces in Italy 1943-45
ISBN 0-7153-92123

Kleinfeld & Tambs, Gerald R & Lewis A
Hitler's Spanish Legion - The Blue Division in Russia
ISBN 0-9767380-8-2

Delaforce, Patrick
The Black Bull - From Normandy to the Baltic with the 11th Armoured Division
ISBN 0-75370-350-5

Taprell-Dorling, H
Ribbons and Medals
SBN 0-540-07120-X

Pettibone, Charles D
The Organisation and Order of Battle of Militaries in World War II
Volume V - Book B, Union of Soviet Socialist Republics
ISBN 978-1-4269-0281-9

Pettibone, Charles D
The Organisation and Order of Battle of Militaries in World War II
Volume V - Book A, Union of Soviet Socialist Republics
ISBN 978-1-4269-2551-0

Pettibone, Charles D
The Organisation and Order of Battle of Militaries in World War II
Volume VI - Italy and France, Including the Neutral Countries of San Marino, Vatican City [Holy See], Andorra and Monaco
ISBN 978-1-4269-4633-2

Pettibone, Charles D
The Organisation and Order of Battle of Militaries in World War II
Volume II - The British Commonwealth
ISBN 978-1-4120-8567-5

Chamberlain & Doyle, Peter & Hilary L
Encyclopedia of German Tanks in World War Two
ISBN 0-85368-202-X

Chamberlain & Ellis, Peter & Chris
British and American Tanks of World War Two
ISBN 0-85368-033-7

Dollinger, Hans
The Decline and fall of Nazi Germany and Imperial Japan
ISBN 0-517-013134

Zaloga & Grandsen, Steven J & James
Soviet Tanks and Combat Vehicles of World War Two
ISBN 0-85368-606-8

Hogg, Ian V
The Encyclopedia of Infantry Weapons of World War II
ISBN 0-85368-281-X

Hogg, Ian V
British & American Artillery of World War 2
ISBN 0-85368-242-9

Hogg, Ian V
German Artillery of World War Two
ISBN 0-88254-311-3

Bellis, Malcolm A
Divisions of the British Army 1939-45
ISBN 0-9512126-0-5

Bellis, Malcolm A
Brigades of the British Army 1939-45
ISBN 0-9512126-1-3

Rottman, Gordon L
FUBAR, Soldier Slang of World War II
ISBN 978-1-84908-137-5

Schneider, Wolfgang
Tigers in Combat 1
ISBN 978-0-81173-171-3

Stanton, Shelby L.
Order of Battle – U.S. Army World War II.
ISBN 0-89141-195-X

Forczyk, Robert
Georgy Zhukov
ISBN 978-1-84908-556-4

Kopenhagen, Wilfried
Armoured Trains of the Soviet Union 1917 - 1945
ISBN 978-0887409172

Made in the USA
San Bernardino, CA
05 June 2015